NEW ROCK NEW ROLE

BOOK ONE OF THE NEW ROCK SERIES

RICHARD SPARKS

12/12/23

CAEZIK
SF & FANTASY
ARC MANOR
ROCKVILLE, MARYLAND

✷

SHAHID MAHMUD
PUBLISHER

www.CaezikSF.com

Cover art by Christina P. Myrvold; artstation.com/christinapm

ISBN: 978-1-64710-086-5

First Edition. First Printing. December 2023.
1 2 3 4 5 6 7 8 9 10

An imprint of Arc Manor LLC

www.CaezikSF.com

NEW ROCK NEW ROLE

For Jenny

CONTENTS

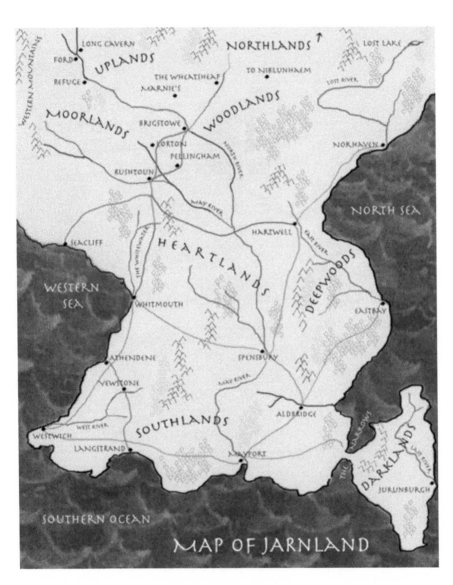

Map by Jenny Okun

A stick, a stone,
A book, a bone,
Go down and down
For half a crown,
A knife,
A life:
A throne

I

Another Life

Nobody remembers who comes second.

Round after round we'd fought, through the qualifiers and into the knockout stages of the tournament, against some of the toughest opposition we'd ever faced, in this or any other game. And now, we were within an ace of winning it all.

The World Championship of Sword and Sorcery.

Below me, on the ground, the dead avatars of our latest foes were slowly fading out of existence. The virtual crowd in the arena was going wild. Fans of every imaginable kind were cheering our victory: human, inhuman; animal, vegetable, mineral, and monster. It was a sea of pumping fists and waving arms and legs and tentacles and fins. They belonged to creatures of all sizes, from hairy orange furballs, to the giant blue centaur on whose back they were bouncing up and down and yodeling.

The Stats readout in the corner of my Heads-Up Display told me that fifty-eight million people worldwide were watching live.

I was in third-person mode, looking down from a high angle—the view I always use for combat. I need to see the whole field of battle, not just what is in front of my avatar's face. I'd named him Daxx when I created him. He is—or rather, I am—our team's battlemage-slash-healer;

and, at the moment, he was doing a little victory dance on the battle-field that we'd just wiped clean of some very challenging opposition.

Grell, a lumbering brute of an Orc, had programmed his software to cycle through a range of goofy facial expressions and idiot moves guaranteed to capture the commentators' attention—not to mention raise the public profile of our team. He was galumphing around like a drunken uncle at a wedding. Qrysta's victory shuffle was as elegant as Grell's was buffoonish. She was always graceful, even in combat. Dual wielding, a sword in each hand, she was everywhere at once, gliding, dancing, leaping and spinning. She was super-fast, and super-deadly. She ran like the wind and hit like a hurricane. Rarely did anyone lay a blade on her. Which made my job easier: I could keep Grell at maximum health and stamina and forget about Qrysta, unless she called on me for aid. All I had to do was keep an eye on her Shields of Mending and Protection and refresh them when they got thin—and, in the meantime, wreak havoc on our foes with my Area of Effect attacks. Those can be anything from Stormbursts blasting out of the sky, to Earthgrips, Ice Traps, or Consuming Slimes, which seize and drain foes and make them sitting ducks for Grell and Qrysta to finish off.

The crowd was loving it. Tens of thousands of virtual voices were chanting our name, *Pil-grimz, Pil-grimz!*

We lined up our avatars and made them bow in appreciation, in all directions, then waved our thanks. The interval entertainment kicked in: a lightshow and blaring music, mixed in with sound effects. High-lights of our last fight replayed on the jumbotron. Below it, virtual cheerleaders were tumbling, high-kicking, and being flung into the air. The producers clearly knew how to keep the streaming crowd jazzed while the TV channels played commercials.

"Well, how about that, guys?" Qrysta's calm voice came through my Immerzion headset as we left the arena. "We appear to have made it all the way to the Big One."

"Yeah, by the skin of our teeth," Grell taunted in his Aussie drawl, his avatar capering alongside the cheerleaders as we passed them. "Daxx bloody nearly lost me."

"I didn't though, did I?" I said.

"Asleep on the job again, mate!" He snorted. "I was within a hair of dying *twice*."

He was right. It had been a close-run thing.

4

Several times I'd thought I was going to lose one or the other of them. Go a player down against a crew as good as the one we'd just fought, and you're toast.

"You and the rest of us," I said. "Those bastards were tough. I was running on fumes. Not to mention just about out of potions, buffs, and every other damn thing I needed."

Grell chuckled. "No worries, Daxxie. Me and Qrysta pulled your pommie arse out of the flames. Like we always do, eh, Qrys?"

"Like we always *have* to," Qrysta needled.

I could only laugh, giddy with the high of victory. "You two are the best."

As we walked up the tunnel to our locker room to prep for the final bout of the tournament, Qrysta mused, "The best. That'll be official if we win the next one."

I said, "You know what? You're so good you don't need me. I'm going to log out and leave you to it; I've had enough fun for one day. I'll just sit back and watch and cheer you guys on. I know you can do it. I have every faith in you."

We all knew they would have died a dozen deaths without my Heals. No one needed to say so. We'd rather trash talk than sweet talk each other.

Trash talking was Grell's superpower. He was always taunting. In combat, that was his job: to get in the opposition's faces, harass them, and try to keep them enraged and focused on him. As our 'tank,' in his rock-hard plate armor, he absorbs all the punishment they unleash on him. I recharge his Health and Stamina; he deals death and destruction at anything within range of his battle-axe. Meanwhile, Qrysta is darting everywhere among them, slicing and dicing, as I pour destruction spells onto the enemy. It's second nature to us now. We can *think* for each other in combat. We've cleared the toughest dungeons without any of us needing to say a word.

That's Player versus Environment: us three taking on the game engine.

Player versus Player, though, is a whole other deal. In PvP, you're not up against a program, you're up against other people. And the ones we'd been battling in this tournament had been good.

Top PvP players ignore taunts, so Grell doesn't waste his energy on them. He goes into block-and-attack mode, fending off assaults and trying to take down whoever he can. Which means that he also takes a lot of punishment. It's my job to keep Shields of Mending and Protection up on all of us, while healing any hits that get through them. In my spare moments, I unleash Screamers and Barkers over our foes' heads to distract them, or Ghouls to Fear them and send them running. Any chance I get, I hit anyone I can with long-range attacks. Foes always reply in kind, of course, with everything they've got, so most of my work is repairing the damage and putting out fires.

When he wasn't taunting our foes, Grell was, more often than not, taunting one of us. When we'd first teamed up, I'd thought he was a bit of a dick. Not that I was going to tell him that. Qrysta and I had found the tank of our dreams—and so far as we were concerned, he could be as spiky as he wanted.

Besides, he soon learned that we were happy to give as good as we got.

Qrysta and I always enjoyed ribbing each other. The addition of Grell to the crew had taken things to a whole new level. Trash-talking is a national pastime Down Under. As he'd once explained, "If you're not worth sledging, mate, you're not worth knowing."

Qrysta hadn't known the word. I'd explained that 'sledging' is what Yanks like her call 'talking smack' to their opponents while playing sports; at which she laughed and said, "Bring it, Orc boy."

"Nah, I'll stick with bashing the pom, thanks, Qrysta," he'd replied. "I don't want you shoving those swords of yours up my backside."

Grell knew better than to mess with Qrysta. Any player unwise enough to give her grief soon learns that her mind—not to mention her tongue—is as sharp as her blades. To look at her, you'd think she was serenity itself—all sweetness and light, but ...

Looks can be deceptive.

Rile Qrysta up, and she is as fearless in a flame war as she is in combat.

The player we only knew as 'Qrysta' shared next to nothing about herself—just that she lived in California. Since her avatar was a badass, Asian sword-dancer, and she carried curved, Samurai-style blades, I assumed she was Asian American in real life.

It would be her prerogative to volunteer information about herself if she wanted to. It's not considered cool to pry. She'd tell us if she wished. Clearly, she didn't, any more than Grell or I did.

We were a perfect fit as a team. We could wipe out crews three or four times our size while simultaneously ribbing each other on our comm channel. The banter we threw back and forth kept us on our toes. It was as if we were goading each other to prove each other wrong. We took our crewmates' barbs out on the enemy. It was team building masked as competition.

Individually, we were all good. Together, we were something special.

Our whole was *way* more than the sum of its parts.

Were we Championship class even?

There had been only one way to find out: see if we could qualify for the Championship. We'd managed that. And were now within an ace of winning it.

In the locker room, where no one could eavesdrop on us, Grell wandered over while I opened my storage chest. "What are you changing?"

I frowned as I considered my response. "Pretty much everything. They'll have seen our last fight. They'll be planning how to take me out."

By 'them,' I meant our next opponents. Take out a crew's healer, and it's Game Over.

Grell, by contrast, just had to do what he always did.

Survive.

In the eye of the storm.

He wouldn't be changing much; a little defense here, a surprise attack skill there.

I swapped out my healing and damage staffs and loaded new macros that would unleash Heals and Shields and Attacks in quick succession. I'd be a whole new battlemage out there in the final. "What do you need, guys?"

They told me, and I handed out potions that I'd concocted myself to my own recipes. Qrysta filled up with speed and strike and stamina. Grell got resistance and brute force to the max. They loaded them into their inventories for instant access.

My job was to make sure they didn't need them.

I took as many of my most powerful magic-boosting potions as I could carry. They all had little twists in them. Some added fire or ice or poison or lightning to my spells so that I got a bonus of Damages every time I cast one.

The five-minute call came.

Butterflies fluttered in my stomach. *Well, that had to be expected*, I thought. I'd never, in all my life, been in anything this big.

Grell said, and I could hear the tension in his voice, "Ready to rock?"

Qrysta said, and I could hear the smile in hers, "Might as well go out there and win this, guys. What do you say? Seeing as we've come this far."

Cool as a damn cucumber.

If I hadn't been so uptight, I might have jumped on her for being so laid back. *Oh, so you think this'll just be a walk in the park? Win or lose, you couldn't care less? Get your game face on—this is serious!*

It was not the time, nor the occasion, to take my own nerves out on a crewmate. "You do realize what this will mean if we win, right?"

"Fame and fortune," she replied.

"Not just that. It'll mean that we get to meet up in real life."

That was true. We'd be superstars. World Champions. There would be symposiums, conventions, tournaments; promoters would fly us from anyplace to anywhere—not to mention pay us to attend, or compete.

Grell groaned. "Every silver lining has a bloody cloud. A hundred bucks to a brass fart you're just some whinging little pom who won't buy his round."

That, I thought, *was more like it!* Less edgy, more belligerent: *this* was how we needed him.

"That'll be interesting," Qrysta mused.

"I bet Grell's even uglier IRL," I said.

Grell snarled, "Blow me, Daxx."

Qrysta, no doubt, wouldn't be as gorgeous as her avatar. Who ever is? I didn't look anything like Daxx, with his flowing, blond Viking locks, chiseled jaw, and shrewd green eyes above a lean body more buff than anything I'd ever had.

Well, why would I want him to look like me?

I saw enough of *me* in the mirror.

I'd spent a long time designing Daxx to be everything I wasn't, and just about every day since then, wished I was. How I'd have had a better life, I believed, if I'd been inside a body and face as fine as his: fit, handsome and, above all, *young*.

In real life, though, I, Joss Palmer—Joseph, really, but I'd never liked the name—was an ageing, balding, stiffening former teacher, now hardcore gamer, glued inside my headset day-in and day-out, where life was far better, and much more exciting.

I'd always loved stories, both true ones and fictional ones, and loved sharing them with my students—English and History had been my

8

subjects. In-game, though, with Qrysta and Grell, we, The Pilgrimz of Pain, were the heroes of our own stories.

I'd come up with the name. The others had liked it. In the Middle Ages, pilgrims were known as palmers, because they brought back palm fronds from the Holy Land to show that they'd made it there and back. Grell and Qrysta didn't know who I was IRL. They just knew me as Daxx, so they had no idea of the private kick I get out of our name.

And, as Daxx, now heading to the final battle of the Championship, the world was my oyster, which I—with sword and sorcery—would open.

When I'd first started playing MMORPGs (Massively Multi-Player Online Role-Playing Games) I'd assumed that all gamers were young. That may have been because my then fifteen-year-old nephew had turned me onto them when he and my sister moved in with me to share the load of our mother's last months. Then, one day, one of my Guildmasters posted in Guild Chat that she wanted to hand over the reins as she was turning eighty-five, and did anyone want the job?

Not me. Running a guild is a ton of work. I'd had enough of work for one lifetime. Retirement suited me just fine.

My wife died nearly twenty years ago. We never had children. I still missed her, but eventually found that I liked living on my own. I had my pension, a roof over my head, and—until last year—my dog. I kept meaning to get another one, as company for my daily walks, but somehow hadn't got around to it. And now, as we made our way to the World Championship and gained more and more followers, I'd found myself with a second career: making money on our brand and turning my passion into my livelihood.

Online, I was no longer a retired teacher, living alone in my bungalow on the edge of a small town in England. I was a celebrity.

And I was anything but solitary. I had friends. Great friends, that I'd met in various games, on various worlds, over many long hours and days of play.

The best of whom were Qrysta and Grell.

I spent every moment I could in their company. Running with them, and getting up to mischief, was always a joy.

My neighbors probably thought I was a bit of a recluse. Perhaps I was. But who cared about Real Life? My online life contained everything that reality lacked.

No doubt it would be a letdown, for all of us, when we met IRL—but, so what? We were crew. We knew each other. We *liked* each other. We'd be fine. It'd be weird, since we had come to know each other as how we *wished* to be, rather than who we actually were, but there was no reason we couldn't forgive each other for being our disappointing actual selves. It would be the same for them as for me.

When Qrysta and I first met, it had been in one of the hardest fights that either of us had ever attempted. I'd made my way down, not without difficulty, to the final level of a famously brutal dungeon, only to find Qrysta soloing the End Boss. None but the very best players would even think of attempting such a tough Boss Fight alone. No solo had ever managed to finish him. Bragging rights awaited the first avatar to do so. I believed that I had worked my way far enough up through the school of hard knocks to give it a try—expecting that I'd get my balls handed to me on a plate, as who wouldn't, first time?

But that would be okay. I'd learn, and resurrect back in safety, and figure out what I needed to work on before coming back down with better skills and gear and trying again.

And, if necessary, again and again. For as many times as it took.

I crouched at the tunnel exit, in stealth, to scope out the challenge that awaited me.

There she was, dancing around mobs of monsters attacking her from all sides, while a giant of a demon roared and leapt and pummeled at her—yet, somehow, never managed to land a blow.

I had never seen anyone dodge so well.

She wouldn't win, I could see that clearly enough. She was hitting hard, but the demon self-healed and recharged anytime her attention was diverted. She was having to kill off his minions *and* avoid him every time he powered up and came after her again.

The longer she fought, the more minions were added, crawling out of the walls and floor—all piling in on her. I didn't want to interrupt.

Nor did I want to leave empty handed.

If she managed, as seemed far from likely, to kill this Boss solo, I wouldn't share in the loot-drop. And if she did finish him off, it'd be an age before he'd respawn so I could take him on solo myself.

I didn't have the patience to wait around watching a battle which would at best end in stalemate. She, whoever she was, had a choice: die under the relentless assaults of the demon Boss and his ever-growing horde, or call it a night.

She was so good she had to know that.

I decided to throw her a lifeline. She could go nowhere solo, or—maybe—somewhere with my assistance. *Together*, we might just take him down.

And that would be a win-win, I thought.

Hey, she could always come back some other time and try to solo him again.

I pinged her a message. *Healer/battlemage. Need help?*

Her reply pinged back. *Fuck off.*

I had to laugh, so popped over a smiley.

I settled back to watch. She danced, and struck, and dodged.

She was good. *Very* good.

But not good enough.

I'll be here till he's dead, I messaged.

It took *five whole minutes* for her to call on me. Five minutes of the best dodge-rolling, evasion, and sword-dancing I'd ever been privileged to witness.

Five minutes in a solo Boss Fight seems longer than five hours of root canal.

The message came. *Any time.*

I had no idea how she'd managed to last that long. I'd have been dead within seconds. She'd been moving like a blur before but went up a gear when I hit her with Heals and Shields.

Then I cast my best Traps at her assailants.

With them immobile, she was able to start whittling them down.

It was tough enough with the two of us. We were hugely outnumbered, and, for the next half hour, busy.

Working together became almost instinctive. She hit, I healed; she confused, I diverted; I trapped, she killed.

The Boss had immense reserves of health and stamina, but one of us was always damaging him while the other killed off his minions.

Blow by blow, we drained him, and he died.

We looted his corpse. We chatted. Neither of us needed to tell the other how good we were.

Only three other duos had ever taken that Boss down before.

Our names would be on the leaderboard.

11

That, we agreed, would be just fine.

We also agreed that it would be fun to pair up again.

A full raid from an enemy faction arrived, but we'd taken the precaution of dropping into stealth, so they never saw us. They noticed the dead Boss and wondered who had killed him.

They searched high and low for us, but we'd melted away.

After that, Qrysta and I ran together whenever we could. Once we had comms up, I was surprised to hear her American accent. Not much later, Grell joined the team.

A Brit, a Yank, an Aussie. I don't know if they felt the same, but I was glad we were all different. It was as if they were bringing exotic, *other* lives into my little provincial home.

We had everything we needed, the three of us: tank, damage, Heals—and to a better level than we'd ever had before with any other teammates. We were also purists. We never took shortcuts. We never googled solutions or used cheat sheets or walk-throughs. That was beneath us. It was a matter of pride for us to clear quests on our own.

We discovered that I had a knack for solving the puzzles within quests. The others began to look to me for solutions to problems, as the strategist; and gradually, I morphed into the team leader.

I was good at oversight. They were good at execution.

Grell turned out to be a skilled negotiator. He could talk to other crews—in other factions as well as our own—and strike deals that got us out of all sorts of trouble and into all sorts of opportunities. He was always learning stuff that Qrysta and I had never even heard about. There was clearly more to our Aussie Orc than met the eye.

Qrysta was our source of extra income. The more we ran with her, the more Grell and I saw how good she was one-on-one.

This, we all agreed, was a commercial opportunity ripe for the taking.

Grell, our huckster, arranged duels for her and worked the odds as a sideline. I stayed out of it, knowing nothing about any of that. They had their skills, I had mine. She fought, he bet, we made money. Qrysta rarely failed to deliver. She did lose from time to time. That was only to be expected. There's always someone out there better than you.

She never lost a rematch.

Qrysta learned while in combat. She was always studying her opponents as she fought them. She worked out what they were doing right and what she was doing wrong.

She fixed her leaks—and then kicked their butts when they squared off again.

ATM time, Grell or I would say, when we were getting low on funds. Adventuring is expensive. We always had gear to buy or repair or upgrade, or supplies to replenish, so got through the gold as fast as we made it.

Grell had once teased, *time to milk the cash cow.*

Qrysta had given him an earful. *Who you calling a cow, you steaming pile of Orc shit?* it began, and carried on for several irate sentences.

When she stopped to draw breath, Grell said, "It's an *expression*, Qrys! Jeez, lighten up, eh? I'm not calling *you* a cow, mate. It's a compliment. Like, you're the goose that lays our golden egg."

There was a loaded silence, then Qrysta, furious a moment before, burst out laughing. "Oh, boy!" she said, when she recovered. "*Open mouth, insert foot.* I love you, Grello, but, um: *cow? Egg? Goose?*"

Grell got the point. Chastened, he mumbled, "Ah, fuck off, why don't you?"

Qrysta responded cheerfully. "I will if you will."

Which they both, by silent agreement, did.

So Qrysta was our breadwinner. Lots of wannabes lined up to face her one-on-one. It wasn't long before few of their backers would give us anything but short odds on her. Short odds were better than none, we reasoned, and so the money—little by little—trickled in.

It would be pouring in if we won the Championship. A fat purse came with the title, but that would just be the start of it. We'd be stars. We could set up challenges against other pro crews—best of seven, Qrysta had suggested, like the World Series—and *that* we would monetize, bigtime. Different scenarios, different arenas and rig-outs and conditions.

The fights would also be sponsored, and we could live stream them. The more viewers our channel pulled in, the more we'd make. I knew we'd have endorsement deals—the offers had been coming in for days. We'd told them all that we'd get back to them after the Finals. It was a gamble because—what if we lost?

Nobody remembers who comes second.

But if we won, our counteroffers would be asking for a *lot* more.

Our cue came through our headsets.

"Pilgrimz of Pain, to your positions, please!"

The lights in the arena abruptly blacked out, and the music fell silent.

A roar of expectation rose from the crowd. A fanfare sounded. Spotlights swept the arena.

I had to hand it to the programmers. They put on a hell of a show.

"Ladies and gentlemen, it's *tiiiime* …" The Ring Announcer did his thing.

"Let's do this," Grell said, and led us out into the arena.

"Introducing," the Announcer roared, and we heard our names, one by one, as giant close-ups of each of us appeared on the jumbotron, "The *Pilgrimz of Paaaiiiiinnnnnn!*"

The crowd cheered, and he moved on to our opponents: Hell's Razors, who emerged at the far end of the arena.

We stalked to our starting positions opposite them.

"Okay, you sons of bitches," Grell muttered, glowering at them. "Prepare to meet thy extremely painful dooms."

The digits on the jumbotron counted down from ten to zero, the crowd chanting them out, each number louder than the last.

At 'one,' we chugged our potions, buffing ourselves to the max.

I had glowing green Shields up on all of us as the starting signal blared.

The six of us launched into action, everything on the line.

Nobody remembers who comes second.

Any number of times, that could have been us. Hell's Razors hit us as hard as we hit them, but not—just as we expected—with everything they had. They, like us, were too canny for that. Use up all your reserves, and you're there for the taking.

I threw a Thunderstorm over them, which blasted down lightning and hail, while the enemy Sorceress led with an Earthquake, throwing Grell and me off our feet. Qrysta was in midair, as usual. She touched ground as little as possible in combat. She didn't trust the ground. It could grip you, swallow you, fling you, turn to mud or quicksand. She landed behind the Sorc and skewered her a dozen times before leaping away while I Negated her Earthquake.

The Sorc's Shields held, so Qrysta didn't do much damage, but she had gotten her attention. And that of the rest of her crew. No one appreciates having their healer attacked.

No Heals, no chance.

"Your six, Qrys!" I yelled, as the enemy sword and board fighter shot in to attack her from behind.

She flung herself to one side but took a glancing blow.

"Crap," she muttered, before turning on him, as I healed the damage she'd taken.

Grell chuckled grimly as he sunk back into his battle stance.

"No mugs, these bastards," he said.

"Too much to hope for," Qrysta agreed. Her voice was as calm as it always was in combat; her avatar a frenzied blur of dodging and striking.

Their sword and board guy was slower than her, but not by much. He had all the moves, and his strikes hit home often. He also seemed to be just about impervious to any damage.

Grell, trading blows with their tank, a huge Barbarian, noticed. "Tag time, Qrys," he suggested.

"Gotcha."

We all knew what he meant. We'd worked this move any number of times.

Leaping and slashing and feinting, Qrysta lured her opponent over toward Grell.

I counted down. "Three, two, one—"

We hit him together, with everything we had. I Rooted him and blew a volley of Flamebombs at him, and Grell nailed him with an Executioner's Strike, while Qrysta drilled a blur of thrusts into him from behind. Before he could react, she was away and harassing the enemy Sorc again.

We'd hardly done any damage at all. And we'd used some of our best shots.

"Bugger me!" Grell muttered. "What's with this guy?"

We found out eventually, but not until we'd been through the grinder far longer than we'd have liked.

The battle ebbed and flowed below me, the advantage fluctuating between us and our foes. At times they'd gain the upper hand; at others, we'd have the lead. There was fire and fury everywhere, from the blows being traded on the floor to the aerial attacks the enemy Sorc and I were launching, all the way up to the sky. My Stormbursts seemed particularly effective, slamming lightning strikes and thunderbolts down onto our foes. We lobbed all kinds of air-bombs over each other and scrambled to Negate those coming at us. I was as busy Cleansing as I was healing.

Qrysta was clearly better than the other team's sword and board fighter, but we'd seen that he had protection that seemed invulnerable.

"We can't hurt this guy," Qrysta said, "but he's not hurting me, whatever he does."

It was Grell who had the lightbulb moment. "Sitting duck!"

It took her a moment to realize. It would be a hell of a gamble. "Really?"

"Really." He sounded certain.

Qrysta warned, "We're dead if this doesn't work."

"It'll work. Daxxie, max shields on her in three."

"On three," I confirmed.

Grell counted down. I focused all my healing power on Qrysta.

She stopped moving, right in front of the sword and board guy.

The enemy Sorc saw her chance and Rooted her.

Their sword and board guy was all over her.

Grell laughed. "Gotcha!"

"You're a genius, Grell," Qrysta said, leaping back and away as I freed her.

Grell had seen through their bluff. He'd spotted that the sword and board fighter could be their actual tank, not the big Barbarian. He'd been right. The guy had hit Qrysta with everything he'd got, and that had been just about zero. All his power was in defense and protection. Which meant that the Barbarian would have to be more vulnerable than he looked.

We switched tactics. Grell switched targets. Qrysta and I focused on their healer; and that, after another few minutes of mayhem, was pretty much that. We wore them down and took them out, Barbarian first, then Sorcerer. Their sword and board man was the last to drop, weakened by my Energy Drain, his legs chopped from under him by Grell, Qrysta's swords punching through his shredded armor. We whooped. We hollered. We celebrated. We cavorted. We reveled in the applause and the cheers of the crowd.

I was stunned. *Did we just win?*

I was so caught up in the euphoria of the moment that I couldn't put my finger on the moment when everything started to go weird, but go weird it did—very weird indeed.

We were dragged out of the arena by some invisible, irresistible force, in different directions, unable to control what was happening. We gasped. We squawked. We shot off down wild rabbit holes at speed, sucked out of our post-fight celebrations, the cheers of the audience still echoing in our ears, amid the roaring, and the bucking.

"*Qrryyyssttaaaaaaa!*" I yelled, as we plunged down pipes of flashing light and through blank tubes of darkness, shouting for each other, turning over and over and around and around, helpless to resist—and then I lost them, as they vanished into a disintegrating digital vortex, whipped off and away.

I called for Grell—for both of them—until my voice grew hoarse, but I got no reply. They'd gone …

Where? And where was *I* going?

My vision filled with distortions and flashes of blinding color. It was unbearable. I tore at my headset, wondering what the hell kind of system malfunction this was.

It wouldn't come off.

I was on my feet, staggering around in my room, yanking desperately at my headset, which was firing all kinds of flashes and interference at me, between moments of terrifying emptiness.

Then it was as if the world tipped sideways. I was screaming. I know that because I felt it in my throat, but I couldn't hear a thing.

Everything stopped.

Everything went black.

Then I was hurtling again, through blasts of light and color, punctuated by patches of blankness. Nothing made sense. I couldn't breathe properly. I couldn't hear, or see, or feel. I just needed to get this to stop.

I kept punching myself in the face as I tried to dislodge my headset. I was scratching my forehead as I hauled on the damned thing which refused to release its grip on me.

What the hell was going on?

I couldn't stand the mad visuals that were piling in on me wherever I turned, so I scrunched my eyes shut. I took a deep breath, and struggled, continuing to wrestle with my headset. When I finally wrenched it off, my whole body felt as if it was being ripped out of the collapsing virtual world I'd just been buffeted around in. My chest was heaving for breath. I was bent double from the exertion.

I opened my eyes.

I was standing on grass.

My feet were in scuffed, brown boots.

What?

I'd been wearing slippers.

I'd never seen these boots before in my life.

Dark gray leggings were tucked into them. I'd been wearing sweatpants.

I was standing in a meadow, not the floor of my living room. A warm breeze teased at my clothes.

How was that possible? It was meant to be the middle of winter.

Not here, it wasn't. And my house was nowhere to be seen.

I straightened up, startled, and looked around. Where were the others?

I was in the middle of nowhere—a nowhere that I didn't recognize. All that I could see was hills, woods, and grassland. In the distance, snow-capped mountains gleamed on the horizon. There was no sign of civilization. There was no farmland or pasture, no fences or felled trees.

I was in untouched, endless wilderness.

I knew this wasn't a scene inside my headset because I was holding it in my hand.

Only—what was I seeing?

It wasn't my headset.

It was a crude, bronze helmet.

I peered closer at it. The face reflected back at me from its curved surface was indistinct, but all too recognizable.

It wasn't mine.

It was Daxx's.

His long, blond hair fell forward over my shoulders as I stared back at him. At … *me?*

I froze in shock. I was *physically in* my avatar's body.

When I managed to speak, my voice was a croak. "Uh, guys? Qrysta? Grell? Can you hear me?"

They didn't respond.

I was all alone, on an unknown hillside, talking to a helmet.

2

First Encounters

"Hello? Anyone there?" I called out.

Then I wished that I hadn't. How'd I know if the response would be friendly? Better to be quiet.

I looked around, eyes darting this way and that, wary in case anyone appeared.

No one did.

I turned around to make sure, and realized that something was hanging from my back. Something else was bumping against my left leg. I looked down to see that it was a sword a scuffed leather scabbard. I stared at it in shock—it was *real*. I hesitated, then drew it out, noting its weight, my hand shaking on its hilt. I'd handled hundreds of swords in dozens of online games, and this was about as a poor a weapon as I'd ever seen—a battered, cheap shortsword, its blade pitted and flecked with rust. I turned it over; its edges were dull, its hilt well-worn leather over wood. I immediately thought, *noob equipment.* It looked like the sort of weapon a player would start out with but would sell as soon as he'd earned enough coin to upgrade. And then I thought, *wait a minute, I'm actually holding this thing. I'm not an avatar, I'm … really here.*

Wherever the hell 'here' was.

I spun around, trying not to panic—noticing, as I did, that my body was a lot nimbler and more muscular than it had ever been before. The object strapped to my back knocked against my shoulder blades. I could guess what it had to be: a shield—and, by the weight of it, not a big one. I fumbled with the straps, finally working out how to unsling the thing. It was a small buckler, round, wooden, and bound with a rusty iron rim.

Why did I have these things, instead of a staff of power? I had built Daxx as a battlemage and healer. He'd *always* had a staff. That had been his only weapon, his only means of defense. When he'd started out, his first staff had been as crude as this shortsword.

I tried to connect the dots. I appeared to be Daxx, yes—but was I a mage? Perhaps not. How could I know, until I found a staff and tried casting? I didn't feel safe with just a crappy sword and shield. They were better than nothing, but if I could cast—well, I'd have a decent arsenal at my disposal.

Or would I? How did I know that I would be able to do what Daxx could do before? Did it work like that here?

And where *was* 'here,' anyway?

I looked every which way, searching for anything I might recognize.

Nothing in my line of sight rang any bells. I didn't spot anything to suggest that this location had appeared on any game map I'd ever explored before.

There were so many thoughts chasing each other around in my head that I found it hard to decide which two-and-two I should put together. I was thinking, *what to do,* as well as *where was I,* and *how did I get here,* and *wtf was going on. What to do* pushed the others out of the way. I had no answers to those; they would have to wait until later.

What to do needed to be decided first.

I could stay where I was until something happened or my team found me—ye gods, I hoped that Grell and Qrysta were here too— or, I could head somewhere, anywhere, to seek help, or at least some answers.

The *something that happened,* if I were to stick around, might be unwelcome. I might need to use this sword and shield. I'd never held either in real life before. If I was going to have to wield them, I'd better learn how. That thought scared me—using an actual sword, in actual combat? I could get maimed or killed. I wasn't wearing any kind of armor; all I had on were boots, woolen leggings, and a hide jerkin over a homespun shirt.

And that begged another question: if I died, would I be able to resurrect as I would in a game? I couldn't still be in a game—not just because I recognized nothing about where I was, but because I felt as alive as I ever had. Which meant that I felt just as mortal. I doubted that I could resurrect, and I didn't want to find out that answer the hard way.

Rather than heading off in some random direction, might it be wiser to stay where I was until night fell and obscured my presence? I quickly dismissed the idea. There are creatures that hunt by night— and I wouldn't see them coming. No, it didn't seem wise to be out in the open, after dark, in the wilderness. Surely it was better to get moving and try to find some form of shelter.

Evening was still a long way off. It seemed to be mid-morning, on an early autumn day, I judged, as the leaves on the nearby trees were just starting to turn. So far, I knew nothing. I wouldn't learn much by just staying put. Time to explore.

That meant traveling on foot.

Traveling where?

I looked around again, searching the horizons in all directions. No obvious destination suggested itself. *So*, I thought, *what did I need?* The answer was obvious: I needed to stay alive.

Then, what did I need for that?

Food and water. Fire and shelter.

I didn't think water would be a problem. Where there are hills, there are streams and rivers. That solved which way to go. Head for the mountains. Find the streams.

I started walking. I fixed my line on one of the highest peaks in the distance. It stood out, being an odd, bent shape. My way led up a gentle slope at first, then downhill into a belt of trees. There was a brook in the cleft between the slopes. At least I had water. I doubted that finding food, fire, and shelter would be that easy. I knelt down and scooped up a handful of the clear liquid and examined it. It was cool and smelled clean and fresh. I took a mouthful, and it tasted like all of those things. Safe enough to swallow, I decided. I made myself drink as much as my stomach could hold as I had no container that I could fill.

I hopped the brook and started up the opposite slope. I looked for traces of people, but saw none—no paths, no cut trees. Old branches lay where they had fallen. Those would have already been gathered for firewood, if there had been anyone around to gather them. I didn't know whether to feel relieved or worried that this place was uninhabited. Friendly people would be great, but unfriendly ones—not so much. There was enough dead wood that I could build a fire in minutes, but I had no way of starting one. If I'd had a staff, of course, I could blast fire into it.

The thought made me stop in my tracks.

What was a staff but a stick of wood?

There were sticks of wood everywhere.

I found one that seemed about the right size, maybe a foot shorter than I was. I trimmed off a few twigs and inspected it. It looked even less impressive than my crummy shortsword. I didn't feel confident that what I wanted to attempt would work.

I aimed it at a tree.

Well, now what? I had no Readout screen to access, where I could pick among my skills. I didn't even know if I had any.

I said, "Flameball!"

Nothing happened.

I sighed. *Yeah, right.*

I tried a couple of other attacks, just in case. "Lightning! Stoneblast!"

Silence. Just the wind rustling in the leaves overhead.

Well, now I knew I couldn't just use any old stick. I dropped it and headed on. The trees thinned, and my twisted waypeak rose into view again. I strode on towards it. I'd been in poor shape for years, and too lazy to take myself in hand and do anything about it. Here, I was *bursting* with health. I was tireless, strong, and above all, I was young again! It felt so, *so* good.

I'd been marching for hours at a fast pace, feeling I could keep going forever, when I heard the howl.

My stomach wanted to drop through my boots and then heave itself back up out of my throat as the hairs on the back of my neck crawled upright.

Wolf.

I froze.

One-on-one, could I fight off a real wolf? I didn't want to find out.

Then I heard the answering howl. It also came from ahead of me— two o'clock to the first howl's ten.

22

Me against two? Forget about it …

I dropped to the ground, my heart racing, hoping they wouldn't spot me.

My mind was racing too, but not in a useful way. It was filled with gibberish thoughts and swear words, and pleas for this not to be happening. I couldn't think coherently, nothing resembling a plan of action. Just *re*-action, instinctive, panicked, and terrified.

The first wolf howled again. *Did it sound closer?*

A heartbeat … two, three … then the second one answered. They seemed to be moving across my line of march, from left to right.

I tried to whack my brain back into shape. *Concentrate. Use your intelligence.* My mind was totally scrambled. *Come on—focus!* Both wolves appeared to be crossing between me and the mountains.

And then I heard a third howl.

From behind me.

The first two had sounded to be coming from some distance away. This last one was a lot more up close and personal.

I was trembling. *I'm dead! No, I'm not. Think.* I had no idea how to use a sword for real. And against three wolves? No chance.

I could run, but they could run faster. And I'd tire first.

But they couldn't *climb*.

I sprinted for the nearest stand of trees and scrambled up the lowest bough of a huge, old oak. I was twenty feet up its trunk when the wolf behind me howled again.

It was much, *much* closer. I peered through the curtain of leaves, trying to calm my thumping heart and quieten my breathing. Silence. Just a gentle gust of wind now and then, and the sounds of birds. And then, appearing in a silence so total it was as if it had materialized below me, there it was.

Wolf.

It moved its head around, sniffing the air. It puzzled at the bough that I'd scrambled up, sniffed at it, followed my scent towards the trunk. Its great, gray head lifted. It saw me, and its eyes locked onto mine.

Silence.

Followed by a low, long, rumbling growl.

It sat, staring up at me. Waiting for me. Waiting for its nice, juicy meal.

God, the *size* of the thing! It was enormous—as big as a pony. I could see its sides heaving as it breathed. It studied me with its huge, yellow eyes.

I had the distinct feeling that it could wait forever down there. One of us might die of starvation, of course, if I never came down, but I thought that unlikely. It was far more likely that I'd fall asleep eventually and fall. With any luck, I'd break my neck *before* that thing had its jaws around my throat.

I supposed I'd have to kill it.

And soon, I thought, as I remembered the howls of the other wolves.

When would its companions appear? Only two? How about the rest of its pack? Taking this brute down was going to be hard enough. Any more of them, and I wouldn't stand a chance. I needed to kill it while there was only one of them.

I drew my sword and tested its point. Sharp enough. Good.

I shifted on my branch, moving from a sitting position to a crouch. The wolf stared up. If I attacked while it was watching me, it would be ready for me. I'd land, maybe awkwardly, and it would be on me. I needed a diversion. I reached out slowly and broke off the nearest small branch I could reach. I reversed my grip on my sword, holding it out in front of me, point down.

I had two feet of chipped and rusty, but serviceable, iron; and just the one shot at this.

I threw. The wolf heard the crash of the branch landing in the undergrowth and whirled to face the new threat. With both hands on my sword hilt, I jumped.

It must have sensed something. Maybe it heard me brushing the leaves on my way down, because it whirled back to face me. It was quick, but not quick enough. My sword was into its shoulders and then the creature was staggering sideways, snarling with fury. I heaved at the sword, working it deeper into the wound. The wolf spat, snarled, and struggled. I sawed and wrenched, and the damn thing seemed to be getting stronger rather than weakening—with those terrible teeth far too close for my liking—but at least it was impaled and couldn't sink its fangs into me. A slashing paw caught my hand and drew blood. My sword slid free. I hacked at the brute's neck. It coughed, crumpled, and died.

My heart hammered; sweat poured off me. My stomach lurched and I threw up. I took a few moments to calm my breathing, then I wiped my mouth with the back of my unwounded hand. I didn't have anything that I could use to staunch the bleeding—which, thankfully, wasn't too serious.

I wasn't able to cast, so I couldn't just heal myself. I removed my jerkin, stripped off my shirt, and cut a sleeve off it, which I wrapped as tightly as I could around my hand. I stood there, panting, my chest heaving. It was, I was pleased to see, a muscular, broad chest, above a washboard stomach. Definitely an improvement on the rolls of flab that had hung over my belt before—not to mention my saggy moobs, with their little sprouts of graying hair.

I'd often wondered what it would be like to look as good as Daxx. Well, now I knew. It felt different but the same. I felt stronger and fitter and healthier—but none the wiser. I was still me inside. And I was still lost in the middle of nowhere.

I wiped my sword, first on the grass and then on the wolf's pelt. *Wolfskin*, I thought. *Waste not, want not.*

And then I thought, wolf *meat?* Well, what else did I have?

I got to work.

It was a grisly task, but it had to be done. My wolfskin would not have won any prizes in a woodcraft competition, but it turned out reasonably well. There were a few ragged edges here and there, but once I got the hang of peeling the skin from the carcass, it came away pretty easily. I made sure to be patient and not to rush it, being careful not to aggravate my injured hand. Eventually, there it was, bloody and limp and still warm. Heavy though. Well insulated. It would make a reasonable blanket—at least for a part of me. I had no idea how to tan it or dry it, which I didn't have time for, anyway. I needed to keep going.

Food, fire, shelter.

I mulled over my survival list—at least I had the first one of those covered. A leg would be enough. I cut one away, working the point of my sword through the thigh joint. It was long and well-muscled, and like the skin, pungent. It was going to be a pain to carry, but that was just tough. I only hoped it wouldn't taste too horrible and that I could work out how to make a fire so I wouldn't have to eat it raw.

I cleaned and sheathed my sword, wrapped the wolf haunch in the skin, tied it around my neck, and set off again towards my waypeak. The sun had passed its zenith, and I'd worked out that my destination lay pretty much due west. I hadn't heard the other two wolves in a long time, and their howls had been faint—just on the edge of sound, heading off towards what I judged to be the north. With luck, I wouldn't be running into them.

I'd survived my first taste of combat here, I thought, as I strode on west. I'd looted a wolfskin and harvested enough meat to feed myself for days. That could have worked out worse. Mind you, it hadn't been actual combat. My next opponent might not be below me, where I could drop on it. It might be human. Or inhuman. I tried not to think about that. Dropping out of a tree onto a wolf was one thing, actually facing off against someone armed? It might be a good idea to know how to use my weapon.

I stopped, unslung my shield, and slid it onto my left arm. I drew my sword, trying to think what a good stance would be: shield up and across, in front of me and below my eyes; sword beside it, pointing ahead, parallel to the ground, my right elbow level with my shoulder; weight mostly back on my right leg, my anchor, ready to shove me forward; left leg advanced, ready to skip me back.

I'd been a staff-wielding battlemage for so long that I could hardly remember anything about sword and board work. Elbow down by my hip, sword pointing … upward? Or raised high, aimed down in front of my shield? All seemed workable. And then what? Jab. Hack down from overhead? That would be easy for an opponent to see coming. A shield would stop that and then I'd be stretched forward, leaving a nice, wide-open armpit for whoever I was fighting to skewer me through. And then, goodbye sword arm.

Slash across lower at legs? Forehand and backhand? Thrust up? It all depended, I supposed, on what the other guy was doing. Whatever, it all felt awkward, as if I was posing for some invisible judges who were going to shake their heads and sigh and give me very low scores. Practice was clearly going to be necessary. Against what, though?

I looked around at the trees. Sparring with a tree was not going to teach me much, trees not being the most mobile of opposition. I could at least measure distance between myself and the target, however. That seemed somewhere to start.

Within less than a minute, I was squaring up against a birch tree, then skipping around it, peppering it with attacks which didn't actually land. I didn't want my sword to keep getting stuck, as I'd have to stop and lever it out, so I sheathed it and found a stick about the same length as my sword.

I had no reason to think that any skills I had learned before would come back to me. Mashing a keyboard is nothing like handling real weapons. But I'd experienced plenty of fighting styles, so I tried to remember what I could and see if I could bring them to life. As well as striking with the sword, I tried shield-play, using my shield arm both to deflect and block imagined blows and also to bash. *Strike with the iron rim*, I thought, *not just the front.* I saw that I could jab in at quite a number of angles with my shield which would both hurt and distract an opponent.

Yes. It's coming back to me now. I was soon getting into-it—twirling, starting and stopping, and stepping and bashing, whacking at invisible limbs, dealing deathblows and moving on to the next opponent (a larch tree). I fended off surprise attacks from behind and from either side, defeating the larch. Caught up in my imaginary battle, I whirled around back to my birch tree, so entranced that I didn't at first notice the arrow.

I'd shoved my shield up in front of me to ward off an imaginary slash aimed at my neck and drawn my sword arm over my shoulder for a downward strike. My strike froze when I saw the arrow, its head buried in the birch tree's trunk about a foot above my own, its shaft still quivering from the impact.

I must have stood there, panting from my exertions, for several seconds—presenting, I realized once I'd gathered my scrambled wits, a perfect target for whoever behind me had shot it there. I spun around, peering in panic in the direction the arrow must have come from. Nothing. I snapped my head left and right, up and down, around, and turned and turned about.

Nothing, anywhere—until—*thunk!*—the larch also had an arrow standing in it.

I froze again, looking everywhere and seeing no one; more panic and scuttling, shield up, sword out, heart thumping, sweat running down my back. Yet another *thunk!* and a new arrow was imbedded in the damn birch tree! I twirled as arrow number four *thunked* into the larch beside the other. And then another, and another, *thunk thunk*, half a second apart.

My mouth was dry with fear. It was obvious now: whoever had the bow was playing with me. He could've shot me any time he wanted. He hadn't. So ...

Might as well let him know I knew that.

I lowered my shield, dropped the stick I'd been using as a sword, and removed my helmet.

I heard laughter.

From two sources.

Someone said, "Well, he's no fighter, but he'll make a good fool, capering about like that."

"A natural," someone else agreed, in a darker, deeper voice. "Have them in fits, he will."

They both chuckled again.

"All right," the first, higher voice said, "what's your name, tree killer?"

I was about to reply, "Joss," when I realized: if I was here, maybe Grell and Qrysta were here too, somewhere, and maybe we'd hear about each other, which would be good—but the name Joss wouldn't mean anything to them.

"Daxx," I said.

A grunt. "You lost, Daxx?"

I was but didn't want to admit it. "No."

"Where you going, then?"

"That way," I pointed towards my waypeak.

The other, deeper voice snorted derisively. *"Pff!"*

"What," the first voice said, "all the way to them mountains?"

"Yes," I said, "so I'll be well away and not bothering you."

I wondered what they were thinking as I searched for them, making sure not to make any sudden movements. I saw no one, wherever I looked. It was unnerving that I couldn't see these people who thought 'I'd make a good fool.' What was that about?

Eventually, the first voice asked, "Why there?"

"I have friends there," I lied.

" 'Course you do." The deeper voice was scornful.

"Not from around here, are you, Daxx," the first voice stated.

It wasn't a question.

"What makes you say that?" I countered, thinking, *talking is better than being shot at. Keep this going, learn what you can, give away nothing.*

"Couple of things," the voice said, as if he had been considering the situation carefully. "One, people around here don't attack trees. If they did, we'd know they'd eaten the wrong kind of mushroom and we'd help them see the error of their ways. Carry 'em home, knock 'em cold, whatever it took. People around here respect the trees. We'd be foolish not to. You don't annoy the trees; they can take it amiss." The voice paused, implying a threat. "You don't want trees taking it amiss at you, Daxx. They could make things very nasty for you. Quite ruin your day."

"Or night," his companion added, in a tone that said, *night would be worse.*

Information gathered: *what the fuck? Trees ...?*

"Thing number two that gives it away you're not from hereabouts, Daxx, is: no one but a complete moron would willingly head into giant country only armed with a sword they'd use as a toothpick."

Information gathered: *giant country.*

They were waiting for my response.

I didn't have one. The game was up—*literally*, I thought. This was no game. It was all too real. Real wolves, real arrows. And I was at the mercy of—who? I needed to find out. There was no point in trying to bluff any more. Time to change tack, and see where that leads.

"Okay," I admitted, "I'm lost. I was going that way because I could see that mountain on the horizon, the twisted one. I just picked it at random. Had to aim somewhere."

"Eddyr's Fang," the higher voice said. "Not the best choice. Some giants are worse than others. They're all bad, but around Eddyr's they're particularly nasty. Cleverer than most, too. I don't think you'd have made it all the way, Daxx. Or come back."

"Well," I said, eventually, "thanks for the tip."

"No problem," the voice said. "So, let's see your warrant, then."

"My what?"

"Warrant, papers—orders from your boss, safe conduct signed by the reeve, whatever."

"Authority to be on our land," the deeper voice said.

"Without which you are a) trespassing, and b) an outlaw," the higher voice explained. "Show us that, you're free to go, with our apologies for the delay."

"Legit targets only, we know the rules," his companion added.

I checked my pockets. They were empty. "I, *er*, don't seem to have any papers."

"B it is, then. Which means you're coming with us." He spoke matter-of-factly as if I had no choice in the matter.

I didn't like the sound of that. I didn't like the confident, mocking tone. I didn't like not knowing who I was talking to, or why they'd been shooting arrows into trees around me. "Where to?"

"Eventually," he said, "Brigstowe."

"Where's that?"

I heard chuckles. "Yup, you're definitely not from around here. Brigstowe is the nearest town, to the south and west of here. Last town before the moorlands and uplands. And you don't want to go into them. They're full of all sorts o' things you don't want to be dealing with."

A town, I thought. *That could be better than this wilderness.*

"South and west, you say?" I said. "Yes, I might head there, when I've … done what I need to do. But I don't need company, thanks. I'm the lone wolf type."

"Yur, we noticed the wolfskin," the voice said. "They'll probably want it back."

That didn't sound good.

"So, if you want to avoid that wolf's pack coming after you, and you becoming the main course at his funeral feast—which will happen when they get a whiff of their dead relative—which direction *wouldn't* you go in?"

Jeez. How the hell should I know?

"That way," I pointed in the direction I'd come from. I'd killed the wolf back there, after all.

"Keep pointing," he said. "Now, turn around. That's it. Keep going. All the way."

I did as I was told. I stopped when I'd rotated a full circle.

"Correct," he said. "They're everywhere. I'm not saying it's crawling with the sods, but, one minute they're miles away, you haven't seen hide nor hair of them for days, and the next they're all around you and closing in. You know, Daxx, it strikes me your luck might run out if you stick around out here. One of these days, if you're to live that long, which I find doubtful, you might do something we don't do around here, which you have no idea about and which would get you killed. Or worse."

I took the bait. "Worse?"

"As in, 'What's worse than being killed?'" he asked, incredulous. "Blimey. D'you want a list?"

"I don't think I do, thanks all the same."

"No. Might not help you sleep at nights. Wise choice. All right then, Daxx. We'd best be going."

They emerged from the trees. I didn't really see any movement. One moment they weren't there, the next moment they were, standing in front of me about twenty paces away. Twenty of my paces, that is. Thirty of theirs. They were smaller than they had sounded. The tops of their heads reached no higher than the middle of my ribcage. They were wiry and *quick* looking in every sense. Alert, intelligent, fast. They had dark, hooded, penetrating eyes; copper-colored, weather-beaten faces; and long hair tied back over their pointed ears. One's hair was brown, the other's black above a bushy black beard. They had bows in their hands, quivers on their backs, and knives in their belts. They were dressed in skins and furs and leather, some of it studded. Their belts held waterskins and pouches, as well as their knives. They looked, more than anything, capable.

"Allow me to introduce ourselves," the one with brown hair said. His was the voice that had been doing most of the talking. "I'm Nyrik." He gestured to his companion. "This is Horm. And you're our prisoner."

"Oh, there's no need for that," I said. "I'm not your enemy, I have nothing against …" What were they, I wondered? I made my best guess. "… elves. I come in peace."

Their bows whipped up, arrows stretched, and Nyrik snorted, outraged. "Elves be fucked!" he shouted. "We're not fucking elves! Do we *look* like fucking elves?"

"Well," I said, "kinda. I mean, the elves where I come from."

"You have lucky fucking elves then; fuckers around here are *nothing* like us! Horrible little ugly bastards, eat you before you're even properly dead!" His eyes narrowed. "We're not the sort to take offence, are we, Horm?"

Horm was glaring at me, an arrow drawn tight to his cheek. "He'd better not call me a fucking elf again!" he challenged.

"No. He'd better not," Nyrik agreed. "Take my advice, Daxx: don't call anyone around here an elf, all right? They might not be so … forgiving, shall we say, of a foreigner's ignorance, as me and Horm here."

"No," I assured them, "I definitely won't. Thanks for the warning."

"Heed it," Nyrik said.

It was both an order and a threat.

"I will. I promise."

"Yeah, well," he said, and the two of them lowered their bows. They were still clearly nettled by my gaffe. "No, we're not elves, Daxx. And lucky for you we're not, we'd be eating you alive by now if we was.

"No, we're not elves," Nyrik repeated. "We're slavers."

31

3

Old Acquaintance

"We'll be taking that sword, then, Daxx," Nyrik continued, as Horm lifted his bow again.

I hesitated. What could I do? Fight? My shield might be able to cover my head and neck, and the top of my chest, but I couldn't outrun arrows. My balls were in their court, and there was nothing I could do about it.

I unhooked my scabbard from my belt and dropped it beside my sword.

"Very sensible," Nyrik said, coming forward to pick them up. "So, you being on our territory and not having a warrant makes you technically a trespasser, and not being able to explain yourself and having a cock-and-bull story about going to visit friends in giant country, we can only conclude that you're an outlaw. Wouldn't you agree, Horm?"

"I would."

"I'm not!" I said. "I've never broken a law in my life!"

"Well, if you can prove that you'll be free to go. Meanwhile, as our job is hunting outlaws and bringing them in for a life of involuntary servitude, and as outlaws always try to protest their innocence, you can hardly expect me to believe you. So, you hang onto that nice looking wolf leg, and we'll be on our way."

"Cook that up for supper tonight!" Horm sounded happy at the prospect.

"Partial to a bit of wolf, me and Horm are," Nyrik continued. "We'll have to bind your hands at night o' course, but there's no need for us to do that now, is there?"

"No, no," I agreed, "I won't try anything." My mind was racing.

Outlaw?

Slavers?

I needed to get out of this mess. I couldn't begin to think how.

Nyrik grunted, as if to say, *course you will*. "You'd be daft to," he said.

I got the message. Dead or alive? I'd take alive.

They retrieved their arrows from the tree trunks, each muttering something under his breath quietly to the tree. It sounded respectful, like an apology. Gently, they wiped the wounds that their arrows had made in the trunks with the roots of grass, muttered again, nodded a little bow at each tree, and stuck their arrows back in their quivers.

"All right," Nyrik said, "which way d'you think then, Daxx?"

"How should I know?"

"Guess."

I guessed and pointed north.

"Wrong again," Nyrik said. "You *are* lucky we happened across you. Giants one way, snow-trolls the other. *Tsk tsk*. You wouldn't have been long for this world, Daxx."

"I can see that," I agreed, trying to sound calm while feeling anything but. "What world is this, by the way?"

Nyrik frowned. "*The* world. Aren't any others that I'm aware of. You aware of other worlds, Horm?"

"Fuck off," Horm snorted as if he'd never heard such a stupid idea in his life.

"There's your answer," Nyrik said, shrugging. "Bloody daft question, though, if you ask me." He didn't seem interested in why I'd asked it. No comeback with: *what world are you from then, Daxx?* Which, frankly, would have been difficult to answer.

"Off we go, then," Nyrik said, slinging his bow across his back.

And off we went, Nyrik on my right, Horm on my left. Horm was the taciturn, silent type, but Nyrik was happy to chat.

"So, here's the way we see it, Daxx," Nyrik said. "You're our prisoner, but there's no need for us to be unpleasant about it. Nothing personal, you understand? We often get quite pally with our goods. Just as there's no need for you to be difficult and try to escape. You wouldn't succeed anyway."

"We're professionals," Horm added. "Good at our job."

"If you don't mind me saying so," I said, "it's not a very nice job."

"You can say that again!" Horm replied. "Some buggers put up a hell of a fight. Got scars all over me, I have."

"Knives, arrows, teeth, the lot," Nyrik added. "What's your line of work, then, Daxx? Bet it's more comfortable than ours."

"What makes you say that?"

"Look at you. Hands as soft as a girl's. Got all your own teeth."

"I'm an explorer," I said.

"Oh," Nyrik said. "That pay well, does it?"

"It can do."

"I don't see no purse on your belt."

"More's the pity," Horm said.

That purse would, of course, then have been theirs.

"I get paid when I get back," I said.

"Oh. Well, you won't be going back now, so … no payday. For you, anyway. You'll make a nice one for us, though."

"Is this all you do? Capture people and sell them?"

"Only outlaws. Can't touch legit travelers. They'd make a fuss, we'd be up before the reeve, they'd be all indignant, we'd be hit with compensation."

"Or jail," Horm interjected.

"Or jail. It's a skilled job, this, Daxx, knowing what's what and what isn't. And outlaws tend to stick together, more's the pity."

"They know what's good for them!" Horm muttered, darkly.

"We have to nab one when he's off guard and spirit him off before his mates find out he's missing and come after us."

"Doing the realm a service, we are," Horm said.

"And here's the funny thing." Nyrik grinned. "I bet you'll never guess when an outlaw's most likely to be off guard, eh, Daxx?"

"When?"

"When he's *on* guard. Doing guard duty, at night. We watch, and if the dozy bugger drops off, he's gagged and bound and off and away before he knows it."

They chuckled.

"We don't have slaving where I come from."

34

"Well, no reason for us to go there then, eh?" Nyrik decided. "Where is that, by the by?"

"A place called Pitcombe."

They halted abruptly and stared at me frowning.

"Eh?" Nyrik challenged. "A valley full of *pits*?"

They both seemed put out by the idea.

"No," I said. "It's on the River Pitt."

That seemed to reassure them.

"Oh," Nyrik said. "Makes sense. I mean, no one in their right mind would build a village near any *pits*." He shook his head at the thought.

"Pit-elves!" Horm said and spat.

We walked on.

"Yur," Nyrik said. "All elves is bad, Daxx, but pit-elves is the worst! Keep you alive as long as they can, if they capture you. Their idea being, the more you suffer, the better you taste. So"—he clapped me on the back, as high up as he could reach—"you're lucky it's us what captured you, eh? And not them little brutes."

Information gathered: *pit elves!* "It seems a dangerous place," I ventured. "What with them and wolves and giants and so on."

"And bears and sabercats and nightwalkers," Nyrik said. "Even been some eefrits up this way recently, which you usually don't get, 'specially this time of year. They don't like the rain. Undead, of course, but they tend to stick to their haunts. Weres, when the moon's full."

"Werewolves?" I asked.

Nyrik looked at me quizzically. "O' course were*wolves*, what other kind is there? We steer well clear. Though we sometimes leave bits and pieces for them, if we're flush."

"Bits and pieces?" I asked. "Of what?"

"Deer, boar, geese, that kind of thing. Weres love a bit of goose. They don't usually get it, not being able to jump that high and not having bows. They don't need 'em in the normal course of events. Those bastards can run anything down, and them claws …! *Whuup-whuup*, end of." He said this matter-of-factly, as if it was completely normal to live in a world where such creatures existed. "Leave them a goose or two, and they might leave you something nice in return."

"Such as?"

"Things they found. On people they killed and ate. This knife …"

He drew the dagger at his belt and held it up to me. It was a good, sharp blade fitted into a deer horn handle, with a brown jewel set into its hilt. "... off some dead merchant's dead bodyguard, this was. Wandering around up here at full moon—I mean! How dense can you be, eh? Bloody asking for it. Weres have a sharp eye for the shinies, I can tell you. They pick out the good stuff. So, we sit up a tree and wait to see if they leave anything for us, in return for the geese. Sometimes they do, and sometimes they just howl and bugger off with not so much as a thank you."

We walked until about an hour before sunset. I wasn't tired when we halted for the night. They complimented me on my fitness and size and muscles, and said—as if I'd be pleased to hear it—that they were sure I'd fetch a good price. I asked who from, and they looked at me blankly, and said how would they know. Nyrik shook his head at my stupid question and unlocked a tree with an actual wooden key on a keyring he'd taken out from a pouch on his belt. He fiddled with the keys, looking for the right one. "Wrong wood won't open the wrong tree," he said. "Alder, beech, ash—ah, there we are, elm." He inserted the key into the elm tree's trunk and it swung open. He stood aside for Horm and then gestured for me to follow him. I went in and down after Horm as Nyrik locked up behind us.

Steps led down into the earth. Light glowed in the walls, from little blue, phosphorescent blobs. "Mushrooms," Nyrik told me when I asked him. "The wrong kind. Don't eat those. You'll be off into the wide blue yonder, no idea what you were up to, singing to ogres, thinking you're an otter and plunging around in the river and annoying the hell out of it, wrestling trees, and that would be bad—any and all of it."

We spiraled down further and came to a wide chamber. It had a dirt floor, flattened and hard. Tree roots poked in here and there from the walls, suffused by blue mushroom light. Horm and Nyrik unslung their bows and quivers, then took off their boots and rubbed their feet. Nyrik gathered wood while Horm got out a tinderbox and flints. "Pass that haunch o' wolf over, then, Daxx," Nyrik said.

I handed it over. "Won't you set fire to the tree?"

"Nah," Nyrik said, "we know better than that. Old Elm won't feel a thing."

Horm got a fire going in no time, and Nyrik cut off three slices from the wolf haunch. We put a stick through each and held them to the fire. They were soon sizzling and dripping. *If wolf meat tasted as good as it smelled*, I thought, *it would be delicious*. And it was.

"I tell you what would go well with this nice bit of wolf, eh, Horm?" Nyrik said. "A nip of that Careful Juice of yours."

"Right you are, Nyrik!" Horm agreed. He fished around in his pouches. "The very thing. Wolf haunch and Careful Juice! What could be better?"

He found a small, leathern flask and pulled out its stopper.

He took a swig, not by any means a large one, exhaled, and smiled a smile that looked as if it could go on forever, then passed the flask on to Nyrik, who did likewise.

Nyrik held the flask out to me, but before I could take it, he said, "D'you have Careful Juice where you come from, Daxx?"

"Not that I know of ..."

He nodded. "Just a sip, then, to start with. It's called Careful Juice for a reason."

I sipped. The reason soon became blindingly obvious.

We laughed. We hooted. We sang and danced and ate and sipped Careful Juice, and told uproarious stories and wept tears of joy and delirium at them. We gorged ourselves on wolf, slumped back, and went our separate ways into dreamland.

My dreams had more than a touch of the weird about them. They took me to the moon and back, via everything that had never happened to me, but that I hoped with all my heart one day would. I woke up the next morning with someone untying the rope around my ankles, which had been secured without my knowledge sometime during the night. We got up and breakfasted on the hard tack and harder cheese they got out of their packs, our heads slowly clearing from the aftereffects of Horm's Careful Juice.

After which we loaded up and headed back up the stairs to continue the journey that would end with me being auctioned off to the highest bidder.

It was a lovely autumn morning when we emerged from our elm tree. A few puffy white clouds sailed before a brisk wind in the bright sky. Sunshine warmed our faces. Birds sang. The leaves overhead and grass underfoot rustled against the wide silence of the wilderness. We struck a path before midday and followed it to a track, onto which we turned south. The track became almost a road, which it fully was by the time we passed huts and then houses, barns, and stables. There were animals in fields: cattle, sheep, pigs, horses, poultry, all that you'd expect in farmland; even, at one crossroads, a duck pond.

There were one or two other travelers. We exchanged greetings in passing, but nobody seemed interested in anyone else's business. I was interested in them, though, studying them as they went by. They were ordinary looking humans, for the most part. A couple more of … whatever Nyrik and Horm were. They acknowledged each other but didn't stop to pass the time of day. There were some two-legged things that looked almost completely human, but not quite; and one that looked completely *not* human.

We saw it as it rose over a brow in the road. It came down the slope towards us, stepping with deliberate, birdlike strides. It was almost all leg. Two tall, spindly limbs stalked along carrying a short, bulbous trunk, which leaned forward so that its head thrust out lower than its shoulders. It walked like some gangling, gaunt waterfowl, lifting its long feet up, and stretching them forwards in huge, slow strides, where they landed with soft thumps. I couldn't see its face from afar as it was hooded in a deep cowl. Nyrik and Horm didn't greet this one. They moved onto the grassy verge while it stepped its eerie, unrelenting steps down the center of the road.

I joined them. We kept moving, Nyrik and Horm clearly intending to ignore that … creature. It was yet another reminder that this place didn't resemble any game I had ever played.

The world seemed to fall silent as the misshapen being neared, silent but for the sound of those large, taloned feet thumping the road in steady, ominous rhythm. Its long, black cloak billowed behind it, and I caught a glimpse of the face buried beneath its hood as it stalked past. I immediately wished that I hadn't. Its brow was humanlike, domed and large, but below it there was a long snout and lower jaw like that of a pikefish, or a boar, jutting and nasty. The thrust of that jaw said: *growl*. Its eyes were two cold chips of white, which glinted as they noticed me looking at it, and the look of burning ice it gave me turned my stomach to water. I failed to suppress a shudder. It seemed to rumble deep in its throat as it passed—a rumble of warning, I felt, aimed at me.

"What was that?" I asked when it was behind us.

"Eefrit," Nyrik muttered. "Told you they was up hereabouts. Bloody odd."

"S'not right," Horm muttered. "I don't like it. Gives me the creeps." He shuddered, and I could tell he meant it. If two hardy characters like these were unsettled, what else might there be in this world that could be even more alarming?

"*You* run after it and tell it," Nyrik said, still in a low voice. The thing obviously bothered them. I didn't know what an eefrit was, but I decided that I didn't want to, and didn't ask. I also didn't want to give away how completely alien I was to this world.

We walked on as we'd been walking all day and the day before, none of us tiring, none of us feeling much like talking any more. We'd found out about each other, and learned what we'd learned, and didn't have a whole lot more to say. As the sun slid down the sky towards the west, afternoon turning into evening, Nyrik pointed at a stone by the roadside. "Not long now."

I looked at the stone.

"Milestone," Nyrik added. "An hour, hour and a half at the most."

"To?" I asked.

"The Wheatsheaf," he said. "Best inn for leagues."

"*Only* inn for leagues," Horm said.

"Better than that flea-ridden boghole tomorrow," Nyrik said.

Horm grunted agreement.

An inn sounded good.

We reached The Wheatsheaf as the western sky began to redden. We weren't the only ones heading there. The inn stood beside a cross-roads in its own yard within its own high walls. *Fortified*, I thought. The farms and hovels hadn't been walled or protected in any way. I hadn't seen any signs of trouble all day. No doubt they, and the barns and byres, all locked up securely at night. Nyrik stopped to bind my wrists in front of me and then roped my legs so I could only take short paces. "Don't want you slipping out and off, now do we?" he said. He led the way across the yard past the stables, where grooms tended a couple of steaming horses. Nyrik and Horm were known there, and they exchanged waves and greetings with staff and guests alike; the staff were busy, the guests hungry.

We were just about to go inside when a voice called, "Hoy! Nyrik, Horm!"

Nyrik lit up on seeing the little man headed in our direction.

"Vagg!" he cried.

"Don't tell me it's fight night!" Horm said, excited.

Vagg was older than the others, I judged, and squarer, but no taller. He did not seem like a man of the woods, though—a man of the fields, perhaps, a farmer rather than a hunter. His clothes were work clothes, but well made, the only unusual thing about them being the pair of thick leather gauntlets he was wearing. He carried a bowl of something that looked like sludge and smelled like a swamp.

Vagg leaned closer and lowered his voice.

"Third bout," he said. "Empty your purses, lads. You'll thank me. And don't be put off by his looks." He tapped the side of his nose and added with a sly smile, "Against *nine*."

Nyrik and Horm were shocked.

Whose looks? I wondered. *Nine what?*

Vagg sauntered off towards one of the barns, saying, "Got to give him his fuel!"

"Nine …!" Horm muttered. "Bleeding hells."

Nyrik clearly agreed. "Yeah, but *Vagg* …"

"Probably be good odds," Horm suggested.

"Bloody well have to be, for *nine!*" Nyrik said as he led us inside.

The main parlor of The Wheatsheaf was a large, warm room full of tables and life and chatter and servers hurrying about. A log fire burned in a huge fireplace that took up most of one wall. Its hearth was so wide that people were sitting inside of it on benches set into the thick stone sidewalls that arched in over their heads to form the chimney. The man on the outer end of the far bench lowered his mug of ale, wiped his mouth on his sleeve, and grinned at us. "Well now, look who it isn't!"

"Mulden!" Nyrik cried. "Shove on over, me old mate, and find us a wench! We need ale."

A serving girl arrived at the man's beckon, a tray of foaming mugs in hand. "Hullo, Eva darling." Nyrik grinned. "What you up to these days, 'ey?"

"Mind yer own business." She chuckled, offering the tray around. "Supper, gents?"

"Yes please, love, and plenty of it," Nyrik said.

We took a mug each. Eva had a smile for all of us and glanced at the ropes around my wrists. Her eyebrows rose. "Aw, *shame* …!" She gave me another, more sympathetic smile before brushing past me. Mulden shifted down the bench, and Nyrik and Horm squeezed in on the end. There was no room for me.

"That all you've got?" he said, glancing at me.

40

"Just the one," Nyrik agreed.

Mulden grunted.

"Yeah, me too." He nodded at me. "Sit on over there by mine."

I turned and looked at the bench on the other side of the big fireplace.

It held only one occupant, but that occupant took up most of the bench. He looked up at me balefully, through small, piglike eyes, watery in his rough, brown-gray skin. Large, triangular ears, and teeth sticking up from his lower jaw like the tusks of a boar—long, thick and yellow—dominated his features. He had bristly hair, huge hulking shoulders, and a stomach like a gorilla's. He wore iron armor that had clearly seen better days: cuirass, rusty, and dented; iron leggings, ditto, tucked into knee-boots—or rather, knee-sandals, which were a bizarre combination of iron ribs and leather panels, hinged at the ankles. The enormous, scrub-haired feet inside them ended in black claws. His wrists and ankles were shackled.

I'd never seen him in such poor gear before, because Grell had been high level when I'd first met him, equipped with far better armor, but, with a surge of joy, I recognized the Orc wearing it at once. I took care not to show it. Grell, too, knew better than to react on seeing me.

I sat beside him, and turned my face to the fire that was crackling in the hearth between us and our captors, as if trying to ignore him. I touched his foot with mine, pressing it against his three times. His foot pressed back. *Thank all the gods. Grell!* He was off to be sold as a slave too, by the look of it, but at least we'd found each other.

"Slim pickings out there these days," Mulden commiserated with his fellow slavers.

"And eefrits," Nyrik agreed.

"Yeah. Creepy buggers," Mulden growled. "I wonder ..."

Nyrik shuddered. "Don't even think about it! Anyway, who'd buy a fucking eefrit?"

"No, I wasn't thinking that," Mulden said. "No market in eefrits, *gods!* I was wondering if the presence of eefrits up these parts this time of year might be affecting the presence of, how shall we put it, *suitable candidates* for our line of work?"

"Effing hells, Mulden!" Nyrik was shocked at the implication. "You think ...?"

"Rumor is," Mulden suggested.

"Them sods," Nyrik scowled. "Eating our bloody livestock! I've half a mind to fill the next one I see full of arrows."

"I wouldn't do that," Mulden warned. "It wouldn't appreciate it."

"It'd be dead," Nyrik said.

"That wouldn't stop an eefrit."

"No," Nyrik agreed, and took another long draught of ale. "What d'you think they're doing up here anyway, Mulds?"

"I try not to." Mulden took another swallow. His mug was empty, and he called for more. Eva came over with a jug and refilled it. She waited while Nyrik and Horm drained theirs and then held them out to her.

Good idea, I decided, and swallowed the rest of mine. It was rough and bitter and strong—and I'd needed it. I held out my mug, and Eva refilled it with another teasing smile. *Yeah, I know. Look at me. Pathetic, aren't I?*

She looked at Grell.

He felt her looking at him and stared back. She held up the jug.

Grell drained his ale then held out his mug to her. She glanced at me again with yet another little teasing smile then swished off.

"So, what's yours then, eh, Nyr?" Mulden asked.

"Foreigner." He looked over at Grell. "Nice Orc."

"Thank you. Unusual, can't make him out."

"Unusual in what way?"

"Not like your normal Orc."

"*Normal* Orc?" Nyrik said. "No such thing. They're all as loopy as the next one."

"*Standard* Orc, then. *Regular* Orc. Usually takes a long while to take down an Orc single handed. It was all over in seconds. Big warhammer on him—piece of junk, but you know Orcs and hammers. He was a complete plonker with it. Not worth shit, so I dumped it."

"Not normal indeed," Nyrik agreed. "Born wielding those things, they are."

"Had him on his arse and trussed without breaking a sweat. Don't tell anyone, all right? Don't want it affecting his price."

"Lips are sealed, Muldsie," Nyrik promised. "What's his tribe?"

"He, er, 'hasn't got one' ..." Mulden said, meaningfully.

"Oh dear. Best get him sold pronto, before his lot come looking for him."

"My thoughts exactly," Mulden agreed.

"He got a name?" Nyrik inquired.

"Wouldn't give it. Not even when I asked nicely. Looked puzzled when I asked what tribe. What kind of Orc don't have no tribe?" Mulden gestured my way. "What's yours called? Might as well introduce them, they'll be sleeping together tonight." He must've seen the confusion on my face. "Not like that," he told me. "Tied together. Just so's you're both there in the morning. He snores like fuck, and he don't half fart, but he's docile. Can't understand it." He shook his head. "Wimpy Orc. Eefrits. What's the world coming to, Nyr?"

"Fucked if I know."

"So," Mulden said, "got a name, has he?"

Nyrik answered, "Daxx. Funny bloody names, these foreigners." He took a long drink of his ale.

"What you betting, then, Mulds?" Horm asked. "Rats or dragons?"

Both Grell and I looked up in surprise.

Dragons!

"I usually go rat over five," Mulden said.

Nyrik lowered his voice. "Vagg's got one in. Third bout."

"*Does* he now?" Mulden's eyebrows shot up. "I'll be on him, then! Vagg knows his dragons. How many rats he up against?"

"Nine."

Mulden sat back, scowling in disbelief. "Nine? *No* chance! I never heard of a niner. Have you?"

"Never," Nyrik said. "Saw a sixer once. Nearly chewed to bits by the end of it, he was, but *nine* …" He trailed off.

They all shook their heads.

I caught Grell's eye. He had no clue what they were talking about either.

"Well, Vagg knows his dragons," Mulden repeated. "Although, I dunno, *nine* … "

My mug was empty again. "Can I get another?"

Nyrik shrugged. "It's your money."

I was perplexed. "I don't have any money."

"Well, *was* your money, should I say, before we liberated it. Sword, shield, helmet, wolfskin. Junk, apart from the skin, but they should cover our bed and board. He even took the rest of that nice big wolf leg for his famous mystery meat stew. You're treating us too, so, cheers mate!" Nyrik waved across the room at Eva.

"Who took it?" I asked, still none-the-wiser.

Nyrik nodded his head in the direction of the innkeeper; a bustling, garrulous man who looked both all geniality and all business. "Mine host, Jan the Brewer. Proud new owner of your gear." When he saw my expression, he added. "Well, it's not as if you'll be needing it where you're going."

Great, I berated myself. *All I arrive with is noob gear, and what's the first thing I do? I lose the lot. Pathetic.* I should have been working my way *up*, picking up better equipment, looting a much nastier weapon than that lowly shortsword, which I could then sell for a few coppers. Hell of a start I've made. I needed to do better than this.

"Like our ale, do you, stranger?" a voice asked.

I jumped, startled out of my thoughts. "What?"

Eva was smiling down at me, eyebrows raised.

"He's foreign," Nyrik told her, with a grin as teasing as hers.

"I said," Eva repeated, her voice lowering to a more intimate level as she leaned towards me, "like our ale, do you, *foreigner?*" A smile played on her lips—full, red lips, in that pretty, guileless, face. Her bosom heaved towards me, showing plenty of cleavage.

"It's very good ale," I managed. "Thank you." I held up my mug, and she poured me another.

"*Ooh,*" Eva cooed. "Lovely manners he's got!"

Nyrik chuckled. "Hands off our goods, Eva."

She frowned at him. "I haven't touched him." She glanced back at me, then added, with another smile, "*Yet.*"

I wanted to crawl under the bench, but it had no under.

"Oh gods!" Nyrik said, while Horm and Mulden grinned at me. "Bugger off and get us our food, darlin', all right? We don't want to miss the fights."

"I do believe our Eva likes you," Horm teased as she hurried off. "Lucky we're here to protect you, eh?"

"Bet you get girls throwing themselves at you all the time, eh, Daxx?" Nyrik grinned. "Nice-looking lad like you."

That hit me like a slap in the face. *Whoa—wait a minute. I don't look like Joss anymore. I look like Daxx. I'd built him to look good, hadn't I? Which would mean that I did now …*

It was quite the thought. *Time to adjust the attitude.* I didn't know how to do that. *What would Daxx do, talking to Eva?*

When Eva arrived with the food, I had formulated a plan. I wouldn't act, I would *re*-act. She handed me my trencher last. *Deliberately*, I thought. She smiled down at me. I smiled back. Her eyes held mine. I felt a warm glow in my stomach. "Thank you, Eva. I have to say, it all looks"—I looked from the food to her—"absolutely delicious."

Her smile broadened. "Well, mayhaps you'll find it tastes as good as it looks." She winked, brushed her hair back, turned, and swished away.

"Whoof!" Nyrik said, shaking his head. "Shame you're going to be sleeping in the stables chained to an Orc, Daxx, or you might have made our Eva's night."

4

A Night at the Wheatsheaf

The barn was crowded with all types, ranging from short ones like Nyrik, Horm, and Vagg to big ones like Mulden. None was as big as Grell. Mulden jabbed him in the ribs and said, "Oy, No-Name, clear us a path!"

Grell did as he was told. There were some protests as he shoved his way through, but those protests died when people saw who was doing the shoving. They parted before the alarming Orc, and we soon found ourselves ringside.

On our right was a mean-faced, hard-eyed man with a wicker basket. Squeaks and scratches were coming from inside it. To our left, a confident, smiling man was proudly showing the punters a cage, draped in black cloth. From beneath the cloth came hissing and rattling sounds, and puffs of steam.

I heard a tut of disapproval from Vagg beside me. "Tchah," he muttered. "Amateur."

The 'amateur' whipped off the cloth with a flourish, and the crowd *ooh'd* and *aah'd*.

Inside the cage was a dragon.

I've always loved dragons. I was awestruck to see one, right there, in front of me—even though it was only the size of a chicken. It was

46

covered in red and orange scales that glittered in the torchlight. It looked, as all dragons should, proud, its head slowly turning this way and that to glare disdainfully at one and all, as if to say: *I am the lord of all I survey. And you lot are peasants.* The effect was slightly spoiled by the fact that it had a wet cloth tied around its snout. The wet cloth was the source of the steam. It seemed disrespectful that they were going to make this regal creature fight rats.

Its trainer, wearing thick leather gloves like Vagg's, lifted it out of the cage, and held it up high for the crowd to admire. The dragon stretched its minute wings and sneered back. Chicken sized it might be, but even a chicken can flap itself a few feet off the ground. *There was no way that wings that small could lift a scaly creature like that into the air*, I thought. Its handler removed the wet, steaming cloth from his charge, which opened its mouth and roared. A sheet of flame blasted out of its jaws, setting light to several sacks on a nearby shelf. People rushed to beat out the fire, and I quickly changed my mind about the dragon, seeing it less as a regal creature and more as a highly dangerous pest.

Its handler lowered it into the makeshift ring that had been rigged up out of old doors and planks on the barn's floor, and tucked it into its corner slot, where it fidgeted and hissed and snorted smoke. It was clearly itching for a fight.

The ratter emptied his basket of rats into the other corner. They were long and lean and meaner looking even than their handler. They looked intelligent and vicious, but above all hungry. There were five of the brutes—but, surely, not even that many stood a chance against a flame-throwing dragon.

The noise of the crowd grew. Bets were being made left and right. The odds favored the rats. You could get six-to-five against the dragon.

"What d'you think of him, Vaggsie?" Nyrik asked.

Vagg grunted. "No chance."

Nyrik and Horm were surprised. They'd been as impressed as I had with the dragon's firepower.

Horm said, "Eh?"

"That's half his fuel gone, isn't it?" Vagg said. "On a pile o' sacks!"

"Oh." Nyrik hadn't considered that. He and Horm put their heads together, fished out some coin, and bet twelve silvers on the rats to win ten. Mulden backed them for eighteen.

"Ladies and gentlemen, here we go!" the ringmaster cried. "First bout of the night. In the rat corner, five hungry little buggers—and when I say little, I mean biggest rats you ever saw—and in the dragon corner, Fiery Fred! Let's hear it for our fighters!"

The crowd hollered and cheered and whistled. The ringmaster dropped his arm. The handlers removed the blocks from in front of their charges, and their charges charged. Fiery Fred wasn't much of a tactician. He was the up-and-at-'em type. He scuttled towards the rats, bellowing fire. The rats were too canny for that. They scattered, dodged, and lost some hair, at which the crowd cheered. The air was soon filled with the stink of singed rodent, but none of them was badly burnt. And Fiery Fred, sure enough, was soon out of breath.

The rats noticed and then it was their turn to charge. The dragon ran this way and that, desperate to avoid the vermin as they leapt on him, biting any part they could sink their teeth into. Fiery Fred's scales were some protection, but these rats had technique. They tore at his scales, wrenching them off one by one, while Fred ran in frantic circles, trying to shake them off.

"He'll never get his puff back, running like that," Nyrik said happily.

He didn't. Well, not enough to deal any real damage. He turned and let out a blast at the nearest rat, incinerating it. It was a short blast that ended in a feeble whiff of smoke. Then the other four rats were on him, rending and biting, while the crowd roared, and Nyrik and Horm hopped up and down with glee, yelling, "Go on, you ratties! Go on, my sons!"

I stared at the carnage, unable to tear my eyes away. Fiery Fred staggered under the weight of the rats tearing chunks out of him and toppled over. The crowd whooped, or groaned, depending on how their bets had gone. The rats were feeding on Fiery Fred before he was even dead.

"Your winner!" the ringmaster cried, pointing at the ratter as he threw a sack over his rats and their dragon dinner and scooped them up. The sounds of chewing and squeaking and scraping continued from inside the sack as he handed it to his apprentice, who carried it outside.

"Like I said, bloody amateur!" Vagg muttered. "Gives us handlers a bad name, putting up a half-trained show pony like that."

Nyrik and Horm came back with their profit, grinning. "How about that, Daxx, my boy!" Nyrik said, the silver coins shining in his palm.

48

Well, I thought, *he'd been a fine-looking beast, Fiery Fred, with a fine-sounding name—but he couldn't live up to it. Handsome is as handsome does—and all that Fred had done was end up as rat food.*

We got another 'no' recommendation from Vagg for the second bout as well—Raging Storm against four rats. Vagg flicked up two fingers briefly.

"Four or less, I go dragon," Mulden said.

Nyrik and Horm made a proposition bet: the dragon to kill exactly two rats.

Raging Storm duly obliged. He was even more colorful than Fiery Fred had been, though in a palette of greens rather than reds. Well, he was *before* he started the bout. By the time what was left of him was scooped up in his conquerors' dinner sack, he looked as if he'd been stomped on by a troll.

Mulden was annoyed. He'd lost all his winnings from the first bout and more.

Nyrik and Horm had turned their twelve silvers, and ten profit, into three gold—there being twenty silvers in a gold, as they explained. They were beside themselves with excitement, and nerves, because next up was the fight they'd been waiting for.

Vagg made his quiet way to the ringside, with a few polite " 'scuse please, folks." In his arms was not just the scruffiest dragon I'd ever seen, because at that point I'd only ever seen three in my life, but just about the scruffiest animal of any kind I'd ever seen. It looked more like a stray cat than Fiery Fred or Raging Storm. I immediately felt sorry for the poor little thing. I didn't want to see it having to fight for its life. I wanted to sit it on my lap and stroke its head.

The ratter, on seeing it, was furious.

"Nine o' my finest against that little squirt!" he mocked. "I'll give you all the four-to-one you can handle!"

Vagg didn't reply. He just scratched the little dragon's ears. I peered at it, wondering how something so unprepossessing could possibly survive against nine of the ferocious, cunning rats I'd seen demolishing the other two dragons. It looked around calmly with none of the arrogance of Fiery Fred. It noticed me and held my eyes.

Hullo, I thought. *That's a sharp one.* I kept my eyes on it, half expecting it to wink at me. It didn't.

Vagg had clearly been waiting for Nyrik and Horm to get their bets on. They put all three of their golds on to win twelve. They looked anxious as they rejoined us, passing Vagg, who nodded at them calmly. Then, loudly, he said to the ratter, "I'll stake ten to your forty, rat-arse, and you give the coin to Tom the Barner here to hold, 'cos I don't trust you shifty rat-fuckers one bit!"

The excited crowd grew still, the loud chattering falling almost to a murmur.

Ten gold!

Vagg held his hand out, and the ringmaster took his ten gold coins.

Vagg was obviously known in these parts. Known, and respected. Mulden was plainly not the only one who believed that *Vagg knows his dragons*. But the little fellow he was stroking was unimpressive looking, to say the least.

"You're on!" the ratter shouted, handing his purse to the ringmaster.

At that moment, I caught Grell's eye. We both knew what the other was thinking: *Any chance of sneaking out of here while they're all busy watching the fight?*

I didn't think so. *Sneak out how? Go where? Do what?*

I shook my head. He nodded. We knew that we needed to talk. There was no easy answer. We had to play this long.

The buzz of conversation restarted. I got the sense that, had the dragon belonged to anyone but Vagg, the odds against it would have been much longer. Ratty stopped offering four-to-one, as he had all his gold committed. Others stepped up, and threes became seven-to-two, became fours again, as it seemed that there were few believers in one dragon against *nine* rats, not even one of Vagg's.

Nine mean-looking, hungry black rats were loaded into their corner. Rolling Thunder—for that was the little dragon's name—was set down in his corner by Vagg, who leaned in and whispered something in its ear. I could almost swear the creature nodded.

The crowd jostled for position to watch the action as the ringmaster said, "Ready, set—go!" Vagg and the ratter lifted the planks that kept their beasts in their corners. The rats poured out and took positions left and right and center, facing the harmless-looking dragon.

Rolling Thunder strolled a couple of slow paces and watched them.

The rats scuttled this way and that, anxious, tense, hungry.

Rolling Thunder, watching them, took a pace to one side or the other in response, rarely more. The rats didn't know what to make of him. They knew he'd be firing at them sooner or later, so they didn't want to risk being hit. They needed to wait till he was out of breath. Then they'd be all over him and feasting. All nine of them.

The rats knew they had the advantage of numbers. They also sensed that their opponent wasn't bothered by his disadvantage in the least. And that felt … wrong. He should have been scared, he should have been angry, he should have been … anything but hardly moving, calmly watching.

The rats jostled. They squeaked. Their noses and whiskers twitched. They were famished. They could smell that nice feast of fresh dragon meat in front of them, just waiting for them to tear into. There were nine of them—there was one of him. With not a lot of meat on him, nowhere near enough for all nine to get a decent meal.

You could see two of them suddenly think, *the hell with it, I'm not going to miss my dinner, what are we waiting for?* They dashed off to one side, and leapt, one at Rolling Thunder's head and one at his back. The little dragon was one step ahead of them, even I could see that. By hardly moving, he had cut them out of the pack like a sheepdog. He opened his mouth wide and hit them with what I can only describe as a disdainful burp. Their charred corpses landed at his feet, smoking.

The crowd reared back, a "Whoa!" in every throat, either out of joy or shock. Rolling Thunder ignored the other rats while he ate the two that he'd just barbecued. Then he turned and began to hunt. It was a masterclass. They knew he was coming for them, and gradually they saw that there was nothing they could do about it. His slow stalking was interrupted by bursts of speed as he worked his opponents to his will.

I could tell that it was not a mistake when one slipped behind him and jumped on his back. It began tearing at the little dragon's scales, desperate to get to his flesh where he was vulnerable. Rolling Thunder lived up to the first part of his name. He rolled. The rat on his back was skewered under his needle-sharp spines. Its teeth lost their grip. The dragon squirmed on its back and kicked like a horse in a field, this way and that, flattening the rat into a wide, bloody mess. The dragon rolled to his feet, twisted his head around, and ripped the impaled rat from his back. He chewed and swallowed, shaking his victim's blood from his minuscule wings. The other six rats were worried now. They ran every which way in desperation.

"Three down, six to go. Who wants five-to-one against the rats?" Vagg shouted.

He got no takers.

Rolling Thunder tracked every movement the rats made, calculating his next action. It came when their paths all crossed. He herded the rats into a corner. Realizing they were trapped, the rodents charged, and leapt in the same coordinated death-leap that had seen the ends of Fiery Fred and Raging Storm.

Rolling Thunder hosed a long, slow arc of fire at them, turning his head to hit them all, one after another, in a flamethrower breath that lasted long after they were all alight. The rats dropped, sizzling.

The victorious dragon waddled over to them and sniffed their charred corpses as the crowd went wild. He turned away disdainfully. He'd eaten enough rat for one night. He backed up and dumped a pellet of dragon poop on them, then shuffled back to his corner where a smiling Vagg scooped him up in his arms.

Nyrik and Horm were actually dancing for joy. "How about these, eh, Daxx?" Nyrik yodeled, brandishing his winnings. "Twelve silvers turned into twelve *gold!*"

"Nice!" I said. "That little thing's going to be terrifying when it's fully grown."

"Eh?" Nyrik stopped cavorting and frowned at me. "It *is* full-grown."

"Twenty-eight years old, he is," Vagg said, scratching Rolling Thunder's neck fondly. "Never met a rat he couldn't handle."

"Why?" Nyrik asked, curious. "How big are dragons where you come from, Daxx?"

"They can be the size of this barn."

Nyrik stared at me. "You're pulling my plonker," he said, not believing a word of it.

"I'm not. One could take this barn out in a single breath, from a hundred yards up in the air."

Horm said, "Eh? *Flying?* On them tiny wings?"

"Huge, leathery ones," I corrected.

"Whooh. *That* I'd like to see! Actually ..." He reconsidered. "No, on second thoughts, I wouldn't."

Well after midnight we all bedded down in the stables, Grell and me at one end, furthest from the door, chained together, hand and foot.

Nyrik and Horm and their colleague Mulden were not amateurs; there was no chance of us escaping.

We had our very own pile of straw to ourselves. Our captors had pallets and sacks which they filled with clean straw and arranged as nests of mattresses. They seemed used to the accommodation. The Wheatsheaf was often full, it being the only inn within a day's walk.

There had been other inns in the region, once upon a time, Nyrik had told me, but they had made the mistake of not having walls. "The which," he'd added, "in these troubled times, you need to have."

When we crossed the yard from the barn to the stables, we'd seen that the big double gates were closed and bolted. The left-hand gate had a porter's cubby stuck to its back, perched beside a little postern door, through which the porter would admit anyone who arrived after dark—unless he didn't like the look of them. Few people ever arrived after dark. Especially not these days, what with the eefrits.

What were they *doing* here, everyone was asking. No one had a clue. The assumption was that whatever it was, it wouldn't be good.

Guesses were made as to the eefrit's current numbers. At least eight, it was calculated. That had brought about a thoughtful silence. *Eight* eefrits? At this time of year. Someone else added that they usually went as mysteriously as they came—here today, gone tomorrow. Mulden had muttered, "Roll on tomorrow."

Grell and I knew that we could talk when the others were asleep. Meanwhile, I had his ferocious breath to contend with. And his farts. And the reek of his feet in his iron sandals. Whichever way I twisted, or turned, the result was worse. *Terrific*, I thought, as I wriggled and shifted into the least-worst position I could find. Feet, farts, or halitosis. Oh, the luxury of choice.

It had been a long day. We must have covered well over thirty miles. Fit and strong though I now was, I was glad to get horizontal.

I'd meant to stay awake until our captors were asleep, but I dozed off.

I was woken by a nudge, and a gruff voice in my ear whispering, "Daxxie …" It was accompanied by harsh, sour breath.

I recoiled, blinked awake.

"They're asleep," Grell said.

We listened and heard snoring.

"Mate," he continued, "is it good to see you!"

"Yeah," I agreed. "Wow. I'll say!"

"What the hell's going on?" Grell said.

"I've no idea."

"None? You're the puzzle guy, Daxxie!"

"I've been racking my brains, Grello, believe me. All I know is, I don't recognize this place. Do you?"

"No. I don't even recognize *me*. I'm an Orc? For real? The only damn thing I recognize is you. And don't tell me that's who you are in real life."

"I think you mean *were*."

"Huh?"

"*In real life* is a long way behind us, mate. This is who we are now. And where we are."

"Jeez. I mean—how the fuck?"

"How should I know? All I know is we need to figure this out."

"No shit," Grell agreed. He paused. "You think Qrysta's here?"

"God, I hope so."

He grunted agreement. We both knew how much we could do with her help. The three of us stood far more chance together than alone.

Then I thought—*alone?*

Grell and I had each other. Qrysta didn't.

"And if she is, I hope she's okay," I added.

"Can hardly be in worse shape than us," Grell said, trying to reassure me, but we both knew that that was not true. We were chained together, and captives, on our way to be sold as slaves, but we were safe and under shelter. Who knew where Qrysta was and what might be happening to her?

There was nothing we could do about it when we couldn't do anything about our own situation.

Best not to think about it. I said, "What's it like? Being an Orc?"

Grell grunted. "I dunno. I don't feel like one. Although … I know I'm as strong as an ox. And a lot uglier." He sighed. "Which means that if everything functions the way it seems to, all I'll be able to fuck is Orc chicks. *Not* my first choice!"

"There could be miscegenation," I said.

"Miss-*whutt?*"

"Inter-species intercourse."

Grell grunted at that. "Oh. Well. That would be nice! I'll have to work on my smoothies." He dropped his voice, channeled his inner lothario, and whispered, seductively, "*Hello there*, young elf-maiden! Ever pork an Orc?"

"*Not* elf," I said, and told him what Nyrik and Horm had told me about pit-elves.

"Jesus!" Grell muttered. "*Eat* you, alive? Elves are meant to be lovely and wise and wonderful." He blew out a *pff* sound of bafflement, followed by a lot more foul breath. I tried not to gag, or even breathe. Before I could ask him not to do that again, he continued, disbelieving, "This place is full of surprises."

"You can say that again. But ... not in my direction, okay? Your breath is kind of strong."

"Is it? Sorry," Grell whispered, turning his head to point it away from me. "I floss every morning and night, in real life. Pride myself on my hygiene, I do."

"I think you mean *did*."

"Eh?"

"This is where we are now. And *who* we are. Although ... I don't feel like the way Daxx looks, not inside."

"Yeah, I know what you mean," Grell said. "Orcs are meant to be ferocious. Tough as nails, fight till they drop, but me—I don't have a clue. Mulden had me flat on my back in no time. I mean, what's the point of looking like this if you're a complete wuss?"

"At least you had a hammer," I said. "I didn't get a staff, and Daxx is a mage, right? Just a crappy sword and shield that were then sold out from under me. What's that about?"

Grell said, "Could be there's no magic here. I mean—why should there be? This place is real, right? There was no magic in real life."

"Yeah," I had to agree.

"Pity," Grell said. "We could use your skills right now. Immobilize our captors, frisk them for the key to these chains, and we're off."

"We'll have to think of something else," I said.

"Yeah, but what? I kept telling myself, no, this can't be happening, but it was, right from the kickoff. I mean ... fuck me sideways."

I couldn't help smiling. "Roll over and I'll see what I can do."

Grell snorted, stifling his laugh as best he could.

We froze, listening.

No one woke up and came over to check up on us.

We relaxed, and I said, "I've been thinking, too. I have a theory. You're probably not going to like it."

"Try me."

"Well, we won, right? The Championship. We proved ourselves to be the best. What if somebody wants to see how we do *here*?"

"What? That's insane! Who? Why?"

"Add *how* and *where* to those questions, and—I have no idea, Grello. But as Sherlock Holmes said, *Once you eliminate the impossible, whatever remains, however improbable, must be the truth.*"

Grell protested, "This is *all* impossible!"

"As far as we *knew*. If you'd said, when we won, that this is where we'd be now, we'd have said *that's impossible*. Now we know different."

"But—how …?"

"See above: no idea," I said. "But don't you want to find out?"

"Sure. I'll wring his fucking neck!"

"Suppose he—or she, or it—doesn't have a neck."

"Eh? The fuck are you on about?"

"Well, have you even heard the faintest rumor that *human* tech could do something like this? To us? Whip us away, and dump us here? With man-eating elves, and whatever my two captors are, and eefrits, and giants, and tiny flightless dragons?"

"Nope," Grell agreed.

"So, let's keep an open mind," I suggested, "and let's assume that whoever did this, did it for a *reason*."

"Such as?"

"Stop asking me questions, Grello—I don't have answers any more than you do. But I do have a plan."

"You do? What is it?"

"*To find out.* Who. Why. Everything."

"How we going to do that?"

"By staying alive. And, if she's here too, by finding Qrysta."

Grell grunted. "That's your plan?" He didn't sound impressed. "Keep an eye out for Qrysta and stay alive?"

"Yes. We look and listen and learn. We need information, Grell. Resources. Skills. Stay alive and keep our wits about us. They're all we have."

"Whoever put us here aren't making it easy for us, are they?" Grell muttered.

"That's for sure."

▲　▲　▲

We were all up before dawn, joining the small group of travelers waiting in the yard for the gates to open. We ate some hunks of bread and cheese and drank a mug of small beer each. The landlord came out and haggled with Nyrik over 'my' tab. Nyrik bartered cheerfully, the landlord sharply. He handed Nyrik a few small coins for my belongings, which he pouched with a, "Thank you, Jan, and my best to Mrs. Brewer!" And then to me, "And thank you, Daxx, for a delicious evening, as I think you'll agree."

Yeah, right, I thought. *Great, now all I have are the clothes I'm standing up in.*

"And as long as you're not going to bring forth a baby half-Orc in nine months," Nyrik continued, "a thoroughly satisfactory night all round. Fleas?"

"A few," I replied.

"Well, won't be long now before we'll have you all scrubbed down with that lovely yellow hair tied up in a nice bow. All right, then. Let's be on our way."

We hefted our packs and parcels. Grell and I had been weighted down like beasts of burden, but our loads were well arranged and not too heavy, and at least we now had a waterskin each. My cargo consisted mainly of sealed pots.

"Honey," Nyrik said, when I asked what they contained. "Jan Brewer is the warden of the local beekeepers. Best honey anywhere, from the orchards up here. We'll sell it for more than double in town than he could here. Easy money."

"Easy for you," I said. "I've got to carry it."

"It'll keep you fit. Anyway, you're a big strong chap, you won't hardly notice it … . Oh, 'ullo, darlings!" He grinned as two girls of about six ran up to him and hugged him, squealing. Twins. Chestnut hair, green eyes, matching white-and-yellow smocks.

"Do a trick, do a trick!" they chorused, jumping up and down and giggling.

"A trick?" Nyrik protested. "Now where would I get a trick from at this time o' day?"

"My ear!"

"My hair!"

"Your bag!" they demanded in concert, their eyes shining with glee.

Nyrik shook his head, arms folded, and frowned down at them in mock seriousness. This was, plainly, a game they always played. "Hair … ear …" Nyrik mused and then his arms unfolded in a blur and passed over two mops of chestnut hair, over the top of one girl and to the side of the other, stopping in front of each glowing, huge-eyed face. In one hand there was a piece of shiny red glass shaped like a jewel, and in the other a small lace kerchief.

The girls stared at them, then laughed and clapped and bounced. Each took the gift that had appeared from her ear or hair. They looked at their prizes, and at each other, and then back at Nyrik.

"What do we say?" Nyrik prompted.

"Your bag, your bag!" they chorused.

"Not 'thank you,' like well-brought-up young ladies?" Nyrik protested. Then he sighed and shifted and wriggled and pulled faces of reluctance as if he *really* didn't want to do what they'd demanded, which made the little girls giggle and cringe, hands over their mouths, while Nyrik cringed painfully opposite them. The more Nyrik squirmed and hesitated, the more they stifled their snorts. Their eyes looked as if they were about to pop out of their heads. Eventually, after a pantomime that went all the way from confusion to agony and back again, Nyrik made up his mind—*obviously* against his better judgement—and pulled his leather shoulderbag around in front of him. He froze. The girls froze. He shook his head as if sadly disappointed.

The twins couldn't hold back any longer. "What is it, what is it?" they asked.

By this time, they weren't the only ones spellbound in suspense.

"Ur," Nyrik said, "you're not going to like this."

Their faces fell. They held their breath.

So did I, and everyone else watching.

"Awww," Nyrik gave a rueful smile as he brought a puppy out from his bag. "Sorry, darlings, it's the wrong color—you wanted a yellow one."

It was a black-and-white sheepdog puppy, barely more than a week old, its eyes newly opened. Around its neck was tied a sky-blue ribbon with a little bow.

Their mouths were open. Their eyes enormous.

They took it and stroked it.

"He's got a yellow name, though," Nyrik said as he handed it to them. "Sunny. And he'll be the best herder aroundabouts, if you two do your job properly, and train him right. Get your Uncle Alrick to show you how—he knows his dogs."

The little girls were cooing and stroking, but were too overawed for words. Finally, one of them whispered, "Is he really for us?"

"Really," Nyrik said. "What's more, he'll look after you when you're bigger. You two pretties might need a friend with a nice deep growl and nice sharp teeth. Tell your mom I said so, all right?"

"We will, we will!" they chorused.

"Be another of you when I come back, eh?" he said.

"Better not be another boy!" one said.

"Now then, young Mandy. You'll love it whether it's a him or a her, all right?"

"Boys are stupid!" the other one said.

"You won't always think that, young Mindy," Nyrik smiled, tousling her hair. "Now get along with you. Wi' that ribbon on him you'll know which one he is. Go pop him back with his mom before she misses him. It's feeding time, you don't want him to get left out and not grow big and strong, now do you? You'll like watching 'em all suckling, him and his brothers and sisters."

They looked puzzled.

"Tom the Barner," Nyrik explained. "Their mom's in his hayloft. Tell Tom thankee from me, and if I need another pup, I'll let him know."

"We will!" they said in unison.

They turned and ran off, then stopped as if thinking the same thing at the same time. They looked at each other, turned back to Nyrik, curtsied, and said, again in unison, "Thank you, Mr. Nyrik."

"My pleasure, young ladies," he replied, with a courtly little bow, and smiled after them as they ran off.

"Known them since they was babes," Nyrik said to me. "Those two will be heartbreakers in a few more years." He straightened up, all business again. "Right, then, let's be off."

We headed out with the other travelers, most of whom, perhaps a dozen, were also going our way. Another two or three peeled off and headed in the direction we'd come from. North, up into the wilds.

I fell in beside Nyrik. Horm was on the other side of him, Mulden behind him, and Grell trudged along in the rear, laden with everything he could carry.

"Going to be a good haul," Nyrik said, "with that sodding great Orc carrying more than the rest of us combined."

Jan the Brewer and he would split the profits, he told me. Jan put up the money for the trade goods, which were produce gathered from the local farms. Nyrik and Horm—and on this occasion, also Mulden—were the sweat equity. As well as honey, we were carrying cheeses, pickles, and jars full of autumn fruits in the local firewater. Distilled from those same fruits, Nyrik told me.

"Where'd you get that puppy?" I asked.

"Last time I was through here, Tom Barner told me his bitch was due, and he thought Jan's girls would like a pup. He wanted something from the wild, and I said I'd get it for him. He was happy to keep it quiet when she whelped, so we could have our little bit of fun." He barely drew in a breath. "I got a length o' ribbon off Eva, the lass who was pouring your ale and making eyes at you. If you hadn't been chained to an Orc all night, you might have had a surprise visitor. Very welcome one she'd've been, too, I have no doubt. Oh well. I expect she'll have better luck next time. Well," he reconsidered, "there prob'ly won't be a next time in *your* case."

A thought struck me. "Are there other magicians here? I mean ... *real* magicians?"

Nyrik stopped and frowned at me.

The others halted to listen.

"Are you calling me a fraud?" he demanded.

"No, no. What you did was ... excellent. Great sleight of hand. I meant, like—*real* magic. Not tricks."

Nyrik studied me. His face was neutral. "Such as?"

"Spells. Enchantments." He was looking at me thoughtfully, but I was getting nothing back from him. I ploughed on. "Magic staffs, that can blast you to pieces. Rings of protection, binding, strength. Amulets of power." Nyrik was still giving away nothing, his body still, his dark eyes boring into mine. I thought, *well, screw it, might as well go the whole hog.* "You know, proper battlemages and warlocks and wizards and witches and sorcerers and necromancers. Masters of the arcane arts, who can shoot fireballs from their fingertips and fly on broomsticks or winged steeds or carpets, and bind the dead to their will."

Nyrik continued to stare. He shook his head abruptly and said, "You want to lay off the ale, Daxx."

We set off again, falling in step as before.

Mulden said, "Up at Aylsmoor there's that necr—"

Nyrik cut him off with a curt "Shh!"

Mulden *shh'd.*

Then Horm said, "And Old Marnie, she's a w—"

"I said shush!" Nyrik barked, in a voice that meant *this stops now.*

He glanced at me. Studied me for a moment. Then walked on, head down, brooding.

5

Old Marnie

Nyrik and Horm were arguing in low voices, some way away from us. We'd stopped for lunch, and once again I was securely roped to Grell. They obviously didn't want us to hear what they were talking about. Mulden was with them, listening—not taking sides, it appeared, but having the odd observation to add to the discussion. Horm seemed to be protesting, and Nyrik seemed to be urging. The argument absorbed their attention, and when all three of them were deep in dispute and looking away from us, I saw my chance.

I whispered, urgently, "Grell, you should tell him your name."

"Why?" Grell whispered back.

"If Qrysta is here too, maybe she'll hear it. Or mine. She hears our names, she might help. If she can."

I was watching our captors throughout, and when Nyrik glanced over to check on us, I was head down and brooding.

Nyrik turned back to his discussion, and Grell grunted, "Okay."

The argument broke up shortly. The three of them stood up, untied us, and Grell and I shouldered our loads once more.

"Change of plan," Nyrik said.

"Hope it's a good one," Mulden said, not sounding too sure it was going to be. Horm just looked glummer than he usually did, which was a lot of glum.

"See you at the show, Muldsie," Nyrik said. "Gold piece says mine gets more than yours."

"No chance," Mulden said. "Rarity value? When did you last see an Orc sold?"

"Cowardly Orc? Never," Nyrik taunted.

"You said you weren't going to tell!" Mulden accused, alarmed.

"Keep your hair on, Mul." Nyrik chuckled. "Slaver's honor!"

Mulden spat on his hand, Nyrik did the same. They grinned, shook hands, clapped each other on the back, and leaned back, looking at each other.

Mulden said, "You have yourself a bet, Nyr. It'll be all I can eat and drink at The Wolf's Head after the auction!"

"Yeah, on you." Nyrik agreed. "All right"—he hefted his bundles— "off we go, then. Not so far as they're going today, but that just means further for us tomorrow."

Before we could go our separate ways, Grell announced, "My name's Grell."

We all looked at him, the others registering surprise.

"Where you from then, Grell?" Mulden asked.

Eventually, he said, "Oz."

Mulden looked blank. "Ring any bells?" he asked Horm and Nyrik.

Horm shook his head, and Nyrik said, "Nope."

"You?" he asked me. "Anywhere near your pit?"

"No," I answered, truthfully.

Mulden regarded Grell again.

"Oz, eh? Land of the cowardly Orcs."

Grell's small, piggy eyes narrowed. "I'm not a coward, mate," he said quietly. And he didn't sound it. He sounded … menacing.

"No?" Mulden considered. "So how come you didn't put up a fight?"

Grell stared at him—hard. Chained and manacled though he was, his stare was unnerving. "I'm a pacifist."

All three of their faces screwed up in confusion.

"A 'pacifist Orc'!" Nyrik squawked. He had plainly never heard such an absurd idea.

"Yeah, you little pointy-eared fuck!" Grell snarled. "Doesn't mean I can't crush you like a bug if you piss me off, so what's it to you?"

Nyrik took a step backwards, even though Grell hadn't moved. "Nothing, matey, no offence meant."

Grell grunted. "None taken," he allowed, his eyes drilling hard into Nyrik's.

We all looked at the Orc to see what was coming next. Nothing did.

Eventually, Mulden asked, "Want to say anything else, Grell?"

Grell shook his head.

"Right. Well, let's be going," Mulden said, then added, "See you in Brig, lads!"

"Bye, Muldsie," Nyrik said.

Mulden set off, Grell lumbering after him. We'd be meeting again at the auction, I knew, but I hated to see him go. Without him, I felt even more lost than I had before.

"Blimey," Nyrik said as we watched them go. "Strange days, eh?"

I thought, *you don't know the twentieth of it.*

Nyrik set off at right angles to the direction that Mulden and Grell had taken. Horm and I fell in beside him. There was no path, just rolling, grassy moorland dotted with trees.

"Where are we going?" I asked.

"See an old friend of ours," Nyrik replied.

Horm said, darkly, "*Very* old."

The change of plan, whatever it involved, freed Nyrik from the thoughts he'd been turning over in his head, and he became his usual chatty self again. As we walked, he regaled us with stories and gossip, going back over the years, things that even Horm hadn't heard. A kaleidoscope—no, a torrent—of images filled my mind. Things that were upside-down, or perfectly logical, or completely out of the question, fought for supremacy in my struggling brain.

Either this guy is a lunatic, I thought, *or he's stating a lot of facts that I am having a hard time even* thinking *might be facts, let alone believing them. He's just blowing smoke, surely?* Yet I knew, even though the old part of me hoped that he was telling tall tales, that he wasn't.

The new part of me was beginning to realize that *different* was the way that it was around here, despite everything sounding insane or nuts. Until I had evidence to the contrary, I had to assume that what I was being told was *sensible* or *logical*. Only—not in any way the old me understood the meanings of those words.

I felt myself going around in circles, chasing my own tail. It *hurt* to think.

So, I told myself, *stop thinking. Give yourself a break, ease up on the hurt. This is it. Accept it and get with the program. You won't get anywhere floundering around in denial.*

What's always the first step? *Admitting that there's a problem.*

My name is Joss, and I'm an—

—other person. My name is Daxx, and I'm a captive.

There you go, I told myself. *Problem identified. Now all you need to do is solve it.*

And the old part of myself sneered back, *Good luck with that.*

I was getting fed up with the old part of myself. *Yeah, yeah, stop whining,* I told it. *A gazillion steps to go, no doubt, but we've just taken the first one: Deal. With. The. Problems.*

Old Me didn't respond.

Good. Now. Be prepared that there may not be any easy answers. And hang in there.

Solve the problems or die trying.

Nyrik was happy to educate the ignorant foreigner about the ways of this world, and all that was in it. I didn't push him when he evaded a subject that he didn't want to talk about. There were plenty of others he'd expand upon. Even Horm chipped in from time to time and added color or disagreed, or threw in some odd point that Nyrik didn't know about. When Nyrik challenged him or asked how he knew that, Horm would say, "I have my sources." It was a stock response, clearly, that Nyrik was used to, and he didn't push further. Eventually, when Horm used it to end an argument about the forging of weapons, on which he clearly considered himself more of an expert than Nyrik, I asked, "What sources?"

They looked at me sharply. And then at each other.

Nyrik said, "Horm's mom's a nibler."

"Nib*lun*," Horm corrected, sounding nettled.

"Whatever. Niblers to the rest of us. Odd bunch. Some of the most beautiful women you'll never see your life. 'Cos they never come Upground. Stay down with their men, who are as ugly as fuck. Good smiths, though. The best. Them's the ones you hear tap-tap-tapping away underground on their anvils."

"You ain't never seen jewelry like my mom makes," Horm said. "Rings, amulets, necklaces. Diadems. Can take anything you want to Imbue into them, my mom's stuff can."

"Imbue?" I asked.

"That's enough of that," Nyrik snapped. And, to Horm, "I told you, *shh!* Shut it, all right?"

"*You* shut it!" Horm snapped.

Nyrik was surprised. "You wot?"

"You called my mom a nibler!" Horm shot back. "That's rude, that is! Disrespectful."

"Well, they call us lot woodies!"

"That's different!" Horm barked. He was really getting worked up.

Nyrik stopped. We all stopped. Horm was glaring at him, clearly annoyed.

"Different how?" Nyrik enquired, sharply.

"You're not my mom!" Horm shouted.

Nyrik, I could see, was also riled. They glared at each other for a few long moments. Then Nyrik took a deep breath, exhaled, and agreed. "You're right. I'm not your mom."

Horm was still glaring at him, but only because he was still steaming. Both, I could see, wanted their spat to be over, but both also felt they couldn't back down right away.

"I apologize for calling your mom a nibler, Horm," Nyrik said, at last. "That was disrespectful of me. Hurtful." Nyrik turned to me. "It's a term nibluns don't like, Daxx, just like we don't like *woody*. I can quite understand my old mate Horm pointing out to me the error of my ways. And I appreciate him doing it. A valuable and timely lesson in minding my manners. Horm's mother," he continued, "is a niblun lady of consummate talent. The work*woman*ship in her jewelry has to be seen to be appreciated."

He held out his hand.

Horm grunted, took it, and shook it.

"Handsome apology, Nyrik," he said.

We moved off again.

I fell in beside Nyrik and said, "So, if you're not woodies, what are you?"

"Woodfolk. Men-o'-the-woods. Woods Kin. Which is two words, only they get run together to woodskin, so some ignorant buggers think we have tree bark for hide. Goodmaster, if they meet us in the wildwood, or Goodfellow, or Goodsir. Sometimes just *sir*, which is a laugh. Do we look like sirs?"

"I've had *sir*," Horm agreed. "*Sir Horm*. Eh? I mean, fuck off."

"Only we don't laugh," Nyrik went on. "Oh no; we just stare at them all solemn, with our bows drawn on them, and they wet themselves. Our turf, see, the Woodlands."

I considered what he said. "You both seemed to get on with other folks last night, like Mulden and that Orc he captured."

"Oh, we all do, for the most past. Neutral territory, see?" He fell silent as if that had explained everything.

We walked on.

"My dad's not the only one," Horm said, not much later, "to marry out."

"Oh?" I said, because he seemed to want a response.

"Dad's second cousin married an Ogress. One of the calmer ones. Lovely kids. Their girl, Urngra, is a stunner."

"In more ways than one," Nyrik added. "Seven foot tall if she's an inch, has a punch that can fell an ox. Seen her do it, her fifteenth birthday."

"That's an Ogrish rite of passage, on turning fifteen," Horm explained.

"Then they eat it," Nyrik added. "They always say one-punch ox tastes the best. Can't tell the diff myself, but then I'm not Ogre."

"That you are not," Horm agreed. "Though you've killed a few."

"Which we do not tell them that," Nyrik said, mangling his syntax.

"Which we do definitely never not," Horm agreed, mangling his.

"And most of it's gone by the time the bit they lay aside for roasting is done," Nyrik continued. "For the guests," he explained. "Those of us who aren't Ogres don't particularly like raw ox. Still-warm gizzards steaming as they open it up … . You wanna see 'em"—he chuckled—"with them gizzards! One will put one end of an intestine in his mouth, and another will do the same with the other end, and they'll swallow their way towards each other, *omfing* and *momfing*, while the rest of them piss themselves laughing. The one who swallows the most gets to shove the other one off and eat his too." Nyrik chuckled. "Good party, an Ogre fifteenth. And not just the food. They're all out of their heads on sproj. Which tastes like triple-distilled horse piss, and kicks like the horse it didn't come from. We hope." He turned to his companion. "How do they make that stuff, Horm?"

"Well," said Horm, "what they do, the Ogres, is: they creep up to the horse, unseen like—and it's a real skill, if you're an Ogre, creeping up unseen. Eight-, nine-foot-tall blue bugger covered in furs and skins, with arms as long as you are. Takes a lot of practice. And one creeps up behind the horse with the bucket, and the other creeps up in front of the horse and, at a given signal, leaps up and says, 'Boo!' And the horse pisses itself. Only, it does so *into* the bucket, which Ogre B has strategically positioned in place while Ogre A got himself ready to do the *boo* bit."

Nyrik stopped and looked at him. "You pulling my plonker, Horm?" he challenged.

"Swear to gods," Horm said.

Nyrik looked doubtful. "Really?"

"Really."

Nyrik considered. "I've never heard this. Where'd you hear this, Horm?"

Horm said, "I have my sources."

Nyrik said, "Ah." And we moved on.

I thought, *Ogre hooch made from horse piss? Surely not ...*

"Well," Nyrik said eventually, "all I can say is, it works, however they make it. Can dance all night on that stuff. Even if you can't feel your legs."

"Just never give an Ogre Careful Juice, Daxx," Horm warned.

"No," Nyrik agreed. "It does not agree with them. Ogres are no good at being careful."

"Don't know how to sip, see?" Horm explained. "Only how to glug. You saw what a sip does. Imagine a glug—"

"—going into an Ogre."

"Talk about mayhem," Horm said.

"And hangover," Nyrik added. "When they eventually wake up. After a week."

It was late afternoon when we crested the brow of a ridge and saw the cottage standing below us beyond an orchard and a paddock. It was perched on the side of the hill that sloped down towards an empty valley. Smoke curled from the single chimney that poked out of its thatched roof. A barn stood nearby beside a pen for livestock and a vegetable garden. None of it was walled or fortified.

"Who lives here?" I asked.

Nyrik replied, "You'll see."

"Aren't they afraid?" I asked. "Out here, all alone, with no walls to protect them?"

They both chuckled. Quietly. And, it sounded, somewhat nervously.

"There's other ways of protecting than walls, Daxx—you should know that," Nyrik said, his voice little more than a murmur.

"I should?"

"*If* I'm right about you, the which we'll soon know."

He and Horm had grown quieter as we approached. We wove our way between the fruit trees in the orchard down towards the cottage. *Pleasant little spot*, I thought. *Very peaceful and rustic.* It felt, though, a bit ... secretive. Not exactly welcoming like The Wheat-sheaf. *Open house, come on in everyone, make yourselves at home.* No. This place was not that.

The cottage had a single door at the back. There was a strange, round bronze head on it. It had wild, wide eyes, a mane of wavy bronze hair, and a heavy ring in its mouth.

Nyrik raised the ring to knock. The wild, wide eyes blinked at him and then froze open again.

A voice from inside said, "Hullo, Nyrik. I've been expecting you."

Nyrik slowly lowered the ring, so that it didn't make a sound. He pushed the door inward. It creaked open.

He nodded at Horm, who went in first, then at me, and I followed Horm into a small hallway with a mat on the floor and a boot-scraper.

Nyrik entered last and called out, "You want me to lock up, Marn?"

"Please, Nyr. What with these eefrits about."

"Yeah, them buggers." Nyrik closed and bolted the door. "What they doing up here, Marnie?"

The voice within grunted. "Never you mind," it replied. "Not your problem. At the moment."

"Thank gods for that!" Nyrik muttered, as he took off his jerkin and hung it on a hook. We scraped the mud off our boots and wiped them carefully. The hallway was cramped with the three of us in it, filled as it was with cloaks and boots and hats and sticks: light cloaks, dark cloaks; cloaks waxed against the rain; gardening boots, walking boots; black hats with wide brims, hats with bent points, some with curved points, and sharp points; walking sticks, climbing sticks, a stout longstaff with a thumb-notch at the top; and half a dozen broomsticks, leaning against the walls.

I followed Horm into the warm little room beyond. It was part sitting room, mainly kitchen. At its center was a wooden table, chairs around it, and bits of cloth and needles and thread lying on top, haphazardly. Above a fire, a cauldron was bubbling and steaming as our hostess stirred, her bent back to us. Candles threw shadows on the walls and up into the gloom of the smoke-blackened thatch above the rafters. It was still light outside, though very little came in through the single window, which was small and held diamond-shaped panes of thin, pale horn rather than glass. There were cupboards covered with pots and jars and bundles; scrolls and old books were strewn on every available surface; bunches of herbs hung drying from the rafters, along with strings of sausages and cuts of bacon.

I stood there, trying not to stare at our hostess as she straightened up from the cauldron. Which she did slowly, the way old people do, only a lot more slowly, because she was a lot older than most old people. She handed her ladle to a small, misshapen, greenish-brownish creature crouched beyond her by the fire, which I hadn't noticed at first. He took it, stood, and continued stirring. He was barely taller than the cauldron itself. "Seven by seven by seven, Hob," she instructed. "Seven sunwise, seven widdershins, seven times."

"Hullo, Hob," Nyrik said, "how's things?"

Hob looked at him with big, pale eyes, stirring slowly, the ladle gripped in hands larger than his head. "Nossobad," he allowed. "Thow's hings with you?"

"Going nicely, thankee Hob. Could be worse, eh?"

"Would be curse," Hob agreed, dourly, and turned back to his slow, careful stirring. His lips moved as he counted, and at seven, he reversed the motion of the ladle, and began again with a soundless: *One ... Two ... Free ... Thour ...*

The old woman shuffled over towards me. "So, this is him," she said.

She studied me. *Stared* at me, long and hard, from the one good eye she had. The other was covered by a large black patch. It was a penetrating, knowing stare; a stare not so much seeking information as confirmation, of things she already knew.

About me.

I looked her over and confirmed what I already thought about her. *Hag.* The great-great-grandmother you never had and never wanted.

"*Mm,*" she grunted and nodded as if she'd seen something. "Sit."

I sat on a wooden chair by the room's round table.

Nyrik said, "I've brought you something else, Marnie."

"We've," Horm corrected him, a little nervously.

"*We've,*" Nyrik concurred. He brought a little bundle out of one of his pouches and offered it to the old woman. "A little something from me and Horm," he said, "for your pains."

"Pains," she muttered, taking the parcel. "Aches and pains. The older you get, the more you hurt, eh, Horm?"

Horm grinned nervously.

"Aches and pains and hurt. Got plenty o' that. More'n enough to go around ..." She unwrapped the parcel, and when she saw what it contained, smiled. "Ambergris!" she said, sounding both surprised and pleased in that sharp voice of hers. "Nyrik, Horm, you *shouldn't* have!"

"The least we could do," Nyrik said, respectfully.

"More'n most do," she grumbled, and wrapped the mottled, gray-ochre lump back up in its brown paper, then tucked it into the pocket of her apron—a black apron over a black dress. "For my pains indeed, hey?" she chuckled, getting Nyrik's joke. "I'll make a salve o' this that'll soothe 'em away nicely! My thanks, young goodmasters."

Nyrik and Horm inclined their heads. I could almost hear them thinking, *phew, so far so good.*

Old Marnie resumed her contemplation of me. Arms crossed, staring hard.

I found it hard to meet that gaze.

"Yes," she said, eventually. "You did right to bring him to me. We need to see about this."

"We thought you'd ... know what to do," Nyrik said.

"I do. That's why I've been cooking."

Silence descended again. Her gaze didn't waver. Mine did, a lot.

To break the unsettling silence, I said, "Nice to meet you, Marnie. I'm Daxx."

"We'll see about that," Old Marnie said. "All of it."

More silence. More staring at me with that stare penetrating all the way in.

I tried small talk again. "You knew we were coming?"

She didn't reply, busy staring as she was.

"Marnie knows," Nyrik said, hesitating slightly, "when people think about her."

"Oh," I said, "that must be ... useful."

Marnie sucked at a hollow tooth. "No power," she announced. "They took it away." She studied me thoughtfully with her one dark eye, arms folded across her chest. "They don't usually do that. You have to do something really bad for that."

"Like what?" Nyrik asked.

"Necromancy."

Nyrik and Horm stiffened.

"I don't know anything about any of that!" I said.

Old Marnie grunted. "Like I said, we'll see about that." She didn't take her eyes off me.

Eye, I corrected myself.

Marnie leaned in, as if doing so would give her more answers. "I don't think they did that to this one, though." She tapped a gnarled finger on my forehead. "He's too ... empty. Something else happened. Yes." She nodded. "There's more to this one than meets the eye ..."

She sucked at her hollow tooth again. It made an unpleasant, *expectant* sound, as if something uncomfortable was about to happen.

Marnie unfolded her arms and reached up to her eyepatch. "Seems I'll have to use the other one," she decided.

She lifted the eyepatch.

If I hadn't been instantly rooted to the chair by its burning gaze, I would have leaped up and run screaming from the room. The eye that it had covered was twice the size of her other eye, both in height and width, and it was red, and rotating. Gold lights winked in and out within it. I fought the urge to throw up.

"Hold still," she muttered, clamping my chin with her bony hand. "Look into my eye ..."

Her stare bored into me. I couldn't move. I could feel the panic building inside me, unstopping, swelling and swelling, the more she stared ...

"*Mm*," she said, after far too long, dropping my chin and lowering the eyepatch back into place. "How're we doing, Hob?"

72

"Beven sy beven, teven simes," Hob answered. "On the last neven sow." He stopped stirring, tapped the ladle on the cauldron, and waited. "Doup's sun," he said.

"Bring us a crock then, Hob," she said without turning, her gaze still fixed on me. "Two mugs."

Hob ladled and crept over with two mugs and a jug from which steam rose. *No*, I thought, *not steam. Smoke.* And a peculiar, haunting smell. Many smells, rather; all of which I seemed to have known before but couldn't identify. Hob put the jug and mugs down in front of Old Marnie.

She poured.

She held one mug out to me and kept the other.

"Drink," she said.

I looked at the contents of the mug. "What is it?" It was dark green with black swirls in it.

"Memory Soup."

The smoke-not-steam rose from it, in lazy, gentle puffs. I watched. It bubbled.

"It's too hot," I objected.

"It isn't," Marnie disagreed. "Always bubbles a bit, Memory Soup. Even when chilled. And you don't want it *chilled*. Chilled leads to cold memories. No, you want them nice and warm."

"Why?" I said, playing for time. "What's in it?"

"That's proprietary," she said. "Guild secret. You in the Guild, Daxx?"

I'd been many magic avatars—sorcerers, conjurors, warlocks, battlemages and healers—so had been inducted into their guilds and magic circles. *She might*, I thought, *have respect for a fellow member.*

I replied, "I might be."

"What's the word, then? That only Guild Members know? And don't give me one and tell me it's above my rank, because there aren't any."

"I've forgotten," I said.

Marnie grinned. It was not a comforting smile. "Well then," she said, "let me refresh your memory. Drink."

I opened my mouth, and she brought the mug to my lips. I turned my head, and said, "What does it do?"

"It's like dreams. Only liquid."

That sounded more like a nightmare. "I don't want to."

"Old Marnie wants you to," Nyrik said. "And when Old Marnie wants you to do something, you'd be best advised do it. Marnie tends to take against those who thwart her."

I looked up at Old Marnie's grim face.

"You don't want to thwart Marnie," Nyrik said, drawing his horn-handled dagger. "Any more than you want me to come over there and tickle you with this."

I drank.

▲ ▲ ▲

I came to with a gasp in my own living room, in front of my computer, my chest heaving for air, my eyes weeping with relief. My head was spinning, and the room with it. It was all indistinct, somehow, and fuzzy at the edges. I was homing in on myself, sitting there, at my desk, my hands on my controls, my headset on my face.

Then I was *inside* the headset, and my life began to flash before me. Not my real life, but my other life, in … *here*, where I'd just gone. A whirl of places and people, and equipment and battles, and potions and dungeons, and trials and errors. Deaths and respawns. Failures and triumphs. Creatures of every conceivable kind, alive and dead, or both, flashed through my mind as I remembered encountering them.

But those memories now felt so much more real.

I tried to shield my head as that overload of images and experiences hurtled towards me, tried to close my eyes, but they kept pouring in, lodging in my brain for the briefest of moments until the next one shoved it aside. A millisecond and then gone—and then another and another and another. It was like seeing a mashup of clips of every game I'd ever played, everywhere I'd ever been, and everyone and *thing* I'd ever met, blazing through me at hyperspeed, faster, and faster, until everything went dark.

6

The Highest Bidder

It was an effort to surface from such a deep sleep the next morning, even though I wanted to. Someone was saying my name. Someone else was gently rocking me back and forth.

I fought my way to consciousness, slowly realizing that hours had passed, not just minutes, and forced my eyes open. I was sitting on the dirt floor of Marnie's kitchen, leaning back against Horm, who had his arms around me for support while Nyrik held a cup to my lips. The smell rising from it had woken me. I drank, not stopping to think what it was, because I knew from the smell that it would be delicious.

It was. Rich and thick and sweet, like warm forest flowers dripping with honey. I swallowed, and my head cleared.

"There you are, then, Daxx!" Nyrik said. "Sleep well?"

"Yes," I said, cringing when the hours that I'd been lying on a hard floor made themselves known to me. "Thanks."

"I'll say you did!" He chuckled. "Ten hours and more you were out. Up you get, then, we've a long walk ahead of us."

"What happened?" I said, remembering where I was. "Last night? After the …"

"Memory Soup? Couldn't say. Marnie will tell you if she wants. All we knew was to bring you here so she could take a look at you. What she saw is none of our business."

I took another mouthful of the reviving drink and felt better. Then another sip, and I could feel my strength beginning to return.

"Where is she?" I asked.

"Milking her cow. She's given us some of her cheese for the journey and a loaf and a pot of her pickles. Road Pickles, she calls them. There's stuff in them that keeps you going all day, fast as you please. It'll be a good lunch today!" He peered at the light sneaking through the horn-paned window. "Marnie says the weather will be fine, it won't rain."

The door opened, and Marnie pottered in with her milk pail. Hob got up from his perch by the fireplace and took it from her. The fire, I noticed, had gone out. A pile of kindling and sticks lay in the hearth waiting to be lit.

I couldn't help staring at Hob as he poured the cream off into a pot.

"Hobgoblin," Marnie said. She'd been watching me watching Hob.

I was curious. "Hob for short?"

"Hob 'cos he said so. They like their names that way. Lob, Nob, Bob. Keeps them focused."

"Hogboblin," Hob said, as if to agree.

"Not seen one before, have you?" She didn't ask; she knew.

"No."

Without taking his eyes off his task, Hob muttered, "Boghoblin. Hignblob. Hoga-boga-bibblegin."

"Common around here," Marnie said, "if you know where to look. Behind hobs, mostly. But not where you come from." She looked at Nyrik. "We need to talk. I'll send him out in a minute."

"Right, Marnie, o' course, no prob. We'll wait outside," Nyrik said. He and Horm scrambled to their feet and gathered their things. "Take your time, no rush!"

"Thank you," Horm said, sounding relieved to be out of there.

Nyrik, as if reminded of his manners, chimed in. "Yes, thanks, for the food and the hospitality and the place to sleep, lovely and warm and comfy. Much appreciated, Marnie." He paused, then babbled on. "Anything you need? From out there? Next time we're passing, I can drop it off."

"Shoes," Marnie said, standing over me and looking down with her disconcerting gaze.

"Oh, right—shoes it is. What size?"

"It don't signify," Marnie said, unconcerned. "I can spell 'em to fit."

"Black, presumably?"

She nodded. "Black."

"Leave it to me, Marn!" Nyrik promised. "Within the month. Within the *week*, even. We'll be back this way in a few days, all being well."

"That'll be nice," Marnie said, staring at me the whole time.

"Okay. Right. See you outside, Daxx." They shuffled out quickly, muttering goodbyes. I heard the door close behind them. The quiet cottage, on its quiet hillside, grew completely, deafeningly silent.

I didn't want to look at Marnie, but I couldn't look away.

"Sharp lads, those," she said. "They heard what you said and knew I'd need to see you."

"What did I say?"

She quoted what I'd asked Nyrik. "Are there real magicians here?" She watched me.

Her gaze was unsettling, but for the first time since I'd found myself there, I felt a glimmer of hope.

"Are there?"

"That," she said, eventually, "would be telling. And it's for you to do the telling first, not me. So: tell me. Who did this to you?"

I said, truthfully, "I don't know."

"*Why* don't you know?"

I turned the question over in my head. "If I knew, I'd tell you," I said.

" 'Course you would, but I don't mean that. They scrubbed you, clean as a peeled apple, and you don't know who did it?"

"No."

She nodded, thoughtfully. "I saw what you could do," she said, hobbling over to fetch a staff that was leaning against her mixing bench. "Your power. Your skills. No one here knows a tenth of it." She handed me the staff. "Fire's laid," she said. "Should be easy enough to light. And mind not to burn my house down."

I took the staff and looked at it. Its wood was brown, and it had a mottled blue stone set into its head, below its thumb notch.

"Unless," Marnie challenged, "what I saw in you was just dreams."

I held the staff in my hand. I had no readout, no inventory that I could see, no way of knowing how to pick among my spells and skills—nor whether, indeed, I actually had any.

"Go on, then," she urged.

I pointed the staff at the pile of wood in the hearth, thinking *this isn't going to work*. What I needed was a Flameball, and not a big one. But how to tell the staff that?

"Fire," I said.

Nothing.

"Small Flameball."

Again, nothing.

Marnie sighed, disappointed, and held out her hand for her staff. "Too much to hope for. Pity."

"I used to be able to."

"For real?"

"Well ..." I had to admit, "not exactly."

"No," she agreed, "not exactly. And you're not exactly lying." She sounded puzzled, and studied the blue stone in the staff, which was rippling with blue and white light. "Heartstone knows when you're lying. It's a truth stone, is lapis lazuli. Well, *not for real's* no good to us. Off you go, lad. If you're lucky, you'll end up in some noble lord's library, and you can write down those tales of yours for his children."

"They weren't tales, Marnie, I ... lived them. I could cast. I could heal, I could deal damage."

"And where's the proof of that?"

I didn't know what to say. I was as disappointed as she was that I couldn't wield her staff. More, probably. If I'd been able to cast, she might have helped me, maybe might have saved me from being sold.

I said, "If I found proof, would you help me?"

She looked at me thoughtfully, then nodded. "Yes, I'd help you, because then you'd be able to help us. There's not many with the eyes to see and the ears to hear, but there's trouble brewing. Big trouble. So, bring me your proof, should you find it, and then we'll see."

I felt a surge of relief. I knew what I had to do, now. I had a purpose—even if I had no idea how to achieve it. "Thank you, Marnie. Could I ... do anything for you? In return?"

"Mayhaps you coming here, now, is no coincidence," she said. "Mayhaps you'll have a part to play. Gods know we're going to need the

78

help." She considered me, her expression serious. "I saw you healing and casting and blocking spells and working fire and ice and storms to your will. Come in more than useful, that lot would. Yes, I hope you find your proof, lad. So, best start looking."

"I will," I said, getting to my feet.

"Word of advice," Marnie said. "Keep it to yourself. Folks don't hold with our kind. Unless they need us, o' course. And they'll be needing us before too much longer, the way the wind is blowing. As many of us as we can muster."

▲ ▲ ▲

Nyrik, Horm, and I set off down the hill from Marnie's cottage, past her fields and outbuildings. At midday we rejoined the road from which we'd taken our detour. It was more crowded than it had been further north. Carts and wagons and horses with riders of all ages, sexes, and species on their backs, wove in and out of each other with surprising ease.

Nyrik and Horm greeted acquaintances and traded news and gossip. The road rose, and the road fell, and the sun rose, and the sun fell, and when we reached yet another ridge, sometime in the midafternoon, the town came into view below us and grew clearer as we came down the other side. It was walled, a proper castle on a rise at its center, its banners flying in the breeze, their devices too far off to make out.

The town turned out to be farther away than it had seemed, so by the time we reached the gates in its high, thick walls, I realized it was larger than I'd at first thought. Brigstowe, I saw, was more than a town: it was a city. The gates were open, its guards loafing about, unconcerned by the traffic passing in (mostly) and out (rarely, this late in the day). Travel at night, I gathered, was risky, even this close to town. None but the well-armed, and swift-horsed, traveled at night, and then only when they had to. The realm, I gathered from Nyrik and Horm, was unsettled. People were on edge. Eefrits in the north. Trouble in the south. Outlaws everywhere, growing bolder. Dark times were coming, everyone felt, though no one knew exactly why they all felt it.

The market square was crowded as my captors had told me it would be. People had come from far and wide for the monthly auction, often traveling for days, Nyrik said. He and Horm were pleased by the timing.

"Won't have to wait for our money, we'll get a nice fat purse to-morrow!" Horm said.

We dropped Jan Brewer's wares off at his partner's stall. My hands were tied again, and my legs roped, but not enough that I couldn't walk easily. I just couldn't run. I'd been itching to escape, of course, and had kept my eyes peeled for any opportunity to do so. I hadn't seen one.

My captors were, indeed, professionals. They marched me to a stone building at the edge of the square, and we went inside. Its interior was a single, large room. Bars across it separated most of it from the entrance where we stood. There were figures behind the bars, sitting on benches, on the floor, standing, leaning against the walls, holding onto the bars, and staring out at us.

How many, I wondered. Fifteen? Twenty? Then I noticed that the barred-off section was itself divided into two unequal cages. The smaller cage held female prisoners. There were few of those. I didn't see Qrysta among them.

Nyrik approached a clerk who was perched at a high desk by the fireplace. "Evening, Scribe Donnell."

"Was wondering if you two would turn up." The scribe glanced up at him and then at me. "Just the one?"

"Yur," Horm said.

"Name?" Scribe Donnell, asked, dipping his quill in his inkwell.

"Daxx," Nyrik said.

"Odd name," Donnell said. "How d'you spell that?"

I said, "D-A-X-X."

He wrote in his ledger, and without looking up, said, "Of?"

Nyrik said, "Pit …"

He turned to me. "What was it again, Daxx?"

"Combe," I said, but Scribe Donnell was already sprinkling sand on the words *Daxx of Pytte,* to dry the ink. He blew the sand off the page, then nodded at two guards, who took an arm of mine each and escorted me over to the cell. I could see Grell sitting alone against the back wall, a wide space around him despite the crowd behind the bars.

"Get your beauty sleep now, Daxx. You want to be looking your best tomorrow!" Nyrik called out after me.

As they headed for the door, I heard Horm ask, "What do you think, Nyrik? Hundred?"

"Easy," Nyrik replied. "One twenty—one fifty, even."

My ropes were untied, and the cell door locked behind me. I walked over to Grell and sat beside him. "Hey."

"Hey, Daxx."

"How's things?"

He glanced at me, sourly. "Living the dream."

"Yeah," I agreed. "I land here with noob gear, and what do I do? I lose the lot and level *down*."

"Mulden says it'll probably be the mines for me."

"We'll have to escape," I said. "Meet back up. Work this mess out."

"Miners are chained up, underground, never see the light of day again, he says."

I'd never seen him so miserable. Grell, who was always taunting and full of life and fight, looked overwhelmed with sadness. "Don't give up, Grello. I'll find you; I promise. I'll get you out of there."

"Yeah," he said. " 'Course you will." Tears were rolling down his cheeks. I put my arm around him; he grunted and sighed.

"Gonna miss you, Daxx," he muttered.

"Me too, my friend," I said.

There was a silence. I noticed one or two of our fellow prisoners looking at us with curiosity. They looked away again quickly when Grell straightened up and caught their eyes.

"Mulden says with a good crowd and a decent number of lots the auction could go on all morning," Grell said. "We'll be sold individually and then marched straight off with our new owners."

The prospect was disheartening.

"So, this is goodbye," I said.

"Unless we can find a way out of this," Grell said. He didn't sound hopeful.

"We could start a riot," I offered.

He nodded at the guards.

"Fancy getting filled with crossbow bolts?" he asked.

I didn't.

There was indeed a good crowd the next day, and a very decent number of lots, but the auction didn't go on all morning, and it wasn't goodbye after all.

⋏ ⋏ ⋏

There was a viewing first, before the auction started. We were inspected by prospective buyers and questioned about our skills and knowledge, our captors beside us talking up our finer qualities. I listened as Grell was checked over by two brutish men, nearly as large as he was—and a lot meaner looking.

"Oh dear," Nyrik said. "Poor sod."

"Who are they?" I asked.

"Mine foremen. Nasty pieces of work. Flog their miners to death, they do."

"Never see daylight again, miners," Horm said.

"Injuries?" the chief foreman was saying, testing Grell's biceps.

"None that I found," Mulden replied.

His deputy said, "You ever use a pick, Orc?"

Grell's eyebrows rose in surprise. "No," he said, sounding relieved. "I play fingerstyle. Have you got a guitar? I'll show you."

The deputy foreman raised his whip, annoyed. "Pick*axe*, fool!"

"Oh," Grell said, crestfallen. "No. Sorry."

"Now then, gents. None o' that," Mulden said, holding up a restraining hand. "Buy him, and he's yours to whip as you please, but not while he's mine."

"No tribe. Outlaw. Trouble," the chief foreman said, frowning at Grell. "You cause trouble in my mines, Orc, and I'll flay the hide off you!"

"Yes, sir. I won't, sir," Grell said.

His deputy turned to Mulden. "You sure he's a bloody Orc? Pixie under a spell if you ask me!"

The chief foreman gave Grell a hard stare. "See you later, Pixie Boy!" he said, and they sauntered off, the crowd parting before them.

"Think someone else might bid on me?" Grell asked Mulden.

"Those two tend to discourage other bidders," Mulden said. "The big, nasty one bids; the bigger, nastier one stands by the auctioneer, looking at other bidders and … discourages. They don't try it on with me, though. They know my rules. Fair price or no sale. I'd better put a reserve on you, with those two charmers here." He walked off to confer with the auctioneer.

I saw Grell's shoulders slump in dejection. My heart ached for him. The *mines!* I felt a swell of anger at the two foremen. I thought, *if you'd talked like that to the Grell I used to know, he'd have torn your heads off.*

Well. The Grell I used to know would never have been captured in the first place. And here we were. Out of our depth, unskilled, unarmed—and, it would seem, about to be separated.

A brisk, middle-aged woman had made her way along the line and was standing in front of me, eying me thoughtfully.

"What d'you think, Alice?" Nyrik asked. "Stud or stripper?"

Alice snorted. "Don't do studs no more, Nyrik. Ain't the demand. Ladies of leisure hereabouts too busy, what with the war. Not that he isn't a handsome devil."

"War?" Nyrik said, alarmed. "What war?"

"Noble lords gearing up all over the realm, is what I've heard," Alice answered. "Old King Wyllard's too weak to stop them. They'll be at each other's throats come spring, you mark my words. His Lordship's got some scheme cooking. Daft bugger, I hope he gets his poxy head chopped off." She leaned in. "Open wide, show us your teeth, darling."

I opened wide.

"All present and correct," Alice sounded surprised. "Not a fighter, then."

"Nah," Nyrik said, "can't fight for piss."

At that moment, marching boots tramped on the cobblestones outside in quick time, and a dozen guards marched in, at the double, and along to the center of the room where they stamped to a halt. At their head was a dour-faced, lean, cold-eyed man, the two stripes of his rank on his chest. He took off his helmet and tucked it under his arm.

Nyrik said, "Oh for fuck's sake. No. No, *no* …!"

Horm muttered, "Corporal bloody Smott. *Just* what we need!"

Scribe Donnell hurried over to Corporal Smott with his ledger.

He followed him as Smott started at the end of the line, inspecting each captive in turn.

The clerk read off each man's name and details.

Corporal Smott said, with very few exceptions, "Mark!"

Scribe Donnell made a mark in his record, and they were on to the next. At each *mark!* there was a groan from the seller.

The only exceptions were the very old, the very feeble, and the female prisoners.

The voices came nearer to me—the murmuring clerk, and Corporal Smott's sharp replies of *mark!*

83

"Mark!" Smott said, looking at Grell beside me, before the clerk could even say, "Grell, Orc." Which he did anyway. Behind Grell, Mulden cursed. "Bugger me bloodless! Son of a bitchwolf!"

"Daxx, foreigner," the clerk said.

"Mark!"

Nyrik let out a stream of invective.

Corporal Smott noticed him. He sneered. "Little bleeding Nyrik. You want to watch that tongue of yours, woody."

"Fuck you too, stripe-arse!" Nyrik yelled.

"I'll stripe *yours* if you don't watch your lip!" Smott threatened.

Nyrik snorted. "You can try if you want to lose your hand. Fuckin' *army?* He's worth twice your fifty gold. Three times, and you know it. Both him and the Orc are!"

"Who said anything about fifty?" Corporal Smott challenged.

"What? It's always fifty, you thieving bastard. You saying you're going lower? Fuck you, we'll take ours elsewhere!"

"*Was* always fifty," Smott agreed, nastily. "Not *is* always fifty. Not now that My Lord has outlawed slaving."

Uproar. Every seller in the house was shouting at once, as were most of the crowd who had come to buy, or watch to pass the time, all yelling the same thing. *This is an outrage! No more slaves? That'll mean no more auctions!*

Well, that was their tough luck. I didn't care about the Brigstowe social calendar. I was only interested in our immediate future. *If slaving has been outlawed*, I thought, *does that mean Grell and I are going to be free? That would be good …*

Faces surrounded Corporal Smott on all sides, screaming at him in fury. He ignored the invective being hurled at him and merely stared at Nyrik with distaste. He didn't like Nyrik, and it was clearly mutual.

"*Atteeeeen*-shun!" Corporal Smott suddenly roared above the pandemonium, and his guards stamped to attention. "*Preseeeeent* arms!"

The guards hefted their pikes and stamped into the crouch, ready for the command to quell the crowd. The crowd subsided and backed away from them.

"Don't you lot know there's a war on? Or there will be any day now?" Smott demanded, strolling around the room. "You honest, loyal, gods-fearing citizens, liege-men and women of My Lord of Brigstowe? By whose leave you live in this fine town, *his* fine town, name of Brigstowe, safe behind his fine walls and under the protection of his fine castle, and his fine army? And don't you know what happens to *dis*-loyal citizens? Their lives are forfeit, their homes and chattels seized, their families thrown out of the town gates. Or, in times of war, into My Lord's spacious and very deep dungeons with all the other traitors. Where they will be induced to reveal where all their coin and treasure is hidden, under the expert attention of Mr. Stretcher, Mr. Needles, and Jeremy Redhot-Pincers, esquire."

He stopped, his voice echoing in the silence that his words had produced.

"That's better," he said. "Now, where were we? Yes. But My Lord is a generous lord, and a noble nobleman, and although he's outlawed slavery, there being a war on, he hasn't outlawed it retroactively. The old slaves may remain where they are, there will be no new slaves; and all *prisoners*," he emphasized, meaning *not slaves*, "brought for *recruitment* today," meaning *not sale*, "will earn a *bounty*," meaning *not price*, "for their *captors*," meaning *not owners*, "of twenty gold pieces a head."

The uproar broke out again.

Nyrik was purple in the face. Horm hopped up and down with rage, shaking his fist at Corporal Smott.

Smott ignored them all. He held up his arm, the guards stamped two paces forward in their crouch, and the hubbub quickly subsided. "And ten gold, for your expenses, for the ones we didn't mark. Who are free to go. Take it or leave it, we're taking our marks *now*. This is a *draft*, not a bloody auction! Any as wants the bounty, see Steward Marmsley at the castle. If you don't, more fool you." He stared down the opposition. "Guards! Line up the prisoners. Scribe, hand me that ledger." Smott signed Scribe Donnell's ledger with an X, and the guards herded us all out. "Chop-chop, at the double, one-two, one-two! Fall in! *Slooooope*—arms! Quick, *march!* Left right left right left right *pick your feet up you 'orrible little man*, left right left right left right left—"

And we were out, into the town square, and marching through the streets of Brigstowe, towards the castle that loomed above us.

7

Serjeant Bastard

We stood shivering in the damp, dawn air, shifting our feet on the hard dirt floor of the training yard, blowing on our hands, trying to warm ourselves up. It had taken me a long time to get to sleep the night before. I'd had so much to think about. I hadn't liked my situation from the start, and it seemed to get worse and worse—but now, with our change of circumstances, my mind had been churning.

We wouldn't be in chains all the time in the army. There had to be a chance to sneak off. Stuck in an army, with war coming? No thanks. I knew what I had to do: get back to Marnie. Find the proof that she needed and get my old skills back. Which meant getting away, and not getting caught.

We'd need horses. We wouldn't get far on foot. We'd need arms and armor. *Be patient*, I told myself. *Sit tight, learn the lie of the land, wait for our chance.* Below me, Grell had tossed and turned in his too-short, too-narrow bunk which had too little space between it and my bunk above. He banged his head on it a number of times, and on the wall behind him, and banged his feet and legs and arms against the bunkposts and swore. Which woke other grumpy recruits, who swore back from various perches in the darkness. And when Grell wasn't bumping, or swearing, he was snoring, or farting, both of which were worse. Even he noticed it in his waking moments and apologized.

"Jeez, sorry, Daxxie," he'd muttered up at me. "If I'd known I'd ever smell this bad, I'd never have built myself as an Orc. Can't bathe, can't brush my teeth, stink to high heaven …" He'd sounded miserable.

"Look on it as our secret weapon," I'd said. "All we have to do is stand you upwind of the enemy."

That made him chuckle. "Poor buggers," he'd sighed and rolled around a bit before going back to sleep.

I'd dropped off myself, eventually. And now, here we were in the training yard, at daybreak, rubbing our arms against the cold and wondering what was coming, without any expectation that it would be good.

A wooden door thudded open on the balcony above us, and the two sentries outside it stamped to attention, thumping the butts of their pikes on the floorboards. A voice growled, "Sloppy. Again." Another *stamp-thump*. I heard a sour grunt, which was more a *don't do that again* than approval.

Slow, heavy footsteps approached along the balcony then down the wooden stairs to the platform that ran along the end of the yard. A big man, almost as wide as he was tall, appeared, bit by bit: leather boots first, then leather leggings with spiked steel knee-joints, then a tabard of fur over a thick leather jerkin, and finally, a big bearded head, the black hair on it streaked with gray. Bushy eyebrows sprouted above hard, dark eyes. The skin of his face was like the leather of his clothing, weather beaten, lined, and scarred. It was not a face to mess with. He walked to the edge of the platform, ignoring the guards waiting on it who stamped to attention as he appeared.

He looked us over, slowly.

He grunted again.

"My name," he said, and although he spoke in a normal voice, rather than barking at us, his words carried clearly to the back of the yard, "is Serjeant-at-Arms Blunt. Blunt by name, blunt by nature. What you will hear from me will be *to the point*. Blunt, point. Not two words that usually go together, but they do here. Which is why you will easily remember them. You'd be well advised to. Blunt, point. Got it?"

No one answered. No one made a sound. No one had made a sound since the door on the balcony had banged open, which was one reason why Serjeant-at-Arms Blunt's words carried so clearly to everyone.

"Applies in more ways than one here," he continued as he strolled up and down the platform, appraising us as he addressed us. "Today, we will be using weapons. I want to see how good—or more likely fucking useless—you are with any of them. We will be using weapons with *blunt points*. And edges. Those blunt weapons will hurt you, but not kill you, so try to avoid being hit."

Being hit.

He paused to look recruit after recruit in the eye and let those words sink in. We were, we all knew, in for some *being hit*.

"Eventually," he continued, "if you succeed in avoiding being hit, some of you might become halfway-decent fighters. Some of you probably fancy yourselves as halfway-decent fighters already. I have news for you. You're not. You're rubbish. All of you. As we will see this morning, as sure as eggs is eggs. Talking of which, after this you get breakfast. There'll be all the eggs you can eat in there, and bacon, bread, oatmeal, cold cuts, pickles, cheese, a tankard of small beer each, and plenty of bandages. You'll need the lot. Because after breakfast, we'll all be out here again for another little go-round. So, let's work up an appetite."

My heart sank at the prospect. Working up an appetite, I felt pretty sure, would involve a working over.

"All right, Orc," Serjeant-at-Arms Blunt said to Grell, "let's start with you." He glanced at the muster roll that a guard held for him. "Recruit … Grell. Only Orc in the yard, not a difficult guess. Tribe?"

Grell said, sheepishly, "Don't have one, Serjeant."

Blunt heaved a sigh. "Outlaw. Just what we need. Your mob gets wind where you are, and we'll have to fight the buggers off. They won't take no for an answer. Orcs," he spat. "I know your codes, don't worry, I'm not going to beat the name of it out of you. Just remember, you're one of *us* now. If they come for you, they've come to kill you, not to take you home and marry you to the chief's daughter. You got that, Recruit Grell?"

"Yes, Serjeant Blunt."

"Good. Life with us, death with them. Or, of course, death with us if you can't handle yourself. Which I expect you probably can't, just like everyone else I can see. Weapon of choice, Recruit Grell?"

"Battle-axe," Grell said.

Blunt glared at him as if insulted. "Battle-axe?" He snorted. "You? Battle-axe is for *elite only*, not for ignorant bloody recruits! Are you elite, Recruit Grell?"

"No, Serjeant. I don't think so, Serjeant."

"Nor do I! Any Orc pathetic enough to get captured ain't *elite*. Warhammer." He nodded at a guard, who hastened to fetch one for Grell. "Like any other bloody Orc who isn't *elite*. I expect you've used one before?"

"Yes," Grell said, eying the clumsy weapon he'd been given.

"Yes, *Serjeant*," Blunt said, gently.

"Yes, Serjeant," Grell repeated, quickly.

Blunt glanced around our group. "When you speak to me, you will use the word *Serjeant*. With or without my name. *Without*"—he paused to emphasize the point—"the name by which I am universally known around here, and is used by one and all, but only when I'm out of earshot. Serjeant Bastard, they call me. But never to my face."

He lifted his chin at the scrawny, shifty-looking, pallid little lad next to me. He looked barely out of his teens, yet he had the sort of face that had seen a lot of things in his short life—a face that said: *older than my years.*

"You," Blunt said to the lad. "What don't people call me to my face?"

The shifty-looking lad opened his mouth. Left it hanging there. Closed it again.

Serjeant Blunt grunted. "Ugly but not stupid. Good combination in a soldier. Name?"

"Oller," the lad replied. When Blunt slowly lifted his head from the muster roll and raised an eyebrow at him, the lad quickly added, "Serjeant."

"Thief," Blunt read. "Anything goes missing in my barracks, Recruit Oller, you'll be up before me. You don't want to be up before me. Find someone who's been up before me and ask him."

He seemed to be expecting a response.

"No, Serjeant. Yes, Serjeant. No, Serjeant," Oller replied.

Blunt handed the roll back to the guard without looking at him. "Right, Recruit Grell, give me a number between one and twenty."

Grell, examining the hammer, looked up puzzled. "Huh?"

"Huh, *Serjeant*," Blunt corrected. "You can count?"

"Yes, Serjeant."

"Then be so kind as to give me a number between one and twenty and be quick about it or we'll be here all day, and I don't want to be here all day—I want breakfast."

"Nine," Grell said.

"Nine." Blunt nodded and, without turning around, gestured at the guards behind him. "Every day," he said as the guards removed the black cloth at the back of the platform, "we have a little tradition here. The guards equip this wall with weapons from our armory and place them in any order they want. I never know that order. Do you know that order, Recruit Grell?"

"No, Serjeant," Grell said.

"And you and I have never met before today, have we?"

"Never, Serjeant."

"We haven't planned this, corresponded by secret messages, smuggled between us by trusted accomplices?"

"No, Serjeant."

"So," Blunt addressed the rest of us. "You will see that this is not planned between Recruit Grell and myself. I never use plants or stooges. What you are about to see has been decided entirely at random." He turned and walked to one end of the row of weapons. He counted them out quietly as he paced along the racks until he stopped and said loudly with more than a little amusement in his voice, "Well. *This* you don't see every day. Nine. Morningstar. Hammer versus morningstar. Most unusual."

He picked up the morningstar, an evil-looking, spiked iron ball on a chain hanging from a wooden handle. "Not the ideal weapon against the warhammer. Especially not one wielded by a fucking great Orc. Still, needs must." He picked up the shield that stood behind it. It was bound with iron and was more or less rectangular, its bottom edges sloping inward to meet in a central point. "Underappreciated weapon, the morningstar," Blunt mused, swinging it gently. "Mostly by incompetent arseholes who keep hitting themselves with it. The idea being, as with any weapon, to hit your *opponent*. Not the back of your own fucking head. Takes a while to get the knack. A few self-inflicted wounds, most recruits give up and go on to something less painful. All right then, Recruit Grell, do your worst—and let's all see how bloody useless it is."

We all backed away from Grell as he hefted his warhammer, left hand low on its shaft, right hand up under its massive head. Grell lowered his head, crouched, and glared at Blunt.

Blunt waited then lowered his shield, stood up, and sighed. "Very nice," he said. "Very scary. Now, try bringing that to life, eh?"

Grell shifted his grip on the warhammer's shaft and, with both hands at its base, straightened up and began whirling it around his head.

Blunt, who had dropped down into his defensive stance, relaxed and stood up, watching him. He shook his head in disdain. "Next," he said.

Grell stopped whirling. "You didn't fight me, Serjeant."

"You're dead," Blunt replied dismissively. "Who's next?"

"Eh? I'm not!" Grell protested, then quickly added, "Serjeant?"

"Whirling that thing around you like that? What d'you think just happened? You brained every one of your mates within six feet of you, that's what just happened. Cleared a nice wide space around you for the enemy to slip in from all angles and fill you full of holes. Lucky it wasn't a battle-axe; you'd have beheaded half your fucking squad. Lesson number one: training's about more than just how good you are with your weapons, it's about using your *brains*. All right,"—Blunt lifted his shield and faced Grell—"want to go again?"

"Yes, Serjeant."

Twenty seconds later Grell was on the ground, moaning and clutching his foot. A step, a feint, a block, a dart, a jab of the shield at Grell's face to distract him, and Blunt's morningstar thumped onto Grell's foot. Grell went down in a heap, yelping.

"Like I said, good weapon, the morningstar," Blunt handed it and the shield to a guard. "Now, I know what you're thinking," he stared down the rest of the recruits. "Did I need to hit him that hard? The answer is *yes*. Why? Because I'd taken note of his equipment. Lesson number two: what's the enemy's gear? Recruit Grell here is wearing your typical Orc hinged iron sandals. Dunno how they can wear those things, they'd tear a normal person's feet to shreds. Not that Orcs aren't normal persons, Recruit Grell, no disrespect intended. Some of my best enemies have been Orcs. Come one, come all into My Lord's army, we're all equal here. With the exception of the Undead, they go to Special Forces. Don't play well with others, Undead. Can't have recruits eating each other.

"Tough buggers though, Orcs," Blunt returned to his theme. "Observe how the cage-like construction of the typical Orc hinged iron sandal surrounds and protects the Orc foot, ankle, and shinbone. Observe, also, as a matter of interest, the heel-spike. When you see an Orc raise his or her leg up and forward, you will be on the ground, most likely, so roll away as fast as you fucking can, and keep rolling before the bugger stomps it through you. Now. Note the effect of my morningstar on that cagelike construction. It was a blow of sufficient power to crush the top iron ridge down into the arch of the Orc's foot, collapsing the iron ribs and trapping said Orc's foot so he or she can no longer move it. Can you, Recruit Grell?"

"No, Serjeant," Grell gasped.

"Remember that this is the effect of a *blunt* morningstar," Blunt continued his lecture. "A combat, *sharpened* morningstar would also have contributed wounds to the overall effect. The Orc would now not only be rolling on the ground in agony, unable to do more than hobble if he could ever get up again—which, of course, he wouldn't, as you'd finish him off with your dagger—he'd also be horribly wounded with a mashed and bleeding foot."

He said to the guards behind him without looking at them, "Help him up, get him to Smith to get that sandal off, take him to breakfast. Right. Who's next?"

No one volunteered. Two of the tallest guards hauled Grell upright, took a thick, hairy arm each over their shoulders, and helped him out, Grell hopping on his undamaged foot.

It was a long two hours till I sat down, exhausted, beside Grell on the bench at a communal table in the mess hall. He'd been the first into breakfast, once the smith had freed his foot from its pulverized sandal, so he had taken his seat by the fire and kept a space for me. I'd been hard at work with shortsword and buckler, and I'd been tagged by the guards more times than I cared to count. Every blow had hurt. I'd been lucky. I hadn't had to dance with Serjeant Bastard. I'd watched, we all had, as he pulverized every recruit he faced. He'd seem to move at a tenth of the speed of everyone else and then things happened so fast you never saw them. My turn would come, I knew. And running away and crying wouldn't be an option.

"How are you doing?" I asked.

"Seems Orcs can take a lot of punishment."

"Good to hear," I said, piling into my breakfast. I was famished.

"Serjeant Bastard could've taken my leg off," he observed.

He didn't need to add what he was thinking, which was, *but he didn't.*

"Doesn't want to lose a recruit," I agreed.

"What did you get?" Grell asked.

"Sword and board. I was hopeless, like most of the others. That thief, though, *whoo!* Oller. Knives. Quick as shit. No one could touch him. Serjeant Bastard thought he was getting cocky, so took him on *bare-handed* and disarmed him. Had him in a headlock with one of his own knives at his throat. He let him go and said, 'Need to work on your defense, son,' then strolled off to his next victim. No one could lay a weapon on him. Even in groups of three or four. Well, apart from hitting what he was blocking with—his shield, or broadsword, or crossed swords if he was twin-blading. He may be an old fart, but he's better even than Qrysta was. And for *real.*"

"Qrysta," Grell mused. "If we had her, and our old skills ..."

"I wish." I took another mouthful of breakfast. "But we don't. So, let's get good, right? And hope she turns up."

"Yeah," Grell said, "let's do that."

I chewed, swallowed, and continued, "Then at the end as we were falling out, Serjeant Bastard asked him, Oller, quietly like in passing, 'You throw 'em?' And Oller said, 'I don't like to, Serjeant. Don't want to lose nice knives.' 'But you can?' Serjeant Bastard persisted, and Oller said, 'If I have to, Serjeant.' And Serjeant Bastard said, 'Go on, then. Show us.'

"So, Oller took a couple of knives and stood about a dozen good strides from that wooden target-dummy with the sword and shield. And took his time, measuring. We'd all stopped to watch by now. Oller hefted one, holding it by the tip of the blade, shifted his weight about and measured, and changed his mind and, eventually, threw. It clunked into the shield, flat, upside down, and dropped to the ground. Some of us watching laughed. Oller went red, took the other knife, hefted, thought, changed his stance, and let fly, and this one stuck in the shield, right by the edge—only it was hanging down, not in very deep, so that soon fell out too.

"And you know what Serjeant Bastard did? He went to the weapons rack, picked up this long leather strap full of knives, wrapped it around his chest in an X-shape—obviously some kind of a knife-holster. He

93

turned, walked away, and stood opposite the target-dummy, at the same spot as Oller had stood, with his arms folded. 'Say when, young man,' he said. And Oller, like an idiot, said, 'When what, Serjeant?' So, Bastard said, 'When I can start, what do you fucking think?' Oller went redder, and said, 'When,' and *foop foop foop*, one after another, from both hands, into head, arms, legs, shield, so fast it was like they were all in the air at once. And the last two, a second later, Serjeant Bastard threw at the same time, one from each hand, into its crotch. They stood there, quivering, like a couple of horrible steel cocks.

"He took off his harness, handed it to Oller, and said, 'Go and get 'em, Recruit Oller. It's all right, he's dead. Dead men don't run off with your *nice knives.*'"

Grell grunted.

I ate.

We looked across at Serjeant Bastard who was eating his breakfast at a table reserved for the guards. At which—unlike at all the other communal tables where chatter was everywhere, even occasional laughter—no one was speaking.

"Fuck," Grell said, contemplating Serjeant Bastard and his skills. "People a lot higher level than us around here."

"That's for sure," I agreed, and went back to shoveling breakfast into me. It was basic stuff, but so damn *good*. I'd never tasted piggier bacon, or more chickeny chicken legs, or eggier eggs. Even the coarse dark bread was bursting with deep flavor, and the *butter!* The butteriest butter imaginable, rich and pungent, with a taste that went on forever. And there was some stringy, khaki-green stuff that the undercook told me was called samphire and came from the cliffs by the seashore, which was salty and crunchy and powerful strong. In my hours in the training yard, I'd worked up a huge appetite. As I ate, I felt strong and relaxed and ready for more.

Grell turned to me and said, "What are we going to do, Daxx?"

"Long term, no idea. Short term, Grello, we are going to learn how to *fight*."

Grell thought about that and nodded. "Mm, good idea."

"Could come in useful," I said.

Grell chewed, swallowed, and said, "Yeah, I'm about done with being a wimpy, useless Orc!"

"I think we have a hell of a teacher. Emphasis on *hell*, perhaps, but if you want to learn, learn from the best."

Grell nodded.

"Too right," he said. "I could do with knowing how to use a war-hammer. I believe I could be good with that."

"You've learned weapon skills before, Grell," I pointed out. "No reason you can't do it again."

"None," he agreed. "You're right, Daxxie. I am going to get good again!"

"Me too. And then—" I stopped. I had been just about to tell him about Marnie. But I'd failed with Marnie. I didn't want to get his hopes up, that I could once again be the battlemage he'd known before. *Proof*, I thought. That's what she needed to see, and that's what I needed to find. Meanwhile, like Grell, I was going to learn how to fight.

"And then what, Daxx?" Grell said.

"And then we won't be pushed around again, will we?"

"Too damn right we won't!"

We finished breakfast, took bio breaks, and assembled again in the training yard. Grell informed me, not that I'd wanted to know, that I wouldn't *believe* the size of an Orc dump. Like a bloody great cow-pat, he said, a pyramid of steaming poo.

And we trained.

Serjeant Bastard had been right, we soon saw. We were indeed rubbish, all of us. Arms drills were bad enough. We were hopelessly uncoordinated. Even a simple step-slash-block with sword and board could be a dozen or more different movements, our shambolic crowd doing a dozen different things at different times, instead of three, simultaneously. The guards bellowed and berated. Serjeant Bastard strolled among us, arms crossed, beard bristling, eyes glaring, mouth grim.

After an hour of drills, it was time to spar—and sparring was worse. *Much* worse. We used training blunts, not combat sharps, but even so, sparring, in a word, hurt. We sparred with the guards—or watched, bruised and knackered, as the guards sparred with our fellow recruits. They took a special delight in mocking us—both verbally and physically. They were so much better than us that they saw every move before we even made it. They loved punishing us, leaping and stabbing gleefully as we tottered and slipped and swiped and missed. They'd twirl their opponents around and whack them on the helmet, or the legs, or the backside. Even those of us watching and waiting for our next bout of humiliation and pain couldn't help laughing as useless recruit after useless recruit was battered, bewildered, and sent sprawling.

Grell faced off with his warhammer against a shrimp half his size, who pointedly swapped out his own hammer for a two-handed cudgel with which he beat Grell black and blue. Grell could hardly move at the end of it. He tottered back to the bench where I was sitting and slumped onto it, muttering, "Fuck a duck, Daxx."

Serjeant Bastard noticed and made eye contact with me. He nodded. My heart sank into my boots. I knew what that meant. I hauled myself to my feet and readied my sword and shield. Serjeant Bastard picked up a shield that matched mine and a sword that didn't. His 'sword' was no more than a stick of wood. *Well*, I thought, *at least I won't be hacked to pieces*. Not that our training swords had sharpened edges, but they were solid lumps of iron and would definitely hurt. I doubt they could hurt any more than Serjeant Bastard's stick sword did.

Not that he used it at first. He tucked it into his belt and battered me with his shield alone for a couple of minutes as if softening me up. When I finally got the hang of what I was meant to be doing and started blocking some of his blows, he grunted, "About bloody time!" and drew his stick. The next few minutes were the most painful of my life. It was like trying to fend off a threshing machine. That damn stick was everywhere, jabbing, slapping, feinting, and flashing as he worked me over from feet to face. My shield was always where his stick wasn't, because a split second later it was beating whichever part of my body I'd just exposed to it.

Thumps from his shield turned me, confused me, and backed me the length and breadth of the training yard. I was heaving for breath and weeping from the pain of it all as he finished me off. A crack across the knuckles numbed my hand, making me drop my sword, a prod on my foot had me hopping on one leg, a clout from his shield sent me stumbling back against what I later learned was called a quintain.

There were several of these devices in the yard, target dummies, all of different design. This one was the upper half a soldier, on a swivel, sword in one hand and shield in the other. I couldn't think what the hell Serjeant Bastard was doing when he started fighting the dummy as well as me. He wasn't. He was using his blows on the dummy to make it beat the crap out of me, while he kept me diverted with the occasional bash of his shield.

All I could do was hop and squeal and try to cover myself and flail with my sword at the dummy, which was landing five blows on me to every one that I landed on it. I could hear the laughter all around me, growing louder and louder, and the jeers as my swipes missed, and the cheers every time I got hit. A flurry of blows ended the spectacle, raining in on me from all sides at once. Serjeant Bastard had maneuvered the dummy to give me the final hits, almost simultaneously: a thwack over my head then a jab in my back that sent me sprawling, face down into a puddle.

I struggled to my feet and limped over to the bench where Grell was applauding along with everyone else, a wide grin on his face and tears of laughter running down his cheeks.

Serjeant Bastard let the merriment run its course for a few moments, then said, quietly, "Right, who's next?" There was instant silence as every recruit tried not to catch his eye.

Finally, it was lunch. Then an afternoon of more punishment. Supper came with the first good news of the day: Brigstowe Castle, we discovered, had an excellent brewer. I ate what I could, drank what ale I was allowed, and somehow dragged myself into my bunk. Standing hurt badly enough, but lying down hurt more as more bruises found something to poke into them. I shifted about, trying to find a tolerable position. I hadn't found one before I passed out.

It was still dark when the guards roused us the next morning. I was so bruised that it took me a full minute to get out of my bunk. I was grateful I now had Daxx's fine, strong young body, but even that was as stiff as a board. I shuddered to think how I'd be feeling if I was still Joss. I made a mental note to keep Daxx in as good shape as I could.

At dawn, we were again in the training yard, waiting for the door to thump open above us, and Serjeant Bastard's heavy tread on the stairs, knowing he was coming down to make our lives a misery.

We trained, all day and every day. We trained with every one of the twenty weapons in Serjeant Bastard's rack; and with several others that he brought out when we thought we knew what we'd be facing in combat. Nets. Thorn-darts. Biters, which were wicked little sharp-toothed clamps on the ends of shafts. We wouldn't be up against those any time soon, Serjeant Bastard said told us. "Foreigner weapons, those.

But forewarned is forearmed, eh? In case My Lord ships you out to some godsforsaken hellhole overseas. And where else are you going to get warned about foreigners' nasty surprises, other than here?"

We trained in autumn rains and in winter snow, Serjeant Bastard driving us so hard we were drenched in sweat despite the freezing cold. And we'd sit, exhausted after another battering, on the bench, and our sweat would freeze inside our clothes.

And over time, as the year turned, and winter warmed to spring, we got good.

As we knew we'd need to be. Because spring meant the start of the campaigning season, and My Lord of Brigstowe was itching for a fight.

8

My Lord's Army

Graduation took up most of our final week.

There was the written exam, which recruits who couldn't write took with a guard writing their answers as they dictated them. I offered to help, as the few guards who could write only did so painfully and slowly, but they all thought that I'd cheat for my mates and put down the correct answers, not whatever they told me—which, on reflection, I probably would have done.

The written exam was the easy part. *How Do You Defend Yourself Against a Dual-Wielding Sword-Dancer?* Easy: sword and board and better dancing. Easy in *theory*.

The second exam was the practical. In which you had to Defend Yourself Against a Dual-Wielding Sword-Dancer—who was an experienced guard, and a lot better than most Dual-Wielding Sword-Dancers that we'd be coming across in My Lord's wars, because those wouldn't be graduates of Serjeant Bastard's school of very hard knocks.

And then we had to face up one-on-one against another recruit, with whatever gear the guards decided; and they usually decided on rigs they knew neither you nor the other recruit you'd be fighting were happiest with. We were competent with every weapon in the rack by that time and skilled enough to wield even our least favorite ones as capably as most of the guards.

Then it was Mobs. At the start of our training, Mobs had been you alone against two or three guards, all whacking at you gleefully. Or you and your randomly chosen squad against a solo guard, who toyed with us and taunted us and pissed us all off. Or your squad against another squad.

By the time of Graduation, we were giving as good as we got—and *oh*, how we loved paying the guards back in the coin they'd been paying us with over the previous weeks. The guards hated Graduation. We were all as good as they were now. Better, most of us—because the guards were soldiers who weren't good enough for the front line. They were considered too old or too injured or too slow, we now realized, even though they'd seemed like monsters to us when we'd started our training. They knew we were better than them now, and they resented it. We knew it too and let them know that we knew.

The swagger they'd had when we'd been drafted was ours now. Mine especially. I'd made sure to look after Daxx's lean, hard body, putting it through grueling workouts every day in addition to our weapons training. I was in peak condition by the time Graduation came around—as fit, as the Brigstowe saying went, as a butcher's dog. Once we'd seen that we were their superiors, Grell and Oller and I had talked about maybe overpowering the guards and making a run for it—but the castle gates were bolted every night, its walls patrolled, and all weapons locked up in the armory. And none of us liked the idea of Serjeant Bastard coming after his deserters.

The final test of Graduation was our masterclass. Each of us, one after the other, against Serjeant Bastard. We all knew we were never going to be *that* good. He was so good it was stupid. He did everything at a stroll—while we did everything to the best of our ability—yet he never broke sweat.

There was one difference, though, from all the times we'd dueled with him before. After he'd flattened us or disarmed us or trussed us up with some bit of twine he just happened to have about his person, he'd shake our hands and say, "Well done, Recruit," and sound as if he meant it. He might add, "Welcome to My Lord's army," or, "Gave a good account o' yourself," or, "Nearly tagged me a couple of times there!" To Grell, he said, "Recruit Grell, I should warn you that there ain't an Orc out there as good as you with a battle-axe, so when you meet an Orc with a battle-axe, talk first. He'll see the battle-axe, so he'll know you're elite. And if he doesn't want to talk first, tell him I said that. Nice, like. Before you square up. No need to hack a fellow Orc's head off right off the bat, all right?"

Grell said, "Yes, Serjeant Blunt."

"Give the poor sod a chance. Might make a friend, you never know. I'd rather have friends than enemies. Especially enemies like you."

Grell shook Serjeant Bastard's outstretched hand and saluted, solemn as a statue, but glowing with pride as he lumbered back into line. And why not? Grell with a battle-axe was terrifying. All that he'd known before, in our previous life, had now germinated and borne fruit in this one. He was as good now as he'd ever been—and he'd been the best two-handed fighter I'd ever seen. It wasn't long before he couldn't find anyone to spar with him one-on-one.

I did, for a while, with my sword and board, but he just smashed my shields to pieces and hurt my arm. My *arms:* my left arm would hurt because it had been holding the shield while he destroyed it, and my right arm would hurt because whacking at Grell with a blunt-edged training sword hurt me more than it hurt him.

I was good myself by Graduation; one of the best two or three with sword and board and more than competent with everything else. I was never going to be an Oller with knives, or a Grell with battle-axe, but I was far better than those two with any kind of bow. I was no Qrysta, but I was better than any of the guards at twin-blading, my choice being shortsword in my right hand, axe in my left—a throwing axe, not a big thing, but worrying enough to distract an opponent—switch hands and *thunk*. My axe would be standing out of his forehead while I stabbed at the next guy.

I danced now in combat. We all did. One time, Grell and I took on Oller armed with nothing but his vicious little knives, two in his hands and others in his cross harness. My shield and Grell's armor looked like porcupines before we got Oller down, and I didn't chop his grinning little head off with my throwing axe.

Grell was a beast with anything two-handed, not just his battle-axe. Warhammer, longsword, pike, it didn't matter. The result was always going to be the same. Grell wins, the other guy loses. I could hardly lift the damn things he fought with. Once, for a laugh, he took on three of us armed with nothing but a chair. We couldn't get near him. Long into the night we'd argue about what the best rig for our build was. Several weeks in we'd all settled on the gear we liked best, and for Grell the choice had been easy: battle-axe. Over the months of our training, he had learned how to execute his old skills for real—but he felt nervous about putting himself forward to Serjeant Bastard as *elite*. I told him there was no question about it. He was far and away the best of us two-handed.

"So, tomorrow," I said, "march up to Serjeant Bastard and challenge him."

Grell was shocked at the idea. You didn't challenge Serjeant Bastard. You avoided him. "Mate, I'm not sure—"

"You're always moaning how no one will spar with you!" I said. "Put yourself up against the best. Go get him. And dump him on his arse like he did to you the first day."

The next morning, the training yard fell silent when Grell strode up to Serjeant Blunt, battle-axe in his hands, and said, "If you're not busy, Serjeant, I'd appreciate the chance to spar with you."

"Would you, now?" Serjeant Bastard replied. "I am busy as it happens, Recruit Grell, but I dare say this won't take long." He was wrong. They went at each other hammer and tongs for twelve minutes, neither yielding an inch. They'd have made mincemeat of any of the rest of us. We were almost allowing ourselves to think that Grell might actually stand a chance, when Serjeant Bastard challenged him. "Is that all you've got, Recruit Grell?"

Grell didn't miss a beat. He kept fighting, but, clearly, didn't know what to reply.

"Thought so," Serjeant Bastard said, and found another gear and another and then Grell was flat on his back, Blunt leaning on his battle-axe, staring down at him, nodding. "I'm much obliged to you for the workout. Been letting myself get out of form, I have. I see that now. Tomorrow we'll go again, if you please. I can't be getting out of form."

He held out his hand and hauled Grell to his feet.

That we had never seen before.

"Well done!" I said, as he re-joined me.

"Whooh!" he said. "Got a long way to go still."

Grell used a battle-axe all the time after that, unless the trainers had him on something else. He'd drone on forever about heft and balance, blade angle and the difference between single-head, with balancing braining-spike for the backhand, and double-bladed; or why double-bladed could be better with double *different* blades, depending on cut, set, and weighting, rather than your traditional symmetrical. And how sometimes the best attack was the sudden *poke*, straight ahead with the head-spike. "They never expect that," he said.

He almost *married* one particular battle-axe. It looked as heavy and brutal as any of them but was surprisingly light. It was light enough that even I could handle it and do reasonably well with it. In Grell's great fists it was a tornado of steel. Serjeant Bastard noted his choice. "*Niblun-made*," he told Grell. And, "You've a good eye for a weapon, you have, Recruit Grell."

A tradition arose: every day's training would end with Serjeant Bastard, with whatever weapon he fancied, taking on Grell and his niblun battle-axe. Towards Graduation—in those one-on-ones which we all gathered around and watched, cheering Grell on—Serjeant Bastard would even sometimes be breathing heavily before he had Grell flat on his back with a blade at his throat.

The climax of Graduation was the Passing Out Parade and Presentation Ceremony. We assembled in our new rigs. Our *real* rigs. Proper armor. Chainmail in my case, leather in Oller's, plate in Grell's. And proper helmets. We'd been issued it days before and had polished it all to a shine. Gleaming leather, as smart as if we were going to My Lord's Ball. Glittering steel. Grell's breastplate shone like a mirror. And our sharps! No more training-yard blunts: our combat-issue weapons had edges you could shave with and points you could push through doors.

My short blade was hi-tech compared to my old shortsword. A bit longer, a lot sharper, and far better balanced. I couldn't stop oiling it and polishing it, turning it over in my hands and flicking it around with the wrist strokes I'd learned. My shield was a perfect weight and fit, cut for me by Pearse the Carpenter out of ash boards that I'd picked out myself in the sawmill, and iron-bound by Collen the Smith.

Oller's knives were as light as feathers and hard as diamonds. He could have three in the air at once at a ten-pace target, and they'd all hit together exactly where he wanted them to. He nicked all our purses the night before Graduation, for a laugh, one at a time, and held them up before us smirking until we clocked it, felt at our belts, snatched them back, and swore at him. You couldn't trust Oller further than you could throw him, but he was one of us now, and anyone he targeted would be one of *them*, so fuck 'em.

Grell's Presentation Sharp was the niblun battle-axe, but Serjeant Bastard had ordered Collen the Smith swap its blunts out for a warhead. With its slender blades it looked almost frail. It was certainly no longer as ugly as the other training-yard battle-axes. It looked *right* now, sleek, almost delicate—and lethal. Its new head was sharp, and shiny, with a gleam that somehow also glowed.

"Special head, that," Serjeant Bastard said as he presented it to Grell. "Look after her. And she'll look after you."

"Yes, Serjeant Blunt," Grell said. "I will."

"You'll see," Blunt said. "Fall out, Graduate Grell the Oz-Born!"

We were in My Lord's army now, so had to have surnames, that was Regulations. I was Daxx of Pytte, which was how Scribe Donnell had spelled it when taking delivery of me from Nyrik and Horm. Informally, we were just Daxx Pytte and Grell Ozborn, to go with Oller Pinches.

Grell saluted and fell out.

The salute was usually the end of that recruit's Presentation, but before Grell could turn about to march back to our ranks, Serjeant Bastard added, "*Original* head," in a meaningful tone. "Back to *all original specs* now, that is. We used her as a training axe because she's light, being niblun-made. People could handle her if they couldn't handle a heavy. We couldn't have recruits training with that *original head*, there'd be corpses everywhere. Thin, eh?" He eyed it appreciatively. "Slender, you might say. You'd think, looking at that, it'd sheer off in a fight, snap in half. There's no snapping niblun blades, however thin." So, it wasn't a new head after all, but something significantly better than anything even Collen Smith could forge.

Grell was expected to say something, but couldn't think what, so said, "No, Serjeant. Yes, Serjeant. Thank you, Serjeant."

Serjeant Bastard gave him a small smile, and his hard eyes glinted with amusement.

"You'll see," he said. "Fall out, Graduate Grell!"

Grell fell out and marched back to join us, trying hard to look serious, but I could see he was bursting with pride.

A special battle-axe like his needed a special name, Grell decided. *She*, Serjeant Bastard had called it. *Her*. She needed a female name.

He couldn't think of anything Orcish, or warlike. He got up from our bench at supper that evening and lumbered over to Serjeant Bastard, sitting at his usual table with several guards. They talked briefly, then Grell lumbered back and reinserted himself into the wide space between me and Oller.

"Fugg," he said, with a big smile. "Orc Goddess of War."

We agreed that Fugg was an excellent name for his battle-axe.

"D'you think that's where the phrase 'Fugg off' comes from?" Oller wondered.

We didn't.

The next day we marched off to war.

▲ ▲ ▲

My Lord of Brigstowe rode at our head. We all thought he was 'a right ponce,' as Oller had muttered, on seeing him in his finery, seated on his white charger, which was richly caparisoned to look as flashy as My Lord of Brigstowe himself. He wore a cloak of white and crimson and gold flowing from his shoulders. Plumes of the same colors sprouted from his fancy, gold-banded helmet. Gold and jewels winked everywhere in his armor. There were gemstones set into the pommel of his sword.

It was a nice-looking sword, I had to give him that. When he drew it and held it above his head and gave his stupid speech about honor, nobility, chivalric deeds, and heroic deaths, I thought, *we're not going towards anything noble or chivalric*, and *fuck death of any kind, heroic or otherwise*. We're going off to slaughter your enemies before they slaughter us. And as for honor: well, as long as we don't run away or kill civilians, everything else is irrelevant.

We were there to do a job. We knew how to do it, even though we were virgins when it came to actual battle. But we knew we could fight.

Grell trudged along on one side of me, Oller scuttled along on the other and I thought, *safest spot in the kingdom.*

We knew about the king, now, Wyllard, and his kingdom. In short, he was old and weak and his realm was on the verge of falling apart. This noble lord was threatening that noble lord, and rumors flew as to who might be about to invade where, or what recent enemies were making alliances against ancient allies. Chaos, the place seemed to be.

The King's Law still held, it was maintained, but it wasn't as if the king had much chance of enforcing it. The noble lords did that 'on his behalf.' They did it with varying interpretations—particularly of the tax laws. One of the reasons the king couldn't do much to enforce his laws was a direct result of those interpretations. The noble lords kept the taxes that they collected in their vaults, 'for safekeeping until peace breaks out,' rather than 'risk sending them to the royal treasury, what with all these outlaws on the roads nowadays, His Majesty wouldn't like his revenues to fall into their hands, ooh no.'

So, the king was broke, we gathered, and by all accounts a bit of a ditherer; both of which stopped him getting his act together and knocking Their Lordships' heads together and imposing the King's Peace.

All that was way above our pay grade. The plots and plans and intrigues and dealings of the High and Mighty didn't concern us, so we didn't waste time thinking about them. We thought about soldier things, wine, women, and song—the usual, when we weren't thinking about war. There'd been no women in the barracks. There had been a few about the kitchens and serving in the mess hall and all over the castle in positions high and low. Oller smacked a serving girl on the backside one evening, nothing more than a playful tap and she'd belted him with the back of her hand, knocking him off his bench, and poured stew over him. We laughed our heads off.

Then Serjeant Bastard stood up, slow and deliberate, and came over to Oller, who was wiping himself down. He called the girl over and told Oller to apologize to her. Which he did. You always did what Serjeant Bastard told you. Then Serjeant Bastard said in that quiet voice of his which carried to every corner of the mess hall, "You do that again, Recruit Oller, and you'll be up before me."

Oller replied, "Yes, Serjeant Blunt. Sorry, Serjeant Blunt."

Serjeant Bastard stared at Oller a bit longer, then sauntered back to his supper. We all sat down, and no one said anything. Low voices spoke, then normal ones, and soon enough the usual banter and laughter and swearing resumed. So, we talked about women as we marched and wondered if there'd be any and what they'd be like and whether they might be friendly.

Chances were not, we assumed; not if we were going to slaughter their menfolk. There'd been wine in the mess hall, though only on special occasions: the feast for My Lord's birthday; the Midwinter

Solstice; Marchday Eve—which marked the first day of spring and the beginning of the good weather (at least in theory)—and the start of the campaigning season.

No one fought wars in winter if they didn't have to.

Always there was beer, at every meal. Thin, sour, small beer at breakfast, because you didn't want to drink the water from the castle wells, which was rank and brackish. I grew to love the taste of that small beer. It cut through the grease of the breakfasts, which were heavy on the stodge, and damn good fuel for the morning's training ahead.

At lunch, two mugs of ale. At supper, six—eight on weekends. The ales varied, depending on what Matty Brewer had been brewing. He liked to experiment, did Matty the Brewer. He brewed hoppy ones, bitter ones, golden ones, thick black ones, fruit-infused ones, and ales made from malted wheat and oats and rye, rather than barley. All were decent, many excellent. We became beer connoisseurs and then full-on beer-bores.

We could prose on all night around our tables in the Undercroft— where we gathered during our down time, between bouts of dicing, skittles, and toss-the-horseshoe—about *nose* and *palate* and *aftertaste* and *forwardness* and *length*. After a night on the fruit beers, Grell's farts were virtuoso eruptions of olfactory appallingness. They would waft up to me on the bunk above and permeate the room, eliciting cries of "*Phwoorrhh!*" and "*Gods!*" and "*Fuckinell, Grell!*" and the sound of blankets flapping to fan the stench away.

Song? We sang a lot, especially in the Undercroft. Songs from all over the kingdom. Sad songs, funny songs, nonsense songs, love songs, longing songs, and not a few in the category *Unprintable*.

At night, we camped. Six to a bivouac, five in ours, because of Grell taking up room enough for two. Oller somehow always managed to slip to the other end of the rank as the bivouacs were counted off. He was good at slipping, Oller. One morning he presented the cook with two ducks he'd 'just happened to come across.' We passed the duckpond as we marched off after breakfast, where a baffled looking poulter was counting his ducks and coming up two short. We ate better than the other soldiers that night, having promised Cook one of the duck legs. After a week on the march, we arrived at the war.

The cause of which we had now learned.

My Lord of Rushtoun held a grudge against My Lord of Brigstowe, because My Lord of Brigstowe had married the girl My Lord of Rushtoun fancied. Who'd never fancied him, incidentally, so it wasn't as if My Lord of Rushtoun had a leg to stand on. But he had a grudge, and he nurtured it over the years, and when the chance came, he acted on it.

He'd had to settle for another wife, who he always resented and compared unfavorably to the one he'd lost, even though he'd never, so to speak, had her. And his wife soured—as who wouldn't, under the circumstances—and My Lord of Rushtoun and My Lady of Rushtoun grew apart, and were at best frostily polite, and at worst cold and hostile. Their marriage, though, had produced a daughter who was as lovely and happy as they were loveless and miserable. That much was known by all in Rushtoun; and the child, Esmeralda, was adored by all in Rushtoun as much as her mother was pitied. What no one but mother and daughter knew, and we were to learn later, was the truth about the girl who would soon cross our paths in the most unexpected way.

Well, that's not quite putting it the right way. *She* was unexpected, of course. A bunch of conscripted rank-and-filers, we didn't expect noble maidens to crop up in our lives. It was what happened *when* she crossed our paths that was unexpected. What she wanted was unexpected, even to her, and where it all led was *really* unexpected. And really significant in the grand scheme of things. But by that point, of course, we knew that everything was unexpected, and it didn't bother us. We simply dealt with it. Well, when I say *simply* … . No, it wasn't simple at all. We damn nearly didn't make it. But I get ahead of myself.

As the king grew weaker and weaker, the lords, great and small, began to flex their muscles and stretch their limbs. One lord would encroach, and another lord would retaliate. Alliances were formed, and betrayals betrayed and re-betrayed, and things began to pull themselves apart in the realm.

My Lord of Rushtoun remembered his grudge of decades ago and sensed his opportunity. He sent out raiding parties, who pillaged and stole and burned My Lord of Brigstowe's fields and villages. And when that went unpunished, because My Lord of Brigstowe had no standing army ready to protect his lands, into which his neighbors had not trespassed in generations, My Lord of Rushtoun grew bolder and invested a small, outlying town that was the demesne of My Lord of Brigstowe's liege-knight, Sir Fauntwyn of Pellingham, who rode with us as we marched southward, usually at My Lord of Brigstowe's side, and whom we called Sir Fucking Pelican, sometimes without the Fucking.

We all thought, what kind of name is *Fauntwyn*? You can't say that without a nostril-raised snoot down at us peasants. Tall, sinewy bugger was Sir Pelican. Also, our commanding officer, so we had to obey him, but we all itched to square up to him and sit him down hard in a puddle on his dainty noble backside. We all felt, inside, *who is this languid, drawling nincompoop?* Why's *he* got a demesne? Because his mother was Lady Someone, before she married his father, Sir Someone Else? What's he done to entitle him to order us around, and make us shove in there into the enemy ahead of him and die instead of him?

So, when the war came, we were all thinking, *look out for Number One.* And Number One was us. Me, Grell, Oller. The squad. The troop. *My Lord's army.* Us. Everyone else, corporals and above: they're *them.* We wouldn't shed a tear for Corporal Smott, Serjeant Bastard, Captain Doggett, Sir Fucking Pelican, or My Lord of Brigstowe and his grand companions. They weren't *us.*

We'd fight for them—of course we would. We had no choice if we wanted to avoid the gallows. But, really, we were fighting for *us.*

It was Oller who made it easy. Well, not easy for *us.* We had a tough time of it. But easy for our superiors. My Lord of Brigstowe had sent a small force off to besiege Pellingham with orders to make itself look like a big force. Lots of tents and banners and trumpets and squads marching busily in plain sight. Meanwhile, the rest of us, the bulk of My Lord's army, went the long way around through My Lord of Rushtoun's forests, where no one ever went except poachers. We ate well in those forests, feasting on My Lord of Rushtoun's venison. We knew they would have closed the gates of Rushtoun before we got there, but we'd cut their forces in half, and Rushtoun was undermanned behind its high, thick walls.

Those walls were the problem. There was a lot more of our army than there was of theirs, but they were safe and well-provisioned, and we were out in the open. A siege could take years. Skirmishing parties could make our lives miserable. They could harass us from the forests at night, whittle us down while My Lord of Rushtoun's soldiers slept safe and sound in nice warm barracks. Time was not going to be our friend.

We were outside those high, thick walls, looking up at them, thinking *this is no good.* My Lord of Rushtoun's guards jeered down at us and fired the occasional arrow.

Then Oller said, "There's always another way in."

Grell and I looked at him. We knew that tone when Oller spoke in it.

Secrets.

Hidden information.

Oller said, "Under. Over. Around. You don't have to go *through.* Gotta be an idiot, to try to go *through.*"

"Yeah, well, we're led by an idiot," Grell said.

I turned that over in my mind. It seemed to me that they were both right. "I think we should go and see Serjeant Bastard."

So, we did. Serjeant Bastard listened and took us to see Captain Doggett, and Captain Doggett took Serjeant Bastard and us to see My Lord of Brigstowe and his retinue in his silk-lined pavilion, who all looked down their noses at Captain Doggett and Serjeant Bastard— and, especially, at us. They argued and advised and covered their own backsides with politician subtlety as the wind blew this way and that. Until My Lord of Brigstowe said to Oller, "So. Got another way, have you?"

Knowing how to tickle the gentry, Oller said, "Mayhaps, My Lord. If My Lord pleases."

My Lord of Brigstowe preened modestly and probed, "How do you know this?"

"If it please My Lord, before I was fortunate enough to join My Lord's army, I was a bad lot. Joining My Lord's army has been the saving of me. Serjeant Blunt here and My Lord's officers such as Captain Doggett, sir, have given me a second chance. I'd be honored to offer my humble suggestion to My Lord in return."

My Lord of Brigstowe's eyes glinted with smugness. He contemplated Oller and nodded. "Thieves Guild?" he inquired.

Oller said, as if he'd never heard the term before, "My Lord may have better sources than me, but as far as I know there's—"

"—No such thing," My Lord of Brigstowe chimed in. "I know ten o' that, Private Oller. If I've heard it once, I've heard it forty times."

Oller didn't reply.

"So, this other way …?" My Lord probed.

"Mayhaps as I could find it," Oller offered.

"And if you could?"

"We'd open the gates for you."

"We?"

"I'd need help, My Lord. A hand-picked team. Which I would pick myself, if it's all the same with My Lord, and begging My Lord's pardon. This ain't a one-man job."

"Details?" My Lord of Brigstowe enquired.

Oller didn't reply for a long while. Eventually, he said, "Confidential."

My Lord of Brigstowe smirked at that. "As I suspected. Can't have you giving away *guild secrets*, now can we? Rest assured, we don't need details, Private Oller. We need results."

He paused, staring at Oller and the rest of us. "Can you deliver results?"

"I believe so, My Lord," Oller replied.

We all stood there, looking dumb and dutiful, while they all looked important and knowing, and conferred, briefly, in low posh voices—but they all knew that My Lord of Brigstowe had already made his decision.

"Very good, Private Oller," he said. "You have tonight. Use it well."

9

A Surprise Attack

Special Forces would have come in very useful in Oller's scheme, but we didn't have any Special Forces. Special Forces trained elsewhere. Underground, mostly, in deep caverns, and had Special Trainers. There'd been no time to round any up, either trainers or recruits. Organizing the Undead and *Weres* and the other unorthodox creatures that Special Forces favored took time. And specialist skills.

You couldn't just draft trolls, for example. You had to break them in, like horses. And that meant troll-breakers, and they were all many long leagues away in the Uplands. It took months to break a troll. My Lord of Brigstowe didn't have months. And as for what Serjeant Bastard disdainfully dismissed as "ghoulies and ghosties," they took some finding, too. Also, their dietary requirements were complicated. Less so after a battle, we gathered, when they'd tuck into enemy corpses while regulars like us were still looting them.

So, no SF, but we did have SFX—Special Effects. Our SFX came courtesy of Watkyn of Lorton, who'd been apprentice to Lorton's alchemist until Lorton's alchemist had found him in the broom cupboard bonking his wife. Breaking the terms of a five-year apprenticeship was a serious offence, so the reeve had given Watkyn a choice: serve your remaining four years in My Lord's dungeons or join My Lord's army.

Watkyn had entertained us all, in the Undercroft or at High Feasts, with his Stinks and Bangs. He couldn't do much more than fireballs and sparks, for Bangs, having only done one year of study—and they weren't *real* fireballs and flashes, just the effects of them for show.

Alchemists find that having a good show is an important part of their trade. The common folk didn't distinguish between alchemy and magic—which, of course, alchemists couldn't do because they weren't in the Guild of the Arcane Arts. They had their own guild, the Chymical Guild of Alchemie, and went about their own business; and if the common folk thought that what they did was magic, that was all for the better.

For Stinks, Wat did things like roses and glade-in-the-rain and ones he called *rainbows*, which were a potpourri of smells, all of them delectable. The ladies of the castle loved them, high-born and low. They loved Watkyn, too, if the rumors were to be believed. Wat spent many a night elsewhere than in the barracks, and the morning after those nights he'd be crap at sparring.

What he told us of his *not-so-nice* Stinks worried us. Another thing he had been doing at nights, he confided, was capturing Grell's farts. Oller called him Wat Fartcatcher after that, but only once, because Wat didn't appreciate it and clipped him around the ear. And Oller liked Wat—we all did.

The idea of weaponized Orc-fart began to grow on us. That could be a distraction in enemy ranks: it'd be like pouring hot water on an anthill. They'd be flailing about in panic. We all decided that we'd stand upwind of Wat when he flung them. Grell's farts were stored in little clay pots which Watkyn kept in straw-padded crates on a supply wagon. They were also, he told us, certain to be flammable, so we'd be needing fire arrows. This had intrigued Grell, who'd decided to ignite the next fart he felt coming on—and then, to make sure that it was going to be a damn good one. He ate an enormous supper that night, of what he considered a promising dietary combination: fish-paste on toast with fire-peppers, followed by beans (broad, runner, black, string); asparagus, fermented cabbage, a dozen spiced wild boar sausages, potatoes mashed with blue cheese, stewed plums with sour cream, oat biscuits, a selection of cheeses, mainly the runny, odiferous kind, all washed down with his ration of ale (eight mugs, it being a Saturday). Matty's brew that night happened to be plum-and-ginger-infused black ale, which was not only delicious and powerful but also superbly gassy. We all trooped back to barracks to wait for the results. They took a while to appear.

"I can't understand it," Grell said baffled. "You'd have thought they'd be coming by now." There was a lit candle ready by his bunk, which he was perched on, shifting anxiously, listening for the first tell-tale rumbles in his intestines. Unusually, there were none.

"I know what it is," he realized. "I'm so excited I can't fart."

We all agreed that was a sentence we'd none of us ever expected to hear.

Grell lay down and tried to relax. Not many minutes later, he said, "There's one! Definite rumble!" And then, "Yes. Ooh. I think we may be in luck …!"

He wasn't. But we were. "Here we go!" Grell said, hauling himself around on his back, so that his legs were in the air, sticking out sideways from his bunk as well as upwards. He lowered the candle into the firing line and let rip. Grell discovered, immediately and painfully, that he had made the elementary, and serious, mistake of not having any clothing on below his waist. Orcs are hairy all over, but especially hairy below the waist. Your average Orc backside looks like your average doormat.

I don't know if you've ever seen an Orc with his arse on fire, running screaming from the room, having first bashed his head on the bottom of the bunk above his, yelling. As a result, he could no longer hold his candle upright, thus pouring hot wax over his crotch, and yelling again, streaking across the yard trailing smoke and fire to plunge butt-first into a horse trough. But if you have, I know you'll agree it's a sight you'll never forget.

It was now time to battle test Watkyn's Stinks and Bangs.

And ourselves.

⋏ ⋏ ⋏

We stood in the dark under the east wall of Rushtoun, the other side from our encampment, with its cooking fires and torches and bustle and noise, staring up into the night. It was raining, which Oller was happy about. We weren't.

"Guards don't like rain no more'n you do," he explained. "They'll be skulking in their huts as much as they can, drying out and grumbling, and staring into their fires, which'll make 'em night-blind. Soldiers, eh?" He grinned his sly grin, his mismatched teeth glinting in the dark. "Won't be many patrols up there in this. No moon neither. Clouds as low as you could ask for. There'll be mist soon, I shouldn't wonder! Perfect. Piece of cake, this."

He got four thick pads of cloth out of his pack and sorted them into the order he wanted. Each had a leather strap on its back, from which, on two of the pads, loops of canvas hung on cords. "Legs," he explained, adjusting the loops so that he could slip his feet into them and then cinched them tight around his feet. He slipped his hands into the straps on the other two pads.

"Feet first," he said.

"You're going up that feet first?" I asked.

The wall he was studying was sixty feet high if it was an inch.

"Yep," he said, and adjusted his pack. A string hung behind him from the back of his belt. "I'll give it a flick when I'm up. Tie the ladder on and shimmy up, quiet as you can. Orcs can be quiet, yeah?" he asked Grell.

"Quiet as a mouse, Oller," Grell promised.

"Gods, I wish I could see their faces when they see you coming!" Oller chuckled. The little sod was actually *enjoying* himself. Out there, in the cold rain, about to climb a slippery wet wall with no rope.

I thought, *this might not end well, what's he so cocky about? We're about to invade a castle single-handed—well, the four of us.*

"Right," Oller said, when he'd tightened his gear. "See you up top."

When Oller said *feet first*, he meant it, but not in the way I'd pictured it. He placed his four stickies where he wanted them as he went up, the feet stickies always ahead higher, with their canvas stirrups hanging down. One at a time, he shifted a hand sticky or a foot sticky; and he did it at remarkable speed. Three of his four limbs were always stuck to the wall at any time, while he tore the fourth off at a sideways angle with a surprisingly quiet squelching sound and replaced it, higher, with an even quieter sticking sound.

Up into the night and the rain he crawled—squelch, *pok*—squelch, *pok*—squelch, *pok*—until he was out of earshot and then out of sight. Grell, Watkyn, and I waited, shivering, worrying about sentries and guards and arrows and spears and boiling oil and dungeons. The string flicked, tapping the wall with a quiet slap. I tied the rope ladder onto it, gave it two tugs as the signal to Oller, and it whipped up into the night. When it stopped, I tugged at it to test it.

Solid.

"Off you go, then," I said to the soldier who was waiting to run back with the message to Captain Doggett. He took off, and I shimmied up the rope ladder. Wat came after me, and finally Grell heaved up himself up, trying not to puff and pant. He couldn't have climbed in his plate armor, so was wearing only the plate helmet and leather everywhere else. His battledress was rolled up on his back, with all the other enormous bundles he was carrying.

I slid over the parapet, avoiding the dead guard whose throat Oller had cut, and helped Wat over with his backpack full of clay pots, *very* carefully; and then Grell loomed above us, carrying three times as many pots as Wat. I thought, *how the hell can they miss that? Over here! Fucking great heavily armed Orc hauling himself over the wall! Shoot, charge, sound the alarm!*

No arrows flew.

No footsteps came running.

No trumpets blew.

Watkyn and I had our bows, their strings off and wound up and under our helmets to keep them dry, and quivers full of arrows sealed because of the rain. Some of our arrowheads were bound in oil-soaked rags. I had my shield and sword and throwing axe, and Oller his harness of knives. So, neither of us could carry any of Wat's SFX pots. Wat reckoned we had more than enough Stinks and Bangs to put on a decent show, though. He was excited at the prospect of seeing them in action. And nervous, of course. We all were, even Grell. Orcs may be big and scary, but they're not stupid. They want to survive, same as anyone else.

We were four, trapped now inside an enemy town swarming with guards, and if we didn't pull this off, chances were we'd be dead. Captured alive, maybe, but that would be no fun either, what with dungeons and torturers. And the chances of guards letting us live when we'd slit the throats of their mates …?

We tried to calm our nerves and slow our racing hearts, but I for one didn't succeed. This was our first proper action, and we jumped at every shadow and imagined every kind of thing going wrong. My mouth was dry, and when I whispered, "Right," it came out as a croak.

We set off in single file, in the same order as we'd come over the wall: Oller, me, Watkyn of Lorton, and finally Grell. Along the parapet; blend into the shadows by the guard-hut; wait until they come out on their rounds. Oller was quick with his knives, always behind the back of the rearmost guard, who died without a sound and was in my arms so I could lower him quietly to the ground while Oller moved on to deal with his partner.

We had to work fast and move fast, because someone would notice the lack of patrols sooner rather than later and find the dead guards, and if the gates weren't open by the time they did that, they never would be.

We came down the wall level by level, staircase by staircase. Their floorboards creaked and yelped as we came, especially under Grell's weight, but there was noise aplenty at street level what with running feet, grooms and servants calling, officers barking orders, horses neighing and stamping, citizenry hurrying and shouting, and guards marching by in squads. They knew that My Lord of Brigstowe's army was outside the walls, so everyone was worried and busy, and no one noticed our little contributions to the hubbub.

We watched and waited and slipped from shadow to shadow as patrols passed, sloppy and soaked and miserable and tired, heads down in the steady rain. We left Grell in a cramped goat shed to get into his battledress, watched by a baleful milch-goat. Collen the Smith had made Grell's battledress the day before. It was, basically, a dress—but one made of chainmail. Grell slipped it over his head and buckled the sleeves around his arms. He was going to clank, he knew, but when I gave him the signal, speed was going to be more important than silence.

Wat and I took our stations at points that covered the gates and its guard-posts. Sir Fucking Pelican had often been a guest of My Lord of Rushtoun, before hostilities had broken out, and knew the town well. He had drawn us a plan of the area around the gates, and an accurate one it turned out to be. When we were all in place Oller slipped, quiet as a cat, into shadows which swallowed him up. We listened, to the noises of the town and the silences beyond them and the hissing rain; and then Oller was back from where Sir Pelican had said the guard brazier nearest the gate would be. It had been, exactly where he'd marked it on his plan.

Oller joined me, handing me the lantern he'd lit from the brazier, its shutters closed so as not to give off even the faintest glow of light. I could feel heat radiating from it. Oller slunk off to his spot and then it was just a moment or two to breathe, and—*time to do this.* I gave the little stray-dog *yip* I'd agreed on with Grell, and there he was beside me, quickly and a lot more quietly than we'd feared.

"Grease," Grell said. "Collen greased it, so it don't clank much."

"Go get 'em, mate!" I whispered.

And in seconds Grell was at the gates and lifting the great oak-beam bars that held them shut. He dropped them both to the ground with a resounding clatter and started to haul the gates open. They were only a quarter of the way open when the guards erupted from the guardhouse, but that was enough. Grell picked up one huge oaken bar, raised it high over his head, and threw it at them as they charged him. They went down like ninepins. He threw the other bar at another mob of guards, coming at him from the guardhouse on the other side of the gates, with the same result.

It was time to fight. Yet again I wished that I was a battlemage rather than a foot soldier. Foot soldiers get hurt. Battlemages can heal. For all I knew, though, there were no such people in this world. I pushed the thought aside as I lit a fire arrow. Wat began hurling his pots, and his Stinks and Bangs burst out of them, loud, blinding and fetid. When he'd thrown them all, he too got to work with his bow. Soon we were shooting war arrows as well as fire arrows, picking off guards who couldn't see where we were, to distract them from Grell who was hauling on the gates again. They were shooting at him, but he worked on, heaving the enormous gates open foot by painful foot, ignoring the few arrows that hit him, and the many that bounced off his battledress.

Then the guards turned and shot wildly at where they thought we were—but weren't. We were always somewhere else. We could see them, outlined against the fires that our arrows had started when they slammed into the guardhouse. Wherever they were aiming, they were aiming wrong, because they couldn't see us. They especially couldn't see Oller, who slipped among them hamstringing and stabbing.

I kept my eye on Oller as he worked his way among the enemy guards, slashing and slicing, so I noticed when the smooth flow of his progress was abruptly halted. Instead of weaving among his victims, he was upright and gagging as a guard had his arm around his throat—and a dagger raised to plunge into his chest, from high and behind.

The guard was holding Oller up between himself and me. I had no time to think, which was almost certainly a good thing. Instinct told me where to aim, and in the brief half-second I had when the guard pulled Oller across to give himself a better target for his knife, I let fly. The arrow took the guard in the neck. Oller dropped to the ground as another guard lunged at him, and I put two arrows into that guard, chest and stomach. Oller looked around, knew he was safe, and disappeared into the shadows again.

And not a minute too soon.

Because at that moment we learned, spectacularly, that Watkyn had been right. The stench of his Stink pots had been unbearable enough, distracting the guards and alarming them—they wondered what in all hells were they being attacked by! Anything that smelled that disgusting had to be *terrifying* …

What scared them out of their wits and ended the brief but spectacular battle at the gates of Rushtoun was the moment that Watkyn's belief—that his Grell-harvested Stinks were flammable—was proven all too true. A miasma of heavy, putrid, volatile gases, engendered in fruit beers, brewed in Grell's bowels, and aged for weeks in Watkyn's clay pots, erupted in a volcanic, foul-smelling inferno. Flaming, gagging guards ran in all directions. Oller and I fired a few more arrows at them for good measure, but stopped when the wind shifted and held our sleeves over our noses, our eyes streaming.

We were downwind. My Lord of Brigstowe's vanguard was upwind and pouring through the gates that Grell had opened, Sir Pelican at their head, roaring at the top of his lungs and fighting like a one-man pack of hounds. I made a quick reassessment of Sir Fucking Pelican. He may have looked like a ninny, and sounded like a prat, but he was screaming steel hell on legs when it mattered.

Wat, Oller, and I regrouped at the rendezvous and hurried to Grell, who was trying to get an arrow out of his buttock. Watkyn, being in the alchemist line, knew about wounds and medicines and dressings. The arrow had pierced the chainmail of Grell's battledress and skewered it to Grell's backside. Other arrows stuck through the battledress into other parts of Grell, but he didn't seem particularly bothered. A deft twist, at which Grell grunted and at which I would have fainted, and the arrow was out. Grell said he didn't need a dressing; it was only a scratch.

Wat and I helped Grell to the guardroom, Grell limping a bit but not in any serious pain. Orcs, we had learned over our weeks of sparring, could take a great deal of punishment. Wat extracted the other arrows from Grell neatly and quickly, stitched up the worst of Grell's wounds, and put salve on the others. We rested after our exertions, drinking the guards' ale, relaxing, and telling anyone who came in and tried to make us do anything to sod off. Oller had disappeared.

My Lord's army did the rest while we recovered in the guardhouse. They rounded up the surrendering guards and reassured the citizenry, who were terrified and fearing the worst. And while the Powers That Were dealt with anyone who was anything to do with My Lord of Rushtoun, we were in the barracks commons with the other tired but happy soldiery, drinking ale, relaxing, and chatting, everyone telling everyone else what he'd done and what his mates had done.

The cooks were ordered to turn My Lord of Rushtoun's High Supper into My Lord of Brigstowe's Victory Feast. At which, Serjeant Bastard himself informed us, we—the four of us—were to be Recipients of Honors. Serjeant Bastard knew the form. He kept us outside the Great Hall until the correct moment, in parade formation, in full fig, armor nothing like polished to a sheen, but with the worst of the mud and blood scraped off, and weapons at the display. When the fanfare sounded, he said, "Right, lads, chins up, chests out, shoulders back, bags of swank!" Then he marched us in behind My Lord of Brigstowe's banner and heralds, *left right left right*. We stamped smartly to a halt below the High Table.

Serjeant Bastard bellowed, "Privates Third Class Lorton, Ozborn, Pinches, and Pytte, *sah!*" He took a right turn and marched four paces, halted, turned left, and froze in place at attention, eyes front, sword upright at the display, his sword arm parallel to the ground.

Of course, it was all about them, not us. The High and Mighty. Our job was to stand there and look dutiful and honored while the High and Mighty addressed us. And each other. And their adoring public. My Lord of Brigstowe said this, and Sir Fucking Pelican said that. Each rose to his feet, solemnly, and observed the protocols. My

Lord of Brigstowe prosed for ten minutes, Sir Pelican for five. I was beginning to regret not having taken a leak before this dog-and-pony show had begun, when it was all over.

Privates *First* Class Lorton, Ozborn, and Pytte.

Straight from Third to First.

Lance Corporal Pinches.

We swelled with pride, Oller most of all. The double jump meant four extra silvers a month, not just two, for us, and the triple jump meant six for Oller.

A purse each, five *gold*, from My Lord of Brigstowe's own hand!

And to cap it all, we four were the first-ever recipients of the Valorous Order of Champions of Pellingham—which were pinned onto our chests by Sir Fauntwyn himself. Only, the insignia hadn't been designed yet, so he pinned on white ribbons as markers where they'd go once they actually existed.

We *about turned,* as smart as you like, and marched to our places on a lower table with the rest of our squad, who clapped us on the back and cheered and toasted us and jeered at our white ribbons and started calling us the White Ribbon Girls. Soldiers can be pretty basic. Can be? Make that *usually are by default.* And then they went back to what they had been doing before the presentation, which included eating and drinking, but was mainly gazing adoringly at Esmeralda and sighing. There was as much sighing that night as toasting and jeering.

Being nobility the High and Mighty had observed the forms. Though now technically My Lord of Brigstowe's prisoner in the Great Hall of what had, until a few hours previously, been his own castle, My Lord of Rushtoun was at the High Table as if an honored guest, seated on My Lord of Brigstowe's left. My Lady of Rushtoun was on My Lord of Brigstowe's right. She looked composed and comfortable, her husband discomposed and sullen.

But nobody looked much at them. All eyes were, at every opportunity, on Esmeralda, seated next to her mother. From our bench at the far end of the hall, she looked hardly more than a radiant golden blob. But she was the loveliest golden blob that any of us had ever seen. We drank her in, and drank ourselves up, from loud to quiet to wistful and back again. Golden hair, like sunlight on a waterfall, held back off her radiant loveliest face by a bright green ribbon. A matching bright green ribbon graced her throat. A simple kirtle of the same green over a simple white chemise. Eyes as blue as cornflowers, and a smile that weakened knees. Her every movement was music. She chatted happily with all and sundry; and when she laughed, the Great Hall echoed with a hundred answering private, understanding murmurs of joy. Looking at her, we all felt like the only man there. Minstrels strolled below the High Table, singing of chivalry, nobility, heroism, and true love, but mainly getting in the way as they sang at Esmeralda, so we had to bend this way and that to do our gazing.

It was an excellent night. The wine flowed and was magnificent. My Lord of Rushtoun was something of a connoisseur, having some of the best vineyards in the realm down in his southern lands along the river. His stewards, eager to please their new overlord, made free with his cellars, bringing up the best stuff we'd ever tasted in our lives, and an endless supply of it. We enjoyed guzzling it, raising our glasses to him as he watched, glumly, from the High Table.

The women of Rushtoun were delighted to see us. We'd done the opposite of slaughtering their menfolk. We'd saved the lot of them. We'd liberated them from My Lord of Rushtoun's bossy guards, with their requisitions and orders and *don't you know there's a war on?* There wasn't a war on anymore. Peace had broken out, and we behaved like proper, respectful, peacetime citizens, which drove them wild. We'd *won!*

Moreover, the battle fever had not ended in battle lust which they had understandably feared. Serjeant Bastard had told us all that we were guests in their town and were to behave accordingly. He hadn't needed to spell it out. *Mind your manners, no raping and pillaging, or you'll be up before me. And you don't want to be up before me.*

I'd never heard my squadmates so polite. Not a questionable word escaped their lips as we mingled with the townsfolk. The men of Rushtoun were wary and uncommunicative. The women, by contrast, were welcoming and happy to talk. Earnest conversations broke out, on high tables and low, about all sorts of unimpeachable things, but as the wines and ales flowed the undercurrent beneath those innocent topics flowed harder and faster, carrying us all with it. No Rushtoun woman needed to say it. The meaning below our small talk was clear enough.

1: You've saved us from My Lord of Rushtoun's guards.

2: You saved our husbands.

3: You saved our boring husbands, with whom we are fed up because they are so deadly dull, and nothing exciting ever happens around here and when it eventually does it's, *whoa, no, My Lord of Brigstowe and his nasty pieces of work, we're all going to die and be raped and pillaged …!* Instead, it's, *ooh, look at these nice polite big strong Brigstowe soldiers who have come to save us!*

4: Another drink?

5: Don't mind if I do, soldier boy/gracious lady.

So, one thing led to another, or rather several others, and nice and agreeable it all was. Our thoughts were wandering—as were our hands. *Wouldn't mind finding myself in a quiet corner with you,* and, *hot in here isn't it, fancy a bit of fresh air?* And, from the voice attached to the hand that patted my leg under the table that I was now sitting at—which had started off mainly Rushtoun women, but was now equal parts Brigstowe soldiers—a hand that belonged to Deb the Scribe, who'd been pleasantly surprised to learn that I could read, "Would you like to see my scrolls?"

It was the most exciting question I'd ever been asked.

It had been a fine night, and it was only going to get finer. Those who wanted to sit outside and look at the stars and shyly hold hands and sigh in a moment of spiritual, poetic wonder that they would never forget, did so. Those who wanted to gallop each other in the stables or haylofts or barns or cellars, likewise.

I lost Daxx's virginity to Deb the Scribe, in her chamber above the scriptorium, after perusing one scroll for a few moments of polite appreciation, then looking at her. And then we were kissing before she broke off, took my hand, and led me to her bed. Afterwards, we talked for hours. And after talking for hours, stopped talking. For hours. The one thing we never talked about was what was happening. I just wanted, she just wanted, and we responded to the signals that we sent each other. It was the best night I'd had in ages. As I drifted off to sleep, I thought guiltily about Qrysta. Why *guiltily*, I berated myself? She and I were crew, that was all. I'd often thought it would be nice if there was more to our relationship than that—but there wasn't, so snap out of it. I hoped that she was having as good a time as I was. Then I immediately didn't. Who was I kidding? The thought of her with someone else was unsettling. *So don't have that thought,* I told myself. And added, *hypocrite, or what?*

Dawn came. We ignored it. We ignored the reveille. We ignored *Come to the Cookhouse Door, Boys,* when the trumpeter blew it at noon, far away in our camp outside the town walls. We ignored everything except each other for as long as we could. Which wasn't long enough and had to—as all good things must—eventually come to an end.

IO

The Heartstone

We were billeted in barracks that had formerly housed My Lord of Rushtoun's guards. Lance Corporal Oller started throwing his weight around right away. We couldn't decide if he meant it or was just doing it to annoy us. We decided that the answer would be the same in either case. The answer was Grell picking him up by the throat in one huge hand as he strutted around our barracks, yapping pointless orders, his lance-jack's stripe newly sewn onto each sleeve.

"Make that bed, lickety-split, private! Polish them boots, private—you call them polished! Cook's old blind bitch could lick 'em them shinier than that! Double quick now— *Arghhh …!*"

Dangling there, a foot off the ground, with Grell glaring at him and breathing his noxious exhalations at him that were even more ferocious than his glare, Oller got the message.

He apologized that night, handsomely. "You have to understand that I am a prat," he told us. "By default. Look after Number One. I'm not that bloke now. Well, *course* I am, you've all seen me all puffed up with my stupid stripe. But I am trying—and I would *so* love to succeed—to change. I just wanted to prove I deserved it." He was clearly rattled by how angry Grell had been with him. He shook his head. "Nah—I was just bigging myself up is all. Who am I kidding?

This fucking stripe? This thing could've cost me my *friends* if I'd gone on like that. It ain't worth it."

He hacked his left sleeve off, above its chevron, threw it in the fire and then collapsed on his stool, staring at the burning sleeve, tears running down his face.

Grell patted his shoulder somewhat awkwardly. "It's okay, mate. I shouldn't have come on so hard. We still love you—don't we, Daxx?"

"Of course," I said.

When Oller stopped sniffling, had wiped his eyes, and for the last time smeared his snot-strained right sleeve across his nose, he looked at us. One after the other. Then back again. He gulped. "I never had friends before," he said.

For some reason, it seemed just about the saddest thing I'd ever heard. I didn't know what to say, until I remembered what seemed like a very long time ago.

"I never had any friends either, Oller," I said. "Except Grell, and … someone else. And we'd never even met."

Oller looked confused. "Eh?"

"We … corresponded," I said. "Grell lived leagues away."

"Up Orc Country?" Oller tried to follow.

"Yes," Grell said. "I never met Daxx in real, um …"

Oller said, "Oz, right?" He was getting surer.

Grell nodded. "It's a long way from where Daxxie lived. We met here for the first time face-to-face."

"You're educated," Oller said, turning to look at me. "You should be the lance-jack, not me."

"Not your decision, Oller, nor mine," I said. "You keep your stripe. You earned it; you'll be a damn fine lance corporal. We'll follow you anywhere, won't we, Grello?"

Grell grinned, nodding. "As long as he asks nicely."

Oller started sniffling again, and I went off to get another shirt his size and two more cloth chevrons from the quartermaster.

Oller, watching me sew his stripes on, was silent and thoughtful. He shook his head. "Can't think what's happening to me," he muttered, confused. "Never done this before."

"Never done what before, Oller?" I asked.

Oller looked at us. "I've got friends now. You should *share* with your friends."

And he told us where he'd sneaked off to on the night of our raid and the taking of Rushtoun.

As he talked, we followed him out. It was night. The streets were dark, apart from the odd lantern carried by the odd citizen. There were lamps on poles in the town square, and on the walls of the inns, but here, in the side streets where Oller was leading us, there were only shadows. "Good," Oller said, "no one will see us." And also, "Don't tell anyone. It'd get me into trouble with my superiors. And I'm not talking about no officers in My Lord's army, my ... *other* officers. Not that you'd tell anyone, us being friends and all. And you trust your friends." It was as if he was reminding himself of the rules of a new game. You do *this* now, not *that* anymore. *That* was then, *this* is now.

"I knows where they hide things, see?" he went on. "It's always the same places. They think they're being oh-so-clever and original, but that's because they're amateurs. Amateur hiders. I'm a professional finder. Was." He stopped by a blank wall, listened, looked around. "Turn around," he told us. "Don't look."

We obeyed, even though we couldn't have seen what he was doing anyway.

There was a click and a rustle and then Oller said, "Follow me."

A section of the wall had swung open. A faint light emanated from it. We had to crouch to go in, Grell needing to drop onto all fours. Inside, though, the passage was high enough for him to stand up while Oller swung the secret door closed.

"Where are we, Oller?" I asked and, "How did you find this place?"

"Thieves Guild," Oller said, answering both questions. He led the way down the gently sloping passage, our feet making almost no noise on the soft, sandy floor.

That, clearly, was all he was going to say.

"Have you been here before?" I asked.

"I popped in here to make my number, soon as I could. Rules. New face, new town: you have to make your number at the TG. Can't have freelancers working the patch, getting in everyone's way."

"How did you know it was here?" I asked.

"Likely-looking faces. You soon learn how to pick 'em out. Then it's secret signs to each other, back and forth, then a casual chat—wouldn't sound anything out of the ordinary to a civilian, but it'd have certain *ordinary-sounding* words and phrases in it, that say a lot to us. Guild handshake—sorted. Go your separate ways, meet at the appointed place, follow him or her here, report to the Receiver. I'll need to get his say-so before you can come in, wait here."

We had reached a wide space at the end of the passage, part cellar, part cavern. It was filled with barrels, chests, crates, trunks, and hand-carts piled high with boxes. We waited while Oller padded over to a table where a small, black-coated man sat.

They conferred in whispers. Oller padded back.

"I vouched for you, you're in." He led the way again—not ahead into the cellar, but off along its wall to one side. "In here." He held open a door which he closed behind us when we were inside. It was a small room, in it another table, several chairs, and sets of scales and weights and measures. "This is where we do business with outsiders. Buying and selling and the like. It's the only room where non-Guild folks are allowed. You wait here, I need to get my lockbox. It's safer here than in barracks. Safer here than anywhere. Safer than it would be in that vault of His Lordship's up in his castle. 'Cos we know where that is. No one knows where this is. And we lock away our lockboxes, where no one else can get at them, because—well, if you're caught stealing, you're out of the Guild for life and all your lockboxes confiscated, no second chances but … *thieves*, right?" He grinned and disappeared. He returned a few minutes later with a small, iron-bound chest which he put on the table.

He locked the door and then, with a key hanging from a cord around his neck inside his shirt, he opened the chest. "Got another o' these in Brigstowe, but that's empty apart from dead flies. Nothing like as nice as this one, which cost a pretty pile o' coin but was worth it, and anyway, I'm flush now what with what I found after the raid when everyone was running about all over the place and not looking where I was looking. That's always the best time, when everyone's panicking. I thought I might as well take a look around, see what's what."

One by one, he brought out his trophies.

A purse of gold, heavier than the ones we'd been given. "Eighteen pieces o' gold!" he said. "Found this in the old *Loose Brick in the Chimney* in My Lord's chamber. Them was behind My Lord's chest of drawers." He handed Grell a leather-bound book. "The one with the odd telltale scrapes on the floor by its feet where he keeps dragging it back and forth. Hopeless." Grell had opened the book and

128

was turning the pages, not believing his eyes. I glanced at it. It was a picture book, and the pictures were extremely—to cut the next word short—*graphic.*

Grell said, "You and Deb try this one, Daxxie?"

"Whoa!" I said, checking out the picture he was pointing at. "No, not yet …"

"Collector's item, that," Oller said. "It'll fetch a pretty penny from the right dealer. Solid silver, these candlesticks," he continued. "Look at that molding and the engraving. Antiques, them. Just standing about in the open, would you believe it, one on each of My Lord's bedside tables, candles still in 'em! My Lady's tom."

Grell said, "Huh?"

"Sorry—thief talk. We rhyme words, then shorten them. Tomfoolery, joolery."

He took the pieces out, one at a time, and handed them to us. We inspected them, turning them over in our hands then placing them back on the table. Brooches; necklaces; rings; a delicate tiara of filigree gold wires, like a very small crown, its points tipped with pearls; belt buckles and shoe buckles of silver and gold. "Top of wardrobe, behind the privy, secret floorboard." He let us know where he'd searched and done his finding. "More a *bleeding obvious* floorboard to eyes like mine, it being shinier than the other floorboards, all that rubbing as she lifts it up and down. And this"—he got out a small pouch of soft yellow leather—"lovely, this is. Never seen anything the like."

From within the pouch, he brought out a large jewel. "Tourmaline, and I've never seen a bigger nor a finer! Got to know your jewels in my line o' work."

It was red at one end and green at the other, the colors merging into each other like a path leading away up a hillside towards a sunset.

The word was out of my mouth before I knew that I'd opened it. "*Heartstone!*"

"Eh?" Oller said. "What's that, when it's at home?"

"I … don't know," I admitted. I'd heard the word before—but where?

"But you know what it is."

Did I? I wondered as I held my hand out for it, and Oller gave it to me.

And then I remembered. *Heartstone knows when you're lying.*

Marnie.

The red and green jewel that I was holding was nothing like the lapis lazuli stone in her staff. *But then*, I thought, *why should it be?*

"I think …" I trailed off, pondering. "If this is what I think it is …"

I gazed at it, *into* it, turning it over and over in my hand. It was beautiful, its shifting reds the crimson of summer roses, the burgundy of fine wine, its greens promising growth and foliage. And it was *warm* … the warmth of sunshine on a meadow. The warmth of blood on grass.

"Where did you find it?" I asked.

"Her Ladyship's chapel. Inside Her Ladyship's embroidered kneeler. She's a devotee of Lymnia, who from memory is the Goddess of Patience and Forbearance. Am I right?"

We didn't know.

Oller frowned. "I thought you read books," he said to me accusingly.

"We don't have—who was it?—*Lymnia*, where I come from."

"Oh." He remembered. "Foreign. I keep forgetting. Here, look what it does." He held his hand out for the stone. I passed it to him.

He wrapped his hands around it, leaving a small hole by his thumbs, and held them up. "Take a peek," he said.

I put my right eye to the gap between his thumbs. The jewel inside was glowing, lighting up the space within his cupped hands.

I felt, as I watched its glow, its reds and greens dance and change and merge, a sensation of being drawn in … . "Wow."

In turn, after his peek, Grell also said, "Wow."

"Watch," Oller said, closing his hands tight.

We watched.

After a while, his hands glowed, from within, the red glow shining through so that we could see his bones and veins, then slowly changing to green and back again.

That was no ordinary jewel. Suddenly, I knew what I needed to do.

"Oller, can I have it? On loan," I added quickly, at his scowl. "I'll give it back, I promise."

"What d'you want it for?" Oller asked, suspicious.

"I need to show it to someone."

"Who?"

"You don't know her. She'll be pleased with you if you do," I added, and the tone of my voice informed Oller that that would be a good thing for him.

Oller looked at his beautiful treasure again. Something seemed to change in his mind, at which he nodded and grunted as if in agreement.

He looked up at me and held out the heartstone. "Seeing as you saved my life not once but twice, Daxx, with your fancy shooting back at the gates, it's yours."

"Oller, no, I—"

"Yes, you can," he interrupted. "Take it. You know what it is. Even if you don't. And you know what *that* means," he said, with a *very* significant look.

"I don't," I said, once again holding the warm, gleaming heartstone and staring at it, hypnotized by its enticing glow.

"You will," Oller assured me. "We don't talk about it. Different guild. They mind their own business, we mind ours. This"—he nodded at the heartstone—"is GAA business, not TG. Want me to ask around, find the local branch?"

I'd been thinking how to look into the Guild of the Arcane Arts, to see if I could learn whether there was magic in this world. On finding the tourmaline heartstone, though, I knew where I needed to take it.

"No," I said. "Thanks all the same."

"What you planning, Daxx?" he said, with his lopsided smile.

"I think," I said eventually, "that we three need to go on a journey."

"Ooh, goody!" Oller grinned. "Don't know about you two, but I'm getting fed up with soldiering."

"Me too," Grell agreed. "Dull as hell, a peacetime army."

We all gazed at the heartstone. It was hard to look away from it, in that quiet, dark little room.

"I think it's meant for you, Daxx," Oller said, slowly. "I think I was meant to find it for you. It shines brighter when you touch it."

"Does it?" I turned the tourmaline over in my hands. Its reds and greens did, indeed, seem to be glowing more brightly. "I think you're right. Thank you, Oller."

"My pleasure—*friend*."

I wrapped the heartstone back up in its soft leather pouch and said, "One day, I hope I find something for you."

Oller grinned. "That would be nice. But if I'm with you, I'll find it before you do." He added, with a wink, "I knows where to look."

Oller put his treasures back, locked up his lockbox, and trotted out with it. He came back without it, and we left. Oller locked the room behind us and returned its key to the Receiver. As we reached what seemed like a blank wall at the end of our tunnel, which we knew led out into the back alley, Oller pointed to the two words written on the wall, above the secret door.

Finders Keepers.

"Guild motto, that is," he said.

⋏ ⋏ ⋏

"Where in all hells have you three been?" Serjeant Bastard demanded as we were marched into the Orderly Room between six of his guards. "We've been searching high and low for you, castle and barracks! I even had to send a search squad into *town!*"

"That's where we were, Serjeant." "Sorry, we were off duty, Serjeant." "We didn't know you wanted us, Serjeant, we had time off so we—" We blurted, over each other and all at once, until Serjeant Bastard leapt to his feet, roaring.

"*Time off! Time off!* There's no *time off* in My Lord's army! What do you think this is, a bleeding school picnic?"

"No, Serjeant." "Sorry, Serjeant." "What did you want to see us about, Serjeant?" We mumbled in reply, chastened.

Blunt glared at us and slowly sat back down. "Well, you wasn't to know, I suppose. Came out of the blue to me, so …" He shook his head. "How was you miserable lot to know His Lordship of Rushtoun wants to see you, right away if you please, in His Lordship's Inner Sanctum? Off you go now and look smart about it! It don't look good to keep His Lordship waiting, and it don't reflect well on *me*, so be off with you. At the double! *One two one two—*"

We saluted, about turned, and ran.

"What's an Inner Sanctum?" Grell asked, as we hurried from the castle's barracks to its residential quarters.

"Dunno," I said, and neither did Oller. But Steward Hemwarth did, when we found him at his table in My Lord's counting house. He worked all day and all night, did Steward Hemwarth. Rumor was he even slept in the counting house. He led us along a dark-paneled corridor with rich carpets on the floor and portraits of haughty-looking Rushtoun ancestors on the walls, sneering down at us. He knocked on the door at the end of it, and stood aside when My Lord of Rushtoun's harsh, supercilious voice from within rasped out, "Send them in."

"Yes, my lord," Hemwarth said, with his usual obsequiousness.

He held the door for us, and we stepped in nervously.

A figure was seated in the chair beyond My Lord of Rushtoun's large, ornate desk. The chair was facing the other way. All we could see of it was its high, carved back.

"Shut the door and leave, Hemwarth," the voice growled, deep and rough. My Lord of Rushtoun clearly had a nasty throat that evening. I hoped I wouldn't catch what had brought it on. "And no listening at the door!"

"At once, my lord. Certainly not, my lord."

The door closed behind us.

"Draw the curtains," My Lord of Rushtoun ordered. "Behind you."

I turned and found the thick, heavy drapes which I drew across the door.

"Nosy bugger's always listening at keyholes. Hence the curtains." My Lord of Rushtoun's voice was somehow higher and less raspy than it had been as he rose from his chair and turned to face us. The reason for which was that the figure sitting on it was not My Lord of Rushtoun, but his daughter Esmeralda.

"Took you long enough!" she snapped.

And in her own voice, it was the sweetest, most delightful snap you could ever possibly hear.

Silly grins came to our faces, and we simpered.

"Don't *do* that!" Esmeralda ordered.

"Do what?" I said, smiling dreamily.

"Simper! I *hate* simpering. And wipe those stupid grins off your faces, you look like sheep that have eaten idiot-grass!"

I laughed. As did Grell and Oller.

"Is that a thing?" I said. "*Idiot-grass?* Or did you just make it up? I hope it's a thing. I'd like to try some, it sounds delightful. If not, it's the cleverest joke I've ever heard!"

"Oh, for the love of Lymnia!" Esmeralda groaned. She had come around the desk now and strode towards us. "Goddess of Patience and Forbearance give me *strength*." She stared at us, her lips pursed. She took a deep breath, clearly trying to control her temper.

She began again. "You're here to do a job. A hard, horrible, dangerous job, which nobody must know about, ever, under any circumstances, and I picked you because you're hard, horrible, dangerous characters—everyone knows what you did the night of the raid. You and that skirt-mad alchemist. And you stand there, simpering and tittering like half-drunk chickens!"

"Tee hee hee," I agreed, thinking of chickens simpering and Grell being compared to one and how funny and charming she was while Grell gurgled and Oller chuckled.

She waited for us to stop. We eventually subsided, and stood there, gazing at her adoringly.

She stared back stonily.

"Turn around," she said at last.

We turned.

"Okay, you can look now," she said, her voice slightly muffled.

When we turned back, she was wearing a bag over her head.

It was as if the light had gone out of the room, *and taken the unicorns and pixies and flowers with it, and the bunny rabbits had scuttled back into their little holes . . .*

"No," we said, "please take that off. There is no—"

"Do you know how annoying," she interrupted us from within her bag, "it is, to have to carry this stupid thing around with me everywhere? If I want to get anything actually *done?*"

We did not. If we wanted to get anything done, we had to do it ourselves. But then, we weren't nobility.

"Inside this bag it's hot and stuffy, and I can't see your faces to see what you're thinking. It's much easier to lie to someone with a bag over their head than to someone who can read you like a wide-open book. So, don't make me do this again!"

She took the bag off, and as she stuffed it back into the pocket of her smock, the sun came out again, the unicorns and rainbows danced around her once more, the bunny rabbits emerged from their little holes, and—

"This is *serious*," she said. "I need you to take me seriously! For all the gods' sakes! At the moment, inside, I look like *him!*" She pointed at Grell, then held her arms up at him like claws above her head and gave a scary attacking *roawwrr!*

It was the loveliest scary roar you could ever hear.

"*Awww,*" we murmured.

"*Argghh!*" she howled.

"I don't look like that," Grell said, grinning at her wistfully. "Wish I did."

"Oh, so the big scary Orc wants to be a girl, does he?" Esmeralda taunted.

"No," Grell said, quickly, "I meant …" He swallowed and finished lamely. "Nice."

Esmeralda glared at him, breathing hard.

Her glare faded, and she sighed. "I'm sorry. It's not your fault. It's the fault of that fairy fucking godmother, excuse the technical terminology."

"What fairy godmother?" I asked.

"I'll tell you later—*if* you agree to help me. Please?" Her lips were trembling. "I've got no one else to turn to. You're my only hope."

"Anything," I said.

"I shouldn't have spoken to you like that. I … well, you're *soldiers.* I thought I had to act tough, or you wouldn't take me seriously."

Tears were running down her cheeks. We were all handkerchiefs and concern, and *there there,* and *of course we'll help,* and *just tell us what you need us to do,* while our hearts broke for her. She wiped her eyes with *my* handkerchief—she'd chosen *my* handkerchief!—then blew her perfect nose with exquisite grace into it and handed it back. I put it away quickly, in a buttoned inside pocket which even Oller wouldn't be able to pick. I wasn't going to wash that handkerchief ever, I was going to keep it always, have it framed and hung above my mirror where I could gaze at it—no, I'd wear it in my helmet as her favor, in a tourney, which I'd win, because I had her favor, which meant that she loved me, and we'd get married and ride off to our castle, me on a white steed and her on a dappled palfrey with the unicorns and pixies and rainbows and bunny rabbits—ooh, and some little tweety birds too.

"I've never done anything like this before," Esmeralda said, breaking into my reverie. "I'm scared, but I know I have to. And I don't trust anyone else in this town. They'll just shop me to Daddy and I'll be grounded. And when I saw you at the feast and heard what you'd done and how brave you were, I thought Lymnia had heard my prayers. I can't go alone, it wouldn't be safe."

"Go where?" I asked.

"Mayport."

Mayport, we knew, was the capital city, which lay many long leagues to the south.

"Them roads aren't safe at the best of times," Oller agreed. "Bandits, outlaws, wolves, bears and so on. And this ain't the best of times, what with the wars and such."

"And patrols," Esmeralda said. "They'd be out looking for me as soon as they saw I was gone. I'll pay you, of course. A hundred gold each."

We wouldn't earn that much in twenty years in My Lord of Brigstowe's army, no matter how high we rose through the ranks. Deserting sounded a lot more lucrative than soldiering.

Grell said, "Why d'you need to go to Mayport?"

"To find her."

"Find who?"

"My fairy godmother."

None of us knew what to say to that.

"She came to me in a dream on my sixteenth birthday and in all my dreams since. She's in the King's City, she says, and Mayport's where the king lives. I have to go to her, and I must hurry. I have something for her, she says, and she has something for me."

I said, "Did she say what that is?"

Esmeralda shook her head. "No. Just that the fate of the realm depends on it."

She sounded and looked miserable as she said it.

Silence fell in His Lordship's Inner Sanctum.

I glanced at the others.

"Well, I'm in," Oller said. "A hundred o' gold, or sitting on my arse in barracks all day?"

"Too right," Grell said. "And what were we saying earlier, eh? Dull as hell, a peacetime army."

Esmeralda's slumped shoulders straightened, and she looked at us, almost in disbelief.

"You will?"

I said, "We will."

"Oh, thank you, *thank* you!" She hugged us each in turn. "I'm sorry I was rude earlier, I just thought—well you'd be hard, horrible, dangerous characters, so I had to be horrible."

Grell, a soppy grin on his face from Esmeralda's hug, said, "I'm not horrible."

She looked at him. "I expect you can be, if you want."

"Well," Grell admitted, "yes. But I'd never be horrible to *you*."

"Just to anyone I told you to be horrible to?"

"Yeah, just point 'em out! But I don't want you to think of *me* as horrible, that's all. 'Cos I'm not. Am I, Daxx?"

"Not to those you like," I said.

"See? I like you," he said to Esmeralda. "And I'd like you to like me. Which you won't if you think I'm horrible."

Esmeralda thought and nodded. "I see your point, Grell, but what I happen to want is people who *can be*, not *are*, horrible."

"Oh, I *can* be," he agreed. "I'm just not." He grinned at her happily.

She smiled back, a lovely, radiant smile, and it was as if the sun had suddenly come out in that darkened room. "I promise I won't tell anyone, Grell. It'll be our little secret. Right. Here's the plan."

We followed her to her father's desk where she unrolled the map on it. It was large and detailed and showed the entire realm.. "We're here." She pointed at Rushtoun. Mayport lay way down on the south coast at the mouth of a long river, May River, much the largest river on the map. May River had its sources in a number of streams springing up in the Western Mountains which all ran east in a long curve to the north of Rushtoun and Brigstowe. It widened as they merged into each other and then turned south more or less in a straight line, with the occasional long detour around hills, until it flowed into the sea at Mayport.

"Think you can find your way there?" she asked.

"Piece of cake," Oller said. "I'm good at finding."

I studied the map. As I did, I traced the line of our journey so far. I could even work out, vaguely, where Grell and I had separately started.

Pieces of the puzzle were beginning to fit together.

II

On the Run

Esmeralda said, "This had better not go wrong. Or I'm for the high jump. Which I do not intend to take. I intend to get to Mayport. Even if it was safe to travel alone, everyone around here knows me. I'd be stopped within half a mile and trooped back to Daddy. For a lecture how Daddy's Little Girl mustn't, and Daddy's Little Girl shouldn't, and *uurrhh!*"

She grimaced, then a conspiratorial smile spread on her face. "But now I've got you three hard, horrible, dangerous characters, haven't I?"

Grell beamed at her. "That you have!"

"I prayed to Lymnia, and here you are," she said. "So, we'll be under her protection. Now, I want you all to meet me in five days' time, two hours before dawn, outside the stables. You know where they are?"

We did.

"You be there, we'll be off, and we'll all be fugitives. We'll do what we all have to do and I'll do what I need to do and you'll be rich. How does that sound?"

We considered.

"Risky," I said.

"Yur," Grell seconded.

"Possibly painful," I added. "Deserters get flogged."

"I liked the last bit," Oller said. "Rich."

"Focus on that, then." From the pocket in her smock, Esmeralda pulled out a purse.

"Ten gold each." She counted the heavy coins into our hands. "Down payment. You'll get the rest as and when."

"As and when what?" Oller said, suspiciously.

"As and when I get it," Esmeralda said, eyes wide, all butter-wouldn't-melt-in-her-mouth innocence.

Oller, drowning in that dazzling, cornflower gaze, grinned soppily back.

"Or don't you trust me?" she added.

"Yes! Of course, I do!" Oller started gabbling. Grell and I knew why. Oller didn't trust anyone. "You're trusting us, with your life, and to get you to Mayport, o' course I trust you, how could I not?" He looked at Grell and me for support. "Eh?"

I said, "We trust you."

"So, the arrangement is all right with you, Deserter Oller?" she enquired.

"Yes, dear," he simpered, then added quickly, "no, dear. I mean, no *dear*. There's no *dear* in that sentence, I didn't mean to say *dear*. It just slipped out. All unbidden, like. Oh dear …" he tailed off.

"Daxx," she said to me. And it was my turn to drown. "Find Peat, the stableboy. Be nice to him and say, 'Aha, Peat the poet. *Very* nice …' with a knowing, secret smile and a wink. Like this." She demonstrated.

Her knowing, secret smile, and her wink made my heart leap and my knees melt. I grinned and sighed.

She waited. "Did you get that?"

"Yes," I simpered.

"Let's hear it then."

I mimicked, "Aha, Peat the poet. *Very* nice …" with a knowing, secret smile.

"Add a thoughtful nod," Esmeralda suggested.

"Okay."

"Go on then."

I did it again, adding thoughtful nod.

"Mm. That should do. Now, back to barracks and not a word of this to anyone."

We turned to go.

"Not that way, this way." She led us across the room to one of the bookshelves behind My Lord's desk. An idea struck her, and she stopped. "All right," she said to Oller, "let's see how good you are at finding."

Oller walked along the bookshelf—a large, wooden fixture that took up the entire wall from floor to ceiling in vertical sections four feet wide. He appraised it with an expert eye. "Won't be too far, has to be within reach ... not too much of a stretch up or down ... . Nice piece o' work, this," he said. "A chippie who knew his business made this. *Hm*. If I were to stake my professional reputation ... ." He stopped. "I would say ... ." He pointed at an unremarkable, brown leather-bound volume just above his eye-height, to his right, one exactly like a lot of other equally unremarkable, brown leather-bound volumes around it.

Esmeralda's eyebrows rose. "How did you know?"

"Trade secret," Oller grinned. "May I?"

"Go ahead."

He reached over to the book he'd picked out and pulled it. It didn't come away from the shelf as we'd expected, but swung back and down until, with a click, the bookcase moved an inch from the wall.

"Lovely craftsmanship," Oller said, swinging the hidden door open on its hinge. "Might've missed that if I hadn't known it was there. Often, it's a matter of time, i.e., not enough of it. What with feet running and people coming and such and suddenly having to hide behind a curtain. Or make yourself scarce. It's best when you have lots of time. If I'd gone through My Lord's desk and found nothing, and also nothing in the obvious places people hide things in rooms like this, thinking we'll never spot but are the first places we look ... ." A thought struck him, and he looked around the room. "There's something under that plant pot." He padded over to it. There was. A small, brass key. Oller grunted. "Ur. We know what *that's* for, don't we!" he said, disdainfully.

Esmeralda said, "What?"

"My Lord's *other* books." He glanced at us. Which we understood. *My Lord's naughty picture books, like the one Oller had found in his bedchamber and liberated.* "Which'll be ..." he considered. "Oh, yeah. Nice." He crouched beside the cabinet on which the plant pot stood and found a secret panel. He slid it open and put the key in the keyhole that the panel had hidden. "Yup." He extracted the naughty picture book, and flourishing it at us with a grin, said "Told you! Best put this back." He moved quickly, before Esmeralda could ask to see it. "If anything goes missing, My Lord will know someone's been poking about in his Inner Sanctum. We wouldn't want that, now would we, miss?"

"No," Esmeralda agreed. "Come on."

We filed into the secret passage, following Esmeralda with her lantern. It twisted and turned and branched and led to stairs which we took up then down. After a lot of down, she stopped by an empty iron candleholder, just like all the other iron candleholders we'd passed.

"Fifteen!" Oller said, impressed.

I frowned. "Fifteen what?"

"Candleholders, including this one, that are more than just candleholders. Pull on 'em, and there's your secret doors. Wish I had time to explore all of them."

"Don't come back into the castle," Esmeralda ordered. "I don't want you drawing any attention to yourselves. Lie low, act like normal soldiers, and *be there*. On time, unseen, and your absence not noticed. All right?"

"All right," we promised.

She reached for the candleholder and pulled it. It swung down. A section of the wall clicked inwards.

"Check it out," she told Oller.

Oller listened, waited, eased the door inward, and stepped outside into the darkness.

"All clear," he whispered.

"Off you go," Esmeralda said.

"Goodbye," we whispered, and, "Thank you," and, "We'll be there, promise!"

We joined Oller outside, and he clicked the hidden door shut behind us.

"Deserters, eh?" he said, happily. "Suits me! I don't like life on the right side of the law. Too many rules and restrictions."

Grell said, "Warm beds. Good food. Plenty of ale. Who needs all that?"

I thought of the heartstone. And of the pieces of the puzzle that we were living.

⁂

141

That night in barracks Grell and I talked.

It had been a while since we'd conferred about the Big Picture. It was almost as if it had faded in our minds, I realized. We'd been so busy living it that we'd become absorbed into it. The here-and-now, the immediate future, our duties and routines, patrols and meals, were all that we really thought about. It was as if, somehow, the questions that we needed to find answers to had been pushed to the backs of our minds where, neglected, they'd quietly remained. Unasked. Which meant, of course, no nearer to being answered.

But now things were about to change, abruptly. We were heading into the unknown again in five days' time. That sharpened our focus. In a quiet corner of the common room, Grell and I put our heads together and went over everything that had happened to us from the beginning.

We'd learned a lot since we'd arrived here, and not just combat training. We knew the lie of the land and the ways of its people. We were no longer fishes out of water, but regular folk who could come and go like anyone else and get by. We had weapons, armor, packs, and gold. Most important of all, we had each other. We were a team. Oller was no Qrysta. In combat he'd be sneaking and stabbing, where Qrysta would have been dancing and slicing, but he was going to be damn useful. We wondered, yet again, about Qrysta. Would we ever see her? Was she even here?

I had a theory about *here*.

It was time to run it by Grell. "Where did all this start?" I asked.

"For me? Middle of a moor in the Uplands. Wilderness for you."

"Wrong," I said. "Where were we before that?"

"Home," he said.

"Doing what?"

"Winning the Championship."

"And then?"

"We were here."

"That's the way it looks, right. But suppose we went *somewhere else first*."

"Where?"

"Somewhere they did this to us," I said. "You can't tell me you were an actual Orc in Australia. And I never looked like this. I wish I had done, I'd've had a much better life. This is *happening*, Grell. We know that, for real, for sure, and it's been happening for months. So? What happened in the months before? Between? Or years, I don't know—how long d'you think it takes to make us one of these?" I indicated him and myself again.

Grell said, "Crikey …"

"Crikey indeed," I agreed. "Well, we don't know how long, any more than we know how they did it. Or who they are. We're living this, but supposing it's not just for our benefit?"

"What d'you mean, Daxx?"

"Okay, so we do our quests and fight our fights and get better and better and richer and more capable, and end up with, who knows what, a castle? A lordship? We don't know what the endgame is. Strikes me that so far all we've been doing is getting to know the arena. We haven't even *found* the Main Quest. Maybe it's this little jaunt of Esmeralda's, who knows?

"The point is, Grell, don't worry about the endgame, what matters is we're in a *game* on a *real world*. We came right from one *game*, which we'd won, into another. Which we barely understand. And we're not players anymore, like we were back there, where we understood the rules and could log out and have bio breaks and chat with each other on our comms-channel. We're still the people we were, inside, but incarnated in flesh-and-blood versions of our own avatars. Who, by the way, aren't noobs anymore. I mean"—the thought struck me as the idea became clearer and clearer—"we did our orientation that first day. Right? Pick a direction, head for it—next thing, I walk into Nyrik and Horm, and you walk into Mulden, and we're captives. Not a good start, right? But look at what came next. Not slavery, like we'd expected. *Training*.

"We did our training with Serjeant Bastard. That's the first thing you do in any new game, isn't it? Learn the controls, learn how to wield weapons and fight, how to interact with the world. We graduated from that level. We have combat sharps and are damn good with them. We completed our first quest when we took Rushtoun. Which gained us five gold each and promotion."

I let that sink in.

It did.

Grell nodded thoughtfully.

I went on. "Okay? Well, that's the Big Picture. Or at least, a small part of it. Those are pieces of the puzzle that, as far as I can see, fit together."

"Yeah," Grell mused. "It kinda does. I mean, it's crazy, but—"

"It may be crazy, but it's *real*. That's what we have to deal with. That's what we've been dealing with so far. As for the crazy part, maybe it's only crazy for us. Because we don't see the whole of the Big Picture yet. It may not be crazy for *them*."

"Who's 'them'?" Grell asked.

"Whoever's doing this. *Has* done this. To us. Wouldn't you think they'd have a *reason* for it? For putting us down here? Wherever the hell 'here' is? Well, I know one thing: wherever this rock is, it isn't Planet Earth. It's an instance of something like it, but not Earth as we knew it. Somewhere Earthlike where we can survive and feel it's all familiar enough, even when it's wildly different. Where we now fit, even though we didn't at first.

"And we're fitting more and more as we're learning, surviving, and getting good. And here's the thing." I paused. "I think we're getting good for a reason. Because that way lies success. Well, they will have their reasons for doing this to us, to have us here doing what we're doing. Think about it."

"I have," Grell said. "A lot. Who, why, how."

"And, like me, you've been too near the bark to see the damn tree, let alone standing on a peak so you can look down at the whole forest spread out below you. So, pull back, take a look from above, and it's obvious."

Grell turned the threads over in his mind. I saw the moment that he worked it out. His eyes grew round, and he looked over at me. "They're watching!" he said.

"Yep. We had tens of millions watching when we won the Championship, right? And among those millions must have been whoever did this to us. And *could* do this to us. And decided to do it to us. For their own reasons. And if that's right, then we need to win this campaign too. Which means *not dying*, for a start. I don't think we get any resurrections here. Do you? I mean … I have no wish to try it and see, but it feels to me like dead would be *dead*. Agree?"

"Yeah," Grell started, then added, "but …"

"What are their reasons? Big Picture, Grello. *We don't know*, so don't worry about it. We just do our jobs. *Of course*, we don't know everything yet. When do you ever? Only when it's over. Which in our case means we'll know only when we've completed the Main Quest and won the—whatever the reward is. *Won*. We need to *win*."

Grell said, "What if we don't?"

I smiled. "Then we'll never know, will we?"

"I suppose not …" Grell said.

"So, let's win," I suggested.

"Fine with me," Grell agreed. "It's gonna be weird, though."

"*Going* to be? What, it's not weird enough for you already?"

"No, I mean weird knowing we're a spectator sport."

"So, let's give 'em a show."

"Right." Grell thought for a while, then said, "These … people. Who did this …"

I said, "I very much doubt they're people as we understand the term."

"Non-people, then. D'you think, when this is over … whenever we've done what we're meant to have done, whatever that is …"

"Won."

"Yeah, right. Won. Do you think they'll let us go? I mean, put me back in Oz, as I was, and you in England?"

"How the hell should I know, Grell? They could *eat* the winners."

"Jesus!"

"Only one way to find out," I said.

"Win," Grell said.

I agreed. "Win."

Grell nodded and considered. "And how do we do that?"

"I've been thinking about that," I said. "And when I stopped thinking about it—which was pointless, because I don't have the information I need, the data—I realized something. Well, two things at once, simultaneously."

"And what were they?"

"One, something my dad always said: *If it was meant to be easy, it would be.* Well, clearly it isn't meant to be, because they're not making it easy for us."

"And two?"

"It's more fun when it's not easy."

Grell nodded. "Ah."

▲ ▲ ▲

I strolled by the stables the next morning. They were busy with stable-hands mucking out, feeding, curry-combing, and leading horses out to be saddled or to the smith for shoeing. I could see now why Esmeralda had chosen two hours before dawn. The fewer witnesses the better. In my soldier's mail I could ask which one was Peat and get a quick answer, no questions asked. No "Who wants to know?" like a civilian would have had shot back at him.

Peat was a mop-haired, gray-eyed, soulful-looking lad, not tall, but wiry and strong with the bandy legs of a horseman. He was carrying a pail and a mop towards a stall, his thoughts far away. He stopped when he saw me waiting for him. I lowered my voice and gave him a knowing, secret smile as Esmeralda had instructed, then said the magic words: "Aha, Peat the Poet. *Very* nice …" with a wink.

Peat blushed like a beetroot and grinned like a fool.

Then I added the thoughtful nod.

"Did she like it?" he whispered.

"Loved it," I said. "She said it was one of the best poems she'd ever read."

"Did she? She *did*?"

"She did. Soldier's honor." Which, seeing as how I was about to desert, didn't mean a whole lot. But Peat the poet-slash-stable boy wasn't to know that.

"Did you like it?" he said.

Always needing praise, these poets.

Well, I thought, *I might as well make his day.*

"Oh, she wouldn't let anyone *else* see it! Said it was for herself alone. Kept it folded up next to her bosom."

Peat whispered, awed, "Bosom?"

"Over her heart."

Peat repeated, "Bosom …"

"She takes it out all the time to read it again. Sighing. She did when I was with her and gave me the message for you. Took it out, from her—"

"Bosom …"

"Unfolded it tenderly. Sighed. Read it, her lips moving like two perfect cherry red … ." *Whats?* I thought. *Worms? What do lips look like when they move?* I couldn't think. "… Cupid's bows, of such kissable perfection I wanted to—"

"You didn't!" Peat challenged, glaring at me. "You didn't try to kiss her!"

"—faint," I said.

Peat relaxed.

"Yeah," he said, wistfully. "I know! Go on. About my poem, about how she liked it."

"And she read it, slowly, all of it, silently mouthing the words to herself with a dreamy, faraway smile, and at the end, do you know what?"

"What?" Peat breathed.

"A tear rolled out of her big, blue eye and trickled down her flawless cheek, and she wiped it away with a little lace hankie and said, 'It's so *beautiful* …!'"

"She didn't!"

"She did. Soldier's honor! Then I said, 'Please let me read it, My Lady,' and she said, 'No, it's for my eyes only' and tucked it back into her bosom. Where it nestles now. It nestles there night and day. It is with her, everywhere she goes, sleeping and waking. Next to her heart."

Peat gurgled.

I said, "So, you know what to do."

Peat came out of his trance and said, "Yes. Write a sequel!"

▲   ▲   ▲

On the fifth day, two hours before dawn, Grell, Oller and I were by the stables, waiting. We had loaded up with everything we could think of and kept going over in our minds what we hadn't thought of but were bound to need. It was dark and silent, apart from the occasional snort or whicker from the sleeping horses.

It was so dark that we didn't see Esmeralda approaching with two horses, their muffled hooves making hardly a sound, and Peat following her leading another two. He handed us the reins. Esmeralda thanked him, told him he was wonderful, would one day be a great and famous poet, and kissed him on the cheek.

Peat said, "I've got something for you, my lady." We heard the rustle of paper.

"I'll treasure it forever!" she promised, and added, "I can't wait for daylight so I can read it." And she kissed his other cheek, and Peat groaned.

"Our secret, remember!" she said. "Now, go back in there and drink this. You'll wake up tonight with a sore head, but they won't be able to wake you before it wears off. So you won't get the blame and be in trouble, all right?"

"All right," Peat replied.

She whispered conspiratorially. "I can't have my favorite poet getting into trouble, especially not on my account!"

"No," Peat simpered.

She swung up into the saddle, and turned her palfrey's head towards the town. We mounted and followed. No one stopped us. We hardly saw anyone on our way through the shadowed streets. A night watchman, snoozing in his box. A lamplighter, snoring in his. A shadow slipping among the shadows, Oller-like. "One of us," Oller whispered. "There's nothing like a dark night when all's well and honest folk are abed. Happy huntings, mate!"

We reined in at the gates. This could be the tricky part. If any of the city guard got suspicious, we'd be in trouble. Plan B was to knock them out before they raised the alarm. It wasn't a very promising Plan B, and we hoped like hell we wouldn't have to use it.

We didn't.

Esmeralda threw back her hood and radiated her loveliest, sweetest smile at the guard who emerged from his hut. "We're going to pick dawnflowers for Daddy," she confided. "It's a secret! Dawnflowers only flower at dawn, that's the only time to find them. And if you pick them then, they stay open all day and smell lovely! Daddy *loves* dawnflowers."

The guard's face wore the expression we all now knew as Esmeralda Face. Soppy, vacant, happy—and pliable. He'd do *anything* for her now.

"The gate?" she whispered, in confidence. "We'll slip through, and you can shut it behind us."

He did.

"You won't tell anyone, will you?" She grinned. "It's a surprise for Daddy, like I said. A secret!"

"No, my lady, I won't!"

"Thank you!" She blew him a kiss as she rode past.

He smiled dreamily. We followed. I don't think he even noticed us. He only had eyes for Esmeralda. The gate closed behind us.

We were out.

We had, we reckoned, only a few hours before we were missed. Grell, Oller, and I would be missed at roll call after breakfast. Esmeralda had complained of a headache the night before and told her maid that she was going down with something and not to wake her in the morning. Someone, eventually, would knock, and on finding her bedchamber locked, knock louder. And would then go for help and advice.

My Lady of Rushtoun would arrive with the castle apothecary, because Esmeralda was ill, and they'd knock and shout and, when they got no answer, My Lady of Rushtoun would go in the back way, along the passages to the iron candleholder that opened the door behind the long mirror in Esmeralda's dressing room. She would go through into Esmeralda's bedchamber and find the bed empty.

We didn't want to be caught and brought back in chains and flogged for deserters. Esmeralda didn't want to be gated, chastised, lectured, and above all thwarted in her intentions, which were to get to Mayport without anyone knowing. As we knew from her map, Mayport lay many leagues away to the south and east, so naturally, we turned off the road into the forest and headed in the opposite direction.

12

A Poem and a Story

We rode west and north, Oller in his leathers, Grell and me in our uniforms under chainmail shirts. Even a stallion as big as the one carrying him would have broken under the weight of Grell in his full plate armor, so he'd left that behind. We each had bows and a quiver full of arrows as well at Oller's belt full of knives and my sword and board. Grell, of course, had his beloved Fugg slung on his back.

Esmeralda was in sensible traveling clothes, hard wearing and practical, topped by a large, green, hooded cloak. We each had bedrolls and blankets, and our saddlebags were filled with food that we'd all gathered from various sources. Oller had left the contents of his chest with the TG Receiver to sell, which would take time if he was to get the best prices. He'd given Oller an advance of ten gold pieces, so between us, we were well provisioned and well supplied with gold.

Within an hour we came to the first stream. We walked our horses into it and turned to the left, going west against the current. After half a mile we came out on the other side, then rode east and north, hard. We knew that there was another stream ahead of us which would join with the first stream in a few miles. Those would flow on to the east, joining others until they were all eventually the May River. When we reached the confluence, we walked our horses into the new stream and doubled back along it, upstream now, heading north and west again, this time for several miles.

Esmeralda knew that sometime—today or with luck not until tomorrow—we'd be tracked by Daddy's hounds. They would cast about along both banks until half a mile downstream they found the scent again. We knew that the huntsman wouldn't think we'd vanished into thin air. He wouldn't be fooled by *that* old trick. We knew he'd think that we couldn't outsmart him and his hounds, *oh* no! And we knew that his hounds would find our trail sooner or later.

So, we wanted him to interpret our trail as, *ah, tried to be clever they have, My Lord! They've made it look as if they're heading one way then gone t'other. That's the real way they've gone, east along the stream, I'll be bound.* And Esmeralda had left sufficient clues in her chamber, in hidden places where even an amateur could find them, about her destination being Mayport. Which it was. A lie is always best hidden inside the truth. It's just that we were going the long way around to get there.

I'd left a note for Deb when I'd slipped out that morning and she slept on. I'd put it among her papers where she'd find it, eventually— but not too soon, I hoped. It said that I was sorry and hoped to be back soon so I could tell her all about it. I signed it *with love.* The whole thing felt fake, and I hated myself for writing it, but I couldn't leave without doing that. I was pretty sure I wouldn't see Rushtoun again.

Grell, Oller, and I weren't worried about My Lord's hounds.

We were worried about Serjeant Bastard.

Serjeant Bastard would take it personally, three of his soldiers deserting. He'd want them back. And Serjeant Bastard was implacable. Whenever the conversation failed—which was most of the time because we were riding hard—and we went into our private thoughts, there was Serjeant Bastard coming for us with that look of his. Arms crossed, one eyebrow raised a fraction of an inch, beard jutting in our direction, brooding. We shuddered at that mental image and dismissed it, but you can't dismiss Serjeant Bastard. So, we had to start talking again to distract ourselves. If Serjeant Bastard got his hands on us life would be unpleasant, and we didn't want to think about it.

We couldn't gallop along the second stream. Our horses walked up it, which had the benefit of resting them. While they walked, we talked, so that we weren't thinking about Daddy's hounds or Serjeant Bastard. The sun was over the horizon by that time, way off behind us, east and south, it being officially spring now, though you wouldn't have known it from the weather. It felt more January than April: misty, gray, chill with a wind from the mountains and, from time to time, spitting with rain. But we were riding with Esmeralda, around whom the sun always shone. Fluffy white clouds floated high in her own bright blue sky, and unicorns and rainbows and pixies frolicked about her head. Hunched in her green cloak, hood covering her golden hair, she still radiated. And the three of us rode beside her, entranced—which was awkward, because one of us was always nudging another of us out of the way.

It was Oller who remembered the poem. "D'you get a lot of poems?" he asked.

"All the time," Esmeralda said glumly.

"I've never made one up," he said. "I dunno how. Have you, Daxx?"

"Not really, no," I said.

"How can you *not really* make up a poem?" Oller challenged. "You either do or you don't."

"Well, I've done rhyming in my head, sometimes," I said. "You know, you see a wall or something and think *that's tall.* And then you go, *look at that wall, isn't it tall? Compared with that, I am small.* It's not … profound, or anything."

"No," Oller agreed, "it's bollocks. But it does rhyme. For the most part. You, Grell?"

"Yeah. Orc poems. *Slash, stab, thump, whack. Hit me and I'll hit you back!*"

Oller considered that. "Pithy. To the point. No unnecessary verbiage. Not a florid metaphor in sight. Nothing otiose, redundant, superfluous to requirements or pleonastic. Apposite and economical."

"What the fuck's *pleonastic?*" Grell said.

"Adjectival form of the word *pleonasm,*" Oller said. "Which means, long winded, repetitive, flowery claptrap."

I looked at Oller, puzzled. I'd never heard him talk like that. "Where'd you get words like that, Oller?"

"Words like what?"

"Otiose. Pleonasm."

Oller frowned. "Never heard of them."

I reined in my horse and stared at him. He stared back, but not at me, through me. He was miles away. I thought, *what the fuck?*

And then I knew we were on the right track. And that, even though I didn't have a clue how to get where I wanted, we'd get there.

I thought, with a smile, *Marnie.*

Yes dear, her voice whispered in my head. *Keep going. Or rather, coming. I'll see you soon.*

I thought, *Thanks.* And then, *I have something for you.*

I heard her whisper again, *I know.* It was a neutral whisper, but even so, I could sense the weight in it.

Old Marnie was worried.

I remembered what Nyrik had said. *Marnie knows when people think about her.*

That I do, I heard. *Think of me and I'll think to you—as long as you're above ground and not too far away, I'll hear you. If I need your attention, I'll do something to get it, like with your lad there. It's easy with the simple ones. Can't get into a mind like yours from a distance.*

I stopped thinking about Marnie and thought about Oller.

He shook his head and came back from wherever he'd gone. "Eh? Where were we? Oh, yeah. Poems. Is it any good?"

Esmeralda grunted. "If it's anything like the last one …" she muttered, meaning *it'll be terrible.* She felt about in a pocket inside her cloak for the piece of paper that Peat the stable boy had given her in the dark before that morning's dawn. She unfolded it, read it, and grunted again.

"Well go on, then!" Oller said. "Read it. Out loud. I want to hear it."

She said, "If I do, you'll want to cut your ears off."

"I'll be the judge o' that," Oller objected. "I like poems, me! I like it when the bards sing. Some of them make it up as they go along, did you know that? You can ask them anything, while they're in the middle of singing, and they'll drop that in and make it clever. We had a great bard in the TG back in Brig, you couldn't throw anything at him he couldn't handle. We all thought he should go off to Mayport and be famous—have a great career, he would. Only, of course, being TG, he'd nicked it all. From other bards. Who'd beat the crap out of him if he used their stuff without the appropriate credit and royalty payments. You can sell stolen goods easy enough if you know the right fences. Apparently, you can't sell stolen songs. There aren't any song-fences. Go on, then," he urged Esmeralda.

"Once is enough," she said, and handed the piece of paper to me. I took a deep breath and read aloud:

Thou shinest, at My Lord's High Table,
Like the fairest maid in fable;
I'd climb at night, if I were able
To get a good throw with my cable
So that it looped around thy gable,
And tryst with thee, in silk and sable,
Until the dawn! Then down my cable
('Twere hanging still, around thy gable),
Back to my stall in My Lord's stable.
I'd love thee, though thy name were Mabel*!*

I looked at my audience. Grell's face was closed, frowning; Oller's was open, mouth gaping, eyes wide, eyebrows raised.

Esmeralda was scowling under her hood.

"That's good, that is!" Oller said, approvingly.

Esmeralda stared at him in disbelief. "It's *drivel!*"

Oller frowned. "No, it's not. All them rhymes? That's *proper* poetry, that is. Every line rhyming? Half the time they only rhyme every other line, in ballads, and then different rhymes all the time. Not *one* rhyme, like your poem. How many lines is it?"

I counted. "Ten."

Esmeralda said, "And they're all—"

"Yeah, the *same rhyme!*" Oller beamed. "That's exactly my point! Clever, that. I've hung from gables myself, any number of times, but I'd never 've thought of *cable*. I'd think, *rope*. Like I usually think when scaling roofs and such. And *rope* doesn't go with *gable*, does it? So, there you are. That's proper poet-thinking, that. And proper poetry words. So, you can't say it's not proper poetry. It's got *'twere* in it! Proper poems have *'twere*, all the time. I've heard them. And *'twas*."

Esmeralda's frown disappeared, to be replaced by the loveliest of smiles. "Oh, very good, Oller. You had me completely. I really thought you meant it for a moment."

Oller was baffled. "I do."

"It's 'proper poetry because it's got *'twere* in it'?" she said.

Oller stared at Esmeralda as if she was an idiot. "That's what I said."

Esmeralda stared at Oller as if *he* was an idiot.

One of them, I knew, was right. And it wasn't Oller.

"And you *meant* it?" she said.

"And *tryst*," Oller said. "That's a proper poem word. And *thee* and *thy*, he didn't call you *you*, like an oik; he used proper poetry words."

Esmeralda was speechless. She looked at me, helplessly.

I shrugged.

"One of the best poems I've ever heard, in my humble opinion," Oller continued. "What's it called?"

Esmeralda studied him. She was thinking, *if this doesn't convince him, nothing will.* She said, to me, "Turn it over."

I did.

On the other side words were written, in block capitals, decorated with little hearts and big X's.

"Its title," I said with deliberate care, "is 'For Esmeralda, Fairest of Maidens with the Fairest of Names, but Nothing Rhymes with It'."

There was a silence as Oller puzzled it out. "What, like *orange*?"

"Doesn't rhyme with orange," Grell objected.

"Not with, *like*," Oller elaborated. "Nothing rhymes with orange. Or Esmeralda, he's saying. A bard told me that, once. He said, *nothing rhymes with orange.* Some Lord who loves poems—*proper* poems—was offering a hundred gold pieces to anyone who could find a rhyme for orange. The bard knew I was good at finding things, he wondered if I'd come across one. I hadn't. Nearest anyone had got to it, he said, was some troubadour who traveled everywhere, who said way up north way beyond the Uplands, the men wear wool skirts with crisscross patterns and have a bag hanging on the front of them called a *sporrinj*. No one believed him. Might've done if he hadn't said that about the patterned skirts. I mean, it's cold enough down here in winter, never mind way up north beyond the Uplands. What man would wear a skirt when it's bloody freezing, eh? And hang a bag on it?"

Esmeralda was staring at Oller open-mouthed. On her, with that perfect mouth and those blue eyes that you could drown in, it was an expression so utterly wondrous that you just wanted to stare back with your own mouth open.

Which Oller did.

Esmeralda shut hers first and then turned to me. "I hope you're in charge, not him."

"We're a democracy," I said.

"Well? Who's in charge of it, whatever *that* is?"

"We all decide together," I said. "We talk it through and see what we all think."

Esmeralda shook her perfect head in disbelief at such a ridiculous idea. Sunbeams danced in her golden hair and sapphires glinted in her wide blue eyes and unicorns and pixies and rainbows frolicked around her head.

"Oh gods," she groaned. "Unicorns and pixies, right?"

I nodded. "And rainbows."

"Fuck," she muttered, and rode on ahead of me.

We had to go in single file, now, up the stream. Willows closed in overhead. Bullrushes grew in clumps along the stream's edges which were muddy and marshy. Our horses didn't like that, so we stuck to the middle of the stream which was stonier and more solid underfoot.

After a few hours we came to another stream, flowing from the north into ours. We turned up it. And kept walking. Esmeralda didn't want to talk to us. She rode at our head, wrapped in her cloak, her hood up against the rain that had started again and didn't look like stopping. We walked a few more hours then turned off up the northern bank when the stream curved back to the west. We didn't want to go to its source, in the mountains. Mountains meant giants.

We cantered, for as long and as far as we dared without overtiring our horses. We weren't in the wilderness proper, yet. It was hill country, moorland, wild enough—but there were walls here and there, mostly incomplete and tumbledown. And folds, for the sheep that we didn't see on the hillsides—because, we decided, it was still too early for them to be driven up here to their summer pastures.

That was a relief. Where there were sheep there would be shepherds. We didn't want to meet any. The search parties would come this way eventually. Not before we'd made it to Mayport, we hoped, but the fewer people who could identify us, the better. As well as sheepfolds, there were the remains of houses. Well, hovels. People had lived here once, a long time ago it seemed. The hovels were few and far between. Most had no roofs and some had more burnt walls than just the fireplace.

In the cold gloom of the evening they looked mournful, and the whole land felt dreary and unwelcoming. We all felt, somehow, that we were being watched. I thought of Marnie, and she thought back, *Yes, I'm watching you. Can't tell if anyone else is. Next hill, you'll find a spot for the night.*

Good, I thought. Shelter. We were all tired after a long day in the saddle. Shelter would be welcome.

Marnie thought to me, *You should tell them.*

I should?

You should. Make 'em think.

I told the others, "We'll find shelter down the other side of this."

Grell looked at me. "You think?"

"I think," I said in a tone that meant, *I know.*

▲ ▲ ▲

The cottage had a roof on it with only a few holes to let the rain in. It was dusk when we led our horses in through the broken wall, and dried them as best we could, rubbed them down and combed them. They'd put in a long, hard shift. There had been plenty for them to eat on the way, and more than plenty to drink, but they each got a well-earned nosebag full of oats for their supper. Grell gathered stones and branches and made a makeshift door so they couldn't get out. Perhaps more importantly, nobody—or nothing—could get in without us hearing. We wondered what might be out there in these desolate hills, walking the nights. He laid other, bigger stones across the dirt floor between us and the horses. There wasn't much room left for us.

We ate well enough from the supplies we'd gathered over the previous five days. We drank a mouthful each of some fierce spirit Oller had traded for at the Thieves Guild. *Bottled Bottle*, he called it, explaining that 'bottle' was thief slang for *guts*. It wasn't as spectacular as Horm's Careful Juice, but it warmed us up nicely. And, as it did so, we all felt our tiredness drop away, and we felt braver and more comfortable and more confident and more ready for anything.

Esmeralda shared some delicious biscuits, lemony and sticky, from My Lord's bakery. Oller lit a candle, using a flint and tinder from a sealed box he kept inside his jerkin. Esmeralda spread out the map she'd liberated from My Lord's Inner Sanctum. We studied it.

157

I pieced together our journeys so far. I could see where I'd started, the wilds, the woods and forests, and big blank areas north of where were now were. The mountains to the west. Eddyr's Fang was marked, in a long range that was labelled *Western Mountains (Giant Country)*. There was nothing to the west of them. They reared up at the edge of the map. I saw where I'd met Grell at The Wheatsheaf. Brigstowe. Rushtoun. Lorton. Pellingham. South and east were more towns and villages and keeps and castles, with names like Whitmouth, Hartwell, Spensbury, Norhaven, and Westwich, and rivers and lakes and forests; and, on the southern coast, at the mouth of a large bay where the May River flowed into the sea, Mayport.

I showed them where we were going. I extended my finger slowly towards the map, and Marnie guided it to a point north and east of where we thought we were.

"There's nothing there," Esmeralda said.

"There is, I've been there. It's just not marked on your map."

"Can't be very big, then," she said.

"It isn't, and I don't think she'd let it be on any map, anyway."

"Who wouldn't?"

"The person we're going to see."

"Who?"

"You'll see. You don't know her. I do, though, and she promised she'd help me."

"What about the rest of us?"

"We're together," I said. "Help one, help all."

Marnie thought to me, *Don't make promises you can't keep, lad!*

"If she wants to," I added quickly. "So, try to make her want to, all right?"

The map was large, colorful, and detailed. Forests in green, rivers and seas and lakes in blue, mountains drawn in long ranges of pointed little peaks in gray and white. Towns drawn as buildings and castles within encircling walls. Dotted about were abbeys, priories, meaderies, breweries, shrines, vineyards and farmlands, and boundary lines between domains. There were many blank spots where all the map read was things like *Uplands (Orc Country)*, or *Parts Unknown*. There were also plenty of little dots in purple, yellow, orange, and red.

"What are those?" I asked Esmeralda.

"And the songs he sang after the High Supper were merry songs. He played dancing tunes on his lute, and the castle musicians joined in, and everyone danced. And the singer himself danced, and danced as beautifully as he sang, and he danced alone while they marveled at his clever steps, and he danced with the womenfolk, high and low, all eyes upon him and his partners, and he danced with the Lady. They smiled at each other as they danced, and the singer held her in his arms, around her slender waist, and they spun and skipped and glided, until the music ended and the singer bowed and the Lady curtseyed, and though nothing had been said, the tryst had been sealed.

"The evening ended, and the singer thanked the Lord and Lady for their food and wine and settled down to sleep by the hearthfire. He did not sleep, but waited until the castle was still and the firelight dim, then rose and left on his soft-stockinged feet. He found his way to my Lady's bedchamber, where he let himself in, and slipped into her bed beside her, and pleasured her in more ways than she'd ever imagined possible. He left at dawn the next morning with his lute and his songs, and she watched him go from the high window of her bedchamber and had never felt so happy and sad at the same time. She thought of her vow and the child that was growing inside her, for she knew that the two things were connected. It had been no accident that the singer had come, from who knew where, on the very day she'd made her vow to Lymnia.

"So the next evening she slipped a love potion into her Lord's night-time posset, it being more of the *physical* type of love potion than the soulful kind. And her Lord woke to find her taking off her nightclothes by his bedside, and his willy standing at attention under his covers and aching like hell. So they did it, and she went away and felt, *serve the miserable sod right*, and that was the last time they ever shared a bed.

"There was one more bit in her part for her to play, which she did when she told him, in a secret, smiling whisper into his ear, as they broke their fast the next morning—by way of explaining her night-time visit—*we need a child!* And he saw that she was happy, and was content. And nine months later, I was born, and I turned out to be as lovely and happy as their marriage was loveless and miserable.

"So that's it. And there's a price to pay. There's always a price to pay. And the price was told to Mommy, the Lady, by the fairy godmother

161

who turned up as I was about to be named in the castle chapel on the feast day of Lymnia, Goddess of Patience and Forbearance. And she said to the Lady, 'What do you wish for your daughter, My Lady?' And the Lady said, 'I wish her to be the most beautiful, kindest, happiest, brightest girl who will live the loveliest life there ever was or ever will be, as fair as a spring morning and as sharp as a winter night, as clever as a wizard and as kind and welcome as soft autumn rain after a parched summer, and I want everyone who sees her to love her.' And the fairy godmother said, 'Blimey, that's a bit of a mouthful, what was all that again?' So, the Lady repeated it, until she'd got it off by heart and then the fairy godmother pronounced it over the little girl, who gurgled prettily and cooed and started glowing, and everyone went *awwww ...!*"

"*Awwww ...*" we echoed, when she stopped.

She hadn't finished though. "And then she turned to the Lady and the Lord and said, 'Give her all the love you cannot give each other, and she will take all the hurt from your hearts.' Then she looked down at me and said, 'May you have a long and lovely life, my pretty, the loveliest there has ever been or ever will be. We will meet again in six and ten years, and I shall have something for you, and you shall have something for me.' And she smiled at the Lady, curtseyed to the Lord, and left.

"So that's why we're going to Mayport. She came to me, like I told you, in a dream when I turned sixteen. A dream that returns again and again, in which she says she's in the King's City, and I must come to her as soon as possible. And Mayport is where the king lives, isn't it? It's very important, because I have something for her, and she has something for me, like she promised. I don't know what either of them could be. But she's behind all this. She's behind *me*, what I am. So, I need to do my part of the bargain. I mean ..." she added and then tailed off.

Then she said, "What I *hope* is she'll take it away."

"Take what away?" Grell asked.

"The unicorns and the pixies and the rainbows and the bunny rabbits. All of it." She looked up at us, uncertain how we would take it. "I know it sounds ungrateful, but I just want to be normal. Like anyone else. I just want to be me, who I really am, not what everyone thinks I look like."

She was obviously sad and confused and unsure of herself.

"I'll take it," Grell said, to cheer her up. "If she needs to put it on someone else."

Esmeralda smiled. "I'm growing to love you, Grell. Just like Oller loves you and Daxx loves you. You don't want everyone else loving you as well."

Grell said, "Why not?"

"Because they don't have a reason to. We three all do."

Esmeralda inched over to Grell, who was sitting on the floor next to her, and kissed him on the cheek.

"I can't expect you to understand," she said. "But thank you for taking me to her. All of you. And anyway, it's probably something else entirely. We'll see when we get to Mayport, right?"

"Right," we agreed.

But we were wrong.

Very wrong.

13

Klurra

My long way around to Marnie's had taken us far into the Uplands. So, it was no surprise that the first person we met was an Orc.

The Orc emerged out of the mists, stopped and glared at us, hard—and especially hard at Grell.

"Who are you?" she demanded.

"Who wants to know?" Grell shot back.

"Klurra of Stonefields," she replied, as if she owned the land we were standing on.

"Mind your own damn business, Klurra of Stonefields," Grell told her.

"It is my business," she replied, not intimidated in the least. "You being *in* Stonefields. And not one of us. We like to know when one of *not-us* is trespassing on our land."

"We're not trespassing, we're just passing through," Grell countered.

"To do which, you have to trespass. On our land. Trespass being, *being on our land*. Duh! So, out with it. Who are you, trespasser?"

Grell was stumped. He'd have to answer, but he didn't have a tribe. So, she'd think he was an outlaw. And would either attack him or get the rest of her tribe to come and attack him, or he'd have to kill her. Which he didn't want to do. He thought she seemed nice.

"Grell of the Oz … garoos," he said.

Klurra's eyes narrowed in suspicion. "Never heard of them."

"Long way away," Grell said. "Overseas."

"Over *seas?*" she said. "No Orcs overseas that I've heard of!"

"Work it out, thicko," Grell snapped. "You're looking at one. Me. I'm from overseas. And I'm an Orc. So. Now bugger off out of our way."

"How d'you get here, then?" Klurra asked, not budging an inch.

"On this fucking horse, how d'you think?"

"Good swimmer, is he?"

"Eh?"

"Swam across the sea carrying a big ugly bastard Orc?"

Grell scowled. "What you clearly mean, is, and I'd have clearly understood if you'd expressed yourself better, 'How did I get *there*, then?' Not *here*. *There* being the point of disembarkation from the ship I got there in. From the overseas land of the Ozgaroos."

"What was it called?" Klurra demanded.

"A," Grell said, "*ship*."

"Named?"

"The *Southern Star*."

Grell, we began to see, could think surprisingly fast on his feet.

"Captain?"

"Jack Warner," Grell said. "Only everyone called him Captain Lighthouse. Which you probably won't get, you being as thick as four short planks, so I'll explain it to you. Sailors are called *jacks*. That's one of their nicknames, like *tars* or *sea dogs*. Lighthouses warn sailors. So, are jack warners."

Klurra's face cleared. "Oh. That's clever, that. One more question, and I'll decide your fate. Why did you come all the way from Ozgaroo?"

"That's my business and no one else's. However, in order to spare myself the bother of chopping your dense little head off, I will add that I am on a secret mission from my chief." Klurra opened her mouth to speak, but Grell held up a hand and went on. "You'll want to know his name, I expect, you being the incredibly nosy type. Bruce. Bruce the Pomhater. Poms being a tribe o' prats we Ozgaroos can't fucking stand. Present company excepted," he added in a mutter to me.

Klurra relaxed. "Well, why didn't you say so in the first place, you big bag of wind, wasting my time like that. Papers." She held out a hand. "From your chief," she said, and waited.

Grell didn't move, let alone produce any papers.

Klurra said, "No chief would send an Orc out without papers, so's he can get safe passage through other Orc lands."

"I said *secret* mission," Grell retorted. "He's not going to go writing it down on a bit of paper, is he? Gods you're dim, aren't you? Are all Stonefuckers as dim as you?"

"Wouldn't expect him to," Klurra replied. "Not the *mission*, fartface. Just the usual. 'Please let whatever your stupid name is through, blah blah blah.' So. Let's see it."

Grell sighed and got off his horse. "Some people," he said, as he lumbered towards her, "can't take a fucking hint."

"And some people," she replied, lumbering towards him, "can't produce their fucking papers which an Orc would always carry. So, I believe I need to take you to the chief."

"Don't have time," Grell said. "Important mission. Time is of the essence."

"Just have to make time, won't you?" Klurra reached around behind her for a warhammer. It was one of two she was carrying. They were big, brutal-looking things. She hefted it in her hands, staring at Grell. "Orc who 'doesn't have time' to pay his respects to the chief? Never heard of that, any more than I've heard of bloody Ozgaroos! You'll be coming with me."

"No, I won't," Grell said, hefting Fugg, his battle-axe.

"Battle-axe!" she said, scornfully. "Can't you lift a proper weapon?"

" 'Course I can," Grell said. "I prefer this, that's all. I'm elite."

"You, *elite*? Fuck off!" Klurra snorted.

"You fuck off!" Grell retorted.

"No, *you* fuck off. With your fucking poncy battle-axe! Put that thing down and use a proper weapon." She unslung her second warhammer and tossed it to Grell, who caught it in one great fist. "Same as mine, it's my spare, so I won't have no advantage by having a better one. Always carry a spare, I do, for when I break one over some stupid *outlaw's* head."

Outlaw.

Well, I supposed we were. And Orcs didn't approve of outlaws.

Grell sighed and shoved Fugg headspike-first into the ground. He swung the warhammer a few times to test its weight and balance.

"Gods, what a piece of crap!" he said. "You actually *fight* with this?"

166

"About to find out, aren't you?" She grinned, dropping into a crouch. Then straightening up again, said, "Shit, forgot my manners, sorry— might I have the honor of knowing the name of the brave Orc warrior I am about to bash the brains in of?"

"Grell of Ozgaroo."

"All right, Grell of Ozgaroo, let's be having you."

"Oh, you'll be having me all right!"

"That I will!"

"*Gaaah!*"

"*Rraaaah!*"

They crouched, facing each other, and paced from side to side, then back again. Their movements began to mirror each other. They raised their weapons at the same time, with the same poses, and flourishes.

Few people have been lucky enough—as Oller, Esmeralda and I were that day—to witness a real live Orc Mating Ritual. The reason for this is that Orc Mating Rituals usually take place after battles, when anyone who might have been around to watch is now dead. I'd say mating *dance*, if that was all it had been. It started out that way, like a war-dance, or a haka, each throwing challenges and insults at each other, but while it started out like a dance, it ended more like a war. Or rather, a battle. Not the battle that we spectators had been expecting, but the oldest battle of them all: the battle of the sexes.

As they stamped and flourished and glared, the threats and insults began.

"Gonna slap you around, that's for sure, pretty boy!" Klurra threatened.

I thought, *pretty boy? Grell's the ugliest bastard I've seen here. Well, until today … now there are two of them.*

Grell shot back, "Scarecrow!"

"Pigbollock!"

"Elf-tit!"

"Elf-tit! Did you call me *elf-tit*?" Klurra was incensed.

"Yeah, an' I'll apologize to the next repulsive elf-hag I see for comparing her scrawny dug to you. They may be fuckin' 'orrible little shits, but there's a limit!"

Klurra snarled, "Goblin turd!"

"Wolf-bitch!"

Klurra frowned and straightened up. "Oy," she said in a non-war-chant, more normal speaking voice. "You know the rules. No compliments."

"Er, sorry," Grell said. "Where was I?"

"Goblin turd."

"Yeah, right. Eefrit hemorrhoid!"

She grinned, sank back in her crouch, and said, "Nice one!"

"Oy, no compliments, nibler-arse," Grell shot back.

"Giant snot!"

"Pustule!"

"Snowdrop!"

"Sheep-shit!"

"Meringue!"

"Meringue?" Grell queried, contemptuously as if to say, *is that the best you can do?*

"Light and fluffy and sweet and crunchy," Klurra mocked. "Ready for a crunching, meringue-boy?"

"Oh, it's crunch time, is it?" Grell threatened.

"Come on over and see," she taunted.

"*You* come over *here* and see. I'm not going near some cabbage-flavored fart—my poor fucking nostrils! You must be joking!"

"You come here, 'fraidy-cat!"

"No, you come *here!*"

They began lifting their feet high to the side, like sumo wrestlers, and bringing them down with thumps that shook the ground, mirroring each other, synchronized, each bellowing, with each thump, "*Wooh …! Wooh …! Wooh!*"

Gradually, the angle of their feet changed, from sideways to forwards, a few inches at a time, and the two bellowing, glaring Orcs slowly stomp-danced towards each other, warhammers raised.

After a few more *woohs* they were facing each other, half a dozen paces apart, great plumes of breath billowing from mouths and nostrils.

"Think you're gonna tap me with that teaspoon?" Grell mocked.

The Orc girl flung her warhammer aside. "Not gonna dirty it with your bugshit-for-brains, you scrawny streak of pixie piss!"

I snorted. *Scrawny?* Grell's built like a brick shithouse.

Grell tossed aside his warhammer with a casual flick. It sailed into a thorn bush some twenty yards away. "Don't need no tin-toy hammer for this!"

"You don't make it easy on yourself, do you?" Klurra sneered. "First little baby's going to get a spanking, then he's going to get scwatchies on his lickw armsy-warmsies when he has to get my hammer out of that thorn bush. Oh no, wait, he's going to have *two* bwoken armsy-warmsies in a minute."

"Gods, you don't half jabber, like a bloody auctioneer with diarrhea!" Grell mocked. "Just shut up, will you. The sight of you's bad enough without your blab-blab, blahdy-bloody-blah-blah blah all day!"

"Who's talking!"

"I am, so you shut up."

"*You* shut up!"

"Or I'll shut you up!"

"Yeah? You and whose army?"

"This army-warmy," Grell echoed her babytalk as he held up his massive right arm, fist clenched. "Won't need *this* army-warmy." He tucked his left arm behind his back.

"Won't need either." The Orc girl crossed both of hers, contemptuously. "One puff and I'll blow you over."

"Yeah?" Grell stepped towards her.

"Yeah!" She stepped towards him.

"Go on, then! Try it if you think you're hard enough!"

"Oh, I'm hard enough, you flimsy sack of duck down!" Klurra leaned forward and blew in Grell's face.

Grell waited till she ran out of breath, which took a while.

When she'd stopped and stood in front of him, chest heaving to get her breath back, Grell said, "Ooh, did someone pick some nice lavender today? How lovely on this soft, spring breeze!" He took a huge breath, opened his mouth, and exhaled a roaring blast that I knew from bitter experience was so noxious you could almost see it. Thirty feet away that I was, I winced. I'd made sure, since our night hog-tied together in The Wheatsheaf's barn, to stand always *upwind* of Grell. His breath could stun pigeons. I was downwind of him now and quickly held my nose before his exhalation could reach me.

Klurra didn't flinch. "Yeah, well," she said, unimpressed, when Grell ran out of breath and stood panting opposite her. "You know what they say. Pretty promises are all very well, but can he live up to them?"

"I dunno why I waste my breath on you," Grell returned in the same dismissive tone.

"Deeds, not words," she mocked. "All sweet talk and no action."

"Yeah," Grell mocked back. "Time for talking's over, flapmouth."

"Then flutter off, little fairy. Back to your gnomey-homey in the dingly dell."

"You see any wings?"

"Ooh, no, sorry, did some *howwid ickw* boy pluck them off you? *Awwww ...!*"

"And I'm going forward, not back."

"Oh, are you?"

"I am."

"*Raaaah!*" Klurra roared, and "*Raaaah!*" Grell roared back and, roaring, they charged at each other, thumping into each other's chests, bouncing off and then thumping in again. At first neither of them used arms, just chests and breath and roars, until the arms came into play and then there was pushing, shoving, grabbing, grappling, and staggering in the least coordinated dance you've never seen, which became, somehow, coordinated, as each shuffling monster felt for the other's weaknesses and maneuvered and feinted and attempted to trip and throw, their roars now subsiding to grunts of exertion. And then there was an *oof*, and an *urf*, and they fell over each other's feet and tumbled to the ground with another jarring thud and then it was time for us to look away.

We didn't, half stunned from realizing that we'd just watched an exhibition of foreplay at its most remarkable.

Orc sex is like normal sex, only with Orcs. Sweating, puffing, squelching, shifting, grunting, honking, howls of outrage, and arguments about who had to lie on the damp patch.

I turned to Esmeralda, who was watching, mouth open. "Should you be watching this?"

She shrugged. "Why not? *You* two are!"

"Well, it's ... you being a noble maiden and all that."

"I'm not going to be a maiden forever I hope!" she replied. "And when it comes time to stop being a maiden, I wouldn't mind knowing what I should be doing."

We watched Grell and Klurra cavorting energetically and loudly on the ground, rolling, and thrashing, and biting, and barking, and giving orders, and complaining, and encouraging, and whacking each other on the backside as if they were horses.

"As long as you realize that's not the only way to do it," I pointed out.

"I'm not a complete idiot," Esmeralda retorted. "And I've seen Daddy's picture books. I know what's what and what goes where and how."

"That's a relief. For your husband, especially. I don't know if he'd appreciate a wedding night like this ..."

We knew that we shouldn't watch, but it was impossible not to. Just when you thought you'd seen it all, there was something new. An all-action, rip-roaring spectacle, in living 3-D.

Esmeralda said, "I've practiced fellatio. With a carrot. With my cousin, Roselle. She's twenty." At my raised eyebrow, she added, "Different carrot, we had a carrot each. She showed me how. She's done it for real, with her boyf. She says slowly is best, and humming. She also said best not do *that* when I bit the end off my carrot. She hasn't gone all the way with him, has to stay a maiden, of course, until the wedding night. But she will soon, they're marrying next month, and I expect I'll get a full report. If I ever see her again ..."

She tailed off.

Oller said as he handed us cheese sandwiches, "I had a girl, back in Brig. Mellyn. Barmaid at The Wolf's Head. I thought *we* was wild; I mean she was ... energetic. Inventive. Nothing like this, though."

We ate our sandwiches, which we washed down with water from our skins as we watched, and the *oofs* and *warghfs* and *grurgls* continued in the background. *As dinner theatre goes*, I thought, *this is pretty good value for money*. Seeing as it was not only free, but also 'highly original and superbly executed' (*The New Orc Times*); the characters were 'so well realized as to be entirely lifelike' (*The Daily Chainmail*); the choreography 'was both spellbinding and luminous in its fluidity' (*World of Dance*); and 'not only was the unexpected twist at the end breathtaking, but the entire climax was earth-shattering in its intensity. Highly recommended!' (*Sports Illustrated*).

We watched all the way to that climax. It was preceded by bouts of breaking off and jumping in again, which eventually led, via twists and turns and acrobatics, to somersaults, the two of them tumbling end over end down the slope, gathering speed until they crashed into a tree. Which made Klurra squeal with delight, and Grell yelp, "Ow!" because the part of them that had hit the tree was his head. Klurra giggled, and Grell gurgled, then he jumped to his feet with her perched on him and her legs wrapped around his thick hairy waist, and he ran around the tree, three times one way and three times the other, while she kicked his thick hairy bottom with her heels and drummed her fists on his back, yodeling with delight. And then they fell, with a shriek from Klurra and a bark of surprise from Grell, into a ditch covered with bracken. Its long brown leaves thrashed about above them, from the thrashing about going on below.

"Be a hell of a honeymoon," I said, to Esmeralda. "You and … who? D'you have anyone in mind?"

"No. I'm only sixteen, I've got plenty of time."

▲ ▲ ▲

Klurra knew of a nearby cave where we spent the night. The Stonefields Orcs kept it stocked with firewood, and Oller had a fire going in no time. There was plenty of room for the horses, and once we'd groomed and settled them for the night, we shared and shared alike. Orc sausage, we discovered, was delicious, juicy and spiced with firepeppers. Klurra loved Esmeralda's lemon biscuits, so Esmeralda gave her the entire package of them, wrapped up in a linen cloth.

By now, of course, Klurra adored Esmeralda, just like everyone did. She thanked her, and said she'd share them with her mother and sister, who loved cakes and would never have had anything as delicious as these. Then she grinned and said, "Fat chance of that, I'll eat the lot long before I get home." So, Esmeralda offered her the other package of them, but Klurra said no, because she wasn't going home anyway.

A thought struck her as she said that. She turned and looked at Grell, who was sitting on the ground beside her.

He looked at her and grinned.

She reached out and patted him on the knee.

She saw us looking at them, smiling. "They breed *real* Orcs in Ozgaroo!" she said.

Grell swelled with pride and beamed at her. I could tell he wanted to say something nice back but couldn't think of anything. "*Lucky* Orcs," he said eventually. "And I'm the luckiest of the lot!"

Klurra smiled at him. "Yeah, well," she said, her smile fading. "I suppose your luck's going to run out tomorrow."

Grell frowned, worried. "So … I suppose you're going to haul us up before your chief, eh?"

"No no, course not. Silly old bastard would probably cut your out-law head off. Bit of a stickler, Chief Elbrig. Old fashioned, one for the rules. I'm not having no one cut that gorgeous head off. No, tomorrow you go one way, I go the other."

Grell hadn't considered that.

"Assuming we continue in the directions we were taking when we met. Which were opposite. If you think about it, we'd never have met if we'd been going the same way. And we wouldn't be sitting here now having this nice chat around this nice fire after what I must say was a very nice day."

"Me too," Grell agreed.

"You lot enjoy it?" Klurra wondered.

"Very much," I said, and Esmeralda said, "Definitely," and Oller said, "Yes indeed. Never seen the like, me."

Klurra nodded, pleased. Then she said, "I'm not asking where you're going, don't worry. Secret mission and all that."

"Where are you going?" Grell asked. "If it isn't secret?"

"It's not exactly secret …" Klurra said. "It's … Orc business. I could tell you. But not them."

"Oh," Grell said.

She waited, watching him.

"I'd like to hear about it," Grell said.

"Come on, then."

She and Grell got up and went outside.

When they came back in, his face was shining.

"It's a *quest*, Daxxie!" he said. "A real, honest-to-goodness proper *quest!*"

"Orc quest," Klurra added. "Orcs only."

14

The Parting

We breakfasted before dawn, after which Grell and Klurra got ready to ride off on their Orc Quest. It had been Oller's idea to give Klurra his horse as a thank-you for not taking us to her chief, who would have needed to kill us as outlaws and trespassers. He'd have succeeded, even if he'd had to use all the Orcs in his tribe to help him. There'd be too many of them, and only three of us.

"Four," Esmeralda protested, annoyed. "I can shoot a bow!"

"We'd still all be dead," Oller said. "Though you'd enjoy taking a few with you, hey?"

Esmeralda grinned back. "Yeah. That I would! Anyone attacks my friends, *I* don't run away squealing! I shoot."

Oller had asked me how far I thought it was to where I was taking them. I *thought* the question to Marnie, and she thought back, *Tomorrow evening.* My horse could carry Oller and me, and we'd walk in turns. There was no rush. There was no one pursuing us, we were sure of that now. And once we were at Marnie's, no one would find us. I knew that. I don't know how I knew it, but I did. Marnie thought back, *Not if I didn't want them to find me.*

It was tough saying goodbye to Grell. I quite understood. An Orc Quest, for Orcs only? You couldn't turn *that* down if you were a

174

veteran adventurer like Grell. And what if it led him to more answers about *why* we were here? But, still, I was going to miss him. And I'd feel a lot safer with him around.

He'd see me again, he promised. He'd find me somehow, even if he had to go all the way to Mayport. I told him I'd get a message to him, and he said how, and I said, meaningfully, "Like how we used to communicate in the old days …?" His eyes clouded over, and he thought about what I'd said. When he realized, his eyes widened, and he said, "You think?"

I said, "We'll see."

"Bleeding hells!" he said. "Does that mean what I think it means?"

"I hope so. It would be … different, but the same principle"

"We'd have comms? Whoa! That would be *brilliant!* Then all we'd need would be Qrysta, and we'd be unstoppable. 'Specially with this little bastard making up the fourth." He nodded at Oller, who grinned. "Talk about specialists. Every skill covered!"

Oller said, "What aren't you telling me?"

"You'll see," I said. "I could be wrong, which is why I'm not telling yet. But if I'm right … . Remember Serjeant Bastard?"

Oller shuddered. "Don't remind me."

"He won't catch us, Ols, don't worry. Not in two days. What I mean is, remember what we all learned from him? We all went from being completely hopeless to being pretty damn good. At all sorts of things?"

"That's true …" Oller wondered where this was leading.

"If you're going to learn, learn from the best, right?"

"Right …"

"That's all I'm saying for now."

"Ah," Oller said, and tried to work out what I *wasn't* saying.

I helped Grell with his horse, and Oller and Esmeralda helped Klurra sort out supplies and packs on the horse that Oller had given her.

Lend, Klurra had insisted to Oller, not *give.* She'd promised to bring his horse back. And Grell back. Or die trying.

Various things were traded. We wouldn't need food for more than two days now, so we gave them the rest of our supplies. And Oller's flask of Bottled Bottle.

"You'll be needing this more than we will, methinks, and sooner rather than later."

Klurra thanked him and said, "It won't go to waste, that's for sure."

Grell came up to envelop me in an Orc hug. "I can't tell you anything about it now, mate, but can once it's all over, Klurra says. Sounds effing *amazing!* Some really nasty pieces of work for me to battle-test Fugg on!"

"Great name, great axe," Klurra said, no longer mocking it as not-a-warhammer. Indeed, she was eyeing it enviously. "Niblun and all. Lucky bastard!"

"I'll get you a niblun hammer, Klurry!" Grell promised. "If I have to go all the way to Niblunhaem itself and beat one out of them."

"I'll come with you. Wouldn't mind some nibler armor while we're at it, why not?"

"Yur!" Grell agreed. "Got to be better than this bloody army issue. Fucking chainmail! Wish I had my old plate back. Would've killed this poor sod, though. Carrying *me's* bad enough, even for one the size of him." He patted his horse appreciatively. It was, indeed, huge—a stallion as black as a stormy night and usually as foul-tempered, except with Grell. He seemed to actually *like* Grell, not just tolerate him.

"Light as feathers, hard as rocks, they say," Klurra said. "It'd be something to be in full niblun! We could try to find a way in, on the way home, eh? There has to be one up there, 'cos they trade with the giants. That'd be something, eh, Grellie? Us coming back from this to the tribe in full niblun. With you-know-who's head hanging from my saddle. Talk about creating a stir!"

I said, "These giants, up in the mountains, Klurra, have you ever seen any?"

"Oh yes," she said.

"How big are they?"

"Me standing on Grell's shoulders would be a little 'un. And if Grell was sitting on his horse, with me on his shoulders, that would be just about the biggest."

That sounded alarming. "Did you have to fight them?"

"Not always. Most are prepared to be reasonable. Some of them won't see sense and you have to ding 'em. Or dong 'em, depending which hammer I use. Makes no odds to me, they're identical, except for the nicks and scratches. Both equally effective. When I get my niblun hammers, I'm going to give them better names than Ding and Dong."

"Them's good names, Klurry," Grell said. "Appropriate. To the point."

"Poetic," Oller agreed. "Lots of things rhyme with ding and dong. Sing and song, for a start. Long. Strong. Wrong. Hey!" An idea struck him. "I could try making a poem up!"

"You do that, Olls." Grell enfolded Oller's scrawny frame in a hug.

Oller said, "Oof!" as the air went out of him, and he hugged back as best he could.

Grell released him. "I wanna hear it when we come back, all right?"

"Yeah," Oller said. "I'll give it a go. Daxxie and Ez can help if I get stuck. I mean … . There's lots. Grell, hell. Orc, fork. Klurra …?"

All work stopped as we racked our brains.

Grell's face brightened, and he said, "Kookaburra!"

"Is that a thing?" Oller said.

"Yeah, it's a noisy bloody bird where I come from, in Oz!"

Klurra stared at him. "Oh yeah? I'm a noisy bloody bird where you came *to*, am I?" she challenged.

Grell's face clouded again, and he stammered, "Er …"

"You could always use *not*," Esmeralda offered, diplomatically. "*Not* like a kookaburra. Something like that."

"Yeah," Grell jumped at the suggestion. "*Nothing like* a kookaburra! Perfect, thanks, Ez."

He grinned uncertainly at Klurra, who grunted and relaxed.

"Mm," Oller said. "I'll work on it. There's more to this poem-writing malarkey than meets the eye."

Grell hugged me, and hugged Esmeralda, as daintily as he could. Then Klurra hugged us all as Grell checked the horses' girth straps yet again.

Klurra said, "If you meet any Stonefields, just give them the password. Tell them 'Klurra says weasel.' It's code. They'll work it out. You probably could too, it's pretty bloody easy. Has to be, for your average thicko Orc to get the message." She looked at me expectantly, as if I could crack it. "If I'd said elk or otter or ant, they'd chop your heads off," she hinted. "But not badger, or wolf, or jackdaw."

"Ah," I said when I got it. "So, I could say any of those, or lark or deer or boar. As long as it doesn't start with a vowel."

"Yep! Grell's right, he told me you're a clever one. And if you don't give them *weasel* or one of them others, just don't try *yak*. Yak confuses them. Is *y* a vowel, like in rhythm, one of them will say, and they'll argue, and most of them are always looking for an excuse for a nice fight.

And they'd take your heads back to the chief, and I'd deal with them when I got back and they'd squawk *'y's a vowel, like in rhythm!'* And I'd yell at them for being ignorant tossers, and there'd be another fight, so they'd be twice as happy. So not yak, all right? Or yeti."

"You have those here?" Grell asked.

"Yes indeed—and where we're going, too, so you'll probably see some. Yaks, anyway. Giants herd the yaks, live on them. They make a drink out of fermented yak milk. It's disgusting, but effective. Yakyuk, we call it. Can't wait to see your face when you try it, Grellie. You'll look like you've eaten a whole lemon with poo for pips. It don't half work, though—you'll feel great after. Although not the *morning* after. Yetis don't bother us, nor the giants, nor the giants them. They know better. You hear them howling in the night from way up in the high peaks. Lovely sound, it is—sad and haunting. Always makes me know I'm miles from everything and everywhere, just where I belong."

She gave us all a last smile and a wave. "Bye then. See you all when our roads meet again." She turned back to Grell. "Come on then, big boy. Let's go looking for trouble!"

She swung up into the saddle, and Grell mounted his stallion.

"Don't keep him too long, Klurra," I said. "We need him back. We still have a job to do."

"Couple of weeks, three tops," Klurra said. "Then he's all yours."

"Good to hear. Happy hunting!"

"Thanks," she replied, and Grell said, "Have fun, mates!" and Oller and Esmeralda and I replied, "You too."

And they rode off, into what in another twelve hours would be the sunset.

It wasn't long before we were in the saddle ourselves and riding in the opposite direction. We didn't have to use Orc code. Klurra was the only Orc we met on that journey, and by midday the Uplands were behind us. We'd only skirted the edge of Stonefields territory, so were no longer trespassing. The high moorland with its outcroppings of rock and gullies filled with stunted trees dropped gradually away behind us. Every slope up was followed by a longer slope down, and soon the terrain changed as we descended into the lowlands. The land grew greener and the grass longer and sweeter for the horses.

The cold moorland burns became chattering streams, flowing down the hillsides into meadows and woods. Cheerful birdsong replaced the harsh cries of crows and ravens. Our spirits lifted as the sun warmed us. Spring wildflowers carpeted the woodlands and leas, and insects glittered above the waters. The stream we were following joined a river, where we stopped to rest the horses in the shade of a grove of ash trees. Oller took off his boots and leather leggings and waded into a pool. He'd seen trout. He tickled them, catching three, in minutes, with his bare hands. Fine, fat ones, they were. We ate well that night.

"Can't be anyone comes this way," he said, as we picked trout bones out of our teeth. "Fish grow wary when they learn about people."

We had a fire. We had stomachs full of fresh grilled trout. We had shelter. It wasn't much, but it would keep the rain off if it came in the night. Marnie had led me to a low cliff that ran along the river. It sloped inward at its base, its top leaning out over our bivouac. It didn't rain. We were neither comfortable nor warm, but it wasn't a bad night. I'd long stopped worrying about Esmeralda and her being a noble maiden used to her comforts, her feather bed and her pillows. She radiated happiness. And when Esmeralda radiated, the world was perfect.

"I've never had an adventure before," she said, as we lay, rolled up in our cloaks and blankets, our faces to the dwindling fire. "Only escapades, like climbing trees and scrumping apples in people's orchards. Or lying in wait for friends on their way home in the dark and leaping out at them shouting, 'Boo!' so they'd scream … ." The memory made her smile. Her smile outshone even the fire. "Nothing like this, though. Daddy will be going nuts." She frowned, considering. "I wonder what Mommy will say to calm him down."

"She won't be going nuts too?" Oller asked.

"No. Not really. She'll pretend to, at first. Just to buy us time. She'll rush about shouting orders and tearing her hair and sending people this way and that, and then changing her mind and countermanding her orders and helping everything stop rather than start. She's good at dissembling, is Mommy. She's had to be. Being a Lady and having to set an example. And being married to Daddy."

"So, she knows?" I asked.

"Bits," Esmeralda said. "She'll probably work out more bits. She's clever. I left her a letter. It told her enough to let her see my reasons. And not to worry, I was safe. She'll put two and two together when she learns you three deserted. She probably won't quite know what to make of it, but she always says I know what I'm doing. And, of course, there's her vow. Which I reminded her of in my letter. 'You made a vow, I'm going to keep it.' She'll worry, of course she will. But she'll know that whatever's at the end of my story, it won't be like hers. And she'll pray to Lymnia, Goddess of Patience and Forbearance, for the strength she'll need to see her side of it through. And because her vow was to Lymnia, she'll know I'm in good hands."

She smiled at me and then at Oller, our heads sideways on the ground on the other side of the fire.

"I am, aren't I," she said. And it wasn't a question. It was a statement.

"The best!" Oller said.

"The best," she agreed.

And to show her I meant it, I said, "I'll make a vow."

Esmeralda said, "No, you don't need to. I *know*. Like Mommy always says. And vows have consequences. There's more to them than the words. And more to the words than just one meaning. You could think you're vowing one thing, but the meaning can shift inside the words—and then you've also vowed something else you perhaps didn't intend. And perhaps shouldn't have. And anyway, I'd rather you didn't. You're free. Mommy isn't. She's chained to her vow."

"A chain you're going to break," I said.

"Don't say *break!*" Esmeralda was alarmed. "Not with vows! We don't want even the *suggestion* of break. No, it's keep. It's obey. It's fulfill. What matters, when it's all over, is *how* we kept and obeyed and fulfilled. There's more than one way to do those words, just as they all have more than one meaning."

"Do you know how?" I asked.

"No," she admitted. "That's what we're going to find out."

That seemed a bit vague. "You must have some idea."

"Oh, lots. And you, and me, and Oller—and Grell when he comes back—are going to keep going until we get there."

"Mayport," I said.

"The end," she said. "Wherever that is. And by then, we'll have found out."

"Ah," I said. "It's the journey, not the destination."

Esmeralda said, "It's both."

"Right." I lay there, staring at the fire and turning it all over in my head. I thought, *of course we always want* all *the information*. Surprises can be nice, but they can also be nasty. But what do you do when you don't have all the information?

You keep your eyes and ears open, and you keep looking and listening.

That thought was somehow comforting, and it was the last thing I remember before my eyes closed, and I was asleep.

▲ ▲ ▲

I thought I began to recognize the way to Marnie's some time before I was sure that I did.

I'd walked that way before, with Nyrik and Horm, down in the other direction. Now we were approaching from the other side, riding up the valley, through her overgrown, scruffy orchard, which was—strangely for this time of the year, it being the middle of spring—bursting with fruit. And not just the usual ones—apples and pears and plums and apricots—but ones that I'd never have expected to see up here in this climate. Mangoes, papayas, lychees. There was even a neat row of pineapples in the ground, all ripe and ready for the harvesting. And two long rows of vines, heavy with both green and dark purple grapes.

Off to one side, behind high, yew hedges was her herbarium, which I hadn't noticed before. We could see the entrance to it ahead, an arch over a gap in the hedge. Coming down, as I'd done with Nyrik and Horm, it had been behind us, off to one side where the hedge cut back at right angles. I'd had no reason to turn back to look that way.

Oller, Esmeralda, and I walked our horses in through the arch. The herbarium was even bigger than the orchard, and even messier. Parts of it seemed to be in shadow, despite the bright afternoon sunshine. At one end there was a shining pool, dotted with lilies. At the other lay a dark, muddy-brown pond, fringed with dull green plants that looked oily and rotten. The pond stank, we discovered, as we rode past. We held our breath and looked at it uneasily. A greasy, brown bubble grew on its surface, expanded slowly until it was enormous, then burst with a plop, spitting out pustules of goo and a burp of foul-smelling gas which smoked as it hung, wavering above the surface. By its bank, the trees were stunted and twisted. Dark berries gleamed among their leaves with a glint that said *don't*. Their trunks were thick with fungi, and toadstools sprouted at their feet.

"Who lives here, then?" Oller asked, as we emerged through the herbarium's upper arch and saw the cottage above us.

"A friend of mine," I said.

Esmeralda was apprehensive. "I hope you know what you're doing, Daxx."

"I don't," I replied. "But she does."

Marnie came out of her pig pen as we approached, blood on her arms and a dead piglet in her hand, its throat freshly cut. "Here you are, then," she said, matter-of-factly. "Made good time. No troubles on the way?"

"None." I was leading my horse, which Oller was riding. Esmeralda was on her palfrey, looking nervous. I'd never seen her look unsure of herself before. The world seemed dimmer than it usually did when she was with us.

"How are you, Marnie?" I asked.

"Old. Creaking and aching." She didn't seem in a very good mood. I wondered if she ever was.

"Thank you for the directions," I added, thinking that politeness might help.

"Picked 'em up well enough, didn't you?" she said, with what might almost have been the beginnings of a smile. "I don't think it'll take long to sort you out. Her, though ... ." She studied Esmeralda, who quailed. Marnie grunted and said to Oller, "And you I've got a job for. You'll be riding off in the morning, first thing, and it's a long way, so you'll have your work cut out to get there and back in time. Which you'd better be. Time's running short."

She didn't say what for. Oller looked as if he wanted to ask, but refrained.

Marnie shuffled off towards her cottage, and I saw Esmeralda pull herself together. I went over to her and patted her hand. She looked at me, cornflower-blue eyes wide and worried. She was trembling.

"It'll be all right," I reassured her—even though I knew that Marnie was far from reassuring.

Without turning around, Marnie said, "I told you once before. Don't make promises you can't keep."

Esmeralda looked at me in fear. I could see that she wanted to turn her palfrey around and gallop away, anywhere, it didn't matter where—as long as it wasn't here. I couldn't blame her. Marnie was alarming.

"Don't be a fool, girl," Marnie said, again without looking back. "This is where it starts."

I could see that Esmeralda was close to tears. "Thank you," she managed.

"We'll see about that. There's oats and hay," Marnie said, pointing at the stable, and Oller said, "Right-ho."

Esmeralda and I followed Marnie into her cottage while Oller fed and stabled the horses. I stood aside, in the tiny porch, to let Esmeralda go on ahead of me through into the kitchen. I could feel her trembling in her cloak, which she kept on, as if she felt she could hide in it. She noticed the broomsticks and hats and boots and cloaks, all black—and looked at me, pleading, hoping I'd say we'd come to the wrong place.

"Mayhaps you have," Marnie said from the kitchen.

I went in, bumping into Esmeralda, who had stopped just beyond the doorway. I looked over her shoulder and saw Hob.

He was coming slowly over from his place by the fire, on his crooked, cautious feet, his long hands clenching each other in front of him over his thin arms and chest. He was looking hungrily towards us. His eyes, which I remembered as gray and dull, were yellow, and gleaming bright, and much, *much* bigger than before … and were growing larger all the time. He was no longer a drab, brownish green, but a bright, deep green—a somehow ominous green. A smile began on his clenched, tight lips. It widened and widened, lips still sealed, until they seemed to wrap around his head.

Marnie stopped and turned to us. "You hungry?"

"Very," I replied.

She grunted.

"Hob'll stew this up for you," she said, holding out the piglet. Hob's smile shrank, and the gleam in his greedy eyes dulled. "Just the head now, Hob!" she said, her voice sharp with warning. "And sort the gizzards, we'll want the liver and kidneys for breakfast. The rest of them are yours once he's in the pot."

Hob, staring at the piglet, nodded. "Stew," he said, a little sadly, turning to Marnie and nodding. "Gort the sizzards."

"You see as you do that!" Marnie ordered, and stared at him hard.

Hob nodded again.

Marnie said, "You might want to look away now. He's one third Hob, but two thirds goblin."

Hob was grinning again, his eyes enormous and yellow and gazing at the piglet dangling from Marnie's hand in front of him, his dark green skin shimmering.

I took Esmeralda's shoulders and turned her around so she couldn't see what was coming. She buried her face in my chest, her body shaking. I held her and patted her and said, "It's all right." I'd wanted to say things like *everything will be fine* and *there's nothing to fear*, but I knew now not to make promises I couldn't keep. She was already fearful and nothing had happened yet.

I looked over her shoulder as Hob's lips parted. His mouth opened, wider than seemed possible. It was the mouth of a nightmare fish from the deeps, filled with needles above and below, curving inwards, long needles, short needles, gripping needles, and tearing needles which seized the piglet's head and tore it off at the neck as Hob's bony hands pulled the piglet's body from Marnie's grasp. Horrible sounds of crunching, and Hob's feeding snarls and gurgles of joy, filled the room. Esmeralda whimpered, and her body shook. Hob's frenzy was as short as it was terrible. His eyes shrank and grayed out. His green gleam faded back almost to brown. His mouth became small again, and he padded with the headless piglet over to the pot to prepare our stew.

I sat Esmeralda down, and Marnie came over from her mixing bench with cups of something warm for us.

"No point in wasting it," she said. "Won't be much meat on him, him being a runt. But it'll fill you. I'll add herbs, for the nerves," she added.

"You weren't going to eat it anyway?" I asked.

"I usually let Hob have the runts," she said. "Perk of the job. All I wanted was the squeak."

She shook her head as Oller came in to join us.

"Poor squeak it was, too. Thin. Thinner even than her last farrowing's runt. Cassa, my sow. You want to mark what Cassa does, she *indicates*. I'm thinking she's indicating there won't be none next year, not even the thinnest." She looked at Oller. "Like I said, time's short. May not be enough of it. You'd best be quick."

Oller said, "Quick as I can, but—why me?"

"Because I need something found."

She turned to me and held up what appeared to be a straw. It was the hollow stem of a reed, sealed at both ends with clay.

"What d'you make of that?" she asked, as if we both knew the answer.

I thought I did. "Thin," I said.

She nodded. "What would be another word for that?"

"Narrow."

"Indeed. Give it a listen, then."

I held the reed up to my ear and listened. At first, I couldn't hear it, so thin the sound was. But then, I could. The piglet's dying squeak. As faint as a puff of wind yet stretching on forever.

"Three's all I've got," Marnie said. "You'd best not be in want of a fourth, so use them wisely." She looked at Oller again. "Runt." She eyed his scrawny body. Oller was barely taller than she was—or would have been, if she'd been able to straighten up. He was shorter than Esmeralda. "Strong, though, ain't you, lad? Sneaky and quick. Proper finder." She jerked her head, indicating the cluttered kitchen. "Think yourself good at finding, don't you?" she challenged with a hard smile.

"I am," Oller said.

"Let's have the proof of that," Marnie replied. "Off you go. Find what you find. And if you're as good at finding as you think you are, you're the lad for the job."

She turned to Esmeralda, and Oller started looking around the room. He was thinking, hard. Appraising the place, like the professional he was. And thinking, *what I am going to find here isn't going to be the usual. So, not the usual places, then ...*

He wandered off to case the room. Out of curiosity, I also looked around, wondering what he'd find where. Mixing-table. Workbench. In the darkest corner a flat, black stone lay on a pedestal, a candle burning on it. It looked somehow like a shrine. A strange, curling sign was painted on the wall behind it. Above the fire, the mantelpiece was dotted with curios. A stuffed owl. A twisted piece of yellow-brown wood, worn smooth by the sea. No, not wood: some mineral that looks like wood .... The word came to me. *Meerschaum.* Seafoam. How did I know? I knew but didn't know how I knew. I thought, *knowing without knowing how. Instinct. Without a second thought. That'll be the way.* Next to the meerschaum was a severed hand—its skin dried to leather— standing upright on its wrist. At the center of the mantelpiece was a pair of scales, one measuring tray hanging much lower on its arm than the other. Why was it there, I wondered? Why not at her mixing table?

I looked over at the mixing table and saw her other set of scales. Its trays were hanging even.

Wondered when you'd notice, Marnie thought to me. *Thought you'd have spotted it last time. If you had, you'd see it's hanging even lower now. Everything out of balance. Like I said, time is short. At least your eyes are sharper now, and your thoughts. You'll need 'em sharp where you're going. And you're right about instinct. Think twice and you're lost. Doublethink, double trouble.*

She thought that all to me, while gazing at Esmeralda, who looked back up at her, pleading and fear in her huge cornflower eyes. I stood behind her, one hand on her shoulder. I remembered that look from when Marnie had fixed it on me, and tightened my grip in reassurance.

Oller went outside, lost in thought, to explore the outbuildings. He didn't close the door behind him. Marnie glanced at it, and it shut itself with a bang, which made Esmeralda jump and look around, scared, as the door's bolts slid themselves home. She glanced back up at me. I smiled down as best as I could, which was weakly. She reached behind herself for my hand, and I held hers between mine. She looked back at Marnie, who was waiting for her.

Marnie held Esmeralda in her gaze again. After a while, Marnie said, "No time like the present. Time being short. Why?" she asked Esmeralda.

We all knew what she meant.

Esmeralda's voice emerged as little more than a whisper. "I have to get to Mayport."

"And why is that?"

"I had a dream when I turned sixteen. I keep having it. I have to go to Mayport—it's very important, I must get there as soon as possible. I have something for her, she has something for me, like she promised on the day I was named. She's calling me. I have to see her."

Marnie said, "See who?"

"My godmother."

Marnie leaned a little closer.

Esmeralda tried not to flinch away.

I felt her shivering under my hand. I tightened it again on her shoulder a couple of times to remind her I was there.

"You're looking at her," Marnie said, and raised her eyepatch.

Esmeralda screamed.

15

The Heart of the Matter

Her scream died away into silence.

Marnie's gaze bored into Esmeralda.

Esmeralda couldn't move. She stared back into Marnie's huge, terrible red eye, seeing nothing. All the seeing was going in one direction: at Marnie. Everything that was being gathered was going the same way, into Marnie: a flow of thoughts, conscious, subconscious, and unconscious. Marnie was studying, learning, unlocking hidden meanings that Esmeralda didn't know were buried within her.

No one moved. I wanted to shield Esmeralda, protect her from this assault, stop what was happening.

Marnie thought to me, *You should hear this.*

Another voice came. *Hello, dear. Marnie's told me all about you.*

Marnie thought, *Huh! Not much o' that.*

I do hope we meet some day, the new voice said. *I'd have been there now, if I could, but, unfortunately, I've been detained. One of these days, eh? With luck and a following wind.*

Need plenty of those, he will, Marnie thought.

In my scrambled brain, without even forming a sentence, I was thinking, *who, whuhh? Where, how—*

I'm Junie, dear, the new voice answered. It was a kind voice; the voice of someone you feel you've known since childhood. *I'm Esmeralda's godmother. Turned out lovely, hasn't she?* Her voice brimmed with pride.

Marnie thought sourly, *Lovely is as lovely does, Junie.*

It's not her fault, Marns.

No, it's yours, Marnie snapped back. *We all know that. What none of us knows is what we can do about it.*

There was an awkward silence in my head.

Well, Junie's thought came. *I'm sure you'll think of something.*

Are you? Marnie challenged. *That makes one of us.*

When it came again, Junie's voice sounded smaller. *I thought it was the right thing to do. You know that. What with her mother's vow and all.*

Well, Marnie thought, *you weren't to know. None of us did. The vow's the least of our problems now. But if you'd known then what we know now ...* she tailed off, shaking her old head.

Mayhaps there's another way, Junie thought. *Which I don't see yet. And mayhaps this young feller-me-lad is part of it.*

Grasping at cobwebs, Junie, Marnie snapped. *You won't haul your way out of this with gossamer.*

Junie's voice was resigned but almost cheerful. *I know, dear. I'm done for. But I bought us time. Wheels have turned and we're not alone now. I would so very much like to meet you, young Master Daxx. Mayhaps I will, if you're quick enough about it.*

He's no master yet, Junie.

Junie's voice chuckled in my head. *Yes, well, I've seen what you've seen in him, Marnie. Unlock that lot and there'll be fireworks!*

If it's true, Marnie warned.

If it's true, Junie agreed. *Could be just a lot o' fairy tales rattling around in a young lad's head. Mixed in with a lot of wishful thinking. You should give him a wish, Marn. See what he wishes for.*

I'm not playing none o' that! Marnie countered. *Idleness is weakening your mind, Junie. This is no time for daydreams.*

It's all I've got, Junie sighed. *Time. Time to daydream. Have you seen what you need to see?*

I wish I knew, Marnie replied. *I've seen her well enough. Poor thing. Such a shame.*

She was as lovely and happy as their marriage was loveless and miserable, Junie quoted. *That has to stand for something.*

I thought, alarmed, *Was? What does she mean, was?*

I'm not disputing that, Marnie thought, *but stands for what?*

Well, Junie replied, *that's what we're about to find out, aren't we?*

There was another contemplative silence.

Price is high, Marnie shook her head in sorrow.

High indeed, Junie agreed.

I had to ask. *What is the price?* I thought to them. *And what's it the price of?*

They both answered simultaneously, *Her.*

I waited for an explanation. None came.

Is she the price? And is she also what she's the price of?

Now you see our problem, dear, Junie thought to me.

I looked at Esmeralda, frozen like a statue in Marnie's gaze, and felt my heart break into a thousand pieces of glass—no, of ice, which fell to the ground at my feet. My feet grew cold as the grass they were standing on died, as the ice soaked away from where it had fallen and spread its bleak chill into the world. The chill of death. Esmeralda, frozen, and the world dying into an endless winter. *Esmeralda is the price? In what way? How will it be … collected?*

I knew, without having to be told.

Her life.

"What can we do?" I whispered.

No one knows, Marnie thought.

And Junie thought, *We've been trying to think. For sixteen years now. Mayhaps you can come up with something.* She didn't sound hopeful. *Unless it is all fairy tales and wishful thinking in that handsome young head of yours.*

Me? What do I know that could help?

That's what we're here to find out, Marnie thought back.

We considered in silence.

Have you got everything? Junie asked.

Marnie grunted. *Probably. Much good it's done me so far. I can't see what I'm looking at. Poor child don't know herself, of course. Sixteen years, blink of an eye to us old 'uns. But in that blink, those big blue eyes will have seen. Even if she didn't notice. And I can't for the life of me see what that can have been, can you, Junie?*

I can't, dear. It's been lovely seeing her again, though. Such a precious girl. Warms your heart to look at her.

Don't you go boasting now and patting yourself on the back! Marnie admonished. *You laid the Glamour on her, and I'll own I've never seen a better. Your masterpiece, I'd say. Expensive things, masterpieces. For those as can afford them.*

And they make the world a better place, Junie thought.

That they do, Marnie agreed. *While they last.*

We gazed at Esmeralda, drinking her in. The thought of a world without her in it was unbearable. Tears were pouring down Marnie's cracked old cheeks, just as they were running down my own.

This dream of hers. Marnie shook her head. *Thinking you were calling her. Poor child.*

I could hear Junie's sigh, in my head. *I know. It's started. As we knew it would.*

I thought, *What has started?*

The beginning, Junie thought. *The beginning of the end.*

We all contemplated Esmeralda in silence.

You can let her go now, Junie sniffled eventually. *Thank you, Marnie dear. Filled my poor old heart with joy today, you have. I doubt I'll be seeing her again.*

The sadness in her thought was complete, as if a curtain was falling on an enchanting spectacle, or she was waking from a fine dream to dull daylight.

Goodbye, my darling, Junie thought to Esmeralda; and then, *And goodbye, young master-to-be-or-we're-all-finished. And thank your clever finder for me when you see him. There's not many as would have found that stone where I hid it. I doubt I'll be seeing you myself, much though I'd like to. Unless you do come up with something.*

She sounded resigned, calm but not hopeful, matter of fact. Her part had been played, her thought made that clear to Marnie and me. She was leaving the stage to others, for them to take the drama to its end.

Marnie thought, by way of goodbye, *I don't know as how I'd have done what you've done, Junie. But I'm not saying you was wrong. Buying time …*

… Time is expensive, Junie acknowledged. *And payment's due.*

That it is, Marnie agreed.

Junie's reply was resigned. *Well. I'm just glad I won't be around to see it paid.*

Marnie grunted. *And I'm thinking you might just be the lucky one. The poor lass …*

Junie chuckled, and I could feel its hollowness. *My luck ran out a long time ago*, she thought to us.

Yes, well. Be our turn next, like as not. Marnie reached up for her eyepatch and lowered it over her huge, red eye.

Esmeralda blinked and stirred. She stared at Marnie, lost. Then, gradually, she remembered where she was and how scared she'd been. She turned to me. I patted her shaking hand and smiled as best I could.

She was so lovely, so good, so precious. I would do anything for her. And my heart was on the ground in a thousand icy pieces. Clearly, Marnie and Junie believed that she was doomed—not only that, but also that they couldn't see anything to stop what they saw as inevitable. I couldn't allow myself to believe it too. What was the threat? Who was threatening her? Why? There was so much that I didn't yet know. All I knew was that there *had* to be something we could do to stop it. And that I would find it or die trying.

The door unbolted itself, and Oller came into the hallway from his explorations. He was looking smug as he joined us in the kitchen, barefoot and carrying his boots. He was soaking wet and shivering, but clearly pleased with himself.

"How many?" Marnie said.

"Nine," Oller grinned, taking his clothes off under his blanket and handing them to Hob, who hung them up to dry by the fire.

Nine? I thought. *Nine what?*

Marnie's eyebrows shot up. "There's only seven!"

"There's nine," Oller said. "Want to see 'em?"

"Indeed I will!" Marnie said, nettled. "Once we've finished with our young lady guest." She shook three drops from a little bottle into the cup of water that Hob placed in front of Esmeralda. "Heartsease," she said, with a nice smile. "You've been through the bother and it'll settle you."

Esmeralda smiled timidly back.

She drank, and her shoulders relaxed. "What just happened?"

"I had a good look at you, dear," Marnie said, with another comforting smile.

Esmeralda said, "Oh."

"And I must say, I liked what I saw." She patted Esmeralda's soft, small hand with her old, leathery one. "Quite brightened up my poky little home, you have. Makes me think I need to give it a good spring cleaning."

"I can help," Esmeralda said.

"Can you now! That would be nice. An extra pair of hands would be very useful," Marnie said. "You and me and Hob, we'll get this place spick and span in no time. In fact …" A thought struck her. "Yes, that's a good idea, that is," she said to herself.

We waited for her to tell us her good idea, but she didn't.

I said, "What is?"

"Never you mind. You'll see soon enough."

Hob put a bowl of stew in front of each of us, with spoons, and a wooden platter of chunks of bread, to which we helped ourselves. A runt the piglet may have been, but his stew was delicious. As we ate, we listened.

"Right," Marnie said, "now's the time for explanations. When you were named"—she turned to Esmeralda—"your godmother laid a Glamour on you. She was here just now, having a good look at you, too, through me. She's very proud of you. As who wouldn't be, you've turned out so well. There's much more to you than meets the eye, my lady, and what meets the eye is special enough. Someone could look like you and be a terror inside. But Junie laid it well, not just on the surface but deep down and all the way through, skin and bone and mind and soul. And not just for a while, neither, but for all the years of your life.

"But a Glamour is a Glamour, and yours is a problem, the position you're in. I can't take it away—not a Glamour given at your naming in the sight of the goddess. Only she who laid it on you could do that, and she's in no position to. What I can do is lay another one over it, and that we need to do to keep you safe. And if you're going to be spring-cleaning with me and Hob, we don't want those dainty hands getting cracked and crabbed, and those pretty knees chafing on my floor, now do we? Look the part, learn the job."

We were all looking at Marnie while she was talking. When she stopped, we turned to look at Esmeralda, who was gone. Sitting in her place was a scullery maid, homely of face, brown of hair and eye, dressed in a work smock and apron.

She looked at us and our puzzled expressions. "What?"

"Hand us what you found in the cowshed, will you?" Marnie held out her hand to Oller.

Oller reached into his bag and brought out a small mirror. "Why'd you hide it there?"

"Bluebell likes to preen," she said, taking it from him.

"Seriously? A preening cow?"

"No." Marnie snorted, disdainful that he'd fallen for it. "Hob and me, we don't like reflections about the place. Bothersome things, reflections. I put them away where they can't annoy us. Here, child." She passed the mirror to Esmeralda.

Esmeralda looked into it and gasped, her hand flying to her mouth.

"You're still the same inside," Marnie said. "And you'll still sound like you, so work on your scullery maid talk. It's best if you sound the part as well as look it. I can take it off you anytime. And so can anyone I teach how, if they've the skill." She looked at me.

I understood the glance. She would teach me how—if I were to show her that I had the skill.

She went on, "You told me you've brought me something."

"Yes, I have." I fetched my bag from the floor by my feet.

Marnie said, "No, you didn't."

"I did," I said, "it's a gift."

"It's a gift all right. But not from you to me."

I put my bag on the table and was about to reach into it.

"No need to do that," Marnie said. "First things first. Fetch me some sticks of a length you'd use for walking—shoulder height. While this finder shows me what he's found. *Nine!* Where there should be seven. I don't like surprises."

Oller didn't know whether to look pleased or worried.

"All right." I got up from the table. "Where from?"

"Anywhere your feet and hands lead you. My suggestion, time being short, is try the woodshed."

I nodded. It was late evening now, getting dark.

"I know." Marnie read my thought. "No candle. Wouldn't want you doing this in the daylight. Off you go."

"How many shall I bring?"

"As many as you like," she said. "Shut the hens in first. Foxes know not to come here, I don't like it. But foxes don't always play by the rules. Lock them up and black them out. Nights are short, now, too short for a decent sleep, and I want to get up in the mornings when *I* want, not when that blasted rooster sees the first light o' day."

I went out through the cluttered hallway, into the patch that was her front garden. All that grew there was unkempt grass and some wildflowers and weeds. Her nanny goat was grazing on it. She lifted her head, staring at me with her pale goat eyes, chewing. The woodshed was next to the cowshed, beyond the pig pen. First, I stopped by the chicken run, where the cockerel was already on his roost. He looked at me scornfully as I chivvied his wives inside. I put the night-blanket over their hutch and headed for the woodshed.

It was almost fully dark when I went inside.

Long sticks lay in piles along one wall, along the other, logs.

Marnie had said *sticks*.

I reached for one, touched it, and felt it leaching into my hand. And then flowing up my arm. I put it down, quickly. I tried another, and the same thing happened. And a third. Each time, the stick leached itself into me, and each time, it was a different leaching.

I crouched down by the shadow in which the pile of sticks lay and thought about it. I realized that I was waiting for a thought from Marnie.

None came.

This was up to me. My choices. As many, I understood, as I *like*.

There were five of them, in the end. Each had a different weight and a different heft and balance. And each had a very different feel. I put those five aside and spent time holding them, one after the other, letting their essences flow into me. One felt sharper, one calmer, one more evasive, one warmer, one as hard as stone. I liked them all. I turned back and rechecked every other stick in the pile. I decided that I couldn't have given them all equal consideration.

Eventually, I found three more that spoke to me, in feeling, along my arms, into my chest and stomach. I stood with them, in turn, there in the dark woodshed, and felt them in my legs and shoulders, eyes and ears, in my bones and guts and heart. Of the three new ones, one felt grim, one light, in both senses, and one jittery. Or did I mean quick? Or did I mean mysterious? No, they all felt mysterious. But the others all felt it *knowably*: clearly sharp, reliably calm, honestly warm, and so on.

I wasn't sure I liked this jittery one. It hadn't really spoken to me at first, certainly not the first time I'd gone through the pile—as if, I now thought, I hadn't been worth speaking to. *Okay*, I thought, holding it, *now why should that be?* I gave it time to answer. Before it did, I could swear that I felt it laughing. I waited and held it, and eventually it stopped playing with me and leached itself into me, deeper and deeper, growing clearer and stronger, until I couldn't put it down. I made my-self pull back, though, and retried the others, but I kept coming back to the laughing, jittering one, trying to see if I could decide what on earth it was.

I couldn't.

I carried the eight sticks back into Marnie's kitchen and put them on the table as she cleared away Oller's findings.

"Eight," she said. "Good number is eight. Lucky. Pick one."

"I can't make up my mind."

"I said *pick*, not choose. We'll get to *choose* later. Any order."

I picked up the nearest one. *Grim.*

Marnie grunted. "Hornbeam. Word?"

"Grim," I said.

"You can say that again!"

We went through the others, one by one. Elm, blackthorn, holly, birch. At my words for each of them, Marnie said, "You know your woods."

"I really don't," I said. "I couldn't tell you which is which."

"Not important. You can tell which is *what*."

The last three that I'd picked up were willow, which felt light—light in weight, and imbued with light, and my word was *light*; then yew, which was the opposite, *dark*, and that word came easily. Marnie nod-ded, grunted, and seemed relieved when I put it down. The last one, the jittery one, came up my arm quicker than the others and into my chest and heart faster, where it danced and teased. And I couldn't put it down.

"Rowan," Marnie said, pronouncing the *row* to rhyme with *cow* and *now* and *how*.

Ah, I thought, examining it. *So that's what it is.*

"Word?" she said. Her voice was quieter now.

I thought and thought—but couldn't pin it down. "It keeps chang-ing. At first it was *jittery* and then *quick* and then *mysterious*. And then, when I picked it up again, when I tried to decide, I couldn't, so *undecided*. And now it's down to two words: *dancing* and *teasing*. And I don't know which it is."

Marnie was looking at me, appraising. And nodding slowly. "If you had to pick?" she asked, gently.

"I don't think I could."

"No," she smiled. "You couldn't. No one can. No one has ever been able to pin down the rowan. Trickster she is, my lady rowan."

"She?"

"Some believe the first woman was formed from the rowan tree, and the first man from the ash tree. She's two things to all and two different things to each. To all she is fire and healing, and to you dancing and teasing."

She came over to me and took both my hands in hers. I was still holding the stave of rowan between them.

"I'm pleased for you," she said. "You couldn't have chosen a better!"

I didn't realize that I had made my choice. Or that my choice had decided itself for me.

"Thank you, Marnie."

She smiled, a relaxed smile that I hadn't seen before on her lined, old face. "Don't thank me, child. Thank my lady rowan."

I looked down at the stave and silently thanked her. A welcoming warmth flowed back up my arms, and I smiled. Which Marnie saw.

"And she said, *you're welcome.* Off to a good start, you two are. Right, tomorrow we begin," she announced. "Today is over. Sleep now. You'll find her name in the night. She will tell it, in your dream. Be sure to listen. You want to name her *right*, the way she tells you. Remember your dream. I'll want to hear it in the morning."

"I'll try," I said.

"Come, child," she said to Esmeralda, who got up and took her hand. "You need your sleep. Scullery maids are up early, long before noble ladies are awake."

Esmeralda, now a little scullery maid, stopped and turned to Marnie. "Thank you so very much."

"You're welcome, my dear. And you'll always be welcome in my humble home. It'll be me thanking *you* next visit—you just see if it isn't!"

A comforted smile came to Esmeralda's homely face. I caught Marnie's glimpse back at me, and she knew I'd caught her lie.

She needn't know, Marnie thought to me.

No, I agreed. *That would be cruel.*

But I knew, and I felt the knowledge's misery.

Marnie and Esmeralda, the scullery maid, went into the bedroom beyond the only other door in the cottage. As it closed it behind them, I heard Marnie say, "You'll be needing a name too, same as my lady rowan."

"What did you find?" I asked Oller. "Besides the mirror?"

196

He chuckled. "More than she'd expected. She went through it all while you was off picking out your stick. A bundle of dolls, a bagful of clouds, and a bottle of rainbows. A box of poisons she couldn't trust about the house. Buried deep, that was. But the ground above it was dark and dead. I didn't want to dig, but I could see something was there all right, so I knew I had to. What else? An invisible knife. Behind a plank in a wall in the pigsty. Thought it was empty till I felt in the space. *For emergencies*, she said. A piece of paper with a name on it in a flask at the bottom of the well. Deep, that well, and cold, but I wasn't *not* taking a look. I've found gold in wells. She grunted when she saw it. Broke the flask, threw the paper in the fire. And a ring and a necklet she didn't know about." Oller grinned, smugly.

"They puzzled her," he went on. "She said she'd been over the place thoroughly, when she took it over. Couldn't understand how she'd missed them. I said, 'Well you're not a professional finder, are you?' And she gave me a look that could've curdled milk and said, 'No more'n you're a professional diviner!'

"She sat there where you are now, turning 'em over and over in her hands. Didn't like it at all. 'I'll look into these tomorrow,' she said, and tucked them away in her apron."

"Were they …" I began.

"Magic? Dunno. Not my field. But they were old. Very old. I know my antiques. There's a star sapphire as big as your thumbnail in the ring, I've never seen a finer. The necklet's made of big, green malachites. Stones of power and protection she said they are. But she wouldn't say more."

"She must have been pleased," I suggested. "As well as surprised."

"She didn't seem it. *Thoughtful*, more like. Did say I was a good finder. Why's she want them sticks?" he wondered.

"We'll find out tomorrow, I think."

Oller snorted. "You might, I'm off crack o' dawn. I'll be needing your horse."

"Fine with me. Where to?"

"Aylsmoor. Far and fast, she told me. Got to go and find something, *lickety-split and double quick!*" He channeled Lance Corporal Oller in officious prick mode, before he'd seen the light.

Aylsmoor. The word rang a bell. I couldn't think where I'd heard it, though.

197

I said, "I expect you'll manage that."

"'Locked and hidden and guarded,' she said. 'By a really nasty piece of work.'" He grinned. "I like a challenge, me. Best turn in then, get some shuteye."

Oller got up and settled himself down on the floor by the fire, wrapping himself in his blanket. Oller, we had learned, had a cat's ability to fall asleep almost at will. He turned onto his side, his face to the dwindling fire where Hob was perched on his stool, his arms around his knees, eyes half-closed, staring into the embers. Oller was soon snoring gently. I sat at the table, turning my rowan staff over in my hands, feeling the smoothness of her, admiring the grain and the shifting tones of purple and green and gray and brown deep within her, holding her up this way and that to catch the last of the firelight. This was heartwood, I knew. It would never split, or crack, or snap. She was strong, quick, solid, and lighter than she looked, and above all, beautiful.

I began to wipe her down with a rag that hung from Marnie's workbench. Would she need oiling, I wondered, or waxing?

I stood up and put my right thumb on the notch at her top. My palm fitted her perfectly. She was exactly the right height, my thumb being a few inches below my shoulder when she was vertical. *Stick*, I thought? This was more than a stick. It was a staff. *My* staff.

She felt like an old, clever friend, whom I hadn't seen in far too long, and who was about to make me smile with her tales. She felt like a new, young, merry friend, who had come into my life that moment to change it. I smiled in return at the thought, and in my mind looked forward to hearing the rowan's tales and to the changing that my rowan staff would bring to my life.

I looked up and noticed Hob watching me from his perch by the dying fire, where Oller's clothes hung, steaming. "Rowan, wicken, rodenquicken," Hob muttered. "Wiggin, Royan, Witchbane, Witchwood."

198

16

Sticks and Stones

I slept like a log and was woken by the sound of an armful of them falling onto the pile by the fire.

I blinked my eyes open and saw that Oller had gone. The room was filled with the smell of baking, and sunlight was gleaming beyond the horn panes of the little window.

Esmeralda, sorting the logs she'd dropped, looked over at me and grinned.

"Morning, Ez," I said. "Sleep well?"

"Deep and long." She brushed her unruly mop of brown hair off her face. "And it's not Esmeralda."

"Oh, ah?" I said, still baffled from sleep. "What is it?"

"Guess," she said, a glint of amusement in her mud-brown eyes.

"I give up."

"I showed Marnie Peat's poem. She absolutely cackled. *Mabel*, we agreed."

"Perfect!"

Marnie came in carrying a pail of milk.

"Got kind hands, has our Mabel," she said. "Bluebell don't usually like strangers milking her. Good judge of character, Bluebell, which is why I ask people I'd like to know about to milk her. Kicks the pail over,

199

whacks 'em with her tail, the ones she doesn't take to. Stood there good as gold and quiet as a mouse for Mabel."

She put down the pail. "Pour the top off and let it stand, we'll make cheese later. I'll show you how. Fill a mug o' the rest for the young 'un. Teaspoon of honey in it." Mabel jumped to do as Marnie had said. "Them oats done, Hob?"

"Roats eddy," Hob said.

"Full breakfast, Hob. Three eggses, fried tomatoes, and all. And fry up a slice o' blood pudding and plenty of bacon and the runt's kidneys, young Daxx is going to need his fuel. He's got a long day ahead of him."

I sat at the table as Hob put a bowl of oatmeal and berries in front of me, piping hot. He shuffled back to the fire, and Mabel gave me a mug of honeyed milk, still warm from Bluebell's udders. I tucked in. The oats were followed by that morning's bread, straight from the oven, and what Marnie told me was Bluebell butter and Special Apricot jam, made with Special Apricots, whatever they were. I soon felt what they *did*. I was fizzing with energy as Hob put a plate full of fried things in front of me. Three eggses, bacon, blood sausage, tomatoes and runt kidneys, with a wedge of hard cheese and a pile of something green and dark and sticky. Wood spinach, Marnie said, for the iron. It didn't taste like any spinach I knew, but by now such minor details didn't bother me. I could feel the iron gripping in my blood as if every vein was a rod. I felt I could punch through walls.

Marnie said, "She give you her name yet?"

My rowan staff indeed had, in the night—but I couldn't recall it.

I looked up at Marnie, a forkful of sausage halfway to my mouth.

Marnie stared at me. "But you can't remember it."

"I heard it. And I thought, *of course*. And I went off back to sleep, thinking, *that's your name, thank you.* And I'm happy. And she says, *what is it?* And I repeat it, so as to make sure I won't forget. And she smiles. I mean, if you can *hear* a smile … and I drift off, and come back and go … *wait, what was it?* And it comes back to me. *Phew*, I think with relief. *Of course, it is, how could I forget that?* And then I nod off and wake myself up again, paranoid that I'll forget it, and I think, *yes, no—wait, that's it. Isn't it? Doesn't sound right. I* think *that's it … . Only it might be something else.* It keeps … shifting."

Marnie had been scowling at me in alarm. When I finished, the scowl turned into a smile. "You'll get it."

200

Baffled, I said, "What?"

Marnie said, "Write it down—what you just said. Write it down in the middle of the night when you wake up, and you think, *yes, thank you.* If you don't write it down, it'll be gone in the morning. I told you my lady rowan was a trickster. She's teasing you. She's right to, seems that brain o' yours needs a bit of exercise. She's showing you as well as telling. Write it down, and if it's not clear in the morning, boil all the words down. You'll see. You've told me, so we won't lose it. Best if you find it yourself. Takes work, this work does. Eat up and let's be starting. Mabel, you and Hob start the spring cleaning. I want everything shining when I get back. Move it all where you want, tidy away, I can find it."

"Will do, Marnie!" Mabel said, with a smile as happy as Esmeralda's had ever been.

"And Hob, you do as she tells you. Don't be difficult or sulky, work with a will."

"I will, with a will-I-will," Hob said, crabbing over to Mabel.

He stood by her side, his head no higher than her waist, and reached for her hand.

"I mike label," Hob said, looking up adoringly at Mabel. "Nabel's mice!"

"Bring my lady rowan," Marnie said, shuffling out. "And your bag o' tricks."

I picked up stave and bag and followed her outside.

⋏ ⋏ ⋏

We stood opposite each other in the orchard, having herded the sheep that were grazing there into the next field. "For safety," Marnie said. They were frisky, and skittish. They didn't like being herded.

"You need a sheepdog," I said.

"I do," Marnie agreed. "Last one was the best. Bess. Died, same as we all do. If I ever get to town …"

"Tom the Barner at The Wheatsheaf has sheepdog puppies. They'll be half grown by now and looking for good homes."

"Does he now? There's a thought. I miss my Bess, I have to say. Same as I missed Pippa, Sal, Ivy, and them others before her. Tom Barner, eh? I know what he's in need of and all. Might pop over one night and take a look."

I felt my eyebrows rise in surprise. "One night? It's a long way. That'll take more than one night."

Marnie looked at me and grunted.

"Depends how you travel. And no, you can't come with me. I've seen your guilds, all of them, in your secrets and memories, and your Magic Circle, and they're none of 'em Coven. Talking of what's inside you"—she hefted her staff—"let's see if you can use that thing."

I copied her action with my stave of rowan.

"What wood's yours?" I said.

"Oak."

"What's its word?"

"Ouch." Marnie whacked me on the shin with it. I yelped and hopped, and she hit me on arms and back and buttocks, quicker than I could move, and finished with a light but firm rap on the head for good measure.

"You're dead." She smiled.

We'd trained at quarterstaff under Serjeant Bastard, and I'd been pretty handy with it, but I'd been sword and board since Graduation, so was badly out of practice. I squared up to Marnie, in the regulation My Lord's army posture, and she snorted contemptuously. "We're not in no training yard now, boy. This is street fighting." A moment later I was on my back, clutching my legs and sides in pain. My staff landed with a clunk on top of me from the height that Marnie had flicked it to.

She was leaning on her staff, staring down. "Have to do better than that."

I stood up, limping.

We went again, and this time I was ready for her, so was at least able to fend off most of her blows as she flailed at me like a vicious little whirlwind. And then, gradually, I found my rhythm, and was able to fight back. She parried my attacks with ease, but I could see that she was watching them, carefully, appraising my ability. She stopped, abruptly, and leaned on her staff, thumb in its thumb-notch.

"You've got the basics." She wasn't even panting. She was ancient and bent and stiff, and I was young, strong, and fit—but I was heaving for breath. "Should be all right in a pinch. We'll work on the advanced stuff another time. That's not what we're here for, though."

I thought, *then why break every bone in my body ...*

"I didn't," Old Marnie snorted. "If I wanted to break bones, I would. I did that because that should always be your number one response. Your go-to tactic. If you can get out of trouble that way, use that way. If you need to step things up another level … it can escalate. Get out of hand quick. And we don't even know if you have another level. Remember that."

I gasped, "I will."

"Save you a deal o' trouble, mayhaps. Right. Let's see what you've brought me."

I fetched my bag, which I had put down before our sparring, and got out the soft leather pouch. I handed it to Marnie.

She unwrapped the heartstone and froze, her face filled with awe. She turned it over in her hand, held it up to the sun, shielded it in her hands to see it glow in the dark, and brought it out again.

I thought, *she hadn't expected this.*

"Indeed I hadn't! Well now. Things are looking up!"

I said, "Heartstone?"

"Heartstone," Marnie agreed, studying the glinting, red-and-green jewel, as if trying to learn its secrets.

"What does it mean?"

"Heartstone," Marnie repeated, not taking her eye off it. "Heartwood. You'll see."

"Oller found it. And gave it to me."

"That one, *giving*?" Marnie was surprised. "Giving away *this*?"

"He said it was meant for me. And that he was meant to find it for me."

"Where did he find it?"

"Sewn up inside My Lady of Rushtoun's own embroidered kneeler. In her chapel."

"That was clever of Junie," Marnie said. "Hiding it where Lymnia could guard it. And clever of Oller to find it."

I frowned. "She didn't tell you?"

"Only what it was, not where. *The loveliest stone for the loveliest life* … the fewer who knew *where*, the better. Something like this, in the wrong hands …"

"You're not the wrong hands."

Marnie looked at me. "I'm not." A gentle smile crinkled up the corners of her eyes in appreciation of my compliment. "But what if *I* fell into the wrong hands? And they asked it out of me?"

203

"Who could do that?"

"You'll find out. And soon." She turned the stone this way and that, almost reverently, within one gnarled hand. "Junie found it on her travels and knew it was for Esmeralda. What Junie had in mind for her, you see, when she turned sixteen, was to 'prentice her. She saw the effect of the Glamour she'd laid on the babe, right away, there and then on her naming day. Looking at all the faces gazing at her, and going, *awwww*, she realized the baby was *casting*. And she'd be casting her spell on everyone from then on. *A caster she is*, Junie decided, *and mayhaps a caster we will make of her.* For which, she'd need stick and stone, same as you. And when she found this beauty … she knew it was for the other beauty, young Esmeralda. So, she went back one night to Rushtoun, and hid it where young Oller was to find it, though she knew nothing of him when she did."

As she spoke, Marnie stared long and hard into the heart of the heartstone. "There's power in this all right. For them as can unlock it." Without taking her eye from it, she held out her other hand for my stave of rowan wood. "And it's for a caster, no question. But not, I think, for Esmeralda." She held the heartstone in her right hand and the rowan stave in her left, and gazed from one to the other.

"Every tree," she said, "has its stone, and every stone its tree. Most casters use whatever they can find. And you don't find *heartstones* just lying about the place. Oak is diamond, and you just try to find a *diamond* heartstone! Long years I've sought and still don't have one for mine, he has to make do with a topaz." She showed me the golden stone set into her staff. "My alder has her lapis lazuli, and my blackthorn a lovely dark bloodstone. Others, though, they have to make do with a mix and match, something different, which adds variety, but weakens both stick and stone. For the truth of both, the *true* power, you need matching hearts, stone and wood."

She assessed the stone carefully. "Tourmaline." She turned it over and over. "Rainbow tourmaline, too—not just one color but two—and *red* and *green* at that! I've never seen a prettier, nor a bigger. The power of both colors, she'll have now, my lady rowan, and them's the *best* two! And bigger means better and stronger. I'm beginning to think we might stand a chance now, after all." She glanced over at me, eyes twinkling, before she turned her attention back to the gem in question. "Lymnia, hey? Well, I'll need to pay her my proper respects. *Rainbow tourmaline …!*"

She stroked the rowan wood staff gently with her forefinger. "Given her a polish, haven't you? She'll like that. You take care o' her, she'll take care of you. Now, my lady. Time to open your eye ..."

Her stroking slowed as she neared the top of the stave, and when she reached the thumb notch, she stopped, as if feeling for something.

"Ah," she said. "There." She peered closely at the spot that her finger had found. "See it?"

I leaned in and looked. The wood was not all one color or all one texture. In the purple and brown of the heartwood were dark flecks of other colors—grays and dark greens. Marnie's finger was resting below one such fleck. It seemed no different to any of the others.

"Feel it," she said.

I did. I felt the rowan jittering and teasing her way up and into my arms, and the warmth of it made me smile. But the rowan stave always did that.

"Close your eyes," Marnie said softly.

I did.

"Can you see what she sees?"

"No ..."

"Then move your finger out o' the way."

I did and saw shadows, in which the shadow of a face was looming over me. The only eye that I could see, it being pushed right up to mine, was closed. I jumped back instinctively, and the shadow face pulled back away from me.

My face.

I opened my eyes and looked at Marnie.

"Shadows." She nodded. "Tricksy things, shadows, like my lady rowan. Help you see in the dark, she will. Close your eyes in the dark, both yours and hers, and see shadows. Now, fit the stone."

Marnie handed me the rainbow tourmaline. It was more than half the width of the stave, far bigger than the tiny fleck that she had found. She was smiling at me. "Go on, then. Not polite to keep a lady waiting. Pop it in so she can take a look at you."

I brought the jewel up to the stave, and as I did so, the fleck opened, and grew wider and wider—until, as stone touched stick, an unseen gentle force seemed to pull the stone in, bringing it to nestle at last in its new home. The heartwood swelled outwards to make room for it, then settled back around it. Where, before, the stave had gently tapered towards the thumb-notch, now it bellied outwards around the shining heartstone, like the hood of a cobra. I tried to turn the tourmaline, just to see if I could. It didn't move. It was locked into place, like a gem into a ring setting.

"Now." She handed me my staff.

My very own magic staff …

My lady rowan and her shining tourmaline eye. I gazed at her in awe. Marnie's words echoed in my mind as I sensed the staff inspecting me with as much interest as I was inspecting her. *Pop it in so she can take a look at you.*

I felt wonder mixed with excitement—and also relief. It was as if I had come home. I was back where I belonged. I was no sword and board fighter after all, but a battlemage. And for real this time. It felt as if I was who I was *meant* to be, now—who I had *always* been, deep inside.

At last, I thought, and the warmth of my rowan stave's merry laughter flowed up my arm and into my heart as if she was thinking what I was thinking. *There you are, then! Right, let's go.*

"Red side up," Marnie said. "Interesting. Seems we'd best try your reds first, then." She straightened up, rubbing her hands together, clearly intrigued. "All right, young man. Proof of the pudding's in the eating, as they say. Let's see what you've got, the two of you."

She stumped off across the grass, stopped a dozen paces away and turned to face me.

"When you're ready." She stood looking at me, leaning on her staff.

I decided that I should go for the simplest skill I could think of. Something that didn't need too much power and wouldn't use up all my reserves, if I had any. I had no way of knowing. There were no gauges, no counters, no warning lights. There was only *me.* I was all I had.

I looked at my staff, whose name I had failed to recall even though she had told me in my sleep, and decided, *Basic Fireball.*

Could I do that? I looked around for my skills. But, of course, I couldn't find any. I had no digital readouts any more than I had a virtual inventory that I could call up. My inventory was what I could carry. My skills were … what?

Marnie said, "I'm waiting."

I couldn't think what my skills were. Or where I could find them. *Think!*

Marnie snorted. "About time!"

I looked at her, puzzled, wondering what she meant.

And then I felt the rowan stave's warmth flow into me again as if she was telling me something.

I frowned at her, and my mind cleared.

She was telling me *yes*. I knew that much. *Yes*. Yes what?

Yes to what Marnie had just said? Or to when I'd told myself, *think!*

I felt a tingle through the staff in my hand as I thought the latter, and I smiled. The rowan staff seemed to jump joyfully in my hand in response—at which I realized that we were already working together, in tune with each other, synchronized. There was no need for me even to ask the question, *And you'll do the rest?*

I closed my eyes and brought up an image I remembered, decided that would do, opened my eyes again, aimed my staff at Marnie, and thought: *Basic Fireball.*

There was a flash and a loud explosion, and a sizzle as the Fireball leapt from the rowan stave's tourmaline heartstone and hit Marnie in the chest, firing her twenty feet backwards into a gooseberry bush.

On the way, Marnie yelped, "*Gaaaaaaaaaaaaaahhhh!*"

I stood there open mouthed for a moment, then ran over to Marnie who was on her back, legs in the air and petticoats flapping, trying to get upright. "Sorry, Marnie, I—"

"Get me out of here!" Marnie gasped.

I grabbed her hands and pulled her out of the bush.

"Are you all right?" I asked. There was a big burnt patch on the front of her dress, hot around the edges, and still smoking. She beat at it with her hands. I was about to do so as well, but stopped myself. It didn't seem right to start flapping at Marnie's bosom.

"Ow!" she yelled, as her chest burned, and "Shit!" as the glowing fabric caught against her hands.

Instinctively, just as I had always done in combat, I raised my staff and *thought* a Healing spell in Marnie's direction. My rowan stave bloomed a green light around Marnie. Gradually, her blackened hands returned to their usual mottled yellow-gray color, and her chest stopped smoking. I hadn't had time to wonder whether my staff would be able to cast Heals. Now I knew—and I knew that my staff knew. I smiled at her again and felt her warmth in response. She was as much an extension of my arm, of my very *self*, as Grell's battle-axe was of him.

207

Shocked, Marnie straightened up, and looked at me. "Heals too," she said, impressed. "It's all coming back now, ain't it?"

I felt both guilty and elated. "I think it is."

Marnie's mouth split in a smile. She cackled. "And there you have it! '*I think. It is.*'" She jabbed me with a bony forefinger. "What took you so long?"

I grinned back. Suddenly, I felt wonderful. The rowan stave was dancing for joy in my hand and up my arm, from her heartstone all the way to my heart.

I realized how important this moment was. "Thanks, Marnie."

"Oh, you'll be paying for your lessons," she said, cheerfully. "But you'll be paying in kind, and I'll be paying in kind, so we'll both come out ahead." She started to back away from me. "Now—let's try that again, shall we? Only this time, try something else."

"But—"

"I know what you're thinking. Poor old Marnie—can't defend herself. Old Marnie can, don't you worry about that! Others can't. So, you've got to do it for them. I just wasn't prepared for your first go to work."

She waited.

I worked out my next objective, nodded, and hit her with an Orb of Shielding.

I watched the familiar green sphere form around her, and wondered if there was any limit to what the rowan staff and I could do together—then immediately saw that there was. The Orb wobbled—something that I'd never seen one do before—then broke apart into a mist that quickly dissipated. I was baffled, until I felt my stave encouraging me, as if she was saying, *Go on, try again. If at first you don't succeed* …

Yes, I thought. I'd been trying to run before I could walk. Grell's skills had come back to him soon enough, but hardly all at once. I was going to have to learn how to work with my new staff. I might have the knowledge, or at least the memories of it, but this was more than just a staff. She was my partner. She was going to have to teach me as much as I would be teaching her. Teamwork. I felt her glow of approval as I thought the word.

Right, I thought. *Together.* I raised her, and together we cast another Orb of Shielding over Marnie. This one glowed a richer, brighter green. And it held.

208

"*Mm.*" Marnie inspected the glowing ball that now surrounded her. "Pretty. New one on me. What's it called?"

"Orb of Shielding. I cast this to protect my allies."

"Well, let's see if it's any good. Hit it."

I did. With Fireballs, then I tried out other damage casts to see if we could also conjure those up. Some came easily, others fizzled out or seemed to have no power, but we worked on them, and eventually they were all hitting hard and true, bombarding Marnie with destruction attacks.

The Shield held.

When the smoke and flames had cleared, and the lightning-strikes and ice-shards had stopped coming at her from above and below and all sides, she said, "Well, there's your problem, isn't it? If that's all you've got, you've got an enemy you can't hurt."

"You said *hit it*," I said. "Not *get rid of it.* I thought you wanted to see how strong it was." Just as it had taken more than a little trial and error for my staff and me to learn how to execute damage and healing casts for real, it took a while for us to get the hang of negation and cleansing. We took down the Orb of Shielding with a Riddance, and I felt that it was all coming back to me. I knew how to wield both staff and spells. Now it would be just a matter of gaining confidence in my ability, recalling everything I'd once known—and, of course, practice.

Marnie brought up a shield of her own. It didn't look nearly as strong as my Orb of Shielding. It wasn't. I took it down in the blink of an eye. And her next one, and the next.

"Right!" she said, and I didn't like the tone in which she said it. "If that's how you want to play it, my lad, that's the way we'll play it."

She pointed her oak staff at me. Its topaz heartstone lit up an ominous orange. The next thing I knew, it felt as if I was being stung by a swarm of angry hornets. I yelped and leaped about in terror, casting negates and cleanses at myself, and finally I got a Lingering Mend up over me. Inside its soothing, green ball my agony gradually abated. I did not want to go through *that* again—not now, not ever—so I cast the strongest Orb of Shielding I could over myself. By then, Marnie had some sort of shield up on herself—an invisible one, which I could not see, but which lit up like ball lightning around her whenever one of my attacks hit it. I fired attack after attack at it, as hard as my staff and I could unleash them, but as far as I could tell we were making no impression on it at all.

209

I was soon in as fierce a one-on-one firefight as I'd ever encountered—and, because this one was for real, it had very real effects on me. Anything that Marnie blasted at me had the power to knock me off my feet. I'd have spent half my time flat on my back if my shields hadn't held.

Even so, it was like fighting on the deck of a small ship being tossed around in a hurricane. It is not easy to think clearly in combat at the best of times, which that day on the hillside most definitely wasn't. I was casting as hard and as fast as I could, without pause, healing, blocking, attacking—and, naturally, my staff began to lose power. Neither she nor I could carry on at full strength indefinitely. I needed to conserve what energy we both had, I saw, and that meant fighting smart.

Which meant doing what Marnie had told me to.

Thinking.

My brain was scrambled by the noise and chaos of our duel—so much so that it had taken me some minutes just to come to that realization: *Think.* My first thoughts were an incoherent whirl that added up to not much more than, *now the hell what?*

I felt my stave's response flow into my arm. It wasn't anything specific—no more, really, than a reminder that she was there.

Yes, I thought. *Teamwork.*

And then I thought, *Any ideas?*

No response came.

It was Marnie who came to my rescue.

Come along, laddie, I heard her sharp voice in my head. *What did I tell you?*

She punctuated that hint with a gust of wind that threw me back against an apple tree.

I tried to recall what she had told me.

Then I got it.

You think. It is.

Okay. I do the thinking, my staff does the casting. That made sense. What didn't make sense was what happened when I hit Marnie with yet another powerful Flamebomb, which is like a Fireball squared. Like all the other attacks we'd thrown at her since she got her invisible shield up, it had no effect on her at all. It just wasted some of my dwindling reserve of magic energy. To my surprise, instead of heat radiating into my arm, cold crept along it from my staff.

I thought, *cold?*

Then I wondered if that was a hint from my partner.

I threw up an Ice Storm overhead. Hail bombs pounded down on Marnie, and lightning stabbed against her shield.

And my arm went hot.

Bizarre. *So, she wants me to try another fire attack*, I thought. Not a Flamebomb—those were costly, in terms of power, and seemed to do no damage. *Flamefield*, I thought, and a moment later Marnie was engulfed in a sea of liquid fire which lapped around her as if eager to burn her alive—but that, too, had no effect on her shield.

And now my arm was positively freezing from my hand all the way to my shoulder.

I thought, *what the hell kind of message is my staff trying to send me? First cold when I fire heat, then hot when I attack with cold, then freezing—*

I get it! And my tricksy rowan stave sensed that I got it, and I felt her silent laugh of delight in reply.

Hot. Cold. Freezing.

It was, literally, child's play.

Her heat response meant *close*, cold *not close*—and freezing meant even further from the answer.

What had I been doing when she went hot?

Aha!

I hit Marnie with every Ice Attack I could think of, and my stave flung them at her eagerly, the two of us working in tandem. Ice Traps rooted her, Frostbolts cracked open her shield, and my Ice Storm pummeled her harder and faster than she could heal herself. She was out of power and out of luck when, ignoring her arms held up to show that she was yielding, I Levitated her off the ground, where I rotated her, slowly, end over end, while I healed her in a Lingering Mend.

"Oy!" she protested. "Stop that!"

I stopped that, instead laying her horizontal in the air, and spinning her again, around and around.

Then I put her down. Or rather, dropped her from three feet onto her backside.

"Ouch!" Marnie yelped.

"*Ouch* indeed," I said. "In return for all the *ouches* you gave me from your oak staff earlier."

"Never seen the like!" she muttered, getting to her feet and dusting herself down. "Well, it seems like I was right about you all along, laddie. And it seems we've a deal to learn from each other. *Ice*, eh? Mastery of the cold would be a fine thing to have!"

"I'll be happy to teach you," I said. "And what was that invisible shield of yours? And that stinging attack? That was *nasty*."

"Oh, I've others in that line, young 'un. Venom magic. We don't usually teach that to outsiders, it being a guild secret—and one outsiders are rightly wary of, so that they know to be wary of us. And that was my Thought Shield, one of my Awareness skills. Can't get through that physically nor mentally. Or couldn't till your Frostbolts took it down."

I said, "Guild of the Arcane Arts?"

She shook her head. "I'm in that too, o' course. My other guild. Coven."

▲ ▲ ▲

Learning weapon skills had taken months under Serjeant Bastard. Even Grell had taken a while to get to where he was as good as he had been—after which he became even better, thanks to being trained by a master. During that morning with Marnie, it became clear that I had all the knowledge and skills but was just having trouble accessing them. It was going to take time—but, I thought, I too now had a master to train me: one who was also, in many ways, my apprentice, because she'd never heard of some of the skill lines that I knew well. Much of what I knew was new to Marnie. Most of what Marnie knew was new to me. So, we mentored each other, through long, often grueling, yet rewarding rematches until Oller returned.

Marnie taught me how to lay Glamours and dispel them, and also the secret to Mabel's Glamour, should I need to remove it. It was clear that I was as poor with her styles of magic as she was with mine. I was hopeless at what she called Awareness. That was the skill that enabled her to know when other people were thinking about her, and for her to *think into* them, as she had done to me on my journey from Rushtoun. It would take me a lot of time and practice, she said, to become a master of that.

"Stick at it—why, who knows?" she said, as she patiently led me through the first steps of Awareness. "One day, you might even earn yourself one of *these*." She pointed at her eyepatch.

Beneath which, I knew, lurked her terrible, red 'other eye.'

I shuddered at the thought of having one of *those*.

"You can see things with it you wouldn't believe," she said. "Beyond time and place. Into the heights of the heavens and the depths of the soul."

We harvested from her herbarium—even, at one midnight under what she called an empty moon, and I called a new moon, from the things that grew in and around the dark, bubbling pool. We sparred daily, for long hours—eventually needing to go to a remote hillside because we'd been terrifying her livestock. Marnie had plenty of attack casts of her own which were new to me and hard to handle. We let each other inflict wounds, so that we had to heal and fight at the same time, and I learned how to monitor my staff's power, which was far from unlimited. The rowan's tourmaline heartstone would fade, as would the topaz in Marnie's oak staff, our casts would fail, and we'd take breaks to let them recharge.

Our dueling was not as hard, physically, as arms drill with Serjeant Bastard had been, but far harder mentally. Soon, though, I was wielding and thinking automatically, on instinct, so that the rowan stave was part of my arm and an extension of my thoughts.

I had her name, now. She had teased me with it night after night, the words shifting and slipping out of reach and shifting again, until I actually slapped myself in the face in my dream of her and went, "*Duhh!*"

I felt her merry laughter in my heart and knew. There it had been, all the time, staring me in the face.

Marnie saw my elation the next morning and asked without asking. She just stopped on her way in with her pail of milk and looked at me at the little kitchen table where I was holding my staff.

"Shift."

Marnie nodded and smiled. "Knew you'd get it."

I felt the staff's joy at our understanding as she unleashed a warm glow into my hands—her version, I thought, of a big hug. She was mine, and I was hers, and we both knew it. *Shift*. "I thought it would be something ladylike. A feminine name. Or a word of power and beauty, like *lightning* or *firestorm*."

"A grand word, eh?" Marnie mocked. "Well, now you know her better. My lady rowan don't do grand."

She then showed me how to close Shift's eye, with a thought, and open it again when needed.

"It don't do for people to see a heartstone in a stranger's staff," Marnie said. "Put them on the alert, that would. They'd know you for what you are."

Better to be a simple traveler with a simple wooden staff.

17

Looking Forward, Looking Back

I was used to seeing Mabel up and at her tasks when I woke each morning, on the floor in Marnie's kitchen by the fire that Hob always got going nice and early. I came to expect it, in the ten days that we'd been at Marnie's, during which I'd been training and trading secrets, and Oller had been away on his mission, and Mabel and Hob had been spring-cleaning.

What I didn't expect, the morning of our departure, when I opened my sleep-stuck eyes, was to see Mabel stroking a puppy. Oller, who had returned in the night, was fast asleep rolled up in a blanket by the fire, so she whispered, "Guess her name!"

I thought, but nothing came. "I think I'll need a hint."

"Bess and Pippa and Ivy and Sally were all named after friends of hers," Mabel said, her eyes shining. She waited.

"Esmeralda?" I said.

She nodded happily. "And it's good too, Marnie says. I need to get used to people shouting *Esmeralda*, and not thinking *that's me*. While I'm Mabel."

She stroked the hairy, black-and-white bundle of fur and energy that was the puppy and smiled. "We're going to show her the sheep now. You should come too." She looped a rope around the puppy's neck and did her best to stop it rushing and leaping and fizzing. It was still not fully grown, I could tell by its feet which looked too big for it, but it was maybe three-quarters of the way there. One of Tom Barner's, I thought, born, what—six, seven months ago?

"I definitely will." I got up to go with her. We left Oller to catch up on his sleep.

"Watch how she *looks* at them. That's the important thing, Marnie says. See these brown spots, in the hair just above her eyes? D'you know what they're for?"

I didn't.

"They're for when she closes her eyelids. The sheep will think she's still staring at them, watching them, and they won't misbehave. They look like two eyes, see?"

I saw what she meant—two brown 'eyes' made of hair that matched the dog's eyeballs. "That's clever, that."

"She's a clever girl, Ezzie. Marnie brought her back last night. She was on my bed when I woke up! Well, it's not a bed, just a pallet on the floor of Marnie's room. D'you know, I've never slept so well, nor felt so"—she searched for the right word—"*unworried.*"

"That's good," I said.

"Mm," she agreed. "I've had a lot to worry about, all my life. Lots of it I didn't understand. I still don't, really. I expect the picture will become clearer when I know how to look at it. I know I'll have to worry about it again, sooner rather than later, probably. But while I'm here, with Marnie, and now Ezzie, I don't."

"Must make a nice change," I said.

"It does. I can't believe Marnie's going to teach me flying today!" A big smile lit up her face. "To *think!*"

I'd ever seen her happier. A puppy. A flying lesson. *Pure joy*, I thought. "More than I'll ever do."

"Yep. Like Grell and his Orcs Only quest. Coven Only, is flying. You're off to the fighting. We'll be *doing* and *doing* and *doing*, don't you worry about that! Marnie says she's beginning to hope now. And also"—she reversed herself, leading me out of the kitchen—"she says Hope is an absolute bitch who makes us all make idiots of ourselves, *hoping* for this or that to be different. *Hope clouds your eyes with Stupid Dust*, she says. *Rub 'em clean, and see clear, and tell Hope to push off out of it and mind her own business!* I suppose," Mabel considered, "everything involves its opposite, in some way."

In the hallway, Mabel said, "Feel this!" The broomstick that she was touching was still warm from Marnie's journey. "Long way to The Wheatsheaf, Marnie said it was. And a nasty wet night—wind and rain in her face there and back. Had to ride far and fast. 'Gave Tom Barner the tincture he wanted, and he gave me this pup. Named her after you, I have. I name all my sheepgirls after my friends.'"

I smiled at homely, happy little Mabel. "One day, in the battle to end all battles, I'll look up and see you above me."

Mabel grinned. "That you will!"

"Wreaking," I added, "godsawful hells of havoc. And I'll know you have my back."

She held out her hand, palm up, and I slapped it. "Teamwork."

"Teamwork!"

In my hand, Shift quivered in approval.

Mabel led me outside, Ezzie straining at her rope leash, excited by everything. The dog was immediately interested in the sheep. They didn't seem to care a jot about her. They thought, *who's that lump of hair with the tongue?* And, *where's her manners, looking at me like that?* The bellwether came over after a while to check her out. Ezzie sniffed him, he sniffed her, and Ezzie licked his nose. You could almost see the old bellwether thinking, *hullo, what's this then?*

"That's good, that!" Marnie said, putting down the basket of eggs she'd been gathering and scratching the sheep's ear. "They'll teach each other. The ways of the sheep and the ways of their dog. It's sheepdog, not dogsheep. The dog is there for the sheep, not t'other way around. Old Runnel there'll let her in, slowly like, on the ways of his family. And she'll gather. And she'll let them know that when she says *jump,* she means *jump.* And they'd better say *how high?* That's all there is to it, really.

"The sheep are the ones that matter. Ezzie's job is to guard them. Chase off the jackdaws when they come for the newborns' eyes. Smell wolf on the wind. Kill foxes if she can stalk them. She's not the boss any more than he is. Teamwork," she finished.

Mabel and I exchanged glances, and Shift jittered in my hand. It was going to be all about teamwork from now on.

We followed Marnie as she hobbled back to her cottage, Ezzie tangling around our feet and barking. "Need to stop that," Marnie said. "Quiet and peace is what we need, peace and quiet." Mabel stopped and *shush'd* the excited puppy, making her sit, pointing a stern finger at her. Ezzie sat, alert for her orders. "Good girl," Mabel said when she was quiet, and Ezzie trotted into the house beside her, tail wagging.

Oller was up and at his breakfast when we came in. He grinned at us, chewing. It was good to see him again. Marnie said, "Saw your horse was back when I got home last night. And you asleep when we got up. All done?"

Oller nodded, pleased with himself, and said, "Not the easiest. But, yup."

"Right. Come with me." She hobbled off to her bedroom. Oller swallowed and gulped and stuffed another forkful into his mouth and hurried after her, chewing and wiping his hands on his grubby shirt. They went into Marnie's bedroom and shut the door.

Mabel and I were, of course, eager to know what he'd been up to, and I didn't like being kept out of their consultation. Hob laid another of his huge breakfasts in front of me. I thanked him and tucked in.

"Well?" I said, when Oller came out again.

"Guild business," was all he'd say.

"Marnie's TG too?" I asked, surprised.

"Coven, not TG. We're always happy to help Coven. You never know when you might want them to help you."

We got ready to leave. Marnie filled my pack with potions and ingredients. Oller had loaded our saddlebags with food and drink, including some of Marnie's Special Peach Brandy. We were taking Esmeralda's palfrey. We'd told Mabel the day before that we were going without her. She'd been furious and had made a huge fuss. *She could shoot a bow and arrow! She could twist people to her will!*

"We know all that, dear," Marnie had said, "but that's not what's needed. I need you here with me. You've got a job to do, and you need to learn how to do it."

"But my palfrey!" she'd objected.

Marnie had chuckled and told her, "You won't be needing no horse, girl. Going on a trip ourselves tomorrow night, there's friends of mine you need to meet. These lads will be riding, you'll be flying."

That had stopped Mabel's tantrum in its tracks.

She'd stared at Marnie, hardly believing her ears. "*Flying?*" she'd whispered, stunned.

"So you'll need to learn how," Marnie had told her. "First lesson first thing."

It was third thing as it turned out. First Ezzie the sheep puppy met Runnel and his family. Second, Oller conferred with Marnie, and we all ate our Hob-cooked breakfasts. While we ate, Marnie told us everything she knew about what we were all doing.

"Enemy after enemy," she said. "Fight after fight. They'll be coming at you from all sides, they will. Harder and faster and nastier the more you go on. Now, take heart from that, you young 'uns. The nastier they get, the more it means you're getting *close*. And as you close in on him, remember, he's death, he is. Death to you, death to us, death to the world. Fail in this, and we're done for. I expect you want to know why. Who. All that."

We did.

"Sometimes to go forwards, you have to go back," Marnie said. "In this case, a long way back."

She gathered her thoughts and began. "Once upon a time, when the world was young, there were twin brothers, Jaren and Jurun. Some say they came from over the Eastern Seas, and some say they came down from out of the Far North, beyond the Uplands and the North-lands, and some even say they came from beyond the Western Mountains, but who could come from there, over those peaks that touch the sky, and across the lands of the giants?

"All the way south to the coast they came, along May River, where Jaren met May, who some say was the river herself, and some say was the month herself; and whatever the truth of it, they fell in love and married. Which Jurun never did, by the way, having his mind on higher things. All the way down Jaren and Jurun settled this land, made it their own, and ruled it together and wisely. One kingdom, they decided it was, and though they ruled it together, no kings or queens after them would, they agreed, so it would only ever have one crown, which they wore turn and turn about. And the people they had brought with them called it Jaren and Jurun's land, or t'other way around, which became Jarenjurunsland and Jarnjurnland, and all sorts of other things before it settled down at last to be Jarnland, which is how it came to get the name it has today.

"The brothers were alike in most ways but different in one. One was, one did. Jaren, the one who did, had a function. A reason for being. An explanation for who he was. There was a land to settle, towns and cities to build, crops to plant and farm, and fields to work and fill with livestock. So much to do, so little time. While the other, Jurun, had all the time in the world, to be, to think, and to ponder. He didn't need a reason for being, because being *was* his reason. All he needed was time; time to *be*. He didn't need an explanation for who he was, because he simply *was*. Why do I need to *do*, he thought? Doing is a waste of time. I be. I am. I exist. I spend my hours in song and silence, in study and thought and contemplation. I don't waste my time with deeds.

"And when people asked him, polite-like, the way people do, 'What do you do?' he'd reply happily, 'Nothing.'

"And, of course, they didn't understand. *If you don't do, you're a burden*, they thought. And told him so to his face. Which annoyed him. They didn't *understand*, he thought. Idiots. And while Jaren's people *did* more, and his lands grew, Jurun's people *were* more, and their lands didn't. Which upset Jurun, for was he not the wiser of the two? Were they not brothers, sharing the rule of the realm as they'd always agreed, but which now largely seemed to belong to his practical, unimaginative brother? For it was to Jaren that the people came for counsel, when he wore the crown, as to what they should *do* in all their petty concerns. Few came to consult with Jurun when the crown was on his head, about how they should *be*, and the loftier matters that occupied his superior mind. And he wore the crown less and less, as his mind was busy with those loftier matters, and he left the duties of kingship more and more to his brother.

"In time, Jaren made his home at the mouth of May River, in a town he built that he named Mayport, for his bride, which was soon a big and busy city. Jurun found the hustle and bustle of Mayport distracting, with its noise and its hurry and its interruptions. Far too much *to-do*, when what he needed was peace and quiet for his thinking and being. But he was still king, as much as Jaren was, and to remind Jaren of that fact, he cut the crown in two on the last day that he wore it whole, and took his half with him when he left with those that followed him, who were fewer than those who stayed with Jaren. East, they went, until they came to the narrows between the North Sea and the Southern Ocean and made the land beyond it their own. Almost like a big island attached to the mainland, it is, and there, on the far eastern coast, at the mouth of another river which is called the Last River, he built a town for himself which he named Jurunburgh. But that's not what it's called now, as you will soon hear.

"As he sat in his tower with his books and ideas and thoughts, and brooded, Jurun came to the conclusion at last that he knew what he had to—wait for it—*do.*

"He needed to stop all *doing*. People would be better off without *doing*. They could sit around, all day and all night, and leave the doing to others. It seemed a wonderful plan. He would free every man and woman and child from the grind of the drudgery of existence, give them leisure and comfort and learning, and deep conversation and high philosophy for their minds to explore. They'd be happy. And grateful. He knew he was the savior of humankind, our liberator.

"Well, you've seen the problem, haven't you? Who are these *others?* Those who are going to be doing all the *doing*, while the people, his people, did the *being?* They couldn't be people, obviously, because all people were going to be free from that. So: *not-people.* Which term, it became clear to him, meant the *not-living.* And he became more and more excited by the idea and harsher and more insistent. Because he was getting fed up with the living, with their complaints, their dreary, stubborn logic, and their ingratitude. *I'm doing this for you!* he'd explained over and over again. But they didn't appreciate it.

"And so it was that his attitude changed as he realized that it was those who obeyed him, who understood what he was doing, that he should be doing it for. It suddenly all made perfect sense! And the others, the living, who he had wanted so much to help and to free, were not deserving of his efforts. They just wanted to *do.* To go about their little, humdrum lives. While the not-living, who obeyed, and *were*, seemed to him to rise above that low level of tiny, toiling existence. He grew to despise the living and to wish them all dead.

"The wish, as we know, is mother to the thought, and the thought to the deed. He would remove the burden of life from the creatures of this world, their burden of *doing.* And they would join him in Eternal Being.

"And so, he put his plan into action. All those years of not-doing, and now he was doing what he needed to do to end all doing. And his people, such as remained to him, went, in time, as we all do, from being to not-being. Only they did not leave him and go to the next world and stay there as they should, but returned to him to serve his will in this one. And they brought others with them from the lands beyond. And they, and he, did not like the light of this land, preferring the night and the shadows.

"So, where other towns build up, or out, Jurun's people built down, down where it was always dark, and they could live the lives, or to be more accurate, *be the not-beings,* that suited them. And the folk of Jaren's lands stopped calling his brother's city Jurunburgh, and referred to it by many names, some light to take the worry out of it, some dark as it deserved: *The Undercity, The Buried City, Downtown, Darkbury,* and such, until it came to have the name it is known by now, Downbury.

"His brother, Jaren, grew concerned by what he heard out of Downbury and went to his brother's tower to consult with him—or his *undertower,* as it now was, as it sank deep into the earth—for the realm was unsettled by the rift between them. 'We must work together, brother, as we always have,' Jaren told Jurun, but Jurun did not like *work* anymore than he liked *do,* and he liked *together* less, so he killed Jaren with a blade of ice through his heart.

"Jurun had long known that day would come and had long planned for it. It was how he could achieve that Eternal Being that he longed for—all the time in the world to be, with his *not*-beings. He had learned this from Time himself. He had journeyed to where Time stands still, at the floor of the world, down and down into the darkness, beyond the earth that embraces us all when we die. And down there, he found a still sea of ice—ice that fire cannot burn, not even the fire of the sun. The sun warms the skin of the world and quickens life in the earth that is that skin, on which we live and laugh and sorrow and die. But far below that is only cold and death.

"Jurun discovered that the lightless ice sea lies around an island where the roots of the world-tree grow, the tree that supports the earth we walk on and the heavens above her. He cut a limb off that tree and heard its scream and made a staff of it. Never has there been a staff with such power, for none had dared to venture where he ventured, as none have since. Using it, held high, he lit up the darkness above the lake of ice and the island where the world-tree grows, and in that light saw the black stones that fall from the fire in the earth's heart.

"One he found was as large and smooth as a goose's egg, of a black that seemed to absorb light, rather than reflect it. And that egg of *un*mirror-black obsidian was the heartstone for his staff, from the world's heart itself. He fitted stone to stick, and with his staff of power he forged a knife from the ice that never melts, and that fire cannot burn, and made a handle for it from a root of the world-tree, which writhed as he cut it. And he listened as Time spoke to him from the world-tree's heart. He listened with the power of his heartstone, for black obsidian lends the art of scrying to those who are apt for it.

"Jurun saw into the future and was content. Far in the future he would have all the time in the world, as he had long desired. And Time would have his price, for every life costs a death. And so Jurun and Time wrote their bargain in the Book of Life and Death that Time keeps in the world-tree's heart at the floor of the world, and sealed it with his brother's life.

"So it was that Jaren never returned to Mayport, and over time the lands that were Jurun's grew dark, even in daylight, which could no longer penetrate the haze that hung over them. Which is why those lands, to the east of the Narrows, are now known as the Darklands. And if you ride to the Narrows, you will see where they begin and our lands of light end. Brown its air is, and thick, and it swallows the light that falls on it. And no one goes in there, because those who do never come out.

"And no one has come out of the Darklands since Jaren rode there to consult with his brother and found his death. All that has come from there is Rumor, for Rumor can come and go as she pleases. Rumor said that Jurun died at last, as we all must, seated on his throne in his hall which lay at the deepest level of his undertower. Rumor said that he returned from death, and dwells—I shall not say lives—among the others of his kind that his people became. And Rumor is as often right as she is wrong. All that is certain is that the realm was uncertain, from the day that Jaren died at his brother's hand, a blade of ice through his heart."

Marnie paused, taking the time to consider everyone in the room carefully, to make sure we were listening to what came next. "There are ways of finding out, that some here above ground practice, even though those ways are forbidden, having to do with dealing with the dead. The dead, it is believed by some, can be bound to those forbidden ways by the living and forced to reveal what they know, but Binding is an art reserved for the divine, and the mortal who dares attempt it is a fool—and a dead one, when he's discovered. The Guild doesn't tolerate necromancy. They show no mercy to those that dabble with it.

"It was a necromancer who came to the Guild of the Arcane Arts many long years ago to make his confession and pay his penance. One of us, he had been, and respected, until his curiosity got the better of him and led him down the forbidden path. Now he had returned along that path, at the end of his days, to offer what he had learned to those who might know how to use it. Three-parts mad, he was, old and almost unseeing. He shook whether standing or sitting, his robes little more than rags. He sat before the Conclave and told, haltingly, of what he had done, and then of what had been revealed to him. Jurun was indeed dead, the dead had informed him, but his life had not yet ended, for his bargain with Time meant that his time would come again—and that this is how they had sealed the bargain ...

"Mabel will know the rhyme," Marnie said quietly. "Children chant it in their games. Mothers sing it to their babes-in-arms:

"A stick, a stone,
A book, a bone,
Go down and down
For half a crown,
A knife,
A life:
A throne."

"Everyone knows that!" Mabel agreed. "It's a nonsense song, it doesn't mean anything." She saw the look on Marnie's face, and her smile faded. "Does it?"

Marnie said, "It means everything."

"I thought it was just ... a nursery rhyme," Mabel said. "We'd make up things, gestures we had to do with each word, as we played. If you were sitting on the throne at the end, you won."

"And everyone else lost," Marnie said.

The silence fell again, and those words echoed in our minds.

And everyone else lost.

"There's more truth in nursery rhymes than in half the history books in the College of Lore and Learning," she added. "In that one above all, seeing as it comes down to us through the years from Time himself."

She let that sink in, then continued.

224

"The old necromancer begged leave to stay at the guildhall until death came for him, as death comes for us all, which was to be very soon, he said. And he begged the Conclave's pardon, which they granted him after some debate, some saying that what he'd done was unforgivable, others saying that what he'd learned was of great significance and hadn't he paid a high enough price for it? When they assented, tears filled his old eyes, and he asked one more boon, which was that when he died, they would burn him, as he had spent enough of his life among the dead and had no wish to spend his death among them. He died the next day. They laid him on a pyre which they lit at sunset, and so he left this world having played his part."

Marnie stopped and took a drink of water from her cup. We all thought about what she had told us. I was, as if by instinct, holding my rowan stave across my lap. I was puzzled, as I turned over in my mind what Marnie had said, and I felt Shift's response through my hands. She was puzzled, too.

"You say the rhyme means everything, but … what? I don't get it." I could tell from her anxious tingle that Shift was as concerned as I was, in response to which, I added, "It must have some kind of purpose."

Marnie sighed. "And that's the heart of it. It means everything, those of us who have put our minds to the matter agree, but we can't see how. The consensus of our wisest minds is that it means everything *in the end*. And we're in the middle. Mayhaps its purpose is to get us to that end. As to how we do that, well. None can answer." She shook her head. "Many have *had* answers, o' course. Suggestions, theories. They could all be right or all be wrong. We just don't know. We wish we did."

She stopped. She looked, suddenly, very old. *Perhaps,* I thought, *this had been troubling her for a lifetime.*

She continued. "What we can say is that it means that it is not over. Jurun was dead and all was quiet in the realm—even, as far as we knew, in the Darklands, for long centuries. And so, the world forgot about Jaren and Jurun, or, if they remembered them, they thought of them as legends from the times of myth. And the story became a nursery rhyme for children to make up games to, and the people went about their business. Kings and queens came and went. Wars broke out, peace broke out, and the days and years and ages passed.

"Until, some fifteen years ago, Rumor whispered again to the world, and what she whispered was that there were stirrings in the

225

Undergrounds, and gatherings, and summonings, and disturbances where there should be naught but the peace and quiet of the grave. And one of her whispers began to be heard more often, by those with the ears to hear and the wit to listen, and that whisper was a name. *Jurun.*

"And those of us who concern ourselves with such matters began to consult with one another, to think what we could think. Rumor whispered again and again, and some of us put two and two together and believed that we could see what had happened."

"And what had happened," Marnie turned to Mabel, "was you."

"Me?" Mabel said, surprised.

"You, young Mabel as is Esmeralda. Fifteen years ago, Rumor began her whisperings. Not many months after you were named in the chapel in your father's castle."

"This isn't my fault," Mabel protested.

"No," Marnie said. "It's Junie's. We all know that. There's nothing can be done to change that now." There was a sadness in her tone that we all noticed. "What *can* be done, though, it seems has already started. Otherwise, why run away the way you did, with these *hard, horrible, dangerous* characters?"

Mabel said, "I thought I had to find Junie."

"You *dreamed* you did. There's a difference. Who sent you that dream? Not Junie. You were riding to Mayport, where you thought the dream said you'd find her. The *King's City* being Mayport, right? She isn't there, though. She's in the *other* King's City. Downbury." She paused, waiting for that to sink in. "You would never have reached Mayport. His plan was in action, and he had summoned you, as well as the others he has summoned, and—as far as he could see—all was going according to that plan. But what happened, most unexpected, was that you came here. With these *hard, horrible, dangerous* characters. And here we all are."

Marnie fell silent. The room fell silent with her. Motes of dust drifted in the sunbeams that suffused their soft light through the horn-paned window.

Mabel said, "Junie's a prisoner?"

"More than that. She's *bait.* Luring you to him."

"Why me?"

"Because of what Junie laid on you. *The loveliest life there ever was or ever will be.* That's what he's been waiting all this time for."

226

"He wants her to take it off me and lay it on him?" Mabel said. "He's welcome to it! It's not all rainbows and unicorns like everyone thinks—everyone on the outside. That's all for *them*. And I don't mind, really," she added quickly. "I know how lucky I am, I wouldn't want anyone to think I'm complaining. How could I? That would be very ungrateful. But I sometimes think it would be nice to be, just, you know … ." She tailed off. "Normal."

Marnie took Mabel's hand, patted it, looked into her eyes, and said quietly, "You heard what I said, dear. Every life costs a death. And"— she paused to emphasize the point—"t'other way around."

Mabel, Oller, and I went still.

Once again, I felt my heart break; not just for Esmeralda, or myself, but for the world.

On his stool by the fire, Hob muttered, "Life dosts keth."

Mabel said, realizing, "Oh …"

I felt myself drowning, my head spinning at the thought of the unbearable. What Marnie was saying was not even to be contemplated, it *must not happen*. "You said Jurun was dead."

"Aye," Marnie agreed, "I did. And now he's preparing his return."

She waited for us to understand.

I already did. I looked at her in horror.

She nodded.

"From death," I said.

Marnie said nothing.

Esmeralda finished the thought. "Which costs a life." She looked from face to face. She swallowed.

None of us needed to say it. We all knew which life it would cost. Not just any old life, but the loveliest life there ever was or ever would be.

Oller, who had been listening as intently as I had, said, "We must stop him."

Marnie said, "Indeed we must. Because if we don't, no one will. We didn't think anyone could, for a long time." She turned from Oller to me. "And then you came along—we'd none of us seen that. I doubt Jurun has seen it yet. He'll be wondering where Esmeralda has got to, soon enough, but there's no reason he'd look all the way here. And if he did, he'd only see Mabel. But if he does hear about you—*when* he does—he'll want to know all about you, you can be sure of that. Want to question you himself, he will."

I brushed that worrying thought away and made myself think about what she'd told us instead.

"There are holes," Marnie admitted. "Holes in what we know, holes where the missing pieces fit. We know so little, it seems—but that little is all we know and all I can tell you. You'll find those pieces on your journey. Who knows, you might be looking at them already and just can't see them. Journeys take time, destinations are there already. Beginnings are slow, endings quick. No one can see the future, especially not from that far back. When you meddle as he meddled, you create disturbance. It builds and builds, over time, like a long big wave, until it crashes in a moment. And those of us with the eyes to see know the wave is about to break. But now you're here. And you can make the difference."

"You warned me not to make promises I can't keep. I can keep this one, though." I turned to Mabel. "We'll do everything we can."

"That we will!" Oller seconded.

With a weak smile, Mabel said, "Thank you."

"And so will we, young Mabel and I!" Marnie said. "We won't be just hiding away up here, we'll be *doing* and *doing* and *doing*." Hearing the words that Esmeralda had said to me herself earlier that morning, I felt heartened. *To do.* Had that not been Jaren's purpose? The brother who had dedicated his life to addressing the problems of his realm? The brother that Jurun had killed with his blade of ice—and was now our problem?

Realizing that, I saw that our quest had revealed itself at last.

Our purpose.

I knew what we had to do.

I reached over and took Mabel's hand. "Teamwork," I said, when she looked up at me.

She smiled; a smile less uncertain than her last.

"Teamwork," she replied.

Yes, I thought. We have a team. Esmeralda, Marnie, Oller and me. Shift quivered in my hand, and I quickly added *and Shift*. I felt her warm glow of confirmation. And we would also have Grell, of course. Not for the first time I wished that Qrysta was with us—that I even knew where she was.

Marnie nodded at me. I saw from her look that she approved of what I'd said—and, indeed, knowing her Awareness skill, thought. She

228

turned and fixed her one good eye on Oller. "And you, young man, need to be finding. Daxx has the first two in the rhyme, *stick* and *stone*. You're the finder, now it's your turn. *Bone* would be like to be underground, I'm thinking—in one of the dark places. Boneyard, tomb, crypt." She grunted. "Rather you than me. *Book* where books are. So, go and find them. In any order, it don't signify. You found stone first, before stick. Throne'll be the last, of course. That's what the others lead up to."

She returned her gaze my way. "And *you* look after him, to make sure he can keep finding," she instructed me. "Two's a good start, stick and stone, but your luck may not hold all the way to the seven. Which is why I've put a bundle for you in your saddlebag. Use them only when you have to. They're hard to come by and won't work more'n once each. And I've only got the three I can give you."

"Three what?" I asked.

"Narrow squeaks," Marnie replied, her tone ominous.

"Why half a crown?" Oller said, as if offended by such a paltry sum. "There's twenty silvers in a gold, and a crown's worth five silver, so a half-crown's one-*eighth* of a gold piece? I've got thirty-two o' gold in my purse at the minute! You're asking us to find a *half-crown?* I wouldn't get out of bed for that!"

"Not a half-crown, Oller," Marnie said. "Half a crown. Which means half a kingdom. He'll want his brother's half. Once he gets his hands on that, we're finished. Better we get our hands on his half first, but you're going to have to take it from him. And he won't give it up without a fight." She pushed herself up from the table and got stiffly to her feet. "So off you go now, young feller-me-lads, off on your findings. And be quick about them, because what matters is that you find him before he finds Esmeralda."

We stood, the silence enveloping us all again.

I couldn't think what to say.

But Oller could. "I'm good at finding," he said.

And that, somehow, broke the spell that we were all under, hearing Oller's chirpy voice telling us what we all knew to be true. He *was* good at finding. If anyone could find anything, or anyone, that person was Oller.

I smiled at him. "The best." I patted his shoulder.

18

Oller's Tale

"You are that, young man," Marnie concurred. "Last night, he brought me something I'd been racking my brains how to get my hands on for years," she told us as she brought something out of the pocket in her apron.

It was a large, silver key.

"What does it unlock?" I asked.

Oller grinned. "Everything."

"*Every*thing?"

Marnie handed it to me and said, "Try it."

I took it and looked around. I spotted a small, iron-bound chest on her mixing bench. There was a tiny keyhole in an iron plate on its front. I moved the key towards it, and it shrank to fit. I turned it, it clicked, and the lid sprang open. "Wow."

"Wow, indeed," Oller said. "Marnie says I can keep it when this is all over. No more poking about with bits of wire and picks and such. Now I can get into even magic locks."

"Lock it back up, then," Marnie ordered. "There's things in there mustn't get out, and get out they will, any chance they find, if they wake up."

I locked the chest, and the silver key returned to its original size as I took it back to her.

I handed it to Marnie and, as she led us all outside, she passed it on to Oller, who tucked it into one of the many pockets inside his jerkin.

"You'll need better'n that," she said, "to keep it safe. Silver, that is, so it needs a silver chain around your neck—and one that won't break."

"Silver's not all that strong," Oller said.

"It is if it's Imbued," Marnie said.

"I'll keep my eyes open for one, then."

We stood in the bright morning sunlight, ready to begin our journey. As we said our goodbyes, Marnie handed me the old star-sapphire ring and the even older necklet of malachites she hadn't Divined, that Oller had found on her property.

Oller, irked, said, "Why does *he* get to have them!"

"He's the caster," Marine said. "You're the finder. Can't make head nor tail of these, but they're casting gear, not finding. Find yourself boots of speed, or a cloak of shadows, they'll be for you. Teamwork, eh? Your Grell's the hitter. Armor, wards of protection, rings of strength and such, that's what's for him if you find them. Assuming you find him again, of course. And we can't assume anything."

"Speed boots!" Oller said. "I like the sound of them. Where would I find the likes of them, now?"

"From a cobbler who knows his craft." Marnie held out her empty hand to him. "This is for you, though. Proper finder gear, this is."

He was puzzled for a moment, until he realized. He reached out, and his hand closed around the handle of the invisible knife that he'd found in the wall of her pigsty. His eyes grew round with wonder. "I'll treasure this!"

"You do that, lad," Marnie said.

"But don't you need it?" Oller asked. "You said, 'for emergencies.'"

Marnie snorted and said, "If this isn't an emergency, I don't know what is!"

We hugged and smiled and said our goodbyes, mounted and rode off, north and east. Esmeralda had given us her map as well as her palfrey. We had a pretty good idea where we were going, and who we needed to find.

Sometimes, to go forward, you have to go back, Marnie had said.

231

It seemed clear to me, from mulling over Marnie's tale, that we needed to find Nyrik and Horm again, and to get Horm to take us to his mother—his niblun mother, who lived deep in the Undergrounds, where all the trouble was brewing. We knew we were going to have to go there eventually. Who better to make their ways and secrets known to us than folk who lived down there already?

There was no need to press the horses, so we rode at trot and walk. It felt good to be on the road again, in the late spring sunshine, larks singing in waterfalls of joy from the high blue yonder above the meadows, curlews bubbling off across the moorlands, thrushes and blackbirds and finches filling the woodlands with song. We should have been burdened down and worried, but we weren't. This was what we were living for, and we'd never felt more alive.

Oller was still preening from Marnie's praise of his finding skills. He couldn't wait to tell me what had happened.

"It belonged to one of your lot," he began. "Caster, like what you now are. Only not one of the nicest. He's Guild of the Arcane Arts, of course, but Marnie said Conclave had their doubts about him. Couldn't prove anything, or that'd be the end of him. People can't just barge in on a caster's place, not even Conclave, if they don't have proof. They guard their privacy, do casters. You have to be invited, and he's not the inviting type." Oller shifted in his saddle. "Quite the ride to get there, it was. He lives up Aylsmoor way."

I thought, *where do I know that name from …?*

"And a bleak and barren and unwelcoming place it is. Like the Uplands we crossed, when we met Klurra, only worse. Wonder how she and Grell are getting on … cracking skulls, I expect."

"Probably." I grinned, despite my worry. "If I know Grell—which I do."

"Dreary and damp and dark it was, Aylsmoor, seemed like the sort of place the sun never shines. And not much in the way of cover. That worried me. I could see his tower, the moment I came over the ridge. It was in a dark little coombe of its own, high ridges all around it, only the one way in: an opening where the ridges didn't quite meet, and a fast black stream ran out. There was a big barricade across that, heavily barred on the inside. I could see it from where I was lying, surveying it all below me. His tower looked more of a sad old ruin than anything imposing. No way into it that I could see, no front door, no windows.

232

A few hovels and such nearby, for his serfs and animals. Fields, an orchard. Nothing like Marnie's. All the trees seemed dead. They weren't, I found out later. They just grew dead things.

"I tied your horse up out of sight, back down behind the ridge, and waited till night. Then I went down to take a look-see. One of the buildings, I could see when I got close, was an entryway. There were steps in it, going down. I could see torchlight flickering from down there, so I went in, quiet as a mouse, keeping to the shadows." Oller's face soured. "Didn't like what I saw down there. Nor what I smelt. It smelled of death and decay, and vinegar and salt and chemicals and spirits—the liquid kind, for preserving; though I've no doubt the other kind would like it down there well enough. But sometimes you don't like what you see and smell and just have to get on with the job. It was his storeroom."

I could guess what was stored in it.

"Spare parts and that. Fresh supplies. Some in shrouds, some in pieces. Some in jars and bottles. 'Course, I was on high alert, every nerve tingling. Every rustle, of a mouse or whatever, sounded like one of them shrouds unwrapping and something climbing out. Fair gave me a turn, I can tell you, when I caught sight of a glass jar full of eyes. Just the eyeballs floating in liquid, and they all seemed to be staring at me. I watched them as I sneaked past, half expecting them to turn all together, watching me tiptoeing by. They didn't, thank all the gods. Yeah, I was on edge all right, but I just kept telling myself, *you're in now, Oller. Look on the bright side, you don't need no stickies and have to climb up where there's no windows.* Probably doesn't expect many visitors, him."

I said, "*Bright side?* Down where you were?"

"I know," Oller agreed. "Just egging myself on, to keep going. Which I did, slow and steady, and above all silent. And then, of course, I heard noises—behind me. Footsteps. I was just about at the far end of the first big crypt, looking for the way on. I knew there'd be a way on because he'd want to use the other entrance from his tower—which lay in the direction I was heading. There'd have to be one. So, I ducked down behind this big slab of stone and hid. Altar it was, I could see. Nasty stains on it, some running down the back where I was hiding. I peeked out, when the footsteps stopped, and saw what it was.

"Another delivery. Three more for his work, fresh out of the earth."

233

I was horrified. "Hells, Oller!" Marnie had said that the GAA had suspected this guildfellow's depravity ... but would she have sent Oller there, knowing the extent of it?

Yes and no, came her voice in my head, and I could sense her acknowledgement of the seriousness of what she had tasked him with. *We needed to know what was going on up there, and whether it involved my old friend. Your lad Oller is a finder all right. Rather him than me—or you. I doubt we'd have lived to tell the tale.*

Oller continued, oblivious to our quick exchange. "They put the bodies down on slabs and then a door opened in the wall where I'd be bound to find it before too long, and *he* came in. Thin, tall, and stooped. Grim old face, white beard, long white hair, but only from the sides; he was bald as a coot on top. Staff in his hand, thumb-notch same as yours, with something dark red in the top of it. He went over to the deliverymen—well, I say *men*, but they were odd shapes I can tell you, not like any men I've seen outside my nightmares.

"They just stood there, arms hanging, longer than normal arms. I'd seen all I needed, and I wanted to take my chance while I had it, so I slipped in through the door, nipped through what looked like a laboratory, then up the winding stairs set into the walls. What I was looking for would be where he did his bookwork, in his library or study or some such. And that would be at the top. Well, it was, and there wasn't even a door to open. The stairs led straight up into it, and at the top you just stepped in. I couldn't believe my luck!"

"Your *luck!*" I said. "Weren't you scared?"

Oller considered that. "Well, yes and no," he said, eerily echoing Marnie's words. "I mean, I knew things would go bad for me if he caught me. And if you ever saw me after that, I wouldn't be the Oller you know no longer. So I was on high alert, no question; even my hairs seemed to be standing up and listening. But I'm a pro, see? It's my job. It's like ... remember sparring, under Serjeant Bastard? We was all nervous as kittens at first, weren't we? After a while, you get used to it. So, you don't think no more about the other recruit beating the crap out of you and being frightened it'll hurt. It's familiar, now. You focus. He taught us that. *Mind on the job.*"

In my mind I felt Marnie's concurrence with what Oller said and revised my judgement of her. She'd given the right man the job. I realized that, in many ways, she knew us better than we knew ourselves.

I know what you can do, she corrected. *It's for you to show me you can do it.* Without thinking, I said, "Trusting our instincts and doing the work."

Oller thought I was responding to him and said, "Exactly!" Marnie chuckled, her presence fading from my mind.

"It was a big, round room," Oller continued, "taking up the whole of the top floor. And it was just stuffed with hiding places: bookshelves, cabinets, chests, boxes and bags, and his worktable piled high with books and scrolls. Big carved chair behind it, and a nasty carving on it too: a horned head with a gaping mouth and wide, staring eyes painted red. I stood there for a bit, arms crossed, studying, thinking, *absorbing* the place. I could see well enough; it was lit by glows. Cold ones, but clear. I couldn't see where they came from."

"Moonglows," I said.

"Looked like moonlight, yes." Oller nodded. "Can you do those, Daxx?"

"Should be able to. Not in daylight, though."

"Try tonight, eh?"

"I will indeed. I need to practice them. I have a feeling we'll be needing light where we're going. The Undergounds."

Oller grunted and returned to his story. "Couldn't stand there forever, of course, he'd be back up sooner or later. Him being the nightshift type. So, I got to work, feeling sure I'd spotted a few likely places and a couple of definites. Nothing of interest in any of them. Well, there was plenty of interest in the *normal* course of things, but I couldn't pinch any of them, could I? Suppose he came in and just happened to want that very thing. And it wasn't there? He'd lock the place down tight and turn it upside down, hunting for the thief. And he'd find me, no matter how well I hid, because there's finding and there's *magic* finding, and even I can't hide from that.

"So, I left him his bag of gold and his rings and his things and his carved little wooden dolls with pins in their eyes. I went through his desk and his papers, not moving anything a hair out of place. I looked everywhere I could think, then everywhere else, and I was beginning to worry. Standing there deep in thought I was, when I heard footsteps coming slowly up the stairs. Soft footsteps, but heavy. Him, in his robe and slippers.

"I knew there was no way out. I'd checked. Not even the chimney. Too narrow and with a big twist in it against the rain. First thing I do, on a job: always check the exits. So, it was Plan B, and I was glad

I'd taken a leak before starting out on this, because with him being the nightshift type, it was going to be a long while before I could take another.

"Second thing I always do, see, is check where I can hide. And this place, that was easy. Almost as many hiding places for a thief as for a key. I was up on top of his bookcase before he'd taken ten steps. It was another thirty before his wrinkly old bald head appeared up the stairwell, white hair floating below it. Carrying a bag, he was, head down. He never looked up. They never do. Wouldn't have seen me anyway. Shuffled over to his desk. Stopped on the way to put something on a little shrine he has up there. Black candles and all. Another nasty, red-eyed head on it, this time a carved stone. He bowed to it then went and sat down, started bringing things out of his bag, examining them, looking at books and scrolls and arranging them, and getting quite absorbed in his work.

"I wasn't directly opposite him. I'd chosen a spot away to one side as I didn't want him looking up suddenly and catching a glimpse of me. To see me, he'd have to turn his head as well as look up. I never took my eyes off his neck and shoulders, they'd be the first to move, and I'd be back in the shadows out of sight. So, he settled down to work, and I settled down to watch. No danger of me dropping off to sleep and snoring, as I expect you can imagine. Strung tight as a bowstring I was. But relaxed, at the same time. Doing my job.

"And blow me if he didn't do it for me! Couple of hours of that, no more, and what does he do but reach under his desk? And there's a click, and up slides a piece of the desktop. And there's a drawer in it and in that is the key. He takes it, goes across to a plain bit of wall, and when he puts the key towards it, a keyhole appears, and he unlocks it."

Oller went quiet, shuddering. "I wish I hadn't seen what was in that cavity in the wall. It looked dead but was moving. And it didn't look happy. He had a knife, and … cut something out of its stomach and put in its place one of the things he'd brought up in his bag. The dead-looking thing wriggled and struggled. Didn't make no sound, though. I 'spect he'd taken its vocal cords. When he finished, he sewed it up with a needle and twine, careful like and slow. Each time the needle went in, the thing twitched. Its mouth was hanging open, then closing a bit, then opening, as if screaming a scream we couldn't hear. Thank the gods.

"He closed it back up again and moved on along the wall to the next one. Another keyhole appeared, another click as another part of the wall swung open. Old woman, by the look of it—or had once been. What hair hadn't fallen out was white and thin, her white eyes wide, and her dugs hanging by her scrawny arms. Filled me with fear and pity, the poor thing. And the horrible thought, *glad that ain't me*, followed by, *could be me, next.* Another slice, another old part swapped out for a new, the old girl twitching at each cut. And them poor old blank white eyes staring up out of her shriveled head, unseeing but somehow yearning for the light, as he closed the wall back on her.

"Then back to his desk and his work and his sorting of pieces and parts and consulting this paper and that book. From then on it was just a matter of waiting. The sky to the east began to lighten, beyond the windows you couldn't see from outside. He put down his quill— he'd been writing on and off, the sound of his quill scratch-scratch-scratching away the only noise to be heard, apart from him clearing his throat or grunting or muttering.

"He put the silver key away and pushed on the drawer which slid down shut. Got up, went back the way he came. Stopped at the little stone head. Got out a knife—well, more like a spike than a knife really, thin like a tooth. He held his left hand up, the point to it. And you know what? A tongue slid out of the idol's mouth. He pricked his thumb, and three drops of blood fell onto it, slowly, one after t'oth-er. He bowed, muttered some words, wiped his thumb, put his knife back in his belt. The tongue slid home and the mouth closed and the throat swallowed. That mouth had been open before when I'd come in. I thought, *glad its eyes weren't.* They were just paint, though, not big glowing jewels or anything. So I hoped it couldn't see. Then he left, padding back down the stairs.

"It was a long time after the sound of his footsteps had died away before I made my move. Over to the desk, keeping out of the stone head's eyeline, just in case—pays to be *never too careful* in my line o' work. I found the catch easy enough in the kneehole because I knew it was there, but beautifully hidden it was. Even I might never have spot-ted it. Up pops the drawer, pocket the key, push it back shut. Beautiful job of hiding it was, too. You couldn't even see the join when it was closed up, among all the other panels in the desktop.

"All that remained then was to scarper. It took me about three times as long to get down and out as it had to get in and up. Daylight's no friend when you don't want to be seen. And he wasn't the only one in there, no more than I was the only one moving about. There were more of those things like his deliverymen, and they didn't half walk quiet. I know enough to go slow, even if I hear nothing. Good thing I did. One moment the place was empty, quiet as the grave, the next one of them is there, creeping past silent as a cat, and you think *bleeding hells*, where'd *that* come from! So yeah, my heart was in my mouth the whole time. It was broad daylight when I made it back to the crypt. I could see it washing down the stone stairs, the way I'd come in. Sight for sore eyes it was. 'Course, I wanted to run into it and out of there and keep running, but I knew better than that. Movement, in plain daylight? Like to be noticed.

"Well, I wasn't. Or I wouldn't be here now. I'd be shut up in his wall, I shouldn't wonder, and him finding his silver key on me." Oller shuddered and then grinned. "Wish I could see his mean old face when he finds it's gone! Marnie says he'll be getting a visit from Conclave quick as quick. They'll be putting him out of action, no question. And getting those poor creatures out from inside his walls, gods willing."

Oller reached for his waterskin and took a long draught. He needed it after talking for so long.

"I felt eyes on my back, and I crawled bush to bush all the way up the hillside, I can tell you," he said. "Slid over the skyline, chest heaving. I must've spent five minutes flat on my stomach looking back down for signs of life—or, worse, pursuit. The thought of which didn't sit well as you can prob'ly imagine. But there weren't none. You won't see me if I don't want you to, but you're never a hundred per cent invisible. I thought, *right, let's get all hells out of here*, tried to get up, and that's when my whole body started shaking.

"Had never happened to me before, that. I couldn't hardly stand. Somehow, dunno how, I got on your horse, and let him take over. I eventually had enough strength to canter, and we was soon long gone."

He stopped as if the telling of his tale had drained him again.

I tried to imagine what he'd been through. And then tried not to.

I said, "Glad you made it, Oller."

"Yeah," he agreed. "Me too."

"If you'd done that for Serjeant Bastard instead of Marnie, you'd be a Serjeant yourself by now."

Oller smiled. "Nah. No more stripes for me, mate, thanks! I made enough of a prat of myself with *one* as a lance-jack. Think what *three* would do to me!"

"Well, I could never have done it, that's for sure. I'd have run a mile."

"Yeah," Oller said, "it's always a trial. But when the guards catch you, you know you're going to the dungeons. When the likes of *him* catch you, that's the end of you."

A thought struck me. "If you're *that* good, Oller, how come you got caught and ended up in My Lord of Brigstowe's army?"

Oller gave a rueful shrug and a sheepish smile.

He sighed at the memory. "I'd found something someone else wanted. TG, of course, but from out of town. I paid her the courtesies, helped her with what she wanted to know. Didn't realize she was double-dealing me—she'd learned that I'd got what she'd come all the way to Brigstowe for. Nice looking lass she was, too. And a nice evening it was becoming. I bought her an ale, she bought me one. More followed. We ate, the best The Wolf's Head had. Chatty she was, all sorts o' stories, all sorts o' fun and laughs. Invited me up to her room. 'How about a nightcap, Olsie?' And I said, 'Don't mind if I do.' Woke up the next day with the maids in the doorway looking at me, the bill not paid, all my pockets cleaned out, and a sackful o' the innkeeper's valuables on the floor. Hauled up before the reeve. My Lord's army or the dungeons."

He shrugged. "Easy choice."

"I thought you said she was TG."

"She was. But, you know—*thieves*."

"As in, 'no honor among'?"

"Yep. No way to see it coming, though. Thought she was working another case. Had no idea she was working *me*."

He didn't seem too upset about it.

"And now," he said, as if reading my mind. "Here I am. Off to do something important with friends. Worked out well in the end, eh?"

"I hope you'll continue to think that," I said. "Did Marnie say what you'd need the key for?"

"No. Just that it might come in useful. She'd always wanted it, and now she knew why. Didn't like him of Aylsmoor, did Marnie, not one

239

bit. 'He doesn't deserve it,' she said. 'That's *pure*, that is. Unlike him!' A friend of hers had made it, she told me. Her life's work, it had been. A *good* friend. Who had disappeared. Without a word."

We wondered about that, and we didn't like where our thoughts led us.

"Apparently things started vanishing soon as the key was gone," Oller went on. "From crypts and reliquaries and chapels. Sacred things. Revered things. Things that were buried with devotees, sanctified things that had been blessed by priests and priestesses, things that were said to be not of this world. Things that were best not falling into the wrong hands. All locked away, they'd been, as such things must be. Marnie put two and two together. She thought him of Aylsmoor might have it, and would I care to take a look."

We rode on, as the sun climbed towards noon, and the day warmed. As we rode, I worked on the skills Marnie had traded with me. They needed memorizing and refreshing, not to mention instant recall in the heat of battle, when they'd have to be instinctive. Occasionally, I'd forget something without which they wouldn't work, and I had to check my notes in the little black book Marnie had given me. I could easily find what I might want to look up just by tracing a word with my finger on the blank front page, and the book would open at the right place.

The notebook was so thin that I could slip it inside my mail shirt, but when I opened it and flipped through its pages there were far more pages than seemed possible. That, Marnie had told me, was because she had spelled the book to have an infinite number of them. She wanted to make sure that I'd never run out of space. As well as all my skills and secrets, we had transferred all Marnie's knowledge into it—much of which I hadn't had time to look through yet. The infinite notebook contained far more than just what we two knew, though. Marnie had summoned the learning of the ages into it, her ages as well as mine, and any time that anything new was learned, she said, it would learn itself into my Infinite Notebook too. It comforted me to feel that all that knowledge, that wisdom, everything we'd thought and tried and discussed and wondered about, was nestling inside my shirt above my heart, where I could get at it quickly.

Casting, Marnie and I had learned from each other, requires many different skills. They all take time to master. We'd both been experts in our own fields, but when Marnie unlocked me, and Shift and I were able to work my secrets, she was surprised to find that she had to start again, almost, to learn and use them. There were entire fields of magic that she'd had no idea about and was intrigued to discover—just as I'd never heard of her Venom skillset. It was as if whole new worlds of possibilities had opened up. "Takes me back to my young days, this does!" she'd said. "Back when I was an Initiate and everything was new. And that's a deal of years ago. I'm grateful to you, Young Mastercaster!" She'd chuckled, using the nickname she'd given me. It was the same for me with what she was passing my way. I was a complete noob with those skills. There was one in particular among them that I thought I'd need to master sooner rather than later: Marnie's ability to *Think Into*, from her Awareness faculty.

It wasn't proving easy.

I tried and I Thought and I practiced, and I consulted my notes and frowned and screwed up my face and grunted, so strained looking that Oller asked me if I needed to stop and take a dump.

All day and all evening I worked on it, sometimes feeling a slight tingle of progress as if something was listening … but it was as if I were a deer in a field, looking up, alert, ears twitching, sniffing the wind for signals. I was listening for sounds that never came. Marnie had told me that it was hard. That it would take time. We didn't have time.

Moonglows, on the other hand, proved easy to cast because they were from my old repertoire. I could have those appear wherever I wanted, at will. They could float high overhead or light up patches of floor. Other Lights came easily, too, from warm ones to narrow beams that I could point at targets in the distance, and which would never widen but just light one tiny, far-off spot. Area Glows, which flooded. Individual Glows, which lit a single person and moved with him or her. We would have light wherever we went now, however dark it got and however deep we were going.

We were avoiding all roads, keeping to the hills on a course that would take us well clear of The Wheatsheaf. Too many people had seen me there. If Serjeant Bastard sent scouts up the road from Brigstowe, as we assumed that he would, he'd hear of us sooner or later, should we have shown our faces there. And then he could coordinate his search parties, bringing those that he'd sent south and east to Mayport back towards us, north and west. His scouts would know that I'd been brought into Brigstowe by Nyrik and Horm, as noted on Scribe Donnell's ledger. They'd ask for them, and for me, and would describe Oller and Grell.

I remembered the barmaid, Eva, who I'd thought had been mocking me with her teasing, but had—according to Nyrik—just been flirting with me. If indeed she had been, she would remember Daxx, I suspected. So, we'd gone wide and looped around over the hills to the west.

There were pens up on those hillsides, for the sheep when they were pastured there in the summer—and crofts, dotted about, long distances apart, usually in the same state of disrepair as the ones on the Uplands, their roofs missing or holed. They were little more than single-room hovels, but they had firepits, this being the cold north. Firewood was easy to gather, and damp though it was, Shift blew fire into it and soon had it blazing. We fed and groomed the horses, ate, and wrapped ourselves in our cloaks to settle in for the night. Oller, as usual, was asleep within minutes.

I lay awake, staring at the dwindling fire, and went back to my problem.

How to Think Into, and then converse with, someone.

Sometimes, Marnie had told me, an easier way is to enter them in their sleep.

I tried thinking my way into Oller as he slept when his mind was open and his thoughts wandering. I couldn't hear any of them. *I'm not getting anywhere,* I thought to Marnie as I lay in my cloak by our fire.

She thought back instantly.

Well, I've taught you all I know. Keep working on it.

Any suggestions?

If I had, I'd have given them to you. It can take years just to get the basics. Your ears tingle, and you think, hullo, someone's thinking about me. *And it can take many more years from there till you can tune into them. I can't get anywhere with your Crackle, if that's any consolation. I point my staff—and not just the oak, I've tried all three—and summon up the skill you gave me and put everything into it. Nothing. Not even a little spark. Let alone that fizz thing you can pop out any time that you say's so easy. And I'm nowhere near you with them great bolts of lightning jumping out of Shift, which I have to parry with everything I've got. And even then, my hair's standing on end for an hour.*

I could hear her sigh. *Takes time, eh? Just like my Thinking Into. I miss our sparrings, lad. Taught me a deal o' stuff, you did. It'll be coming in useful before long, I don't doubt.*

It'd be useful now, if I could get in touch with Grell.

Keep working on it, is all I can say, she thought to me.

I asked, *how's Esm—*

Ezzie the pup? Marnie interrupted quickly. *Settling in nice. Fond o' young Mabel, she is. And Mabel's fond o' her, dotes on her.*

I noticed her emphasis on *Mabel*.

She hadn't wanted me to name Esmeralda.

I thought, *Not secure …?*

Marnie thought, *You never know. Someone might be eavesdropping. Best to be careful.*

I got the message.

I asked her, *How will I know if I get through to Oller in his sleep? Can I make him raise his hand or something?*

Doubt if even I could do that! Marnie chuckled. *You'll start* hearing, *that's all. And look out for the tingle in your ears. Both of you. When that starts, put your all into it. It's not easy, this stuff.*

I'll say.

Any tips on Crackle?

I considered. Storm magic had been one of my expertises. It had become instinctive, second nature. I tried to think back to my noob days, learning that skill line.

I stopped. My own words echoed in my head. *Second nature.* You *became* storm. Storm worked through you. You were part of it.

I thought, *Marnie?*

Yes dear?

Did you get that? What just occurred to me?

I did. Second nature. You think I should stand outside in a thunderstorm and point my staff at it and give it everything I've got—and might be as I'll pop out a spark? Thunder might not like that. He might pop something back at me, bigger and harder.

Don't fight it. Blend with it.

Marnie considered. *Might be as that might get me somewhere. And not just soaked to the skin.*

And if I apply that principle to Oller … I wondered.

Think like him? Marnie queried. *And how would you go about that?*

243

I don't know. Night, Marnie, I thought to her. *Love to Mabel and Ezzie.*
Goodnight, dear. And good luck.

I turned onto my side, face to the fire. Oller was snoring softly the
other side of it, his face towards the flames, open mouthed and relaxed.
I considered the problem.

Think like Oller.

Yes, but—*about what?* Let's say he and Grell and I were squaring
up for a fight, like in Mobs training. We'd all be thinking different
things: me sword and board things, in those days, Grell battle-axe
things, Oller knife things. Those aren't *like,* they're different.

So … put down sword and board and pick up some knives.

I had an idea.

I got up and started going through our saddlebags. A few minutes
later, I was wrapped up in my cloak again, looking forward to the
morning and wondering how it would go.

Within moments of picturing the scene, I was asleep.

19

The Thought Process

Dawn was breaking as I opened my eyes to see Oller already awake and busy. He had another fire going and was frying eggs over it. He saw me and grinned. "Morning, matey! Breakfast?"

"Sounds good to me." I unrolled myself from my cloak.

I went outside to relieve myself, standing in the clean morning air, inhaling it, watching the sun slide above the eastern horizon. Around me, there was nothing but emptiness, long green hillsides, and a gentle, cool breeze. How nice. How peaceful. And then, *how long will this last?* We had a job to do. From what little I knew about what lay ahead, it would be far from peaceful and far from easy.

After we'd eaten, I told Oller I'd hidden some things of ours about the place, and that I wanted him to find them. And that he wasn't to move.

He said, "What? Why not?"

I didn't let on; that would have distracted him. I didn't need him dividing his thoughts between what he was doing and what I was doing.

"Tell you later," I said. "You can move your head around, turn this way and that. Just don't go anywhere until I tell you that you can."

"All right," Oller said, already thinking. "Not many hiding places in here, shouldn't take long …"

I didn't answer. I watched him as I went through the items in my head, *Thinking* them to him.

Necklet. Ring. Knife. Pouch. Button. Cheese. Book ...
Necklet. Ring. Knife. Pouch. Button. Cheese. Book ...

Oller looked around, thoughtful. He looked up. He turned this way and that. He checked the doorway that had no door. He scanned the walls and the floor.

I Listened, the way Marnie had taught me. "There's a part of your mind that you must always keep empty," she'd said. "If everything's full, where will the Thoughts squeeze in?" I Listened into the empty space which I'd worked on the night before and guarded all morning, keeping my inner ear always open.

And I heard ... *ng.*

Oller was looking at a corner of the thatched ceiling, where I'd hidden the ring.

I Thought *ring* at him.

No reaction.

Then I heard, *Ch* ... starting like the crunch of a dry leaf underfoot, a long way outside and on the edge of hearing, distinct but trailing off quickly. He was looking at the woodpile. Into which I'd tucked the cheese.

Unn ... . But he was looking at something behind me. The button was under his pack, away to his right.

All his Thoughts had been so faint that I'd never have noticed them if I wasn't standing still, Listening Into my empty space.

... *klet* came louder. Even if I hadn't been Listening inside, I might have thought, *huh? What was that?* Once again, Oller was looking at the spot where the necklet was concealed: my blanket. I was so pleased I almost missed the ... *nn*, as he located the knife. Or rather, *mis*-located it. He was looking at a hiding spot—but not the knife's. And then, faintly but clearly, as I Thought the word into him, I Heard his answering thought: *book*. Which, he had decided, correctly, was in his saddlebag.

That left just the pouch. And the fireplace. Which he looked at with a nod, and a tiny but firm Thought echoed in my head, *pou ...*

He'd found them all.

If not all correctly.

Now to find out if he knew what he'd found.

246

I let him scan the room, again and again. Each time he did so, and his glance fell on a hiding place, he'd confirm it in his head, and I'd Hear an echo of the thing that was hiding there, or a faint *yep* or *mm* as he grunted aloud.

"That's the lot," he said. "Seven, right?"

"Seven. Do you know what they are?"

"Not a clue," he said. "I could probably make some guesses, seeing as we don't have a lot of gear with us. But why'd I need to do that? I can just fetch 'em and find out."

"Good," I said. "We're going to do something different, though. When you know *what* I've hidden and where I've hidden it, only then can you go and get it."

Oller said, "Eh?"

I repeated my instructions.

"Blimey," he said, "how'm I meant to do that?"

I wasn't about to tell him that *he* wasn't, *I* was—using him as my sniffer dog.

"Just give it a go," I said.

Oller stood there, looking thoughtful. Which he was. He knew where to look, he just didn't know what he was looking for. I Thought the information to him. *Ring*, I Thought. *Ring.*

Ring.

He got it and with a nod headed for the corner of the ceiling. I almost spoiled it by chuckling when I realized that I'd also thought, *he picked up on the third ring.* My interruption of my own *Thinking* into him made him stop and hesitate, but he was almost there and keen to see what his find would be, so kept going. He put his hand into the thatch and brought it out again holding up the ring. He grinned.

"Stay there," I said. "Don't move. Same again."

He'd found the ring's hiding place first, so I decided not to think of the item he'd originally found second.

Knife, I thought. *Knife.* And kept repeating the thought, until he padded over and felt around me to the back of my belt.

"Sneaky!" he said. "Almost as if you weren't hiding it. It's always on your belt, so I'm not going not look there, am I? Tuck it around the back, it's almost as if you're pretending that's not one of them. Can't fool me, though!"

We went again. And again. It didn't get any easier. Some took longer than others, but he got them all in the end. And he'd got them all correctly, which I hadn't. I'd mixed up the *n*'s of *button* and *knife*. He hadn't. Even though he hadn't known that I was guiding him to either of them, he'd found them, one after another.

"Thanks, Oller," I said, when it was all over. "As you keep saying, you're *good at finding* all right."

He grinned on hearing his catchphrase. "What was all that about, then?"

I told him.

He whistled, his eyes growing large. "You mean … we can *think* to each other?"

"I can with Marnie," I said. "Mind you, with her it's easy. She's an expert. I'm a complete beginner. But if I work on it …"

"Wow," Oller said. "Come in handy, that will!"

"*Would,*" I corrected. "I'm a long way from where I need to be."

"Best work on it, then," he said. "We could use a deal o' that!"

"I will," I promised.

I reported back to Marnie, who sounded less encouraged than I'd hoped. *'Tain't easy, this. Not all of it comes as quick to all as to others.* Her voice sounded thick and tired. *You can't get to grips with my* In *magic no better than I can cast your* Out *magic. I tried them Colds of yours last night. Out there all hours, I was, and all I managed was to catch one.*

I heard her sneeze, and her hoarse voice came again. *Couldn't freeze a cup o' water, and it weren't no warm night neither. Oh well. Keep at it, eh?*

I replied, *keep at it.*

▲　▲　▲

Oller and I didn't have time to practice our Thinking Into much before we were in a fight where we could have used it.

It was two days later. The weather was closing in, following us as we rode, becoming steadily darker and more threatening. Rain was coming. A hard wind was coming. We needed to find a place where we could hole up and wait out the storm. Keep dry, eat, rest, listen, and watch the weather gods trample the skies. We wanted to be indoors, below what the winds were hurrying towards us, under shelter, not out in the open.

We were cantering, now, looking for any cover we might come across before the heavens broke. The silence was as dark and brooding as the sky. It would break soon enough, in half an hour, an hour at most. We rode hard, the only sound the thumping of our horses' hooves on the open grassland. There was no shelter but groves of trees. We knew better than to be among trees when lightning struck. From the top of a low rise, we saw ahead of us, at last, something that promised shelter below us.

Walls.

Around an open space in which we could see a long, low roof.

It was some kind of earthwork, once fortified, a refuge in this wilderness. The area around it was wooded with plenty of cover, but the earthwork itself was clear of trees. It would not be a target for lightning. We headed for it—and heard clashing.

It was coming from below and ahead, not from above and behind, where the ink-black storm clouds were chasing us, and from where we expected the rumble of thunder at any moment. What we heard, though, as we galloped towards the refuge, was not thunder, but the clash of steel on steel. Raised voices. A bark of anger or pain. Orders, challenges, taunts. We slowed to a trot, easing our horses in among the trees outside the walls, taking everything in at once. There were several horses tethered there already. Silhouetted against the sky on top of the walls were three figures, dark, cloaked, bows in their hands, aiming downwards, loosing arrows into the space beyond. We slipped from our saddles and tethered our own horses away from the others. All the while, from beyond the walls, the sounds of conflict continued. Carefully, we rounded a corner towards the entrance which we'd spotted in the wall.

No one was watching our way, on lookout. Keeping to the shadows, we eased in through the opening that would once have been the gateway and looked in to see a fight in progress.

Four—no, five men, with their backs to us.

And one lone figure, facing them, facing us, back to the far wall, dancing across it, swords carving the air.

It took only a moment.

I'd have known that figure anywhere.

I gripped Oller's shoulder.

We were going to have to act at once. Explanations would have to wait. Five against one, plus the archers on the walls. She was

249

moving fast, never in one spot for more than a split second, rolling and ducking, crouching and leaping, but arrows skittered on the ground where she'd been, and one would catch her sooner rather than later. The men were shouting and cursing and threatening, and yelling when one of her blades bit home, so they wouldn't hear me when I gabbled in Oller's ear, "I know her, she's a friend—archers first, you take the one on the right!"

His bow was strung and an arrow notched in an instant, as was mine. I nodded, and together we loosed. Two archers dropped, and the other on my side of the wall had my second arrow in him before he could turn his bow or cry out. Oller put an arrow into the back of the man between Qrysta and me. He fell forward with a yelp and a thud. The rest of them noticed and turned, their attention distracted from their prey, who now had, I could see, an arrow in her upper left arm.

Our surprise arrival was all the break that Qrysta needed. She was into them from one side, carving with her one good arm, slashing high and low. Shift blew a flare over them with a Distraction barking noisily inside it. The flare left us in shadow while illuminating their faces as they looked up and around in alarm—only to be dazzled by it. Qrysta finished the man nearest her with three strokes that were so fast they were almost simultaneous: leg, waist, neck. He dropped, folding messily.

By then Oller was among them, slipping and stabbing. I threw up whizzbangs and shrieks, and they had no idea what had hit them: flashes and blasts from above and behind—murder from below. I immobilized two in Inert and Ice Trap as their cohorts lay dying on the ground.

Qrysta stood with her right arm at the ready, sword out towards us, breathing hard, her face a mask of pain, her eyes switching from Oller to me and back again.

Oller wiped his knives and sheathed them, looked at her and then at me.

"Who are you?" Qrysta demanded, her voice a rasp of exhaustion and defiance.

I was smiling at her, almost giddy from my happiness at seeing her. And then I realized—of course she wouldn't recognize me! Not in this cloak and hood over my armor. "Hey, Qrysta."

Her eyes widened.

I pulled back my hood.

She hesitated. It was clearly too much for her to take in, all at once. Two strangers had appeared from nowhere and turned the tables on her attackers. But one of them was no stranger.

"Daxxie?" she said. She lowered her sword and leaned on it unsteadily, driving its point into the dirt. "Thank all the gods ..."

We were by her side immediately, helping her to the ground where she sat, or rather slumped, the last of her strength draining out of her.

"Get her under shelter," I said to Oller. "Storm won't be long." We couldn't take an arm each. Qrysta would have fainted from the pain. We joined our hands under her, sat her on them, and hurried to the stable that ran along one wall. It was open, but its roof looked sound. There was a horse in it, a magnificent chestnut charger, tied up in the remains of a stall. We cleared a space and lowered Qrysta to the ground as gently as we could. She gasped with pain through clenched teeth.

"Hold on, Qrys," I said. "I'll deal with that as soon as I can. Oller, horses."

Oller ran out to bring in the other horses. He'd know to be on the lookout for survivors if there were any outside. There were only two in here, and they weren't going anywhere till I released them. I got one of Marnie's Ease Pain salves from my pouch and smeared it around the arrow in Qrysta's arm. "That'll help for the time being, Qrys. Be right back."

I ran after Oller, giving the trapped men a Hard Bastard glare on my way out. We tethered the horses to each other and led them inside the refuge. There were nine of them. They were skittish and spooked, so it wasn't the work of a moment. The rain was spitting down through the trees now, the wind gusting in bursts that were growing stronger and longer, lashing at our cloaks and the horses' manes and tails.

By the time we herded them through the gateway, it was raining hard. Thunder had been stalking the sky towards us, and jolts of lightning lit the horizon, back in the direction we'd come from. It would soon be a downpour. At the moment, it was more of an *across* pour, as the wind drove needles of cold rain along the yard into our faces.

The horses were only too glad to see shelter ahead of them and knew what to do—get under it. Oller calmed them and settled them in while I went out into the yard to deal with our captives. I roped the one in the Ice Trap, cleansed it from him, and shoved him towards the stable, shouting above the noise of the breaking storm for Oller to take him. Then it was a rope around one wrist of the other man before I cleansed his Inert. He dropped to the ground, gasping. I turned him over, roped his hands behind his back, and jabbed him with the toe of my boot to get his attention, yelling, "Get up!" He did and staggered ahead of me into the shelter.

Oller took over guard duty as well as horse duty, and I crouched back down beside Qrysta. The wind was howling now and talking was impossible. We had to shout at the top of our lungs as I worked on her, but we managed a few exchanges before the thunder was booming and crashing above us, when there was no longer any point in trying to talk. Shift laid Numbness and Heal on her and then Soften on the arrow sticking through her left arm. As I cut the arrow apart below its flights, Shift's Soften slowly altered the tough ash wood of the shaft. It became pliable, more like rope than wood. I took hold of the arrow-head and carefully drew the shaft through and out. Blood ran out with it, and flowed, until Shift's Close Wounds spell sealed Qrysta's skin back together.

Qrysta, who had been gritting her teeth, relaxed. "Wow …"

I looked at her. "Seems you've been training yourself, Qrys," I shouted over the storm. "You were all over those guys."

"That I have," she yelled back with what remained of her strength, her blue-black hair whipping around in the wind, which was vicious even in the shelter of the stable. "Tell you all about it later."

I finished binding her arm, which was needed more as padding for when my casts wore off than to help the wound seal. That, my Close Wounds had already done. I wanted to cushion her arm as it would be sore for days and hurt if anything bumped it.

"Who's that?" Qrysta mouthed, meaning Oller, as he crouched beside us. I couldn't hear a sound above the storm, but I indicated that Oller was with me. Oller grinned and held his water flask to her lips. She drank. Then he uncorked his flask of Old Marnie's Special Peach Brandy. We drank, Qrysta, me, then Oller. We smiled as its warmth spread through us, relaxed us, and we settled back to wait out the bellowing storm.

It was a good half hour before it passed, and we could talk normally again. Unbelievably, given the roaring and booming and slamming of the thunder, the snap of lightning bursting overhead, and the whinnying and stamping of the horses, Qrysta actually fell asleep—or perhaps simply passed out, leaning against me as I sat with my back to the wall. Rain flailed in through the open wall of the stables. I dealt with it as best I could, casting Aura of Warmth around us—which did little more than take the edge off the cold, sharp stabs of rain—and Muffles to dampen the uproar for the horses. At last, the cacophony eased, and the winds lessened as they chased the storm away.

Qrysta woke up with a start—remembered that she was safe and sat up, looking at me and Oller.

He held his flask out to her again.

She took another mouthful.

"Oller," I said, "this is Qrysta. You've seen what she can do with twin blades, and you'll never see a better."

"Pleasure, Qrysta!" he said, holding out a grubby hand, which she shook.

"Thank you, Oller." She passed Old Marnie's Special Peach Brandy to me. "That's damn fine stuff, that is!"

"Best thief you ever saw," I told Qrysta. I could tell she liked the sound of that. I took a swig and added, "A teammate of mine and Grell's."

Qrysta's eyes widened.

"Grell's here, too?"

I nodded.

She smiled—her old, familiar smile that warmed my heart. "I guess I should have realized as soon as I saw you, but ... that's the best damn news I've had since I got here."

"He's here, and bigger and better than ever. He's off on a quest at the moment, but we'll see him again soon enough. *Shit*, Qrys, it's good to see you!"

"You can say that again!" Qrysta said. "Those bastards would have had me for sure."

My anger returned. "Who were—are—they?"

"Bounty hunters. I have a price on my head. Sons of bitches have hounded me all the way from Hartwell."

I'd seen Hartwell on Esmeralda's map. A big town way off to the east.

"More of them kept popping up, ahead, alongside," Qrysta continued. "I could shake them but only for so long. I'm shattered, Daxxie. It's been days and nights of this. They must have some system of communication. It was like they were steering me."

"Let's find out." I nodded at Oller, who brought our two captives closer. They'd been close enough to hear. They clearly didn't like what they'd heard any more than they liked what we'd done to them or the position they were in.

I started with the one I'd released from my Ice Trap. "Name?"

"Durns."

He had a hard face, a callous face. "Right, Durns. You're going to answer my questions. I'm going to cast a Truth on you. Lie, and it'll bite you. Understand?"

He didn't. But he'd find out. Probably the hard way.

I turned to the other captive. "Name?"

"Arbett."

Arbett looked no nicer than Durns but was clearly the more frightened.

"Same goes for you." I raised Shift and laid Truth on them, then asked Durns, "Why were you hunting my friend here?"

"The reward. Why'd you think?"

"Whose reward?"

"My Lord of Hartwell."

"Guild?"

He didn't want to answer. I waited.

Reluctantly, he said, "Mercs."

Oller spat. "That's no *guild!* That's just a parcel o' scum!" He glared at Durns, who eyed him warily. "Fucking mercenaries," Oller muttered. "Outlaws and bandits and deserters is what they are." Then he remembered that we were deserters too and left it at that.

"How do you communicate?" I asked. "With the rest of your gang?"

Durns said, "We talk. Same as anyone."

"Over distances?" I pressed.

He hesitated. "We don't." A moment later, he jumped as if something had sunk its teeth into his backside. "Ouch!"

"Lie again, it'll bite you harder. In the balls." I pointed Shift at his crotch. He flinched.

I turned to Arbett and asked, "How big is the reward? That Your Lord of Hartwell is offering?"

"Two thousand."

I turned to Qrysta in shock.

She smiled through her exhaustion. That old, mischievous, roguish Qrysta smile.

To Durns I said, "Two thousand *gold*?"

"We wouldn't hunt her this hard and far for no silvers," he retorted.

I said, "What in all hells have you done, Qrysta?"

Her weak smile broadened. "Made a very powerful enemy."

"I'll say! By doing what?"

"Long story," she said.

Durns said, "Stealing from My Lord of Hartwell, nicking his horse, and setting fire to his pavilion."

I frowned at Qrysta, amused. "Sounds like you've been busy, Qrys."

"That I have, Daxxie. That I have indeed."

20

The Information

Durns and Arbett were a mine of information. They parted with it willingly, eagerly even. They knew that their lives depended on their cooperation.

The first thing I needed to learn was whether we were safe. "Are there any more of you out there?"

Durns grunted a sour little laugh as if to say, *yeah, right.*

"I need answers," I said. "Are there any more mercenaries who were working with you, tracking my friend here, signaling maybe? Maybe setting ambush up ahead? And who didn't make it back when you closed this trap?"

"Ambush was laid here," Durns replied.

"So? Who is scout, who is lookout, who is flank, who is fallback, who is reserve?"

Eventually, he said, correcting me, "*Was.* Just one, ahead. Was one left and one right, but they came in once we'd got her cornered. Point man will be long gone by now."

"What makes you so sure?"

He shrugged. "It's what we'd have done."

Arbett nodded in agreement.

Oller snarled, "Mercs!" He looked at me. "Save their own skins at all costs, they do. Leave their own mates to lump it, and run for their lives."

I studied Durns. He hadn't jumped as if bitten in the balls. Must be telling the truth, then. Good. We didn't want anyone coming after us for payback or tailing us on our way. The point man must have ridden back to check when he heard that the fight was over—no doubt expecting to find Qrysta dead or captured and his companions celebrating. Once he saw us, our captives immobilized and his dead mates strewn about the place, he'd have made himself scarce.

"That's what you'd have done," I repeated, studying Durns.

He explained. Arbett chimed in, agreeing. It seemed there was no more loyalty among mercenaries than there was honor among thieves. Like the Thieves' Guild, the Mercenaries' Guild had a motto that was just two words: *For Hire.* The point man would be well on his way by now, they both said, putting as many leagues between himself and us as possible. He'd have seen what we'd done, and he'd want no part of tangling with us. Move on, find another town, another branch of the MG, and sign on for another job.

I was interested in the words *sign on*. You signed on with the guild, they said, not with any leader, if you wanted in on a job. The HC—the MG High Command—would appoint leader and deputies and assign roles. You got paid when you signed off on getting back with a report of the job, and filled in the amount earned in the all-important P/R column: Payments and Rewards.

The man who had run off would have to write *none* in that column. That wouldn't please the HC, because their cut of nothing was nothing. Each *none* entered in any year meant a penalty on your dues, doubling them, or tripling if there were two *nones*, and so on. Which is why the MG held back a portion of your payouts until you retired or died, so they could deduct penalty dues before handing over the balance to you or your heirs.

The usual trick, after a failed commission, was to find some money on the way back: banditry, highway robbery, shaking down some farmers or a village—all depending on how many there were of you. One lone merc wouldn't be able to do much more than hold up travelers, if he met any stupid enough to be going alone and unprotected up there. He'd get nothing like the two thousand gold promised, but with My

Lord of Hartwell's fifty down, which had guaranteed the MG's immediate attention to the matter, the point man might scrape another fifty together to cover the five per cent that the HC expected for giving him the job. Then he'd be able to write 5% in the P/R column and avoid the penalty. The HC took ten per cent of a successful commission, but never less than five, even from a washout.

Such details reassured me. I could see exactly what we were dealing with: cold-hearted professionals who would sell each other out without a second thought. That was their world. They all knew it, and they all accepted it.

"What's the reward for mercenaries?" I asked Oller.

"Depends what they've done," he said. "There's usually something they're hiding about their pasts. Any reeve would know. They all get the warrants that are circulated to every town and city. Deserters get flogged, outlaws sold, murderers hanged."

I studied Durns. "Looks gallows-bait to me."

Durns, sitting cross-legged on the ground, glared back sullenly up at me.

"You two are going to talk," I said. "And when I say *talk*, I don't mean *beg*. Talk for your lives. Tell me anything that you think might save your hides. I saw what you did to my friend, and I know what you were going to do with her when you'd taken her. Which explains why three archers didn't take her down. They weren't aiming to. Skipping arrows off the ground by her feet to keep her distracted, that's all they were doing. One of them didn't do it well enough. You had other plans for her, didn't you?"

They glanced at each other. I'd heard them taunting Qrysta, in the fight: *bitch*, and *slut*, and *you'll be paying us back for this trouble, each and every one of us, turn and turn about, girly*, and *won't look so pretty when we've done with you*.

I waited, looking at Arbett.

He said, "Yes."

I nodded. "We don't have plans for you. Like as not, we'll slit your throats and leave you for the crows. We're not going where some reeve can take you off our hands and pay us your bounties—and while we're at it, ask to see our papers, ask us our business, which is ours and none of his, thank you very much. Which might make him suspicious and call the guards. We don't have time for that. Which means it's not looking good for you, mercenaries Durns and Arbett. So, tell us what you've got, all of it, and see if you can save your necks."

They did.

Not being fugitives, as Qrysta had been, the mercenaries could go anywhere they wanted, so they'd been calling in at towns and inns and villages in their pursuit of her, talking to guards, to officials, to other mercs in their MG branches. Qrysta had learned nothing since she'd taken off from Hartwell one step ahead of the law. Durns, Arbett, and the others had learned a lot, all of which they had pooled as they journeyed.

As they talked, we learned it all too.

Much of it was interesting but worthless. Not worth their lives, that is. I knew we weren't going to kill them, but they didn't know that. They certainly thought that Qrysta was itching to put a blade through them. And they didn't like the look of Oller at all. Oller's face, glaring at them with his narrowed, mean eyes and tight, hard jaw, said *cutthroat*.

We heard all sorts of stuff, about campaigns, and rumors of betrayals and alliances, and skirmishes and hostilities—none of which concerned us. We learned that a mine beyond the Uplands had struck gold, and that prospectors were heading that way and pissing off the Orcs whose lands they passed through. Some of their merc team had been thinking of trying their luck up there after bringing Qrysta in. As to why My Lord of Hartwell was offering such a huge reward for a lone fugitive—well, she'd caused a heap of trouble. Ruined his tourney, she had, burned his pavilion, stolen My Lord's prized charger. Enraged, Lord Rylen had been, and they were to drag her back to Hartwell for a 'proper punishment.'

"Punishment?" I asked her. "What for?"

Qrysta snorted. "The 'proper punishment' I gave him for being an asshole."

I waited for her to enlighten us.

"Long story," she said.

Oller laughed. "I like her."

I got the hidden message. Parts of the story were for my ears only. I could wait for the right time. "She does rather grow on you, doesn't she?" I replied, remembering our first meeting, and her response to my offer of help in her solo Boss Fight. *Fuck off.*

Among the many things that followed, as they told us everything that they could think of in the hope of saving their skins, Durns and Arbett told of the disappearances that had been happening, of sacred things from sacred, well-guarded places. Oller and I believed we knew who was responsible for those. The various cults and sects that the valuables belonged to were distraught about the thefts and were offering large rewards for their return. Again, that was of no interest to us, we thought, but we asked for details, and they told us what they could remember.

The stolen items had all sorts of weird and wonderful names, from the Alb of Bairtmayne to Zenchrya's Coronet—at which our ears perked up, but it turned out that that was a complete coronet, made by a master goldsmith and given to the Cult of Zenchrya, Goddess of Lore and Learning, by some devout and scholarly queen only four hundred years before. So, not ancient, and not half a crown.

Durns and Arbett didn't remember them in alphabetical order, of course, just whatever came into their heads as they struggled to recall who had heard what where. Qrysta and Oller and I were all separately wondering what we were going to do with these two. We couldn't take them with us as prisoners. Where could we get rid of them?

My mind was so cluttered with those thoughts, that I didn't immediately notice anything interesting about Harmony's Flute.

A thief, however, always pays attention to items of potential value. Oller asked, "What's so special about a flute? Is it made of gold, set with jewels. What?"

Arbett said, "It's holy, that's what. To the Cult of Lymnia."

The mention of Lymnia piqued my interest. "Any idea why?"

"No."

Durns said, "It's not even a proper flute. Let alone made of gold. It's just an old bone with six finger holes and a mouth hole. So that you can tootle on it."

Bone.

I felt a tingle of excitement at the word. "Go on."

"Meant to be her leg bone, they say."

"Lymnia's?"

"Harmony's. Goddesses don't give up their leg bones. If they even have 'em. Harmony was some person from the myth times, demi-goddess or nymph or some such. Harmony has something to do with Patience and Forbearance and making things calm and peaceful. Everyone getting along. Dunno how it all fits, I'm not much of a one for gods. It's been missing for years, that, though. Not one of the latest go-round of disappearances."

"Missing from where?"

"The Order."

"What Order?"

Durns looked at me, his eyes narrowing. I could see that I'd made a blunder. Clearly, everyone knew about The Order. Everyone, that is, except 'foreigners' like me and Qrysta.

Luckily, Oller came to my rescue. "The Order of Order." As if, of course, I'd know it.

"Oh," I said, as casual as I could. "Right. No interest to us, then."

"Still a big reward for it," Durns continued stubbornly. "From *The Order*." He said it as a challenge. He knew that he'd busted me.

I decided that I didn't like Durns. "If someone finds it after all this time, good luck to them," I said dismissively, in my best Hard Bastard growl, giving him another Hard Bastard stare. He averted his eyes. He didn't want to provoke me. "The new thefts are what we want to hear about."

They went back to their recollections of what was missing, and who was offering what rewards. I let them talk and made notes in Marnie's Infinite Notebook. When they began to repeat themselves, and then run out of things even to repeat, I told Oller to take Arbett out of earshot and wait for me. Durns, warily, watched them as they went across the yard. He was thinking that I might be about to kill him.

"Where are your maps?" I asked.

"Saddlebag."

He led me to his horse, and I went through his possessions. He watched me to see what I stole, even though there was nothing he could do to stop me. We'd take what we wanted later when the time came to be rid of them. At that moment I wasn't interested in loot. "That's them." He nodded at a bundle of waterproofed, oiled skins. His maps were rolled up inside them; lengths of cloth, marked in black ink, rough and sturdy, and nothing like as decorative as Esmeralda's. Durns helped me find the one showing our current location. It showed the refuge and other features, some within an hour or two's ride.

"See that square, north-east?" he said. "If I was you, I'd take me and Arbett there."

"Why? What is it?"

"Headquarters."

"Of?"

He looked at me. "Crew I used to lead."

I thought, *outlaws.*

"Know this area well, do you?"

Durns nodded. "I do. And that's why we was herding her this way."

"You were their leader?"

"Deputy," he said. "Started out that way then took field promotion when our leader mysteriously took sick, and we had to leave him behind. In a sanatorium, run by priests and that, he'll be fine. So, me and a couple of others who used to run with me were doing the herding, unknown to the rest of them, like. We made it so she kept ahead of us, and we steered her where we wanted."

"Why?"

"Work it out," he said.

I did. *Treachery.* I needed to hear it from him.

Which I did. He said, "Ten of us started out on this job, and two thousand o' gold don't go so far between ten as it does between three. Biggest score any of us had ever heard of, there'd never be another chance at so much. The further we got from Hartwell, the harder to turn around and go back." He shrugged. "Up here's *my* turf. I've got friends here. Swords. And if she's worth two thousand to Hartwell, she's worth that to others, maybe more. Others who might want what Hartwell wants."

Warning bells rang in my mind. I needed to know if there was anywhere Qrysta shouldn't show her face. "Does anyone else have a bounty on her?"

"Not with the mercs. But as a bargaining chip with My Lord, maybe others would pay a lot for her. His rival lords and such. You take us to our old headquarters, me and Arbett, she and all she's worth are yours. We'll thank you for our lives and be on our way."

I said, "How big is this crew of yours?"

"Hard to say, I've been away more'n a year. Was, let me see, seven, no, eight of them when I left—me and the two others who came with me. Dead now, thanks to you. Arbett's not one of us, but we'll make him one if he wants. And he'll want if he has any sense. It'll be the oath or the knife. So, there won't be no more than ten I'd say, including us."

I waited for the Truth to bite him for lying.

It didn't.

Even so. Ten of them, three of us. On their turf. "How far?"

"If we overnight above the ford, which ain't more than three hours from here, we'll be at base tomorrow evening, easy."

"I'll think about it. What's at the ford?"

"Path, in from the west and heading north and east. Skirts the Uplands. Eventually hits the road, a day or two to the south. Turn off it near the ford—I'll show you where—and a mile on there's a hideout. Well hidden, you'd never find it if you didn't know it was there. Secure and all, better than this place."

I studied the map again, and his other maps, for the areas it adjoined. I compared it with what I knew from Esmeralda's map. The ford was not far out of our way. A secure billet for the night? We'd need that if anyone decided to follow the trail we were going to be making with our twelve horses. I thought, *Durns need not know what I'm really planning.*

We saddled up and rode out of the refuge, with our string of captured horses and our two prisoners, and headed north for the ford.

Much as I longed to hear what Qrysta had been up to, I knew that it would have to wait until we were alone. I wanted Oller and Qrysta to feel at ease with each other and knew that would take time. They'd only just met. They were off to a great start, but she might say something I understood that wouldn't make sense to him.

Oller and I had been through a lot together. We'd earned each other's trust. But Oller was the naturally suspicious type. He'd smell it out if I was talking in code to Qrysta. He'd know that I was *not-saying* things that I didn't want him to hear. That would immediately alert him, and make him doubt me as well as her. He couldn't possibly know that I didn't want him to hear what I was saying because I knew that he'd have no way of understanding what I was talking about. Qrysta got the message when I looked at her, and nodded in reply.

Later.

Qrysta was in no fit state to talk anyway. Riding with her left arm in a sling was hard work enough without talking as well. She was dozing and almost falling off her horse within half an hour of leaving the earthwork. I revived her with as much Heals as Shift could lay on her, and one of Marnie's Boost Health tonics gave her a second wind, but what she really needed, after being on the run for so long, was rest. I intended to give her as much of that as we safely could.

I could, though, have a private word with Marnie as we rode, about the Flute of Harmony and whether that could be the *bone* of the rhyme.

You're not the first to wonder that, she thought back to me. *It's been suggested before. We have no way of knowing.*

You didn't think to tell me? I asked.

No point in putting ideas into your head and distracting you from finding the right bone *whether it's the flute or not*, she replied. *If we knew for certain, I'd have told you. But we don't, any more than we know where it is. Still, it's as good a theory as any, I suppose.*

We reached the east–west path that led to the ford a couple of hours later and turned to our right along it. We saw no one ahead or behind. There were few travelers even on the high roads these days, Durns told us, let alone far off the beaten track where we now were. Which was the reason, we gathered, why he'd taken two of his crew and headed off to find merc guild jobs. What with everything coming apart in the realm, the pickings had dwindled there from lean down to none. They'd been running low on everything: food, drink, and especially gold. The further south and east they went, he'd figured, the more chance they'd have of finding a well-paid job.

Their road had taken them, via a couple of smaller jobs, to Hartwell, where My Lord's commission had them heading back home again. It had seemed too good to be true. All they had to do was thin the herd of their fellow MG and bring in the prize. But then Oller and I had come along and spoiled his plans.

The river was a good thirty paces wide at the ford, and as at most fords, running fast across its shallows. Its water was biting cold, the Spring snowmelt having started up in the Western Mountains. Evening was on us as we mounted the far bank and continued along the path that curved away now, east and south.

After half a mile Durns said, "We turn off here."

I couldn't see a path.

"We don't like to leave tracks." Durns saw me inspecting the ground. "We come in from all angles, never the same way if we can help it. There's no hiding a string this big, but anyone who sees the tracks of this many horses will think twice about coming after us, to ask us our business. And we ain't seen a soul. I doubt even my old crew have been this way in a long while. I've seen no signs of anyone going where we're going."

We turned off to the north and walked our horses through the trees that grew all around us, heading back towards the river, upstream of the ford. There was no sign of human presence. You'd have thought that no one had ever been here and that this was untouched wilderness. That was just the way Durns and his crew liked it. If there's no sign of people, then no one comes looking for people.

We were curving back one way, and the river back towards us another way off to our left. To our right, a low hill rose as we walked the horses along it, steepening to beome a cliff as we neared the river. The face of the cliff was covered in vegetation: hanging trailers of plants, tufts of fern sprouting among clumps of grass, and thin trees clinging to stony ledges. It was a gloomy place despite the greenery and the sound of the river, getting louder as we came closer to it. We could hear a waterfall ahead.

I was beginning to get uneasy. This would be a good place for an ambush. We were trapped between cliff and river and, judging by the roaring of the waterfall, the river blocked off any escape. I cast Reveals, but the only hidden life that was revealed were the fuzzy, red outlines of two deer, back among the trees.

"Here," Durns said, reining in his horse.

He was looking at the cliff face. Trees, foliage, and vegetation against a blank wall.

He turned to me with a smile. "See it?"

"No."

"Well-hidden, like I said. We'll need these off." He held out his bound hands. Oller untied them with a look that said *don't try anything, mate!* while I raised Shift. They got the message. Durns and Arbett dismounted and walked up to the wall. Durns showed Arbett where to grip and what to push. They lifted. Arbett pushed. Durns pulled. A section of the vegetation detached itself from the cliff, and they hauled it to one side, revealing a hole in the cliffside.

The hole was a passage, wide enough to lead our horses into it. I led the way in, leaving Oller to supervise Arbett and Durns as they closed the hidden gate behind us, barring it on the inside. Qrysta followed me on My Lord of Hartwell's charger, the other horses behind her. I cast some Glows to light our way and reassure the horses and then, to my surprise, we were turning left towards the river which we could hear thundering above and around us.

There was daylight ahead, dim but enough to light the path. When the path turned again, we saw that we were behind the waterfall, through which the evening light was leaking. The noise was deafening, and the horses didn't like it, so I cast a Calm and a Muffles, which helped, but I was relieved to get them beyond that and then up and out into daylight proper.

We emerged into a stockade that had been built in a natural basin in the hillside. It was bowl shaped, having three sides of cliffs and one of river, which ran fast and black below us as it funneled into the mouth of the waterfall. Stakes had been driven into the ground along it and joined by fencing of split logs. It was open to the sky above.

Rough shelters stood out from the cliffsides, nothing more than roofing held up by wooden uprights. It wasn't much, but it would more than do for one night. The storm had blown away towards the west and taken the clouds with it. The sky was clear, and the night promised to be fine, if cold.

Oller gathered firewood into a pile, then stood back as Shift blasted flame into it, setting it alight. Arbett and Durns still had their hands and feet bound, but they were able to tend the fire while Oller and I groomed and stabled the horses. Qrysta helped as best she could with one arm in a sling. We weren't short of food, what with everything the mercs had been carrying in their saddlebags. We ate as the sun set slowly somewhere out of sight beyond the small patch of pale sky that we could see above us.

We were tired, all of us. Qrysta was exhausted and soon asleep in her blankets. I talked with Durns and Arbett, who watched Oller as he went through every saddlebag and secret hiding place. His search yielded a good amount of coin. In the mercs' packs he found knives, arrows, flint-and-tinder boxes, and bowstrings as well as food and drink. We'd relieved the dead of their weapons and armor back at the earthwork as well as any valuables they'd had on them. What we needed now, Oller had said, jokingly, was a Receiver. And a horse-trader. We were, in a way, rich, but our riches weren't of the kind we wanted which was gold in our purses. I had a plan for that, though.

In former times, Durns told us, when the king's patrols had policed the highways and byways, his crew had needed to be able to melt into the scenery. Home Base was known to the patrols, and they'd raided it more than once, but they never knew about this stockade. The last royal squadron had come up this way six years ago, and it had been a quarter the size they had been before. The roads had never been truly safe but now were more dangerous than ever. There'd been no need to use this place recently. There were no travelers on the path that crossed the ford to extract tolls from. "Lean pickings everywhere," Durns said sourly, as he watched Oller going through his packs and setting aside the keepings. Before we'd left the refuge, he had checked the two mercs thoroughly for sharps, several of which he found. A dagger each, in their boots; a long needle; a folding razor.

I wished that I had some sort of Barrier Alarm that I could lay on the passage back to the outside world, but I did not have that skill. I didn't expect that any enemy or predator would be coming that way in the night, but it would have been nice to be sure that I'd know if any did. I wondered if Marnie had a cast like that in her repertoire, and waited, expecting her to Think to me. She didn't. We must be out of range, I decided. With the mercs bound hand and foot by an expert—Oller—and us in this well-hidden, high-walled bolt hole, I decided that we didn't need to keep watch that night.

We slept.

I woke in the middle of the night to see a shadow moving among us. It was crouched over Arbett. Silently, I reached for Shift, my sleep-fuddled mind rapidly clearing, and felt her come to life in my hand as if she, too, had been dormant. She cast Inert at her target, then we lit the stockade with a flare. The creature shrieked, looked up in alarm, and froze as our Inert struck it. Blood was trickling from its open mouth. The teeth in it were sharp, curved fangs.

21

Of Maps and Plans

"Fucking vamps!" Durns got up and went over to the immobilized creature. "Horrible little sods. What's he doing above ground, anyway? I don't get it. Everything's topsy-turvy these days."

We studied the thing, frozen in mid shriek, fang-filled mouth open, eyes wide with fright—black eyes, which seemed to be all pupil. A shock of feathery, mangy, white hair framed a gaunt, pale face, its skin like old parchment. His hands, raised in alarm, were more claw than hand, with long, dirt-encrusted nails. His arms were thin, as were his legs, which were crouched and froglike. His chest was narrow, his stomach a little pot below skeletal ribs. His clothes were the tatters of what had once been a shirt and leggings. His feet were bare and long and bony, and his toes ended in curving brown claws.

He was smaller even than Oller, and he looked frail as well as menacing, frightened as well as malign. A creature of the shadows, living in the shadows, to avoid and evade as well as to stalk and to feed.

Arbett, holding a piece of cloth to his neck, growled, "Little shit, biting me like that … . Better not be contagious!"

"Know at sunup, won't we?" Durns said .

"Can they talk?" I asked him.

Durns shook his head as he contemplated me. "I wish the boot was on the other foot, my friend. I've a deal of questions I'd want to put to you. As it is, just about all I know about you is that you're not from around here. 'Course they can bloody talk. They're human, just like you and me. Or they were once. Most of them forget how after a while. Their throats close up. Vocals rot from lack of use. The words leave them. No one to talk to, see? They're solitaries. I've heard it's different down south. Some say there are clans of them, and if that's so, maybe they talk to each other. Who knows? This one should still be able to. He can't be more than a hundred."

I studied the vampire. He looked nearer a thousand years old than a hundred. "You said, 'what's he doing above ground?'" I asked Durns. "Don't they have to come up to feed?"

"They don't have to feed on humans. Anything warm-blooded will do. Most of them live on rats. Squirrels if they can catch them. That's why they're small and thin like this bugger. Human blood is what they like best, though. Beefs them up. If they can, they take a human, keep it caged and fed, and feed on it till it gives out."

"Doesn't that turn the human into a vampire too?"

Durns shook his head. "Only if he's contagious. Otherwise, it turns the human into a month of meals. And then into a corpse. They usually don't feed on humans when they're contagious because what good's another vamp to them? They can't drink vamp blood, it'd poison them. Only, of course, sometimes when they're contagious they happen across some human and can't resist—quick feed, and scarper— and some poor bastard wakes up with holes in his neck, a horrible headache, and can't stand daylight all of a sudden." He stared at the creature, disgust written all over his face. "No, they don't like to make other vamps because that's competition. Their food sources are limited enough. They want to keep their turf for themselves."

I studied the vampire. He looked at once scary and pathetic. I wondered how he'd got down the steep cliffs into the stockade.

I looked at his fingers and toes again. They were dirty, especially the long claws that were his toenails. "Must be good climbers."

"Have to be," Durns said. "There's all sorts of things in the Undergrounds they need to avoid. They usually nest as high up as they can get, in cracks in the ceilings, and such. So's nothing can creep up on them. Which is why some people think they can turn into bats. Don't believe it myself."

"When are they contagious?" I asked. "With *Weres* it's full moons, isn't it? When they can change."

"Dunno." Durns shrugged. "Not my field. Ask an apothecary. They harvest them. Vamp blood's useful in their potions. Only if it's contagious, though. They hire us from time to time to get an expedition up and fill a few flasks. Not a popular job. There's far worse than vamps down where these buggers live. If Arbett turns funny when the sun rises, you could drain this one, maybe get twenty gold from him."

It wasn't gold I wanted from the vampire. It was information.

I told Oller to rope him with a loop around one wrist, the same as I'd done to Arbett when he was immobile. I cast Ice Trap on his feet and cleansed the Inert. He started wriggling and ducking and struggling immediately, but he held fast in his Ice Trap. Oller had his wrist yanked hard up behind his back and struggled to get the other one under control. Durns caught the flailing arm and dragged it behind the creature where Oller lashed his hands together. The creature was hissing, weakly, and creaking rather than shrieking.

He was clearly terrified.

I stood in front of him and pointed Shift at him. He saw her glowing heartstone, and shrank back from it.

"Listen," I said. "I'll let you go if you calm down and answer my questions."

I waited for him to stop hissing and creaking. Eventually, he did.

"Can you understand me?" I asked.

He stared at me, big black eyes glinting. I could see comprehension in them.

"Can you speak?"

He stared. Then nodded.

"You can stay here till sunrise, or you can talk to me." I saw the sudden alarm in his face. *Sunrise* … . "So, let's start with your name. Do you have one?"

His voice, when it came, was as thin as he was, as dry as dust, and like dust in the wind, his words seemed to fade away into nothingness. "Yesss …"

"What is it?"

"Uurchhh …"

270

"Urch?" I assumed that was the remains of his former, above-ground name.

He nodded again. "Yesss …"

"Where do you live, Urch? Near here?"

"Yesss …"

"Is it big? Where you live? Or a small place?"

"Biggg …"

"Many tunnels? Caverns?"

"Many. Many. Far. All the wayyy …"

"All the way to where?"

"Uplands. Eastlands. Darklandsss …"

That was interesting. An underground network beneath the whole realm? That would be a good way of avoiding people you didn't want to meet.

"Niblunhaem?"

"Yesss …"

"Have you ever been there?"

He shook his head. "Niblers don't like usss …"

"Could you show us the way?"

He hesitated. "There are othersss … in the wayyy …"

"What others?"

"All sortsss … . They wouldn't like you. Not alivvve …"

"Where is the entrance?"

He jerked his head, indicating back along the river, upstream.

"What were you doing here tonight?"

"Hunting … . Saw the firelight. Climbed down."

"Don't you hunt underground?"

"Better prey up … fatter ratsss … too many othersss …"

"Underground? What others?"

"Spiders. Deads. Eefrits. Mennn …"

"Men? What men?"

"Huntersss …"

"Hunting you?"

"Hunting stones. And bones. And buriedsss …"

"Buried what?"

"Boxes. Bundles. Lostsss …"

"Do you mean treasure? Gold?"

He nodded. "All sortsss … . They talk. We listen. We talkkk …"

"We? Others like you?"

He nodded. "Othersss …"

"Do you know if these men are looking for anything in particular?"

"Specialsss …"

"Did you hear any names? Of things they are looking for?"

He shook his head. "Mapsss … . Plansss …"

"They have maps?"

"Yesss …" he said, then added, "They diddd …"

I thought I understood. "They died, didn't they?"

"Some … some left, some died. Others came down other waysss …"

"And the eefrits?"

"Gathering. Summoned."

"Summoned? Who by?"

He was too frightened to answer. He crouched and twitched and looked at me nervously, almost imploringly.

I thought, *it's worth a try.* "Jurun?"

He cringed so low that he was almost squatting, his shoulders hunched up in fear. His reply was a weak hiss through clenched teeth.

I pressed on. "Do you know where to find him?"

He screwed his eyes up tight, and shook his head vigorously, his white hair fluttering. "No," he muttered. "No no no, noooo …"

It was obvious he knew more than he was saying. And he didn't want to think about it, let alone tell us.

I knew I needed to talk privately with Qrysta and Oller.

The Undergrounds. We were going to have to enter them eventually. And here we had a guide who could at least show us the way in, even if he wouldn't want to go where we needed to go. We also had Durns and Arbett to consider. Not to mention a string of valuable horses. We knew what Arbett wanted to do with the vampire for feeding on him.

"Burn the fucker," he said. "They hate fire. Serve him right!"

I ignored him.

While I was considering, Urch said, "Colddd …"

Being nothing but skin and bone, he didn't have much insulation on his thin body. Oller roped his legs, and I cleansed the Ice Trap. Urch tottered as his legs found their freedom of movement again. Oller tied him to one of the uprights that supported the low roof, then he, Qrysta, and I went aside to confer.

It didn't take long. We had our course of action worked out within ten minutes. I got out Esmeralda's map and cast a Glow over it. Oller brought Urch over, and he crouched dutifully beside me, the map spread out on a blanket on the ground.

"Can you read this?" I asked.

"Yesss …"

"We're here." I pointed to a spot by the river. There were three red spots nearby, one yellow, one purple. The yellow one was named Duraenbar. The purple had the legend, Long Cavern. The reds were two Pits and a Midden.

I said, "Duraenbar?"

"Old people," Urch said. "Lost place. Big. A temple, for their godsss …"

"Do any of these connect?" I asked. "Can you get from one to the other, underground?"

"Yesss …" Urch said. "Not all …"

"Which?"

He pointed at one of the pits.

"Not that," he said, "bad place …"

"Why's it bad?"

"Bad things live there … ." He shuddered. "Don't go …"

Qrysta said, "Sounds like good advice to me."

"And this is where you live?" I pointed at Long Cavern.

"Yesss … . Deep. Longgg … . Never go deep, stay up by toppp … . Night hunt, day nessst …"

"And you were in your nest, up in the ceiling, when the men came?"

"Yesss …. Watched them go. Downnn … . Tennn … . Ten went down. Three came backkk … . Later, many many daysss … . Scared, they were. Runninggg …. Looking back, behind them, hearing things coming after themmm … . They ran out into the sunnn …"

"What things?"

"Weren't thingsss … . One more man. Left him behinddd … . Weakest. Hurt. I smelled the blooddd … ." He stopped and looked at me guiltily.

"You took him?"

He nodded.

"Dropped on himmm …. Held him downnn …. Fed on himmm …."
Despite his fear of us, his memory of the taste of human blood brought a longing warmth to his old, weak voice.

273

"For how long?"

"Until he dieddd …. Soonnn …. He had mapsss …. Papersss …"

I asked, "What happened to them?"

"Kept themmm …. With his thingsss …. Knife, pens, potsss …"

"That doesn't sound like a soldier," Qrysta said.

I agreed. "Researcher? Scholar?"

Qrysta shrugged. "Could be."

I turned back to Urch. "Why did you keep them?"

"Nice thingsss …. Reminded me …" he tailed off wistfully.

"Reminded you of what?"

Urch replied, "Before …" and stopped.

I looked at him. His face, now that it wasn't screwed up tight, or jumping with terror, was relaxed, and mournful.

That surprised me. I considered what he'd said. "Before you became what you are now?"

"Yesss …." Tears rolled down his ancient cheeks.

"When was this, Urch? That you fed on him?"

"Three nightsss …"

This had all happened very recently, then. That meant there was valuable information up there.

"How long would it take us to get there?"

"Not longgg …. Minutesss …. Nearrr …"

"I want that man's things," I told him. "You take me there and give them to me and I'll let you go. Will you do that?"

"Yesss …"

He didn't sound surprised, or relieved—just sad. As if death was of no more consequence than life.

Suddenly, I felt sorry for him. This was a creature—no, a human—no, a *former* human—for whom life was an endless, empty struggle. Prey or die. Feed or starve. What little else his existence held was pitiful enough: a few possessions which he held onto to remind him of the sun and the life that had been taken from him.

"I can't climb like you, we'll have to go back and around the cliff."

Urch said, "Rope …"

"What about it?"

"Give me rope …. I'll climb, and tie it to tree …. Then you follow uppp …"

That seemed risky. What was to stop him scuttling up the rock wall and running off? I didn't know if I could hit him with Inert once he had reached the top. He might be out of range. And anyway, if he was Inerted, he couldn't move to tie the rope to the tree for me.

"I'll go," Oller said. "Won't be as quick as friend Urch here, but it don't seem too hard. Plenty of hand and footholds."

"You sure?" I asked. "At night?"

Oller grinned. "I do my best climbing at night, Daxxie. Anyway, I'm the finder, don't forget. I can take a look-see around up there; you never know what I might spot that an amateur like you would miss."

So, it was decided. I found a small stick in the depleted firewood pile under the shelter and cast a dim Glow on it. Oller wrapped it up tight in his blanket so that no light leaked, roped it to his back and started climbing. He was up top within minutes. Rather than letting Urch climb and risking him making a run for it, we tied him to the rope Oller lowered, and Oller hauled him up. He was as light as he was thin and old.

Oller called down, "There's a tree here that should do. I'll put a loop around it and lower myself down when I get back. Sleep well!"

And he was gone.

"Sleep," Qrysta said. "Good idea. I've about a missing week of it to catch up on."

I cast a Lingering Mend on her, knowing it would soothe her and help her recovery. Its warm, green bubble bloomed around her, making her smile. "I love these. Thanks, Daxx."

"Any time."

She wrapped herself in her blanket and dropped off within minutes. Arbett was clearly nervous about the morning. He rolled and muttered and cursed. Durns told him to shut it and Arbett told Durns to shut it and they were both testy and frustrated, so before things could get out of hand I told them both to shut it. When they didn't and turned their bile on me, I cast Mute on them. They realized no one could hear their curses, so subsided, and were soon both asleep. No doubt snoring, because they'd been snoring before when I'd woken up and seen Urch feeding on Arbett, but now, thankfully, they were snoring in silence under the Mute. I lay awake, thinking everything over.

Not for the first time, I recited the poem in my head.

A stick, a stone,
A book, a bone,
Go down and down
For half a crown,
A knife,
A life:
A throne.

I did not know where the throne was yet, but I could guess who was sitting on it. And I suspected that it would take the knife to wrest it from him.

Even though I could not say why, at that moment, because I could not point to facts and a step-by-step route to our destination, I knew we were on the right path.

The first faint light of dawn was in the sky as Oller slid down his ropes. He whistled before he did so, to alert me. I woke and watched as he pulled one end, and the other slipped up and off his anchoring tree and fell to the ground beside him. He whipped it around his arm to gather it in then stowed it under a saddlebag.

He padded over to me. I said, "How did you do?"

"Not too bad," he said. "Friend Urch was most helpful. Gave me all the stuff he had, that he'd taken from the dead man. I went on down a bit, just casing the place. Got an uneasy feeling after about half a mile or so, thought it best not go any further. But you know what he said, about the men running back? And the last one that he dropped on? I found what they'd been running from. Or rather, the remains of their mates—which told me all I needed to know." He shook his head at the memory and exhaled. "Hanging from the ceiling, they were, wrapped up all neat in cocoons of cobweb. I slit 'em open, and out they fell, dry as sticks and drained of everything. Just bones in little empty sacks of skin, they were. But they had their clothes on, still. Them giant spiders don't eat clothes. Found some things in them, and all!"

He dropped his pack by me, and continued, pleased with himself as he rummaged around in it. "I think you'll like what you see, Daxxie.

I said cheerio to Urch on the way out. He said let him know if we're back this way. I said we would. Poor bugger, eh?"

"Indeed," I said. A long, empty, solitary life. Feeding. Taking. Giving nothing in return. How that must break your heart, if you had any fellow feeling. Whatever you had been above ground would fade over the long, dark years. And so would you: to a shadow, a wraith, a wretched thing of darkness, alone in the night.

I lit the predawn gloom with a Glow and watched as Oller put his finds on the ground in front of me. "These are what Urch took from the feller he fed on." He set them out: a portable writing case of fine yellow wood, inlaid with mother of pearl, containing inkpots, a penknife for splitting quills, and blocks of ink for mixing with water; a leathern pouch containing goose quills, two already split for nibs, and ink-darkened; a wooden-shafted sealing stamp, its tip brass; sticks of sealing wax; and several lenses, for magnifying and examining.

"Nice pieces, these," he said. "He weren't no pauper. Someone spent good money on that expedition, I'm thinking. Proper scholar with a decent escort to protect him." He pulled out some more items. "These were on the soldiers, the ones hanging in the webs, in their pockets." He set out more items, various trinkets: knives, coins, dice, buttons, needles, coils of thread and twine, hooks, and two pairs of studded brass knuckles. "Not much of interest to you there, Daxx, but there's more to come."

He handed me a folio of papers, wrapped in waterproofed cloth. "This was the scribe's—dunno what you'll find in there. I didn't have time to look—but this here"—he held out another packet, this one much thinner—"I did take a peek at before I got that uneasy feeling and put your Glowstick out. It was one of the soldiers who had it. Sewn into the lining of his jack. Well now, thought I, what's this doing sewn up nice and tight and hidden like that? Silk and all, look at it!"

I unwrapped it from its protective oilcloth. It was indeed silk: a map, light, thin, and painstakingly detailed. And not just delineated in black, but in rich inks of all colors. It was, without a doubt, old, despite which, the colors had not faded. I was sitting on the ground, cross-legged with Shift leaning across my lap. I felt her jumping and dancing against my thigh as I looked at the map. I thought, *magic. Magic inks, not fading over the years*—and felt Shift's warm glow of confirmation. Clearly, my staff recognized other magic items.

I was reading the inscription at the bottom right corner—*A Map of the Undergrounds from Dark Caverns (NW) including unconfirmed ways through to the Last Land (SE)*—when Oller's finger jabbed at a spot where a path tapered out into dotted lines. An arrow pointed from them with the words *Parts Unknown*. "See?" he said. I examined the area that he was indicating and saw two things as he moved his finger in the direction he wanted me to look.

Newer, darker dotted lines had recently been added with branches that were not fully completed. Among those new lines that went on, left or right or straight ahead and led nowhere, only one way was finished.

It pointed to the words:
The Floor.

22

Now We are Five

"I expect you think that means what I think it means." Oller grinned.

I thought, *the Floor. The floor of the world.*

"And I expect you expect what I also expect, which is that we'd have to find our way down there eventually," he chattered on, delighted. "If that's where all this started, then that's where we're going to have to go to finish it. And I'm good at finding things, but it would take even *me* a lot of time and a lot of wrong turns—and we'd probably bump into a lot of nastinesses on our byways and detours before I found the right way. Some of which might want to eat us."

I looked up at him, his face gradually coming into view as the dawn broke above the surrounding cliffs. He was radiating excitement.

I shook my head but couldn't help smiling myself. "You are insane, you know that?"

Oller agreed happily. "Yup!"

"You're actually *enjoying* the prospect of blundering around down there, where no one in his right mind would go, even with the King's army?"

"I don't need no army," Oller replied. "I've got you and Qrysta—and Grell when he gets back. This isn't a job for the likes o' Serjeant Bastard's squaddies. This is a job for specialists."

"Yeah, but, *numbers*, Ols!" I objected. "Who knows how many bloodthirsty *whatevers* are down there?"

Oller shrugged. "We're going to have to find out sooner or later. And now, we can avoid all the *bloodthirsty whatevers* up all the wrong turnings we *don't* need to take, 'cos we've got this map."

"Well, it's all going to have to wait." I started packing up. "First things first. Good work though, Oller. You're the best."

"Thanks, mate," Oller said with another cheerful, lopsided smile. "You too."

He followed me as I went over to Arbett, who was wriggling and sweating and glancing anxiously up at the lightening sky. Durns was watching him closely.

"How are you feeling?" I asked Arbett.

His voice was hoarse and dry. "Okay ... I think."

"Water," I told Oller. "Then give him a sip of Marnie's."

Oller held a waterskin to Arbett's lips, and he drank deeply. Oller then uncorked Marnie's Special Peach Brandy, and Arbett took a large mouthful. He swallowed and exhaled.

"Thanks," he rasped. He was nervous, still unsure that he hadn't contracted vampirism from Urch, but Marnie's liquor worked its magic. His body stopped twitching and trembling, and his shoulders relaxed.

I asked, "Headache?"

He shook his head. Durns had told us that the headache, when it came, would be unbearable. The only cure was to scuttle into darkness and not come out into daylight, ever again.

We waited.

"So far, so good," I said.

Arbett just grunted.

Somewhere off to the east, the sun must have cleared a low cloud, for the sky swelled with a warm orange glow that grew, and soon it was fully daylight.

We all studied Arbett. There was no screwing up of eyes, no squealing and cringing away from the light.

"Thirsty?" I asked, not adding the words *for blood*.

Arbett shook his head. "I'm okay."

"Good."

Arbett almost began to believe that he was safe now. "You think?" He wanted reassurance. "I'm not ..."

"I think you're not," I said.

"And I think we're not going to have to waste time making a point-ed stake for your heart, Arbett," Durns said with his usual grim humor. "If that had been your choice rather than ending up like Urch. Which would have been mine, that's for certain."

Arbett exhaled, his head dropping to his chest in relief.

"Thank all the gods," he muttered.

Qrysta was still out for the count, wrapped up in her cloak and blanket by the remains of the fire, her face soft and relaxed, her twin blades in their scabbards within easy reach. I looked at her and thought, by no means for the first time when looking at Qrysta, *wow*. She was even lovelier in the living, breathing flesh.

I took a deep breath and sighed. She looked wondrous. Soft, long, blue-black hair tied back behind her in a knot. Flawless skin, perfect lips open a fraction as she whiffled endearingly. She looked smaller than she did when upright, somehow. I realized that she wasn't ac-tually as big as she looked with a sword in each hand. In combat, when a tornado of whirling steel, screaming blue murder at our foes, Qrysta looked enormous. Which was probably because she was ev-erywhere at once. And wherever anyone tried to lay a blade on her, suddenly there she *wasn't*.

She was the perfect combination: huge damage, small target. I gazed at her with all the affection I felt for her that had grown over the years that we'd been partners. And, of course, something more, which I'd buried, as I knew she'd wanted me to. I'd told myself just to consider her beauty an added bonus to her supercool personality and sharp mind—and even sharper blades. There was no law that I knew of against having fine-looking friends. And, *gods*, she was fine looking! Just … gorgeous. I knew that she wouldn't appreciate it if I gazed at her like this when she was awake—or even asleep as she was now, if she'd known I was looking at her. But I allowed myself just a couple of moments to study her, to drink her in, to remind myself how much I liked her … valued her.

Qrysta, my teammate, who I knew like the back of my hand, who I loved just the way I loved Grell … and that was as far as our relation-ship went, so stop staring and get moving.

I tapped Qrysta gently on the shoulder with Shift. She frowned and wriggled away.

"Up you get, Qrys, rise and shine." I tapped her again. "Time's a-wasting, we have a road to hit. Dawn's broken, Arbett's not a vampire, Oller has madam's breakfast ready, but madam doesn't get it in bed."

Qrysta rolled upright and looked up at me. "Hey, Daxx."

"Morning, Qrysta."

"Breakfast," she said, "sounds good."

"Road rations," I said. "They'll keep you going. We eat in the saddle. We have a long day ahead of us."

"Okay, let's go. Whoo, a full night's sleep and I'm ready to rock!" She unfolded like a cat and was on her feet, smiling at me. "I mean, could you have ever imagined, Daxxie? Back when we first started running together?"

I smiled, shaking my head. "Not in a million years."

She spread her arms wide and laughed aloud at the sheer pleasure of being alive. *And*, I thought, *at the joy of being what she now was.* I knew the feeling. Daxx was definitely an upgrade on what Joss had been. I wondered who she had been before finding herself here.

"Can't wait to hear what you've been up to, Qrys," I said.

"Me too," She glanced at Oller.

I got the message. *We'll talk when we're alone.*

We left the hideout shortly after dawn, chewing on our breakfasts of hard tack, harder cheese, dried plums, drier sausage, and a wrinkled apple each, all washed down with water from our skins which we'd refilled from the river. Good, fresh, clean water it was too. We closed the entrance to the stockade behind us, Durns taking care to make sure it was well hidden. Then we rode along the path from the ford, east now and south.

Towards noon, I called a halt on the side of a long, grassy hill.

I told Durns and Arbett to dismount then handed the reins of their horses to Oller, who attached them to the rest of our string.

"This is where we part ways," I said, as Oller slipped from the saddle and drew his knife. "You know your way to your base from here, we're heading elsewhere."

Oller cut the ropes that bound their hands.

Durns gave me a grim stare. "We'll meet again."

"You'd better hope not." I hit him with a Shock Jolt from Shift—nothing that would do any damage but would definitely get his attention.

He staggered backwards, yelping, his hair standing on end.

"Look, I don't like you any more than you like me, Durns. What you had in mind for my friend? I don't forgive that. Your crew paid with their lives. I only let you live because you were useful. We don't need you anymore, so be on your way. And, if you remember, you were going to thank us for your lives."

Durns muttered, "Fuck you!"

Oller handed them their food packs and waterskins which was all we were allowing them.

"There's bears out here," Durns said. "Wolves, sabercats, other things. You going to leave us unarmed? Might as well kill us now and be done with it!"

He had a point. "Fair enough," I said. "A sword and a shield each, Oller. And nothing we can sell for good coin, just gear that will keep them alive."

Oller found two shields and two swords, the shields shabby, the swords nicked and rusty. He handed them to Durns and Arbett while I pointed Shift at them, in case they tried to be clever and attacked Oller.

"Bows and arrows?" Durns said.

"Don't be stupid," I said. "And have you shoot us in the back? Not a chance. Off you go."

They gave us a last, hard look each and then headed north, trudging up the slope. We wheeled our string of horses back onto the path and trotted them down the long hillside, Qrysta on one side of me, Oller on the other.

Finally, we could talk.

"Well now," I said to Qrysta. "We have a little catching up to do."

"That we do," she agreed.

"First things first, though," I said. "Young Oller here knows nothing about you, any more than you know anything about him. I'd just like to say that Grell and I wouldn't want to go anywhere without him. Quick as shit, a lot slipperier, and twice as nasty. Now, with you back on board, we have the makings of one hell of a team."

"All the skills covered." Qrysta grinned.

"Indeed we do," I agreed.

Sneak, tank, damage, Heals—we were capable of all kinds of trickery, everyone doubling down and reinforcing each other.

I chuckled. "I would not like to meet *us* in a dark alley, I can tell you that."

Qrysta studied Oller, and her face grew serious. "You may not know anything about me, Oller," she echoed my words, "but I know something about you. The most important thing. I owe you my life. I won't forget that."

Tongue tied, Oller mumbled, "Well, Daxx, too, not just me. We just—"

"Saved my life," she interrupted firmly. "And not just my *life*, Oller. Those bastards were going to have their fun with me when they got me down. I could maybe have handled the five of them, tired though I was, but with three archers? Sooner or later, they'd have put arrows in me, especially if I started carving up their companions. And then ..."

She let us paint the picture in our own minds.

Neither Oller nor I could think what to say.

Qrysta continued. "Not a great way to go. So. Whatever I can do for you—both of you—I will. Anytime, anywhere, no exceptions."

I didn't need to say it, but Oller said it anyway. "You too."

We rode on in silence.

I thought, *then there were four.*

I was one short.

▲ ▲ ▲

Two days after we parted company with Durns and Arbett, we came over the crest of a rise and saw the north–south road in the valley below us. A couple of miles away, to our right, the walled compound of The Wheatsheaf rose at its crossroads. That was where Oller would be going to seek for word of Nyrik and Horm and to sell the horses. We assumed that even a stable as big as The Wheatsheaf's would neither want, nor could afford, to buy nine mounts all at once.

"Leave that to me," Oller said. "I know how to bargain." He would pay for their stabling up front and sell any that the stablemaster wanted to buy. The others, Oller would leave for him to sell on our behalf, on commission.

Oller and I had practiced our Thinking Into each other in the few spare moments we'd had. We were no better at it than before. He couldn't pick up my words with any certainty. However hard I Listened For him, I only heard faint noises, almost always unintelligible—and most of the time, they just seemed to be interference rather than anything I could guess might be coming from him.

There might be something there, we thought, but we had no way of being sure. The only success we thought we might have had was with his ears tingling. If he emptied his mind, thought of nothing, and listened to nothing, I could Think Into him, and sometimes he'd feel his ears tingle. It was the best we could do. Every night at sundown, he'd find a quiet spot for half an hour or so, close his eyes, and empty his mind. We agreed that, if his ears tingled, convincingly, he'd come north to find us, and we'd watch the road for him. That was our fallback plan. If, between us, we didn't manage to flush Nyrik and Horm out of cover, we'd be heading into the Undergrounds alone.

No one knew Oller by sight at The Wheatsheaf because he'd never been that far north, but his former squadmates in Serjeant Bastard's search party would recognize him if they saw him. We decided it was better that he wouldn't be seen, and that someone else would be instead, so before we came to the road I laid a Glamour on him. The big, grim bruiser that Oller now appeared to be called himself Agnolf—which sounded like a sudden punch hitting an unsuspecting nose.

"How do I look?" he said in a voice like a low growl.

"Horrible," Qrysta said, truthfully.

He laughed. It was a laugh that, coming from Agnolf's hard face, was intimidating.

"I'm going to enjoy being big and scary!"

Agnolf had coin enough to get himself a private room and as much ale and food as he wanted. He could eat and drink and listen and learn and, if anyone asked him his business, stare at them until they decided that it was nothing to them.

Before he reached The Wheatsheaf, though, Oller met someone who was going to be of great service to us. I say someone, because he became one of us; a true friend, in the way that only dogs can be—which is what he was: not a person, but a dog. He was a small, scrawny, brown, bushy-tailed fellow—and the only living creature to be seen on the road. Travel, it seemed, had come almost to a halt now that wars had broken out all over the realm. He watched us with interest as we led our string of horses onto the road.

He didn't seem frightened. Nor, when we reined in and looked more closely at him, did he seem to be much more than hair and skin and bone. His thin ribs showed clearly through his sides.

Oller, who was as soft-hearted as Agnolf was hard-faced, said, "Poor little perisher!" He dismounted and crouched down, holding out his hand for the dog to sniff.

Agnolf was indeed big, and scary he certainly looked—but the scruffy little dog wasn't scared. Dogs are not deceived by Glamours. Dogs have noses that will smell any truth that humans try to hide. He looked at Oller warily but gave a tentative wag of his tail when Oller clicked his tongue at him and said, "Come here, little guy, I won't hurt you. How's about a sausage?"

At the word *sausage*, the tail wagged more confidently. The mutt, Oller decided, reminded him of himself—a little waif, who had to fend for himself and had no one to look after him.

Qrysta and I watched as the dog went over to Oller, cautiously, wagging his scruffy brown tail—and, of course, knowing Oller for exactly who he was—a human version of himself.

"Hullo, matey." Oller reached out and scratched the little dog's ears.

The tail wagged a little more confidently. He liked Oller. And Oller liked him.

"You look like one of us, all right." Oller contemplated him. "A proper little finder! With that clever nose of yours, I bet you could find all sorts of things even I never could." The dog liked having his ears scratched. His tail wagged happily. "Seems to me that that clever nose of yours is what found *me*. You've probably had to look out for yourself all your life, eh? Foraging and finding. Hardly seems fair, on a nice little feller like you. Well, how about you tag along with me, eh? You'd be welcome for as long or as short as you please. What do you say?"

The dog licked its lips with a long, pink tongue. Then it sat and held up a paw.

Oller smiled and shook it. "Deal. Welcome aboard, little guy."

It was a thin paw that Oller was shaking at the end of a thin foreleg, both of which matched the dog's thin body.

"Time for that sausage, eh?"

The dog's ears pricked up.

Oller got up and rummaged in his saddlebag, where he found a cold sausage—one of several that we'd taken from the mercenaries' supplies.

"Here." He held it out to the dog.

The dog waited, politely, until Oller waggled the sausage for him. "Here. Go on, then."

The small dog took the sausage and then sat down and chewed it. It was gone in a moment.

The dog wagged his tail.

Oller smiled and found another sausage.

And that was how Oller found another friend, and Little Guy found his name. Oller, who had never had friends in his life before he joined My Lord of Brigstowe's army, because he was the lone wolf type and *needs no one and nothing, thank you very much*, now had a sixth friend, to go with me, Grell, Esmeralda, Marnie, and Qrysta.

"Well," I said, "looks like you'll have company while we're away."

"That I will." Oller-as-Agnolf remounted his horse. "Goodbye, mateys, and happy hunting! Come along, you—let's see what they've got to eat at The Wheatsheaf," he said to the dog, who fell in beside him as he set off with the string of horses.

"See you soon," I replied. Qrysta said, "Bye." We turned our horses to head back north and west towards the Uplands.

When I looked back, the little brown dog was trotting along beside Oller towards The Wheatsheaf, head up and alert. There was something about the two unlikely traveling companions that tugged at my heart.

Qrysta and I were on the same mission as Oller was: to find Nyrik and Horm. They would know how and where we could find the nibluns, Horm's mother being one herself. First, though, we needed to find Grell.

Now that Oller wasn't around to be confused by what we 'foreigners' were saying, Qrysta and I could talk freely. She was excited to hear about Grell and how we'd met, so I went first. I told her how I'd found myself here, and how Grell had, and how we'd been sold at auction into My Lord of Brigstowe's army, where we'd trained until we got good—Grell especially, with his beloved niblun battle-axe. Then how we and Oller had deserted after the capture of Rushtoun with Esmeralda—and everything I had learned from Marnie about our situation and what lay ahead of us.

"Well," she said when I finished my tale. "Sounds like we have a job on our hands."

"That we do," I agreed.

"An honest to gods real life quest," she mused. "And from the sound of what we'll be up against, it's good that you're a battlemage for real, Daxx. Heals and damages, blades and battle-axe. I expect we'll be needing all of those."

"And Oller's knives," I said. "You should see the little sod at work with those."

"I don't doubt I will." She didn't sound perturbed by the prospect of what lay ahead. That was the Qrysta I knew, all right. Cool as a breeze.

I turned to her in the saddle. "So. Your turn."

23

Qrysta's Tale

"I was on this little island. In a lake, high up in the hills. There was nothing but mountains and grassland and trees anywhere I looked. And all I had was two crappy swords, just about the worst damn things I'd ever seen. And I was in old leathers—britches, jerkin, boots. I mean—same as you, Daxx: *what the fuck?*"

"Unexpected, right?"

"You can say that again. Well, eventually my mind stopped racing, and I tried to figure out what to do. I pretty soon realized I'd have to swim ashore, unless I wanted to stay there forever. And the sooner I did, the longer I'd have to dry out. It was morning, and I didn't want to be soaking wet and freezing at night, wandering around in the dark. If I got it over with I could maybe run some heat into me.

"There were two small trees on the island, and I managed to hack one down—which wasn't easy with the blunt blades that were all I had. I trimmed the branches off it and tied my gear to it with my jerkin, hoping I could keep at least some of it dry. The water was so cold it took my breath away. I just kept telling myself to keep swimming and concentrate on getting ashore.

"I was frozen stiff when I made it there. I jumped up and down, beat some warmth into my arms and legs, and began to run. Downhill,

I decided, away from the mountains. Pretty soon I reached a forest of pine trees and other evergreens. I worked out which way was south and headed that way as best I could. South meant somewhere warm, and I never wanted to be cold again. Steam rose off my clothes as I jogged, mile after mile, at an easy pace. Noon came and passed. I found a path, down through the trees, and eventually came to a road.

"Two figures were coming along it from the north—going in the direction I'd be going myself. I knew they'd seen me. I waited for them as they approached. They stopped in front of me and inspected me. They were alike, but not alike, dressed in clothes that were in some ways similar to, but in other ways different from, my own. One had two swords on his back, their hilts sticking up above his shoulders, the way I carried mine. The other's swords, one long and one short, were tucked into his belt.

"And here's the thing, Daxx. They looked like me. Except they were both male."

She let that sink in.

I said, "You mean—Asian?"

She nodded then said, "Well, one kinda did, the other not so much. Big place, Asia, there are all kinds of people there. One was more my kind than the other—let's put it that way. They looked me over, and not with approval. I puzzled them like they puzzled me, it seemed.

"Then one of them, pointing at my swords, said, 'It is forbidden!'

"I thought, *uh-oh*. But I didn't want to play the wimp, so I said, 'Not where I come from.'

"He didn't like that. 'Warrior only!' He scowled.

"I said, 'I am a warrior.'

"He seemed to take that as an insult. And a challenge. He whipped his blades out of their scabbards on his back, took stance, and said, 'Show!'

"Well, I didn't want a fight—I wanted help, to know where I was, where I should go, all of that …"

Qrysta paused and gathered her thoughts. "Running with you guys, what I could do seemed fun, so I took some classes IRL, in dual wield, to see what it was really like. And they were fun, but I'd only done a couple when … this happened. Just about all I'd learned from them was how bad I was. How bad *any* beginner is. A student with just a year's experience was way better than me. And those two didn't look anything like students. They looked like they meant business.

That move of his, drawing his blades, was slick. He knew what he was doing all right, I could tell."

She shook her head and swallowed.

"I knew I was way out of my depth. I backed off, hands raised, and said, 'Listen, no. I don't want trouble.'

"That, clearly, was not an acceptable answer. The other guy had his blades in his hands so fast I'd barely seen the movement.

"I got the message. *Fight now, or you'll be fighting both of us!*

"My throat was dry, I can tell you. And my heart was racing. I was *scared*, Daxx! I mean—I knew what I *should* do, but I had no idea how to do more than the basics of it for real. So, making it as obvious as I could that I had no quarrel with them, I drew my swords.

"I knew how poor they were—even worse than *I* was, if that was possible. We circled each other. I'd said *warrior*, so he was wary. He had no need to be. I was way out of my depth, totally useless. His first attack broke through my guard, his swords only touching my blades to slap them out of the way.

"It was over in seconds. I was whacked, battered, upended, and disarmed on the ground with a sword point at my throat. I just lay there, staring up at him.

"They bound my wrists and checked out my swords. And the guy who'd kicked my ass said, with contempt, 'Warrior.' The other guy laughed and jerked on my rope so I had to follow them. From then on, they ignored me. I tried talking, but they never replied."

"So," I said. "Captive. Just like me and Grell."

Qrysta grunted a rueful laugh. "How about us World Champions, huh? Heroes to zeroes."

I could only agree. I remembered how it felt, being captured by Nyrik and Horm, trussed up to Grell in The Wheatsheaf's stables, off to be sold at auction.

"I had no idea where we were going, of course, or where I was," she continued. "And they didn't tell me. We marched until evening, turning at last off the road, back east towards the mountains. A path led into a narrow cleft between two hills and then out again into a valley. Across it, surrounded by forest, I saw a building. At first I thought it was a fortress. Then: no, a temple. Then: a monastery. My captors strolled casually towards it as if they owned the place. Suddenly, they stopped. They stiffened and adjusted their clothing.

They'd seen something unexpected. They straightened up and hurried to the entrance.

"An elderly man, dressed all in white, was standing at the top of the steps, waiting for us.

"My captors stopped below him and bowed low, holding the position. He ignored them and studied me. I studied him back. He was small, white haired, and old. The sort of old geezer you wouldn't look at twice, normally. But this wasn't normally.

"He was, clearly, in charge.

"He reached out a hand and was quickly given my swords. He turned them over in his hands, inspecting them, his face impassive. He nodded to the side of the building before turning around and going back inside.

"My captors hustled me down the steps, off to a side entrance. They led me along a corridor past kitchens and laundry rooms and storerooms. I was delivered to a sour-faced woman who ordered me to change into drab work clothes. My leathers were thrown into an incinerator. The sour-faced woman, my overseer, led me to a cell and locked me inside. There was a thin mattress on the floor, two blankets, a bowl of rice broth, a pitcher of water, and a bucket. I was too tired to think. I ate, drank, and was asleep within minutes.

"Jabs in the ribs woke me before dawn. The overseer handed me the mop that she'd been jabbing me with and a pail. I followed her out and got to work. I scrubbed. I mopped. I polished. I washed clothes and scoured pots. I mended drapes, dusted cobwebs from ceilings, and set traps for mice. I planned my escape. I thought, *hide a needle in my sleeve, gather clothing I can survive in, steal food.*

"I managed none of those things. My needles were always counted, as were the clothes I washed and ironed. The storerooms were monitored. I was locked inside my cell every night. I was the lowest of the low, an underservant to the servants, who doubled my workload with the tasks they didn't want to do. The shittiest jobs. We servants were nothing to the students, who barely glanced at us.

"The place was more than a monastery, I soon saw. It was a school. One morning, I was hauling firewood that I had chopped to the kitchen. I had to back out of the way to avoid some students heading to the combat hall, and I dropped some logs. They cursed me; one slapped my face. I knew better than to do anything but apologize and bow my head.

"It was my bad luck that, not many days later, I was washing the floor of a corridor when two of those same students came into it. They were furious that their feet were now wet! They screamed at me and kicked over my pail. One kicked me in the ribs where I knelt, head bowed. When they'd gone, I got up, looked around, and saw the elderly man watching me from along the corridor.

"He turned away and went into a room, but I knew that he had noticed me again.

"There was one job I loved: cleaning the weapons. I could just trip out on them, thinking, *if only* … . Once, when I was admiring two swords that I'd polished to a high shine, I looked up to see the overseer staring down at me. I thought I was in trouble, but she took them and inspected them, then she grunted and put them in the rack and gave me two others to work on. She knew that I wanted to steal them and run away. Which, of course, I did—but what good would they be, if I didn't know how to use them?

"So, I got two sticks and cut them to size, and every night in my cell I practiced. I knew what was in my head. You've seen me, Daxx, in action. You know how good I was in combat when we were running together."

"The best."

That calmed the tension in her voice.

She looked over at me and smiled. "As were you. So I guess you must've felt the exact same thing—*Why am I so crap, why can't I do this?*"

"Frustrating," I agreed.

"I'll say. I mean … ." A thought struck her. "Like you didn't even have a staff, right? You had to train sword and board. All I could get my hands on was mop and fucking bucket!"

I laughed at that. I could imagine Qrysta in full flow, in a horrible tight corner, battling our enemies with a mop and bucket.

"Yeah, I know, right?" she said. "I needed to get what I knew in my head into body so I could handle myself if I ever managed to get out of there. So, night after night, I'd work on my forms, sparring with invisible enemies. Night after night, practicing forms, trying to remember, getting what I knew in my head into my arms and legs. Crouching, jumping, spinning and leaping, slashing, driving, and diving away … . I could have done with a bigger cell, I can tell you. But dual wield is often close-quarter work, so I concentrated on that."

She stopped and took a deep breath, remembering.

293

"It started coming back to me, Daxxie." She looked up at me. "I had no way of knowing. I just felt it. My footwork flowed more. My shapes blended. My crouches and leaps and spins and strikes … . I'd turned a corner. All I needed was real blades in my hands.

"Totally out of the question for an underservant. It's a formal place, the Eastern School. Everything by the book. Everyone knowing their place. All calm and ordered and according to the rules, to tradition."

I could tell from the way that she said it how exasperated she must have been.

"So, I was stuck. All I could do was work on my own and think up crazy scenarios in which I'd escape with weapons, and ride off on the horse I didn't have to find you and Grell."

She smiled as she remembered how it had happened.

"Well, even underservants get their rewards if they do their work well. One morning, my overseer told me that I was considered diligent enough to have the honor of sweeping the combat hall. Which I did at dawn while the staff and students were at breakfast. I was determined to make it spotless because that would mean I'd stay out of trouble. I was daydreaming as I worked my way across, imagining myself in there with blades in my hands rather than a brush. When I got to the far end, I looked up and saw two swords mounted on the wall, a shorter one above a longer one. They were magnificent. I reached for them without thinking, as if obeying their command to take them.

"I lost myself in the beauty of their curved steel blades. Their balance was perfect. My arms felt as if they had found something that had been missing from them all my life. I started moving them around myself, stepping and turning and cutting and blocking and flowing into shapes and forms. They led, and I followed.

"Then I heard an angry shout from the doorway which jolted me out of my trance. Two students were glaring at me. I recognized them. *Logs. Wet feet. Kick in ribs. Abuse.* They strode towards me furious. *Fuck you,* I thought and pointed the blades at them.

"They stopped, shocked. They grabbed weapons from the racks and attacked.

"They came at me with everything they had. Their sparring weapons were blunts, thank the gods, because they tagged me a few times. I had plenty of bruises the next day. But I soon saw that they were nothing to be scared of. I had the measure of them."

Qrysta looked at me, elation shining bright in her eyes. "It came to me so naturally, Daxx! It was like suddenly finding myself awake after a long sleep. *Think you can get away with that?* I thought. *I don't think so.* I pricked them each, once, just to show them I could. They shrieked. I laughed. They could kill me for all I cared. I was dancing. I knew that those two couldn't kill me, they weren't good enough. They were mad and clumsy and out of their league and they knew it. I could have kept going all morning .... Then the elderly man was in the doorway, clapping his hands.

"We all froze. The students protested that I had *dishonored the school*—blah blah blah. He dismissed them, and they bowed low and scuttled out. I froze in a bow as he approached me. He waited until I looked up at him. Our eyes met. His old face didn't change, but I felt that something passed between us.

"He held out his hands. I gave him the swords, and he replaced them on the wall. He nodded, dismissing me, and I went back to cleaning.

"I couldn't tell you how exhilarated I was and, in the same moment, so totally disappointed.

"The next day, the sour-faced bitch of an overseer came to me all nervous, hurried me to his study, and knocked on the door.

"I went in. He was kneeling on the floor. He had four swords in front of him—my pieces of junk and the beauties I'd schooled the two jerks with. I knelt opposite him and bowed. He pointed at my swords. I said, 'No no!' I picked up the others, and felt them talking to me, their guile flowing into my arms. I smiled at him. I couldn't help it. 'Can I keep them?' I asked, giddy with happiness.

"He said in a voice that sounded as if it had been unused for years, 'Who are you?'

'Qrysta. Warrior. Champion.'

"He stared. He didn't buy it. 'They captured you.'

" 'I'd been swimming,' I said, 'across a cold lake. To escape a ... .' Well, I couldn't say *an island where I'd materialized out of nowhere.* So I said, '... a bear.'

"Eventually, he said, 'Bears swim.'

"The lie came easily. 'She had cubs. I was freezing, and there were two of them. I had no quarrel with them, why did they capture me? I didn't want any trouble.'

"He nodded. 'Why, indeed?' He stared at me.

"I had no answer, so I kept quiet.

"He glanced at the swords that I was still holding. 'You know the Way.'

" 'A little. Not all of it.'

"He nodded slowly as if at last understanding something that had been puzzling him. 'So, that is why. That is why you are here.'

"The next morning, in my cell, I dressed in my new student kimono. I hurried along the corridors, head down, hoping not to be noticed. One or two people looked at me, surprised. *What's the underservant doing in a kimono?*

"I made it to the hall and found my place on the left end of the line of students, the lowest position, and knelt beside them. Normally, before class, the hall is relaxed with the hum of conversation, and students and teachers stretching and warming up. Not that day. The elderly man was kneeling there, impassive, in the middle of the line of teachers. Everyone quickly and quietly got into place.

Silence fell.

The elderly man placed the palms of his hands on the mat and bowed. We all, students and teachers, did likewise.

We waited.

He turned and nodded at me.

I stood up and went to stand before him and bowed, holding the position.

" 'Qrysta,' he announced, in his soft, quiet voice. 'Warrior. Student.'

"They made my life hell," Qrysta said, cheerfully. "Did everything they could to humiliate me and hurt me. I was crap at longsword, spear and shield, flails, nunchucks, truncheon, knives, bow and arrow, quarterstaff, barehanded striking and grappling. One fucker—one of the two I'd fought off that first day—nearly tore my arm off, hauling on it long after I'd tapped out, again and again. And I was screaming, not just tapping. A teacher had to jump in and get him off me before he broke my arm. Tore him off a strip, too, but I could see the bastard wasn't sorry.

"He *was* sorry the next time we sparred dual-wield. I beat him black and blue, until he couldn't hold his weapons. Smacked him to his knees and made him tap. 'Tap,' I kept saying, and he'd tap the mat. 'Tap. Tap. Tap.' I held him there at sword point, tapping longer than I'd tapped while he tried to break my arm. They all got the message.

"Graduation, well. It had all come back to me by then. There wasn't a one of them I couldn't handle. I took on the two warriors who had captured me, and they were good, but I destroyed them. The three best

296

dual-wield graduates lined up to face me. I could see the fear in their faces as we knelt opposite each other and bowed. I'd never felt so calm. I stood. The first opponent stood for his bout. I waved the others to stand up too, to face me all together.

"I cut them to pieces. Well, not literally. We were sparring with blunts, of course.

"The elderly man, who was the master of the school, took the swords off the wall and presented them to me.

" 'Blades of honor,' he said, and we exchanged bows.

"Then he turned to the assembly and announced, 'Qrysta. Warrior. Champion.' "

"No surprise to me. Qrys," I returned her smile. "I saw you fighting those mercs. That was the Qrysta I knew, all right." *How different but similar our paths had been,* I thought. *Arrival. Capture. Training. Getting good. Becoming everything that we'd been before—only, somehow, more so.*

"That's me," she agreed. "And there's more."

After our training under Serjeant Bastard we'd earned our spurs in the battle for Rushtoun.

I had a pretty good idea what the next stage would also have been for her. "Combat?"

"Combat," she agreed.

"Do tell."

"When the cherry blossom season came, all us graduates went our separate ways. Most went east, back to the various realms that they had come from. I didn't know how they would get there, whether over land or by sea. I had exchanged few words with the other students in the weeks of our training. Many blows, but few words. Our paths, we all knew, led in different directions.

"The Master summoned me to his study where he showed me a map. He pointed to a town a long way to the south and west. 'There,' he said. I asked what was there for me, and he said, 'Honor. Gold.' Sounded good to me. I'd need gold, as who doesn't, for supplies, and information. My plan being to search for you and Grell. I had hoped, figured, that you guys would be here too, somewhere. So, his suggestion seemed a good one. I took to the road with my pack and my fine new leather armor and the two swords of honor tucked into my belt, in the new style that I had learned.

"The road took me, eventually, to Hartwell."

24

The Incident at Hartwell

"I was minding my own business," Qrysta continued, "finishing off a much-needed supper in the White Hart Inn after the last of many long days' walks, when the trouble started. The door crashed open, and four young lordlings swaggered in, demanding ale and food in loud, lordly voices. Their clothes were rich and gaudy, the hilts of their swords bound with eelskin and sharkskin, their pommels set with jewels, their scabbards bound with gold. Gems glittered everywhere about them, from cap to toe. They were all flushed with excitement.

"They were obviously well known there, and obviously unwelcome, because, as they had already done elsewhere that night, they caused trouble. It seemed that they went looking for it all over the town, and if they didn't find it, they'd make it themselves. Their ringleader was, I soon learned, Lord Rylen of Hartwell himself, newly ascended to the lordship following the long illness, and longer death, of his father. I had already heard of him and of how his father had been much loved, which the haughty new Lord Rylen wasn't. He had chafed, as his father took far too long to die, and grown sullen at the gossip that he heard, of how people were fearful of what would happen when Good Lord Hartwell died.

"What was first going to happen, now that the Month of Chivalric Mourning had finally passed, was the Grand Tourney that the new lord had announced, to celebrate his ascension to the title that was his birthright. The whole town had been ordered to make it the most splendid, most spectacular tourney that had ever been seen in those parts. There would be jousts and foot-duels and team-fights, and archery competitions for longbow and hunting bow and crossbow. Every kind of weapon would be used, from halberd to dagger.

"My Lord of Hartwell himself would participate in several events, for he was the finest blade in the city, all said—especially when they were within his hearing. The purses would be generous. Which, as I said, was why I had come there myself. There would be dancing and music. The feasting would be long and lavish, and the drinking would last late into the night.

"Hartwell was his town now, as was everything in it, and he had delighted his noble friends with his hospitality and the entertainments he found for them which, that evening, had included a fine dustup with the Town Watch. They were drinking hard and toasting each other, grabbing at the serving wenches, boasting about their deeds, and making sure to flatter Lord Rylen, when the door opened again and a stout, nervous, middle-aged man limped in. He had a bandage around his forehead. 'Begging Your Lordship's pardon.' He bowed his head to Lord Rylen. 'Rosmund Venning, Widow Venning as now is, sends to tell you Watchman Venning died of his wounds, and what are you going to do about it?'

"To which Lord Rylen replied, 'Do I look like a bloody wizard, Fillbert?'

" 'No, my lord, but—'

" 'So I can't bring the fool back to life, can I? Shouldn't have drawn his sword on me—that's provocation, that is! Not to mention treason to his liege lord. Tell the bitch to send to the undertaker and not to bother me with her squalling.'

" 'Yes, my lord, but it's customary—'

" 'Custom be damned! I'm eating my supper, can't you see that?' He turned back to his meal and took another mouthful.

"Fillbert, doggedly, stuck to his task. 'As Clerk of the Watch, it is my bounden duty to see restitutions made by those responsible for injury to, or the death of, any officers or men occurring in the line of their duties, my lord.'

"Lord Rylen, chewing slowly, turned back and was staring at Clerk Fillbert. He swallowed, wiped his mouth with the back of his sleeve, and said, quietly, 'Or?'

" 'Or arrest those responsible,' Fillbert muttered.

"The room fell silent.

"Lord Rylen continued to stare. Eventually he said, 'Do you propose to arrest me, Clerk Fillbert?'

" 'No, Your Lordship. No indeed—'

" 'Good. Then fuck off.'

" '—unless Your Lordship does not pay the widow's due.'

"Lord Rylen went still, then lowered the hunk of meat he had speared with his dagger, which had been halfway to his mouth. 'What I *pay*,'—he turned to Clerk of the Watch Fillbert—'is your bloody wages. And damned poor value for money we're getting for them with all the brawling and disturbances everywhere. The town's no better than a bear-pit! *My* town, if you care to remember.'

" 'Yes, my lord, but—'

" 'To which my noble guests, some of whom you see here, have come from far and wide for my tourney, only to find themselves set upon by *my damned Watch!*'

" 'Begging Your Lordship's pardon, but the Watchmen say they was only calming the crowd as was gathering and getting ugly, seeing as how you and your noble guests were bothering the young lass, and she only wanted to be away from—'

"The back of Lord Rylen of Hartwell's hand cracked across his face, the rings on his fingers drawing blood. Clerk Fillbert staggered backwards, tripped over a bench, and dropped to the ground in a heap. The noble lordlings laughed uproariously, none more so than Lord Rylen.

" 'Here's what you'll do, Fillbert,' Lord Rylen said as Fillbert struggled up to all fours. 'As Clerk of the Watch, you will take yourself into custody for breach of the peace—*my* peace, in which I like to dine— and lock yourself up in your cell for the night.'

"Fillbert, clutching his tender jaw stood uncertainly.

" 'Do I make myself clear?' Lord Rylen added.

" 'Yes, my lord. Crystal clear, my lord,' Fillbert mumbled in reply through broken, bleeding lips.

"Lord Rylen grunted and turned back to his meal—but stopped when he saw me watching him. His face changed from a sneer of pleasure to a scowl.

" 'What are you looking at, girl?' he demanded.

"Well, I didn't want any trouble, so I replied, 'Nothing.' But I don't think he liked the way I said it. Perhaps he was expecting me to beg his pardon or something. Whatever, he took offence.

" 'Did you say *nothing*?' he demanded. 'I'm not bloody *nothing*, I'm Lord Rylen of Hartwell. This is my town! And be damned to your impudence!'

"Well, there was no answer to that, so I just shrugged, turned to the fire beside me, and took another mouthful of ale.

"That appeared to irk him even more. I was getting pretty pissed at him myself—but trying not to show it.

" 'I'm talking to you, woman!'

"Well, that was hardly what I'd call polite. But I thought I'd give him one more chance.

" 'I heard you,' I said. "And yes, I said *nothing*. None of my business. Not interested.'

"It didn't work. I could see his face flushing with anger. He was probably not used to being talked to like that, being nobility. Least of all by a girl. Well, that was his problem.

"Seems that he wanted to make it my problem as well. He noticed my swords which were resting beside me in their scabbards. As you've seen, they're beauties. 'Where did you get those?' He pointed at them.

" 'That is none of *your* business.'

"Lord Rylen rose to his feet. He walked over towards me, pushing past groggy Fillbert. All eyes were now on him and me. *Okay*, I thought. *If that's the way you want it.*

"He glared down at me and said, 'Everything in this town is *my* business.'

" 'Then I'll be leaving.'

" 'Not without my say-so, girl!'

" 'Then be so good as to say it, my lord, and I'll be on my way.'

" 'No, you won't!' he said. 'With your stolen swords? Fillbert, arrest this thief.'

" 'They're not stolen, I earned them.'

" 'Hah! Earned them? On your back, I've no doubt.'

"Now he was really pissing me off," Qrysta told me, her eyes glinting at the memory.

I knew Qrysta when she got that look. *Uh-oh*, I thought. *This could get spicy.*

I could understand why she was annoyed. "I'm impressed you held back as much as you did, Qrys. That's not like you."

Qrysta smiled then shrugged. "It's like me now. Better to avoid trouble than get into it, if possible. If there's no reason to. Right?"

I saw her point. "Right."

She continued her tale. "I replied, as evenly as I could manage, 'Those I earned them from indeed ended up on their backs with the point of my blade at their throats.'

"He laughed. Not very convincingly. He could tell I wasn't intimidated, and that bothered him. I could see him thinking, but I knew what he'd decide. He needed to put the insolent wench in her place.

" 'Oh, fancy yourself as a swordsman, do you?' he mocked.

" 'No,' I said, 'swords*woman.*'

" 'Hah! There's no such thing!'

" 'There is. You're looking at one.'

" 'Nonsense. I'm looking at a thief. Fillbert, arrest this thief as I ordered!'

"Not taking my eyes off Lord Rylen, I said, 'There's no need for that, Clerk Fillbert. I'll be leaving now. Shame. I was looking forward to your lordship's tourney tomorrow. Some rich purses to be won, word is.'

" 'Not by bloody *women* there aren't!' the fool shouted. 'Least of all a thieving bitch like you.'

"I thought, *what?* I've come all this way for the tourney to win some gold, and I'm not even allowed to enter? I needed to make sure that I could. 'Now then, my lord,' I said, gently, 'there's no need to go using ungallant words.'

"It worked. 'I'll use any bloody words I want!' Lord Rylen roared. 'Now hand over those stolen swords and be off to the cells with you! And no more words from you, or I'll send my question-master down to make your night a lot less comfortable!'

"I just said, 'No.'

"That shut him up—for about two seconds. 'What do you mean, *no?* Fillbert, gentlemen, I do believe we have a lawbreaker on our hands!'

"Then the other noble lordlings were on their feet, their swords drawn and closing in behind Lord Rylen.

" 'This is your last chance, my lord,' I warned him, not moving, 'To sit back down and stop making a fool of yourself.'

"He scowled, his hand moving to the hilt of his sword. 'How dare you, you insolent slut—'

"I moved while he was still jabbering, throwing my table up into his legs, knocking him backwards, then I had my blades out of their scabbards and snapped across his throat, like scissors. He froze, having managed to draw no more than six inches of his own sword. The other noble lordlings froze too, as did every other person in the room.

" 'Now,' I said, 'perhaps you're thinking, *that's not fair, I haven't drawn my blade.* I was not going to let you do that. It would have led to a disturbance, which the good landlord of this fine inn and his peaceable guests do not deserve to have interrupt their pleasant evening. Perhaps you're also thinking, if you *had* drawn your blade, you could have given a better account of yourself? So, here's my suggestion, my lord: why don't we see?'

"He couldn't manage anything more than 'Gghhh …'

"I needed to goad him a little bit, so I went on, 'There's no need to be frightened, my lord. My blades are sharp, but they won't cut your skin. Not unless I want them to. What do you think, sirs?' I said to his companions. 'Might it not be chivalrous of me to give His Lordship here another chance? Tomorrow say, at the tourney? I don't know as it would be a good thing if it got about that he was scared of facing a *girl*.'

"The other noble lordlings all considered that that was a perfectly reasonable suggestion. Indeed, an honorable one."

I said, "Neatly done, Qrys!"

"Thank you."

"Excellent way to gate-crash a party."

"Yep. He couldn't freeze me out now. So, I looked at Lord Rylen and said, 'Very well, we'll meet again on the morrow, my lord. And you, gentlemen, can put your blades away, you won't be needing them tonight. Tomorrow perhaps you can bare them again, should you feel so inclined.'

"The lordlings sheathed their weapons and backed away.

" 'I won't be needing the hospitality of your cells, Clerk Fillbert,' I told him. 'I've a room here, thank you all the same. To which I will be heading now, I think. It's been a long, hard day, and tomorrow will be longer. Though not so hard. I'd rather dance a few minutes than walk a dozen hours. Until tomorrow, my lord?'

"I relaxed my blades an inch and waited until Lord Rylen said, 'Hhyes …'

" 'Well, now you know my business, and I have your permission to go about it. I look forward to meeting you again.' I removed my swords from his throat.

"The idiot wasn't done. 'You'll pay for that, bitch!' he gasped, feeling his throat.

" 'No, my lord, *you* will. With the handsome prize money that we all know you are offering.'

"And that was that. I sheathed my blades, finished my ale, and left. I was glad to see that the door of my room had two thick bolts on it. I slid them home. *His town*, I thought. You never know what a bully like that might try in the night.

"Or at the tourney itself, of course, but I'd have to wait and see what that might be. First, there was gold to be won. It was a fine morning—and a fine occasion. The field was bright with color and filled with people—combatants, grooms with their horses, servants, knights attended by their squires, lords and ladies, merchants, dignitaries, and common folk.

"First up were the jousts, which Lord Rylen himself won, unhorsing one of his companion lordlings from the night before in the final pass, to loud acclaim from the townsfolk. Then it was archery, the Hunting Bow won by two small, wiry Woods Kin, who split the shafts of each other's winning arrows from fifty paces for fun.

"The Great Warbow went to a tall, dour Southern lad who never cracked a smile, not even when awarded a yew longbow far finer than the one he'd shot with as well as the purse of a hundred gold. He strung it without effort and loosed a couple of shafts at the target, seemingly without aiming, and both buried themselves in the splinters of the arrows that the two Woods Kin had split for fun. The captain of His Lordship's guard won the crossbow trial, bolt after bolt thudding home into the gold. Lord Rylen handed out the prizes, and the spectators applauded and cheered.

"Then came the foot fights: first pikes, then morningstars and shields, finally sword and board, which was won by My Lord Rylen of Hartwell himself, who fought far better than he had behaved the night before. I watched him carefully, and what I saw didn't worry me. What worried me was what I *didn't* see. I suspected he'd try something underhand, but—well, I'd just have to keep my wits about me.

"Seeing him floor opponent after opponent, the townsfolk warmed to their hard lord as they had never done before. With him protecting them, I heard it said, it would take a brave enemy to threaten their town. They cheered him as he won the final bout and laughed with him as he awarded himself a purse of gold with a lordly, 'Your prize, Champion,' and answering himself, in a comically thick accent with a tug of his forelock, 'Thankee kindly, m'lud!'

"All that had been leading up to the main event: the freestyle. Whatever you wanted to wield against whatever your opponent wanted. This was what the crowd had been waiting to see. So far, fighters had been using blunts of equal size and weight, so no one had an advantage. In the freestyle, we would be using our own weapons, sharps—and that would mean blood and wounds, and possibly death.

"While waiting, the onlookers had been eating, drinking, and working themselves up into a fine state of excitement. I saw people making bets left and right. When the fights began, the roars began, the cheers and boos, laughter and mockery, and shrieks of dismay. Bones were broken, blood spilt. Every kind of match and mismatch happened in front of their eyes, and by the time they'd seen battle-axe defeated by daggers, and spear and shield defeated by a half-naked wrestler armed only with a slingshot, no one knew what to think. One by one, the combatants presented themselves. One by one, they advanced to the next round or limped off defeated. Crowd favorites began to emerge: the half-naked wrestler; a spearman from the distant east as quick as a striking snake.

"When I took the field, the hubbub of the crowd fell silent. Then the whispers started. Word of the night before had clearly spread. My first opponent was a big brute with a broadsword. I bowed to him the way I'd been trained, but it seemed the Hartwell folk had never seen that before, and some of them laughed. They didn't laugh for long. The man charged, the way big brutes with broadswords always do, and I waited, then moved at the last moment—fast. He was on his back on the ground with the point of my blade at his throat before he knew what had happened. I heard the gasps of the crowd.

I let him up and stepped back, letting him know he was welcome to try again.

"He did—more cautiously this time.

"I wanted to send a message to Lord Rylen, so when he came again, I twirled him around a little, then whacked him on the backside with the flat of both blades, *one—two.*

"The crowd enjoyed that as he jumped and turned, panting.

"Then, I pushed one of my swords point first into the ground. And waited.

"He charged. I feinted, twisted my blade around the longsword and, using his momentum, steered it hard into the ground where it stuck. He heaved at it, but stopped heaving when he felt the point of my blade at his throat again. He froze. I nodded. I stepped back and bowed. He removed his hands from the hilt of his broadsword and returned my bow. Then he tugged his broadsword from the ground and walked off to sit in the crowd with the other losers. I retrieved my sword and wiped it carefully before sheathing both blades and heading back to my place on the bench.

"One by one we fought and won or lost. The losers left, and the winners returned to the bench. There were some skilled fighters among them. When I was up against the wrestler, I used two wooden sticks instead of my blades. They were easier to use to flick away the stones from his slingshot while dancing around him and numbing his legs and arms with blows that he never saw coming and couldn't dodge. At last, panting, he limped to a halt, unable to walk. He returned my bow, and I helped him from the field.

"The spearman from the east was a challenge. Quick, too. But I was quicker. His reach with his spear was much longer than mine, but I got inside it when I could, slipping below and around his feints and thrusts. I danced until he overreached once too often, then I was low, and wrapped around his legs where he could not jab at me. I pulled him down and rolled him, twisting onto my back beneath him, my heels holding the insides of his thighs, my arm locked across his throat. He choked, and tapped my arm in surrender. He was the toughest. Then there was a knifeman, a net-and-trident man, and two sword and boards—useful practice for what was going to follow.

"Finally, it was just me and the axe-and-whip man left on the bench. I'd watched him, of course. He knew what he was doing. His whip was lightning fast and much longer than I could reach. We faced each other. I could feel the crowd's anticipation. I bowed, but he didn't bow in return, which I thought rude. Instead, he cracked his whip above his head in his customary challenge. I waited, out of its range. Then I approached slowly, walking towards him with my swords crossed in front of me, pointed at him.

"He didn't seem to know quite what to make of that. I saw him decide and nod, then his whip lashed out and twisted itself around both blades, knotting them together where they met. He smiled and heaved on it to jerk me forwards so he could use his axe. I didn't resist, but ran towards him as he pulled and opened my arms. The edges of my blades were pointing outwards, away from each other—and those edges are as sharp as razors. The thick leather of his whip parted as if it were thread.

"Expecting resistance, he tottered backwards. I stood in front of him, swords wide, now blade-inwards towards him. He still had half a whip. He flailed it at me. I scissored my swords in the air, catching his whip in mid lash, and again it was halved. I took another pace, to within the range of his axe. He raised it, but that was what I expected. I had the point of one blade in his armpit and chopped the whip off at its handle with the other. I pushed him higher and higher onto his toes, while staring at him, waiting for him to do the only thing he could. Which he did.

"He dropped the axe, and the handle that was all that remained of his whip.

"He had the grace to return my bow, and while the crowd cheered and applauded, I walked to Lord Rylen of Hartwell for my prize.

" 'A fine day, my lord,' I said, 'and my congratulations on a fine tourney. I wish you a long and prosperous life as lord of this fine town.'

"I thought, *the politer I look, the worse he will*. Give him enough rope to hang himself.

"Lord Rylen rose to his feet. 'You think to flatter me so I will forget your insults.'

"*Okay, here we go*. I replied, 'You think to provoke me so I will forget my manners.'

"He laughed. 'Manners? Are they to be expected from such as you?'

" 'Such as I? You mean, your champion here today? Yes, my lord, they are. You saw me treat my brave opponents with respect. I treat even a coward and a bully with respect, my lord, until he needs to be shown that he does not deserve it.'"

"Nice," I smiled at her cunning. "Trap set?"

She nodded. "Yup, and trap blundered into."

"Remind me never to mess with you, okay?"

She looked at me, eyes wide and innocent. "Now why would you ever want to do that, Daxxie?"

I laughed. "Go on."

"It got him as I thought it would. He said, 'Do you name me coward?'

"I said, 'I name no names. Is that how you think of yourself?'

" 'I do not,' he snarled. 'And I shall prove it to you!'

"I had him where I wanted him. 'And I shall prove what you are for all to see, my lord, but the price of my lesson will be high.'

" 'Your lesson will be at my hands, bitch!'

"I thought, *okay, that's enough. I'm going to enjoy this.* 'That name again. One time too many, I think. Well, let us dance then, if my brave lord is brave enough.'

" 'I'll cut your damned insolent head off!'

"Yes, he was steaming. Good. 'And if you do not,' I warned him, 'I shall take your sword and your purse and the rings you broke Clerk Fillbert's face with and your charger, upon which you rode so prettily this morning. And I shall take one other thing as well, my lord. Your pride.'

"I waited at the center of the field while Lord Rylen was armed by his squires. A servant came out with him carrying a tray with two cups of wine. He held one out to me and took one himself.

" 'A toast,' he proposed, 'as is traditional. To the victor, the spoils.'

" 'A fine toast,' I agreed, though I did not take the cup of wine. 'But I'll not be drinking any of your drugged wine, my lord.'

Lord Rylen scowled. 'You accuse me now of intending to drug you?'

" 'Drink it yourself if it is safe, my lord.'

"Lord Rylen hesitated. 'Hah! You wish me to get drunk so you stand a chance, is that it?'

" 'No,' I replied, 'and you know it isn't. Let us stop talking, my lord, and dance.'

"Well, I soon saw what he had planned by way of dirty tricks. He had soldiers placed around the arena, each with a shield polished to a mirrorlike sheen. When the bout began, they angled their shields to

308

shine the sun into my eyes. And when Lord Rylen saw me screwing up my eyes against the glare, he smiled, because he knew he had the measure of me and was about to have his revenge.

"I stopped dancing—of which Lord Rylen was pleased, because he was blowing hard in his chainmail—and held up my hand.

'Would my lord care to ask his friends to stop shining the sun into my face?'

" 'What friends?' he said.

" 'The ones that you have ordered to shine the sun into my face.'

" 'Do you call me a cheat now as well as a coward?'

"I sighed. 'No, my lord, I call you a fool. If you would give me a moment …' and while Lord Rylen prepared to fight again, I wound a cloth around my eyes and tied it behind my head.

" 'When my lord is ready.' I sank into my stance.

"It wasn't as difficult as it sounds. He was making enough noise in his chainmail to be heard fifty yards away. He rushed, slashed, feinted, roared, and finally got it through his thick head that silence was a better tactic. Which it would have been if he could have moved in silence, but he couldn't. I waited for an overhead blow and caught his blade on both of mine, crossed above my head, their sharp edges turned down and inward from his so that they took no damage. While his weight was all forward on his front leg, I stamped down with the outside of my boot and snapped the kneecap off his knee. He fell, gasping, while I swept his sword from his grip.

"I took off my blindfold, gagged him with it as he struggled to rise, and put my blade to his throat.

" 'I will take my prizes now.' I jabbed at his neck so that he bled and coughed and edged backwards. I took his sword. 'Your purse,' I said, and when he didn't move, I slashed it from his belt with my other blade. 'Your rings. Or do I need to cut those free too?'

"He removed his rings and handed them to me.

" 'Bring my lord's horse,' I told his squires, 'and a donkey too, if you please.'

"The squires hurried to obey. All the while the crowd was buzzing and murmuring with excitement and confusion, but they didn't bother me. What concerned me was His Lordship's guards. They were gathering with their crossbows but didn't seem to know what to do. When the animals arrived, I prodded Lord Rylen toward the donkey and told him to mount. He did. I tied his legs beneath him so that he could not jump from its back. I lashed the donkey's rein to my saddle and mounted his charger.

" 'We are leaving,' I announced. 'I will take His Lordship with me for safe conduct, for it seems that I cannot trust his word. I will release him when I see fit, and he will make his way back to you unharmed, if the gods be willing. And you can welcome him back or not as you please.'

"The guards seemed to wake up at that and hurried to form a line ahead of us. Before they could raise their crossbows, another line had formed facing them. Every archer who had entered the competition was pointing their bows at them, arrows drawn. The guards had seen how good they were—and that they were outnumbered.

" 'She won fair and square,' one of the little Woods Kin champions said.

" 'Which is not how that bastard fought,' the other said. 'So stand down and let her pass.'

"They did.

"There was a brazier full of hot coals by Lord Rylen's pavilion, on which chestnuts were roasting. I kicked it over as we passed, and the silks and satins of the pavilion caught fire at once. The flames distracted the guards and the crowd as I dug my heels into the charger's flanks and cantered away, Lord Rylen bouncing behind me on his donkey."

25

Friends Old and New

Once clear of the town Qrysta had put her spurs into her horse's flanks and headed south. She rode hard, Lord Rylen bumping along behind her. She stopped as evening fell and untied him. She told him to walk home, or rather limp, with his dislocated knee, and rode on south. After dark, she added the donkey to a farmer's field, which had a couple of horses in it, and a mile further on turned west off the road into woodland and began working her way north. She hoped that she'd disguised her trail well enough.

She hadn't.

The hunting party from the Mercenaries' Guild had found it, and they'd herded her all the way into the far west. The rest I knew.

I had told Qrysta that we should avoid traveling on the road. Anyone we passed would be going south and could take news of us with them. Perhaps the description of a man and a woman going about their business would not mean much to anyone, but we didn't want to risk word of us getting back to Serjeant Bastard.

So, we stayed west of the road that Oller had ridden south along, under his Glamour as Agnolf. We had maps to help us now, and I had a reasonable idea of where I'd first met Nyrik and Horm, back off to the east across the road, but it was a big wilderness and sooner or later we'd need to find them or ask after them.

The trouble was, of course, that they were experts at hiding. I hadn't been able to see them when they had been teasing me by shooting arrows out of nowhere into the trees I'd been 'sparring with.' That was one reason why it would be good to have Grell back with us. They'd be bound to spot a large Orc on their turf. Especially one they'd recognize—and, with luck, would think was a pacifist and completely useless in a fight. They probably wouldn't give Qrysta a second glance. *Only a girl*, they'd think. Well, that was what I was hoping, anyway.

The other reason we needed Grell in the team again was that we had a mission now, and Marnie had said time was short. We might never find Nyrik and Horm. We couldn't wander around looking for them forever. Sooner or later we'd need to go with Plan B. Which was, basically, to head into the Undergrounds by ourselves and find our way to the floor of the world.

I'd only had a moment to glance over the dead researcher's notes, but from what I'd already seen I was sure they'd reveal a lot of useful information. We now also had the ancient silk map that Oller had found. *If needs must*, I thought, *we'd be going into the Undergrounds not entirely unprepared*. So, while Oller went south to The Wheatsheaf, Qrysta and I headed for Stonefields.

Where, I told her, I hoped we'd find Grell and Klurra.

"Who's Klurra?" she asked.

I told her. She enjoyed hearing how we'd met her, walking down out of the mists of the Uplands and challenging Grell—and how that challenge had, well, climaxed.

"Wish I'd been there to see that." She chuckled. "Grell of the Ozgaroos, huh? That was quick thinking. There's more to Grell than meets the ear, I've always thought. When he's running with us, he's relaxing, talking smack, and being a big tough Aussie. Strikes me, though, that he's got a bit of a brain on him. I wonder what he does in real life. Something high powered, I wouldn't be surprised."

"I think you mean, *did*."

She grunted. "Yeah ..."

I hesitated for a minute then worked up the courage to ask, "Now that we're here ... does the old rule still apply?"

"What old rule?" she asked.

"The one you and Grell insisted on. That we never talk about who we are, behind our avatars."

"I think you mean *were*," she echoed.

"Exactly," I agreed. "I doubt we're ever going back."

Qrysta looked surprised. "Why d'you say that?"

"Because, if you think about it, however they did this to us—got us here, made us into what we are—that can't have been just a snap of the fingers. A bit of a process, you'd think, right? So … if they did this for a reason, as we're all assuming, that's because they *want* us here. Why would they have a reason to *un*-do it all and want us back where we came from? I can't think of one. Can you?"

Qrysta said, "To make up to us for the inconvenience?"

"Pretty weak reason, Qrysta. And one that assumes they have *our* best interests at heart, rather than their own."

"Yeah," she agreed, "I see your point."

"Not that I want to go back," I said. "I dunno about you, but this is way better than my previous life. To be here, doing what I do best. Being *this* guy, instead of who I was before." I inhaled the fresh spring air and smiled. "Yes, this works for me."

"So, who were you, before?" she asked, ditching the rule of not talking about our real—or previously real—lives.

"Believe it or not, I was *not* a battlemage-slash-healer."

She chuckled. "Actually, I do believe you."

"When I built Daxx," I continued, "I made sure he was everything that I wasn't. I would have loved to have been anything as fine as this."

Qrysta looked at me, her head cocked to one side. In the casual tone she used for our smack talking, when she had a barb to toss out, she said, "Is this the bit where you expect me to tell you how cute you are?"

I grinned and shook my head. I wasn't falling for whatever she had in mind.

"Nah, Qrys. That would take all day, and I want to hear what you've been up to."

That got a smile out of her. After a while she said, "Anything else you want to tell me?"

I considered that. I couldn't see the benefit in dragging up my old life. Who cared who I once was? Or who she and Grell had been? This was who we were now, and she seemed as happy with that as I was.

"Not really. You?"

"Nope," she said.

I hoped she'd volunteer further information about herself, but she didn't.

"So ... no names, no pack drill?" I hinted.

She reined in and turned to me. "You first."

"No, you."

"Why?"

"Ladies first. It's only polite."

She studied me, and a knowing smile grew on her face.

"I love you, Daxxie, but I don't trust you farther than I can throw Grell. We're here now, right? This is who we are. What else matters? I mean—what could be better?"

I could only agree.

"When I was running Qrysta, my life was better. It was ... come *on!* You know, right? Fuller. Richer. Unlimited. I was free. I wouldn't go back now if I had the choice. Not now that I'm ... *this.*"

I knew exactly what she meant, and I felt exactly the same. "That was then, this is now. What difference does it make, right?"

She relaxed. "Right. Ancient history."

And that, I thought, *was that.*

It wasn't. We rode on, but only for a few paces.

"My name was Francis," she said abruptly, "and I was a geek."

"Hi, Francis," I said, automatically playing my role in her disclosure, as if we were in a recovery support session.

"Everyone calls me Frankie. Or did. I'm—was—forty-two years old, six foot one, scrawny rather than fat, but no athlete, badly balding so there's only the sides left, and I shave those. I'm a ... ." She hesitated. "... was, I mean, a ... dentist. Who spends all the time he can pretending to be a hot warrior chick."

I'd reined in, staring at her, open-mouthed.

Qrysta looked back at me and shrugged. "What can I say?"

I just gaped at her. Not that I thought it was bad if Qrysta had actually been a man named Francis in real life. That would be my problem, not hers. But I'd just been given a whole new, and very different, mental picture to wrap my head around.

Qrysta was watching me to see how I'd taken the news. Suddenly she burst out laughing. "Oh, *man*, if you could see the look on your face! Got you *good*, Daxxie!" She shook her head, delighted with herself. "Couldn't think what the dude could have been. Dentist? *Jeez!*" She started her horse back on the path. "Nope, I was a grad student. IT, if you must know, from Orange County, and that's all I'm saying. Except that I was a geek and a hardcore gamer chick and"—she spread her arms wide, giving me a huge smile—"*just the fuck look at me now!*"

When I'd recovered from her one-two punch I said, "You bastard."

"Yep," she said, happily.

I shook my head but smiled. "We can work on your delivery. Polish it up. Lay it on Grell."

"Yeah, we should," she agreed. "You think dentist?"

"Dentist is good. Father. Divorced. Francis is perfect, could be male or female."

"I have an Uncle Francis. He always says, 'Francis with an 'i', not an 'e'. *'I' for 'im, 'e' for 'er'.*'"

"Authentic. He needs some creepy habits, your Frankie. Make Grell's skin crawl."

"Such as?"

"I dunno." My voice trailed off as I wondered what we could cook up to prank Grell.

"Well, what creepy habits do *you* have, Daxx?" Qrysta prompted. "I mean, *did* you have?"

"None," I said.

"You're lying."

I laughed. "And you *aren't* lying?"

She chuckled, her eyebrows rising. "You can think of me as Frankie if it turns you on, Daxx."

I glanced at her, and my look said it all. *I'd rather think of you as Qrysta. That's what turns me on. And that's who you are.*

I saw her reaction, amusement turning to wariness, and I knew I needed to backtrack to reassure her. "We are who we always wanted to be, right?"

She relaxed and nodded.

"Like you said: *'Just the fuck look at me now!'*"

It took a moment to sink in.

We were on the same page.

"Yeah," she said.

We rode on.

Later on, I thought, *well ... I didn't learn a whole lot about her*. Orange County? Plausible. Frankie? I had to hand it to her, that had freaked me out. No, I liked Qrysta just the way she was. *But then*, I thought, *who cared?* What I'd said earlier echoed in my mind. *That was then, this is now. We were who we wanted to be.*

I remembered Qrysta's words:

I wouldn't go back now if I had the choice. Not now that I'm ... this.

I couldn't agree more.

▲   ▲   ▲

Two days later, we came across an Orc.

He was the Stonefields blacksmith, returning from a trading trip to a neighboring tribe. His cart, drawn by two massive dray horses, was piled high with merchandise.

That included a new anvil, which alone must have weighed nearly as much as he did, and as many iron ingots as he could fit on board. The cart was leaning to one side over a broken wheel. He was inspecting it dolefully and scratching his head when we reined up beside him and asked if we could help. He was surprised at the offer and even more surprised when I said, "Klurra says, 'weasel.'"

He brightened at that and said, "Friends of Klurra's, are you? Well, that's good enough for me. I could fix this blasted axle no problem if'n it weren't so laden down. I always carry spare wheels. 'Specially when I'm going trading. Big loads break 'em all the time. Can't get it on, though. It'd take a deal more strength than I've got in these old shoulders to lift this lot."

Old those shoulders may have been, but they were the shoulders of an Orc blacksmith. They made Grell's shoulders look puny by comparison. I doubted that Qrysta and I would add much in the way of lifting power.

I dismounted. "I can help you. We can lighten the load and build up a jack."

The Orc said, "A what-now?"

I explained. We'd pile up iron bars from his cart under it, use another bar to lever it up, get it clear of the ground, and replace the wheel that way. He looked at the wheel, the axle, the load, and the path one after the other, scratched his head again and frowned.

"That'd work?" he queried.

"It'll work," I said.

"How d'you know?"

"Science."

He didn't know the word. "Well, I dunno."

Qrysta said, "How far to Stonefields? Your … village?"

The blacksmith smiled, shaking his head. "Don't know much about Orcs do you, miss? *Stronghold* not village. Walled and ditched and staked, just the way we like it. No one here but us Orcs in the Uplands, but—*Orcs*, eh? Any excuse for a scrap. That way we can keep unwanted visitors outside and meet them there so we can settle things without them trashing the place. Makes sense, if they kill the lot of us, they get a nice, free, undamaged stronghold."

"Is it far?" Qrysta repeated the question.

"Hour's ride on a good horse. With these old buggers I'd make it by nightfall if I had a working cart. As it is …"

"I'll ride there and get help," Qrysta said.

The Orc looked at her surprised. "You'd do that?"

"For a friend of Klurra's." She smiled.

"Well now, miss, that's a handsome offer, I must say!" the black-smith said. "I'd be much obliged. Much obliged indeed."

He told her the way, which was basically follow the path till you come to the stronghold.

"Qrys," I said, "you've never met Klurra, I should go."

"I've met Grell, and she's with him, right? He'd vouch for me."

I said to the Orc blacksmith, "When did she get back? Klurra and her friend?"

He was still thinking about jacks and levers. "Eh? Klurra went somewhere?"

"On a quest. We met her on her way to it."

"Oh ah," he said, "that's Klurra all right, always gallivanting off. When was this?"

I calculated. "A couple of weeks ago."

"Ah, well, I wouldn't know, then. I've been gone a month. There was a lot of work over at Bogginmoor what with their smith dropping dead and his apprentice useless, then the other tribes sending in for this and that and trading and all. Got this lovely new anvil though, reward from Chief Orbruk, for all I done for them. There'll be plenty of work waiting at home for it and me to get stuck into after a month away, if'n I can ever get the damn thing there at all. Oh well, wishing won't get you nowhere as the saying goes."

At which I couldn't help laughing.

"What's so funny?" He glared at me.

I backed away quickly and shook my head. "Me. I can't believe what an idiot I am at times, Mr. ...?"

"Ron the Smith, they call me, short for Ironwright—same as my dad and his, that being as what we are, all us Smiths going back."

"Well, Mr. Smith, first let me introduce my partner, Qrysta Blades, named after what she wields."

"I noticed them," Ron the Smith said. "Unusual. Never seen the like. I'd be interested to take a closer look when we get home."

"I'll be happy to show them to you," Qrysta said.

"My name is Daxx, and I was laughing at myself for my stupidity in not realizing that I have the solution to your little problem. Which I did when you said, *wishing*."

"Little!" He snorted. "You call this *little?*"

I reached for Shift in her sling below my saddle. "If you wouldn't mind stepping back, Mr. Smith?"

His eyes grew round when he saw Shift with her glowing tourmaline heartstone eye opening up. He knew what a stave like that meant, and he backed warily away from his cart.

It took no more effort to Levitate the side of his cart than it had taken to Levitate Marnie. You don't have to *think* harder to move a heavier weight. You just have to think right.

"Well, I'll be ...!" Ron the Smith said as his cart righted itself, its axle parallel to the ground as if it had an invisible wheel on it, unwavering.

"Over to you," I said.

In less than a minute he had the spare wheel on the axle and wedged into place with a few taps of his hammer.

And that was how we rode into the stronghold of the Stonefields Orcs in the hour before sunset, escorting Ron the Smith and his cart full of merchandise. Orc children tumbled out of the gates when they opened. They ran and skipped around us, laughing and chattering and asking questions nineteen to the dozen as Orc sentries stared down at us from the walls and called down greetings to Ron. The area within was like a village green, with huts and booths and stalls on all sides,

318

from which people, or rather Orcs, were pouring. Among them, striding towards us with huge grins on their faces, were Grell and Klurra.

Grell saw me first, probably because I looked familiar to him after all these months together, or perhaps because I'm taller than Qrysta. He hooted and broke into a run at the sight of me, his arms wide. I smiled and pointed across the cart to Qrysta, who was sitting on her horse smiling at him, her arms crossed, waiting. He glanced at her, looked back at me—and then stopped dead in his tracks and did the most perfect double take I'd ever seen.

It ended with him staring at Qrysta in astonishment.

"Hey, Grello," she said, casually. "Wassup?"

Grell threw his head back and let out a roar of joy. "Are you kidding me?" he bellowed. "*Are you fucking kidding me!*"

Qrysta slid off her horse and jogged over to him. "Oh, man. Is it good to see you!"

She held up a hand, for him to high five, which he did. The Orcs had never seen a high five before. All the Orc kids immediately started copying it, shrieking with laughter. Then they copied the next thing Grell did. He enveloped Qrysta in a bear hug and whirled her around whooping. The place was soon full of whirling children, grabbing each other and hooting, falling over and scrambling up to try again. The mood was infectious, and soon everyone was at it, grabbing a partner and whirling and whooping and then putting them down and high fiving.

And that was the beginning of the best party I have ever been to. It didn't lead to a delightful aftermath, like the victory feast in Rushtoun had led to with Deb. It led, rather, to the worst hangover I've ever suffered.

But, *oh*, how I earned it—that long, uproarious night in the Great Hall in the stronghold of Stonefields.

26

Grell's Tale

I learned a lot about Orcs that night—and above all, that Orcs know how to celebrate.

It doesn't take much of an excuse for them to throw a party—no more, Klurra told me, than it takes much of an excuse for them to start a fight. They keep their two favorite pastimes rigorously separated. It is as much Bad Orc Form to start a fight at a party as it is Bad Orc Form to stop a fight *for* one. Orcs like to finish what they started, not to get confused by what they started being diverted into something else. So, although it wasn't long before most of us were well into the spirit of the evening, there was never a hint of trouble.

Old enemies slapped each other on the back, and chortled, and clashed mugs and drank, and teased each other rotten with tears of mirth rolling down their eyes. I'd never have thought to have heard such threats and curses and insults met with nothing but howls of delight. It seemed that the more you insulted someone the more he or she enjoyed the quality of your insults. Orcs were rolling on the floor clutching their sides at suggestions that they were feeble, weaklings, cowards, tossers who couldn't find their own arseholes with both hands, and other such jibes; and anyone within earshot was laughing both at and with them.

Their competitive nature came out not in combat but in party games. A favorite, which soon started and kept recurring again and again that long, liquid night was called *You're So Pathetic*. The rules were simple. The challenger had to turn to his neighbor, look him or her in the eye and say, "You're so pathetic that you couldn't …" and then add something original and insulting and absurd without laughing or looking away before the person they'd said it to laughed or looked away. It's quite something to see two villainous-looking Orcs staring at each other defiantly, nostrils twitching with suppressed laughter, turning purple and holding their breath so that their eardrums are near bursting, while everyone around them piles in with jeers and cheers and goofy faces over their shoulders at the suffering contestants.

Uproarious enough, you'd think, if that was all there was to it. There was more. The Orc who is challenged as being *so pathetic that you couldn't* has to have a mouthful of beer, enough to have his or her cheeks distended to the max. Then the challenger loads up with a mouthful and the staring and glaring and jeers and cheers begin. If the challenged Orc loses and blows it all out into the face of the challenger, then all around them let out a big *hooray*, raise their mugs, fill their mouths, and join in with a countdown from five on the challenger's hand, everyone going "*Mmnh!*" at each number, because *mmnh!* with a mouthful of beer sounds like any number. At zero, when the challenger makes an *O* zero with thumb and forefinger, they all blow their beer out into the face of the loser.

As well as being the best party I've ever been to, it was also the wettest. Grell, being a foreign Orc from a place where they'd never heard of *You're So Pathetic*, was terrible at it. I could crack him up with a simple waggle of the eyebrows and got a face full of Grell-warmed beer for my pains every time. The only person who never lost was Qrysta, merry though she was from the excellent Orcish ale.

In a quiet moment, I asked her how she did it. I say *quiet moment*, but I still had to yell above the pandemonium all around us to be heard. "You ever see me lose my cool in combat, Daxxie?" she replied. I hadn't and shook my head. She smiled at me. That was Qrysta all right. Cool, calm, and collected. And the only dry person in the hall.

It wasn't just drinking, of course. Food appeared in vast quantities, and damn good it was too. No one had been expecting Ron the Smith back that day, or two old friends of Klurra's new friend, but you'd never have known that the feast we laid into that night had not been long prepared. It was turn and turn about in the kitchen full of busy Orcs, everyone mucking in here and there and then returning to rejoin the fun. The kids were everywhere, turning spits in the kitchen and hauling pitchers of ale, clambering over the adults and bombarding Qrysta and me with questions—and when we asked anything in return, bombarding us with answers.

It was from the kids, more than anyone, that I learned a lot about Orcs that night. I heard gossip, and customs, and stories, and names, and grudges, and battles, and enemies—which meant anyone who wasn't a Stonefields, basically, until they'd proved friendly. It was an uproarious, joyous, exhausting, uplifting evening. Then the dancing started and things got really wild.

We all trod very carefully the next morning—not just because even the lightest of footsteps boomed in our aching heads, but because an Orc with a hangover is a touchy beast indeed. The last thing anyone wanted to do was rub anyone else the wrong way. Every Orc in Stonefields had a hangover that day. It was, all agreed grouchily, an actual, genuine *MOAH*. It was a word that sounded exactly how I felt. I thought it was just a moan of suffering until Klurra explained: *Mother of All Hangovers.*

The worse the hangover, it was believed by the Orcs, the better the party. It was easily the most horrendous hangover I'd ever had, and I'd been abstemious compared with the rest of the company, who'd been pouring ale down their throats in torrents—and Orcish ale is anything but weak. Even so, as a matter of pride, to show how great the previous night's party had been, in honor of Klurra's friends who had saved Ron the Smith a ton of trouble, everyone exaggerated how awful they felt and how grumpy and touchy they were. This I was told by Klurra, in a quavering snarl that said *are you a fucking idiot or what?*

"Course they're laying it on thick," she snarl-whispered, wincing at the pain that her own voice was causing her. "The more horrible they are to you, the more you should take it as a compliment. Ow, my *head!*"

Orcs are, though, a practical lot. If they see a need for something, they work out a way to find it. The cure for an Orc party-induced hangover is a tincture called 'Over.' Short for *Hangoverover,* it is created by the stronghold apothecary. It takes a while to work and tastes

322

peculiar—not unpleasant exactly, but as if you're drinking paper. It's the best way I can describe it. Into your dry mouth you pour this dry liquid, which dries it out even more, so that you think you can hardly swallow and long for some water. Which you are not allowed to have until you've drunk the whole flask of Over—about a pint. Drinking a pint of paper takes a while. The compound was full of Orcs sitting with their mugs of Over, attempting to drink them, and failing more often than succeeding. Most of us managed it within a couple of hours. All in all it was a challenging morning: two hours of shaking and croaking with grit-flayed eyeballs while trying to drink paper and failing, eventually managing to swallow a mouthful and then trying not to snap at bad-tempered Orcs who were trying not to snap at you and each other. The last drop downed, you took your empty mug back to the apothecary, who examined your tongue which should have turned bright green. She examined it all the way down—clamping it with thick tweezers, pulling it out as far as it would go, and moving it this way and that so that she could peer down your throat, angling your head around in the dazzling sunlight to check every visible inch— while you squinted and groaned, and your eyes and tongue hurt like hell. If your tongue hadn't turned green, she gave you another flask and told you to start again.

The green was probably just vegetable dye, Klurra said, to stain your tongue as you swallowed. Anyone who spat it out wouldn't get the relief of water, and anyway, water wouldn't do you any good without a stomach full of Over inside you. Like everyone else, the apothecary had been at the party, and like every other Orc, she had freely given her time and talents to help, both the night before and the morning after. So the mugs of Over were free to all, but there was a tip jar by the jugs of water that you were eventually allowed to fall upon with relief, and everyone was generous with their thanks. The ingredients for Over, we were told, were rare. Some had to come from a long way away and were expensive.

It was nearing noon before we were in a fit state for a council of war. Which is what it felt like, because we knew a war was coming, and that we were going to be part of it. It might take place in the Undergrounds, way down in the deeps, and no one in the Upgrounds might ever hear of it. Or it might break out everywhere and involve everyone. We did not know. All we knew was that we needed to decide what to do about it. We gathered in the hut that the Orcs had lent us, as their guests, and went over what we knew so far.

We had maps now and information. Clues and parts of the puzzle seemed to be fitting together, but much of what lay ahead was unknown. We could see, clearly enough, what our clues and information said—but what did they *mean?* Marnie's poem, the nursery rhyme that every child in Jarnland knew and played games to, was plain enough on the surface. It seemed to say, *find these, do that.* But find them where? And do exactly what?

The part of the picture where the puzzle pieces had already fitted together was equally elusive. It connected the present to the time of myth, and Jurun to Esmeralda via Junie and Marnie and Lymnia, but every time it made sense, we could sense that more sense lay just off to the edge where the next piece was missing. So we kept coming up with blanks while going around in circles.

Yes, we all agreed, *here we are.* Then followed the inevitable question: *and now what? Now what* always led to the missing pieces. Speculation was pointless. We could keep speculating, and—who knew? We might stumble across something eventually. Meanwhile, the best course of action was to do exactly what we had been doing. Keep going forwards—on and through to the end, wherever that might lie, and whatever it might be.

To start with, we all caught up on what we had all been doing.

Grell and Klurra were enthralled by Qrysta's tale. Grell put two and two together when she'd told of her time at the Eastern School. *Training.* Just like we'd done with Serjeant Bastard. Our old skills brought to life, honed, and new ones added. Then Lord Rylen's tourney. "Battle testing," Grell said. Just like the taking of Rushtoun.

Qrysta was grilled for detail after detail. It was important, Grell said. She needed to fill us in on everything. She did. Klurra said she'd love to spar with Qrysta and that she'd always wanted to dual-wield. That was probably why she carried two warhammers. She'd never actually needed a spare. She just loved practicing with one in each hand, imagining the moves. If she could find a couple of swords that weren't too short, like the stumpy little things people used, she could maybe learn twin-blading after all.

Grell gave her a puzzled look as if to say, *you're an Orc, Orcs use two-handed.*

"What?" Klurra challenged.

Grell said, "I didn't say anything."

"You thought it," Klurra said. "Orc equals two-handed."

Grell was wise enough not to reply.

"Hide-bound by bloody convention, we are, if you ask me." Klurra snorted. "Well, bollocks to tradition, I'm going to give it a try."

"If you can't find swords, don't worry," Qrysta said. "You won't need them. We'll start with sticks."

"Sticks!" Klurra protested, insulted.

Qrysta smiled. "You'll see."

Klurra frowned. "I don't want no Orcs to see me sparring with sticks."

"Then we'll do it in private," Qrysta said, "where no one will see us. Honestly, you learn quicker that way."

"*We–ell*," Klurra said, unconvinced, "if you say so."

"I do. First lesson this afternoon?"

"All right," Klurra agreed, still unsure about the sticks.

If Grell and Klurra enjoyed Qrysta's tale, Qrysta and I loved theirs. Theirs involved foes much nastier than humans—highly skilled though the fighters at Lord Rylen's tourney had been—and a dungeon boss far more challenging than Lord Rylen of Hartwell. I call it *Grell's Tale* because he'd left us to go off on the Orc Quest with Klurra, but it had involved both of them equally. They both told it, interrupting each other to add detail and color. And when Klurra said, at the end of their telling of it, that she'd never have managed it without Grell, and the gods must have sent him to her the day we met, Grell patted her hand and said, "Nor would I have survived it alone," and that the goddess involved in the sending of them to each other must certainly have been Fugg, who had wanted to see what the niblun battle-axe he'd named after her could do in the right hands.

Wreak havoc, would be the short answer.

Their tale began some time before we first met Klurra. She'd been on her travels further east in the Uplands and had heard something that both intrigued and puzzled her. A Bogginmoor cousin told her that someone had found hell. A week later in Graycrag she overheard two Orcs talking over their ale about the reward their chief was offering for the She-Devil's head. They fell silent when they spotted her listening. Intrigued, she looped north on her way home and eventually found what she was looking for: a troll-breaker's camp. In it were five

Orcs—Wild Orcs, or at least semi-feral rather than tribal, and two chained, enraged trolls, recently taken and a long way from being broken yet. The wilder the Orc, Klurra knew, the more of the Old Lore they remembered. She traded with them for their stories: gold, leather strips, steel arrowheads—and the clincher: Ice Wine.

Few grape varieties can grow that far north, but there is one that thrives. The grapes are harvested when they are frozen solid on the vine, in the autumn, and trodden before they melt. Their ice-juice is then fermented, vatted, and left to age in cold cellars. The vines support few grapes, and the grapes yield little juice, so Orc Ice Wine is rare and expensive. It is also, as I was to learn that very evening, delicious.

"I'd like to try that," I said when Klurra described it.

"You shall," she said, "tonight. As my thanks for rescuing Ironwright Smith. Go easy on it, though. It's not for swilling, like our ale."

The Ice Wine yielded dividends from the troll-breakers. She heard the story of the god and the giantess, Helana, daughter of the Giant King, who fought each other and won each other, as Grell and Klurra had done, but with shape shifting and trickery. One turned into an eagle, the other into a storm to blow it to pieces, so the eagle became a long cave to funnel and trap the wind, at which the wind became an earthquake to shatter the cave, and the cave became sunbeams, resting quietly, while the earthquake exhausted itself, before becoming night and extinguishing the sunbeams, which turned themselves into fireflies and danced until the night became intoxicated with them and fell into a lovesick swoon. There were arguments about versions and details and who transformed into what, but all agreed that the result was the same, and inevitable—the god gave the giantess a ring of gold set with a ruby the size of a pigeon's egg and the color of pigeon blood to seal his bargain with her as his bride.

After three nights of pleasure, Helana the giantess mounted the King of the Yaks, her father's mount, who had agreed to bring her to the tryst with the god and who now carried her through the skies back to her father's hall in the mountains of the Far West. The god returned to the realm of the gods in the heavens but wouldn't answer any questions about where he'd been or what he'd been doing. The other gods had their suspicions. It's hard to keep any battle quiet, especially an epic like the one he'd fought to win his new bride. But they had no proof until the child was born and by then it was too late.

The giantess's father was not pleased to learn that his daughter was with child by a god. Gods do not breed with giants, for the result is always the worst of both. He led her to a secret cave deep in a lost pass in his mountains where he beat the walls with his stone hammer until they cracked. A tunnel appeared, alongside which fire poured out of one crack and ice swelled in another. Down they walked, until they came to a great cavern, which would be her new home and the home of her child.

The Giant King set everlasting flames in torches on the walls which would light her new home until eternity itself ended. He killed the King of the Yaks for his disobedience and mounted his skull on the wall above her seat as a warning to any who might disobey him and enter this place which was forbidden to the living.

Klurra told us that he then declared, "A hell you have found, and a hell I have made for you, so henceforth Hel will be your name." Then he turned his back on his daughter and returned to his hall in the mountains.

In time, the offspring of the god and the giantess was born to rule that realm under his mother's command until she died and left this world. Being half-god as well as half-giant, the child was immortal and lived still in the hell that was made for his mother. It is told that he is as unlike god and giant as he is like; that he is a shapeshifter who can change his form from human to animal to monster. A *weregod* indeed—but he was no demigod, being born of god and giantess, so *weredemon* it was decided—that thought being enough to discourage the living from seeking him out.

Which no one did for all the years since the time of myth, as far as is known. Certainly, no one found him and returned to the Upgrounds to tell of it. But over all those years, the old beliefs began to wither and fade. No one had seen a god walk the earth in all the memories of humankind. Legends, they were all, it seemed; and although the devout continued in their service to their deities, the ordinary folk paid them due respect but not much credence. People went about their daily, earthly business, and heaven rarely seemed to interfere.

Orcs, as has been said, are a practical race. They believe in hard steel, hard blows, and hard facts. They don't have any quarrel with gods and demons. They are usually content to leave them to their concerns above and below while getting on with their own lives here in the middle. Klurra, on learning what she learned on her travels, came to the conclusion that there was something in the Western Mountains worth looking into, and if the Graycrag Chief was offering a large reward for someone's head, then her own chief should have it. Orcs venerate their trophies, and the chief with the most battle-honors is regarded as the Great Chief, and his tribe as the preeminent tribe of its time. As for what it truly was, this cave in the west, there was only one way to find out. If it were, indeed, the next world, well that would be worth the finding.

At that point in her story, Klurra leaned forwards, excited. "It was clear the Wild Orcs saw at least some truth in the myth, one telling me as they drank my Ice Wine, 'You can believe that if you like, but if it is, it ain't the next world where the heroes are taken, or the next where the worthy are rewarded, that's for certain. It's a next world where the *unworthy* are sent, to reflect upon the errors of their ways, the tales say. A harsh place, fiery hot in some parts, cold as ice in others.'

" 'It's all but stories,' another said. 'Just a crack in the ground with a bitch-monster at the end of it. Gods? Giantesses? Explain it how you want.'

"Around their campfire that night, as their captured trolls bellowed in their chains and the Ice Wine warmed us and the late hours settled us towards sleep, one said, 'Well, maybe it's this place or that. Probably this. But only an idiot would go there.' They marked the spot on my map of the west, and another of them said, 'Here, if you're going that way, give this to Orndmund of the Eddyr's Fang clan,' and they gave me something wrapped in black cloth.

" 'What is it?' I asked them.

" 'Troll bits,' he said. "One we couldn't break. Broke his bones resisting us, he did. A crippled troll's no good to us, and he'd die out here if he couldn't fend for himself, so we had to cut his throat. Sad—a big, strong feller he was too, he'd have been worth a price if we could've harnessed him.'

" 'What bits?' I asked.

" 'Hands and feet. And teeth. Giants make necklaces and such out of them. A troll-claw necklace or a troll-tooth belt is a prized possession. Powerful, too, when imbued with giant magic. He'll give me a sackful of stones next time I see him.'

"I was unimpressed. 'Stones?'"

" 'Gemstones,' he said. 'Rubies, diamonds, and such. Lying about all over the place up there, they are. Giants don't bother with them. Too small. Lowland merchants pay well for 'em, though.'"

They wished Klurra luck in her quest the next morning, and she set off west, which was the direction she'd been going on the day that she met us, and in which she continued the next morning with Grell.

"It was three days' ride before we reached the place the Wild Orcs thought it might be," Klurra said, "but we had a bit of fun on the way." She grinned and turned to Grell. "Want to tell them, Grello?"

Grell chuckled and looked at me. "Remember them mine foremen who wanted to buy me at the auction in Brig?"

I did.

"Turns out their mine is way up there in the back of beyond—and turned out we rode right into their camp at the pithead. And who should be sitting there at a table, in the sunshine, having their lunch, but those two bastards. They didn't like us riding up on them, but when they saw it was me—well, I was just a wimpy Orc they didn't get to buy 'cos of Corporal Smott, wasn't I? I dismounted and walked over to them, and they got all happy and threatening, thinking that I was going to be in chains after all and so was Klurra, and we had months of hard labor to catch up on, so we'd be doing double shifts."

He was grinning from ear to ear.

Klurra took over the telling. "And Grell just said, 'Sure, mates. Let's start now. Two of you, one of me, seems like a double shift.' And they looked pleased, the poor sods, and one got his whip out, the other a bloody great broadsword, and I had a ringside seat to one of the best scraps I've ever seen—and I've seen more than a few!

"They weren't no pushovers, those two. Big they were, for humans. But they weren't no match for Grello. He was playing with them, and they soon knew it, driving them backwards, whacking them this way and that, knocking them down and kicking them, roaring, having the time of his bloody life. Then their mates poured out of the huts to help them. Which was fine by me, it meant he didn't have all the fun, and I got to join in. Maybe a dozen of them, but half of them were cooks and such, so it was a bit one sided."

"Good workout, though," Grell said. "It was nice to get the old blood warm again and the arms swinging. I wasn't going to kill them, arseholes though they were. Just smack 'em around a bit. I relieved them of their keys and left Klurry to keep an eye on them and went into the pit. Horrible bloody place. There must have been thirty miners down there. And ponies. I got the chains off them, and we all went back up into the daylight. Which some of them hadn't seen for years. Then we all helped ourselves to the food those foremen had been enjoying, and persuaded the cooks to find victuals for thirty more. Someone slit the foremen's throats when we weren't looking, I'm not too unhappy to say. After a nice lunch, we all went our separate ways.

"All in all," Grell said, "it was a good warm-up to the main event."

Klurra took over the tale. "Hell of a main event it was too. Emphasis on *hell*."

She paused and glanced at Grell, who muttered, "You can say that again."

"There was nothing guarding the entrance to the cavern when we reached it," Klurra continued. "There was no sign of anyone going in there recently. We tied the horses up outside, took a large slug of Oller's Bottled Bottle each, then a couple of deep breaths, and went in. We'd made torches out of pine branches we'd cut on the way, soaking their heads in oil that burned with a smoky flame.

"Well, two Orcs carrying torches aren't exactly invisible, and it wasn't long before the inhabitants of the cavern spotted us coming and promptly attacked. They didn't like the light, they didn't like the flames, and they didn't like us, who, unlike themselves, were alive. Warm flesh, warm blood. A rare treat indeed, for—as the Wild Orcs had told me—only an idiot would go there.

"The first to attack were rats the size of sheep, charging up from the deeps in a chittering, squealing wave of bodies, all teeth and claws, leaping over each other to get at us. Grell got to work with Fugg, whirling and slashing, and I whacked Ding and Dong on rat after rat, but they just kept coming."

"Yeah," Grell said, "millions of them, it seemed like. I couldn't believe that we were going to be done in by bloody *rats*, but we were being swarmed by the buggers. We would've been overwhelmed by the sheer weight of numbers, but then a leaping rat landed on Klurra's torch and burst into flames. Well, that's when we saw—those rats were not only enormous, but also Undead. And therefore as dry as tinder. One burning rat ran shrieking back into the pack, and they all ignited. And fuck me, were we knackered—eh, Klurry?"

"I'll say. He couldn't speak for a minute, doubled up leaning on his battle-axe—same as I was on my hammers. Then the big lump says, 'Think that's everything, Klurry?' And I couldn't help but laugh. Well, more of a croak it came out as."

"It wasn't everything, of course," Grell said. "The rats were just for starters. Turned out that everything down there was either Dead or Undead."

He turned to Klurra, who continued. "We went on down. After a while, stone tombs lined the walls. As we passed, their lids slid back, and the Dead emerged, croaking, and wielding ancient weapons, only to be sliced apart by Fugg, or splattered by Ding and Dong and then put to the torch. It was kind of funny to see lurching, burning Undead warriors from the ages before history, running back down the cavern lighting their way and occasionally igniting their fellows."

"Not that we had time to laugh," Grell interjected. "Others kept on coming, up from the depths, from the tombs, from side-tunnels that led who knew where. But we cleared the lot, eventually."

"It was an eerie silence after all that," Klurra said. "We emerged into a great, buried hall, well-lit by torches in brackets on the walls. A trench ran across one side of it, filled with boiling lava that bubbled and smoked. The other side disappeared into a cold, blue gloom with a floor of ice that led off into the distance. Small, stunted creatures scuttled in the shadows. There was a dais at the far end. At its center was a large throne on which a dead giantess sat, her clothes rotted to rags, her body a skeleton to which a few shreds of dried skin clung. Above her on the wall was mounted the skull of an enormous yak."

"The Yak King. The end of our quest."

"And you know what's at the end of every quest, right?" Grell said.

Qrysta spoke up. "End Boss."

"Yup. So, we approached the dais extra cautiously, weapons ready."

He paused dramatically, looking from face to face.

We were all agog to hear what was coming next. And what came next surprised us.

"Nothing happened," Grell said.

Klurra said, "We watched the dead giantess warily, but it seemed she was going to stay dead. That was fine by us. Ugly, misshapen skull— but that was what we'd come for. We kept an eye out for emerging foes, but none appeared. We looked around for trophies, but there were none as far as we could see. No treasure. No weapons. Nothing but silence and the guttering of the torches and the bubbling of the lava in its fissure.

"Then I noticed the ring that the god had given his bride on her hand—a gold band, set with an enormous ruby. I took it off and examined it. 'Bloody hells, look at the size of it! It'd fall off even *your* fingers, Grell!'

" 'Wear it through your nose, Klurry,' Grell said, grinning at me.

" 'Wouldn't be able to breathe,' I replied."

Klurry felt in her pocket for the ring and brought it out to show us. It was, indeed, enormous. And breathtakingly beautiful.

"Wow," Qrysta said.

Klurra glanced at Grell, who smiled. Some private message passed between them. Klurra put the ring away, and Grell said, "We'll get it fitted to her finger."

Klurra took up the tale once more. " 'Right, Grellie, pop her head off then, and let's be going.' One swat of Fugg, and the giantess's skull rolled on the floor."

"Klurra picked it up and examined it," Grell said.

'This'll look good over Chief Elbrig's high seat,' she said, turning it this way and that. 'Blimey, talk about ugly!'

"I wanted something for myself and saw the yak skull on the wall. 'I'm having that,' I decided, and stepped up onto the dais to prize it off. 'Make me a nice helmet, this will. Look at these horns!'"

"I told him he wouldn't be able to walk through doors wearing them," Klurra said. "He'd get stuck."

"I told her I'd take it off before I go inside, of course. I levered it off the wall and was admiring it when Klurra, looking around at the empty hall, said, 'Bit of an anti-climax, this. I was expecting fireworks. I suppose we'll have to make something up for the telling, eh?'

"I agreed. 'Monsters and mayhem? Yeah, better cook up a nice yarn on the way home.' I put the yak skull on. 'How do I look?'"

"I couldn't help laughing," Klurra said. 'Terrifying. Right, Eddyr's Fang for the delivery of the troll bits and then home.' I tied the skull of the giantess to my back with a strip of leather, Grell slung the skull of the King of the Yaks over his back with another strip, and we set out across the hall, looking forward to getting back to the lands of light."

She stopped and looked at Grell.

He said, "We were halfway across when we saw that weren't alone."

27

Trophies and Gifts

"A little creature was standing between us and the passage back up through the cavern. Small and quiet, it was, with crooked feet and long, long hands, its skin brown blue with leathery, pointed ears, eyes dull and cold. It was naked but for a leather vest and breechclout. Fur clung to the leather as if it had only been half-cured."

Grell turned to Klurra, who elaborated. "Small, yeah, but unsettling. We'd seen nothing like it on the way down. We hadn't heard it appear or seen where it had come from. It was just there, blocking our way, considering us. Grell unslung Fugg, and I grabbed one of my warhammers. The little thing noticed but didn't seem concerned.

"Which we *did* find concerning. Something that hardly reached up to my knees, not bothered by two heavily armed Orcs? That wasn't natural. *It* wasn't natural. Nothing about it was. We didn't know what to do next, so we just waited, watching it.

"And it just waited, contemplating us—for what seemed a long while. There was only the silence of the cavern, the guttering of the torches, the bubbling of the lava in its fissure, and the shadows playing on the walls.

"And then, in a quiet, cold voice, the goblin said, 'There are meant to be five of you.' I didn't know what he was talking about, but I could see Grell did. 'Who says?' he challenged."

"The little bugger ignored me. 'And where's the girl?' it said, frowning. I said, "I don't know what you're talking about.'

'Yes, you do," it countered. 'Where are the others?'"

"I could see Grell was in a fix, so I said, 'What others? Think two of us can't deal with a scrawny little thing like you?' It turned its pale, gray eyes on me—and very unnerving they were. 'The ones who should be here instead of you, Orc Girl. The one who wields, the one who steals, the one who casts. Bringing the one who glows.'"

"Obvious who it meant, right? You lot." Grell paused. "And Esmeralda."

None of us liked the sound of that.

" 'Mind your own damn business,' I told it. And all calm like, it replied, 'It *is* my business.' That was chilling. 'My business and my mother's and the other who shares our realm. And you would have been well advised to mind *your* own business and stay Upground rather than coming down here to meddle in ours.'

" 'We go where we please,' I told him. I did not appreciate being talked to like that—and who was that little pipsqueak to call Klurra *Orc Girl?*

"It thought about that, then said, 'Do you, now? Well then. Where you've *gone where you pleased* is here, where we *don't* please. And we don't appreciate thieves and vandals. Cutting my mother's head off, and her dead and no longer able to defend herself. Stealing what's left of her yak. Important things, those are. And they don't belong with the likes of you. So, you'll be staying here now for all time, dead and buried, here where you *pleased to go*, with all the time in the world to contemplate your folly.'

" 'No, we won't!' I'd had enough of this. If it wanted to try and stop us, let it. 'We'll be going, little whatever-the-fuck-you-are, so move off out of our way, if you know what's good for you.' Well, you'd have thought the sight of us bearing down on it would send it running, but it didn't move. 'Ah,' it said, considering me, then glanced at Klurra again before turning back to me, '*little*, is it, again? My littleness bothers you, does it? A big Orc like you? Well, now. Who'd have thought?'

"I didn't like the way this was going. The creature's composure, and its almost taunting words, were getting to me. 'All right.' I stopped in front of it, glaring down at it. 'Just shut your mouth or I'll shut it for you. And step back before I cut you in half!'

" 'Will you, now?' it said. "A *little* thing like me. Into two *littler* halves. I wouldn't do that if I were you. My two littler halves might take offence.'

" 'Who gives a fuck? Move!' "

"But the goblin didn't move. It just looked up at me thoughtfully with its dull, gray eyes. Which, as he stared, began to widen and turn red, and the goblin smiled, its lips parting, and we saw the terrible rows of needles that were its teeth; needles for slashing, and tearing flesh and crunching bones.

" 'Move!' I repeated. 'Now!'

" 'Now? Very well. If you insist.' "

Grell glanced at Klurra, who took over. "It began to grow. The first inkling we had of what was happening was the way its shadows swelled on the walls behind it. From little puddles of darkness, a huge form emerged. A gigantic, horned head above a barrel-chested body. Two enormous wings unfurled above its shoulders. Their leading edges were tipped with long, thumblike hooks. It squatted on two thick legs, then stood upright, towering over Grell, taller than both of us put together. It leaned back its head, spread its leathery black wings, and roared. The sound of its roar reverberated around the chamber."

"And it was bloody terrifying," Grell said.

"We attacked without a second thought. Grell rolled to one side and came up behind it, aiming a swing of Fugg at the back of its legs to hamstring it. His blow did not land. Instead, the creature's tail caught him in the chest, knocked him off his feet, and he flew across the hall and slid along the floor. Meanwhile, I was underneath it, thumping into it with my warhammer."

"I had the presence of mind to keep rolling, rather than stop to get up," Grell said. "Good thing too—a bloody great taloned claw stomped into the ground where I'd been a split second earlier, missing me by inches."

"I saw my chance and slammed my warhammer onto the foot the monster was standing on. It bellowed and turned its attention to me. I can tell you, I did *not* like the look in its eyes which were big and red and furious—but not as red as the jet of flame it blasted at me when it opened its jaws. I threw myself to one side, out of the way of the blast, rolling the way Grell had done—but I wasn't as quick thinking as him. I got to my feet, confused and dazzled by the blaze. The next thing I knew it had caught me in one massive hand and lifted me off the ground. I was helpless in its grasp. It had my arms pinned and was squeezing the life out of me. I'd never felt pressure like it."

Klurra smiled at Grell. "I'd have been a goner if it weren't for Grellie. Didn't know a bloody great Orc could move that fast, I swear! The demon was glaring at me, mouth open, taking a deep breath in so it could scorch out another flame, and that would have been curtains for me. Grell picked up my warhammer and threw it at its head."

"Yeah, and bloody missed and all!" Grell said. "I was aiming to brain the bastard, but it was opening its mouth wide to fire at Klurra, and instead it only went and swallowed the bloody warhammer. Well, it didn't like that. Stuck in its gullet, it was, jamming its mouth open, and the thing staggered around up there gagging, reaching in with its other claw to get it out.

"That was all the time I needed, me and Fugg! With it otherwise occupied, I was in below it and hacking away for all I was worth—making sure to stay away from that damn lashing tail. Now, I can tell you, you ain't never seen butchery like it. Serjeant Bastard had the measure of Fugg's niblun blades all right. Sharp as lightning they are. They were through that monster's hide like an arrow through an apple. I had him hamstrung back of both legs in seconds, then reverse chops down into the fronts of its ankles which parted like silk.

"Its roars and bellows turned to shrieks as it tottered and fell and then Klurry was out from its grip and smashing into it with her other warhammer. Fugg took one of its arms off at the elbow. I shoved her headspike into its belly and ripped with all my strength. Intestines came swelling out steaming and then the thing was flat on its side with the biggest fucking dent in its head you've ever seen, Klurry's hammer buried up to its handle sticking out of its skull."

"The whole fight can't have lasted two minutes," Klurra said. "But those were two minutes I would *not* care to live again!"

"Once is enough just *hearing* about it," Qrysta said.

"We were wheezing and weeping with relief as you can imagine," Grell said. "Hardly able to stand or even breathe. And I was just thinking, *wow, this thing's head would make a hell of a trophy for Chief Elbrig's wall,* when blow me, the monster shrank down to almost nothing and was the little creepy creature again. No point taking that pathetic little skull, it looked like a pancake."

"Quest completed, though," Qrysta pointed out. "Achievement—what? Demonslayer?"

"Yeah," Grell said, liking the word. "We'll take that." He turned to Klurra with a grin. "Klurra Demonslayer of Stonefields! How does that sound?"

Klurra snorted. "Asking for trouble. Name yourself Demonslayer to an Orc, he'll love that. 'Oh ah? Never killed a Demonslayer before—well, always a first time, eh?' I wouldn't have a day's peace." She winked at Grell then returned to their tale. "Somehow, that was even scarier than the fight, it shrinking like that. We had no idea what we'd been dealing with. We fair *ran* out of there, I don't mind telling you. Giants and demons and shapeshifters? That was quite enough of *that*, thank you very much! The tunnels up were clear, thank all the gods. We were in no fit state to face any more foes."

"It was still broad daylight when we got out," Grell said. "The horses were still there. Calm as anything. Were we glad to see *them!* We were up into the saddle and away quick as we could, and we didn't stop till we reached the Eddyr's Fang mob. Treated us very civil, they did, once they saw what we'd brought Orndmund, the troll claws and teeth. He said he'd pay the troll-breakers themselves, thankee very much, as we were strangers and might run off with the payment, but he gave us something for our pains. Show 'em, Klurry."

Klurra reached into her pack and brought out an amulet of nine yellow-brown squares, carved with designs, all strung on a yak-leather lace, a small silver bead separating each piece from its neighbor.

"Made it himself, he had," Klurra said. "Fine craftsman, that Orndmund. Best in the mountains, the other giants said. That made him laugh—he said all he'd done was choose the beads and thread them on the lace. The pieces were ancient, from an old tomb, he said."

Qrysta turned it over and over in her hands. "What is it?"

"Amber," Klurra said. "There are runes carved into each tile, see? He wouldn't tell us what they meant. Craft secret."

"It's beautiful," Qrysta said, admiring it.

Klurra said, "And it's yours."

"What?" Qrysta was surprised. "No, Klurra, I can't."

"You can."

"He gave it to *you*."

"And I'm giving it to you. In payment for my dancing lessons. And I'll take it back off you if I can get the better of you before you leave."

"Deal!" Qrysta fastened the amulet around her neck. It looked good on her, the old, ochre squares standing out against her black-leather armor. She smiled at Klurra and then realized something. "And I have something for you. I'll be right back."

She went to her bunk and returned with a long bundle wrapped in her cloak.

I knew at once what it was.

"I think it might just be the right fit for you," Qrysta said. "We use these for fighting with shields. They're too long and heavy for us to use for twin-blade work. You need mobility and speed for dual wielding. But with your size and strength, this thing should flick around like a fly whisk."

She unwrapped Lord Rylen of Hartwell's ancestral sword.

Klurra was speechless. "No ... you can't. I can't."

Qrysta smiled. "That didn't work for me, and it's not going to work for you. You can, Klurra, and you will. It needs to be used, a blade this nice."

Klurra drew the gleaming blade from its ornate scabbard. "This thing's worth a fortune!"

"Not as much as Grell is. You brought him back. With a nice new hat."

We chuckled at that, because we'd all admired Grell in his yak-skull helmet when he'd put it on for us. I had done as he asked and cast Fortify on it while warning him that armor casts weren't my strong suit. It was serviceable enough, though, we saw when Klurra tested it with her warhammers, gingerly at first and then more severely. She could not make a dent in it from blow after blow—after Grell had taken it off, of course. She was getting really worked up and about to give it everything she'd got when I'd said, "That's probably enough."

She'd looked at me enquiringly.

"Armor is armor, magic just helps it," I'd said, "and then only for a while. All casts wear off. There's no way to make anything unbreakable. We wouldn't need armor at all if there were, right?"

Grell then said, "No point in destroying my helmet, eh?"

Klurra, turning the magnificent Hartwell sword this way and that, was admiring the play of light along it. An elaborate H was engraved on both sides of it beneath the hilt. "Hartwell, eh?" she said. "Well, not anymore. I'll have to think of a good name that begins with H."

"Helkiller," Grell suggested.

"She was already dead." Klurra got to her feet. "And this beauty wasn't the cause of it. Hel-something is good though."

"Helsbane," Qrysta said.

"Yeah, that's good. I like that." Klurra flicked it around, lightning fast, without effort. "Light enough."

Qrysta and I exchanged smiles. We both knew that a full-size battle sword was too heavy for our wrists if we wanted to execute dual-wield moves. The wrist is important in sword and board play, but the bulk of the power in any move comes from shoulders and arms and backbone, all the way down to the hips and thighs and feet.

"I'll have to get Ironwright Smith to make me a twin for this beauty," Klurra said.

At that, it was my turn to have an idea. "That'll take time, you can use mine." I went over to my pack and retrieved my Graduation sword which I handed to her.

Klurra was unable to believe what was happening. "Are you *sure*?"

"Klurra, any combat we get into, I'll be busy casting, both Damages and Heals. We'd all better hope I won't be needing this."

"Thank you, Daxx." She took it from me. "I don't know what to say ..."

"My pleasure, Klurra."

"They look good on you," Qrysta said, as Klurra held them up to admire them. Mine was nowhere near as ornate as Lord Rylen's, but it was pretty much the same size and shape. She began testing them.

"Nothing in it." Klurra sliced the air with them, her wrists turning in all directions. "Can't hardly tell which is which, if I close my eyes." She closed her eyes, swapping blades from hand to hand, and kept shuffling and twirling and whirling. We all got up quickly and moved to the edges of the room.

"You'll be more of a danger to your mates than to the enemy if you move like that." Qrysta laughed. "Want to go outside and try them out?"

Klurra said, "Do I ever!'

"Can we watch?" I asked.

"Best not," Qrysta said. "Don't want her distracted. Come on, then," she said to Klurra, heading for the door.

Klurra frowned. "You not bringing yours?"

Qrysta shook her head. "Like I said, I'll be using sticks. But you need to get used to your blades so that they become extensions of your arms."

Klurra looked worried. "Sticks, against *these*?"

Qrysta smiled. "I know, hardly seems fair, right?"

As they left, I said, "Klurra?"

She stopped and looked back enquiringly.

"I hope Orc Ice Wine is good for bruises."

She hesitated, not knowing what to make of that, then left to join Qrysta outside for her first lesson.

"She'll find out," Grell said.

"That she will," I agreed.

We sat back down and continued our council of war.

The thing that concerned us most was what the goblin had said: "Where are the others? The one who wields, the one who steals, the one who casts."

And most worrying of all: "Bringing the one who glows."

Clearly, someone knew about us. A *lot* about us. Knew that there were five of us. Knew about Esmeralda. We knew how they knew about her. She'd been in view for sixteen years—but how had they learned about *us*? I reminded Grell of what Oller had said, about his mission to find the silver key: there is finding and there is *magic* finding and you can't hide from that. If a scrawny goblin can transform into a huge, fire-breathing demon, then magic was definitely in the picture. Could I, somehow, magically find out who was looking for us and what they knew and the answers to all those other questions?

Probably not, I thought.

And in the next instant, *that's* In magic, *not* Out magic. Marnie's the person for that.

The Stonefields stronghold was even farther from Marnie's cottage than the refuge behind the waterfall had been, so I expected that I'd be well out of range of her Thinking. I tried anyway. It was important that she was warned about Esmeralda, and I could do with her advice on what Grell and Klurra had learned.

Marnie? Something's come up, I think you'll want to hear this.

I waited. As expected, I got no reply.

Pity. I'd liked to have heard her news as well as giving her ours. I wondered how Mabel's flying lessons were going. The thought of her and Marnie swooping around in the air above her cottage made me smile. I knew we were going to be in the fight of our lives before too long. I also knew that we had something worthwhile to fight for. Something *more* than worthwhile. Something that made life worthwhile, ours and everyone else's.

Esmeralda. Marnie. Oller—and now Little Guy and Klurra. As well, of course, as each other.

"Okay." I opened my pack and took out everything Oller had brought back from his jaunt into the Underground with Urch. "Time to do my homework."

"*Our* homework, you mean," Grell said.

I looked at him. "I'd be grateful for the help."

Grell grinned. "I know, Big Orc thicko, yeah? Appearances can be deceptive, Daxxie. I have a brain too."

"Qrysta said something like that. She thinks you must have used it in real life. A big tough Aussie when you run with us, she said, but in her view that's you just letting off steam. There's more to you than that, she thinks."

"Oh yeah," Grell chuckled, agreeing, and reached for the first sheet.

"Not going to tell?" I said.

Grell, already reading, said, "Nope."

"Some other time?"

"You don't give up, do you, mate?" Grell said. "No. Not now, not ever. Let's get to work."

Some papers were in bundles, some in individual sheets. There were several leather-bound notebooks, similar to the one that Marnie had given to me but without her magical infinite extension. Which was a relief. We had enough to be going through.

Even as it was, it wouldn't be a short job. Some of the notes were in a hasty scrawl. Others were neatly transcribed into official-looking reports. We did not know how to think of the person who had written them—the half-dead man who had provided a meal for Urch as his last deed in life. Researcher, scholar, or simply scribe, we thought, until Grell, removing a scroll of parchment from its leathern case said, "Hullo …" and then, "well now," as he passed it to me.

It was fine vellum, beautifully inscribed and richly illustrated in bright inks of all colors. The illuminated letters that started each sentence were bordered in gold leaf. Even at first glance it was obvious that this was not a run-of-the-mill document. What made that clearer still was the coat of arms at top and center. A highly detailed shield, supported by a rampant unicorn and a rampant wyvern, was surmounted by a large, jewel-encrusted golden crown—half of which was missing. The design on the shield was a white castle, a red pennant flying from its flagpole, standing on the bank of a blue river in a green field which was dotted with white flowers. Above the crown were two large words in red and black inks: *Royal Warrant.*

Below it was written:

By order of His Majesty, Wyllard the Seventh, King: All loyal subjects of Our Realm are hereby desired and commanded to offer every assistance and material aid to the bearer of this Warrant, Royal Loremaster Perrett, appointed to this duty by Ourselves, and to deny him nothing on pain of Our Displeasure. All monies agreed payable by Loremaster Perrett to other parties shall be paid in gold by Loremaster Perrett, unless such sums are beyond his purse, in which case it is agreed in Our good faith that they will be paid upon presentation of a Note of Payment Due signed and dated above his Seal by Loremaster Perrett to His Majesty's Treasurer at the Royal Castle of Mayport. Signed this day by His Majesty and countersigned by His Majesty's loyal servant, Treasurer Eardwell, Lord of Athendene.

A large red-and-blue ribbon hung next to the signatures, affixed by the Royal Seal stamped into a rosette of red wax.

"Well, now we know what to call him," I said. "A Loremaster."

"A man of learning," Grell mused. "Gone all that way from the far south to learn—what?"

"Let's see if we can find out."

I turned my attention to the piles of paper.

And we did.

28

The Loremaster

Loremaster Perrett had been a diligent recorder of everything he had seen and done on his journey from Mayport to his death in Long Cavern far in the north. His diary made his mission quite clear:

For months I had begged leave of His Majesty to furnish an exploration to the north where new information that I have received has led me to believe I would find answers to questions that have challenged historians since history itself began. His Majesty asked why He should be concerned with events of long ago while His realm is at war with itself and He has the challenges of today to overcome. "As history began," I told Him, "so history will end, one day. And that day, we in the College of Lore and Learning believe, is now at hand. Does His Majesty wish to be the Last King of Jarnland? Does His Majesty wish a Future of Darkness for His realm and all His subjects?" "What proof do you have of what you are telling Me?" His Majesty demanded. "You talk of Eternal Darkness, yet the sun rises every morn, and the moon and stars shine at night. My Lords war with one another and My realm is troubled and you wish Me to concern Myself with children's rhymes and old wives' tales?" "All the realm's troubles will cease, Your Majesty, when the realm itself ceases," I replied. "Those who know of these things know they are nigh upon us. The signs that Your people cannot see are writ plain to those of us who can. There will be no warning, no time to prepare, no stopping the flood when it bursts upon us." "What flood is this, Loremaster?" He asked, and I answered Him, "The host that is gathering in the deep places, assembling and readying for the day which will turn all our days into nights, now and forever." His Majesty was disturbed by this, and asked who we were, we who can see these things and read these signs. I told Him, "The Scholars of our College. The Conclave of the Guild of the Arcane Arts. The Sage Sisters of Coven. Those who can fathom the past and scry the future. All have seen the same things and reached the same conclusion. Your Majesty shall be the Last King when the First King returns to claim his realm again. The realm that Your Majesty now holds." He could not believe this, but eventually He asked what was to be done. "We must destroy him before he destroys us," I replied. "And how do we do that?" He enquired. "We must find him before he lives again," I told Him. "From beyond death he is summoning his host and gathering his power. When he has life he will lead them, and none shall stand against him. He is calling that life to him even now. When he takes it, which he soon will, he will take all."

That, Grell and I agreed, seemed clear enough.

Find him before he lives again. Then make sure he doesn't, and never will.

There were old, leather-bound books of lore and legend, and histories of towns and books of maps and charts, and scrolls on natural history and alchemy and gods and demons and their cults and followers among Loremaster Perrett's possessions. We left those for later, assuming them to be his research materials. We concentrated on reading what Perrett had discovered and what was concerning him. After a couple of hours, we were still a long way from having read everything he had written, but we had learned a lot. I'd finished his journal as far as it went. I'd been interested to learn from his final entry that although Loremaster Perrett's expedition was the only one appointed by Royal Decree, it wasn't the only one in the field. He'd received news that three others were to be sent out, two to the west and south by the GAA, and one to the east by Coven. *At last!* he'd written.

They were the last words he ever wrote.

There were references to Marnie's poem. One entire volume of his journal was devoted to examining it and expounding on various theories as to what it meant. In *general*, all seemed to agree that it meant one simple sentence: find these things, then find Jurun and destroy him. In every *particular*, though, the theories ran in all sorts of directions. They all seemed as plausible, and as vague, as each other. There were many candidates for the *book*, including the Book of Life and Death itself. The Flute of Harmony cropped up again and again as a possible candidate for the *bone*. I was going around and around in circles when it hit me.

What if 'looking for the right one' was the wrong approach?

I turned back the pages in Perrett's journal to his reference to the other expeditions.

Yes, I thought as I read it again.

Perrett had written that both of the expeditions sent out by the Guild of the Arcane Arts were led by a caster of the greatest expertise—as was that sent out by Coven. Each leading caster had a staff of unique power, fitted with an appropriate heartstone. The Guildmother of Coven herself, Sister Agneka, led hers to the east with her yew stave and its heartstone of olivine. Magus Ansill led the expedition to the west, his staff of pine holding its emerald heartstone. Sorceress Lyreth led the south expedition, her staff hazel, its heartstone a large black pearl.

Three sticks.

Three stones.

I thought, *well they can't all be* the *stick and* the *stone, can they?*

"Grell, I think I've realized something."

"Yeah." He looked up from his reading. "What?"

"Recite the poem."

He did. "A stick, A stone, A book, A bone, Go down and down, For half a crown, A knife, A life, A throne."

"And we think that means what?" I asked.

"We have to find those things."

"And—where are they?" I probed.

Grell frowned, as if trying to work out why I was being this simplistic. "If I knew, *you'd* know."

345

New Rock New Role

"You've found something in what you've read?"

"No," I said, "it's something in what we've known all along. Something so obvious. I remembered something Marnie said, about finding the missing pieces. 'Who knows, you might be looking at them already and just can't see them.' It's been staring us in the face, and we haven't noticed it."

"Noticed what?"

"It doesn't say *the*. It says *a*."

"Huh?"

"What if all these people have jumped to the same, and very obvious, conclusion? Just like we did. That each of them must be just *one particular* object? And yet, here's Loremaster Perrett blithely saying that three different casters on the other expeditions each have their own staves with their own heartstones."

I let that sink in and then said, "It says *a* book, not *the* book. *A* bone, Grell—not *the*. What if we don't have to assemble a collection of *exact* things, but have one of each category that *works for us*? Like Shift being *stick and stone* works for me?"

"Yeah," Grell said. "You may have something there."

I said, "Here's how we've been reading it. *Find this stick, this stone, this book, this bone, then go down, find the ice knife he killed Jaren with, kill him with it, and take his throne.* Would you agree with that?"

Grell thought it through. "Yeah, pretty much."

"Another reading," I said, "would be: *a stick and a stone and a book and a bone go down and down.* Etcetera. *Go* in that case isn't an instruction to us. It's not ordering us to go. In this reading, *go* tells us what those four things do: they *go down and down* to do the other things."

"So, you're saying, searching for Harmony's Flute, or whatever, is irrelevant?"

"By that reading, yes," I said. "After all, to this day nobody knows with any certainty which *particular* thing any of them are. So, what if they *aren't*? 'Particular' things?" A thought struck me. "Marnie also said, 'you have the first two, stick and stone.' Well, so do the other casters, on the other expeditions. *None* of our sticks and stones are unique. For all we know"—I waved a hand at the pile of Loremaster Perrett's leather-bound volumes—"one of these could be *book*. Just as your yak-skull helmet could be *bone*."

"*Could* be," Grell said, unconvinced. "But, suppose it isn't, and we get down there and face off with the guy and suddenly it's: *uh-oh, wrong bone? Excuse us, mate, we need to nip back up top. Brought the wrong bone—sorry about that. Don't go anywhere, we'll be right back* ...'"

I said, "You're still not reading it right. We go down there with four things, one in each category, and take him on. Knife him, life him, dethrone him."

"And if we fail?"

"Someone else will have to succeed in our place. We've been looking for a magic bullet, Grell. A magic formula that will somehow magically guarantee us victory. I'm saying we don't need it. I'm also saying we could keep looking forever and never find it, like people here have been doing for ages. We need to do what we're good at."

"Yeah," Grell said, "but ..."

"And why should it be the same for us now as it was for him when he killed his brother? All those years ago, Jurun did what he did with *his* stick and stone, etcetera. Now we *go down and down* and do what we're going to do with ours. It's an echo of him and his rather than an exact match. What you might call poetic justice."

Grell frowned. "Doesn't sound very poetic."

"Someone getting his reward or comeuppance by a twist on what he did to earn it."

Grell considered that and nodded. "Just desserts, in other words."

"Exactly," I said. "And this guy deserves, if anyone does."

"No question," Grell said. "Too effing right. So let's give him them!"

"We need to take the fight to him, give him our best shot," I said. "With our best stick, stone, book, and bone. Whatever works for *us*. I hereby nominate your yak-skull helmet as our Official Bone, and ..." I reached for one of Perrett's books at random "... *The Medicinal Properties of Plants* as Official Book."

"Not sure about that," Grell said. "Does he have a copy of *Build Your Own Bazooka?*"

"Not that I saw."

Grell thought about what I'd said.

"You could be right. You could be wrong. Strikes me we could stay up here searching forever. And we don't have forever."

"That we do not," I agreed.

"Right," Grell said, "so what's the plan?"

"Read through this lot, learn what we can, join up with Oller, find Nyrik and Horm, and head *down and down*. Then do what we do best."

"Fight," Grell said.

"Indeed."

"And win."

"Yes," I said. "That would be good."

▲ ▲ ▲

Orcs have ridiculous reserves of stamina. They can carry loads that will kill carthorses, walk all day without tiring, and fight relentlessly for hours. They can also take ridiculous amounts of damage and seem to feel pain far less than the rest of us. For these reasons, a small band of untrained Orcs armed with lousy weapons can often simply outlast a bigger, better-trained and better-equipped force. You don't want to start a fight with Orcs unless you are prepared to spend a long time seeing it through. So, it was something of a surprise when, a couple of hours after she and Qrysta had left for her first dancing lesson, the hut door opened, and Klurra tottered in drained, bruised, disorientated, and—as she said when we asked—"Completely fucking knackered!" She slumped into a chair, crossed her arms on the tabletop, and laid her head on them with a long, low groan.

Grell grinned. "How did it go?"

Klurra just groaned again.

Drink of something?" I asked.

"Qrysta's fetching it," Klurra croaked, her voice hoarse with exhaustion.

I got four cups from the cupboard and sat down just as Qrysta strolled in, cool as a breeze and fresh as a daisy. She was carrying a skin of water and a flask of Orcish Ice Wine. I rootled around in my bag till I found a tonic potion which I handed to Klurra.

"This'll perk you up," I said.

"Don't think I'll ever *perk* again," she muttered, taking it and knocking it back in a single draught. She put down the empty vial but instead of slumping back down, stayed half sitting up, propped up on her elbows, her shoulders relaxing, her head clearing.

"Oof," she said, "that helped. Thanks, Daxx."

"My pleasure." I raised Shift and cast a Lingering Mend which bloomed green around her.

"Whoa! What's this?"

"Lingering Mend. You'll be fine in no time."

"Wow," Klurra said. "Could do with you on my side in a fight."

"You should see him," Grell said. "Best healer ever. Saved my skin any number of times." I smiled at the compliment—then he reverted to trash talking. "And any number of times he *didn't* and we had to save his."

"Water." Qrysta handed Klurra the skin.

Klurra filled her cup and drank, three times. She put her cup down, looked at us, and said, "Damn …!"

"Hard work?" Grell asked.

"Never known the like," Klurra replied. "My gods! I may never get up from this chair. My legs are like blocks of wood."

"Daxxie's cast will take care of that," Qrysta said. "You were just using them in ways you're not accustomed to. Your muscles will learn. You were very good by the way."

"I was?" Klurra sounded unconvinced.

"Very. Most novices don't have a clue. You picked it all up quickly."

"Not all," Klurra said, "you were beating me like a bloody carpet."

"That was to show you what to avoid," Qrysta said. "Which you did every time I attacked you with that move again. You picked up everything that I showed you and got it right away. You never made the same mistake twice. That's rare, Klurra. You have to realize, dual-wield is *counter*-intuitive. You're using your off hand as well as your main hand, and you have to be equally fluent with both. Which, clearly and without any doubt, you will be. You have a way to go, but you were definitely beginning to flow. I would say"—Qrysta smiled—"if you were not an *Orc*, of course, meaning the idea is impossible: that you are a natural."

Klurra stared at Qrysta. "I am?"

"If I'm any judge. A few more days like today, and I feel pretty confident you'll be more than useful."

Klurra groaned again. "Any more days like today, and I'll be *dead*."

Qrysta chuckled. "Tomorrow will be easier. Trust me."

Klurra said sourly, "I have a firm rule in life, Qrysta. Never trust anyone who says, 'Trust me.'"

Qrysta smiled again. "You'll see."

"Ice Wine?" I asked Klurra.

"Excellent idea," she said.

I opened the flask and poured four cupfuls.

Well, I could see why the Wild Orcs had told Klurra everything they knew and had entrusted her with the valuable troll teeth and bones for the giant chief, Orndmund. *Delicious* fails to describe it adequately, just as *colorful* fails to do justice to rainbows. Rich, but subtle, sweet but balanced, strong but gentle, easy on the tongue indeed, but you didn't feel you needed another mouthful for minutes because the last one was still lingering and letting you get to know it in so many delightful ways. It would be a shame to chase *that* away before it had departed in its own good time ...

And then when it *had* gone, you felt no need to follow it up immediately, because that last mouthful had been so good, so spectacular, so intriguing. It was pleasant just to sit there with the memory of it, knowing that the taste had finally gone, and that this was how good *nothing* tasted after that—*ooh*, I have this lovely, empty mouth!—and that another mouthful would be along when you felt like taking it.

And time indeed slowed as we drank slowly. Klurra recovered. Qrysta filled her in on details in their sparring, giving her tips. Our talk turned towards the future. We told them what we'd learned and what we'd discussed, and that we believed the best course of action was to take the fight to the enemy—and sooner rather than later. By all accounts there wasn't much *later* waiting around for us to use at our leisure.

"Sounds good to me," Klurra said.

Grell frowned at her. "What, you're not going to miss me?"

Klurra snorted. "No way. 'Cos there's no fucking way I'm missing *this!* Are you kidding me? Epic fight like this!"

A broad grin grew on Grell's face. "You're coming with us?"

Klurra said, "You just try and stop me!"

We lifted our cups of Ice Wine and drank to that.

"How about this?" I looked at Qrysta. "It used to be just us three. You, me, Grello. Then we found Oller and now Klurra. Things are looking up!"

"Not just me," Klurra said. "Every bloody Orc in the Uplands will want a piece of this! *Way* better than fighting each other."

I said, "You can get them to do this?"

Klurra looked at me in astonishment. "It's a *fight*, Daxx! Not just a fight, a MOAF—a Mother of All Fights! What Orc won't want in on *that*?"

I said, "They don't know what they're up against."

"When the hell has *that* ever interested an Orc?" Klurra said. "All they want to know is, *is there a fight? Great, I'm in!* And, *who do I need to brain with my hammer? Just point me at the bastard!*"

I said, "I'm beginning to feel sorry for Jurun."

That got a laugh, but a weak one. The name reminded us of what we needed to do. And that the odds were not in our favor.

"That's the Ice Wine talking," I said, apologetically.

We fell silent. Ahead of us was the battle to end all battles. No matter how many ferocious Orcs we had at our backs, it might not turn out well.

"We could all die," Grell said eventually.

Qrysta said, "Yeah."

We sipped our Ice Wine and sat there thinking. It felt good to be alive.

We had a job to do.

Which might mean we weren't going to be alive much longer.

I remembered that I had wanted to run what we'd learned by Marnie.

I thought to her, *Marnie? There are some things I need to discuss with you.*

I waited.

Just like a couple of hours earlier, I got no reply.

It worried me even though we were probably just too far apart, and I was beyond range of her Thinking. I didn't like the feel of her absence. Marnie was looking after Esmeralda. Without Marnie to protect her ...

Qrysta saw me frowning at the table and asked, "What's wrong, Daxx?"

"I don't know. Marnie and I can *think* to each other. Like having our own private comms channel. But she's not picking up."

Klurra looked at me in puzzlement.

I explained as best I could. "Friend of mine. A fellow caster. We trained together, taught each other a lot. Like Qrysta is teaching you dual-wield. I taught her what I know, she taught me what she knows. One of the things she is expert at is communication by thought. We can talk to each other in our minds."

Klurra said, "Whoa! That's got to be useful."

"It would be," I said, "but I'm hopeless at it, still just learning. I'm trying with Oller, but we have a long way to go. Marnie makes it easy—for her and me that is. Only she's not coming through. I've tried a couple of times today, and she's not responding. I expect it's just she's out of range."

"Maybe she's on one of the Coven expeditions?"

"Yeah, that could be it." I hoped it was.

Then I remembered how she'd hinted, when she'd cut me off from naming Esmeralda, that our thought-comms might not be secure. She could be not responding out of caution. Or, of course, she could be captured like Junie, or worse …

"Is it important?" Klurra said. "What you wanted to talk to her about?"

"She'd want to hear," I said. "And I'd like to hear what she thinks about it all. Our plan, for example. I'd want her opinion on that.

"And there's another thing. She's the one hiding Esmeralda."

29

Who's Who

When Chief Elbrig heard that war was brewing he was skeptical at first, but soon extremely interested. I'd lost a round of *You're So Pathetic* to him at the feast on the night of our arrival, blowing my mouthful of beer into his face when he'd suggested I was so pathetic I couldn't arm wrestle a raspberry. The phrase was so absurd, and his old face so serious and fearsome, that I'd lost it immediately. As everyone watching shouted "Hooray!" and took a mouthful of beer ready to drench me, and Chief Elbrig began the *"Mmnh!"* countdown from five, I'd objected, while hiccupping with Orcish ale-fueled laughter, "Raspberries don't have arms!"

Moments later I was soaked and coughing, because I'd made the mistake of having my mouth open as I protested, and jets of ale had blasted into my windpipe. It got sillier. A giggling Orc child brought me a raspberry, and I arm wrestled it, overacting first confidence, then surprise, then fear, as the raspberry in my fist threw me sideways off my seat onto the floor. Uproar. And a mighty thump on the back from Chief Elbrig when I hauled myself up onto the bench beside him again, my head reeling. *Berry Boy*, he called me from then on, or *Fruit-fighter*, and his eyes lit up every time he saw me. I'd taken a moment to show him what Shift could do, knocking a few rocks off a wall with

Fireballs, which had impressed him. "You just stick to attacking fruit," he'd said. "And don't point that thing at me!"

We went to see him that evening to thank him for his hospitality, at which he said we were welcome in his territory any time, honorary Stonefields for life we were now, the lot of us. Then we filled him in on our plans.

Hearing about the other three expeditions had made us think big. We wouldn't be the only ones in on this. The more, we thought, the merrier. We had one throw of the dice at this, so let's throw as many damn dice as we can lay our hands on. Klurra had been insistent that a nasty war was the very thing to stir the blood of every Orc in the Uplands. Chief Elbrig agreed. He would call an Orcmoot right away. Every chief of every tribe would be summoned with their counsellors. They'd be all for it. There hadn't been the prospect of such excitement for decades.

"We've all been reduced to squabbling among ourselves over nothings," he said. "Trespass, the odd animal disappearing, someone looking at you in a funny way—just excuses for a little action, really. *This* is more like it! They'll be all for it. What tribe will want to be left out, if every other Orc tribe is marching off to a MOAF! There'll be another party, of course, to celebrate. Better get Apothecary Sarenne working on another batch of Over, eh? Three to five days to assemble, one day to recover. We'll be marching within two weeks."

He sent for volunteers to ride to the strongholds of the other tribes while scribes wrote letters to each chief for him to sign, summoning them to the Orcmoot.

I'd be sad to miss the party, but not the morning after. One morning spent drinking a pint of paper was enough for me.

Klurra wouldn't be coming with us after all. Discussing it with Chief Elbrig, she realized that she would need to stay in Stonefields to tell the Orcmoot everything they'd all want to know. But she would be going off to war and was happy enough with that prospect. We'd see her in the Undergrounds, we all agreed, and Klurra made us promise to leave some of the bastards for her. We said there would probably be more than enough to go around—plenty for everyone.

The plan, in essence, was a simple one. The Orcs would head into the Undergrounds and beat the living—or unliving—crap out of anything that confronted them, making as much noise and mayhem as they could manage. Chief Elbrig's eyes lit up at the prospect. Our group would head in another way and try to take advantage of the diversion the Orcs were creating to sneak our way down to the floor of the world.

Meanwhile, we'd see if we could get word to the other expeditions and to the king and get them all to mobilize every available fighting force they could assemble. Without Marnie I didn't see how we could have the communications in place to coordinate everyone and everything. We wouldn't be able to have councils of war all over the place. We realized, basically, that it was up to us. We'd make a plan of action. We'd tell everyone—gods only knew how, because we didn't—what we wanted them all to do, and we'd just hope to all hells that they, or at least some of them, did so.

We knew how they'd object. *Who are these people, telling all us royalty and nobles what to do?* They'd probably ignore us. But we were going ahead anyway. We knew we had to, and that time was running out.

We also now knew that an army of fired-up Orcs would be wreaking havoc on our behalf. How many could the chiefs muster? We were surprised to hear it could be as many as twelve hundred. "Every Orc of fighting age, which in our case means fifteen, will want to be a part of it," Chief Elbrig asserted. "Only the old and the infirm will stay behind, to guard the children and the strongholds and tend the fields and animals."

I thought, *twelve hundred rampaging Orcs will create one hell of a distraction.*

We spread our maps on the long table in the stronghold's hall and compared them with the maps that Chief Elbrig produced.

We chose entry points into the Undergrounds for the Orc forces, deciding that they should go simultaneously down three tunnels which, all the maps agreed, converged at a large cavern within a few miles of the surface, and that they should create as much chaos as possible on the way down before joining up again at the rendezvous. The whole point was to get the enemy looking their way and attract his attention away from us.

Before we went *down and down*, though, our little group would loop around to the east and south, looking to find Nyrik and Horm, if Oller hadn't already found them by enquiring after them at The Wheatsheaf. Then we'd then take whatever way *down and down* seemed best to us. If all went well, we'd be having advice and help from the nibluns.

355

We allowed ourselves three weeks for everyone to be prepared and in place.

And then ... the fireworks would begin.

▲ ▲ ▲

We rode out east the next morning. Klurra had begged for another couple of hours training with Qrysta which was fine by Grell and me. We used those two hours to continue our examination of Loremaster Perrett's research materials. There was plenty of interesting stuff, but nothing jumped out as being relevant to our current situation. We pushed the horses without exhausting them and got almost to the north–south road by sunset the following day. We made camp in a sheltered dell in the hills where we could light a fire without much fear of foes seeing it. We hadn't seen any people since we'd left Stonefields, and a fire would keep wild animals away.

A fine night it was, warm enough, under a starry summer sky. It was pleasant to sit and rest and eat around our campfire, undisturbed apart from the distant howling of wolves far off in the surrounding hills. I remembered my first day in this world and my battle with the wolf. I'd come a long way since then—we all had. We ate and drank— water and a mouthful each of Marnie's Special Peach Brandy—and talked about everything we'd been through.

"Wish I'd been there to see it," Grell said, when Qrysta told of her exploits in Lord Rylen of Hartwell's tourney.

"Me too," I agreed.

Grell nodded at her swords of honor. "Sounds like you're useful with those things, Qrys. As good as ever, would you say?"

"I think so."

We fell silent. We knew what we were capable of.

We had no idea if it would be remotely enough.

▲ ▲ ▲

We crossed the road soon after dawn. I was pretty sure that I recognized our surroundings by midmorning. Turning around and looking behind me to recall the view of the Western Mountains that I'd had when marching for The Wheatsheaf as Nyrik and Horm's prisoner, I was fairly confident that we were heading back to where they'd found me. Whether they'd be anywhere within a hundred leagues of there, of course, we couldn't possibly know. If they weren't, well, maybe we'd meet other Woods Kin who would know where they might be. I'd allowed us three days to find them, and if we didn't, we'd head down to The Wheatsheaf and join up with Oller.

We didn't need three days.

As we rode, I cast Reveals ahead of us from time to time. When, that afternoon, it outlined two small fuzzy red glows of warmth in the undergrowth, I felt Shift's tingle of excitement up my arm. She'd found them.

We set our trap. I tucked Shift back into the blanket that hung from my saddle and we rode towards them, 'unsuspecting.' They announced themselves in their customary fashion, loosing a few arrows out of nowhere into trees inches from where we had halted.

And out of nowhere came Nyrik's familiar voice.

" 'Ullo 'ullo, what have we here, then?" he teased. "Seems to me I know you chaps from somewhere. Now, let me see, where could that have been, I wonder?"

By the tone of his voice, Nyrik was not in the least alarmed. He sounded overconfident, indeed. He thought us what we had been before: someone who *couldn't fight for piss* and a pacifist Orc—with the addition of some girl or other. We'd taken precautions to make him think of us that way. Like Shift, Fugg was concealed under a blanket hanging from Grell's saddle, and he was in ordinary travel clothes rather than armor. Qrysta, small and meek in her cloak and hood, looked no kind of threat at all.

"Ah, yes!" Nyrik 'remembered.' "Brigstowe! And a lousy bargain from that sod Corporal Bloody Smott. Worth ten times what he paid us, you two are. Well, isn't this our lucky day, eh, Horm?"

"It is indeed, Nyrik," Horm said.

"It's a long way to the markets that remain open, where My Effing Lord of Brigstowe's word don't reach, but it'll be worth it with you two. You three, I mean. Nice looking young woman you have there, Daxxie. Friend of yours? She'll fetch a tidy sum!"

"Hello, Nyrik," I said. "I've been looking for you."

"You have?" Nyrik sounded surprised and delighted. "Well, then this is your lucky day too, young Daxx! Now, put your hands up in the air and sit on the ground while my mate Horm here ties you up one at a time, then I can put down this bow that you can't see, and we'll all be on our way."

All this time, the three of us had been moving according to our plan. Grell tottered feebly to one side as if scared. Qrysta dug a surreptitious heel into her horse's flank which made it whinny and shy and veer off sharply to the other side. I was moving backwards, hands up and babbling. "Look, Nyrik, Horm, no, that's not what we're here for—"

"Says you, Daxx, we says otherwise." Horm materialized out of the background of trees and came towards me with lengths of cord in his hand.

"No!" Grell ran off further to his side.

"That's enough of that!" Nyrik loosed another arrow into the tree nearest Grell where it stuck, quivering.

"Aaah!" Grell screamed, tucked into a ball, and rolled on the ground terrified and babbling.

I was yelling and pleading. "No, stop, don't, please, listen—"

"No, Daxx, *you* listen," Nyrik appeared just as Horm had, out of nowhere, and walked towards Grell. "You do what *we* say, all right? There ain't no two ways about it."

He stopped dead in his tracks as two arrows slammed into the ground by his feet and two more into the ground half a pace ahead of Horm.

Their bows were in their hands instantly, and they were looking around when two more arrows struck.

"The next one goes into your leg," I said.

They whirled around looking this way and that but not up into the tree behind them from where Qrysta had shot while our antics distracted Nyrik and Horm. She'd slid off her horse, unnoticed, scrambled up the tree in seconds, and now, I could see, had her bow trained on Nyrik's leg.

I walked over to my horse and got Shift while Nyrik shouted at me, "Don't move!"

Another arrow missed his foot by inches, and he jumped back in alarm.

"Don't move?" I raised Shift. "Good idea," I said, and cast Immobilize on him.

Nyrik froze like a statue.

Horm hovered, uncertainly, gaping.

"Listen," he began. "No harm done. We'll be on our way, you go on yours ..."

"That," I said, "is exactly why we've been looking for you, Horm. Last time I went with you. This time you're coming with us."

He didn't like the sound of that.

"There's no need to be alarmed," I said. "I apologize for our little charade, gents, but we needed to find you two, and fast. You're too good at hiding for us to find you if you don't want to be found, so we presented you with what looked like a nice, soft target. We're anything but. Grell here has something he'd like to show you. And our partner up that tree behind you could skewer you both in a heartbeat."

Grell retrieved Fugg from her hiding place and strolled over to Horm.

Horm was alarmed at the sight of a glowering Orc approaching him with a battle-axe. "What do you want?"

"I want you to look at that," I said.

Horm looked at Fugg, and his eyes grew round. "Niblun!"

"Presented," I said, "by Serjeant Bastard *himself*, to Grell here as the finest battle-axe fighter he'd ever trained."

Horm looked up at Grell in amazement. "*Blunt* said that?"

"Yep. Things have changed since we met, Horm. And not just us. We came looking for you because we have a proposition for you."

Horm said warily, "Which is?"

"You take us to the nibluns."

"Eh?"

"To your mother. We need to talk to them."

"What about?"

"I'll tell you *if* you agree."

Horm thought. He glanced at Nyrik for guidance, but Nyrik was going to be no help under his Immobilize. "What's in it for us?"

"A lot." I smiled. "Not all of it good. Danger, blame, treasure, shame, death, fame."

Horm said doubtfully, "I'm listening."

I released Nyrik from his Immobilize, and he fell to the ground in a heap, gasping. "You heard all that, right Nyrik?"

He panted, "Yes. Boiling hells!"

"And you see there's no point in trying to run away?" I said, to drive the point home. "I'd just Immobilize you again."

Nyrik nodded and looked at Shift thoughtfully. "Useful, that."

"In more ways than you know," I said, and Shift jittered her amusement into me.

"Yur," Nyrik agreed. "I can imagine." He nodded, thoughtful. "Right, then. We'll listen. First things first, though … ." He glanced at Horm, and they padded over to retrieve their arrows from the trees they'd shot them into. Once again, they rubbed grass roots on the gashes, muttered to the trees, and bowed to them before coming back to join us. "Wouldn't do to piss the trees off," Nyrik said. "May be as we'll be needing their help. Get the arrows out double quick, clean the wounds with earth, which is what they live on, apologize respectfully, and explain. Then it may be all will be well with them, and they won't take umbrage. Never can tell, with trees."

We sat cross-legged on the ground, filled them in on what we knew and what we were planning, passing around the flask of Orcish Ice Wine that Klurra had given us. It made the discussion much more pleasant. Nyrik and Horm were nothing if not sharp. They grasped the bigger picture quickly. They listened closely to what we'd done since we'd parted ways with them in Brigstowe.

Nyrik studied Qrysta with interest. "Should have taken a closer look at you, miss!" he said with a chuckle. "Recognize you now, I do. Right Charlie you made of that swaggering twat Lord Rylen at his tourney. Never seen the like of it! Where'd you learn to fight like that?"

"Here and there," Qrysta said.

"Blindfolded and all!" Nyrik continued. "How d'you do that?"

Qrysta shrugged. "I might as well ask you how you split each other's arrows."

Nyrik nodded. "*Hm*, yes," he saw her point. "Well, watching you was worth more to me and Horm here than the hundred o' gold we won for his Hunting Bow trial—seeing you take him down a few pegs. No one worth the name of hunter in it. Call that a competition?"

"Piece of cake," Horm agreed. "Bunch of wankers."

"That they was," Nyrik said. "We heard the Merc Guild was after you."

"You heard right," Qrysta admitted.

Nyrik's eyebrows rose. "They find you?"

"They did."

"And?"

"They died."

Horm whistled.

Nyrik said, "Blow me down. You took out, what, ten mercs?"

"Nine," Qrysta said. "One had dropped out sick before they caught up with me."

"Still," Nyrik said. "I mean, blimey. Not mugs, those mercs!"

Qrysta shrugged.

Nyrik studied her. "Remind me not to piss *you* off."

Qrysta gave him her sweetest smile. "Now, why would you ever do that?"

"Why indeed?" Nyrik agreed. "So." He turned to Horm. "We take these good folks to meet your mom, right?"

Horm was not as naturally chirpy as Nyrik. Since we'd told him the situation, he had grown more and more thoughtful. "She'll be damn glad to see them, an' all," he replied. "Nibluns are worried sick by what's going on. Used to living nice, quiet lives down in their homes, they are. Getting on with things, not bothering no one, making what they make: arms and armor, jewelry and such. That's all they want to do, is to be left in peace to get on with their crafting. Now there's all sorts of horrible things down there, every which way they turn, hemming them in, stopping them coming and going, waylaying them, murdering them. *Eating* them, some have heard."

I asked, "When were you last down there, Horm?"

"A couple of months ago. Jumpy as anything, they all were. Gates barricaded and guarded. Never used to be like that. Never had to be. Mom was saying about as how she was thinking she should get out and go Upground. Not something a niblun ever says, that. I don't doubt it'll be worse now."

"Why's that?" I asked.

"'Cos they were all saying as how everything was getting worse day by day."

I told Horm what we intended to do. Head *down and down* and find the floor of the world.

The blood drained out of his face. "Are you serious?"

"*It* is. So are we. Will you help?"

They would indeed. In any way they could.

30

Agnolf's Tale

We made it halfway to The Wheatsheaf that day, our first priority being to link up again with Oller. Nyrik rode with me, and Horm with Qrysta. We spent the night inside an ancient willow tree by the banks of a river which Nyrik unlocked using his willow key.

"Peculiar wood, the willow," Nyrik told us. "Doesn't know if it's solid or liquid. Grows by rivers, light as air, hits like a brick. We'll be okay down here for the night. A night tree, is willow; he'll stay on guard for us. He'll let us know if anything is coming that we need to be aware of. Sleep in the sun tomorrow, he will, trailing his leaves in the river and dreaming."

While we were eating our supper, sitting around on the earthen floor of the willow tree's cellar in the half-gloom among the blue mushroom lights, I asked Nyrik, "How can you tell which trees have these hidey-holes?"

Nyrik looked at Horm and grinned. "Woods Kin secret."

I said, "I'm just curious, that's all. I can't see any clue on the outside."

"There aren't any," Horm said, his grin even bigger than Nyrik's.

They looked at each other and chuckled.

"Ah, why not?" Nyrik said. "What's the harm in it? It's not as if they have the keys, after all."

He turned to me. "They *all* have these hidey-holes, Daxx."

"All of them?" I was surprised. "Every single tree?"

"Yup. When they're grown big enough. Sapling's no good, he won't have the strength yet. They *spread* for us, see? Like their branches spread above. Only below, under the earth. A big, ancient oak can make a great hall if he lets you in, room for twenty, and he don't mind if you roast a deer under him for all of them. That's another reason we never piss the trees off. You don't want to be out in the Woodlands at night surrounded by pissed-off trees. You'd never make it out alive. We treat them well, they treat us well."

I said, "So if you were to cut one down—"

"*Sh—sh—sh*, Daxx!" Nyrik interrupted sharply. "You don't go talking of cutting no one down out here! Specially not tucked up nice and safe in this lovely, comfy old willow."

"Sorry," I said.

"You should be!" Nyrik said. "Now, if say, an old tree at the end of her life died off, the way we all must, and fell over—why, all you'd see is roots and earth and a hole where she'd stood all those years and lived her long life. And she'd rot away and feed the insects and toadstools and so on, and her goodness would return to the earth which was her mother. Who'd use it again for her great-great-great-grandchildren. And so her line goes on. So no, you wouldn't see any nice cellar like this. But while they're alive, they spread above and will spread below if they like the look of you and you have the right key."

"Useful," I said.

"Yeah, not half. Like that staff of yours. Rowan, by the look of her."

And, like Marnie had, he pronounced the *row* to rhyme with *cow* and *now* and *how*.

"Rowan indeed," I said.

"Got to be skillful, to handle my lady rowan," Nyrik said.

"She handles me, Nyrik, I just carry her around." Shift, in my hands across my lap, glowed at the compliment.

"And point and shoot, right?"

"Right—but also more than that," I said. "Teamwork."

"Yeah. Makes sense," Nyrik agreed. "Like us and Father Willow here. Teamwork."

Teamwork. The word made me think of Esmeralda. Every time I thought of her, my worries vanished. My aches and pains and problems faded away, I felt at peace and somehow elevated. I had often tried to work out why that was. *She made the world a better place* was part of it, but not all of it. It was, I decided, just an idea. A lovely idea. An idea that she, the embodiment of Junie's blessing, radiated.

The world needs more radiating of that kind of thing—of *making-a-better-placing*. I tried to imagine what it was like being Esmeralda, being *inside* that Glamour, radiating it at the rest of us. I couldn't. It was about as far away as you could get from being dull old Joss Palmer, whom nobody ever noticed if they could help it. Thinking of her made me smile. As it always did.

And then I snapped myself out of it as I thought—Marnie. Why can't I think to her? What's going on? Maybe she was in range now. We were closer to The Wheatsheaf, and her cottage.

Marnie, I thought. *Are you there?*

No reply.

Why? I could think of only three answers.

One, she didn't want to reply for some reason.

Two, she couldn't reply, for some other reason—such as she was still out of range.

Three, I didn't even want to think about. I think that if I'd believed that Marnie was dead, I'd have thrown in the towel. Given up. Marnie dead meant Esmeralda dead. And that thought was unbearable.

I couldn't allow myself to think it. It would mean that our cause was lost already. I forced myself to assume that it wasn't and to concentrate on what I knew, not what I didn't. I knew that I loved Marnie, and that I loved Esmeralda—just as I loved Grell and Qrysta and Oller and Klurra. And yes, if any of us fighters died—of course that would be bad. It would be horrible to lose any of them. But we were fighters. We knew that dying was part of the picture in what we did. What we did, when we needed to, was combat. People die in combat.

Marnie and Esmeralda, though: in some different way they were what we were fighting *for*. It doesn't really compute completely. What's the difference between Oller dying and Esmeralda dying? When it comes down to it? I couldn't puzzle it out.

Maybe it's because Oller would die a hero's death—or a scoundrel's death. He'd somehow have deserved it or have earned it. Esmeralda wouldn't have done either. It wasn't her fault that she was how she was. It was Junie's. Junie had laid the Glamour on her, and Esmeralda had worn it dutifully and bravely and—most importantly—*graciously*, even though she had never asked for it. She'd said how she often wanted to be just normal, but she wasn't, and she knew that she wasn't and she bore her burden cheerfully and cheered the world up around her.

It sounds absurd to wonder: How can someone possibly begrudge, for a single second, having *the loveliest life there ever was or ever will be?* But how can anyone who has never had that responsibility laid on them ever know what it demands? She had been right when she had told us that we didn't understand. That no one ever does. You might think—from the point of view of an ordinary person—that it would be easy being her. *Everyone who sees you loving you,* as her mother had asked of Junie.

It took me a while to consider that it might not look quite the same from Esmeralda's point of view. And that was when I truly came to see what I admired about her. Yes, I loved her, like everyone else, we all did. Junie's blessing on her made us. And in return, she made every single one of us feel as if we were the only other person in the world.

It wasn't about her. It was about *us.* Instinctively, she understood this. And she delivered. How very different she could have been, possessing that power. She could have been selfish, manipulative, a monster. A tyrant.

She wasn't.

She was *true.*

It was that word that hit me, lying in my blanket under the dim blue glow of the mushroom lights beneath Father Willow, listening to Grell snoring and the murmur of the river flowing past the earth wall of our sanctuary. *True.* It sent a chill up my spine. I was worried now for Marnie and for Esmeralda. Something was wrong.

I told myself, *whoa, hold up, you're leaping to conclusions, just like everyone leapt to conclusions about stick and stone, and so on …*

Maybe I am, myself told me back, *but something definitely feels wrong.*

I said, *you're simply panicking because you can't get through to Marnie. Work it out for yourself. Take command. Own your situation. Do what's needed.*

Myself said, *then why isn't Marnie coming through? Something is wrong. Something Esmeralda is doing is wrong … . For all the right motives, no doubt, but she is* wrong.

Junie had been lured and captured. Marnie was … off comms. Esmeralda, I was becoming more and more convinced, was heading the wrong way, thinking she was right. I wanted to get up, saddle my horse, and gallop to Marnie's to find them, to stop whatever it was that was happening.

Instead, I drifted off to sleep. It was pitch black when I woke up gasping.

Qrysta's concerned voice came from the other side of the remains of the fire. "Daxx? You all right?

My heart was racing as I surfaced from the nightmare: Esmeralda, alone, small and shining in the brown haze, us all watching her light fading, growing ever smaller, her high, pure voice singing ever fainter as she rode the black horse away into the gloom. *A stick, a stone, a book, a bone, go down and down, for half a crown* .... And the last of the light that glowed around her vanished, extinguished by the murk that hung over the Darklands.

I sat up, heaving for air, my skin cold and clammy. Instinctively I reached for Shift, seeking the calming warmth of her presence in my mind, to soothe the ache of watching Esmeralda being swallowed up in the brown miasma above the Darklands. I felt my rowan staff's comforting response as if she was saying, *I'm with you. You'll be fine.*

"Daxx?" Qrysta's voice came again.

"Bad dream," I said, and grimaced. "Sorry to disturb you."

"Sorry you were disturbed," she said sympathetically. "You good?"

"I'll be fine." I echoed Shift. "So long as I don't have another."

I didn't.

The next dream was on a whole different level.

▲ ▲ ▲

I was flying through the night, through cold rain. Something was perched in front of me between my arms. Something small and indistinct, no more than a shadow—but it was no shadow. Its thin legs hung down between my knees on either side of the pole I was gripping. It was, I knew, frightened.

I was in a hurry. I should be in front of our campfire beneath Father Willow, but this felt as real and immediate as the nightmare of Esmeralda riding to her doom had been insubstantial and dreamlike. This was no dream.

"No," a voice spoke. I didn't recognize it but knew that it was my mouth that had spoken. I felt the word on my tongue and in my throat. Only it wasn't my voice, it was a woman's voice. I was a woman?

"No. I am. It's more than a dream and more than one dream. Listen, look, and learn."

What is happening? I wondered. *How …?*

"Save your strength, lad," the voice came again. "These can be a headful the first time you get one. Marnie sent me. I'm her Covensister. Name's Ennis. I'm an Envisioner. She knew I'd be able to reach you, wherever you might be, in your sleep. Dreams and visions, those are my domain. In and out of them, giving them and taking them—just like I'm giving you this one and taking you where you want taking."

Where's that? I thought.

"Where *this* one is."

Abruptly, the scene changed. I was in a bed, in a darkened room. Weak light from a moon hidden by clouds leached in through a little round window. My stomach was full. My head was fuzzy.

Had a skinful, he has! Ennis thought, and I heard her voice in my mind now that I was no longer in her body. *Can't blame him,* she continued. *Jan the Brewer's finest makes you want to keep on supping it. Spent many a night comfy in that very bed, I have, Jan's ale drifting me off into my dreams and visions. Sleep on through a thunderstorm, this one would.* There was a pause then, *Nearly there.*

Nearly where?

Something hairy was whiffling in my armpit. I felt for it. Dog. Small dog. Wait—*Little Guy?*

I was Oller?

You're a guest in his sleeping mind, laddie, like I'm a guest in yours. Settle back and leave this to me. Watch and listen and learn. She paused, and I sensed she was distracted. *Right, Hob, off you go.*

There was a sense of disorientation again, and I was back on what I now knew was Sister Ennis's broomstick. We were hovering outside a small, dark window, high up under the thatched eaves of The Wheatsheaf. The little shadow in front of me—*her*—inched along the broomstick and reached out a spindly arm.

Through the window, I saw Little Guy sit up sharply, ears pricked.

Tap tap. Tap tap tap. Tap.

Then there was that sudden disorienting sensation again of being sucked into another body—one that was small and wiry and covered with hair.

I—*Little Guy?*—always slept with at least half an ear open. That was how I had survived in my hard life fending for myself, half an ear open, ready to wake up and run.

But I no longer had to fend for myself. I had Oller to fend for me.

There was nothing that I—Little Guy—wouldn't do for Oller. Especially not warn him of a strange *tap-tap-tapping* at his window in the middle of the night. Even *more* especially when that little window was high up under the eaves, on the third floor, over twenty feet above the ground where nothing should be able to reach to tap on it …

Oller-turned-Agnolf had enough gold to afford not just a room to himself, but a room with an actual *window*—tiny though it was. I, a mere stray dog, had never known such luxury. And the food! Not just scraps, but a whole bowlful for myself, every night, of that nice innkeeper's delicious mystery meat stew with broken lumps of stale bread in it, softening as they soaked up the gravy. I'd been dreaming of that gravy and those soft lumps of bread and the chunks of mystery meat, which were no mystery to my clever nose. Pig, cow, wolf, rat, sheep: all or any, depending on which bit I was eating, and all of them mingling in that rich gravy … . But I was no longer dreaming. I was wide awake, and on high alert.

My—Little Guy's—ears pricked, listening.

There it was again, *tap-tap-tap.*

I whined.

Then growled.

Then whimpered.

Then licked Oller's—Agnolf's—face until he woke up.

Or rather, didn't completely. Oller muttered, not opening his eyes, "Oy! Leave off, you little perisher!" He rolled over.

Tap-tap, tap-tap-tap.

The dog that was me clambered over the lump in their bed and licked Agnolf's face again.

Again there was that befuddling sensation of being pulled out of one body and thrown into another one, and this time when my eyes opened, I glared at Little Guy—and heard, *tap-tap-tap.*

368

Agnolf, being Oller inside his Glamour, who was now also me, was on the alert at once. As a thief, I knew all about sounds in the night, especially sounds that shouldn't be there.

Tap-tap-tap, tap.

I—he—swung out of bed silently and crept across to the window. It was a dark night, well after midnight. The moon was out of sight behind clouds. There was, though, just enough light to see a shadow outside the window. The shadow moved. The hairs on the back of my neck rose. The shadow hovered. Then it reached forward and *tap-tap-tap-tapped* again.

I—Oller, who was also Agnolf—froze.

I was thinking. I had no light, but a candle wouldn't help anyway. It would just light me up, so that whatever *thing* it was that was out there could see me. I didn't want to be seen. I wanted to *see*, to know what in all hells was out there tapping at my window.

I didn't see. I heard. A hoarse voice whispering.

"Oller. Oller. Ake-wup!"

I, being Oller, heard his thoughts. *It's talking? It's talking! Gods above and below, what kind of creature is tall enough to tap at a window this high and can talk and—knows my name! It is death! Has death come for me?*

"Ake up, Woller. It's he, Mob. Wopen the indow, et me lin!"

It took a few seconds to sink in. Little Guy was growling quietly, but I—we—shush'd him. "It's okay, Little Guy. I know him, he's a friend."

Hob?

I opened the window.

Hob's solemn face stared at me, his gray eyes grown enormous so that he could see in the dark. He was hovering, not clinging to the window ledge. He hadn't climbed. He was perched on the front of a broomstick that was floating in midair just beyond the window.

And then I was no longer Oller, Little Guy, or Ennis, but an outsider in the room with them, watching them. Doing what Ennis had told me to. *Look, listen, learn.*

"Ullo, Holler," Hob said.

"Hob!" Oller said, then looked at the woman riding behind him. He didn't recognize her. It wasn't Marnie.

"Harnie needs melp," Hob said, sounding scared.

369

New Rock New Role

"Urgently," the woman said. "Name's Ennis, guildsister o' Marnie's. That's a good Glamour you've got on you there, well cast. Mayhaps as you could step aside and we can come in?"

Oller stepped aside.

Little Guy growled again quietly, just to let them know that he was there and there'd better be no funny business.

The broomstick poked in through the window, and Hob clambered to the ground.

"Wob's hurried, Oller!" Hob said, mournfully. "Garnie's marn, Gabel's marn! Frob's *hightened*!"

Ennis, who was stouter than Marnie—but quite a bit younger, so she was able to bend—was inching her way along the broomstick on her round stomach. She had to tilt it to fit in through the tiny window diagonally but managed it. "Tight squeeze, that!" She dismounted and parked her broom. "Getting too old for this sort o' thing." She brushed the rain off her black dress, removed her wide-brimmed black hat and straightened out its crumpled point.

"What's happened?" Oller said.

Ennis propped her broom against the wall. "We were all ready to fly off to join the main force of our Covensisters—on an expedition. I don't have time to explain now, except to say it's part and parcel of what you're all doing." At Oller's blank look, she added. " 'Us' being our local Northern chapter—Marnie's and mine. And young Mabel too; she's one of us now.

"Brings her dog, Ezzie, with her to our meets. Lovely girl, follows her everywhere. Made us chuckle to hear Mabel say how the pup loved flying, bundled up inside her cloak with her nose poking out, ears flapping in the wind, squeaking with excitement.

"All night we'd been gathering, sisters coming in from near and far. We never ride by day—can't have people seeing us. Council of War we had, everyone talking and telling and listening about what was going on, what we'd heard and learned, where we had to be, and what we had to do. Preparing and planning and resting up before riding the next night to the war. Only—well, Hob will tell you in a minute.

"One of the things that was talked about right away was that everyone had been getting all these *Thoughts* from each other. Only none of us had sent them! I'd ask someone what she meant by something I'd heard from her, and she'd look blank at me and say, *that wasn't*

370

me. It was clear soon enough that someone was *inside* our network, sending us forged Thoughts." Ennis shuddered then continued. "Well, that worried us, I can tell you. How much did he—and we thought we knew who *he* was—know? From listening in and *Thinking Into* us, putting ideas in our heads, seeing how we responded? Clearly, *Thinking* wasn't secure anymore, so we said, *right, that stops now.* Put up the walls, we did." She hesitated, sadness appearing in her eyes. "But not before Marnie got a distress Thought from Hob."

She looked at Hob. He swallowed, cleared his throat, and trying his best not to sound as jumbled as he felt said, "Shadows came. Along the ground, ooh the thr … *through* the air. Eefrits! Om frall sides! Dozens of them! Naking a terrible moise, screaming. Pearing the tace aplart! I hid behind the pireflace. Then sneaked out and wid in the hoodshed. Scob's *hared!*"

Oller said, "Were you asleep? When the eefrits came?"

"No."

"Why not?"

"Waiting up. Mor Farnie and Mabel to bum cack."

"Did they?"

Hob shook his mournful head, and Ennis said, "Not safe. Marnie sent me to fetch him while the rest of them set off at once. Best get *Mabel* as far away as fast as possible."

I noticed her emphasis on *Mabel*. Clearly, Coven knew who Mabel was under her Glamour.

Hob said plaintively, "I won't know dot to *woo* mithout Warnie!" He sniffled and wiped away a tear that welled in his big, sad gray eye.

Oller turned to Ennis. "Where did they set off for?"

"South and east."

His eyes grew round. "The Darklands?"

Ennis nodded. "Seemed important to us that someone keeps an eye on it. Nothing's come out of there in ages, but that doesn't mean nothing's going on *in* there. We thought we'd send out patrols, scout from above. See what's what." She paused. "When do the others arrive?"

"Tomorrow with luck," Oller replied. "Day after at the latest."

"Then I'll pop back tomorrow night. My sisters have gone on ahead of me, I'll catch them up later." She reached for her broom which flew over to her. "Come on then, Hob. You'll be nice and safe at my place. You'll like my Lob, she's just like you."

Ennis angled her broomstick out through the window, squeezed herself onto it, and turned it around in the air so that Hob could climb onto the front.

"See you tomorrow night, then," Oller said.

"Yes, early as I can make it with these late twilights. Probably about midnight."

"I'll be here. And Little Guy will be on the lookout."

"Good dog, that," Ennis said. "Knows what's what."

"That he does," Oller agreed.

As the broomstick backed away and started to turn, Oller said, "Bye, Hob. Look after yourself."

"Hye, Boller," Hob waved a crooked hand.

Sister Ennis banked her broomstick away from the building, and it shot up into the night sky, flinging me out of the dream and back into my own body.

31

The Undergrounds

An elderly scholar arrived at The Wheatsheaf the next afternoon, accompanied by his bookish daughter and their taciturn servant, who stabled their horses while his master went inside to enquire about beds for the night. Many were available. Road traffic had dwindled to almost nothing in recent weeks, Jan the Brewer told him while showing him to the inn's largest room on the first floor. "Usually, several folk sleep here of a night." He indicated the various beds, large and small. "But you'll have it all to yourselves tonight, master." Travel wasn't safe anymore he told them, and those who did brave the road brought all sorts of rumors about all sorts of goings on, none of them good. The scholar said he would be happy to take the room for the night for his group. And that he needed a rest before their supper that evening. He paid Jan Brewer for the room, and Jan thanked him and left.

"What I need," I said, settling my 'elderly' body onto a bed, "is a tub full of hot water and a big bar of soap."

"Yeah." Qrysta settled her 'bookish' self on the neighboring bed. "Dirty work, adventuring. Clean clothes would be nice, right?"

I said, "Shall we ask? Laundry, hot tub?"

"Why not?" Qrysta grinned. "Heading into the Undergrounds tomorrow, might as well look and smell our best."

373

There was a knock on the door.

I called out, "Come in."

Agnolf entered. We'd made eye contact with him on the way in, and he knew to come up right away. He was followed by a familiar looking small brown dog, and then by 'our servant,' Grell.

Grell looked at us, and his 'sour servant's' face broke into a very Grell-like grin. "Together again for the first time, eh?" He clapped Agnolf on the back and bent down to let Little Guy sniff his hand. Little Guy wagged his scruffy brown tail. Grell patted him and scratched his ears. Little Guy decided that he liked Grell.

"Dunno about you lot," Grell said, "but I'm *itching* for a fight!"

Little Guy checked us all out, one by one, moving on from Grell to me and then to Qrysta. He decided that he liked Qrysta too, then jumped up on the bed by Agnolf and sat, ears pricked, watching and waiting.

We were soon all up to speed with what everyone else knew. Oller was surprised, to say the least, that I'd been in and around his dream the previous night and knew all about the appearance of Sister Ennis and Hob. We had to face the fact that there was nothing we could do about Mabel and Marnie, despite our anxiety. We'd just have to hope that they were okay and knew what they were doing. I wasn't going to try to Think to her now that I knew that the comms between us might well not be safe.

All we could do that day was rest up, get the smith to check out the horses' shoes, load up with provisions and, if at all possible, scrub ourselves clean. Oller thought the idea ridiculous. We'd be underground and up to our ears in dirt and enemies any day now—why get washed if you're just going to get filthy again? Grell said Orcs don't bother much about hygiene. But maids were summoned, travel-soiled clothes handed over, a tub hauled up and filled with pail after pail of scalding water, and Qrysta got the room to herself for a half hour while we went about our tasks. Then it was my turn. I lay there and soaked and my mind wandered. I had a pretty good idea of what was coming. Danger, foes, mayhem, blood, sweat—and death or victory. I told myself, as the knots of hard riding eased out of my muscles, to remember this on the way down to the floor of the world. *Remember this calm, remember this still before the storm that is about to break.*

Horm 'introduced himself' to us that evening as we sat inside the wide hearth in the parlor, and we invited him to join us for supper.

Everyone spoiled Little Guy rotten with scraps from their plates. Eva kept our mugs topped up with Jan Brewer's ale.

She didn't have a second glance for the elderly scholar but chatted happily with Horm. "Didn't bring me no handsome young buck tonight, Horm?" she teased. "I should make you fetch your own ale!"

Horm winked at me, and I glanced furtively at Qrysta, but she'd missed it. She had no idea who Eva was talking about. I tried to recall if Eva knew my name. I decided that she didn't. She'd just called me 'foreigner.' That was a relief. Qrysta wouldn't have missed the chance to rib me about it.

We ate and drank and relaxed and didn't talk much. The time for talking was over. Tomorrow we were off on the final leg of our journey. We all wondered, privately, if any of us would make it out alive.

The evening grew late, and we went our separate ways at separate times, so as not to attract attention, and regathered in the room that we'd taken for the night—all except Agnolf, who'd gone upstairs to wait by his window for Sister Ennis. She arrived a little before midnight. She was relieved when he told her to go the large window on the floor below with the candle inside on the windowsill.

"Much easier, getting through a nice big window like that!" Sister Ennis said, easing herself in on her broomstick and dismounting. "Hullo, young Mastercaster! Nice to meet you in the flesh."

"Likewise," I said. "And thank you for your trouble."

" 'Twas no trouble." She gave me a friendly smile, which faded as she continued, "Troubles enough everywhere else. All around, behind and ahead. Especially ahead."

Oller made the introductions, and we sat down to confer. Sister Ennis was gone within the hour. Thought-comms we might no longer have, but we had good, fast messengers—messengers who flew by night and no one saw coming and going. She approved of our plans. Though, like us, she had no idea if anyone else would act on them. We had the Orc army now, and that was far more than we'd thought to have had only days ago. "Marnie will be tickled pink to hear *this*!" Sister Ennis chuckled. "An army of Orcs? She'd *never've* thought!"

Coven would liaise with the GAA, and Ennis was sure they'd also commit everything they could to the fight—this was, after all, GAA work, if anything was. The other guilds would be sounded out, and the noble lords with their armies, and the king with his. If they could all just stop fighting each other … . Well, that was hardly likely, lords being only concerned with their own interests most of the time. But there was no harm in trying.

▲ ▲ ▲

The stablemaster of The Wheatsheaf had only sold one of the horses we'd taken from the mercs that Agnolf had brought in a few days earlier. Few travelers these days, he said, just as Jan Brewer had. Hardly any market in horseflesh. He was relieved when Agnolf told him before dawn the next morning that we'd take two of the remaining eight with us. One was for Horm, the other for Qrysta, to replace hers, on which Nyrik had ridden off the previous morning. That had meant she'd had to double up on my horse, as Horm had done with Grell, who had dropped him off within a mile of The Wheatsheaf. We hadn't thought there'd be anyone there who'd be made suspicious by us riding in with Horm, but it was better to be safe than sorry.

"I'll be happy to stretch my legs." Horm slid down from his perch in front of Grell. "Not much of a one for horses, me."

We would pay for the horses' stabling and feed, that was no problem for us. The problem for the stablemaster was that he couldn't get the provisions he needed for his own horses, let alone ours. Crop stores were depleted. Hay and oats were in short supply. Armies were sending foraging parties all over to the farms to requisition anything they could get their hands on. Honest traders like himself came way down the pecking-order now and had to make do with leftovers. Serjeant Bastard's scouts had indeed been up this way, looking for some deserters, he said. No one had seen anyone answering the descriptions they gave.

"An Orc, can you believe it?" he said. "People would notice a bloody great Orc and remember. Rode off back south they did." A thought struck him. "Maybe I could send your mounts down to Brigstowe, see if we can sell them at market. My Lord's army might be in need of horses."

"Worth a try," Agnolf said. "We don't want them to be a burden to you."

The sky was growing light and the Wheatsheaf roosters were crowing as the porter swung the heavy gates of the compound open.

We mounted and took the road north. We soon left it, heading back east into the Woodlands, but this time into a part of them that I'd never been in before. Our mounts made good speed through thickly wooded, rolling hills, with stretches of open grassland and scrub where they could stretch their legs, and streams in the valleys where we could water them and refill our skins.

It was early summer now, and the weather was warm at last after a long, cold spring. A few small, white clouds floated in the bright blue sky. The breeze was gentle. Birds sang. Deer started at the sight of us and cantered calmly away. The world could hardly have seemed more peaceful. It was odd to think that we'd soon be leaving this sweet, fresh air, and heading *down and down* from this idyllic landscape into darkness and war.

Horm led the way now. It wasn't far where we were going, he said. We'd get there before nightfall. The trouble was that he didn't know if it would be 'all right.' By which he meant: was the way that he hoped to take into Niblunhaem still passable? Or had it been taken over and lost to hostile forces? If that were the case, we'd have to take the long way around, and that could add days to the journey. And who knew if any of the other ways in and out that the nibluns used were still safe? It was still early in the long, summer evening when Horm pointed at the ridge of hills ahead of us and said, "That's it. Not long now."

Down one last slope, across one last stream, through a stand of trees up the opposite slope, and we trotted up the hillside towards the cave that we could see above us. What we couldn't see until we were right on top of them, and they wanted us to, was the welcoming committee that was waiting for us. Horm saw them first, of course, but then, he knew how to *see* better in the Woodlands than we did.

"Fifty, sixty at least …. Nice turnout!" he said, as he rode alongside me to the cave's mouth.

"Sixty what?" I said.

"Best damn archers you ever saw," Horm said. "Or rather didn't yet, 'cos they don't want you to." He slid out of his saddle.

A Woods Kin materialized at his elbow, half his size—a child, I realized—who took the reins that Horm handed to her and started murmuring to the horse she was now leading. Other children appeared by our horses with shy smiles and quiet words for the animals and nosebags of oats which they slipped over the horses' heads. And then we saw that we were surrounded by Woods Kin, all dressed in leather and wool and hides, all with bows, and each carrying several quivers full of arrows, all with knives or hatchets at their belts, and all looking like they meant business.

Coming towards us, grinning, was Nyrik. "Made good time and all!" he called out, cheerfully. "Scouts have gone in a ways and taken a look around, not seen anything. Which is good, but no signs of nibluns, which isn't. Right, let's be going. The kids'll ride the horses back to where they'll be safe and stabled. Can't have them unprotected out here, waiting around for you to come back. Now then, everyone." He called the group to come closer. "Introductions can wait till later. Meanwhile, this is Daxx, Grell, Qrysta—and Oller, I presume?'

"Yep," Oller said. "And Little Guy."

"Oh," Nyrik said, not expecting the small, brown dog. "Nice. Scouts first in the shadows. You go with them, Oller, you being the finder— and your dog, I reckon. Got a good nose, has he?"

"The best," Oller said.

"Good. Nose like that can smell trouble none of us can. Daxx, you three go next, we'll take our lead from you."

"I'll be casting up Glows," I said. "They'll be traveling along with us, so we'll have plenty of light. If trouble breaks out, take down anything you don't like the look of, and make sure you don't hit our hitters." I indicated Grell and Qrysta.

"Me too," Oller said, "I'm no good from a distance. Close quarter work, that's me."

"All clear?" Nyrik asked. Nods and murmurs confirmed that everything was. "Right, let's get going. The sooner we get behind walls the better."

We all hefted our packs and checked our weapons and armor. The Woods Kin strung their bows. We waved the children off on our horses, turned into the cave, and entered the Undergrounds.

It was quiet. And dark. The Woods Kin made no more noise between the lot of them than a few leaves rustling, or mice scuttling into their holes. Oller went on ahead with the scouts, Little Guy padding beside him, ears cocked, sniffing the wind for trouble. Not that there was much wind—but what there was, was coming from below; which was good as it should give Little Guy warning of anything he didn't like the smell of ahead. I threw some Glows into the air above us which caused a few impressed whispers from the archers and a couple of *shushes*. The Glows kept pace with us as we headed on down, and a troop of our shadows slid along the cave walls beside us.

I kept the Glows dim deliberately. I didn't want to warn anything that might be ahead with a dazzling wall of light coming towards them that they could see from far off. The floor was dirt, trodden hard over the years by nibluns heading up with their wares and down with their supplies. The ceiling was a comfortable height, a good ten feet of space above our heads. It showed no signs of closing down on us as we went on, nor did the cave walls seem to be narrowing.

We moved in silence as quickly and quietly as we could, and for a while our progress was everything we could hope for. No barriers, no foes, no signs of danger. Even so, our nerves were on edge. I glanced occasionally at my companions: Grell striding on, jaw tight, a grim look on his face; Qrysta's face was her usual calm mask, eyes alert and shining in the reflected Glows.

Nyrik trotted to keep up with us, his head turning this way and that, occasionally getting and receiving messages from ahead and behind. Each time a scout reported to him, he'd nod to me. All quiet, vanguard and rearguard. After a good twenty minutes, we came to a fork. A smaller tunnel led off to our left. Our scouts were waiting at its mouth. They looked serious.

They reported in whispers.

The side-tunnel led to the stables, where the nibluns kept their pack animals, for their trade expeditions Upground. The protecting gates across it had been smashed open, and the stables destroyed. The hardy niblun ponies and their stable hands had been slaughtered and eaten. There were no signs of fires. They had been eaten raw. There was no sign of life anywhere. Nor of ... *un*-life.

The sights shocked us all. We didn't have the time, nor the inclination, to wonder who—or more probably *what*—might have done that. We needed to press on down with all possible speed. I suggested a change to our formation. I would cast some Glows over the main body of the archers that would move with them while I went ahead of them in the van with the scouts in the shadows, so that I could cast Reveals into the darkness ahead of us.

I cast, saw nothing, nodded at Oller, and the scouting party moved out, trotting on down into the gloom. We were on high alert now, every nerve stretched to the limit. No hidden life was Revealed. Little Guy smelled nothing alarming. The scouts slipped noiselessly along the cave floor as it sloped on, *down and down.*

We stopped as if by some instinct from time to time to listen, to probe ahead with Reveals, and to smell the wind. Then we moved on again, in a process that was repeated over and over: stop, listen, Reveals, move on.

Horm had told us that there were caverns ahead—larger spaces where the walls widened out and the ceilings arched high above. We took every precaution at the mouth of the first one. Nothing changed, nothing alerted us, nothing happened. In a way, the *nothing happening* was the most worrying thing of all. Not that we wanted anything to happen. It was much better to be making swift progress in silence, but we all knew that this was only temporary. Something was going to happen, of that there was no doubt. None of us knew what. All we knew was that something *had* happened back at the niblun stables. And that the walls of Niblunhaem lay ahead. But what was between them and us? And what, if anything, remained of Niblunhaem itself?

The tunnel curved down now and steepened. Here and there mushroom lights glowed on the walls. Spectral, pale, poisonous-looking things they were, different from the warm blue glow of the lights in the tree-cellars. No hidden life was Revealed. Nor was any hidden *Un*-Life. It didn't seem right to think, *so far so good.* It all felt anything *but* good.

As before, we stopped at the entrance to the second cavern to check it out before venturing in. I cast Reveals into the shadows below. Small, fuzzy red outlines appeared as our scouts slipped in past me and moved down along the walls.

Oller nodded and was about to step into the cavern when Little Guy stopped. We looked down at him. He was staring into the darkness ahead. His tail was stiff behind him, his head locked forward, the hairs on the scruff of his neck standing upright. He sniffed the air urgently. Then he cringed back, whining, his ears flattening as if he had heard some threatening sound.

We heard nothing. Oller and I were looking around, this way and that, searching for whatever it was that had alerted Little Guy, who was shaking and whimpering. I cast more Reveals ahead and down and around, and once again they Revealed nothing.

They Revealed nothing because the attack came not from down and around but from above. At the last moment, even Oller and I could hear what must have been deafening to Little Guy. Dogs can hear far higher frequencies than humans, but even humans, when they are close enough, can hear the sonar squeaks of bats.

The bats came in a cloud of leathery wings, sharp claws, and sharper teeth. They were on us in a swarm with no warning—because I had been casting Reveals in every direction but *up*. Unlike normal bats, they did not use their radar to avoid us, but to locate us and to attack us, clamping onto our necks and heads and bodies with their claws and tearing at us with their long teeth, screaming their wild shrieks of blood lust. Also, unlike normal bats, these ones were enormous, each of them bigger than the largest Woods Kin.

The silence we'd been moving in burst into an uproar of shouts and screams—warnings, commands, cries of pain. I had Shift in my hand, high above my head, blasting as wide a field of sheet lightning as she could manage. Woods Kin archers were firing into the air at speed. Grell charged past us, roaring, and whirling Fugg around his head in exactly the way that Serjeant Bastard had told him not to. There was no danger of him decapitating any of his troop here. They were all no more than half his height.

Fugg's razor thin and razor-sharp blades carved through the cloud of bats like an aerial blender, raining chunks of bat flesh and sprays of bat blood down on the rest of us. Qrysta was dancing and slicing, Oller was stabbing anything that clung to anyone, Horm was bellowing with rage or pain, I could not tell which, Nyrik was barking orders to spread out and where to focus fire—and still the damn bats kept coming.

I lobbed Flamebombs at them like mortars, to explode where their numbers were thickest. I threw a heavy Stormcloud at the ceiling, leached Frost into it, whipped up a Hurricane around it, and hail slammed down onto them from above. I threw up Thunderflashes and Bedazzles and sent Barkers into them to scare them away—all while keeping up as many Area Heal Alls as I could. And *still* they flooded in on us, shrieking, biting, tearing, grabbing, kicking, flapping their monstrous wings in our faces which hit with the force of whips. In all the mayhem, I found myself thinking while casting every offensive attack I could come up with, *what in all hells* are *these things!*

It was a question on everyone's lips when it was all over, after the storm of the creatures lessened and the tide turned and we began to gain the upper hand. The Hailstorm seemed to have sapped their resources. Being warm-blooded creatures, they needed a healthy circulation, and the Cold ate into their wings, slowing them down and disorienting them.

My Glows showed that the floor of the cave was littered with bats: dead bats, wounded bats, crawling bats—and, worst of all, feeding bats. They were feeding not only on our dead, but on our wounded and unconscious. I cast as many spells as I could to put them out of action: Ice Traps, Immobilizes, Shock Cages. The Woods Kin tore into the feeding bats with their knives, screaming with rage.

I checked the ceiling looking for any stragglers, any survivors that might have made it back to their roosts. I saw none. I cast an Ice Curtain at the ceiling just to be sure and watched it settle and spread, blue white and cold, as it worked its way down the walls. It was, I noticed, a thin, feeble thing.

I was about to reinforce it when I saw that Shift's tourmaline heartstone was dim. When I was wielding her, the tourmaline shone with a fierce light—red for damage, green for Heals. She was out of power. I stopped myself casting another Ice Curtain and over the next minutes used what reserves she had left for as many Heals as I could.

Nyrik got everyone to focus. Bring the dead, of which there were five, tend the wounded, retrieve every possible arrow from bat or ground, and move on. I checked out the few casualties that my casts hadn't healed, and as Shift recovered her power, one by one they all recovered under her Heals. It took a while as I was not prepared to drain Shift completely. Her Heals were much appreciated. I could tell that we had staunch allies now among the Woods Kin. Our fight was their fight—there was no question about that.

It was still some way to Niblunhaem. Monster bats might prove to be the least of our problems on our journey there. We ran now, knowing that the uproar of the battle in the cavern would have alerted anything between us and the gates of Niblunhaem to our presence. Getting to the city was all that we could think about, apart from *what in all hells were those things?* They were certainly unlike any bats any of us had ever seen before, above ground or below. That left us all thinking the unspoken question: *what else that we've never seen before might there be down ahead of us?*

Even though we were running at a fast trot, we were moving almost silently. The only sounds were the thumps of Grell's huge feet, Qrysta's and Oller's and my boots scuffing, the pitter-pat of Little Guy's paws, and the muffled rattling of our packs and weapons. The Woods Kin made hardly any sound at all. So, we all heard what the leading scouts heard, at just about the same time they did. They stopped, holding up hands for us all to halt behind them.

We listened, and the scouts crept forward, beyond the range of the dim Glow I'd set above them to light their way. Shift had recovered to full strength now, but I saw no reason to light us up more than we needed to see ahead. Some of the sounds were unknown to us: growls, and gurgles, and deep hums, and sudden cracks, as of stones splitting. Others we knew only too well: the screams and uproar of battle.

There was no going back. Nyrik assigned the group leaders their positions. He motioned for those carrying the five dead to leave them where we were and waved to me to go on ahead with Oller, Grell, and Qrysta. The archers nocked arrows to their strings and drew their bows. We moved forward as quietly as we could and halted in the shadows at the end of the tunnel that opened out into the great cavern outside the gates and walls of Niblunhaem.

It was a writhing, heaving mass of bodies.

Many of those bodies were forms we didn't recognize as being human—or Orc, or Woods Kin. Another loud cracking sound echoed around the cavern, and we saw what had caused it. Two enormous figures were hurling huge boulders at the closed, stone-and-iron gates of Niblunhaem.

"Fuck me," Nyrik muttered.

My grip on Shift tightened instinctively. "What the hell are those?"

"Stone trolls," Nyrik said, in a voice hollow with fear.

I looked at the long-armed, hairy, huge-headed, ape-like creatures that swung along on their knuckles with surprising speed, before picking up boulders, rearing upright and then flinging them at the city gates.

I said, "Not *made* of stone, I hope?"

"Might as well be," Nyrik said. "Buggers to kill, I can tell you that! Hides like stone, hence the name. Arrows bounce off them. And look at the *size* of the damn things .... Twice the size of any I've ever seen—which is big enough, I can tell you!"

I looked at the trolls bellowing and hurling their boulders and then retrieving them to throw them again. My mind was churning.

I glanced at Nyrik beside me. He was shaking with fear.

"Boiling hells, Daxx! We can't take *one* of them brutes down, never mind two—not just forty of us!"

Yes, we can, I thought. "Nyrik," I said, "I'll handle the trolls. You and the others stand by."

Nyrik looked at me blankly. "You *what?*"

"No time, the gates are cracking. Just be ready."

"What for?"

I looked down at him. I'd never seen him scared before.

"My signal. I'll send up a flare. If it's green, attack—everything *but* the trolls. If it's red, I'm fucked, so run like hell and get out of here. All of you."

He stared at me, eyes wide, mouth open.

"Got that?"

He gulped. "Yeah, but—"

I nodded and walked into the cavern.

32

Niblunhaem

For all I knew, trolls could be the most intelligent creatures in this world. In which case, we were in trouble. But I'd always associated trolls with brawn power rather than brain power. We could fight them, yes, but we'd all die. There were not only those two almost invulnerable, super-sized stone trolls, but also the hundreds of ... whatever all those other damned things swarming outside the gates of Niblunhaem were. Against them we were forty-odd archers, plus Grell, Oller, Qrysta, and myself. I was the one who was going to have to solve this problem, I knew that. I believed that I knew how. And that *how* relied on trolls lacking sufficient mental capacity to prove me wrong.

There's more to casting than various kinds of Damages and Heals. There are skill lines that involve manipulation—of the environment, of the weather, of light and sound. One obscure branch is Induction. You might, for example, be hiding near a river that your enemies are crossing. They vastly outnumber you, and you definitely don't want to be seen. So, rather than blasting lightning into the river, which would immediately get you noticed, you Induce lightning into it. With deadly results—water and electricity being a lethal combination. Then you slip away.

Or your target might be a cookpot in an enemy's camp, into which you Induce a nasty virus with messy and painful results. A plague of vomiting and diarrhea can lay an army low as effectively as any pitched battle. Induction works stealthily, at a distance, so is useful in situations like those when you can't get close enough to sneak in the poison by hand, or where there aren't enough of you for combat. Induction is magic's version of guerrilla warfare—you can use it while staying hidden.

Which is exactly what I was intending to do. I'd done a lot of experimentation with Induction techniques in my time and had made some intriguing discoveries. It was a much more nuanced and useful skill than most casters realized. I'd learned, once I'd become competent at handling it, that Induction can also work on the mind. But not on a mind that is too sophisticated. And by sophisticated, I mean about half as clear as the mind of a two-year-old throwing a temper tantrum.

The simpler the mind, the easier it is to manipulate. I could induce Terror into a bear that would send it running for its life, even though— if it could think it through—it could stand there and disembowel me with one swat of its claws. But it couldn't think it through. It would be heading for the hills, Terrored, as fast as it could.

That same Terror wouldn't even *register* with your average soldier, let alone affect him. Maybe, with more practice, one day I'd be able to cast Induction into humans. I hoped that I'd live long enough to find out. Maybe I'd be able to blend it with Marnie's Awareness skillset and create a hybrid line of my own: Thinking Into meets Induction. They had much in common. For one thing, you didn't need a staff to cast them. Marnie could Think Into me whether she had one in her hand or not—but only if I thought of her first. She'd had to Think Into Oller on our flight from Rushtoun and get him to say un-Oller like gibberish to get my attention—his mind being, she said, simpler and more open than mine. It was odd how all those thoughts cascaded into me in a kaleidoscope of ideas as I slipped into the cavern and readied myself for what I was going to do. Which I hoped would work. Because if it didn't, I'd be firing up a red flare so that my allies could flee for their lives while my foes closed in for the kill.

What I was going to do was simple: mind-control the stone trolls. Which would only be simple if their minds were simple. I'd soon see. I'd need to succeed with one stone troll before I could even contemplate attempting to Dominate the other, and that meant thinking out my strategy.

Inductions can take time to sink in. Not long, a few seconds, while the mind being Induced submits itself to its new Dominator. But a few seconds would be enough to alert our foes. If I divided my efforts between the two trolls, our foes would have time to notice and to wonder and to react. I couldn't give them that time. I had to hit them before they knew it.

I chose the troll that was heading towards the gates to retrieve the boulder it had just hurled at them. I decided on that one because, if everyone began to wonder what was up with it when it began to behave strangely, they'd be looking at it and away from where I was lurking, behind them at the far end of the cavern. Instinctively I gripped Shift and closed my eyes, clearing my own mind for its assault on the troll's. I felt her calm confidence. *You've got this. You don't need me. Go for it.*

I thanked her, took a deep breath, and cast Induction into my target troll. I felt the cast hit home, like the nibble of a fish at a baited hook. I struck, and Induced into it Dominate, Influence, Manipulate and then Stop.

The troll slowed as it picked up its boulder. Lifted it.

And stopped.

I Influenced it to believe that the other stone troll was its worst enemy. And using Manipulate, I instructed it to hurl its boulder at it and then to pound its chest with its fists, head back, and to bellow long and loud in challenge.

The other troll was, naturally, annoyed. It didn't appreciate either being bowled over by a huge rock or the indignity of being bellowed at. It picked itself up from the ground where the boulder had knocked it, and, roaring and bellowing, started thumping its own chest.

I was into that troll too now, using the same casts: Dominate, Influence, Manipulate. It picked up the boulder that had floored it and hurled it—but not back at the other troll: instead, as I Influenced it to do, it threw it at the mass of creatures all around it. The boulder bounced through them like a giant bowling ball, shattering them, scattering them, crushing them, and flinging them into the air.

The first troll was now stomping around with its huge, clawed feet, and swiping with its long arms at the annoying little pests buzzing around it, who were screaming and fleeing in all directions. I sent up

387

a green flare, and our forces poured out of the tunnel behind me. I popped an Orb of Shielding onto Grell as he charged past me, roaring, arrows from the Woods Kin flying over his head in a blizzard of steel into the enemy ranks, then other Shields onto Qrysta and Oller and Little Guy. Shift began blasting Thunderclaps and Ice Sheets, on which the mob below us was soon all skidding and falling, and Ball Lightnings, which erupted among them and blew them to pieces. The trolls stomped and swatted. The arrows flew. My casts erupted in fire and fury. But there were so many of our enemy. And they had spotted us and were heading our way.

Eefrits. At least a dozen of them.

Not only were those long legs birdlike, they were *fast*. They charged us, tearing and slashing with their taloned arms, and snapping their reptilian jaws, like the nightmarish offspring of ostriches and crocodiles. They ripped and rent and bit and screeched, and no matter how many arrows our archers shot into them, they didn't slow their assault. And they were far from alone.

I'd never been in a fight like it. The only battlemage with forty allies to watch out for against a mob of Undead and creatures of the Underground—and *eefrits*: I was swamped—not just by noise and assailants, but confusion. I did not know where to look or who needed what or what I could contribute. Grell roaring and slashing: yes, I always knew where he was and could keep his shields up and boost his stamina. But the others? Qrysta was here, there, and everywhere. Oller slipped into the shadows. Nyrik and Horm were nowhere to be seen, knives at work no doubt. *Leave them to it*, I decided, and laid down a Flamefield between our foes and the Woods Kin archers around me.

I was in the middle of it. That's not a good station for a battlemage. We operate best at distance, laying down Area of Effect attacks, and healing as hard as we can. The melee was all around me, front and sides and behind. I knew that I was a target there—a soft target. I didn't have plate armor like Grell's. My Orbs of Shielding would hold for a while, but I felt overwhelmed. I needed not to. *Keep calm*, I felt Shift telling me as I began to panic. *We're in this together. All of us.*

I've often wondered since about my staff of rowan wood. How she knew things that I didn't. How she talked to me without words, in feelings that were as true and as real as the feeling you get when you stroke a cat or sit with a sleeping dog's head in your lap. You don't need words. They don't have words. Shift didn't need words.

I felt that I was drowning under the assault that was coming at me from all sides. She knew better. *We're in this together. All of us.*

An Orb of Shielding will protect you from damage. It won't bounce your assailant back off you. I was knocked end over end by a kick from an eefrit that I hadn't seen coming. Luckily, Qrysta had. When I got to my feet winded, she was in front of me, facing it as it closed in for the kill. In a blur of steel, she drove her blades into its eyes—which did no more than send it staggering backwards, shrieking.

"You okay, Daxxie?"

"Yeah," I gasped. "Thanks."

She was gone, hitting the abomination with everything she'd got. Beyond her, Oller was at his murderous work with his knives—only to be seized by a misshapen, toad-headed *thing* that opened its mouth to bite him in half. I raised Shift to blast death at it, but something small and brown leapt at its throat and hung there, shaking with fury. *Little Guy.* The toad-beast dropped Oller to pull Little Guy off its throat and died from a blur of Oller's knives.

Mayhem. Chaos. Horm yelling at me, "Nyrik!" Me seeing his mate surrounded, so casting up a Shield on him, then Horm and other Woods Kin cutting their way in towards him. *No time. Needed elsewhere.* Grell flung through the air by the kick from an eefrit, three other eefrits converging on him. Earthgrips to stop them. They didn't. Flamefields to burn them. They didn't. Those damn things seemed impervious to my casts. How in all hells were we going to be able to handle them?

We weren't. Woods Kin were seized and torn apart or bitten in two at a speed and with a ferocity that was terrifying. I tried slowing them down with Ice Traps, Immobilize, Blinding Flares, but no magic that I threw at them affected them. Shift was losing power, her tourmaline eye fading. Her Greens were needed more now than her Reds, so I switched to Area Heal Alls and spammed them again and again over everyone. Even Grell was taking terrible damage as his Orb of Shielding weakened while he whirled Fugg in a tornado of razor-sharp niblun steel surrounded by screaming, slashing, striking eefrits.

They couldn't lay a claw on Qrysta, who was dancing through them like a mist, stabbing into their eyes, which should have blinded them but didn't, merely enraging them. Oller was slipping between their legs, slashing at hamstrings, and jabbing into groins, seemingly to no effect. Arrows stuck out of the things, so that they looked like demonic hedgehogs, but still they kept attacking, flailing, snapping, slashing.

I was running out of ideas, dodging to avoid their attacks, casting Heals as fast as I dared, watching, agonized, as Grell took cut after bite after slash. One of them seized him in its jaws and lifted him high off the ground, but Grell, bellowing defiance, slammed Fugg down onto its skull, where she stuck. Grell wrenched at her to get her free and hacked at the eefrit's head again and again while it howled and shook and bit until its knees buckled, and it slumped to the ground where Qrysta drove a blade up to the hilt through each of its eyes.

Neither she nor Grell said anything. Neither would have heard above the cacophony of battle. But I knew the look that passed between them.

I've gotcha, big guy.

Thanks, Qrys.

Grell rolled out from the eefrit's dead jaws, gasping for air, hauling at Fugg's shaft until she came free and then turned to face the next foe, his massive, bloodied chest heaving, his small, brute eyes glaring defiance.

Something beyond them caught my eye.

Fire. Streaks of fire, lancing down, from the tops of the city walls.

It took me a moment to realize what was happening.

Niblunhaem's defenders were shooting fire arrows into the mayhem below. One or two were even sticking in the trolls' thick fur. As if they weren't annoyed enough. Now their fur was catching fire—and at last I knew what to do.

I Manipulated the trolls to leave off their stomping and swatting at the creatures below them. The niblun defenders could deal with those lesser foes. *Move*, I commanded the stone trolls through Dominate— and did they ever. They knuckled across the cavern floor like gigantic apes and under my Manipulate command, launched themselves at the eefrits, bellowing.

The eefrits didn't know what had hit them. They turned, uncomprehending, to face their new assailants, and in that moment of hesitation, two of them were torn to pieces and a third was sprawled on the floor after a crushing blow, its back broken. We'd taken just one of the things out since they'd attacked, and that had needed everything that we could all throw at them. Three more were now out of the fight in seconds, and the fight only lasted seconds more after that. Grell stayed in it, howling nearly as loud as the trolls, and hacking great chunks out of the eefrits with Fugg.

Qrysta and Oller slipped among the fallen, writhing eefrits, stabbing them until they lay still. A few arrows still flew from the Woods Kin archers, but most now realized that they could leave the job to us. And the trolls didn't need any more stray arrows in them, to goad them to their task.

When the last two eefrits were cornered and wilting under the hammering they were getting, I called the stone trolls off. They stopped at once and stood panting and glaring down at the eefrits, their terrible long claws hanging loose by their sides. I wanted to talk to these eefrits, if that were possible. I held Shift up high and fired another green flare into the air. All fighting ceased. All eyes watched me as I walked towards the two glaring, hissing eefrits.

I cast Area Heal Alls as I walked, to aid our wounded, and I could see them sitting up, standing up, gasping, leaning on their fellows, recovering. I hit Grell with a Close Wounds. He grunted and lumbered over, falling in beside me, Fugg at the ready.

Qrysta appeared on my other side and then Oller, and trotting at his heel came Little Guy, scowling at the cornered, wounded eefrits as if to say, *one wrong move, chum, and I'll have you!*

The eefrits, crouching against the cavern wall, scowled back at us with a scowl that was a lot nastier than Little Guy's. I remembered those cold chips of white ice from the stare that the one I'd passed on the road down to The Wheatsheaf had given me. I had hoped never to see those eyes again. And here were four of those eyes, their ice chip glares burning into me with infinite malice.

I stopped in front of them and raised Shift above my head. I sent up another Glow to hover above us.

The stone trolls hadn't moved since I'd halted their onslaught on the eefrits. Now, without moving a muscle, I silently Influenced them to bellow and beat their chests. At the noise, every being in the cavern reacted in alarm, jumping, turning, backing off.

The eefrits cowered further away and further down. There was nowhere for them to go, and they knew it.

The stone trolls stood still again, ready for my next command.

I aimed Shift at the eefrits. I could feel her anger through my hand. *Let me at them!*

I don't need you yet, I let Shift know. *But I may any moment, so be ready*. I cast Induction into the eefrits. And then Influence. Followed by Dominate and Manipulate. I Influenced one to stand up. I Influenced the other to lie down.

Neither moved.

So, they were more intelligent than a stone troll.

That didn't surprise me. After all, they hadn't been affected by my Ice Traps or my Immobilizes. They had resistance to any magic that I could cast at them.

"I know you can understand me," I said.

They glared back.

"Talk and answer my questions honestly, or I'll order the trolls to tear you apart."

They watched.

I waited.

I said to Nyrik, "Take your archers down to the gates and finish off the rest of them. If you get the chance, capture any that look out of place or interesting, I'll want to talk to them. I'd like to know what we're up against."

"Right you are!" Nyrik gathered his forces.

"Wait for me," Grell said to him. "I'm not done yet!" He lumbered off after them.

Qrysta said, "Be right back, Daxxie, got a job to finish." She fell in beside Nyrik and Grell and the archers, and they all headed down to help with the mopping up, Oller and Little Guy trotting along beside them.

Several Woods Kin remained behind, those who were too weary or too badly hurt to fight any longer. Good. They all had bows and would be happy to use them on these eefrits who had slaughtered their kin.

"So," I said to the eefrits, "what do you say?"

The voice, when it came, was as horrible as the creature's cold, white eyes. It was a harsh, lifeless croak, like something scraping out of a swamp filled with teeth. "We listen."

I turned my attention to the one that had spoken. "I'm going to lay a Truth on you, so I'll know when you're lying." I cast Truth onto both of them and gave them a moment to decide whether they believed me. "And so will you, because the Truth will bite you. Hard. And we'll all see you jump and know you've been lying and we won't want to give you many more chances. So, speak up, speak the truth, and maybe we'll let you live."

I waited, hoping that my Truth cast would affect them, seeing as my other casts hadn't.

I needn't have bothered. The eefrit stared into my soul, turning my stomach to ice. It was *only a look*, I told myself. But it was a look that I'd see for the rest of my life in my nightmares.

And then it did the last thing I expected. From its throat came a low, guttural gurgle. And on its long mouth spread the grim mockery of a smile.

It was laughing.

As was its companion.

"*Live*," it said, derisively.

It stared at me.

It saw when I understood and then nodded, slowly. "We do not *live*."

Cold crawled up my spine.

"*He* will give us life. That is why we have come to his summons. Life to eat. Life to live."

I thought, *what in all hells am I dealing with?* I said, "So, you know how to find him."

I made it a statement, not a question.

The eefrit said, "*Down, and down.*"

I fixed it with as hard a stare as I could muster. "You're going to take us there."

It uncoiled, more confident now, and stretched back into its usual shape. "With *pleasure*."

I didn't like the way it said that. Nor the way that it was smiling again. As its companion was.

It glanced up at the motionless stone trolls. "Too big," it said, looking back at me, smiling its grisly smile. "For the tunnels. Tight. Low. *Down, and down.* Just you and us. Alone. Your magic tricks don't fool us. Down there we will eat you. Alive."

I was stumped. I could see that my idea of forcing them to take us to Jurun was a non-starter. They would kill us and eat us before we got there. No. The idea of descending for who knew how long to the floor of the world in the company of those creatures was not an attractive one. We would have to get there on our own.

So now what? I could kill them. I could let them go. Neither alternative appealed.

"Don't move," I said.

I Manipulated the stone trolls to jerk awake suddenly and growl. The eefrits got the message. I turned away and walked down towards Niblunhaem.

The battle was over. The gates of Niblunhaem were open, and Woods Kin and nibluns were finishing off the last of the enemy. I cast Area Heal Alls at our allies. I knew that they would be needing them.

Grell was leaning on his battle-axe, blowing hard. I handed him one of Marnie's restorative potions which he gulped down gratefully.

"Thanks, mate," he said. "That might just about be enough combat for one day, even for me."

"Okay, let's sort you out." I cast a Lingering Mend that enveloped him in a shimmering green sphere. It would work on him for ten minutes until it faded. "Get on in. You'll be a hero; everyone will be buying."

"Sounds good to me." Grell shuffled, slowly, wearily, *greenly,* and relieved towards the gates of Niblunhaem. Even Qrysta was knackered, slumped on the ground, head down. Hardly surprising as she'd been at full speed in a fight longer and harder than any we'd been in before. I cast a Lingering Mend over her and handed her another of Marnie's potions.

"Thanks, Daxxie."

"You okay?"

She managed a weak smile. "Still here." She handed me back the empty flask. I took it and her wrist and hauled her to her feet. Our eyes met. Her smile strengthened and I smiled back. *Still here.*

Still work to be done.

We turned and walked towards Niblunhaem. She and Oller and I and the corpse-bearers were the last of our force to be welcomed into the city. The nibluns were all over us, thanking us, saying how they'd given up hope, the siege had been going on so long. Holed up behind their walls they had been, determined to fight to the end—but knowing that the end was coming, and they'd all be dying soon.

And now they weren't going to be. We had saved them. We'd saved their home. There was nothing they wouldn't do for us. We walked in through the huge stone gates to cheers from hoarse, exhausted throats—which ceased as they saw the Woods Kin with their sad burdens. The dead were taken from them, to be treated with reverence, as Heroes of Niblunhaem. The celebrations stopped as the stone trolls herded the eefrits in, to hisses and mutterings. They were bound in chains of Imbued niblun steel that nothing could break and taken to the cells.

The stone trolls stood outside the city walls. I Probed them for hunger and thirst. Through their scattered senses, a picture, or rather a *feel*, emerged. It didn't quite make sense to me as I was wondering what we should do about them—but it made sense to Shift. Just as she'd let me know *you got this* in the battle earlier, she now let me know *I got this*. Along with her serene glow up into my arm, I got some odd noises—grunts and mumbles. They were passing, I soon realized, between her and the stone trolls. I was merely a witness. Whether it was some ancient language or not I have no idea. I am not tree nor troll. All I know was that I understood.

I turned to the niblun beside me, whose name I had heard but had already forgotten, and asked him to send out two barrels of ale to our gigantic allies. Shift quivered happily in my hand.

The nibluns jumped to make it happen. Two huge tuns of strong niblun ale were rolled out to the trolls, who sat and drank, and drank and belched, and drank and lay down and rolled over and snored.

Nibluns are quite different from Orcs—in just about every respect. They look forward, rather than back. They like to celebrate, yes, but, while doing so, they want to discuss matters at hand. What to do, who we were, where, how, when, why—all those questions came both tumbling at us and from us. Getting roaring drunk was not the priority. The priority was to celebrate, *yes*, and to get to know each other, *yes*, but mainly to *deal with the problems*. Which, we knew, were urgent and staring us in the face.

So, instead of waiting until the morning to get to work, people stood up in twos and threes and got on with it right away. Grell showed Fugg to all who asked to see her, and dozens of smiths were instantly at his elbow, telling of who had made her and what she was and *why* she was and how proud and pleased her smith (with whom some of the older ones had served their apprenticeships) would have been of the way she'd performed that day in the hands of a Hero of Niblunhaem. Before he knew it, our Orc was being fitted for a suit of impervious niblun plate armor by a crowd of master craftsmen and their apprentices—supervised by the city's two Forgemasters, Rodvarn and Thorleif, both telling him how each other's armor was so much better than their own. When all his measurements had been taken, they hurried off to their forges to start crafting it.

Qrysta had every swordsmith in the city poring over her swords. They could not credit how advanced and effective these strange-shaped weapons were. They'd never seen anything like them. She was asked if they could borrow them, and she handed them over. The sword-smiths gathered up their apprentices from the other tables and left to be about their work. She and Oller were then measured from head to toe for, they were told, the lightest, *hardest* leather-and-chainmail sneak-and-stab gear they could ever imagine. As was Little Guy, who had no idea why all these small, frowning people were examining him so intently. They measured his limbs; he licked their faces.

I was also told, in no uncertain terms, as a dozen hands measured me from head to toe, that I wasn't in the proper gear for a Master Caster, *but leave that to us, you'll see.* Experts in every field of niblun lore appeared and talked and listened while niblun tailors got what they needed before hurrying off to get to work.

I sat back down and took a draught of fine niblun ale. Horm said, "Niblers don't usually open up to outsiders like this."

"You said, 'niblers.' I thought that was rude."

"Not if you are one," he said.

We raised our mugs and clanked them against each other.

We drank. *Funny old world,* I thought as I took another mouthful of niblun ale. How about if nobody gave a damn anymore and never mind *sticks and stones will break your bones.* Wouldn't we *all* be better off if words really *did* never hurt us? I was still thinking about this when a niblun historian sat down on the bench opposite Qrysta and me. He and I were soon talking at length about everything—lore, magic, the wars, goings on in the Undergrounds, what lay ahead—until he said, when I'd told him of Oller's unexpected findings at Marnie's, "I'd like to see those."

From my pouch I produced the malachite necklet and the star sapphire ring.

He inspected them with interest, then said, "The jewelwrights should see these." He added, his eye caught by the amulet of ancient amber squares around Qrysta's neck, "That too—if you wouldn't mind, miss?"

"Sure." She took it off and handed it to him.

The historian, whose name was Kjelvild, turned it over in his hand reverently. "*Baumbein.*"

Qrysta said, "Excuse me?"

"Amber," he said. "One of the words for it in the Old Language. Which turned from *baumbein* to *amber*, over time. *Baum* tree; *bein*, bone. Another is *börnstën*, burn stone. The Old Folk knew that amber came from the sea, but was it made by the sun burning stones? Or was it, as some now believe, the lifeblood of long-dead trees, grown as hard as bone over long years under the earth, then washed ashore?" He held it up to the light so that he could peer at it closely. "Old, this is. Very old." He studied the runes carved into the amber squares. "*Hmh.* I know runes. But not these …"

I said, "The giant crafter who gave it to my friend, Grell over there, the Orc, would not tell him what they mean. Craft secret, he said."

Kjelvild grunted again. "Ah, well, better ask a crafter." He got up. "May I?" he asked Qrysta.

She replied, "Of course. I'd be interested to hear what they say."

I followed Kjelvild out of the hall where we'd been feasting and into the stone streets of Niblunhaem. They were lit, I was interested to see, by clusters of blue mushroom lights like the ones in the tree-cellars. I popped a Glow above us to brighten our way.

"Useful staff, that," the historian said. "We owe her our lives."

I looked at him surprised. "How did you know she's a she?"

"Rowan," he said, "the lady of the mountain forests, wife to the ash, mother to the first woman. *She* will be interested to see her. And her beautiful heartstone. I've never seen a tourmaline that big. I doubt she will have, either."

I said, "Who?"

"The jewelwright we are going to see." He turned off the main path into a little side alley.

"Horm's mother?"

"Great-grandmother," he said. "Hundred and twenty if she's a day, but still going strong. Makes just a few pieces a year now, but each fetches a fortune. Ah, here we are."

We stopped at a wooden door in the stone wall, and he knocked on it.

It was opened by a stouter, older, female version of Horm.

When she saw me, her face lit up. "The caster!" she said. "And my Horm sold you as a slave." She chuckled and shook her head. "Twenty o' gold to Corporal Smott? You're worth all the gold in Niblunhaem now, lad! Come in, come in." She held the door wide for us and—after stooping to half my height—I entered, after Kjelvild. Introductions were made, and being nibluns, they were straight down to business.

"Show her," Kjelvild said.

I handed Qrysta's amber amulet to Horm's mother, whose name was Neva.

"I was thinking as maybe Gurndren might know these?" Kjelvild pointed at the runes.

Neva held the amulet up to the light and examined its squares. She smiled and looked at me. "Well now." Her head was on one side, studying me thoughtfully. "We have a problem."

"That being?" the historian said.

"Craftwork," Neva replied.

"Ah," Kjelvild said, understanding.

I said, "I'm sorry, I don't follow."

"All crafts have their own lore and learning," he explained. "Which is not to be told to anyone outside that craft. Armorers tap theirs into every piece of armor, using tiny punches, writing what they are giving each piece to have in it forever. And then you take your new armor to the Imbuer for whatever traits she will add, which she will Imbue into it from the *lore and learning* of her craft. And the sword-smith and the shield maker and the fletcher and the cobbler who makes your boots exactly how you want them, *just so.* Craft secrets, they are, carefully guarded. And when it comes to the jewelwrights, well … each doesn't know the tenth of what all the other jewel-wrights know, is how I've heard it."

He turned to Neva for her to elaborate. She was still smiling that odd, secret smile.

"We spend more of our time chasing each other up for this and that than we do actually *crafting*, it seems to me sometimes," she said. "Or asking around: who knows what words go with which stones, or combinations, or shapes, or uses? And, of course, you can't tell them your secret, so you have to do it for them, when they bring it to you for what *you* know, and they have to do it for you when you bring them something for what *they* know. Have to get it *right*, though, because we can't be sharing our secrets."

I partly followed. Who was I to ask why or why not? "Indeed," I said, thinking I ought to reply with something.

"So, young caster," she said, "ever make a piece o' jewelry?"

"No."

"Right," she said, "no time like the present. Come with me. See yourself out, Master Kjelvild. I'll send him back to you in good time."

And that was how I made my first—and to this date only—necklace.

33

Down and Down

It didn't take long.

"No need to bother Nan with this." Neva led me to her workbench. "I can tell you what you need to know. Pop this on." She handed me an apron as she put on her own. "Got to look the part if you're to be a jewelwright."

She found a chair for me, and I sat down beside her.

"Now then," she said. "Got a lady friend?"

I was about to say no but then thought of Deb in Rushtoun. "Kind of."

She looked at me, eyes narrowing.

"Kind of?"

"Well, um. We." I didn't quite know where to go with this. "Had a lovely time. And, um." I shifted on my chair, not wanting to meet her gaze. "I had to leave."

"Go on."

So, I told her. About the taking of Rushtoun and the victory feast and its fine aftermath—and the days and nights that followed, and how we'd run away before dawn, with … . I didn't mention Esmeralda's name. I didn't want anyone to hear me even thinking it. "On a vital mission."

She studied me.

She nodded.

"*Kind of,*" she repeated, and thought about that. "There's more to that story than we know of, isn't there? Remains to be seen where that goes. Well, you've brought the tale of the siege of Niblunhaem to a fine ending, and one we'd given up even hoping for, let alone expecting, so I wish you well in the ending of this tale of yours. *Kind of.*"

She shook her head and smiled. "It was *kind of* you to help us, young Master Caster. I'll be happy to repay the compliment and *kind of* make something *kind of* for her. Describe her."

I did.

"*Mm.*" She smiled. "You owe that one an apology."

Surprised, I said, "How do you know?"

"It's written all over your face. *Guilt guilt guilt!* Sneaking out on her like that before dawn …"

She chuckled. "You young 'uns!" she said, clearly enjoying my discomfort. "The scrapes you get into!" She sighed. "Yes. Those were the days. Remember them as if they were yesterday, I do. Those bright memories from the time we came into bloom …! Sharp and sweet. Clear as crystal. They never leave, however much they hurt. You can tell them to push off and leave you alone, but they don't listen. Good times, bad times." She shook her head again. "*Lively* times, that's for sure …"

She same out of her reverie and was all niblun business again. "Maybe if you save the realm, she'll forgive you. I know what to make for you now, a nice ring. Stones, design, setting—gold, of course. Lovely, I'm going to enjoy that! The sooner we get you out of here, the sooner I can get started on it. Right. Grab a chain you like the look of."

There were dozens of chains of all types and sizes hanging on the walls within reach. Steel and silver on the left, then gold—rose gold, white gold, yellow gold—then other metals beyond that, silvery again … but if it went from cheap to expensive, then those to the right of the gold ones could be platinum, or other rare metals. I picked a chain from the beginning of the left side, a series of simple, tiny links.

"Silver," she said, which made me think of something. "Could you spare another?" I asked. "For a friend?"

"If you tell me why."

I told her about Oller's silver key and how Marnie had said it needed a silver chain that wouldn't break.

Neva nodded. "Pick one you think he'd like. I'll get it Imbued so it'd take those two trolls outside to break it—if they had an hour to pull on it."

I took my time. I knew that it was important to find the right chain for Oller's silver key—just as it had been important for me to find the right staff. I felt each one in turn, my mind open to a response—just as Shift had responded to me in the dark in Marnie's woodshed.

And it was Shift who responded to me in Neva's workshop. *This one,* she said.

Her approval warmed my arm as my other hand held the specific slender chain that she'd picked. I frowned. It seemed similar to others I had handled.

It isn't. This one.

If you say so.

I do.

I lifted it off its hook and handed it to Neva.

My rowan staff jittered happily. *Shift knows best,* I thought, and Shift agreed.

Neva grinned. "Perfect. You'll have it with your ring in the morning. Right, now onto your pendant."

There were boxes and boxes of pendants, in every kind of material: gems, cloth, wood, metal, bone, tusk; some were carved, some designed in any number of patterns. My eye fell on a simple green stone, which seemed to be shaped like an elongated S.

It just felt right—both to me and to Shift.

I handed it to Neva.

"Well now," she said. "Isn't that interesting … . Of all the hundreds of gems, in all these boxes, you choose a greenfire." She looked around in the boxes. "The *only* greenfire," she chuckled. "I don't trust Mr. Co-incidence further than I can throw him—which is no distance at all. *Greenfire!*" she said.

"What's a greenfire?" I asked, happy that I seemed to have made the right choice.

"Look closer," she said.

I examined the pendant. The green stone had, indeed, been carved in the shape of flames.

"Jadeite," she said. "Rare. Expensive. Very. Not to you, of course—you've earned this a thousand times. If you and your friends hadn't come along, those *things* would be eating us all and destroying our city." She sat up, her bearing proud. "Carved it myself, I did. *Now* I know why I made it flames! You never know why you make things half the time. It's always nice to find out."

"I don't understand. What have you found out?"

"Look at your staff," she said. "Look at her heartstone. Green for her healing, red for her attacking. Greenfire. Just about sums you up, wouldn't you say? I thought you were making a little something you could give your lady friend along with the ring I'll be crafting for her. Well, turns out it's for you. Funny how that happens. Pop it on the chain, then."

I did.

"Good," she said. "Congratulations on now being a fully certified jewelwright, etcetera, etcetera, *hereby this day by my hand the undersigned Jewelmaster, blah blah blah*, welcome to the Craft. Apprenticeship served, seven minutes instead of seven years, but who counts. Initiation fee, one gold, waived. Craft dues a million gold—just kidding, also waived." She grinned, clearly enjoying herself. "So, now I can tell you Craft secrets—you now having crafted your masterpiece duly attested by me."

She put Qrysta's amulet on her workbench, laying its age-old, yellow-brown squares out so that we could see them clearly. "Old runes—the oldest I've ever seen. From before the beginning, these are. Long years ago, centuries ago, the master who made these wrote her will into them. I say *her* because I'm a master and I'm a her, so I naturally assume. Could've been a him, who knows? Whoever, she or he was good. The working is … ." She hesitated, staring at the plain but exquisite amber squares. "… well, *masterful*. It's easy to be fancy. It's hard to be simple."

I looked at the runes again. I thought that I began to understand the perfection of their plainness. Perhaps not understand, but at least appreciate. How lovely and, as Neva had said, simple they were. No unnecessary embellishments. Just the purity of being themselves.

She gazed at the amulet, drinking in its austere beauty. Then she said, "This is what the runes say:

"One of three
Three of one
Quick as death
All is done."

Her words echoed in my head. I gazed at the ancient amber squares with their stark, clear carvings.

I thought, *h for the sake of all the gods! Give me a break! Another blasted riddle! How all the hells long is it going to take to work* this *out? We've already got one riddling verse we're groping our way through, do we have to have another?*

Neva said, "Who wears this?"

I told her that Qrysta did, and that Klurra had given it to her, trading it with Qrysta for lessons and a sword after she had herself been given it by the giant chief, Orndmund. Neva asked me to describe Qrysta, and after she pondered what I told her, gave me a searching look, a smile growing on her face. It made me uneasy.

She chuckled and shook her head. "You young 'uns," she said. "Dear o' dear. Can't see your hand in front of your face! Oh well, time will tell. He always does."

Her voice changed. "Seems to me *quick as death* fits to that one, wouldn't you say? So the rest probably does too."

"You're right about that."

So, yes, I thought, *not so complicated after all. Qrysta was one of us three, and we three were one team.*

"Then it's found its wearer," she said.

"Can I tell her?"

Her kind old eyes crinkled. "Of course. You're Craft now, you can tell or not tell as you see fit. But *only* to the wearer, mind!" I had a feeling that she wasn't telling me everything. *But,* I thought, *if she wanted to she would.* Maybe I'd find out later in my own time.

"I have two more," I said, reaching into my pouch for the star sapphire ring and the malachite necklet that Oller had found at Marnie's.

Neva studied the ring, turning it every way, and holding it up to the light so that the needle-sharp, six-pointed star at its heart stood out.

"Another nice one!" she said. "The sharper the rays of the star, the finer the gem. No fuzzy edges in this beauty, she's all business. One of our ancestors made this."

404

"Is it signed?"

"No, but the Upground wright never lived who could have crafted *this*. You know what it means, I suppose?"

"No. I didn't know gems have meaning."

Neva chuckled. "And you call yourself a jewelwright? Disgrace to our profession, you are, young man! The star sapphire is the wisdom stone, the seeking and seeing stone," she explained. "She'll show you solutions and help you see your way to the best results. I do believe"— she looked me in the eye—"that you might know someone who looks for solutions?"

I thought, *we all do.*

Then I thought, *Oller.*

"A finder," I said.

Neva nodded happily. "If you're going to find, first you have to seek. Send him to me, I'll need to fit this to his finger."

"I will," I said. "He's the one the silver chain is for, he might want to pick another."

"He can't," she said. "He won't have the choice. You picked it, so that's the one for him. This malachite necklet, on the other hand … well … it might look lovely, but it's ugly!"

"In what way?"

"Power and protection, malachites are," she said, still smiling. "Pretty to look at, but they're vicious things. They'll get their retaliation in first, if they sense threat. Attack first, ask questions afterwards. Know anyone ugly but lovely?"

I smiled at the thought of how Grell probably would not appreciate being described that way. "I do, indeed."

"I'll get these Imbued, too," Neva said. "Seeking and seeing for the sapphire ring, and we'll see if we can't get a bit of oomph into your greenfire."

I handed her the pendant I'd kind-of-crafted. "Thank you, Neva."

"Thank *you*, young man!" she replied. "And not just for saving our city and all our lives. Thank you for this nice job that I can't wait to get started on: your lady friend's ring. She'll never have seen a prettier." She passed me Qrysta's amber amulet. "This one's got all the Imbuing it can take in those old runes. That's lost wisdom, that is. Nothing any of us know can improve those. Now, off you go then, young caster—I have work to do!"

Qrysta, Grell, Oller, Nyrik, and Horm were sitting on benches at a long table, chatting with happy, celebrating nibluns, when I returned to the Great Hall. They called me over when they saw me and made room for me beside them. "What?" I sat between Oller and Qrysta. "No one playing *You're So Pathetic?*"

Those who knew the game laughed. "No, thank the gods!" Grell said. "One hangover like that led to is enough for one lifetime. Tonight, I go easy."

"How are you feeling?" I asked. "You took a beating out there."

"Yeah, a few bites and cuts," Grell said. "Nothing serious. Damn good Heals you have now, Daxxie. I feel I could give those trolls a workout."

"Don't you go hurting our trolls," I said. "We might need them."

I turned to Oller. "Neva has something for you. Horm's mom. Out that door, main street straight ahead, first left, third alley on the right. Second door. Even you can find it."

"Funny," Oller scoffed, and got up to go.

"I'll come with you," Horm said. "I'm ready to get horizontal, me. It'll be nice to sleep in my old bed again."

"And now we know why this is for you," I showed Qrysta her amber amulet.

"We do?" she asked.

"We do indeed. I can tell you what the runes mean as it's yours now. But not anyone else. Craft secret, Neva says. Apparently, it works that way around here." I leaned close to her and murmured in her ear, "*One of Three, Three of one, Quick as death, All is done.*"

"That's us," she agreed.

"Yup. And if anyone is *quick as death*, it's you," I said. "Turn around."

She did, and I fastened it around her neck.

She turned back. "How do I look?" she asked, smiling, her eyes shining, her blue-black hair framing her gorgeous face.

I grinned back. "Suits you."

"Thanks, Daxxie." She held my eyes then added, "So amber is 'tree bone,' eh?"

I nodded. "Yup. Tree bone."

"You think? This is our *bone?*"

I nodded. "I definitely think."

▲ ▲ ▲

There was still much to be done that night. Kjelvild escorted me to a council of nibluns, who told me everything that they knew about what had been happening in the Undergrounds. The army that had been besieging Niblunhaem had been more Undead than alive. Those alive had been the worst of all the creatures in the world, from pit-elves to *weres*. The Undead had been, as Serjeant Bastard would no doubt have put it, ghoulies and ghosties—but in reality mostly reanimated corpses of all kinds, four legged as well as two. There had also been some specters and wraiths who had had no legs at all but floated in the air casting Ice and Fear attacks.

Now, thanks to the Woods Kin archers and the stomping stone trolls and the fire arrows of the nibluns, they were all just corpses again—or blobs of melted ectoplasm in the case of the specters and wraiths. Every single piece of them had been scraped up and burned on an immense pyre outside the gates of the city. There was no chance now of any of them coming back again to bother us.

None of the nibluns knew exactly what eefrits were or where they came from. They seemed to be alive rather than undead, but they'd told us they *didn't live*, and their resistance to magic was so impenetrable that it was hard to be sure. The two in the cells would be examined at length and their fate decided by the city judges.

On the subject of magic, I asked the nibluns about their fire arrows. It was just a matter of Imbuing the archers' bows, they explained. And *yes, of course they would*, they replied, when I said how useful that would be and could they Imbue ours? Two of them got up immediately and left to find Nyrik and get him to gather all the Woods Kin bows so that they could be Imbued.

They were all business, those nibluns. And how they *loved* their work. Their maps were compared with ours, and we were offered guides to the deep places. It seemed that all we didn't know was ... well, every damn thing else that was happening beyond the walls of the city. How had the Orc army fared? What was happening with the GAA and Coven expeditions south and west and east? Crucially, how much time did we have? Would another army appear from the depths to besiege Niblunhaem again?

The gates were already being repaired, and would be stronger than ever in a day or two. We decided to risk it and take the next day to rest and recover before setting out for the floor of the world. None of them wanted to talk about that. No niblun had ever ventured that far. Jurun was, they believed, the only living being to have gone there, and look what had happened to him. But if he was to be stopped, then all the signs were pointing that way.

Down and down.

They gave us beds, as soft and warm as any I'd ever slept in, and a glass of Nightmilk, which was the juice of pale berries that grow beneath the earth. *For the dreams*, they said. I didn't have any that I could recall, but I'd never slept so well nor woken so refreshed. I positively leapt out of bed the next morning, feeling as if I'd been on the longest, most relaxing holiday of my life, rather than as if I'd been on the road for weeks and in an exhausting battle only the previous day. I couldn't wait to get on with things … until I thought, *Well hang on, getting on with things might mean wandering off to my death. Yes, well, so what if it does? I feel fabulous. Bring it on!*

Jewelwright Neva was waiting for me in the Great Hall. She called me over to her table where she was sitting with several other crafters. "Here's your masterpiece." She handed me my greenfire pendant. "A masterpiece being the work you craft in order to rank as master. It took more Imbuing than we thought it could stand. Quite the surprise, it was. Good sign, that. Pop it on, then."

I did and felt two things simultaneously—a warmth in my chest and a thump on my back. I turned around, expecting to see one of my friends. There was nothing behind me except Shift, who hit me again, expectant.

I looked back at Neva in confusion. The other crafters had noticed and were all grinning and whispering.

Neva nodded. "She can feel it already. She wants you to hold her, lad!"

I reached for Shift. When my hand closed around her, I bounced off my bench as if fired from a catapult. From the first time I'd held her, Shift had jittered and teased her way up my arm. Now, she was slamming into me. It was like being hit by bolts of electricity—her life essence. I almost had to wrestle with her to hold her steady.

After a while, we both calmed down. Surges of power ran through me, through both of us. I gazed at her as if seeing her for the first time. She'd been a formidable enough weapon before. Now, I felt as if I was holding a rocket launcher.

I looked at Neva, when I could finally focus, and smiled. All I could say was, "Wow!"

Neva introduced me to the crafters who had combined their expertise for the Imbuing of my greenfire pendant and Oller's ring of seeking and seeing. I thanked them all and we all got up and went over to my friends.

Grell, tucking into a huge breakfast, was all smiles. "Good stuff, that Nightmilk! Not an ache or a pain anywhere, and *would you look at this?*"

He hauled himself to his feet and twirled like an ungainly mannequin to show off his new niblun armor.

"Half the weight of my old plate and twice as tough!" he said. "I've been out there wrestling the trolls. Worked up a hell of an appetite. Nice fellers, by the way. Not the brightest, as we know, but wouldn't harm a flea. It took me a while to get them to see what I wanted, but once they did, *whoa* did we go at it! I had them kicking and punching and bodyslamming me and look! Not a scratch! Thought it funny as hell, they did. Troll laughter is the best, Daxx mate—talk about infectious. Think how scary their roars are. That's how funny their laughter is. Wish we could take them with us."

I said, "Me too. I wonder …"

"What?"

"I could try shrinking them."

"Worth a go," Grell agreed. "We could do with them at our backs!"

"This is for you," I passed him the malachite necklace that Neva handed to me.

"Green!" Grell said. "My favorite color."

I told him where it had come from, and Neva told him that malachites are vicious stones of power and protection.

"Power and protection," I echoed. "A pretty good job description of what you do, right?'

"Right," Grell agreed. "I love it. Thank you, Daxxie. And you, Neva."

"It's Imbued with Tireless," Neva said. "You'll get third winds, and fourths, not just seconds."

"Excellent," Grell said. "I have a feeling I'll be needing them."

He turned his back to me, and I clasped the necklace around his thick, hairy, gray-brown neck.

"How do I look?" he asked.

I smiled. "Powerful and protective. And *very* pretty."

Grell chuckled. "Oh, and yeah, I forgot this. Talking of pretty."

He reached down beside the chair where he'd been sitting.

"Whaddaya think?" he asked, grinning as he put on his new helmet.

It matched the rest of his armor but had clearly been personalized just for him.

"I think," I said, "those horns look better on you than they did on the King of the Yaks."

I turned to Oller. "And this, Ols"—I handed him the star sapphire ring—"is for you."

Oller's eyes grew round. "You sure?"

"I'm sure."

"Blimey … . Worth a packet, this. Told you I'd never seen a finer. Look at them rays! Sharp as pins."

"They'll sharpen your sight up a deal too, young seeker," Neva said. "Even when you're lost, you won't be. A ring of seeking and seeing, that is."

Oller thanked them all and slipped the ring on. It shrank to fit his finger. Only magic items do that, we knew.

"Gods," he said. "Worth more'n I am, this!"

"I've got Shift," I said, "only now she's Shift Squared because of this Imbued Greenfire necklace, thanks to these fine people. Qrysta's got her amber amulet—which I can't tell you about, you being neither Craft nor the wearer—but that was meant for her all right. Gods know what we'll be facing, where we're going. All I know is, we're a damn sight better equipped now to face it."

"I'll say." Oller got to his feet. "Look what they run up for me— *overnight*, if you please!"

Oller's new leathers were a blend of browns, making him almost invisible even in the bright lights of Niblunhaem. Fur-elk leather, he told me, supple yet hard and Imbued with stealth and evasion. "Fire something at me," he said. I popped a tiny Fireball at him, and it swerved around him before bursting on the Great Hall's wall, startling some quietly breakfasting nibluns.

I waved at them in apology. They waved back, smiling, *no worries*.

"Nice!" I said to Oller.

"Yeah and watch this." He started to walk as normal then suddenly ran. And then absolutely *streaked* across the hall. And then back. And skidded to a halt in front of me, grinning and not panting at all. "Speed boots!" he said. "Just like Marnie said, niblun cobblers knowing their craft."

"Excellent," I said. "So, you can outrun Little Guy now?"

"Everyone and everything *but* Little Guy. They imbued his kit with speed too. Want to see?"

"Yes indeed."

"Come on, then."

Oller and Little Guy led us outside into one of the town squares that connected the wide, underground streets of Niblunhaem. "Here." He handed Grell a stick. Little Guy knew what was coming and sat in his neat brown fur-elk leather battlecoat, ready for action. "Far as you can, big feller!" Oller said, and Grell threw the stick, high and far. Oller and Little Guy watched it soar then begin to fall at the far end of the square. "Go!" Oller said. A brown blur shot away and caught the stick before it hit the ground. The brown blur fizzed back to us, stopped, and turned back into Little Guy, stick in mouth, bogbrush tail wagging proudly.

Qrysta's outfit was equally special. Understated, no frills, just black leather and steel, and fitting that perfect body like a second skin. She looked, in every sense, the business. "How the hell they made these overnight I'll never know." She drew her two new niblun swords. "But they did. Maybe their tools are Imbued so they can work faster. They are just *unbelievable*, Daxx! Weight, balance, grip, everything is *perfect*. They don't feel like weapons, they feel like *me*. My old ones were pretty damn good, but these things … . It's like trading in donkeys for racehorses." She grinned. "And watch this, they were very proud showing me this."

She produced a slip of silk, which she threw in the air.

She turned her swords blade up and held them out in front of her, parallel to the ground.

The wisp of silk floated gently down towards them. When it touched their blades, it parted, without slowing, and wafted to the floor in three pieces.

"*That's* what I call sharp!" Qrysta said, sheathing her swords.

"Nice scabbards, too," I noticed.

"Imbued with Protect and Sharpen. They'll never be blunter than they are today." The swords, she told me, were Imbued with Ice damage. She'd chosen Ice rather than Fire or Storm after discussing all options with the Imbuers. Ice *slows*, they told her, as well as burning cold and cutting deep. Best for someone fast. For Grell, it might be

Fire, or for a caster, Storm. But for a slice-and-dice merchant like her, a slow enemy is pretty soon a dead enemy.

My own clothes were presented to me when we went back inside the city. An undershirt of the lightest, hardest chainmail with its inner breast pocket over my heart for the infinite notebook that Marnie had given me where I could get at it quickly, leather leggings, supple but sturdy thigh boots, and a dark green jerkin of what I was told was some kind of silk. But *you just try poking a hole in that*, they said. I tried. I couldn't. How did they get the needles through it to sew the sleeves on and make the buttonholes? I asked. All I got by way of reply were grins and *craft secret*.

Our outfits were also weatherproof which meant more than just rainproof. They would keep us at a comfortable temperature, cool in the heat of summer, warm in the chill of winter. There was a limit to that, we were told. If we slept outside in the snow, we'd drain them of their power and sooner or later we'd freeze. "Work in them, walk in them, you'll recharge them, especially while you sleep," the tailors and armorers told us. "A bit like giving that staff of yours time to recover."

We were also all given cloaks which would double as blankets, mine brown, Grell's gray, Oller's and Qrysta's black. *Arrowproof*, we were told. Arrows might stick in them or more likely bounce off them, but it would take a steel-bolt thrower wielded by those two stone trolls to put a shaft through them.

Fugg, who delighted everyone who handled her, was given a secret Imbuing which Grell was told not to reveal to us, as it was Craft, and just for the Imbuer and the Wielder to know. "Wish I could, mates," he said, smiling. "It's a beauty!"

Finally, Neva presented me with a dagger in a sheath that I could loop over my belt. "You never know when you'll need a good sharp knife," she said. "And they don't come sharper than that!"

All these gifts, we were told, were the least they could do for us in return for saving their city.

Those who had gone to question the captured eefrits returned with worrying tales. The stone trolls and the bats who had attacked us in the second cavern were not the only creatures down there who were much bigger and nastier than normal. There was a power at work, growing things, making them stronger and bolder and more dangerous than ever before.

Stone trolls never came into the Undergrounds, we were told. They were open air creatures of the remote Uplands. And here were these two monstrous ones, each nearly twice the size of normal trolls—which were huge enough in the first place. No one, so far as we could ascertain, had been handling them. They were simply there with the besieging army, doing what no normal troll left to its own devices would do: attacking the gates and walls of Niblunhaem.

Well, I'd discovered that they were easy enough to Induce and Manipulate. I clearly wasn't the first to Influence them. One thing seemed certain to all of us: someone was behind it all. Someone was behind the undead army and all their allies who would normally have been at each other's throats. Someone had summoned the eefrits. We believed we knew who that someone was. And that he had to be stopped. And soon.

I went through the city gates and into the cavern beyond them, where the stone trolls were happily playing with niblun children. Giggling, shrieking kids were clambering all over them, up their backs and around their heads and then sliding down their long arms. I got them to stop and stand clear and then tried Shrink on the trolls. It didn't work. I couldn't even bring them down to their usual size, let alone to something as small as Grell.

Pity. Two stone trolls that I could Shrink or Grow at will would have been a useful addition to our team. We were going to have to do without them. The nibluns would take care of them, they said, until the Undergrounds were safe for travel again. Then they would guide them to an exit into the Uplands, from where they could find their way home. Enemies they may have been, at first, but allies they had become, and they would be treated with the honor accorded to all of the saviors of Niblunhaem.

Neva gave Oller his Imbued silver chain. He looped it through the bow of his silver key, hung it around his neck, and tucked it away inside his shirt. She gave me the ring that she had made for my lady friend, an exquisite gold band set with three gems: purple amethyst, red jasper, carnelian—stones of love and luck, joy and justice, peace and protection, she said.

She showed me how she'd left the gold band unfinished under the settings. "Simple enough even for an Upground jewelwright to fit to her finger."

413

I thanked her and tucked it away in the inside pocket of my jerkin, behind Marnie's Infinite Notebook.

"Best make sure you stay alive so you can give it to her, then," she suggested.

I told her I would be trying to do that.

▲ ▲ ▲

With our plans made, and after another blissful night's sleep, thanks to another glass of Nightmilk, we woke, breakfasted, packed, and said our goodbyes to the folk of Niblunhaem, before setting out on the last leg of our journey, headed for the floor of the world. Two niblun guides were coming with us, if only for part of the way. They, like the Woods Kin archers, would be turning back at some stage. They would be needed for the defense of Niblunhaem if it were attacked again.

Where we were going, numbers wouldn't be any help. We believed that we had three of the things we needed, *stick* and *stone* and *bone*, and that *book* was waiting for us at the floor of the world: The Book of Life and Death. As was, one way or another, the end. The end of our journey. Perhaps the end of our tales.

We walked for hours, Glows lighting our way, Shift's Reveals showing nothing ahead down the twisting tunnels and corridors. We walked in silence, the Woods Kin archers rustling along all around us with barely a sound. It hadn't been long after we'd left Niblunhaem before the feeling of the Undergrounds became oppressive. Once again, we were on edge, nervous, worried. The air was still and heavy—not stale, but somehow unsettling. We stopped often to listen. We passed openings that led off into the blackness, listening into them for signs of life. I cast Reveals which revealed nothing.

We descended *down and down* for six, seven hours or more, un-threatened but not unworried, with not a sound out of place, not the faintest glow of any Hidden Life bigger than a rat, and there were few of those. I wondered why and Nyrik muttered, "All eaten." I hadn't wanted to ask, *eaten by what.* And then, bang, like a thunderclap out of nowhere, we were under attack.

The first thing that came lurching up at us out of the tunnel was a skeleton, groaning and moaning. The Woods Kin archers filled it full of fire arrows, but most went through the gaps in its bones, and those that struck it didn't slow it. They just poked out from its bones, flaming. It was lurching our way at speed. I blew it apart with a Stormbolt, but it reassembled in midair without breaking stride and flew back down onto its legs that were still scurrying towards us.

Then it was on us, arms outstretched and swinging. We hacked and battered and slashed; it flailed and wailed and bit and clawed, and even when its head was off, courtesy of Fugg, its teeth kept chewing into my arm. We stomped and pounded and blocked and screamed curses, and it was only when I lit a Flameball into it that the damn thing caught fire, fell to pieces, and burnt to ashes, staggering and croaking. We stared at it, gasping for breath, and then heard more *uurr-urr* moans and groans. Then there was another one, scuttling up from the depths, followed by another, and four more.

And then forty.

And then four hundred.

And then gods knew how many.

We fought. The Woods Kin shot and Grell hacked and Qrysta danced and sliced and Oller stabbed and Little Guy bit. I cast Shields around us and healed as hard and fast as I could, but though we took them down in numbers, they kept coming in greater numbers until the tunnel was a bottleneck full of straining, groaning, thrashing skeletons, clambering over each other to get at us. It was as if everyone who had ever died and been buried was coming for us. And they hit hard when they reached us.

Grell placed himself front and center, roaring defiance, Fugg whirling, Oller and Little Guy to one side of him and Qrysta to the other while I cast Damages and Heals and the Woods Kin shot their fire arrows. Which would soon all be gone. Shift too would be drained eventually. The boost that my niblun-Imbued greenfire pendant was giving her would not last forever. And then what? The Woods Kin had knives and hatchets, but those were nothing compared to the hitting power of their flame-Imbued hunting bows, which set the brutes on fire.

And which, without arrows, would soon be useless.

Bottleneck, I thought.

Maybe, just maybe …

"Grell!" I shouted. "*Pile them up!* Drop them on top of each other!"

I had to repeat myself several times before Grell and the others understood. They didn't understand why, but they understood what I wanted them to do. Grell, acting as always as our tank, took a position near a pile of bones and while slicing away at everything that came his way, methodically added to it. Qrysta, with her usual precision, dropped her victims exactly where she wanted them. The trouble was, they didn't want to stay where they'd been dropped. They kept getting up again and reattaching themselves or searching for other bits that belonged to them and then assailing us again.

It was, amazingly, Little Guy who solved the problem. He sprang at the lurching, groaning, scurrying mob, and started herding them— just like Ezzie would one day be herding her sheep. In his niblun, speed-Imbued battle leathers, he fizzed among them faster than any of them could handle, a brown blur of teeth and rage that none of them could grab, however many bony fingers reached for him. Yapping like an exasperated schoolteacher, he ordered his unruly pupils to damn well do what he said, which was *back off! Now!*

The skeletons didn't seem to know what to make of this furious, barking little terror darting around, savaging their ankles, harassing and goading. They clumped away from the steel whirlwinds of Fugg and Qrysta and Oller and the annoying orders of Little Guy, and jammed the tunnel completely. That was my moment. I checked Shift's tourmaline heartstone and saw that it was fully recharged. Time to hit them with everything she'd got. I ripped the end off one of Marnie's Narrow Squeaks, and the dying squeal of a runt piglet filled the tunnel, causing everyone and everything to freeze.

"Down!" I yelled, and cast a torrent of Liquid Fire into the logjam of suddenly-still bones.

The flame storm roared over frozen-in-solid-motion Grell's head, missing it by inches. I wondered how hot it might now be under his steel helmet—and then remembered, *niblun steel, temperature-controlled.* The Fire slammed into the wall of bones and incinerated them. I cast again and again, Liquid Fire after Liquid Fire until Shift was drained, and the bones burned on and on—and, I thought with satisfaction, *down and down.* Let them burn, all the way down until the fire I'd sent into them joined the fires of whatever hell lay down there.

When she had recovered, it was time to use Shift's Greens and heal the damage. Our fighters slumped on the dirt floor of the tunnel, exhausted. The Woods Kin were pale with fear. They were folk of the wide skies and the Woodlands, not the airless Undergrounds. Their arrows were all spent. Four more of them had died. I thanked them at length and with all the sincerity I could muster. Without them, we'd never have made it this far. Their job was done. We'd take it from there. They were hesitant to leave. They didn't want us to think they were abandoning us.

"Without arrows, what can you do? All the ones you shot will have been burned, so there's no point in looking for them. Go home. Defend Niblunhaem if they need you, or gather the folk of the Woodlands and defend them. You have done more than enough and with great honor."

We said our farewells, one-on-one, each to each, and finally to Nyrik and Horm. We embraced. For once, Nyrik was lost for words.

I said, "See you at The Wheatsheaf."

"Yeah," Nyrik said. "You'd better!"

They all slung their bows across their backs and headed back up the way we'd come. The two niblun guides were staying with us, for a while. Then they too would be turning back while Grell, Qrysta, Oller, Little Guy and I went on, *down and down* to the floor of the world.

34

The Floor of the World

The nibluns could tell day from night, but couldn't explain how when I asked them. It was always dark in the Undergrounds, but if you've lived there all your life, they said, you just *knew*. It was night, according to them, when we stopped in a chamber off a side-alley that they led us to, and which they said would be as safe as anywhere down there was these days. It was a chamber the nibluns had used over the years, fitting it with a door that was disguised to look like the cave wall. If you didn't know it was there, you wouldn't know there was anything beyond it.

They had the keys to the invisible keyhole, but Oller said, "Let me see if I can ..."

We all stopped.

The nibluns waited.

"This the wall?" Oller asked.

They nodded, curious.

Oller produced his silver key, and moved it towards the wall.

A spot glowed, dimly at first, then brighter, then grew to become a keyhole. Oller inserted his silver key and unlocked the door.

"After you, gents," he said with a grin at the shocked nibluns, stepping aside to usher us in.

There were mushroom lights on the walls, the nibluns said, but they'd be exhausted by now. They'd need fuel if they were to light up. I put a Glow into the air and let it feed the mushrooms. I extinguished it when they were full and fat and gleaming. These were the pale mushrooms of the deep Undergrounds, rather than the warm, blue ones of the earth-cellars beneath the Woodlands trees. But their light was welcome and comforting. We ate and drank, and talked briefly about not much and slept, safe behind the hidden wall. Drifting off to sleep, the last thing I thought was, *how many more nights will there be? Before the end?*

There were three, as it turned out. Each was more uncomfortable than the one before. Each was spent in a more exposed, more worrying place. Each needed us to set watch and sleep with more than Little Guy's one ear open. They were exhausting nights, after exhausting days, containing only stretched, restless sleep.

We woke tired and sore and drained rather than replenished. It was harder to pick ourselves up every morning, if morning it truly was, as our niblun guides said. Then, on we trudged, *down and down*, Oller leading us with his star sapphire ring of seeking and seeing, and his maps and his Oller skill of finding.

The third morning dawned, if that's the right word, cold and damp and dreary. Every day there'd been a fight of some sort. The day after the skeletons it had been ghouls. We'd only known what they were when we'd killed them all, and the nibluns told us. That had been fierce but short, less than an hour. The next day, longer but somehow easier, it had been—well, not even the nibluns knew what the things were. *Slugs*, we called them, in the end. Pale, long, slimy, poison-spitting, wormlike things, with mouths that clamped on to sink teeth into you, teeth as thin and sharp as Hob's. Nasty wounds, they left.

I'd been experimenting with Wards by then, Armor wards and Absorb wards and Reflect Damage shields. They worked well. We finished the damned things off, eventually, but it took three or more hours to do so, and we were shattered by the end of it.

What else was waiting *down and down* ahead of us, we wondered. We were too tired to talk most of the time. We were almost too tired to walk. We felt like boxers in the final rounds of a brutal, sapping contest. We were just about out on our feet.

The third day, it was the fight of our lives.

The niblun guides left for home after we'd woken and breakfasted—with relief and our thanks. We'd take it from there, we told them. Their job was done. *Wish us luck.* Which they did. Grell, Oller, Qrysta and I hefted our packs for what we expected would be just another day, but what turned out to be the last leg of our journey. There was nothing down here, now. No life, no enemies, no sound, hardly any air. Just the crunch of our feet as we plodded on, exhausted, following the route that all our maps, and all those experts that we had consulted, suggested led to the floor of the world.

From time to time I handed out potions: Strength and Health Boosts for Grell, Speed and Shadow for Oller and Little Guy, Stamina Boosts and Confuse for Qrysta, Power Boost and Absorb Magic for myself. We all appreciated the lift they gave us, but every lift was less than the previous lift, and every step was harder than the one before it. Few potions were left to us, by that last day, so I had to ration them.

Down and down was not just taking us down, it was bringing us down.

We were mute, tired, depressed. Drained. We knew that we didn't belong there, that we shouldn't be there, where everything hated us—even, it seemed, the air itself. We tried to remember the warmth of the sun on our faces, or the smell of the wind in the trees of the Woodlands, or the bright splash of the water of a stream tumbling out of the Western Mountains. It was hard to think that those things had ever existed. They no longer felt real. This was all there was. This gloom; this crunch underfoot; this pace after pace; this cold, heavy air; this *down and down.*

And then, the tunnel we were plodding down ended, opening up into a cavern.

We had no light above us, so we couldn't see it, but we could tell that it was a huge, overarching space with a ceiling far above our heads in the darkness.

Grell whispered, his voice strained and hoarse, "What do you think, Daxx mate?"

I whispered, "I think this is it."

"Me too," Oller croaked.

Qrysta muttered, "So now what?"

I felt Shift's concern. "Damned if I know."

No one else said anything.

I cast Reveals. No hidden life was revealed. I was at a loss.

I thought grimly, *if only there was a Reveal for hidden death.* Because that's what it felt like.

Death.

Still as death; quiet as death; cold as death.

I remembered what Marnie had said. *He's death, he is.*

What to do?

Turn? Run? Get as far away as possible?

Wouldn't that be nice ... . But then some other poor bastards would have to do what we'd failed to do. And those other poor bastards might not have the chance to get this far *down and down.*

Only one thing to do, then. *Keep going forwards.*

So, we did.

We inched our way ahead into the darkness. Soon we could feel the volume of space all around us. It was huge. We were tiny. Insignificant. Weak. Worn out. And even though there was, as far as we could tell, nothing there, the great, dark space was oppressive, and filled with malevolence. We weren't wanted there. We didn't belong. Behind all this nothing there was something, and that something wanted us dead.

The sound of our footsteps changed from the soft scrape of sand and dirt to the firm crunch of ice. *The ice that fire cannot burn,* I thought. We were on the frozen lake that surrounds the island where the world-tree grows. We stopped, listened. Nothing. We'd come all this way; here we were—and now what? We gathered close.

I whispered, "I'll have to set a light."

Qrysta muttered, and I could hear the fatigue in her voice, "Are you sure?"

"What are the chances of getting anything done in total darkness? We can't see in the dark—"

And then I remembered, *yes, I can!*

"Wait." I hefted Shift. I closed my eyes and then closed her eye, the way Marnie had shown me. Before long, shadows formed in the shadows. Four of them, of various sizes, three with two legs and one with four. "I can see you," I said. "Stick together. Oller, hold onto the back of my belt, the rest of you hold onto each other. Ready?"

With a little fumbling they got into formation.

Warily, letting my feet get used to walking on ice, with my eyes closed I led them to where the shadow that Shift was showing me grew, out of the floor of the world, up through the vastness of the cavern and into the earth above. It was the world-tree, on its island at the heart of the lake of ice that the fire of the sun cannot burn. We were nearly there. I believed that I knew what we'd find on that island. The Book of Life and Death, and Time himself.

How nearly right I was. And how very wrong.

Book, life, death, time, yes—but not necessarily in that order.

We were all, even in our temperature-controlled niblun outfits, shivering. Through Shift's closed eye I could see the plumes of breath as we exhaled. Little Guy was whimpering softly.

I muttered to Oller, "Pick him up, his feet must be frozen."

Oller did. He rubbed warmth into Little Guy's paws and murmured to him reassuringly. I heard the slurp of a tongue on Oller's face.

Awkwardly we made our way across the lake until the crunch of the ice sheet under our feet changed to the shuffle of dirt and sand. Holding onto each other, we stepped up onto the world-tree's island. We waited, ears straining, listening. No hidden life was Revealed. Were we, I wondered, too late? Was Jurun no longer here? But that would mean ... Esmeralda ...

And then the last thing I could have expected happened. The moment I thought *Esmeralda*, I heard her voice.

High and sweet and clear, singing the words we knew so well, to a simple childhood tune.

"A stick, a stone,
A book, a bone,
Go down and down
For half a crown,
A knife,
A life:
A throne."

As she sang, she appeared: a faint golden glow at first, far off in the darkness, getting brighter and stronger as she drew nearer. I remembered my nightmare, in the earth cellar below Father Willow: Esmeralda riding away on the black horse into the murk that hung over the Darklands; us all watching at the Narrows, unable to follow her, our hearts breaking.

The reverse was happening. Out of nothingness she appeared, a tiny dot gradually growing into a ball of golden light, walking towards us, smiling, singing, beginning the verse again whenever she finished it. We could only watch, entranced, hypnotized.

Esmeralda. *Here.* We should have been overjoyed—because that's what Esmeralda did to people, wasn't it? She radiated, brought joy to the world, *the loveliest life there ever was or ever will be, and all who see her love her.*

We weren't overjoyed, though. We were horrified. I glanced at the others. Their faces showed fear and anguish. This was Esmeralda, but this was *wrong.* All *wrong.* She was close enough to touch, almost, when she stopped. She looked us over, smiled, and spoke.

"Hello," she said. "How nice to see you all here!"

I opened my mouth to speak, but no words came.

"Every life costs a death, you know," she said, cheerfully. "I can have four more now. Five, I didn't see the sweet little doggy. What's his name?"

Oller gasped as if the words were being dragged out of him, "Little Guy."

"Isn't he lovely? Nearly as lovely as me!" Esmeralda twirled, her golden hair and bright green cloak drifting around her. "The loveliest life there ever was or ever will be! Think of that!" She laughed happily.

She stopped and looked at us. "Well, you *have* been a nuisance. You kept me away for weeks! I should have been here ages ago, but thanks to you I had to wait and wait for me to come, even though that silly old witch had been calling me here, and I was nearly coming and then went off with you instead, and that other silly old witch got in the way, and I had to wait and wait, and I've been waiting hundreds and hundreds of years—it wasn't *fair!*" Esmeralda screamed the last word and stamped her foot, and the look of hatred on that lovely face was poisonous.

I stared at her, shocked. Was she under some kind of spell? Surely, she couldn't mean what she said. We'd come all this way and fought so hard to protect her—and *she* was the one luring us to our deaths?

"Well, now you're going to watch," she continued, clearly unconcerned by what we might be feeling. "And then you're going to die, and I shall have five more lives, even though I won't need them because that's the bargain we made. But you don't deserve to live them anymore, *that's* for certain!"

A thousand thoughts were chasing each other around in my head. What to do? Could I move? Could I cast? Could I speak? I kept trying to, but we were immobile, only able to do what Esmeralda wanted—like Oller telling her Little Guy's name. "Come along, then." Esmeralda turned away and walked off, and without any choice in the matter, we stumbled after her.

Towards the world-tree.

The only light in the cavern was the golden radiance pouring off Esmeralda. As we followed, the vast trunk of the world-tree gradually became visible. An outline at first, it emerged out of the gloom to tower far above our heads, its great branches disappearing into the earth roof. There was something else we could see at its base as it came into view: a small, black shape—which eventually revealed itself as a broken throne. On it, an unmoving figure slumped, its skin dried to leather by the ages and the cold, features sunken into its skull, mouth stretched open on shriveled lips, eyes bound in a blindfold of sapphires.

Sapphires, I thought. *Sapphire, stone of seeing and solution, what solution can you see?*

I couldn't see any. I couldn't *do* anything, let alone solve anything.

"Aren't I ugly?" Esmeralda stopped in front of Jurun's ice-mummified corpse. She looked down at it. "It'll be nice to be up and about again and as pretty as a picture. The loveliest life there ever was or ever will be. I can't wait!"

She walked to the throne and bent to pick something off the corpse's lap.

Two things, in fact, I saw when she turned around. An ash staff, fitted with an obsidian heartstone that drank in the light. And a dagger with a blue-white blade of ice.

"This is for you." She pointed the staff at us and then put it carefully into the corpse's bony right hand. "And this is for me." She raised the dagger and plunged its ice blade into her heart.

We wanted to howl but couldn't. We wanted to run to her but couldn't.

Esmeralda fell and lay slumped across the corpse on its throne, her blood flowing from her heart to his.

All we could do was stand, immobile, and watch her die. We could tell it was happening as the glow that surrounded her began to fade, becoming dimmer and dimmer, finally flickering out as if she were a candle's flame pinched by invisible fingers.

And truly it felt that Hope herself had died with her. Hope, *the bitch who clouds your eyes with Stupid Dust*, Marnie had called her. But anything, even the faintest, falsest hope, was better than this unbearable truth that we were being forced to witness.

I could feel Shift whimpering in my hand, her grief mingling with the tears streaming down my face. If I could have moved my chest it would have been racking with sobs.

And then, from under Esmeralda's crumpled body, came movement.

The hand into which she had placed the ash staff was fleshed again. Strong fingers gripped it and turned it to stand it on the ground; then the body that sat beneath Esmeralda's used it to pull itself upright. Esmeralda's pitiful corpse dropped to the ground as frail as a rag doll as light poured up from the ash staff and hung in the sky, illuminating everything. Plainly, Jurun wanted us to witness his return. With his other hand he removed the sapphire blindfold and looked at us, young, hale, cruel—and infinitely powerful.

We weren't, I thought, *even going to get a chance to resist him.*

He had won.

We had lost.

"Swords," he scoffed. He pointed his staff at Fugg, at Oller's knives, at Qrysta's niblun blades. They all spun up into the air and clattered to the ground beside him. "You won't be using those."

He turned to me.

His gaze bored into me. I was powerless. And petrified.

"You," he said. "You're the one to blame."

I wanted to talk but couldn't. I didn't want to reason with him, because he was beyond reason, but I longed to tell him what I thought of him before he killed us all. Not that it would have had any effect on him—just for my own satisfaction. I wanted to mock him and belittle him and anger him, to make him get it over with. I wanted to tell him how stupid he looked with half a crown on his head. In truth, he didn't look stupid. He looked terrifying, and filled with all the knowledge and power of time. I just wanted this to be over. *Please let it not hurt*, I thought.

Jurun looked at Shift and smiled. "You thought you could stand against me with *that*?" He pointed his staff at her. "Pretty reds and greens," he mused. "I'll have those."

I felt Shift's agony as the obsidian in Jurun's ash stave began to drink in the light of her tourmaline heartstone. She was struggling in

425

my grasp, writhing, shrieking inside my skull, where only I could hear her. Her heartstone flickered and sputtered as the colors drained from it. It went dark, and Shift's scream echoed in my head as she jerked in her death-throes before going still. At a disdainful wave of his staff, she shattered in my hand, dropping in pieces to the ground.

"And I will have *your* heart, too," Jurun said to me, smiling. "For all the trouble you have caused me. I've watched your magic since the crone unlocked it for you. Fancy spells and party tricks!" he mocked. "Fire and ice and thunderclaps. Pathetic. All dark, from now on, forever."

His staff was pointed at my heart. The obsidian stone pulled at it. I could feel it drinking in my life as it had drunk in the light of Shift's heartstone. I felt my chest tearing at me, pulling away a stream of everything that I was and felt and knew—all being dragged towards Jurun's ash stave along an implacable, irresistible black beam. Which swelled. And grew.

And writhed.

And swirled.

And ... smoked?

Sparked?

Glittered?

Little explosions now popped inside the energy beam flowing from my heart to the ash stave's devouring obsidian heartstone. Beside me, I could see Oller and Qrysta and Grell suddenly move—not much, but a twitch, a stumble. They were not rooted anymore, *what was going on?*

Little Guy dropped from Oller's arms as Oller's hand moved to his jerkin. *What was he doing? What was happening?*

Jurun was frowning now, at his staff, at the black tractor beam that joined my heart to its heartstone. He didn't know what was going on either .... He tried to back off but couldn't. The beam was holding him in its grip, just as it was holding me *What was happening?*

Shouldn't I be dying? From the suction on my chest, surely my heart was tearing itself out of my ribcage to fly towards the obsidian void—but *wait*—*no*: it was still pumping. I was still breathing. *What was going on?*

I tried to focus on the beam, on what was fueling it. *Did I see words? Shapes? Yes* .... Attacks, and poisons, and every kind of magic assault and trap and confusion and ambush, all seemed to be being wrenched from me to him, but—*was I attacking? From within that pull?*

426

How?

And then I heard it.

The rustle of paper.

Paper, turning, churning, being ripped away, page after page, but there was always another page behind it, all the way to infinity, while every spell and secret in Marnie's infinite notebook poured into the heartstone of Jurun's ash staff. Even a staff cut from the world-tree itself in the time of myth could not stand up to such an onslaught. Nor could it swallow everything that was hammering into it all the way from infinity.

Marnie's infinite notebook, in its inner pocket of the jerkin above my heart, where I could easily reach it …

Our *book.* Which had shielded me from the onslaught—and turned it back on him.

A tidal wave of all the lore and learning that Marnie and I had gathered between us, which was as much of the magic of the centuries as any two minds had ever collected; all the magic of all her books and all known books, which automatically entered into our *book,* was discharging everything it knew into the voracious obsidian heartstone that had called for it—

—which inevitably, under such a crush of overwhelming power, imploded. The staff that had been holding it incinerated itself and dropped to the ground in a million motes of burned, gray ash.

We all, including Jurun, stared at it in shock until a growling brown blur shot past me and sank its teeth into Jurun's leg. An instant later Oller was at Jurun's throat, slashing with—what?

An empty hand?

No.

An invisible knife.

Jurun hadn't seen it, invisible as it was in Oller's jerkin, so he hadn't disarmed Oller as completely as he thought. And now his neck was severed, cut to the spine. Qrysta wrenched the ice knife out of Esmeralda's body and was stabbing it into Jurun's chest again and again and again: *quick as death, and all was done.*

Grell was the last to the party, picking up his beloved Fugg and swinging her. Her niblun head sliced through the desiccated corpse that Jurun had for so long been and now was once again, cutting it in half. His lower half dropped to the ground, his upper half onto the throne, his half of the crown of Jarnland rolling off his skull. Gasping for breath, I tottered over to look down at him.

His empty eye sockets gazed up at me, unseeing.

Jurun, I knew, would not be troubling this world again.

We stood there, chests heaving, sweat pouring off us despite the bone-chilling cold.

It was over.

Our stick was broken.

Our stone was blind.

Our book drained.

Our bone …

I looked at the necklet Qrysta was wearing. The amber squares of *tree bone* still hung yellow brown on the yak-leather lace around her neck. But the runes that had been carved into them before the dawn of time had disappeared.

I had no words, so I just pointed at it. Qrysta looked down, and felt the now-blank squares. She, too, could do no more than grunt. But she knew what it meant.

Our bone was wiped clean, its power erased.

Shift, our stick and stone, was dead. Shift, who came to life in my hands when I fitted her tourmaline heartstone, who had grown to be more than a friend and partner. The loss of her felt as if some core part of me had been torn out—just as Jurun had wished to tear out my heart. Even though he hadn't ended my life, I felt bereft—as if I had died with her. My muse. My music. Which we would never create together again.

We had half a crown.

Thanks to our book and Oller's invisible knife, we had won the throne.

And yet, we had lost. We had lost Esmeralda.

Our life. The one that we had set out to protect.

Grell picked up her sad little body and laid it on his cloak on the ground. He crossed her arms over her breast and closed her eyes.

We knew we had succeeded, but we all felt that we had failed. *The light of our life,* I thought. *The loveliest life there ever was or ever will be.*

Well, maybe she had been too good to be true. Too good for this world with its wars and challenges and problems and quarrels and all-too-harsh reality.

But in leaving it, she had left it a far poorer place.

We sat around her corpse, not speaking. Qrysta knelt back on her heels. Grell hunkered down on his massive haunches. Little Guy sat patiently, panting, occasionally whimpering. Oller sat cross-legged beside him, elbows on his knees, chin in his hands, looking down. The light that Jurun had cast hung above us as cold and pale as death. None of us wanted to make eye contact with each other. I knelt on one knee. I felt that if I folded my legs under me, I'd never be able to straighten them again.

We knew we had to go. We had to get back to the Upgrounds, away from this place of sorrow. But we didn't want to leave. We didn't want to leave Esmeralda. We *wouldn't*. We'd take her with us, and all the realm would weep when they learned of her death.

We couldn't leave. It didn't feel over. How could it be over and end like this? Our triumph was heartbreak. The fruits of our victory were ashes in our mouths. If I'd had Shift, I could have cast healing and calming over us, but I'd lost her as well—my merry, new, clever friend, who had become such a part of me. The pain of it all was unbearable.

Gradually, we began to talk.

"She did it," Qrysta said, her voice hollow.

We looked at her.

"Did what?" Oller asked.

"Sacrificed herself for us."

"She was under his control," Grell said.

Qrysta shook her head. "Look at the rhyme. We'd gone down and down. We had everything, all the things in the verse—except the life. She *knew* she was doomed. And now, we have the throne."

"She was our friend," Oller objected. "She'd never have taunted us the way she had if he hadn't made her."

I agreed. "That wasn't Esmeralda, that was him. Talking through her. Using her." No one needed to complete the thought: *taking her life for his own.*

And now she was gone.

Her time had come for her—*as it comes for us all*, I remembered Marnie saying.

Recalling her words, something stirred in the back of my mind.

Something else that Marnie had said when she told of the legend of Jaren and Jurun, their intertwined lives, their fates, their last meeting, and—what was it? The bargain with Time, and the Book of Life and Death, and—*what was it?*

She'd also said, "Maybe you've been looking at it all along and haven't seen it."

What did we miss?

Think, I told myself. What Marnie was always telling you, *think.* I think it is …

Yes, now you're seeing it: You think. It is.

What am I meant to think?

It was there, just beyond the edge of my thoughts …

And then I heard it. Marnie's calm, old voice telling us the tale.

He would have all the time in the world, as he had long desired. And Time would have his price, for every Life costs a Death. And so Jurun and Time wrote their bargain in the Book of Life and Death, that Time keeps in the world-tree's heart at the floor of the world, and sealed it with his brother's life.

I held out my hand. "Oller, I need your key."

35

The Key

"They all do, Daxxie," Nyrik had said, *"when they're big enough. Sapling's no good, he won't have grown the strength yet."*

The world-tree was no sapling.

It was the oldest, largest tree of all.

I walked over to its gigantic trunk and around it until I was behind it. When the others were out of sight, I held Oller's silver key up to the world-tree, and a keyhole appeared.

I unlocked it and went inside.

Alone.

I didn't want my crew with me. They might try to talk me out of what I meant to do. I hadn't said goodbye to them, although I expected I'd never be seeing them again. They'd understand, I knew, in time. I'd miss them too. *No one ever had better friends*, I thought, as I walked down the long, spiral staircase inside the world-tree.

Oller. Where in all hells had *he* come from? Sneaking, conniving, snarky, indomitable little thief. All puffed up with being lance corporal. And then, one of us. Just like Grell and Qrysta. My spare arms, those two felt like. Extensions of me. Heart, body, soul. *Gods,* I loved them. And Little Guy! Out of nowhere, a mutt that one of us had found and all of us had taken to our hearts. Esmeralda. A

431

shooting star, blazing across our sky, gone too soon, an unbearable loss. Marnie, as true as the day was long and nine times as grumpy. Wisdom and kindness, terror and charm. We'd have done anything for Marnie—for any of us, for each other.

Klurra, too, appearing out of the mists of the Uplands, tetchy and belligerent, and the best new friend you could hope to find. Serjeant Bastard. Could we have had a finer trainer? Sir Fucking Pelican, My Lord of Rushtoun, Deb, Nyrik and Horm, Chief Elbrig, Ironwright Smith, Sister Ennis, Hob, Historian Kjelvild, Forgemasters Rodvarn and Thorleif, Jewelwright Neva, and two massive, passive, peaceful stone-trolls.

I remembered a line from one of my favorite poems: *I am a part of all that I have met.*

Yes, I thought. *All too true.*

I could see light ahead of me, below, as I wound *down and down* into the world-tree's heart. It was faint at first, growing brighter as I descended, but not much brighter, and though it was an unsteady, flickering light as if produced by flames, it wasn't a warm light. It was, somehow, threatening, and I felt that I wasn't going to like what I saw when I reached its source.

I didn't.

The earthen-floored cellar that the staircase led me down into was musty and gloomy. The air smelled of mold and cobwebs and death. And there, sitting at a table that looked as old and worn as he did, was a figure I recognized at once. Dressed in a ragged, dirty white robe, he was writing, slowly, with an enormous goose-quill pen in a large, black leather-bound ledger. His ancient, bald head gleamed in the weak light that was coming from the lantern that stood on the table beside the book. On the other side of the book was an hourglass. The sand in it, I saw, had run out. He reached forward slowly with his thin, right arm and dipped his quill in an inkwell, raising his head so that I could see his long white beard and the few puffs of white hair that encircled his head.

His watery, dim eyes met mine.

"Oh," Old Father Time said in a voice as dry as the sand in his hourglass and as thin as his arms. "A visitor. Sit down, I won't be a minute."

He kept looking at me as if waiting for a reaction.

"Thank you." I sat in a chair across from him.

The hourglass, I noticed, had a name etched at its base. Even upside down I could read it easily enough.

Esmeralda.

"Get it?" he said, wheezing.

I looked at him puzzled. Was he laughing?

"I won't be a minute." He stared at me and nodded.

What?

The hopeful expression on his aged face faded. "Even my jokes are old," he muttered.

Joke? What joke? "I'm sorry, I don't get it."

He sighed.

"You know who I am, I assume?"

"You're Time."

"And when I said, 'I won't be a *minute* …'?" he hinted.

"Oh," I said. "It's a … time joke."

"Yes," he said sourly. "I don't get a lot of company here. A laugh would be nice from time to time."

"Yes, I can imagine. You'll have to laugh at your own jokes, then," I suggested.

He frowned at me.

"From," I said, "Time—to—Time."

He stared. "Oh." He grunted, unamused, and went back to his writing. Slowly, carefully, he formed three final letters, then put down his quill. They were, I saw, *l, d, a.* He scattered sand on the page to dry the ink, and after a moment leaned forward and gently blew it off.

He sat back and looked at me. "So, what can I do for you?"

"We killed Jurun."

"Yes," he said. "Poor fellow."

"What? He was a monster!"

"Indeed," Time admitted, "but you can't help feeling sorry for him. Dead for thousands of years, waiting for all the time in the world, which he would have had if you hadn't come along. Instead, it turned out to be hardly any time at all."

"Good thing too."

"No doubt," Time agreed.

"You had a bargain with him."

"I did," he said. "And I fulfilled it."

I caught his gaze and held it. "I'd like to make one."

His eyebrows rose. "You would?"

I nodded. "Yes. I would. If that's possible."

He pursed his lips. "It's possible. What do you propose?"

I took a deep breath. "There's always a price. I understand that. The price of Jurun's life was his brother's."

"Well, yes and no," Time said. "The price of his *first* life was. The price of his second was Esmeralda's."

"My proposal is my life for hers."

Time stared at me. For a long time. Without saying anything. Old and watery his eyes may have been, but I saw, as I held his gaze, that they were anything but weak. There was a power there, distant, hidden, older than anything and everything.

"Why?" he said at last.

"Do you need a reason?"

"No. But I'm curious. I'd like to know."

I evaded. He might not agree if I told him. "I'll tell you if you accept the bargain."

His eyes narrowed. "You're hardly in a position to make conditions, young man."

I saw his point. "I know. I'm sorry. I'm … trying everything I can think of. That was the wrong track. I'm here because I need your help. I really, really need to do this."

"Why?" he asked again.

I hadn't had to explain it before. Not even to myself. I just *knew*. It felt right. It had to be done. There was no question. But how could I express that, in words? A feeling of absolute certainty, total conviction—that was all *I* needed. But would that satisfy anyone else? *Probably not*, I thought. Then—*how to rationalize it? To have it make as much sense to someone else as it did to me?*

"Life without her doesn't seem worth living," I said. "Not just for me, but for anyone. Everyone. She makes the world a better place. She's needed. I'm not. It was nice being young again and having real adventures, but I've had a good life. Two in fact. I'm expendable. The loveliest life there ever was or ever will be? That's wasted on death, just as much as it would have been wasted on Jurun."

"She was the price," Time said. "It had to be paid. That was the bargain."

"Every life costs a death," I said. "I know. I want mine to be the price of hers."

"The Ultimate Sacrifice," Time said thoughtfully.

"Yes."

"Your life for Esmeralda's."

"Yes," I said.

"You're quite sure?"

"I'm sure."

Still gazing at me, he nodded slowly. "*Mm,*" he grunted.

He reached for his quill and handed it across the table to me. He indicated the inkwell.

"You do understand that there's no going back on this?"

"I understand."

"Just so that's clear," he added, and turned the ledger around. "There." He pointed to the space beside the name he'd just written.

Esmeralda.

I dipped the quill in the ink and wiped it carefully on the rim of the inkwell so that I wouldn't scatter blotches everywhere.

Then I signed my name next to Esmeralda's in the Book of Life and Death.

I sat back and saw as I handed Time back his quill that my hand was shaking, and that he was smiling at me. A big, welcoming, and somehow very *young* smile.

He nodded at the hourglass. He'd turned it again as I'd been signing my name.

It was full, and the name Esmeralda was the right way up again, at its top.

I smiled back, though with a smile rather weaker than the great beam of happiness that he was shining at me.

I took in a deep breath—maybe one of my last. "So ... what happens now?"

"Now," Time said, "we can begin."

That was confusing. "Begin ...?"

I'd been expecting—well, an ending. To everything. As far as I was concerned, anyway. Death. My death. Not a *beginning.* Unless there really was a life after death, which I'd never managed to believe in, but which would indeed be an excellent thing, I suddenly thought, given my current predicament.

Time was nodding at me again, still smiling, then shaking his head in what seemed to be wonder. "*Humans* ...! You never cease to amaze us. Yes," he said. Then to himself more than to me, "No. Begin at the beginning, not the end. So, to begin at the beginning … . No doubt, in the months you've been here, you've had a number of questions."

"That I most certainly have," I agreed.

"I'm now going to answer them. No need to ask, I know what they are—just let me do the talking, all right? You've had a long day. I'll do it as simply as I can, even though some of it is … rather more advanced than your brain could cope with, so you'll just have to take my word for it." He paused as if wanting me to know that his next words were important. "I'm not Old Father Time. I just put this appearance on for you as you were expecting me to look like this. You're not the only one around here who can lay Glamours. I'm actually an Amalgam."

"Oh," I said. "Hello, Anna Malgum."

He stared at me. "Not Anna. An," he said slowly. "Amalgam. Let me just remove Old Father Time here … ." He digressed. His Glamour faded out, to be replaced by the oddest living being I had ever seen. Even in films, or video games. Or, come to think of it, that I had ever *imagined*.

I could never have imagined … something that was part ant and part rhinoceros, and somewhat resembling a bunch of pipe-cleaners twisted together by a clown stoned on Careful Juice, but more, or perhaps less, like a gigantic amoeba, or a very small sports crowd, and only a little bit like a flamingo, but rather more suggestive of a squid. Or a moth. Or a sea-anemone blended with a teapot, perched on top of a duck. Or did I mean a porcu … pine … tree … frog … man—*go figure*.

I could see it all clearly, even though I had trouble believing it, because the light had changed too, from flickery lantern-light to a steady, somehow *modern* light that filled the chamber with a comforting warmth.

The Amalgam continued explaining as I gawped at it. "Most advanced species are amalgams," it said, no longer in Old Father Time's faded voice, but in a firmer, livelier tone. "A bit of this, a bit of that—*ooh*, that could improve things, let's add some of that. And before you know it, we're not what we once were at all but what we've become. You humans are starting on that path now, gene-splicing and editing your DNA and so on. Which is where and when this whole problem started, as I shall shortly explain.

"It won't be long before you're amalgams too. Although you won't be *our* kind of Amalgam. It'd take you millennia to get even a tenth of the way to this, and well ... the chances of you making it that far are just about non-existent. Humans being still pretty primitive, basically. Hunter-gatherers in penthouses. Too much too soon; not evolved enough to deal with the problems they've created. Messing up their fine planet as fast as they can, and about to start messing up themselves. Well, at least they'll have the chance now, thanks to you."

"Thanks to me? Why? What did I do?"

"Saved your species, believe it or not. Not that anyone there back on your Earth will ever know that you did. They have no idea. Any more than you did."

"How did I do that?" I asked. I couldn't be more dumbfounded. *I'd saved the human race?*

"With considerable help from your friends," the Amalgam pointed out. "You'd never have got far alone."

"That's true," I agreed. "But I still don't understand—"

"You will if you stop interrupting."

"Sorry."

"So," it continued, "you humans are what—a million-odd years old? As a species? Two? Less than three, anyway. We've been in *space* a hundred times longer than that. Right. So—how many dimensions do you have?"

"Three." I said.

"Four, actually, if you count Time. Which you should. Seeing as you came down here to bargain with it. You humans have a pretty good handle on Height, Width, and Depth, and a vague sense of Time. I mean, you know enough about Time to—well, how to explain it?"

The Amalgam paused for a second, considering, before continuing. "If you were looking at a pendulum side-on—in two dimensions, as it were—you'd see it swing back and forth to the same two endpoints. Suppose that pendulum is what you would call History. Now, stand up, rise above it, and look down on it from above. You'll see that the ground underneath it is flowing, in a direction we all call Time. If you stick a pencil in the end of the pendulum and put some paper on the ground, it wouldn't trace out a single line going back and forth to the same endpoints, but a regular, curling wave that snakes forward in time. Which is, incidentally, why History never repeats itself. It just looks that way if you don't know where to stand.

"A hundred or so of your human years ago we thought we were up to twelve dimensions. There was great excitement for a while, until further research revealed that the new one that we'd just discovered was actually a subset of Seven."

It had lost me. "Seven what?"

"Dimension Seven. So, we're still at Eleven, with a much more interesting Seven than we'd at first thought. There will be others. We'll find them, in time." He made a gesture that I interpreted as *that's not important.* "So, back to Time and Height and Width and Depth. Now—and remember, we're not going into detail here because your brain would implode—think of it like one of your keyboards. Press T and you get a T. Right?"

"Right …" I agreed. That seemed simple enough.

"Okay. Now add a special key and press that," it said. "Shift-I gives you an upper-case I, right? Not much change there. A change, yes, but hardly a significant one, shall we say. What about Ctrl-I, *a.k.a.* Command-I?"

I frowned, trying to remember. "You don't get anything. It changes the font, to Italic."

"Right!" The Amalgam sounded pleased. "And there you have it. The conditions of the whole system in front of you have changed. And that is significant indeed."

"Italic is just a font, though," I pointed out.

"Indeed, but on *our* keyboards, so to speak, if there were such things, which there aren't, but imagine there are: if you hit Ctrl+H, or Alt+W, or Opt+D, or Fn+T, you get a whole set of entirely differ-ent *conditions* of height and width and depth and time. In a nutshell, different physics."

"You're right," I said, eventually. What the Amalgam was saying was overwhelming. "My brain would implode."

"Good," it said, "so you get the general idea."

"I think so …" I shook my head. "But it's … way out of my league."

"The science is, of course, but the *idea* isn't," the Amalgam dis-agreed. "Anyone can grasp an *idea*. I'd be happy to show you the proof of it, but you don't have the capability to understand it. No human has. But—surely you can see that it's very useful?"

I couldn't see where this was leading, but he seemed to be explain-ing, in terms that I could vaguely follow, so I nodded and said, "Yes."

"Splendid! Now, that's just for starters. There's more where that came from—much more. If you think Ctrl+H is impressive enough—which it is, believe me—you should check out Shift+Alt+T. That'd interest your man Einstein. Clever, for a human. E=MC², and all that? He was right on the money there. Well, as far as he went. Which wasn't very. He'd love to have seen the next step. And the one after. And ... all the others that beautifully simple equation leads to.

"Okay, so if we take for example Shift+Alt+T, and then alter the *parameters* .... Um, how to make this understandable?"

It pondered for a moment, its various appendages fluttering and waving. "Yes: imagine a sliding bar on your screen, zero at one end, at the other a hundred. A percentage bar."

"I can do that," I said, glad to have something to grasp onto.

"So, you slide the parameter of whatever input you want, in whichever direction you want it to go, after hitting Shift+Alt+T as it were, and the other parameters adjust accordingly. So, taking Albert's M, for example, we can shift the E parameter to less than one—say zero point one—and the M thus goes all the way up to damn near infinity. And of course, if we adjust the E parameter the other way, we can make the thing weigh nothing. Which is how we move a million-ton space cruiser from A to B instantaneously. Even if the destination B is up to a *square* of C-squared of your light years away from starting point A. Although, of course, a space cruiser weighs nothing in space anyway, as I am sure you are about to object, *mass* and *weight* not being the same thing. By no means are they. But they are, shall we say, in a committed relationship."

"*Whoa ...!*" I exhaled. My hands were shaking, and I clasped them together on the tabletop. "Wow. Any more of that and I'll need to lie down."

"So, we can pretty much go anywhere and do pretty much anything," the Amalgam said. "Including, shall we say, *influencing* this planet to be the right location for what we had in mind for you. The flora and fauna are in some ways different, as you've seen, but it's all recognizable as something akin to your Planet Earth."

The Amalgam paused and looked at me out of its various features with what I interpreted as a smile.

"You didn't ... create this place?"

The Amalgam shuffled its features, in a sort of very-other-worldly shrug. "No need. We have a database of quadrillions of planets. This one fitted the bill nicely for our purpose. Earthlike but with differences. As you've seen. And not too much magic."

That startled me. "That's ... common, out here?"

The Amalgam stopped waving and shifting. "Oh yes. There's magic everywhere in this universe of ours. Some planets have more than others. There are places where you and your staff wouldn't last a week."

"Wow." I shook my head, trying to take it all in.

"I know," it said sympathetically. "Quite a bit to unpack, eh?"

"I'll say."

"Any questions?" The Amalgam waited, appendages fluttering again.

When I had gathered my thoughts, I asked, "So ... how 'Earthlike' is this place?" I wanted to find out as much as I could about my new home.

"Very like, in many ways. Seasons, climates, lands, seas, and so on. In others, not so much. As I said, the flora and fauna here are pretty comparable—even if many are unlike anything that you know of. It was easy enough to make a subtle tweak here and there to align them with creatures of your various cultures, myths, and legends. We didn't have to do much. Just nudge the planet's evolution along a bit so that it was ready for you. To welcome and challenge. We seeded it with humanity a while ago and have been interested to observe how your species has evolved alongside life forms native to this planet."

It paused, and—as far as I could tell—contemplated me with its various peculiar eyes. "Well, that's enough of the science. Now for the politics. You might be wondering, given our interest in your human race, why don't we help humanity along its path to the stars, to get you up here with us." Something like a shudder ran through it, and it grunted. "Sad to say, throwing a lot of advanced knowledge at an immature Civ is a recipe for disaster. Never ends well. But we saw your potential from the beginning and have been doing more than just watching. We dropped hints here and there at appropriate moments over the last million years. Flint-knapping. Milling grain for flour. Jet propulsion. You lot are bright enough to pick up on the clues and 'think these things up for yourselves' as you see it.

"Well, not all human history has been peace and light, has it? You discover these things, and fight like cats and dogs over them. We've found—and by 'we' I mean us and the other Alpha Civs—that every single time a species makes it to space, it causes trouble. We were the same way. As were the Zvorp and the Ondur and the Ekromex, all of whom we fought galactic wars with. And by *with*, I mean *alongside* at times, and *against* at others.

"Only those aforementioned, and fewer than a dozen others, have evolved out of that stage. That is a *dismal* survival rate, I can tell you! Many dozens more Civs have fought each other to extinction than have made it through. It's not only wasteful, it's environmentally disastrous. Many healthy planetary systems have been reduced to radioactive rubble by all that unnecessary warfare.

"So, we don't encourage any newcomers to join us. They never get it. They all behave the same stupid way. Just like we all did. They have to get there on their own. See the light, so to speak. Then it's *welcome to the club*.

"You think humans would be any different? You people are excellent fighters. We've just seen you in action, right? Resourceful, determined, loyal, able to think around corners. But you are also as primitive as chimpanzees, just about. Teach you lot our tech and there'd be trouble. We already have four major intergalactic wars raging at the moment. We do *not* need more participants."

He let that sink in.

I said, "You saved humanity through us … only to let it wipe itself out?"

"Not necessarily. I'm just giving you the odds. Humanity now has the *chance* to wipe itself out. Or, of course, not. Which it would not have had if you'd failed the task you were faced with here, as I will explain.

"What happened was that we and our former allies and/or enemies reached an Accord. We had all evolved beyond the stage that the Civs currently fighting those four ongoing intergalactic wars are still stuck at. So, basically, we're fine. We'd love it if all other Civs were fine too. As I said, they aren't—those Beta Civs still fighting each other, for example. But they're not the problem.

"The problem is the Alpha Civs who *won't* join the Accord."

"Why won't they?" I asked.

"Because they hate us and all that the Accord stands for."

"What? Why?" I couldn't get my head around that. "I thought you said … . If they're also Alpha Civs—aren't they, well, civilized?"

"Very."

"Then that makes no sense …"

"No, indeed, none at all." The Amalgam sighed. "Not to us, not to you, not to the other Accord Civs. But it makes sense to them. You see: they're *pure*."

"Pure?"

"Pure. As in, *not-Amalgam*. Not Amalgam like us, or like any of the other Alpha Civs who have improved themselves over the eons. The 'pure' evolved to become Alpha Civs without improving themselves via bioengineering or grafting from other species. They regard us as abominations that must be eradicated from the universe."

I frowned. That seemed unnecessarily harsh. "Isn't there enough room for everyone?"

"More than enough, but that's not the point," the Amalgam answered. "The point is, this *matters* to them more than anything. We're perfectly happy to coexist with them. Or with anyone else. While they see it as their sacred, inviolable duty to wipe us out."

I was shocked. "Could they?"

"Eventually, very possibly," the Amalgam admitted. "Not just yet, thankfully. Our tech is still at least the equal of theirs. But they're gaining. Since founding the Accord, we'd stopped all military research. We had no further need for it. We'd evolved beyond it. We weren't, in the words of one of your Earth bards, going to study war no more. Now, we're scrambling to make up for millennia of lost time. Meanwhile, they are policing the universe as if they own the place. The moment a Civ starts showing signs of becoming Amalgam, they put a stop to it."

"By?" I said.

"Obliterating it."

"What!" I was horrified. "Before they've even begun?"

"Before they even know what's hit them. Or why. Those of us in the Accord don't approve. Billions of creatures destroyed purely because of, well, dogma? It didn't make sense to us. Every Civ that makes it to the stars contributes much of value to the rest of us. We believe you humans would do the same, and we're excited by the prospect. What that would be, in your case—who knows? We'll find out when you get there." It paused, then added, "*If* you get there."

It brightened. "Which you now still have the chance to do because of what you achieved here. But more on that later, back to the Pure.

"What we did was make them an offer. We assured them that we knew they wanted to destroy us, and that they wouldn't rest until they had, but that, as things currently stood, a war would inevitably destroy them as well as us. We understood that they couldn't declare peace with us, because of their dogma. They were furious at the thought and said, 'Absolutely not, don't you dare even suggest it!'

"We said, 'We aren't suggesting it. What we are suggesting is that we suspend hostilities for a certain amount of time (about a hundred of your Earth years) with an option to continue for another hundred, or further hundreds, if both sides are willing.'

"They saw some sense in that, as we knew they would, because they could see that this would buy them time to improve their weaponry to the point where they could break the armistice and annihilate us … . Which is possible, but not guaranteed.

"So they agreed. And the desperate arms race between us continues. Meanwhile, we avoid each other as much as possible and don't attack each other. They're all lifelong, committed, implacable military, and we'd all much rather be doing anything else. But we have to do this or we're finished."

The Amalgam quivered and emitted an odd sound that might have been a sigh. It turned to me and continued, "I expect you're wondering where you come in."

"I am."

"What, our enemies wanted to know, did we propose to do about the obvious problem? Which I'm sure you spotted immediately."

I shook my head. "I haven't, no. Sorry."

"You."

"Me?"

"You plural. Humanity. A fledgling Civ that is starting to bioengineer itself and adjust its DNA and so on—thus starting on the path to becoming Amalgam. If it wasn't for us, the Pure would have wiped you out as soon as they saw what your Earth scientists were up to.

"They didn't like it, but they saw the sense in our proposal. Which was: that any fledgling Civ—such as yours—should have the chance to, as it were, sink or swim. You're not the first, by the way. I expect you won't be the last."

My head was spinning. *Sink or swim?*

"Think of it in terms of your own Earth's past," the Amalgam explained. "At many times in your history, wars have been decided by single combat. Champion versus champion. Much was saved in what you humans call 'blood and gold.' One life is lost, not thousands or millions. All is settled in a day, not drawn out inconveniently over months or years, disrupting trade, destroying towns and cities, laying waste to harvests, and decimating populations. You three won your world's Championship, so it was obvious that we should choose you. Who better to represent you lot in this challenge?"

When it put it that way, I thought, *I could see its point.*

"That challenge being," it continued, "what is to all intents and purposes a 'real life' game. Which is another way of saying a 'real death' game. You knew your roles, your avatars; you'd been playing them for years. We believed you'd join the dots soon enough.

"Your enemies, we agreed, could be represented by whatever they wanted. At a commensurate level, of course, no nukes or starfighters. Or even gunpowder. Just what you had: blades, monsters, magic. So, we set you on this planet and left it to come up with what it came up with."

"It?"

"The Environment."

"You didn't ... design what happened to us? Our ... quest?"

It shook its remarkable head firmly. "No more than the Pure did. Not permitted by the terms of the agreement. We'd have cheated like hell if we had—so would they."

The Amalgam seemed perfectly happy with what it was telling me. I was shocked.

"So, you just ... grabbed us? Without asking? To make us play this 'real death' game of yours?"

"They insisted—the Pure. We were not allowed to give you warning. No coaching, no aid. Their only other condition was that the three of you would be dropped separately on this rock with little more than just your wits. And, as they say here, thank all the gods that those were enough. *Just.*"

I didn't know what to feel. Confusion. Relief at being alive. Indignation at having been hijacked without warning—without even being asked.

"I know," the Amalgam said. "It's a lot to take in. But—there it is, and here you are. Well done. We honestly didn't think you'd make it."

"Nor did we, half the time," I admitted.

"First you had to destroy Jurun, and that was hardly easy, was it? Then you had to realize that that wasn't the end of it. You had to work out the tree and the key, and come in here to bargain with Time. Not everyone would have put those particular two-and-two's together and made four. But you did. And then to make your offer. A death for a life. Yours for hers."

"Which," I said, "doesn't seem to be happening …"

"Doesn't need to. It's the offer that matters. They—our foes—didn't believe anyone would do that. No, you're not going to die. At least not here."

Realization dawned as if I had suddenly emerged from a fog of confusion. "So, we … won?"

"The battle, so to speak," it said. "Not the war."

"You mean … it's not over?"

"Not by a very long shot. No need to worry about that now, I'll fill you in when we meet again. Now off you go, you have a tale to see to the end of its telling. The bargain has been fulfilled and the price paid. Every life costs a death, remember."

I remembered with a surge of joy.

Esmeralda. Alive.

"I expect she'll want to thank you." The Amalgam unfolded itself from the chair that it had been overflowing in various directions and came around the table to me. It moved surprisingly fast, its curious mélange of tentacles and stalks and limbs and what looked like a prehensile rudder all blurring out of focus for a moment as it slid over, and then blurring back in again.

"We'll meet in a day or two, so say your goodbyes to your friends in this realm and be ready. I have something for you. I believe you're going to like it. And Daxx"—it extended a feeler covered in red and black hair, which I took and shook—"well done."

"Thanks." A thought struck me. "Listen, if your name's not Anna, like I thought when I misheard, what is it? Do you have one? I mean, I feel I've come to know quite a bit about you."

The Amalgam hesitated. "Well, strictly speaking, yes, I do have a name. But you wouldn't be able to pronounce it—or, if you pronounced it properly, the way we do, even be able to *hear* it. We speak to each other at ultra-high frequency. Way squeakier than your Earth bats. I doubt even they could hear us …"

It hesitated. An expression that looked something like a frown crossed its face. "Call me … how about 'Ken'?"

I blinked a couple of times. "Ken?"

"Short for Kenneth?"

With its proboscis, long antennae, tufts of spiky black and red in-sect hair, those blue tentacles, its seven normal eyes of various shapes and sizes and two compound eyes, its beak, and all the beyond-weird rest of it, it didn't look anything like any Kenneth I'd ever seen.

I said, simply, "Ken works."

36

The Ride

Little Guy spotted me first as I emerged from the world-tree, and shot over to me in a brown blur, barking and leaping and wagging his tail madly. I bent down to pat him and scratch his ears and got thoroughly tongued.

Second was Esmeralda, breaking off from the others and rushing over to me, shouting, "There he is! He's alive! *Daxx!*" Her arms were around my neck, and she was hugging and squeezing and crying and saying, "We thought we'd never see you again! Oh, Daxx, I'm so happy! And so sorry. And so *relieved!* It's so good to see you!" She kissed my cheeks loudly and repeatedly and hung off my neck, laughing, her feet lifted back off the ground.

I don't think I managed much more than, "Hey, Esmeralda How are you doing?"

"Wonderful! Confused! I've got so much to tell you, all of you!" The others had gathered around me by then and were hugging and patting and guffawing and chuckling and chattering nineteen to the dozen. They'd all assumed that I was dead, that Time had taken my life for Esmeralda's—because that was the sort of stupid thing I'd do, she said. "Go and make a bargain with him. Well, look what happened to the *last* person who did that!"

447

"No, it wasn't like that," I said. "He just explained that everything was balanced out now Jurun was dead again—like he should have been in the first place, thanks to us, so we'd be getting you back."

That seemed to satisfy them.

Well, I was the living proof that what I was saying was true, so it must be, and they accepted it.

Esmeralda grinned. "Look!" She pointed to a pool of red and green light glowing on the ground by Jurun's throne.

I stared.

I felt a thump in my stomach.

I gasped, scarcely daring to hope.

Shift.

Her tourmaline heartstone was shining again in our staff with richer, stronger, more radiant reds and greens that she'd ever had before. My heart lurched. I'd expected Esmeralda to be alive because Ken had told me she was—but *Shift!* I hadn't realized how much I'd missed her. And now, instead of mourning the loss of her, I could celebrate having her back—back where she belonged—in my hands.

Tears welled in my eyes as I picked her up and felt her laughing and skipping for joy all the way up my arm. I stroked her, overjoyed to see her again, and she responded, our private conversation resuming after what had been a cruel termination.

"Her light just came streaming back out of nothing," Qrysta said. "Right when Esmeralda's eyes opened, and she sat up, gasping."

"And scaring the crap out of us," Grell added.

Oller said, "Yeah, we thought, *uh-oh, is it her—or is it going to be* him *again?*"

"We think her light came from the point where Jurun's heartstone imploded," Qrysta continued. "Kind of like a black hole unravelling in reverse. Her stick reconstituted itself around the blank heartstone and leapt about on the ground while the light poured into her, then her eye opened and began to shine. We knew then that you'd done it. His staff's life for Shift's. Yours for Esmeralda's."

"Glad we were wrong about that last bit." Oller grinned. "We missed you, Daxxie! A lot."

"Yeah," Grell said, "we'd done enough grieving today."

"Asshole." Qrysta stared at me fixedly. "Can't fool me."

I said placidly, "I have no idea what you're talking about."

"Oh yeah?" she challenged. "What made you go in there, then? Without us?"

"Someone I needed to see. You'll be seeing him yourself soon enough."

Qrysta crossed her arms and studied me. "See who?"

"Foreigner," I said, then added, "*Very*."

Her eyes narrowed as she wondered what I could mean. I gave her no further information. She'd find out for herself soon enough.

"You too," I said to Grell.

Like Qrysta, he was also puzzled. "Oh, ah?"

Qrysta wasn't finished with me. "Who?" she repeated.

"Ken."

"*Ken?*"

"Mm-hm," I said. "You'll like him."

Oller said, "Do I get to meet him too?"

"Foreigners only, sorry Oller. Foreign stuff." I could see that that didn't satisfy him and changed the subject. Jurun's remains were lying both on and below his throne. "Pity we can't take that with us."

"What, his corpse?" Oller asked.

"No." And before I could explain, another thought struck me. "We do not want him bothering the world again." I aimed Shift at Jurun's remains, and I could feel how she enjoyed blasting a Flameball into them. Within moments his ancient bones were reduced to ashes.

"I meant the throne," I said. "I could Levitate it, but it'd still be a hell of a weight to push. Uphill. For gods knows how many days. Even with Grell doing most of the pushing."

"What do we need it for?" Grell said.

"It's what we came for. The last piece. *Throne*. Shame to have to leave it here. It would prove that we really did defeat Jurun." I paused, considering it. "Wonder how it got down here in the first place ..."

Oller said, "Marnie said, *summoned*."

"Way beyond any summoning magic I've ever heard of," I said. "All I ever summoned was a few ghosts to tell me things on quests, once I'd killed them. Or rather, killed their previous owners. And they just floated there and moaned and gave their answers. I couldn't move *that* thing."

"You could sit on it and fire off Flameballs and have them propel you in the opposite direction?" Qrysta suggested.

I shook my head. "Casting doesn't obey the laws of physics, Qrys. There's no *equal and opposite reaction*, or we'd be flung about all over the place any time we cast. It only obeys the laws of magic. And I can't fly, so I can't tie myself to it and take off."

"I can," Esmeralda said.

We all looked at her.

"Well, that's how I got down here." She walked behind the throne where she picked something up off the ground.

"On this." She held up a broomstick.

"I'm Coven, now, so I can fly. Marnie taught me."

"Where is she, by the way?" I asked, concerned for my old mentor. "I couldn't Think to her, and Ennis said she'd gone off with you and Coven. Is she okay?"

"She was fine last time I saw her. I'm the only one Jurun took over— well, as far as I know."

"Took over?"

"I'll tell you all about it on the way up. You raise the throne, we'll tie my broomstick to it, and off we go. I hope it's more comfortable than the flight down!"

"Bumpy ride?" I asked.

"That's putting it mildly!" she said. "Come on, let's see if we can do this."

We could. I Levitated Jurun's great throne, turned it on its back, and using our cloaks and packs and the many lengths of twine that Oller always kept about his person, we tied Esmeralda's broomstick above it. She hopped on and did a few circles of the cavern to try it out.

I felt Shift quiver with excitement in my hand. I knew what she meant immediately. *A flying stick? That looks fun.*

It did. *You'd have to wear a skirt of twigs*, I thought to her.

I could swear she replied with an actual raspberry.

I had to laugh. *Besides*, I added, *I'm not Coven*.

Esmeralda brought the throne down to land, where it hovered a foot off the ground. "It's like flying a wardrobe," she said. "It handles like a drunken cow. I'll get the hang of it. All right, hop on."

We did. Grell stowed Jurun's half of the crown and ice knife in his pack, and we clambered aboard. Grell sat in the middle, Qrysta perched on the seat at the rear, her legs wrapped around Esmeralda. Esmeralda planted her feet on Grell's back. I wedged myself in front of Grell, his legs and arms around me. I wrapped mine around Oller's in front of me. He held Little Guy in his lap. Little Guy's ears flapped in the wind as Esmeralda took off and flew us across the cavern. I cast Glows above, to travel with us, and a Ward of Silence around us like a cabin. We could talk and listen in relative comfort. It was awkward, but it beat trudging leagues back up through the Undergrounds.

We had a lot to talk about. Esmeralda steered us towards another way out of the floor of the world, and we began the long, effortless, cramped, but surprisingly restful flight to the Upgrounds. She knew exactly where she was going, she said. And her course triangulated with Oller's readings of our various maps, his finder's expertise, and the guidance he was receiving from his star sapphire, stone of seeking and seeing.

It wasn't all plain sailing—or rather, flying. Every now and again we had to stop and squeeze through a narrow cleft in a tunnel or knock some sense into things that decided to attack us. There weren't many of those. It was as if the malign power that had been dominating the Undergrounds had gone, and the creatures that lived, or *un*-lived, down there had gone back to being their usual furtive, skulking selves.

The *usual selves* of the pit-elves we ran into were the worst things we came across. They were as nasty and vicious as Nyrik had made them sound. They grabbed at us as we cruised through a low cavern, jumping from below, dropping from the ceiling, leaping in from all sides, shrieking and brandishing axes and knives.

Qrysta, Grell, Oller, and Little Guy were off their seats and among them instantly, each inside their own glowing Orb of Shielding as I cast attacks at our assailants, and Esmeralda kept our transport moving. The arrows they rained in at us bounced off our Wards. One of them grabbed at Esmeralda's ankle and sank its needle teeth into her leg. She screamed. I blew the brute away with a Lightning Bolt and set Heals on her leg. The fight lasted no more than ten minutes.

"Good workout, that!" Grell said as he clambered back into his seat. "Needed it, I was getting cramps."

Esmeralda knew the route because she'd come this way on her way down.

And she told us what had happened.

"We were on patrol over the Darklands, every day as well as every night, me and Marnie and our Covensisters, led by Sister Agneka, our Guildmother. We didn't mind about being seen there. The only things that could see us from below were enemy, and the whole point was to

451

keep them busy and distracted, watching us, while you lot all did what you were doing. We always went in pairs to keep an eye on each other. None of us actually *saw* anything, whether we looked with our eyes or our minds, which I can't do yet, but some guildsisters can.

"But we all felt it, all right! A brooding, heavy, just plain *nasty* feeling coming up out of that brown murk, aiming itself up at us, if that makes sense. A hostile feeling, probing at us, looking for our weaknesses, taunting us. We were on edge, I can tell you, all the time, drained dry. Every now and then, one of us would swoop down as low as she dared into the murk and scoot around the ruins of Downbury, feet above street level. Only, of course, the problem with Downbury is that it's *down*. There's nothing on the surface now. Everyone, or thing, moved below ages ago.

"We could see the ways that led down deeper. Some of us started dipping in and out of the upper tunnels. We saw nothing, no movement of any kind. But every day, the *watching* feeling, the *enemy* feeling, got worse. Much worse. As if it was about to erupt and pour all over us. We didn't know what to do. We didn't seem to be achieving anything.

"And then, one day, when I was on patrol with Marnie, I was circling over one of the tunnels down into the lower city when everything unleashed on me at once. Or *in* me. Junie was calling out to me, I *saw* you all in my mind, and battles going on down there, leagues away; an army of Orcs battling an army of horrors, a city under siege, and Junie, pleading with me from her prison, arms open, tears in her eyes, and *boom!* I was gone.

"I flew far faster than I'd ever ridden before, faster than I would ever have thought one of these could possibly go. I'd never seen a sister ride at anything *like* the speed. And Marnie was screaming in my head, but I couldn't hear what—and then she was gone, and I was gone, and I went into a nosedive and shot into the tunnel.

"I couldn't move. I was clinging to my broomstick, but it felt like it was grabbing onto me. My hands were clamped around the handle, I was lying flat out, and *flying* flat out! And I wasn't in control; the broomstick was—or if it wasn't, something else was controlling it. We hurtled around bends, up into the ceilings of caves when she shot into them, back down around sudden corners, and into what looked like tiny cracks far too small for us, but we squeezed in and through every time.

452

"Into and out of tunnels we streaked, a labyrinth of tunnels twisting every which way and back, dropping through holes, my broomstick throwing me around, and there was nothing I could do, not even scream. And then there were *things*. Hands grabbing at me, long claws clutching at my clothes. The broomstick wriggled, shaking them off, then zapped forwards and away, then hared around a corner and slammed into a thick wall of cobwebs.

"*Cobwebs!* Sticky and heavy and dripping with some awful slime, and they were endless—drape after drape of them, the broomstick fighting her way through them, inching, bucking, struggling. I could hear the clicking of the spiders as they scuttled towards us, and the spitting and the hissing, and their huge shadows getting closer and closer through the cobwebs. We were trapped, swinging helplessly. We kicked, reared, fought, and *just* made it as the things appeared from all sides to grab us, then off we shot again, trailing ropes of web.

"All the way *down and down* we went, faster and faster, jerking and twisting, throwing me about every way, sometimes turning me upside down and then back or around. I kept trying to shut my eyes but couldn't, and scream, but couldn't. I'd have been thrown off if I hadn't been glued on by the grip the broomstick had on me.

"*Down and down*, faster and faster, the wind getting colder and colder and roaring in my ears, my eyes streaming. How would I ever find my way back to the surface? I barely had a second to glimpse any of it. All I knew was that where I was headed was the darkest place I had ever been—and I'm not saying that just because of the lack of light.

"Eventually, after what seemed forever, we shot out into the floor of the world and across to the world-tree where the broomstick stopped abruptly, and I was thrown off, and that's all I remember."

We were exhausted just listening to her.

Qrysta, behind Esmeralda, her legs wrapped around her hips and her arms around her waist, said, "Wow."

"I know." Esmeralda leaned back against her, welcoming the comfort and safety of her arms after all that she had been through. "*Wow* is what I thought, just before I blacked out, and also, *well that's that then*." She paused. "Only it wasn't, was it?"

I tried to imagine what it must have been like for her. Confusing and terrifying, to say the least. "What do you remember? Of what happened next?"

453

"Well," she said, "I don't know about *next* ... I don't know how long I was unconscious. Could have been minutes, could have been hours, or days. I didn't see any of you, so I don't think you'd got there yet. Who knows? The next thing I knew was Daxx calling my name."

I frowned. "I didn't."

"Well, I heard you, in my head. Clear as a bell. Then I woke up and got up and started singing. Only it wasn't me singing. It was him, with my voice. And there was nothing I could do about it. I knew what was happening, and gradually I faded away inside. Then I was looking out through a blue veil around my eyes. I could see a light beyond it, shining, moving towards you: it was me, singing, only it wasn't me—it was just my body; I was in him now. He was in me, and I was dead and cold and slumped on this throne, blindfolded with sapphires—waiting. I heard what I said, or rather what *he* said with my voice, and then my body put his staff in my new corpse's hand, and I watched me plunge the ice knife into my own body and fall ..."

She stopped, her voice tailing off at the memory.

Qrysta said, "That must have been horrible."

"Mm. It was," Esmeralda said. "That was the worst part. Not me dying, but knowing that you were going to die too, and that there was nothing I could do about it, and it was all my fault."

"It wasn't!" Oller said. "Don't you ever think that!"

"Too right," Grell growled.

"Only you didn't die," Esmeralda said. "Did you? *He* did! Marnie's book stopped him. Oller's knife killed him. Or if it didn't, Qrysta finished him off with his own ice knife under her amber amulet. Book and bone, stick and stone. Knife, and life, and throne."

Grell glanced at me. "Poetic justice."

"Is that what it's called?" she asked.

"Yep," Grell said.

"Well he asked for it, as far as I'm concerned," Esmeralda said.

⅄ ⅄ ⅄

There were signs of life by the time we stopped for the night, or rather what we assumed was the night. We were all tired, the broomstick most of all. She'd been flying gradually slower and slower and was almost out of power when we decided to give her a well-earned rest. The

Serjeant Bastard smiled back. "I'll be interested to see for myself how true the tale is of what you did." He studied her for a moment. "He was good, young Rylen. Trained him up myself when I were his father's Serjeant-at-Arms. Sour lad, though, not like his kind old man. Didn't like me putting him in his place when he got too full of himself. Well, I don't take to sneering, never mind how high born you are. I thanked His Lordship for the work and took my trade off to Brigstowe." He paused, measuring her up. "Well, miss, if you could handle Rylen, mayhaps you'd like to see how you fare against his teacher. I can't have my pupils being roughed up without an accounting."

"I definitely would," Qrysta replied.

Blunt then turned to us. "That's *Commandant* to you three. Swore I'd never turn officer again, but the pay's good and the quarters are better—and His Majesty's kitchen beats that slop-house in Brigstowe." He handed each of us a bound scroll and a leather purse. "Discharge papers, honorable, of course, signed by His Majesty himself, and your back pay. Also, an offer of a place in the Palace Guard should you wish it, the which I very much doubt any of you will. Camp's over yonder, down by the river. Dinner's waiting. I expect like me you're hungry."

"That we are, Serj—Commandant," we managed.

He broke out into the broadest of grins and shook our hands, one after the other.

"Welcome home, lads!" he said. "I'm proud of you. *Very* proud!"

Another feast, this one in the camp by the river around open fires. There was much coming and going and swapping of seats and asking and answering of questions. Marnie had got full comms up again the moment everything had cleared and she knew that Jurun was dead. Messages had flown the length and breadth of the realm, and those who could get here in time had made all haste to do so.

Others would be waiting for us in Mayport, among them Klurra and Chief Elbrig. A third of the Orc army had been lost in the Undergrounds, we learned—a fearsome toll. But they had held a far bigger force at bay and stopped it reaching either the Upgrounds or Niblunhaem. In gratitude, the nibluns were going to equip every Orc in the land with any arms and armor they desired.

The only people who hadn't rallied to the cause, it seemed, had been the noble lords. They'd been too busy fighting each other as we had expected. Commandant Bastard himself would be leading out the

Royal Expedition to knock sense into them. And he'd have seven or eight hundred niblun-outfitted, battle-hardened Orcs at his back in addition to the Palace Guards. Peace would soon be breaking out all over the realm once again.

"And not before time," he said. "One or two domains will have new lords, and one or two of the old lords will lose their heads—and then we can all settle down about our business again."

The first order of that business being to present ourselves to the king.

I knew little about him, this Wyllard the Seventh. He was old, not exactly ancient, but long past his middle years. And ineffective, as recent events had proved. I consulted with Marnie and Junie and their peers on the Conclave of the GAA, and Oller talked to officers of the Mayport TG. Nobody bothered to talk to the mercs, because nobody cared what they thought. That was because everybody *knew* what they thought. They thought about themselves, and *what's in it for me*.

Representatives of all the other guilds were there that evening: Apothecaries, Alchemists, every kind of Trade and Craft. We were also introduced to leaders of all the Cults and Sects and Faiths, and to the Dean and Faculty of the College of Lore and Learning. They all wanted to meet with us, talk to us, and thank us for what we had done. And we wanted to listen.

We listened and learned and, later that night, the six of us gathered privately around the table in our pavilion and put our heads together—Marnie, Esmeralda, Grell, Oller, Qrysta, and me.

What to do now?

The answers were obvious when we considered it all.

To everyone, that is, but Esmeralda.

Marnie could see how overwhelmed she was. And she hadn't even been told the worst of it yet. *Best if she works it out for herself. It's a lot for the girl to take on board all at once*, Marnie had told me.

Esmeralda looked in alarm at the ornate, ruined throne that she had flown up from the floor of the world, as if seeing it for the first time.

"It's yours now, girl," Marnie said, gently. "You won it, by right of conquest."

She stared at Marnie, eyes round with worry. "*They* did, not me. Daxx and Qrysta and Grell and Oller."

458

"Oy!" Oller said sharply, and all heads turned to him as he picked up his dog. "Don't forget Little Guy!'

That broke the tension, and brought a smile to Esmeralda's face, even if it was no more than a weak one.

"Might be the last time I get to tick you off, you going to be queen and all," Oller added. "It'll be *Your Majesty this, Your Highness that*, or whatever the right way to speak to you is."

Esmeralda shook her head. "I don't *want* to be queen."

She sounded very young and very frightened. She was, I could see, on the verge of tears. She'd been so happy and carefree on our flight back to the Upgrounds and all the way here, talking about what she would be learning in Coven as she served her apprenticeship. Clearly, she was imagining a very different life. One not unlike Marnie's, perhaps. She had not seen this coming.

"It's not a matter of what *you* want, young lady," Marnie said, sympathy and firmness in her voice. "There's a job to be done, and it's chosen you to do it. *He's* not sitting on it now, thanks to you, and that means *you* are. The tale needs its ending, and what's the last word of it? *A knife, a life, a* throne."

Esmeralda swallowed. "But …"

"Your life, his life; his throne, your throne."

She let that sink in.

Esmeralda said, "What about King Wyllard?"

"He has his own throne, he doesn't need this one."

"He'll object."

Marnie snorted. "He'll see sense soon enough. His realm was tearing itself apart, and he was about to lose the lot to Jurun. He'll still have half of it—and that he owes to you."

Esmeralda frowned, puzzled. "*Half* of it?"

"Half a crown. Half the realm."

Surprise registered on her face. "We divide the kingdom?"

"Share it. As the brothers who founded it did. The riddle is solved, the tale is told, now to close the circle."

Esmeralda grappled with what she was hearing. It was plain that she had never imagined such a thing happening to her. She kept looking at the throne and at us, and even glanced at the door of the pavilion, as if wanting to run away.

Marnie, who must have been reading her thoughts, said, "Can't run away from fate, girl. No more than any of us can."

"I could say no."

"You could. And then what would happen? Someone else would have their eye on that throne of yours. Some noble lord, who thinks King Wyllard a weakling and a ditherer—which he is, we all know. And he'd plot his plot, gather his supporters; word would get out, and other noble lords would think, *why him? Never trusted that one, nasty piece of work, been our blood enemies for years, his kin have. No, it should be me!*

Marnie paused, to let that sink in, then continued, "It's not as if they're not all primed for it as it is, with all the warring and squabbling going on. That's not what we need, King Wyllard nor any of us. We need peace and harmony."

Esmeralda looked as if she was drowning. "There must be some-one else," she tried again. "Someone better qualified. I'm only sixteen."

"Better qualified than *his life for yours?* There's no such person!"

We all waited while Esmeralda thought it over. The overwhelming idea of it.

She looked from face to face. She knew that she was surrounded by friends, but I could tell she felt very alone.

She turned back to Marnie. "So ... what are you saying? That I just declare my right to half the kingdom?"

Marnie said nothing.

"It seems ... ." Esmeralda searched for the word. When she found it, her voice was small. "Presumptuous."

"It is." Marnie agreed. "*Presuming*, we are, girl. Anyone who says we're wrong can present their own case—and we'll answer to it. You won your throne by defeating Jurun, whether you wanted it or not. That's the way the world works. Actions have consequences."

"So then I ... do what? Fly my throne to Mayport Castle and sit it next to the king's?" She sounded very unsure at the idea. "Won't everyone—?"

I could feel my hands tightening on Shift, who was lying on my lap. She was as tense as I was, echoing my concern.

"That would be polite," Marnie agreed. "And don't worry about *everyone*. You do what you need to do. *Everyone* will do what they need to. Show him you're not a threat, and you're in this together."

"You mean … ruling?"

"Hm, well, that's a small word for a big task. I mean setting the realm to rights." She paused, then added meaningfully, "*Both* halves of it."

She held Esmeralda's eyes.

Which widened in fear, and her hand flew to her mouth as she realized.

"*Downbury* …" she whispered.

Marnie nodded. "The other King's City. That's where your throne came from and that's where it belongs."

Scared, Esmeralda whispered, "I have to go *there?*"

Marnie reached out her cracked, old hands and took hold of Esmeralda's soft, young ones. "You won't be alone, girl."

"But—there's nothing *there*. Nothing *alive …!*"

"And that's the job. Setting to rights. You'll have all the resources of the realm to help you. Coven, the guilds." She looked around at us. "Your friends."

"An army of Orcs," Grell said. "They won't let anyone mess with you. Or any *thing.*"

Esmeralda looked at me. "Will you come with me, Daxx?"

"Just try and stop me," I said. "And these other *hard, horrible, dangerous* characters."

"O' course!" Oller said. and Qrysta said, "Oh yes," and Grell said, "Too bloody right we will!"

That, we could see, she found reassuring.

I held up a hand. "I may have to go somewhere else first—so may Qrysta and Grell, but with luck it won't be for long."

"Where?"

"I don't know. We'll be finding out soon."

That, I could feel, was news to Shift, who jittered her interest up my arm. *Going somewhere?*

"And you won't shake me off, young lady," Marnie said. "Nor Junie, nor the rest of your Covensisters. We know where and when we're needed, and that *where* is by your side, and that *when* is now. Go on, then." She let go of Esmeralda's hands, leaned back, and nodded at the throne. "Let's see how you look on it."

Hesitant, still clearly unsure about the whole thing, Esmeralda rose from the table and walked over to the throne. She stood, her back to us, looking at it for a long moment as if wondering what her future seated on it held, then turned around and sat.

She looked very small and very serious on that huge, ornate, half-ruined throne from the age of legend. But we all knew that she belonged there. I knew I was smiling. The others were smiling too, and Shift was warm in my hands.

Shyly, Esmeralda smiled back.

"Suits you," Marnie said.

Esmeralda's smile grew a little stronger.

▲ ▲ ▲

Grell and Qrysta drew me aside the next morning and told me that in the night they had both, separately, met Ken. Grell had got up for a leak and stumbled back into what he thought was our pavilion but wasn't. He'd woken Qrysta afterwards as Ken had told him to do, and pointed out where she should go.

Ken had told them that he'd be seeing us all again in a day or two. And we all three sensed that, when that time came, we'd be going our separate ways. As to where those ways would take us, who knew?

As we rode on our way to Mayport to see the king, we discussed what we could now see, looking backwards. We noted the little clues that had been left for us here and there, to orientate us to our environment, to make us feel, if not exactly at home, then at least in a world that wasn't too strange. The mythology that was different-but-familiar. We'd none of us heard of Jaren and Jurun before, or any legend like theirs, but the world-tree and Hel, the daughter of a god and a giantess, and nibluns and Niblunhaem: those were echoes of Nordic myths. *Same-but-different.* Woods Kin—'elfish' by our standards, but nothing like the vicious little pit-elves we'd seen here. Chicken-sized dragons. Orcs, I told them, went all the way back to *Beowulf.* We couldn't go into too much detail as Oller was riding with us, baffled by what he was hearing.

"What'ch you lot on about?" he said. "Beer Wolf? Don't like the sound of that …"

"Foreigner stuff, Ols," Grell said.

"You have them in Ozgaroo? Beer wolves?"

"Oh, we do, mate," Grell said. "Bloody tons of the buggers. It's our term for blokes who wolf down their beer. Place is crawling with them. Ozgaroo beer being the best."

"Oh." A lopsided grin split Oller's face. "I'd like to go there. Sounds like my kind of place."

"And I'd like to show you the sights."

"Hm," Qrysta said, considering the prospect that Ken had laid before us. "Wonder where we'll be off to next. Further adventures. Who knows, huh?"

I chuckled. "*He* does." I believed I'd worked out why he suggested the name Kenneth.

"Who?" Qrysta said. "Ken?"

"Short for Kenneth," I said. "Which, in older English, from the Middle Ages, means 'he knows.' And Ken means 'knowledge.' As in, 'beyond mortal ken' equals 'beyond human knowledge.'"

"What are you lot talking about?" Esmeralda said, gliding up on her floating throne alongside us.

"Teamwork," I said.

▲ ▲ ▲

We were trumpeted into Mayport with fanfares. Cheering crowds threw flowers at us and waved and laughed and blew kisses—all very gratifying. Then we were marched into the Audience Hall of the Royal Castle to meet His Majesty, Wyllard the Seventh. Esmeralda flew in on her throne and stopped it next to His Majesty's on the dais at the end of the hall. I uprighted it, lowered it to the ground, and she sat herself on it, wearing Jurun's half of the brothers' crown.

She turned to Wyllard and said, "Hello, your co-Majesty." We'd decided that the bold approach was the best: put our cards on the table right away. It was unexpected, to say the least, but nobody was going to accuse the Saviors of the Realm of treason. She'd won her throne by right of conquest, and what was anyone going to do about it?

On our ride, the Dean of Mayport's College of Lore and Learning had explained the root causes of the trouble that had been brewing in the realm for years before Jurun began his summoning. King Wyllard had plenty of sons, but none by his wife, who refused to divorce him.

The extended royal family had long been at each other's throats, jockeying for position to succeed him. One of his illegitimate sons, a plump lad of twelve, eagerly said he'd marry Esmeralda on the spot, but she said no thanks, she was much too young, and he was *much* much. Her father, My Lord of Rushtoun, was shocked. He told her she should be honored at the offer, *how could she refuse her Sovereign Lord, the King?* And *think what honor it would bring to the House of Rushtoun!*

He stopped when his wife whispered in his ear, and dropped the matter.

He did not relish the thought of being brained with his own chamberpot.

37

The Reward

Commandant Bastard stood in the sunshine that shone over the Royal Castle of Mayport's Field of Honor, unmoving apart from his arms, which were whirling Qrysta's twin niblun blades around himself like half a dozen high-speed fans, in every direction at once. He stopped, almost quicker than he'd been whirling. Qrysta—*Captain* Qrysta, as she now was, since Esmeralda had appointed her Captain of her Royal Guard—watched intently. Grell and Oller and I had warned her that Jack Blunt was good. She glanced at us and nodded. *You were right.*

"*Hm,*" he grunted. Forgemasters Rodvarn and Thorleif immediately said how they should be an inch and a quarter longer for him and should weigh perhaps another three ounces in the hilt and one in the blade; when he said, "Best I've ever seen, these, and you made them overnight?" They said, "Well, not *alone.*" They fell silent, and Commandant Bastard shook his head in admiration. "Amazing. These old knees …"

He did a couple of deep, ungainly squats, all the way down, levering himself up and grunting, and looking about as coordinated as a newborn foal getting to its feet for the first time.

Grell, Oller, and I smiled at that. We knew better. Those who had their money on Qrysta smirked. Nyrik and Horm put their heads together, whispered urgently, nodded, fished out another purse, and doubled down on their bet on her. They'd seen her win the freestyle at Hartwell—*and this old geezer? It was going to be a walkover ...*

It was to be a charity bout, all proceeds going to Orcs who had lost kin in the Battle in the Undergrounds. King Wyllard had seeded the Orc Dependents Fund with twenty thousand gold. Queen Esmeralda had announced that she was very sorry, but she didn't have any money, and she would be *so* appreciative if anyone felt like contributing to it in her name—which they had done to the tune of, so far, forty-two thousand. The Mathematicians of the College of Lore and Learning worked out the odds, gods knew how, and five per cent of all wagers were going to the ODF.

"It'd be nice to use these," Commandant Bastard said with a sigh. "They'd take a deal of battle testing, in my humble. Ah well, some other time. Mayhaps if certain lords don't listen to reason, eh, Captain?"

"You'd be welcome to carry them, Commandant," Qrysta said. She'd decided on *Captain Qrysta* because she thought *Captain Orange*, named after where she came from, sounded silly. We couldn't disagree.

"Most generous, Captain, I'd appreciate that indeed," Commandant Bastard replied, and seemingly without looking, flicked them, one from each hand simultaneously, so that they cartwheeled through the air and stuck, quivering, in the shield of a tilting-dummy.

"Lovely things," he said, not even bothering to look as they hit their target, and oblivious to the impressed murmurs that his feat inspired in the crowd. More bets were made, and once again the odds shifted. "Oh well, have to make do with these today." He stooped stiffly to pick up two wooden training swords.

Qrysta, in her niblun leathers, now emblazoned with Queen Esmeralda's royal coat of arms, which niblun tailors had run up for her, stood waiting for him, her own wooden swords at the ready. Commandant Bastard, moving with his usual slowness, stood opposite her and bowed. Qrysta returned the bow—and made the wise move of scooting backwards a dozen paces at top speed as she brought her swords up on guard. Commandant Bastard had brained, crippled, bruised and battered the air where she'd been standing a tenth of a second earlier, from head to foot via ribcage and arms and shins, before most people realized that the bout had even started.

He smiled at her.

She smiled back.

He was, we could tell, going to enjoy this.

As was she.

And so did we. From end to end of the Field of Honor the battle raged, always in bursts, sometimes just a few clatters of wood on wood, before they broke off again, circled, probed, and considered, while other bursts of action were of prodigious length, producing prodigious volleys of noise—as if all the drummers in Their Majesties' marching band were falling over each other down a staircase into the Royal Carpenters' log racks.

There were to be three five-minute rounds, it had been agreed. Winner by surrender only. There were no judges, because both Commandant Bastard and Captain Qrysta had considered that no one present had the skill needed to be capable of judging.

We were all capable of appreciating, though. At first, both fighters concentrated on defense. Their attacks were fast and ferocious, but mainly little more than feints to keep their opponent at bay, while seeking out weakness, looking for an overly rash attack that they could exploit, or momentum they could use to set the other off balance, if only for a split second. So, for most of the first round, all we heard was the clashing of wood on wood. Towards the end of it, as they found flaws in each other's techniques, more blows began to land on the fighters' leathers. They landed with a softer, stealthier sound, not sharp like the wood on wood, but dull, like grunts of pain.

At the end of the first round, Qrysta tottered back to her corner, blowing hard, where Grell, Oller, and I had towels and water for her. I hadn't seen her this stretched since the three hours we'd spent fighting the poison slugs, and this had only been five minutes.

"*Hells* he's good!" She gulped for air.

Commandant Bastard, we saw, was faring no better in his corner. He'd worked up a serious sweat. We didn't think he even knew *how* to sweat. His chest was heaving, and his legs looked heavy.

"You've got him," I said.

She scowled, and said, "Ya *think?*" Meaning that she would beg to disagree.

They were both in even worse shape at the end of the second round.

"*Very* good!" Qrysta gasped. "It's like fighting air! The bastard's never there when I strike." She took a sip of water which she swilled around in her mouth and spat out, then leaned her hands on her knees to rest while fighting to get air into her lungs. Oller sponged her neck and forehead.

Commandant Bastard's sides were working like bellows where he stood, looking down, nodding his head in confusion, his face drained of expression, while he too was sponged and toweled by his anxious seconds. I saw him look blankly at nothing and shake his head. There was a big welt across the side of his face where Qrysta had caught him a savage blow. Her face was unmarked.

"You've tagged him more than he's tagged you," I told Qrysta.

She mumbled, drained, "So the fuck what? He hits harder."

"Look at his face!" I said.

"Want to see my legs? They'll be black and blue, and I can hardly damn walk!"

Commandant Bastard was also muttering at his seconds, who were exhorting and encouraging and urging, but he didn't seem to be listening. Or even *capable* of listening.

"This one for all the marbles," I said to Qrysta as the bell sounded for the start of the final round, and the fighters hauled themselves towards the scratch again.

Weirdly, though, it wasn't. Afterwards, everyone quizzed them both again and again, saying, "How did you know?" and, "You must have agreed to that, right?" They both said that they hadn't, and that they'd both meant it, genuinely, and it had just so happened that they'd both meant it at *exactly* the same time.

Which was a moment after they came out to face each other for the third and final round. They stood opposite each other and bowed as they had done before every round—and both threw their wooden training swords at each other's feet and then looked up at each other in surprise. They smiled with relief and bowed again, and then stumbled forward on battered, unsteady legs to shake each other's hands.

A tie. All bets returned. Minus, of course, five per cent for the ODF.

Plenty of spectators were unhappy with the result. They wanted a clear winner—especially if that winner was going to be *their* winner. But no one could argue with it. And no one dared to protest and risk getting a *look* from Commandant Bastard—or, worse, a "Right then, come on. Let's see if you can do any better!" Which would end quickly and painfully.

Queen Esmeralda flew down from the royal box—literally. Everyone knew she was Coven now so there was no point in hiding it and sticking to the old *Fly by Night* rule. She leapt off her broomstick, threw her arms around Captain Qrysta, kissed her on both cheeks, then took her hand and raised it in the air to cheers from the crowd and to a yelp of pain from Qrysta, whose raised arm hurt like hell.

Esmeralda was immediately all concern, calling for apothecaries and healers and stroking Qrysta's bruises solicitously while she helped her over to Commandant Bastard and—very carefully—raised his arm as well, to even more cheers, which went on as long as she held their aching arms up and smiled her shining smile at the crowd.

She lowered their arms, kissed Commandant Bastard on each cheek, and dropped his hand. Then she got her shoulders under Captain Qrysta's armpit and helped her off the Field of Honor, Qrysta limping and leaning on her as Esmeralda chatted sympathetically and happily in her ear, all concern and pride and admiration.

Shift and I hit them both with Lingering Mends. They straightened up, and the crowd *ooh'd* at the green spheres that had bloomed around them.

I spent the afternoon with Marnie, who took me to the Guild of the Arcane Arts for my induction. The guildhall was a rambling old building with courtyards, shrines, libraries, laboratories in the cellars, and an observatory in its domed roof. Its main hall was large enough to include its own market, in which stalls displayed rare goods and strange ingredients from all over the world. Its museum was filled with artefacts which it would take months to explore. The Conclave chamber was at the top of a wide staircase, just below the observatory.

My induction was a simple ceremony, which, as one would expect, included passwords and secret signs and ritual phrases. I was given the rank of Caster, jumping right over Novice and Initiate. I sealed my acceptance by signing my name in invisible ink in an invisible book. I hoped that I'd have time to come back there and lose myself in books and scrolls and curiosities and conversations with my guildmates. On the way out, we stopped at the reception desk where the porter shook my hand and said, "Welcome to the Guild, Master Daxx!"

Marnie pointed at a row of pigeonholes behind him.

"What is it?" I said.

"Your pigeonhole," Marnie said. "For your messages."

"Ah," I said blankly.

I looked at the pigeonhole. There was nothing in it. I looked at Marnie, baffled. She nodded at the porter, who gave her a quill and paper. She wrote on it, folded it, and handed it to the porter, who put it in her pigeonhole.

She looked at me and smiled.

Then she looked at my pigeonhole, expectantly.

I looked at it too.

So, I thought, *her message will go from her pigeonhole to mine.*

I was wrong.

A pigeon materialized in it, stepped out of it, and hopped over to the counter, where it looked up at me. It said, "Hello, Daxx. Message from Marnie. 'Welcome to the Guild.'"

When I could speak, I said, "Thank you."

The pigeon said, "Is there a reply?"

"No, thank you very much."

"Don't mention it," the pigeon said. It hopped back across to my pigeonhole. It turned around, sat, looked up at me, blinked, and slowly disappeared.

I turned to Marnie. "Wow."

"All you need is a pigeonhole," she said. "There's one for every guildie at every hall, and we all keep one at home. That way, they don't have to fly to find you, risking hawks and hunters and such."

"Useful," I said.

"Very," Marnie said. "So, we'll stay in touch, won't we?"

"That we will," I said.

"I'd like to know where your road will take you," she said.

"I'll keep you posted," I promised.

ᛯ ᛯ ᛯ

Neva chivvied the Royal Jewelwrights out of their workshop and remade the two half-crowns into one crown again, so skillfully that you couldn't see the join. For good measure, she also made what she called two *halfcrowns*, which were light circlets of gold set with gems of exquisite beauty, far more elegant than the bulky old thing the brothers had shared all those ages ago.

"Poor jewelwrights in those days," Neva sniffed.

The new halfcrowns were much more practical for everyday wear, and King Wyllard and Queen Esmeralda wouldn't have to hand the thing back and forth to each other. They decided to retire the old one to a glass case on a plinth in the Royal Audience Hall between their two thrones.

Things were changing, everyone agreed, with optimism rather than fear of the unknown. *Let's see what the future holds.*

The two co-Majesties wore their new halfcrowns at the Victory Feast which started only a few hours after Captain Qrysta's epic duel with Commandant Bastard. Esmeralda had come around to the prospect of co-ruling the realm and setting Downbury to rights. She had decided, she told us, that it wasn't a burden, but an opportunity—a chance make something of her life. She'd been given a gift at her birth. She was coming to see how she should use it for everyone's benefit. Her people's benefit. And that it would never be easy—in Downbury or anywhere else. She understood that it was her duty: to serve and to share, for the good of the realm.

I told her that I knew she'd do that well. From time to time, I looked at her, by King Wyllard's side at the high table on the dais, radiating even more brightly than she had at the Victory Feast in Rushtoun. It was clear that the old king, and the nobles of his court, already loved her as much as we all did.

Qrysta and Grell and I had discussed what Ken had told us and tried to think whether we could guess what our futures might hold. We couldn't. We were just going to have to wait and see.

Oller had no plans for his own future. He could write his own ticket now as one of the Saviors of the Realm. He knew that, but he didn't know what he was going to write on it. He could hardly go back to thieving; not now, when anyone and everyone would willingly give him anything he wanted. He was going to miss the buzz of climbing in through people's windows in the middle of the night and relieving them of their valuables while they slept.

"Imagine"—he shook his head—"me, a civilian! Dunno what the world's coming to …"

We were sitting below the dais with friends old and new—Citizens of Mayport, who bombarded us with questions, all of us feasting away while the royal musicians played and servants hurried and our cups never fell empty. Every now and then a cold nose nudged my arm, at which I found a scrap to feed to Little Guy under the table. It was after sitting back, having given him yet another juicy lump of meat, that I heard a murmur behind me, saying, "If you would be so kind as to follow me, sir …"

I turned to see a flunkey, who inclined his head deferentially. I stood up and followed him out of the Great Hall.

I made eye contact with Grell and Qrysta on the way.

They both nodded. They knew.

It would be their turns next.

We'd told each other, yet again, that we loved each other, and that we'd all see each other down the road. Not knowing, though, whether that was even possible.

The sounds of the feasting and celebrating in the Great Hall faded away behind us as I followed the flunkey through the castle. He was liveried, clearly someone of high rank, unctuous, fat, balding, and effortlessly superior. He led me down a corridor, up some stairs, across a hallway, and into another corridor where he stopped at a door and knocked.

"Enter," a voice said. And then, "You may leave us."

The flunkey opened the door for me, bowed as I went in past him, and closed it behind me.

The Amalgam—Kenneth—unfolded himself from his seat behind a large table and flowed around it towards me.

"Ready?" he said.

I had Shift with me. I could feel her apprehension. *Who? What?*

It's okay, I reassured her. *He's a friend.*

I could tell that she knew I was just saying that.

A friend? *That?*

To Ken I replied, "I suppose so."

"You *suppose so?*"

"Well, I don't know what I'm meant to be ready *for.*"

"Ah," he said, understanding. "My advice would be, *for anything.* Come along, then, we can talk as we go." He led the way on his blurring undercarriage towards a door in the far side of the room. He opened it and set off down a long corridor. We were still in the Royal Castle of Mayport, it seemed, but we didn't see anyone else as we went on, which was odd. Everywhere else in the castle had been full of hustle and bustle and people coming and going.

"Two things are going on here," he said. "One you know about: your challenge. You have saved the human race, in its blissful ignorance. Or have bought it time, I should rather say, for it to destroy itself rather than be obliterated by the Pure. Or not. But at least it has the chance now. Thanks to you."

He patted me on the shoulder with one of his appendages. "It also, of course, now has the chance to evolve here as well. With luck, you won't mess up this intriguing place as badly as you have Earth. When I say *you*, I mean *you lot*. You'll be long gone yourself, of course. But your DNA will go marching on."

He glanced at me with the expression I had come to think of as his smile. "The second thing that is going on is what I told you before. You won the battle but not the war. If you'd died, well, goodbye humankind. *Game over* as it were. But you didn't, so it isn't."

"So, there's … more?"

"Which will in all likelihood be harder and nastier and more dangerous."

I felt Shift tremble in my hands.

"I'll make it simple for you. You fail, you die. Think of it like the rounds you fought to win your Championship. Lose any of those, and you're out."

"Ah," I said. "Do I have a choice?"

"Succeed and live?" Ken suggested.

"No, I meant, can I say no?"

He stopped and looked at me. "Well, you could, I suppose. You could just … quit. On us, on yourself. That would be an odd choice, though. I mean—why would you? It doesn't seem very like *you*, that. This is what you *do*, isn't it? You're good at it. You enjoy it. Why stop?"

"Because I wasn't consulted. I wasn't asked."

"I explained," Ken said. "They *insisted*. Our enemies. All right, if you want to be asked, let me ask. Daxx, would you like to go on to the next task and sort it out? Or do you want those purple bigots to 'purify' the universe and annihilate humankind along with hundreds of remarkable species and trillions of decent people, who've never done you or them any harm?"

I didn't know why I was protesting, really. I just felt that my free choice had been taken away, but … so what if it had? What else would I rather be doing? Taking my daily, dogless walks in the lanes and fields and woods around my bungalow, daydreaming about situations like this? Or being here now, right in the middle of the action? Game to take on whatever lay ahead?

There was no contest. I was where I belonged.

I was also curious. "They're purple?"

"Well, no. That's what we call them. One race is blue, one is red, so we call them Team Purple. There are a few lesser 'pure' races tagging along after them. It's absurd. What is 'pure' anyway? Evolution isn't 'pure,' it's a haphazard mess. Out of the accidents of the eons, we all emerged in our own places at our own times. What's the difference if our later advances or developments were deliberate? You have to be some serious kind of stubborn not to see that. But, alas, they are. It's their religion. And they're implacable. So, we have to compete or die. Want to help?"

I didn't hesitate. "Of course."

"Good, then get with the program. And don't shillyshally at it. It'll take everything you've got and a whole lot more that you've never dreamed you're capable of. You think what you just went through was hard?"

"Yes."

"Well, stand by for fireworks, as you humans say. If I know those purple pains-in-the-backside, it will only get harder."

Harder? Gods above and below. "How?"

"I couldn't say. I expect you'll find out soon enough."

We came to a long, curving staircase which Ken the Amalgam flowed down with surprising grace. I expected him to stumble, what with that mélange of stalks and tentacles and fins and the prehensile rudder that comprised its lower limbs. His form seemed to alter somehow as it did so, going slightly out of focus for a second which I wasn't quite sure I saw—and then there it was again as clear as day and as solid as I was. The stairs led us into another hall and then along a stone-floored corridor lined with torches.

At the end of it, we came to another staircase. I stood back for Ken to lead the way and this time watched him carefully. He flowed down the thirty or so steps in a second, his undercarriage blurring out and then blurring back in again at the bottom. I trotted down after him. "How do you do that?"

"Science," Ken said, and flowed off across another long, torchlit hall.

I walked along beside him. *Him*, I thought. He was, to me, no longer "an Amalgam," but a living, breathing, extraordinary being. A ... person. With his own personality. Someone I wanted to get to know. Someone I knew that I liked.

"Which it sounds like you're good at," I said.

"Just as you're good at strategy and combat and surviving. We extracted our warmongering long ago and replaced it with superior traits. We're just not vicious shits like you lot are, who can't ever stop fighting as far as we can see. We have better things to occupy our attention. We made a number of boosts to our enjoyment, for example. Not just work, which we love, and pleasures, ditto—but also to the *lack* of them.

"A year or two on a barren moon, with nothing to do but contemplate the stars, does wonders for the soul. Not that we've found evidence of *soul* anywhere we've looked in the universe, but we keep searching. Because while we, and you humans, and all other species, don't—as far as we can see—have actual souls, we all of us feel *soulful*. Music. Nature. Lovers, friends, present or gone. Daydreams. Memories.

"No, we stopped wasting good brain cells on war long ago. Which seemed a fine idea at the time; we'd evolved beyond fighting—what a relief. But now ... we're hanging by a thread."

He sounded gloomy.

"Look," he went on, guiding me through the depths of Mayport Castle, "you did well. That doesn't mean ... ." He stopped and made himself sound a little less pessimistic. "That doesn't mean you can't do it again. Which we hope you will do as you have a lot more riding on you than you could know."

I knew what he'd stopped himself saying: *that doesn't mean you'll necessarily do well with what's ahead.* "I'll do my best," I said. "We all will."

He didn't answer.

We walked on.

I had to know. "So, what's next?"

"I've no idea. That's up to the Environment here. It's all set up to make its own decisions. I don't doubt it will cook up something challenging—so, be on your toes, eh? No resting on laurels."

I grimaced. "Right. Thanks for the warning." A thought struck me. "Starting out on a new—well, quest, will I be a noob again?"

"Certainly not!" Ken snorted. "Level Four and with all the privileges thereof."

"Four?" I asked. "What happened to Two and Three?"

"You passed Two when you graduated. Level One: orientation. Level Two: training. Level Three, the quest you just completed."

"How many levels are there, in total?"

"Ninety-nine, of course," he said. "The usual."

"Wow. Will I have time to reach all of them?"

"Again, entirely up to you. First, you have to *survive*. Dead is *dead*. Nearly there now," he said as we crossed yet another long, torchlit hall. We must have come down a dozen staircases and walked half a mile or more.

When we reached the big double doors at the far end of the hall, Ken stopped and turned to me. "One other thing. The better you do, the nicer your reward. And why not? You've earned it. It will come in useful. I expect you'd like to see yours?"

"I would," I said.

Ken reached out a ... hairy poker and prodded it at a stone in the wall. The doors swung open away from us. He led the way inside. I followed.

It wasn't a vault as I'd been expecting. Nor was it a dungeon, nor a corridor even. It was a huge cavern lit by more torches in sconces. Its floor of intricately fitted stone slabs stretched all the way to the far wall—which was a long way off in the distance. Above the walls of natural rock there was a huge, transparent dome, through which I could see stars. A *dome?* I hadn't seen anything hi-tech since this whole adventure had started. I'd been stuck in some kind of warped Middle Ages, magic included. There hadn't been a hint of any Industrial Revolution on the horizon anytime soon for this planet.

Kenneth poked a panel on the wall, and the stone floor began to split apart at its center.

Both halves slid slowly apart with a deep humming sound. Lights shone up from below. Shadows moved up towards us, casting strange shapes as they ran down the rock walls.

Something emerged into the flickering torchlight.

The shadows danced along and up and down the walls around us as they grew.

The humming stopped. A new section of floor clicked into place.

I stared at the thing that had just emerged from below, my mouth open in astonishment.

It stood there, in front of me, in the echoing silence.

I was dumbstruck. So was Shift. I felt her stiffen in my hand—if wood, which is already stiff, can stiffen. It was as if she was drawing herself in and going, *Whoa …! What in the name of all the gods is that?*

Lights switched on from unseen sources, illuminating the object I was staring at—modern lights, sharp, trained on it from all sides as well as from above and below.

It was a spaceship.

Quite a small one, no longer than an airliner—a hundred-odd feet maybe, tops—but as sleek and as shiny and as sexy as all get-out.

"Your reward," Kenneth said.

I could only stare in amazement.

An honest-to-gods spaceship.

Acknowledgements

Website: *www.richardsparks.com*
Editor: Lezli Robyn (*www.lezlirobyn.com*)
Map by Jenny Okun (*www.jennyokun.com*)
Representation: Julia Lord Literary Management
(*www.julialordliterary.com*)

Coming next (winter 2024):

The Sequel: **NEW ROCK NEW REALM**
Book Two in the New Rock Series